Kingdom of Dreams and Decay

THE ONCE SEVEN KINGDOMS
- BOOK THREE -

ABIGAIL EHRHARDT

Content Warnings

This book contains subject matter that might be difficult for some readers, including death, violence, discussion of past sexual threat, references to past abusive relationship, addiction and sobriety, mention of a past death of an animal companion, and explicit sexual content.

For those who have been forced to dampen their spark. You can light up the world.

PART 1: HEIR

Chapter 1

Dimitri had learned early on there were few things he could depend on. Most of them were unpleasant. Before the past year, there had really only been one good thing on that list: his ability to always have a response.

It didn't matter no one listened to him. His words, his thoughts, his mind, were his and his alone. He'd thought they were the only things that could never be taken from him.

Yet, there he was, his mind completely blank as he stared up at Sylas, the silence only interrupted by the crackle of the Moon King's torch.

"Well?" Sylas asked, holding the cell door open with his free hand. "Are you coming with me or not?"

Dimitri barely registered his words. He felt as though he was trapped underwater, not sure if he was sinking or surfacing—gods, what even was the surface anymore?

How was he supposed to fill his lungs after Deardryn had slammed her glowing palm against Patryclas's chest? How was he supposed to endure when Rayner, the man who had stabilized his crumbling world, had been holding a knife to his back all along?

I won't choose your life over mine.

"This is pathetic," Sylas said, completely unimpressed. "Three months ago, you were storming my castle, ranting of Deardryn's scheme with an impertinence that should have had you arrested. Now, she's tossed you in a cell, shackled you with damper cuffs, and planted her crime on your head, and you do *nothing?* Who are you?"

He didn't know. Patryclas had been helping him find out, but now Patryclas—

Something sharp raked through Dimitri's chest. He hunched forward, choking back a sob as that black wave slammed into him once more.

He couldn't survive this. The way his grief seeped into every corner of his being, flushing him out, consuming him until nothing else remained.

But he'd promised Patryclas he wouldn't turn it off. He'd thought his need for justice would be enough to keep him afloat. But, Crystal spare him, Sylas was practically handing him the opportunity he'd been waiting for, and he couldn't so much as move.

"Look," Sylas said, raking a hand through his hair. "I know you're in pain. *No one* understands that as well as me. But you wallowing in this cell doesn't help anyone. Not you, not Patryclas, and certainly not Analia."

The surprise of hearing her name had Dimitri flinching back, Sylas's black eyes following the movement.

"Yes, remember her?" he asked, stepping closer. "Your friend who helped you escape the Sun Kingdom. The princess who was important enough for you to infiltrate my castle and investigate Deardryn right under her nose. The friend that needs you now."

Images flickered across Dimitri's mind.

Their hours in the Sun Castle library. Her smile when he read an entire passage by himself. Her hand hovering over his shoulder, careful not to make contact. Her hug goodbye.

One by one, the memories sank through the waves, settling in his mind like a collection of anchors.

"She's not here," he rasped.

"Not when you were free," Sylas agreed. "But much has changed since then. And now, you have a chance to do something about it."

Sylas crossed the cell, his arms folding as he came to look down at Dimitri. "I know you love Patryclas. I know you did everything you could. But even though there's nothing else you can do for him, there's still something you can do for her. So, I'm asking you: Are you coming with me?"

The firmness in Sylas's voice had Dimitri wanting to curl in on himself. He didn't know how to leave this cell, to go back to a world where Patryclas—he couldn't think about it.

But there was also Analia.

His friend. The person who had given him everything, who he would do anything for.

Dimitri looked at Sylas's torch, the crackling flame forcing the shadows to the corners of his cold, dark cell. Finally, there was a response on his tongue. "Yes."

"Thank the Crystal." Sylas let his head fall back, giving the ceiling a look of exaggerated suffering.

Dimitri couldn't bring himself to care. Even as Sylas extended a hand to him, flicking his fingers in a hurry-up gesture. Slowly, painfully, he forced his body to uncurl, his legs unstable beneath him as he rose.

But he managed to place his icy hand atop Sylas's scarred one. He managed to keep his footing as Sylas pulled him into the shadows.

One step after another. That was all he could handle as the darkness peeled back, depositing him in a world he no longer recognized.

Dimitri blinked his stinging eyes, finding himself in a large stone bathing chamber. Countless bottles and jars sat neatly arranged on shelves built into the purplish-gray walls, matching those lining the inner ledge of a massive tub. A large mirror hung above a pair of sinks to his left, Dimitri quickly looking away from his reflected greasy blond hair and fraying tunic.

"Where are we?" he asked.

"My bathing chamber." Sylas crossed to the tub and turned on the faucet, water softly burbling forth. "Everything you'll need is either already on the ledge or in the top left drawer below the sinks."

"Why?"

There were endless interpretations of that question, but Sylas decided to go with the most straightforward.

"Because you smell. And I refuse to talk to you further until you wash the dungeon off yourself." He tossed a towel on the counter, barely sparing Dimitri a look as he turned to go. "I expect you to be polysyllabic when you emerge."

Dimitri frowned. But he didn't have the energy to respond as Sylas reached the door, their conversation seemingly at an end. Yet, Sylas paused.

"Oh, right." He turned back, pulling a key ring from his belt with a soft jingle.

Dimitri's eyes widened. He cringed back against the wall as Sylas approached, his eyes locked on the onyx key in Sylas's hand, the grip made from a muted silver.

"I'm just unlocking your cuffs," Sylas said, rolling his eyes.

"No, don't." Dimitri cradled his cuffed hands to his chest, the chain between them restricting his movement. He'd almost forgotten they were there, the absence of his magic a small mercy amid the agony of his cell.

But now, it was going to be released. There would be no hiding the golden flash from Sylas, no way to hide who he was.

"Honestly, Dimitri," Sylas muttered.

Before Dimitri could flee, he grabbed the chain. Dimitri tried to rip his hands away, but Sylas easily resisted, the click of disengaging locks shuddering through Dimitri's body.

"I'm trying to help you," Sylas complained. "The cuffs have to come off at some point, and this is the safest place to do it."

Dimitri's lips parted. And Sylas pulled the cuffs from his wrists and took a large step back.

Immediately, a blinding flash of gold lit up the bathing chamber. Dimitri threw up his arms, trying to shield himself. But there was no stopping the pent-up magic that slammed into him.

It wasn't the blunt pain of the occasional kick from his guards, the pressure when he let his magic build up for too long. This was devastating. It was the torture of every secret, every insecurity and sting of shame, slamming into him all at once.

Dimitri didn't know how he managed to stay on his feet. But somehow, he let the magic pour into his network and back out again, filling and draining him until he was empty once more.

And finally, the golden light faded.

Dimitri sagged against the wall, breathing hard. It took him several seconds to pluck up the courage to look at Sylas, but all he found was a faint crease between Sylas's brows as he slid the damper cuffs into his jacket pocket.

"I'll be waiting outside," he said. Then, he turned and slipped out the door.

Dimitri stared after him, the sudden quiet only interrupted by the running faucet.

There was no way Sylas didn't understand what he'd seen. And he just *left?*

Dimitri closed his eyes, pressing his face into his hands. There was nothing he could do about that now. All he could do was focus on his next step forward.

So, he gave himself one final moment. Then, he pulled off his tunic, kicked off his pants, and moved to turn off the faucet.

It wasn't until he stepped into the near-scalding water that he realized how cold he'd been. He sank down into the tub and tipped his head back, his body starting to shake as his aching muscles loosened one by one.

One step at a time. That was all he had to do.

Dimitri remained in the tub far past what he figured Sylas deemed acceptable. By the time he emerged into a dimly lit sitting room, he was clean, shaven, and dressed in a dark green shirt and pants he'd found in the drawer Sylas had indicated.

He half expected Sylas to have given up waiting for him. But the Moon King sat with book in hand on a dark red armchair, a small cart of covered dishes beside him.

"You should know your dawdling cost you a hot meal," he said, not looking up.

"I'm surprised I got one in the first place."

Sylas grunted as Dimitri crossed the room, coming to sink down on the armchair on the cart's other side. "Did you have Leila bring this?" Dimitri asked.

"No. Like most of my personal attendants, Leila has found herself charmed by Deardryn. I didn't need gossip of my request for a second dinner getting back to her."

Dimitri dropped his gaze. "You know she did that on purpose."

"Of course she did," Sylas scoffed. "From the moment she arrived in my kingdom, she's done everything in her power to win over my staff. But what Deardryn doesn't realize is I have a handful of servants she will never be able to touch, no matter how sweetly the others sing her praises. And one of them brought your meal."

Dimitri didn't want to know what gave Sylas the confident edge to his voice. Selecting a plate at random, he lifted the cover, revealing some form of rice dish. He forced himself to swallow a forkful, barely tasting it, only feeling it stick in his throat.

"So," Sylas said, finally closing his book. "I presume you have questions?"

Dimitri paused midchew. Since when did Sylas offer to indulge other people? He tried to study Sylas's expression, but the king gave nothing away as he rose and headed for one of the many bookshelves.

"How long was I in the dungeon?" he finally asked.

"A week and a half."

That felt about right. Dimitri choked down another bite. "And you're not planning on executing me?"

"If I were, I'd be wasting an extraordinary amount of time."

Fair enough. Dimitri quietly watched Sylas replace his book on the shelf, his hand reflexively going to the black heart on the inside of his wrist.

Crystal spare him, he didn't think he could ask his next question. But he had to know. Had to make it feel real.

"And Patryclas?" he forced out.

Sylas stiffened. Dimitri held his breath as the silence stretched, his heart stumbling in his chest.

He knew what Sylas was going to say. He'd known from the moment he appeared in his cell. But that didn't stop Sylas's cold, flat voice from slamming into him full force.

"He's dead."

The breath whooshed from Dimitri's lungs. He dropped his fork back to the cart with a clatter, his hands shaking so hard it hurt as he brought them to his face.

But that pain was good. It was a reminder there was something more than the grief that surged into him once more, because it was official.

Patryclas was dead. The final chapter was written; the book was closed. But gods, how was this supposed to be the end?

Dimitri swallowed hard, peeking at Sylas between his fingers. He expected to see an icy, bloodthirsty wrath, the type that would destroy the world so it could feel a fraction of his pain.

But Sylas's face was perfectly blank as he turned away from the bookshelf. And Dimitri wanted to be far, far away when that calm finally shattered.

Dimitri didn't know how he forced out his next question. "And Analia?"

"Analia," Sylas said, slumping back into his armchair, "is a far more complicated story."

Dimitri sat quietly as Sylas filled him in on everything he knew. How Deardryn had invaded the Ash Kingdom to lure Analia out of hiding. How she had returned to the Moon Kingdom a week prior with Analia, telling Sylas nothing besides she was to be kept in the dungeon until Deardryn called for her. How Deardryn had spent every day since locked in her study, only emerging for meals.

By the time he finished, Dimitri could actually feel the buzz of his questions through the haze in his mind. But there was only one he cared about.

"So, why is she still here?" he spat. "She killed your husband, imprisoned the one Royal who tried to warn you, and is obviously up to something—most likely with the Crystal, if that's what she stole from Scarsthain. And yet, you're sitting here doing *nothing?*"

"Careful, Dimitri," Sylas warned, shadows rippling across the carpet at his feet. "I have my own reasons for keeping Deardryn here. Don't presume you have the right to pry."

"I do when those reasons involve me."

Slowly, unnervingly, Sylas's black eyes met his. "What makes you think they do?" he asked.

"The fact that you've done your best to smuggle me out of your dungeon under Deardryn's nose," Dimitri replied, refusing to flinch. "And since you're baiting me with Analia, I'm guessing she has something to do with it, too."

An icy shadow curled around Dimitri's ankle. And the classic Moon Royal warning had Dimitri's words coming faster, hotter as his temper finally flared.

"I'm tired of being a pawn on the Royal chessboard. Either you tell me what moves you're making, or you can consider yourself down a piece."

For a long, long moment, Sylas remained silent. He reached for the decanter on the cart, ignoring Dimitri's glare as he filled his cup and took a slow, deep drink. Dimitri waited, silently seething, Sylas not so much as sparing him a glance.

Just when Dimitri was certain he wouldn't respond, Sylas finally looked up.

"You're a Sun Royal bastard."

Dimitri recoiled as if struck. "No I'm not."

"You're not just the Sun King's bastard," Sylas went on, wiping his mouth with the back of his hand. "You're a Sun Royal bastard. For the past twenty years, you've had the opportunity to become the most powerful piece on this 'Royal chessboard.' Why have you made no moves?"

Dimitri's mind scrambled for a response. His entire existence had been dedicated to protecting this secret, from the moment his magic came in at Gritta's. His survival depended on it.

But Sylas already knew.

"Because there are no moves I can make," he hedged.

"Maybe not while you were a servant under Deardryn's control. But you're free now. You spent thirty minutes ranting about her in our first meeting, yet you would rather hide in my dungeon with your damper cuffs than take the opportunity to seek your justice. Why?"

"I thought we were talking about *your* reasons," Dimitri said, his fingers flexing into his armchair.

"We are." Sylas downed the rest of his wine. "Currently, Analia is locked in my dungeon because Deardryn claims she is her biggest threat. Yet, from our first meeting, she has been subtly defaming your character. At first, Patryclas and I assumed it was due to her resentment toward Othin and his affair. But really, it's because your mere existence not only threatens the stability of her political authority but the succession of her crown."

Sylas leaned forward, forcing Dimitri to meet his gaze. "You are the Sun King's Royal bastard. Why do you hide?"

Dimitri wanted nothing more than to shrug him off, show Sylas all of his questions had missed their mark. Yet there was no denying how his voice was little more than a breath as he said, "Because that's not me."

"But it is."

Sylas stared into Dimitri's face, demanding a response. But Dimitri could only fight not to curl in on himself as a deep, familiar ache pierced through his chest.

Sylas's lips thinned. Obviously realizing he wasn't going to get anywhere, he rose to his feet.

"Analia makes for an interesting possibility," he said, suddenly brisk as he wheeled the cart toward the door. "As an enemy of Deardryn, she could be a powerful ally when enacting my 'reasons.'"

Dimitri rubbed his chest, not sure if he was relieved or had emotional whiplash from the change in topic. Regardless, he wouldn't complain.

"So, why is she still in the dungeon?" he asked.

"Timing. At some point, Deardryn is going to realize her prisoners have escaped. And the more time between escapes means the greater my deniability."

"Well—"

"I've arranged for you to stay in a safe location," Sylas went on, ignoring Dimitri as he crossed to a carved wooden cabinet. "There's no way for me to tell my maids not to come to my chambers without rousing suspicion, and there's no place for you to hide in here."

"Wait, hold on—"

"I sent my servant to your chambers," Sylas said, grabbing a decent-sized pack from the cabinet and tossing it to Dimitri. "He collected some of your things. It should be more than enough to get you through the coming days. Now, come on—"

"Stop!" Dimitri cringed away from Sylas's extended hand, his own hands coming up to grip the sides of his head.

It was too much. His grief over Patryclas, his hatred for Deardryn, all his questions regarding Analia, Sylas pulling the rug out from under him over and over again.

He just needed a second to think.

"Dimitri," Sylas said, struggling for patience, "the longer you're here, the greater the chance of someone discovering you."

"I know," Dimitri said, his grip tightening on his head. "I just..."

He was right back where he'd started when he first entered the kingdom. Terrified of being caught by Deardryn. Constantly looking over his shoulder, even when he had Patryclas's protection, Rayner's disguise.

But all of those things were gone. He was alone, defenseless. Only left with the memory of their vows tattooed into his skin.

"Promise me," Dimitri blurted.

Sylas's eyebrows rose. "Excuse me?"

"Promise me," Dimitri repeated, his hands falling from his head as he rose to his feet. "I can't force you to tell me what your reasons are. But I can't help you either if Deardryn finds me. So, promise me with your blade you will do everything in your power to keep me safe."

"You don't trust my word?" Sylas asked.

"Do you trust mine?"

Something like the shadow of a smile flickered across Sylas's lips. "Point taken." With a soft rasp, he unsheathed his scarsworn dagger from his belt, lightly running the tip over his palm. "I swear to you that I will do everything in my power to keep you safe while in my castle—"

"Kingdom," Dimitri interjected.

Sylas's lips thinned. "Kingdom," he amended stiffly. "In exchange, you will co-operate with me and my reasons while I deal with Deardryn."

Dimitri thought for a moment. Finding no treacherous loopholes, he nodded.

"Good." Without further comment, Sylas sliced open his palm. Collecting his blood on the blade, he pulled up Dimitri's left sleeve, swirling his blood across Dimitri's skin.

A flurry of tingles erupted in the blade's wake, racing up toward his elbow, down to his wrist, wrapping around his forearm. Within moments, the path of the tingles had been replaced by an intricate wreath of purple crescent moons, circling around a full moon in its center.

It was the largest tattoo he'd ever received. And as he accepted the blade, feeling the slight sting as he sliced open his palm, he knew it was worth it. Even as his blood became a large purple sun with extending rays amongst the intricate black lines on Sylas's forearm.

"All right then," Sylas said, retrieving his dagger and sliding it back through his belt. "Are you happy now?"

"No."

Just for a moment, Sylas's expression softened. Then, he extended his hand, his voice as bored as ever. "Shall we go?"

Dimitri nodded, reaching behind him to retrieve his pack. Then, Sylas pulled them into the shadows, reemerging a moment later in Sabi's book nook of all places.

"Dima!" Sabi exclaimed, shooting up from her chair. She hurried forward to meet him, something heavy inching from Dimitri's shoulders as she took his hands in hers. "I was starting to think you weren't coming."

"He decided to take his time in the bath," Sylas grumbled.

Sabi ignored her uncle, her clinical green eyes flicking over Dimitri's face. "You're thinner."

"Being locked in a cell will do that to you," he replied. And from the looks of it, he'd traded one prison for another.

He should have suspected as much, though. Sylas needed to keep him hidden from Deardryn, and Patryclas had told him only he, Sylas, and Sabi's team had access to this magically guarded section of the library.

Dimitri's heart flinched at the memory. Patryclas, shooing Sabi away when she'd gotten too close, protecting him even then.

"My servant has been given access to the nook," Sylas said, jolting Dimitri from his thoughts. "He'll be available to bring you whatever you need."

"What about Analia?" Dimitri asked.

"Well, seeing as she's in a cell, I find it hard to believe he'd be able to achieve that—"

"When are you getting her out?" Dimitri interrupted.

Sylas wrinkled his nose. "*If* I choose to get her out," he said, "it will be when I deem it best, and not a moment sooner."

"But—"

"I freed you, Dimitri," Sylas said, taking Dimitri's pack and tossing it on the desk. "Don't push it."

Dimitri made to protest. But Sylas turned away and headed for the exit.

"Deardryn doesn't know of this nook, so you'll be safe if you stay put. And *don't* forget your oath." Glancing over his shoulder, Sylas dipped his chin to Sabi. Then, without so much as a farewell, he passed through the magic and into the library.

For a few heartbeats, Dimitri remained where he stood, completely at a loss. He looked at Sabi, finding her tugging on one of her dark brown curls. Finally, his shoulders slumped.

"Hi," he began.

Sabi yanked him into a hug. He staggered into her, something cracking in his chest as he breathed in her familiar lavender scent.

"You came back," she said, her hand curling into the back of his shirt. "I don't have to start from scratch."

Dimitri let out something that could have been a laugh or a sob. He tried to maneuver his arms around her, but Sabi shoved away, furiously rubbing her eyes.

"All right," she said, pushing back her shoulders. "Uncle Sylas only gave me a few hours' notice, but I managed to get everything set up for you over here." She ushered Dimitri around her desk, her words coming at top speed. "Gathering blankets and pillows was easy, but of course you couldn't sleep on the floor, so I smuggled a spare cot from the servants' quarters. I decided to set it up over here, so you'd be out of the way of my most used bookcases—although if I step on you, it's your fault. Now sit."

Sabi shoved Dimitri down onto the cot, tucked against one of the many bookcases, barely taking a breath as she continued. "Is it all right? Is it comfortable, because I could—"

"Sabi," Dimitri cut in gently, raising his hands. "You're fussing."

"Of course I'm fussing!" Sabi exclaimed, stomping her foot. "My uncle is dead, I've been assisting the woman who killed him to take over our kingdom, one of my only friends betrayed me, and the other has been locked in the *dungeon* for over a week. Fussing over you is the only thing I can do. Now lay back and tell me if it's comfortable."

Dimitri's lips parted, but no words came out. Slowly, silently, he eased back against the mound of pillows, his body growing heavier with every moment.

"It's perfect," he said, looking up at her. "Thank you." He hesitated, his eyes dropping. "Would you like to test it yourself?"

Sabi blinked rapidly. Finally, she sank down beside him, Dimitri making no effort to break the silence that wrapped around them.

"I just don't understand," Sabi finally said, her eyes on her hands. "I've read so many books to try and make sense of people, the world, why things happen the way they do. But none of them can tell me why my uncle had to die, why bad things keep happening. None of them can tell me how to make it stop."

Dimitri had no answers for her. Not when he'd been wondering the same thing for a long time. All he could do was inch closer as Sabi sniffled, their shoulders barely touching. She leaned her head against his.

For a long, long time, they remained like that, neither of them speaking, Dimitri's gaze fixed on the ceiling.

One step at a time. Because while there was nothing he could do for Patryclas, he could still help Analia. He could still make Deardryn pay.

And at the very least, he knew what his next step would be.

Chapter 2

Aaron loved his family. He would always love his family. But that didn't stop him from wondering how much more of them he could handle.

He sat at his dining room table, the smell of bacon and toast making his stomach churn as Surce, Laness, and Branten discussed Talitha's scroll. Aaron, meanwhile, silently counted down the seconds until he could excuse himself, their voices sapping what little energy he had left.

"The problem," Surce said, sifting through her stack of notes, "is the disk isn't a perfect solution. Its magic creates a filter for me to read the scroll through, but it's not written in our common tongue."

"But I thought the creature said Talitha created the scrolls," Branten protested. "Why would she write in a language that wasn't hers?"

"Who said she did?" Surce asked. "From what I can tell, it's written in the forgotten tongue from the Ancient Ones' rule."

Aaron's attention stirred vaguely. Ethelind had insisted he learn the language alongside his other lessons as a child—although he'd only gotten so far before being tossed into the Underground.

He didn't know if that was a coincidence or a sign she knew something. He remained quiet regardless, poking at his food with his fork.

"Well, I guess that makes sense," Laness said, reaching for seconds. "Everything I've heard says our current language evolved right after the Unleashing. So, while Talitha and the other Defiants spent the majority of their lives speaking our language, the forgotten tongue was still technically their first."

"My thoughts exactly," Surce said. "Which suggests one of two things. Aaron, are you thinking the same?"

It took Aaron several seconds to register her question. He cleared his throat, uncomfortably aware of the eyes that had turned to him. "It means either she wrote it early enough in her rule that it was still her primary language, or it's another form of protection."

"Precisely," Surce said. Her topaz eyes stared into his, searching for more. But Aaron had nothing left to give, his shoulders hunching under the thickly veiled disappointment as everyone turned away.

It wasn't the first time they had tried to pull him into their conversations, as if they'd realized an anchor had been severed inside him, sending him adrift. Every time, he could see the hands they reached out to him, trying to reel him back in. But he didn't know how to let them. He wasn't entirely sure he *wanted* to let them.

"At first," Surce went on, "I thought it must be the former, since she already went through so much effort to conceal the message. But then I realized the pieces I could translate were out of order."

"She scrambled it, too?" Branten thudded his head back against his chair.

"You act like you're the one doing all the work," Laness said, poking him with the butt of her fork.

"I'm helping!"

"You're complaining."

The two dissolved into their usual squabbling, neither of them noticing as Aaron bit the inside of his cheek.

It was all too much. Too many voices, too many people, too much sensory information that he didn't have the wherewithal to process. Especially compared to the silence calling to him from his mother's room.

At least that torment was familiar—comforting in a twisted sort of way. But he knew Analia would scorch him—magically or otherwise—if she found out he had withdrawn again.

So, he sat at his crowded dining room table. Not sure if the mental image of her glaring at him made him want to smile or flinch. Because despite all the people in that room, he could still feel the emptiness of her chair beside his.

The dining room door opened. Laness and Branten cut off as Mor stepped inside, midway through pulling on his indigo jacket as he offered a greeting.

"You going somewhere?" Branten asked, passing him a mug.

"Human Kingdom."

"But you just got back last night," Branten protested.

"I know," Mor said, exchanging his mug for a piece of toast as he headed for the entryway. "It probably would have been wiser for me to spend another night there, but I missed being home."

Aaron hadn't even realized Mor had spent the night. He hadn't noticed a lot the past week beyond the swirling shadows in his mind. He picked at a corner of his toast, Mor's voice echoing from the entryway.

"While I'm here, would you be able to make a bead curtain for the Human Kingdom, Surce?"

Surce's eyebrows rose. "I thought the humans preferred to have no magic in their castle."

"They're going to have to deal with it if they keep demanding my presence."

"Is something going on?" Laness asked.

"Not overtly," Mor said, reappearing in the doorway, his boots now on. "But something doesn't feel right. And there's a lot I want to keep an eye on."

The quick glance Mor gave him had Aaron certain he was one of those things. He tore off another piece of toast, his fingers sticky with jam.

"Before you go," Surce said to Mor, "I was hoping you could look at this."

She fished a paper from her stack, Mor coming to peer over her shoulder. After a moment, his eyes widened. "Was this in the scroll?"

"It was."

"What is it?" Branten asked, leaning in front of Laness to try and see.

"It's a drawing of the runes from the creature's chamber," said Mor.

Aaron's fingers dug into his mangled toast.

"Really?" Branten reached for the paper, but Surce pulled it away, turning it around to face him instead. "Crystal fuck me," he said. "It even has all the colors."

Aaron wanted nothing more than to disappear into his seat, ignore this conversation and its implications entirely. But his eyes flicked up, taking in the rainbow lines Surce had carefully sketched.

Definitely the same design.

The shadows in Aaron's mind swirled.

"I found those details interesting as well," Surce said, placing the page on the table. "I didn't notice the specific colors, however, until I started sketching them."

"Why *did* you draw them?" Mor asked, swiping a piece of bacon from her plate.

"Because I didn't trust Branten not to spill anything on the original."

Branten opened his mouth to protest, thought about it, then shrugged and returned his attention to his plate. "So, what's special about the colors?" he asked.

"They're Royal colors," Aaron said flatly. All eyes flicked to him, but he kept his gaze on his plate, those shadows writhing.

"He's right," Laness said after a moment, redirecting everyone's attention to the drawing. "Orange for Ash, gold for Sun, light blue for Mist, navy for Wind, purple for Moon, silver for Star, and burgundy for Sand—that's the red one," she added, looking at Branten.

Branten squinted at the page. "Why not call it red, then?"

Laness cocked her head as if she couldn't tell if he was playing along or not. Branten wiggled his eyebrows.

"Well," Mor mused, "Anna did say she sensed Royal magic in the chamber."

A small, lonely part of Aaron perked up at the sound of her name, but it quickly sank back down.

"Let me get this straight," Laness said, tapping her fingers on the table. "The creature in the Underground was somehow locked up with those runes, which Analia said are infused with all seven Royal magics, and those runes now show up in the scroll that the creature told us about. Which means not only is the creature somehow connected to whatever secrets are in this scroll, but the other Defiants might be aware of what these secrets are?"

"At least some of them," Surce said.

"I hate puzzles," Branten grumbled, rubbing his temples.

"Well, Branten, I hate to inform you that there's still another piece." Surce pulled out a second sheet of paper from her notes and placed it beside the first. "When I realized where I'd seen these symbols before, I returned to the tapestry of the chamber I'd woven. What do you notice about these symbols?"

"Can't you just tell us?" Branten whined.

Surce's eyes gleamed. Before she could respond, Mor cut in, "There's far less silver in your tapestry."

Aaron's mind flashed back to the chamber, Analia's voice echoing through his mind. *The Star magic is so much fainter.*

For a moment, he wanted to latch onto the memory, lose himself in the sound of her voice, let it drown out the sinking feeling in his stomach. He didn't know how he managed to let it go as Surce said his name, verifying Analia's analysis.

He nodded mutely, his mind starting to drift once more.

"We'll have to talk with the creature again," Mor murmured, rubbing the spot where his golden hand met his wrist.

That certainly got Aaron's attention. He sat up straight in his chair, finally sounding grounded as he said, "We're not going back there."

His family startled. They all exchanged quick looks, Surce finally meeting his gaze across the table.

"We haven't reached the point where talking to the creature is our only option," she said carefully. "We still have the scroll, and while my lessons in the forgotten tongue from my years in Ferrin's temple are ancient, they're sufficing for now. But if we reach a point where I've done all I can—"

"We're not there yet," Aaron insisted, his hands clenching around the edge of the table. "Especially since we don't know what information Anna will bring when she returns with the Crystal shard."

His eyes flashed around the table, his magic building in his veins. Laness squirmed in her seat, but once again, Surce was the only one who held his gaze.

"I agree with you," she said slowly. "But at that point, you must also realize what circumstances will follow when she *does* return.

"Deardryn already came dangerously close to our border. And when Analia escapes with the Crystal, she'll throw every resource she has into finding her. Which means we need to prepare."

"That's a lot of conjectures," Aaron ground out, the icy surge of his magic almost suppressing the flinch in his chest. "We have no idea what kind of position we'll be in when that happens, which means our best option is to focus on what we can do right now."

"Our best option," Surce said, her calm beginning to crack, "is to focus on both—"

"Have you spoken with Anna?" Aaron asked, turning sharply to Laness.

Laness jumped. "She's... she's still in her cell."

Starlight flashed across Aaron's knuckles.

"Easy, brother," Branten said, his voice low as he touched Aaron's arm.

Those might have been the most absurd words Aaron had ever heard. How was he supposed to take it easy when she was in a cell? When his own ancestor seemed to have done everything in her power to block their path forward? When his kingdom—gods, he couldn't think about that.

Aaron's eyes darted to the empty chair beside his. Down to his hands, gripping the table so hard his fingers ached.

And somehow, he took a long, steadying breath, forcing every spark of magic, every shred of emotion, back down.

"The creature is our last resort," he said, his voice flat, empty once more. "We keep searching the scroll, we increase security measures around the border, and we wait until Analia returns before making any moves we can't take back."

Branten, Laness, and Mor all silently dropped their gazes. Surce studied him for a long moment, her eyes narrowed slightly. Finally, she gave a short nod.

"All right then." Aaron pushed back from his chair. And ignoring his plate, ignoring the quick exchange of concerned looks, he turned to go.

With every step, the ice in his veins began to thaw, his body melting back into the same hazy darkness he'd been trapped in all week as he reached his room.

Aaron closed the door behind him, his heart aching as his eyes passed over every reminder of her.

Her wardrobe beside his. Her harp. Her vanity tucked in the corner, the black box holding her moonstone ring hidden away in one of its drawers. All proof that none of it had been a dream, but that didn't stop him from feeling like he was trapped in a nightmare.

Aaron sank down on his bed, bowing his head into his hands.

He didn't know how to do this. He didn't know how to go about his life when she was trapped with Deardryn, completely out of reach. He didn't know how to act like everything was fine when he heard her scream every time he closed his eyes. And now there was a threat to his kingdom?

Aaron shifted onto his side, pressing his face into her pillow. He'd retrieved it from her room earlier in the week, back when the reminders of her still felt like comfort rather than salt in the wound. But it didn't even smell like her anymore. Just add it to the list of her possessions that had officially lived in his room longer than she had.

Gods, it felt like a cruel joke. Like the ghost of a promise that never got to be fulfilled.

But she had also promised to come back to him. He just had to hope she could stay in one piece long enough to do so.

Chapter 3

Analia was getting tired of the darkness. She paced the length of her Moon Castle cell, her footsteps softly echoing off the black stone walls.

She'd known she wouldn't be released immediately. This was her punishment for trying to corner Deardryn back in her uncle's chambers. A reminder of where she stood, regardless of her potential to wield the Crystal shard.

And she was having none of it. Especially since, according to the number of meals that had been delivered, she was on day seven of being ignored.

Analia scowled, tugging on a loose thread in her tunic. They were the same clothes she'd put on all those mornings ago in the Starlight Kingdom, the fabric so grimy and worn it no longer felt familiar. But it still retained the smell of smoke, a constant reminder of everything that had happened in that chamber.

The crack as Deardryn's magic broke Aaron from the inside. The gust of wind that launched Deardryn across the room. The overwhelming, soul-consuming wrath of the Crystal's magic. Her sister dead on the floor, Aaron holding her just as he had when they stumbled upon Accalon's corpse, Lucilla's blood on Deardryn's dagger.

Analia bit down hard on her knuckles, stifling her sob. She'd already taken as much time as she could to grieve, telling herself she could fall apart once she was home. But for now, she had to focus on getting out of this cell.

Unfortunately, all her attempts thus far had gotten her nowhere. She'd quickly realized she had two guards monitoring her, neither of them showing her much interest. The second guard in particular seemed to enjoy Analia's questions as much as she enjoyed the slop he delivered—he'd certainly been unimpressed when he found the dagger hidden in her boot.

Normally, she would have melted her cell bars with her flames. But the heavy damper cuffs shackled to her wrists made that plan impossible.

Analia paused her pacing as footsteps echoed outside her cell. She quickly backed up, her door swinging open to reveal the second guard. Fantastic.

"Don't bother," he said, tossing her tray on the ground between them with a clatter. "There's nothing you're going to get out of me."

"I'm sure His Majesty appreciates your discretion," Analia replied, perfectly polite. "But he wasn't the one who put me here. And you have no obligation to obey Deardryn's orders."

"Perhaps I like seeing Royals put in their place."

"You would think disobeying their orders would have the same effect."

"My gods you talk a lot," the guard grumbled.

Something like longing rolled through Analia's chest. Before she could respond, he turned away, starting to close the cell door behind him.

"Don't you think it's odd?" she blurted.

The guard glanced back. Analia took a few steps toward him, her mind racing.

"Deardryn is a queen infamous for her talk of peace," she said. "Yet she locks away one of the very Royals she aims to unite with in a cell. One that has a propensity to talk. What do you think she doesn't want me telling people?"

The guard's indigo eyes glinted in the torchlight. "You are truly desperate to get out of this cell."

"And you have no idea what kind of queen you're dealing with. If she's willing to lock away another Royal, what do you think is stopping her from doing the same to an insignificant dungeon guard?"

The guard's nostrils flared. Now. While he was distracted by his temper.

Analia darted forward, but he was on her in seconds. He shoved her sideways into the wall, stars dancing across her vision as her temple cracked against the stone.

"Know your place," he hissed, leaning in close. Then, with a final shove, he marched out of the cell, slamming the door behind him with a resounding clang.

Analia remained where she was for a few moments, absently rubbing her aching temple. Now what?

Ignoring her tray, she moved to sink down on the haystack that served as her cot. She dragged her knees to her chest, idly fingering the enka bracelet on her ankle as she designed and discarded plan after plan.

She didn't know how much time had passed before she drifted off. She just knew one moment, she was in her dark, empty cell. The next, her eyes blinked open in a softly lit sitting room.

Thick gray carpet covered the space, a collection of dark red armchairs surrounding a long, low table. A pair of wooden bookcases framed a glass door directly across from her, a night-darkened balcony beyond.

"I was wondering how long it would take you to get here," Sylas said, as bored as ever as he lounged on an armchair.

Analia's eyes darted around the room, but they appeared to be alone.

"Where exactly is 'here'?" she asked.

"My dream of course."

"Your 'dream'?"

"Crystal spare me, I'm talking to a parrot."

Analia's blood crackled with phantom flames. "Forgive me," she said. "I don't have a habit of believing unbelievable things."

"No," Sylas sighed, "why *would* you make this easy."

He dragged a hand through his blue-black curls, the picture of suffering. Analia started to protest, but Sylas continued over her.

"Moon magic is not limited to physical shadows. It also encompasses the shadows in a person's mind. And if you're familiar enough with those shadows, you can forge a temporary connection. You can take a look at yourself if you don't believe me."

Analia had countless questions. But she followed his advice, immediately doing a double take.

Her grimy tunic and pants were replaced by her black-and-silver jacket, her phoenix pin in its usual spot against her chest. Her dagger hung from her belt, her hair soft and clean as she ran her fingers through it. Also, no damper cuffs.

Analia looked at Sylas, but he remained slumped in his seat, idly picking at a jewel on the goblet he'd retrieved from Crystal-knew-where.

Well, if he was planning on harming her, he'd wasted the perfect opportunity. So then what was he up to?

"I'm assuming," she said, warily coming to take the seat across from him, "since you had to explain this aspect of your magic to me, the rest of the kingdoms are also unaware?"

Sylas grunted something that could have been an affirmation. He reached out, a wooden side table silently appearing just in time for him to place his goblet on it. Analia's mind buzzed, but she kept her expression impassive.

"So," she said. "What warrants such confidentiality?"

"Plead your case," Sylas said primly.

Analia's jaw dropped. "Now? Was the past *week* too terrible of timing for you?"

"I have my reasons," he said vaguely. "That, and I've grown tired of your servant friend harassing me."

A stack of papers appeared in his hands before Analia could respond, his voice impossibly dry as he sifted through them. "They started off civil enough. 'Dear Sylas, what are you planning to do? Dear Sylas, you're running out of time before the Old Hag makes her move. Dear His Majesty the coward, are you going to use the advantage you have, or are you going to let a foreign infiltrator reign over your kingdom?' And my personal favorite, 'Sylas Ruanega, answer my fucking notes.'"

Well, that certainly sounded like Dimitri.

"Does that mean he's all right?" she asked. Laness had told her that his bracelet had been off for over a week, each passing day of silence having her stomach sinking lower.

"He's irritable and distraught, but that isn't uncommon in my castle right now."

Sylas's gaze darted to the empty armchair beside his, something indescribable in his eyes. Catching Analia looking, he scowled, his bored mask sliding back into place.

"At any rate," he said, Dimitri's letters disappearing from his hand, "I've heard Deardryn's side of the story. I've heard Dimitri's. But I've yet to hear yours."

"What do you want to know?" Analia asked.

Sylas's black eyes met hers. "Everything."

Well, that was a complicated request. But he was also the most powerful ally she could hope to get—as unpleasant as he was.

Analia ran her finger along the plush arm of her chair, taking a moment to collect her thoughts. Then, she began.

She told him everything: the truth behind Accalon's death, her truce marriage, her wedding night, all of Deardryn's schemes. She reluctantly told him that her magic was Accalon's, but she still avoided giving any information about Aaron's identity, keeping the story vague after her coronation. By the time she reached Deardryn's attack on Ash, Lucilla's death, and the unlocking of the first Crystal shard, her voice was hoarse and her heart was aching.

"She then brought me back here to assist in her Crystal research," she finished.

Sylas didn't immediately respond. He thoughtfully rubbed the stem of his goblet, that same wounded expression flashing across his face as he looked at the empty seat beside him. Finally, he placed his goblet back on the side table. "Interesting."

Analia decided to take that as a good sign. "What I don't understand," she said, rising to her feet to pace, "is why Deardryn is still here. There's no way the Defiants would hide two pieces of the Crystal in the same kingdom, and since she's killed a Moon Royal and has all of her rings—"

"Deardryn hasn't killed a Moon Royal," Sylas broke in, the closest she'd ever seen him to surprised.

Analia pivoted on her heel, "What?"

"There have been no Moon Royal deaths since before the last Solstice Ceremony," Sylas told her.

Analia's nails dug into her palms. So, it *had* been a bluff. And she'd fallen for it.

Analia resumed her pacing, her blood starting to burn. "That just means you need to put your family on guard," she said. "Are all of you able to…?"

"Dreamwalk?" Sylas supplied.

Analia nodded. Sylas pressed his lips into a line, clearly reluctant. But he nodded. "I can assemble a group dream to deliver your warning."

Analia perked up. "Are these dreams able to be used offensively?" she asked, returning to her armchair. "If you can pull multiple people in at once, could we try to overwhelm Deardryn in one of her dreams?"

"Don't you think I would have done that already if I could?"

Analia's temper crackled. "Apologies, I didn't realize you had provided study material on your magic and your past attempts."

"Crystal spare me," Sylas muttered. "She's one of *those*."

Before Analia could retort, Sylas continued.

"Dreamwalking isn't the same as accessing a person's mind. It's simply establishing a bridge. Instead of pulling you into my mind or stepping into yours, we meet in the middle of the bridge.

"Consequently, while you could trip during your relentless pacing and twist your ankle here, your ankle would be fine when you woke up. The same goes if I were to try and harm you. I could intimidate, interrogate, or even torture your dream self, and while you would be mentally rattled, you'd wake up physically fine.

"The same goes if I were to try and kill you. The dream would shatter, but you would wake up just fine."

Analia didn't want to know how Sylas knew the last part. She was honestly surprised he'd told her so much in the first place. Although, now that she thought about it, he'd given her numerous glimpses into his capabilities all throughout their conversation.

"So," she said, "you're not able to impact the person directly, but you *can* manipulate your environment."

Sylas stared at her as if waiting for the point.

"Well?" Analia asked, losing patience. "Is that true?"

"Yes."

"So, how do you do it?"

"You imagine it."

Analia's eyebrows shot up. "That's it?"

"Do you have a daily quota of questions you must ask, or are you naturally like this?"

Analia ignored him, imagining a white candle in her hand. The air between her fingers hardened, transforming into a simple white candle.

"Huh." Analia turned the candle between her fingers, finding it indistinguishable from a real-life candle.

"If you're done amusing yourself," Sylas drawled, "we seem to have strayed from your story."

"Have we?" Analia asked innocently.

"You still haven't told me why Deardryn thinks you any more capable of handling the Crystal than herself."

Analia didn't immediately respond. She ran her finger over the candle wick, a small midnight flame crackling to life.

"She needs me," she said, eyes on the flame, "because I have access to all seven Royal Blessings. So, I can presumably not only track the Crystal but also learn to wield it."

Analia waited for Sylas to call her a liar. Gods, she wished she was.

He dragged a hand down his face, looking like a child who was just informed he had more work to do than originally planned.

"Figures," he muttered.

"You believe me?" Analia asked incredulously.

"It was impossible enough you didn't have magic for so long," Sylas said. "Now Deardryn is summoning demons, the Crystal has been broken, and I don't want to know what kind of depravity Accalon was digging into."

Analia winced, her hand automatically reaching for her phoenix pin.

"Your abilities," Sylas went on, "are just one more entry on the list of absurdities I now have to deal with."

He summoned a fresh goblet, perfectly petulant as he drained its contents in one go. But despite his efforts, Analia was starting to get a feel for the king underneath. What he was aiming to do here.

"You know," she said, placing her candle on a nearby table, "instead of *dealing* with my abilities, you could *work* with them."

"Why would I want to do that?" Sylas deadpanned.

"Seeing as you were the one who convened this meeting, I'd say you already have a few reasons in mind. That, and the fact that if you want Deardryn out of your castle, the person she locked in a dungeon might be a helpful ally. Not to mention one less foreign Royal in your castle to contend with."

Analia met his gaze, letting the implication dangle between them.

"Interesting," Sylas murmured. "Accalon has trained you well."

Something sharp sliced through Analia's chest.

"You're no use to me in a cell," he went on, rising and crossing to the balcony door. "I'll send my servants to collect you."

Analia startled at the sudden shift in conversation. "When?" she asked.

"I'll have chambers prepared for you in my guest wing, and we can discuss further actions when you're settled."

Analia's mind struggled to keep up as Sylas pulled a curtain across the glass. "I suppose you'll be wanting to bind this agreement with one of your scarsworn daggers?"

"Not yet. We'll talk about it soon."

"But—"

Analia broke off as Sylas snapped his fingers, and the sitting room dissolved into darkness.

Analia shot upright on her haystack. Her eyes darted around, taking in her stone cell, the cold, everything exactly as she remembered.

It had to have been a dream. But it felt too vivid to be fake.

Analia sank back against her hay, her hand going to the bruise on her temple. She had no way out of this cell on her own. Which meant her only hope... was Sylas.

Crystal spare her, she was doomed.

Chapter 4

Ember followed the reluctant crowd through the Ash Kingdom streets, fighting the urge to duck her head.

Not because of the cold. Not because of the clock tower's summoning chimes echoing around her. Not to avoid looking at the damaged storefronts and broken statues, the patches of churned-up snow still stained pink in the afternoon light.

But because of the eyes.

Ember turned the corner, knowing they would be there. Still, she couldn't suppress her flinch as the Sun soldiers' gazes locked on her from across the street, the murmurs around her rising to a buzz as they spotted the soldiers.

Two men. Different from the two the day before, and the day before that. Yet, the look was always the same: moving first to her healer robes, flicking up to her eyes to check for her markings.

For so long, her robes, her markings, had felt like a badge of honor. They were a reminder that, despite what her fellow healers thought, she was worth something in the eyes of the Crystal and Rosala. But now, they felt like the only armor she had as the guards looked away, continuing to scan the crowd.

After all, she wasn't a threat. She wasn't allowed to be, seeing as she was sworn to neutrality.

Even when an enemy kingdom had invaded her home a week prior. Even when their queen had killed her friend, threw another in prison, and took a third as her hostage.

Ember shuddered, her hand finding her enka bracelet. The three metal charms she'd added dug into her palms, the memories sucking the air from her lungs.

Rosala spare her, how had they reached this point?

Ember was so lost in her thoughts she didn't immediately notice the commotion behind her. She twisted around, the crowd trying to carry her with them as some sped up, most pausing as they searched for the raised voices. But Ember knew exactly where to look.

One of the newer Ash military recruits—a dark-haired man who couldn't be older than twenty—stood below the Sun soldiers' walkway, his arms folded and feet planted as he glared up at them.

"If we wanted gargoyles," he called, "we would have made them ourselves."

The left Sun guard's lip curled. He said something Ember didn't catch over the clock tower's tolls, but the message was clear enough.

But the recruit didn't back down. He drew his sword, his friends closing ranks around him, Sun and Ash voices growing louder and louder as they went back and forth.

Gods, she couldn't watch this. Not again. Just walk away while there was still time, don't let it—

The flash of magic was so quick Ember almost missed it. With a screech, the recruit staggered back, his hands flying to his face.

The crowd around him surged, trying to back out of range. But the recruit dropped his hands and lunged for the walkway's stairs.

The Sun soldiers drew their spears.

Ember's lips parted.

And the recruit's friends grabbed him and yanked him back.

Ember sagged as they dragged him through the buzzing crowd, the recruit cursing and writhing in their grip. But there was no time for relief.

Ember stumbled against the current of people, trying to assess the situation. And she gasped as the recruit lifted his head.

A thick, bloody gash sliced diagonally across his face, starting at the top right corner of his forehead and reaching down to his jaw.

Gods, he'd missed his eye by a hair. This soldier was getting more vicious with his attacks.

"Bring him here," she called, waving down the closest man and ducking into a corner between two buildings. She could feel the Sun soldiers' eyes on her as the group hurried over, but she refused to look up. After all, she was neutral.

Ember wanted to spit the word at them. Instead, she turned to the recruit, who finally paused his struggling as he spotted her robes.

"My name's Ember," she said, her voice slipping into something calm, precise. "I can heal your wound. It will sting, but only for a few moments."

"I know the drill," he ground out.

Ember nodded. Still, she hesitated before reaching for her magic, not used to having her healing privileges restored. Temporarily, at least.

Stifling a frown, Ember touched the recruit's cheek, sending a wave of magic across his face. He winced; the feeling of skin rapidly regrowing and stitching back together wasn't a pleasant sensation. But within moments, the gash across his face had faded to a pink line, then into smooth skin once more.

"Thank you," he said, his voice softening.

"Is there any point in telling you not to do that again?" she asked, bending to scoop up a handful of snow.

The recruit tried and failed to suppress his grin. Ember rolled her eyes, taking pleasure in his yelp as she wiped the blood from his face with her snow. "Get out of here."

Waving off his friends' thanks, she watched as they turned and merged with the last of the crowd heading for the square, the clock tower's chimes still echoing around them. Only once they had disappeared did she bow her head, a cold sweat breaking out across her brow.

So many wounded. Both from the invasion and from trying to test the Sun soldiers' lenience. All of them trying to fight for their home—and who was she to try and stop them? But she didn't know how much more her body could take.

Ember bit down hard on her cheek. Then, she forced her shaky legs to move, following the crowd down the street, continuing forward even when a turn to her left would lead to her apothecary. To her devinroot.

Something oddly similar to longing radiated from her bone marrow. But she had to stay clearheaded. Reaching for her devinroot had been taken off the table the moment she'd stumbled into the healer temple, immediately overcome by the wails of the wounded, the smell of blood and smoke.

She'd been ready to plead her case before being permitted to help. But upon spotting her, Archmaster Hollyn informed her she had temporary privileges and told her to jump in wherever.

From that point on, Ember's days had been consumed by healing what patients she could, occasionally assisting the master healers on the more extreme cases. There were some moments she was so busy she didn't have time to miss her devinroot. But that didn't stop the lingering effects of her detox from clinging to her like a bloodstain, making her bones feel brittle, her mind a collection of fragmented thoughts that couldn't quite fit together. It almost felt like it was getting worse as time passed, rather than better...

Ember shoved the thoughts aside as she finally arrived in the square. The crowd jostled around her, no one wanting to be closest to the Council Building. Not after the first summons a week prior.

Ember tried to wedge herself in the corner between a building and a phoenix statue, but someone knocked into her from the side. She staggered, her shaky legs struggling to stabilize.

"I've got you." Hands latched onto her from behind, steadying her before she could be jostled again.

Ember's heart jolted. She twisted in the person's grip, her blood surging through her veins.

But it was only Rois. The Ash Crystal Guard wore a simple black jacket and boots, his copper hair mussed as he pushed back his hood.

"You scared me!" she exclaimed, shoving his chest.

Rois raised his hands. "Would you have preferred I let you fall?"

"You shouldn't have been able to do either in the first place," Ember hissed. "Does he know you're here?"

"Does he ever?" Rois scoffed with a dismissiveness that was almost believable. But Ember caught the tension in his jaw.

As soon as Deardryn had left the kingdom with Analia, all Ash Royal staff had been rounded up, including the Crystal Guard. To Ember's surprise, they hadn't been executed or tortured for information. They were simply put on lockdown in the castle—although they certainly hadn't been pleased by how long it had taken to find Rois.

Yet, that didn't stop him from sneaking out—Rosala knew how—to meet up with Ember whenever he got the chance. As much as she'd like to be furious with him for putting his life on the line, she couldn't help being grateful for the one sliver of company she had left. Especially after everything he'd updated her on.

Ember started to respond, just to break off as the clock tower finally quieted. Then, the square went completely silent.

"So," Rois murmured, his soft voice unnervingly loud. "Round two starts now."

Ember's stomach did a slow roll. She turned in the motionless crowd, the tension in the air having the hairs on the back of her neck stand up.

But the Council Building's balcony remained empty. Still.

Seconds, minutes ticked past. And only when Ember's nerves were about to fray did the door slide open.

Just as before, the ring of bright blue magic came first. It hissed out across the balcony floor, coming to flicker around the base of the railing. Shielding magic. Closely followed by its wielder, Sun soldiers flanking him on either side.

King Othin Gardelle of the Sun Kingdom. Tall, broad, and with a crown of gilded sun rays atop his dark hair. He wore no armor or weapons, just a luxurious black tunic, its gold threads matching the sun dragon clasp on his white cloak.

It was almost insulting how pristine he looked as he stepped up to the railing, his amber eyes narrowed as he took in the crowd. Then again, why *would* he have so much as a scratch?

He hadn't partaken in the battle. As far as Ember knew, he'd been safely tucked away in the Sun Kingdom until Deardryn summoned him to take her place. Leaving the rest of the kingdom to find out when he had the clock tower signal a meeting the following morning.

Now, he fiddled with the small, magical amplifier pinned to his cloak, appearing almost... annoyed. Before Ember could be sure that was what she saw, his expression smoothed.

"Citizens of the Ash Kingdom," he called, his voice echoing in the silence. "I welcome you to our second joint-kingdom meeting."

Mutters bubbled up from the crowd, Ember twisting to exchange an incredulous look with Rois. He wasn't really going to try this *again...*

"I understand this unification must feel abrupt," Othin continued, raising his voice even more. "It will take time to adjust to our new order. But I've come before you today to provide updates on our continued efforts to prove we wish this transition to remain peaceful—"

Embr winced as a seal seemed to pop around the crowd. People snapped into movement, voices rising as some stumbled back, others shoving closer as if they couldn't believe what they were hearing.

"The fool will never learn," Rois muttered, tugging her back against him and away from the turmoil.

Ember could only shake her head, fragments of their first meeting flashing through her mind.

How Othin had highlighted all the ways they *weren't* tyrant invaders. As if the fact the Ash Royals were being given comfortable arrangements erased the fact that they were locked in the dungeon of their own castle. As if his encouraging Ash citizens to live their lives as usual would normalize the Sun soldiers stationed in the streets, ready to keep everyone in line through whatever means necessary.

He'd barely gotten the words out before the crowd erupted: weapons drawn, magic thrumming, hundreds of voices clashing together. Most were still too injured from the invasion to lash out. But those who did quickly found themselves as bloodied as the recruit she'd just helped as Sun soldiers waded into the crowd.

Ember looked at the balcony, the guards having already drawn their weapons. But even though the crowd still roiled around her, sucking the air from her lungs, it was noticeably more muted than before. Enough so that Othin, his hands tightening around the railing, didn't have to raise his voice as he droned on.

"Othin may not have learned from last time," Ember murmured, "but it looks like everyone else has."

Yet, something bothered her as Othin outlined plans to start rebuilding the kingdom. She'd only had a few encounters with the Sun King after Accalon was killed—none of them direct. But from everything she'd seen, he operated with brute force. He preferred to bluster, bully, or plow through obstacles until he got what he wanted.

She could definitely see a flush creeping around his dark beard as the crowd continued to stir. But his words remained precise. Eloquent, in an awkward kind of way.

"This has to be Deardryn's doing," she said, turning slightly to look at Rois. "This isn't his style at all."

"I know," he said. "But it's also the only reason I'm still alive."

"How come?"

"Think about it, Em. If you're going to invade a kingdom, you can't just kill the ruler and expect the people to get in line. Every person associated with the prior regime—council members, guards, family members—are all potential figureheads for the people to unite around."

"In that case, you all should be..." Ember's throat closed around the word, her hand coming to squeeze his arm.

"Othin would certainly prefer that," Rois said, remarkably unfazed. "But Deardryn has always preached peace. She's decided she'll have an easier time holding on to this kingdom and whatever advantage she gains from it if she can win us over, rather than intimidate us into submission. Especially since she only conquered the central kingdom, meaning the Sun forces have to worry about the rest of the territory trying to rise up."

"A straight, lethal injection to the heart," Ember murmured, her own heart giving a long, aching squeeze.

Gods, this was supposed to be her home. Never perfect, certainly not always fair. But home. Safe.

Now, the king who should have been standing on that balcony was rotting in the dungeon. And according to Rois, his conditions were nowhere near as pampered as Othin claimed. And his sisters, her friends?

Ember looked up into Rois's face, her voice shaking with fury. "She will *never* establish peace in this kingdom."

Just for a moment, Rois tore his gaze from the balcony to meet hers, his russet eyes blazing. "No. She won't. But she's certainly trying. After all," he added, painfully dry, "I'm proof of her good faith."

"Good faith from a woman who invaded us?" Ember demanded.

"I didn't say it was effective," he said. "But by keeping all of us alive, she's at the very least removing potential fuel from the fire."

"Still," Ember said, "how long until Othin decides he's had enough of Deardryn's way?"

"That's the golden question," Rois murmured. He redirected his gaze to the balcony, Ember ignoring Othin's speech as she turned over Rois's words.

She had no idea if Deardryn's strategy was effective, but she had to believe the Ash citizens wouldn't make it easy. She had to believe that there was something *she* could do about this. Not just for her own sake.

Ember's hand drifted to her wrist, Othin's words filtering back into her awareness.

"Throughout this week, I've also been in discussions with one of your Ash political leaders. After countless hours of negotiations and explanations, I can officially report we have come to an agreement. And as a sign of good faith, she has agreed to address you herself."

She? Who was he talking about?

Ember glanced around the crowd, but the outrage had shifted into confusion as people exchanged looks and whispers. She looked back at Rois, about to ask. But her attention was caught by the balcony door opening once more.

And the entire kingdom sucked in a breath as Aeley emerged from the shadows.

Chapter 5

"**N**o fucking way," Rois breathed.

Ember couldn't move. Not as she stared into Aeley's face, finding nothing behind her cool gaze. Somehow still managing to send Ember spiraling back in time. Back to the funeral pyre, smoke stinging her nose, the screams from Accalon's chambers echoing in her ears.

She didn't remember how she and Rois had managed to escape the castle with Lucilla's body. It was all a blur of grief and fear and dark stone passageways, Rois urging her along with every staggering step.

Somehow, they'd made it to open air. And all Ember could do was follow Rois as they snuck out into the kingdom and its endless hidden pathways.

She vaguely recalled stopping to rest in a sitting room hidden in a supply warehouse. But she would never be able to forget the image of Rois settling Lucilla's battered body on the funeral pyre he'd constructed and striking a match.

The two had stayed in that spot for hours as Lucilla burned, Rois stiff and silent, Ember hugging her knees to her chest as she cried.

She was dead. All alone, her family not even getting to say goodbye. Unable to burn in the flames of Mt. Vasolus like every other Ash Royal. She was just... ash.

Eventually, the flames died out. They hadn't tried to stop the wind from carrying her ashes away, but Ember caught the last small handful and dumped it in her pocket, later transferring it into the three phoenix charms on her bracelet.

If she was being honest, she'd gotten the charms with her devinroot in mind. But now, it was because Lucilla deserved to have at least a part of her released by her family. They deserved to get that final moment. Ember had included Aeley in that.

Now, she watched the princess's mother linger by the balcony door. She toyed with the ends of her blonde hair, her blue eyes scanning the crowd as if waiting for the uproar.

But the crowd had gone completely still. Silent.

She finally stepped forward, revealing Ronun, the kingdom interrogator, observing from the shadows behind her with a frown.

Ember held her breath, waiting for Aeley to condemn Othin, tell the crowd what happened to Lucilla, anything. There was no possible way this wasn't a ploy.

Aeley paused beside Othin at the balcony, giving him a quick, sidelong look. This had to be it. It was the perfect moment...

"His Majesty tells the truth," she called, her voice flat, clipped.

Ember felt like she'd been kicked in the chest. She staggered back into Rois, barely able to hear Aeley's following words despite the silence around her.

"We have discussed matters. I agreed to stand by him today. And I tell you, Ash citizens, to follow your king." Her eyes drifted to the side, lingering on a statue of a phoenix perched on a nearby roof. Then, without another word, she turned and strode back into the Council Building, Ronun falling into step behind her.

For a few long moments, the crowd seemed suspended in time. Not moving. Not seeming to breathe. The silence stretched longer, and longer, and longer, until Ember realized it wasn't going to be broken. Not by any Ash citizen.

Eventually, Othin cleared his throat. He quickly wrapped up his speech, his words blunter than before. Then, he too turned for the door, his guards falling into formation around him.

The slam of the door behind them rippled through the crowd.

Slowly, one by one, people stirred, realizing this wasn't a dream. There was nothing to try and wake up from.

All except Rois.

"Fucking traitor," he spat.

A few people nearby turned their heads toward him, looking completely at a loss. That was the mother of their king. The woman they were supposed to respect. The woman who was supposed to stand by them. The woman who had abandoned them.

But Ember refused to believe it. There had to be something they didn't know. There was no way Aeley could side with the family who had captured Cadmus and killed Lucilla.

Then again, look how she'd treated Analia.

"Where's her loyalty," Rois seethed, his body shaking with rage. "Where are her priorities?"

"I don't know," Ember murmured, the crowd thinning around her.

She knew where Lucilla's priorities were, though. She'd sacrificed herself for her family, her kingdom. And Ember had promised her that sacrifice wouldn't be in vain.

Ember squared her shoulders, ready to march off; where, she didn't know. Just as a line of green robes caught her eye.

"Rois," she said, standing on her toes to peer over the crowd, "do you see all those healers?"

Rois looked like he was ready to kick the closest thing that moved. But tightening his jaw, he looked to where she was pointing.

"It looks like all the healers are heading for the Council Building," he said, his tone softening a fraction.

"That's what I thought. I'll meet up with you later—"

"Ember, wait a second." Rois caught her by the sleeve before she could leave. "You've already been pushing it with all of your healing. And you still haven't fully recovered from your dev—"

"Oh no no no," Ember interrupted, pulling out of his grip and putting her hands on her hips. "You're not going to displace your need to worry about someone onto me now that Anna's gone."

Rois looked mildly insulted. He started to protest, but Ember went on, "I told you, I'm all right. But you're not going to be if you don't beat Othin back to the castle."

Rois scowled. "Tell you what," he said. "You manage to walk away in a straight line, and I'll keep my 'worrying' to myself."

Ember scoffed. Tossing her hair, she turned and marched off through the crowd, making a rude hand gesture behind her back as Rois chuckled at her immediate lilt.

She never should have told him about her devinroot. Especially since it was a nonissue now. Even though her entire body longed for fuzzy orange leaves as she headed after the healers.

Ember hovered in the back of the Council Building entryway, a crowd of about sixty healers spread out around her. She'd overheard on her way in that Othin had ordered all healers not working in the temple to gather after the meeting—no one having spread the word to her, of course.

Now, they spoke softly in groups across the white marble room, some standing, some seated on the various chairs and couches scattered about. Ember kept to herself, her mind racing.

Why summon the healers? Yes, they'd just gone through a massive battle, she was sure Sun had injured soldiers. But that didn't require assembling this big of a group.

Ember shoved the thoughts aside as there came the sound of descending footsteps. Her gaze flicked to the central staircase, Othin appearing at the top a moment later, Aeley on his right, Ronun nowhere to be seen.

The healers all fell quiet as the two descended, Ember shrinking away from Aeley's searching gaze.

"Is this all of you?" Othin asked the room at large, reaching the foot of the stairs.

The healers murmured an assent, their heads bowed in respect. Ember ducked her head even lower.

"Good," Othin grunted. "I'll keep this brief.

"After the battle, Ash isn't the only one with injured soldiers. I need healers, preferably two, to come and work in the castle. Heal my people... and others."

A few healers turned and whispered. Ember barely noticed, a heady sort of buzz moving through her veins.

She was right. Othin hadn't summoned this group to find the best healer for his people. He was trying to find the most trustworthy people to deal with his prisoners. After all, oaths or not, he didn't seem like the type to trust easily.

This was exactly what she needed: a way to get into the castle, see what she could do from the inside. But how could she guarantee her selection?

"Normally," Othin continued, slouching against the railing, "I would have Sun people take care of Sun people. But given your oaths of neutrality"—a sharp glance around—"I thought it would be wiser to use the healers in this kingdom rather than bring in those from mine."

She couldn't come off as too eager, that would make him suspicious. But if she was completely disinterested, he would look right over her. Maybe she could subtly get his attention...

Ember inched away from the wall, trying to shift into his line of sight. Just for Aeley's blue eyes to flash to her.

A jolt ran down Ember's spine. She cringed back against the wall, her eyes wide as she looked away.

That was *not* the attention she wanted. Especially since Aeley knew about her friendship with Analia and Cadmus.

How was she supposed to lie around that? Rosala spare her, if Aeley was going to be involved in the picking, and she had truly converted, Ember stood no chance.

"So?" Othin finished, haughtily looking around the room. "Any takers?"

The healers shifted uncertainly. Ember fought the urge to shoot her hand up in the air, Aeley or not.

She really wasn't made for the subtle game. Especially not as her eyes accidentally met his.

"You," he said. Ember didn't know if she wanted to perk up or hide as he crooked a finger at her. "You look half-interested."

Oh gods, what should she do? What should she say?

"My duty is to heal," she said, shifting from foot to foot.

"Yes, as an apprentice." Othin's nose wrinkled. "With only three rings as well."

Not to mention on probation. Ember waited for one of the other healers to bring that up, but perhaps she wasn't the only one that struggled with neutrality. Gods, an apprentice, friend of the king, and stared down by the woman who knew it all.

Ember's mind scrambled, searching for an angle, Othin turning away.

"She might actually be perfect," Aeley mused.

Ember's jaw nearly dropped.

"Why's that?" Othin asked, bored.

"She's a friend of Cadmus," Aeley said, resting a finger against her chin. "She could be exactly what you're looking for."

"If she's his friend," he said, lowering his voice, "then she's the *last* person I want to deal with."

So, this *did* have something to do with Cadmus. Ember ducked her head, knowing silence was her best weapon now.

"If she was any other person, yes," Aeley agreed. "But she's sworn to neutrality. Meaning she might be the only one who can get him to consider cooperating."

Othin looked less than impressed. Ember, meanwhile, was giving herself a headache trying to figure out what Aeley's game was. Regardless, this was the opening she'd been looking for.

"Your Majesty," she said, stepping forward with a bow. "I can't lie: I am friends with His Majesty. I don't wish to see him harmed. But I also understand my oath. If you're looking for him to cooperate, and if by cooperating, he'll be out of harm's way... I fail to see why I can't abide by my oath, my wishes, *and* be of use to you."

Ember stared up into his face, trying to appear pleading, unassuming.

Othin didn't respond immediately. He scratched his beard, Ember wanting to jump out of her skin with anticipation. But she bit down hard on her cheek, forcing herself to stay quiet. Patient. Compliant.

Finally, Othin looked to Aeley. "If she betrays me," he said, "you'll be the one to pay for it."

Aeley held his gaze, unflinching. And Ember thought her knees would buckle as Othin turned back to her and gave a sharp nod.

Doubting he would appreciate a thank you, Ember bowed once more, then scurried back to the wall. She barely registered Othin calling on various other healers, eventually settling on a master healer named Tayla whom Ember had never liked.

Finally, *finally,* she had an in. Now, she just had to help Cadmus, and then he would take back the kingdom, she would get reinstated as a healer, and everything would be fine again. It had to be.

She could do this. Even as her hand absently went to her nose.

Chapter 6

To Analia's surprise, Sylas didn't keep her waiting long. The evening following their meeting, her cell door clanged open, revealing the friendlier of her two guards.

"You're in luck," he said. "You've been summoned."

"By who?" Analia asked, keeping her expression blank.

"His Majesty." The guard beckoned with his torch as he stepped aside, holding the cell door open for her.

Analia hesitated, glancing at the purple pine wreath tattooed above his eyebrows. Definitely a Moon guard. Still, better not to come off too in the know.

Analia slowly rose to her feet. Keeping an eye on her guard, she crossed her cell, finally stepping into the dim corridor beyond. Just to come face-to-face with a trio of maids.

The three wore identical black servant uniforms. The woman in the center was taller, her posture perfect, her light brown hair braided over her shoulder. But it was the two off to the side who perked up as Analia emerged, something like curiosity gleaming in their almond-shaped eyes.

"Hello, Your Highness," the center maid said brightly, leading the others in a bow. "I'm Leila, the head maid of the Moon Castle. His Majesty requested I come and introduce you to Tashia and Letta"—she gestured to the maids in turn—"whom he's assigned to you."

Letta began, "It's a pleasure to meet—oh, ouch." She ran her fingers down her temple, mirroring the spot where Analia's head still ached. "These guards, I swear."

Ignoring the guard's pointed cough, she stepped forward and looped her arm through Analia's. "Come, let's get you out of this darkness."

"I think I smelled the gruel they serve down here when we came in," Tashia said, falling in on her other side. "Absolutely foul."

Before Analia could respond, they bundled her off down the corridor, her guard trailing a few paces behind. Together, the group wound back through the narrow halls, the maids' cheerful voices mostly drowning out the moans and pleas of prisoners as they discussed their shock that a Royal had been left in such deplorable conditions.

They reminded Analia of her maids from the Sun Kingdom. Bie and Nadi had been the first people in she couldn't remember how long who hadn't gawked at her and her lack of magic. They hadn't just treated her kindly, they had treated her... normally. Like she was any other person they could have encountered in the castle.

And that earnest acceptance had contributed to her slowly lowering her guard.

Knowing Sylas, he'd selected her maids for that very reason. After all, alliances only went so far.

Shoving the thoughts aside, Analia allowed her maids to usher her up a steep stone staircase, Leila pushing open the door at the top. Analia cringed away from the sudden light, the door's probable glamor magic tingling across her senses.

It took her several seconds to finally register the castle entryway before her. And once again, Sylas surprised her.

He leaned against a marble fountain in the center of the deserted entryway, his hand lazily trailing through the water. At the thud of the door closing, he looked up, finding Analia in the crowd.

His nose wrinkled. "Why are they always so dirty?" he muttered.

Analia scowled, fighting the urge to pull at her shirt. "I'm sorry," she said. "I wasn't aware there was a bathing schedule."

"Your Majesty," Leila cut in with a bow, "forgive me, but the dungeons are rather filthy. I'm sure Tashia and Letta will run a bath as soon as they reach Her Highness's chambers."

Analia's scowl deepened as Tashia and Letta nodded vigorously on either side of her, but spotting Leila's warning look, she kept her mouth shut. Even as Sylas tilted his head, his eyes scanning over her face with unnerving consideration. Then, with what she could have sworn was a flicker of satisfaction, he pushed off the fountain.

"I suppose that's acceptable," he said, sauntering closer. "I trust her chambers have already been prepared?"

"First thing this morning," Tashia confirmed.

"Good."

Analia stepped forward to meet him, expecting him to want to shadowjump her away. But Sylas slid his hands into his pockets, his gaze flicking over her shoulder to where her guard quietly lingered.

"Tavian," he said. "Remind me, why were you put on dungeon duty?"

Tavian shifted uncomfortably, his chain mail clinking. "I called Captain Byron a jackass during training last week."

"Ah." Sylas nodded solemnly. "You'll be assigned to Her Highness from now on. It's a far more fitting punishment since she, too, doesn't know when to stop talking. You two can battle it out to see who has the higher word count."

Tavian snorted, but Analia was barely paying attention. Her eyes scanned over the entryway, noting all the branching hallways and staircases, the soft burble of the fountain camouflaging any approaching footsteps.

Why were they lingering in such an open area?

"Sylas," she said, "don't you think—"

"*Sylas?*" he repeated innocently.

"Your Majesty," she ground out. "Don't you think we should be going?"

She met his gaze, then pointedly glanced at the wide-open entryway behind him.

"Yes, I suppose there's nothing else to cover." Sylas rubbed his chin with a slow, languid movement that had Analia wanting to jump out of her skin. "All right, Leila, you can return with me. The rest of you—"

"Sylas?"

The blood seemed to drain from Analia's body. She twisted on her heel, her mind a flurry of escape routes and possible explanations as her maids mirrored her movement. But it was too late.

"There you are," Deardryn said, emerging from the hallway to Analia's right. "I've been looking for you. I was hoping we could..."

Deardryn's voice drifted off as she looked over the crowd, immediately finding Analia.

Analia didn't think she was breathing.

The last time she'd seen Deardryn was back in Accalon's chambers. Right after she tried to plunge a dagger into her brother's stomach, piercing through Lucilla's throat instead, her breaths making a horrible wet gurgle—no.

Analia dug her nails into her palms, struggling to force the images back down. Focus. She had to focus.

She stared into Deardryn's face, trying to gauge her reaction. But Deardryn merely tucked a lock of hair behind her ear, appearing as though she were studying an experiment she hadn't expected to play out as it did. And Sylas, looking as bored as ever, barely spared her a glance.

"You needed something?" he asked.

Crystal spare them, he was as bad as Aaron.

Deardryn remained unfazed. "I see you've released my prisoner," she commented, her purple skirts whispering on the ground as she approached.

"I did," Sylas said. "And just in time it seems."

Deardryn paused beside him, her head cocked. "What do you—"

"Look at her face, Deardryn."

Sylas reached out, turning Analia's face with a finger. Analia remained perfectly still as Deardryn stared at her, her eyes widening a fraction as she spotted the bruise on Analia's temple.

"I see," she murmured.

"How astute," Sylas replied, impossibly dry. "Personally, I don't remember seeing this bruise when she arrived last week. Tavian?" He turned to the guard. "Did *you* happen to give Her Highness this mark?"

"No, Your Majesty."

"Interesting. Which means either Analia took up banging her head against the wall in all her spare time, or the guard *you* assigned is responsible."

The second guard was a Sun guard? That at least explained his particular dislike of her. But the fact that he wore a Moon guard uniform was going to make things complicated.

Across from her, Deardryn's eyes narrowed. "Analia has always been clever," she said. "It was likely inflicted after being caught in a scheme to escape."

Sylas shot Analia a look. She shrugged, seeing no reason to deny it. Sylas ran a hand down his face in an obvious look of *Why me?*

"At any rate," Deardryn went on, "I'm surprised you're so invested in the safety of a traitor."

"I'm invested in the condition of our leverage." Sylas finally turned to face her fully, his expression hard. "I know you see her as the woman who killed your son, but that doesn't change the fact she is an Ash Royal. According to the story you told me, you kidnapped her in front of her lover and her brother.

"Do you honestly think they won't try to retrieve her? That their desire for retribution won't be influenced by the treatment she's received?"

"The brother is a nonissue," Deardryn said flatly, squeezing the golden bracelets around her wrist.

Analia flinched.

"I don't see the former locked in my dungeon," Sylas said. "What was his name, Adrian?"

"Aaron," Analia breathed, a fresh crack running down her chest.

Deardryn's gaze flicked to her, and Analia didn't try to straighten her expression. Let her see every scar, every spark of hatred she'd created.

"So, what's your plan, Sylas?" Deardryn asked, running her fingers down a nearby moonstone pillar. "Are you to let her roam free in your castle? Have you decided you prefer to learn your lessons the hard way?"

A muscle in Sylas's jaw ticked. "Were you planning on keeping her imprisoned indefinitely?"

"I was planning on releasing her when I was ready to deal with her."

"Well, I'm ready now. And I have my own methods of keeping her in check."

Without further comment, Sylas unsheathed the scarsworn dagger from his belt. Analia and her maids perked up. Even Deardryn straightened.

"You would bind yourself to her?" she asked softly.

"I would." Sylas motioned for Analia's maids to step back. "I'd be happy to make another if you'd also like one. For your research, of course."

Deardryn's lip curled. Ignoring her, Sylas sliced open his palm with a quick, practiced move, collecting his blood on the tip of his blade.

"I swear to do no harm to you, Princess Analia Valarus, and provide safe lodging in my castle. In exchange for my assistance, you will enact no schemes that could harm my citizens and will cooperate with me when ordered."

Sylas flicked his fingers impatiently. Analia hesitated, running through his words. She hadn't missed how he'd refrained from specifying what "assistance" included, which was a good sign for future aid. And none of her schemes to retrieve the Crystal shard should harm anyone.

But what did he mean, cooperate with him when ordered? That could be interpreted as vaguely as "assistance." Well, at least that gave her maneuvering room.

This was as good as it was going to get. So, she extended her hand, palm up. "I agree."

Sylas slid his free hand under hers, lightly trailing his bloody dagger tip across her wrist.

Immediately, a flurry of tingles raced across her skin, wrapping around her wrist. And when Sylas pulled away, she found a chain of moon phases tattooed into her skin like a bracelet, each purple symbol no bigger than her thumbnail.

"Pretty," Tashia murmured. Leila elbowed her, and Analia glanced back at her with a faint smile.

"It is." Ignoring Deardryn's stare, she accepted the dagger Sylas offered her, hilt first. "I swear as well."

Analia sliced open her palm, her hand stinging as she collected the blood and reached for Sylas. Finding his hand, wrist, and forearm decorated in intricate purple and black lines, she touched the dagger to his unmarked thumb. Her blood seeped into his skin, forming a constellation of a phoenix.

Analia's eyes stung. She handed the dagger back to Sylas, whose brows contracted as he studied his new tattoo. Before she could worry the stars clued him in on who exactly her "lover" was, he lightly ran his finger over the marking.

"I see why Patryclas liked you," he murmured.

Analia was surprisingly touched. Sylas, meanwhile, slid his gaze to the side, taking in Deardryn's folded arms. "Were you hoping to say something?"

Deardryn's flash of temper was so quick Analia nearly missed it.

So, this was the reason Sylas had waited to make their oath. He wanted Deardryn to have no way to object, no way to question what their oath entailed.

Clever. But Deardryn was never one to be outplayed for long.

Ignoring Sylas, she stepped past him, coming to lift Analia's chin with a long, cool finger.

"Your fangs remain sharp, little dragoness," she murmured. "That's good. You'll be needing them. Our work starts tomorrow."

"Your promises sound like threats," Analia informed her, brushing her finger aside with her shackled hands.

Deardryn smiled slightly, then turned back to Sylas. "It's nice to see you around the castle again," she said. "You never know how someone will react to losing their love. It would have been a shame if we had to mourn the loss of not just Patryclas, but your competence."

Sylas's nostrils flared. Analia's eyes flew wide.

Patryclas was *dead?* Could Deardryn have—but why would she kill him when he had no Royal magic?

Deardryn ran an oddly stiff hand down Sylas's arm. Then, she turned and whisked back down the hall she'd originally come from, her flat voice echoing behind her. "Analia's cuffs remain on."

Sylas didn't so much as twitch. Analia's eyes darted to her maids, to Tavian at her shoulder, completely at a loss.

She'd just seen Patryclas less than a year ago at the Solstice Ceremony. He'd survived being poisoned, had managed to preserve his kindness in a political game where that could be used against him, and now he was dead? How many good people had to become casualties?

Judging by the wounded looks around her, this was not the time to ask for details. Especially not as Sylas stiffly turned back to her, his jaw tight.

"Tavian," he ground out, "cut her chain."

Analia reached out, to touch him, to comfort him, she didn't know. But Sylas faded into the shadows, leaving them alone in the entryway.

"Crystal spare us," Leila breathed into the sudden quiet.

Analia could only nod, her heart aching.

Analia's chambers were larger than she expected. Thick, purplish-gray carpet muffled her footsteps as she, Tavian, and her maids stepped inside, Leila having returned to her own responsibilities. Letta busied herself with a cream-colored bedspread as Tashia slipped through a side door, the burble of running water drifting through the chamber a moment later.

The two had sobered considerably since the confrontation in the entryway. Even as Tashia emerged from the bathing chamber, both maids repeatedly offering to stay and assist, Analia could see the relief in their dark eyes as she gently declined and thanked them. They backed out of the room, telling her they were just a shout away if she needed anything. Tavian started to follow, but Analia stopped him with a touch to his arm.

"Tell His Majesty I would like my dagger back," she said. "The one Deardryn's guard took from my boot."

A slow, tired smile curled Tavian's lips. "You're going to cause a stir here, aren't you?"

"Not if my oath has anything to say about it," Analia said, raising her shackled hands, the chain having been cut away by Tavian's dagger.

Tavian's smile grew. Then, promising to find her dagger, he slipped out, softly closing the door behind him.

Left alone, Analia moved to her window. She slid up the pane, taking a deep breath of the night air.

Cold. Fresh. Perfect for chasing away nightmares. But this one had to continue a little bit longer.

Analia sighed. She perched on the deep window ledge and brought her knees to her chest, her fingers finding her enka bracelet on her ankle.

How is everyone? she asked silently.

It was a few moments before Laness's tired reply tingled across her skin. *Hanging in there. Surce is still struggling with the scroll, and I've barely seen Mor with all the time he's spending in the Human Kingdom. But we're all keeping an eye on Aaron.*

How is he?

He misses you.

Which is code for he's brooding. Analia rested her head against the raised windowpane, Laness not trying to deny it. *Would it make things better or worse if I asked you to remind him I love him and am coming back?*

I don't think it could hurt, Laness replied thoughtfully. *How are you doing?*

Well, I'm finally out of the dungeon.

Which means the true game starts now.

If you could just water that down for Aaron when you tell him...

Laness's laugh echoed down their line. Analia smiled, realizing just how much she'd missed the feeling, the sound of genuine laughter.

The two went back and forth a little longer, Analia's eyes wandering across her vanity, her decent-sized bed, the room decorated in the Moon Kingdom's purples and black.

Yes, the game had certainly begun. They'd been playing from the moment Analia discovered her uncle's corpse. But while she'd been a pawn in the Sun Kingdom, while Deardryn and Sylas both thought they'd used her just as easily today, what they hadn't realized was she was constantly learning. Just as she'd been taught.

Analia pulled her phoenix pin from her pocket, her connection with Laness having gone quiet. She ran her fingers along the warm metal, her mind drifting back to Accalon's chambers. How Deardryn had let her keep it to remind her of who she was. But what was she referring to?

The fact she was an Ash Royal? Accalon's family? Or perhaps, the parts of herself Deardryn had learned about first.

Analia's fingers tightened around her pin, a lump rising in her throat. Swallowing it back, she hopped off the window ledge and placed her pin on the vanity. Then, she turned toward her bathing room.

The board was set. And it was her move.

Chapter 7

"Absolutely fucking not," Dimitri seethed. He stood in the center of the book nook, his fists clenched, completely overwhelmed by how the hits kept coming. In the three days since Sylas plucked him from his cell, he'd been trying to stay occupied: binding books, going through Deardryn's order logs, writing his notes to Sylas, and forcing a reluctant Sabi to deliver them. But there was no denying he was still trapped.

His meals were delivered to him. The nook supposedly provided all the entertainment he needed. He couldn't even leave to use the bathing room, instead having been given a chamber pot that had been Blessed—presumably by someone with a relocation Blessing—to whisk everything away. He didn't want to know what Sylas expected him to do about bathing.

He kept reminding himself at least he could do *something* here. But *this?*

Rayner stood in the entrance to the nook, one hand raised defensively, the other holding a tray of food. "I know you don't want to see me," he began.

"So fucking leave!"

Rayner winced, muttering something under his breath. Dimitri couldn't hear it over the roaring in his ears.

He was here. In the book nook, meaning someone had given him permission. He even looked exactly as he had back when they'd first met.

Light brown skin. Perfectly ordinary features, from his dark eyes to his short mahogany hair. Even the stubble along his jaw was the same.

Yet, he'd never seen those shadows under his eyes before. Nor the exhaustion that weighed down his shoulders. And the fact that that was all he could read from Rayner had him wanting to scream.

"I promise, Dimitri," Rayner said, shifting his tray to his other hand, "I'm just here to drop this off and leave."

"You *promise?*" Dimitri exclaimed, the absurdity almost making him laugh. "Because your word means everything, right? Which is why you refused to give it to me throughout the months of you *lying* to me. Betraying me to Sylas and Deardryn—"

"*Not* to Deardryn—"

"Betraying me," Dimitri said over him, "over and over and fucking over again."

Memories played on an endless loop in his mind. Every time Rayner deflected when asked about his oath with Sylas. The look of regret on his face at the Full Moon Festival. The way his eyes darted away when creating Dimitri's Moon Royal disguise.

They were such small moments. But they were there. He had caught them. And the fact that he hadn't put the pieces together stung almost as bad as the image itself.

I won't choose your life over mine.

Dimitri stared across the open space between them, desperate to see even a flicker of regret, shame, *anything.* But Rayner only opened his mouth, paused, and looked away.

"And you still can't even apologize for it!" Dimitri said, throwing up his hands.

Rayner started to reply—gods, please, give him *something.* But he cut himself off with a jerk of his head, and Dimitri didn't try to hide his disgust.

"Look," Rayner said, raking a hand through his hair. "I never wanted—"

"Oh, fuck off." Dimitri turned and stalked around Sabi's desk, putting it between them. "I don't need your shitty attempt at a peace offering. Sabi's already bringing me dinner."

"No, she's not," Rayner said quietly.

Dimitri's head snapped toward him. "Why not?"

"Because," he said, taking a step closer, "Sabi has been requesting leftovers at every meal for the past three days, and people are starting to notice. Not only is it suspicious, but it could implicate her when Deardryn inevitably finds out you're not in your cell."

Dimitri's lips parted, but no words came out. He should have thought of that. After all, Sabi had never gotten a firm grasp on subtlety.

"So then have someone else take over," he said. "Anyone else. The servant Sylas trusted the night I was freed."

"That was me," Rayner mumbled.

Of fucking *course* it was.

"But Sylas said it was a servant," he protested, his hands tightening around the edge of Sabi's desk.

"I might as well be one now. He's been keeping me close since I'm the only one he can trust after..."

Rayner's voice trailed off. And Dimitri couldn't think, couldn't breathe, around the white-hot wave that slammed into him. The fact that Sylas had assigned Rayner to Dimitri after he'd enabled, demanded, Rayner's betrayal? When he *knew* what that had done to Dimitri?

And Patryclas...

"Hey!"

Dimitri gripped the desk, struggling to shove back the grief, the rage, as Sabi swept into the book nook.

"What in the name of the Crystal do you think you're doing?" she demanded.

Rayner rubbed his temple, looking nowhere near ready for a second round. "I'm just dropping off Dimitri's dinner."

"I told you I would take care of that."

"I don't see your tray."

"Because the one I requested is in your hand—"

"You knew?" Dimitri broke in, looking to Sabi.

Gods, the hits just kept coming.

"Yes," Sabi said, raising her chin defiantly. "I found out when he tried to deliver your breakfast the morning after you arrived, and I threatened to hit him with a very heavy book if he tried to step inside. Speaking of which."

Sabi turned to her bookcase. And Rayner, clearly running out of patience, took the opportunity to slip past her.

Dimitri's heart jolted. He leaned away, but Rayner only dropped his tray on the desk with a clatter and retreated, his hands raised. He warily glanced between Dimitri and Sabi, the latter now standing ready with an intimidatingly large book in hand.

"Sylas has ordered I take over Dimitri's meal deliveries," he said, obviously struggling for calm. "I didn't request it; it wasn't my idea. But it makes sense. I have more reasons to be requesting extra meals, and Deardryn will have no reason to connect them back to you, Dimitri, because of my betrayal."

His voice caught on the final word, but his gaze didn't waver as it met Dimitri's. Finally showing him the regret Dimitri had thought he'd wanted to see. But now, all he wanted to do was twist the dagger in that wound until Rayner felt the agony ripping through his own chest.

"You've made your point, Rayner," Sabi said, stepping into his line of sight, book raised. "Now leave."

Rayner bit his lip. He looked down at her, that same regret flickering in his eyes. Then, with a nod, he turned to go. Just before he passed back into the library, he looked back.

"Sylas freed Analia tonight," he said. "He kept it hushed, and I doubt he would want me to tell you. But I thought you should know."

He stared into Dimitri's face, waiting for a response. But Dimitri could only blink, his mind wiped completely blank. Then, before Sabi could hit him with her book, Rayner disappeared back into the library.

As soon as he was gone, Dimitri turned to Sabi. "Is it true?"

"I don't know," she said, seemingly just as startled as he was as she paced around the room. "I didn't see her at dinner tonight, but that ended a while ago. He could have gotten her out afterward."

Dimitri didn't know what to think. He didn't know what to do. Gods, he didn't know anything.

He slumped down in his usual seat at Sabi's desk, ignoring the tray of food even as the smell of meat and peppers had his stomach growling. Sabi paced around him, her book still raised as if she were expecting Rayner to try and return.

"I'm surprised you were willing to risk damaging a book," he said after a moment.

"It was already damaged from Princess Marcella folding the pages. I figured it could handle a few dents from Rayner's head before I fixed it."

Dimitri's lips twitched, even as his entire body ached. Gods, it was such a familiar ache, too.

The ache of rejection. Not being chosen. Forced to dissect every single word for the motive behind it.

He'd thought he'd left that behind in the Sun Kingdom. Yet, there he was, unwilling to believe in the sliver of hope Rayner had tried to give him.

Dimitri looked up as he felt Sabi pass by, evidently deciding the threat had cleared as she replaced her book on the shelf.

"So," he said, drawing out the word. "I take it you're not on friendly terms with Rayner either?"

"He betrayed you!" Sabi exclaimed, looking back at him like he was speaking utter nonsense.

"I know," Dimitri said, fiddling with the napkin on his tray. "But you were also friends with him."

"Until he hurt *my* friend. And logically speaking, if he could do that to you, what's stopping him from doing that to me?"

"Rayner would say it was circumstantial," Dimitri muttered.

"Was it circumstantial when he decided to be your friend?"

That question hurt. A lot. He'd been avoiding that question ever since he found out about Rayner's betrayal, unsure which answer would destroy him more. The possibility

Rayner had befriended him purely on Sylas's orders, or that he'd cared enough about Dimitri to be his friend, but not enough to pull away.

But Rayner's actions didn't make sense with either of those options.

Why help him get into Scarsthain if he was only sent to spy? Why not find a different way to maintain his oath if he'd truly cared for Dimitri? Why care for him at all if he knew he would betray him later?

Well, the answer to that last one was easy: he didn't care. He was just really good at faking it.

Dimitri squeezed his eyes shut, blocking out the memory of a cold winter afternoon.

"Sabi," he said, "what happened in the Wraithhouse after I left?"

Sabi hesitated. Her footsteps approached the desk, her chair scuffing across the carpet as she pulled it out to sit. "I'll tell you if you start eating," she finally said. "I'm all for pettiness, but you're almost two weeks behind on meals because of that cell. Besides, I was the one who requested it, so really, the food is from me."

Dimitri breathed out something that could have been a laugh. Slowly, he straightened in his seat, obediently picking up his fork. Sabi waited until he'd swallowed his first bite before she began.

Apparently, not much had happened. As soon as Dimitri left, Rayner showed the wraiths the top of his tattoo, explaining he had a blood oath with Sylas, who had given him permission to come. After some squabbling about the stolen pulsepearl, he told them they were welcome to call Sylas down there to confirm, which they did.

"At first," Sabi said, "I thought he was stalling to give you time."

"He's spent a lot of time with wraiths, after all," Dimitri mumbled.

"That's what I thought. But then Sylas arrived and he... he confirmed everything."

Sabi's chin trembled. For the first time, Dimitri realized he'd betrayed her, too. Maybe not as badly, not as directly, but he'd certainly betrayed her trust.

Dimitri extended an awkward hand. But Sabi rose, going to fuss over the meager possessions Dimitri had discovered in his pack.

"After that," she said, "Sylas disappeared, and the wraiths let me and Rayner go. And then Rayner walked me back to the castle, refusing to answer any of my questions. He just said he was sorry and left me inside the gate."

Something sharp sliced through Dimitri's insides. So, Rayner could apologize to Sabi, but not to him?

Sabi didn't seem to notice his reaction as she straightened his poetry collection beside his pillow, sending a fresh ache ripping through him. Because Rayner had packed his bag. Which meant he was the one who had made sure that book ended up inside, even though it had been taken from him before he was tossed in his cell.

Gods, it didn't make sense. It wasn't fair. None of this was fucking fair.

Dimitri blinked hard, forcing his vision to clear. Then, he stabbed another forkful and brought it to his lips.

There was nothing he could do about any of that. All he could do was take one step at a time. Forward. Out of the past.

And he intended to do just that.

Chapter 8

Analia woke to a quick knock on her door. Tashia and Letta crept inside, offering hushed greetings and apologies for how early it was, but Analia easily waved their concerns aside.

"So," she said, nodding to the breakfast tray in Tashia's hands. "Another tray?"

The previous evening, she'd emerged from the bath to find an identical tray waiting for her on her desk.

"His Majesty has decided it's best to keep you separated for now," Tashia said apologetically, setting her tray on the vanity as Analia came to sit. "We're to bring you your breakfast and lunch in here."

"You can have dinner with the other Royals, though," Letta said, hefting the garment bag she'd been carrying onto the desk. "Last night was a special circumstance, since dinner had already ended. But Tavian has orders to escort you to the dining room each night going forward."

"And I presume he's currently on his way to escort me to Deardryn?" Analia asked.

Letta winced. "She requested to see you first thing."

Analia smiled at her food, expecting nothing less after her months of early mornings in the Ring Room. "In that case," she said, "I suppose I shouldn't keep her waiting."

Despite her words, Analia didn't rush through her meal. She took her time as she chewed, Letta fussing with the garment bag behind her, Tashia finding a comb in one of Analia's vanity drawers.

After her months in the Starlight Kingdom, she'd grown accustomed to taking care of herself without assistance. But she couldn't deny how her body relaxed as Tashia gently ran the comb through her hair.

Gods, she'd been alone in that cell for so long. But this was no time to get comfortable. Not as she watched Letta pull her gown free in the mirror.

The floor-length gown was a deep black, shrouded in layers of shimmering, dark purple lace. The long sleeves flared at the wrists, the neckline modestly low.

It was completely Deardryn's taste—if not her coloring. And a part of Analia was quietly disappointed she wouldn't be wearing it.

"You don't have to bother with that, Letta," she said, swallowing her last piece of fruit. "I won't be needing it."

"I'm sorry, but Queen Deardryn sent this herself."

"I know. But I already have an outfit for today."

The rustle of lace quieted as Letta looked back at her. Analia gestured to her bathing room with her fork.

Obviously intrigued, Letta let the dress fall to the desk, then headed for the ajar door. Tashia continued her combing, but Analia caught her eyes flicking to the door in the mirror as Letta snorted.

"Princess Analia," she said, poking her head out with a grin. "You are *looking* for trouble."

"I don't know what you're talking about," Analia said innocently.

Letta laughed. She emerged with a bundle of dark clothing, her golden-brown eyes sparkling as she lifted them for Tashia to see.

Tashia grinned. And Analia caught the faint crease between her brows in the mirror as her dark eyes lowered back to Analia's hair.

Analia stepped into Deardryn's new study, Tavian giving her a sarcastic farewell as the door closed between them.

The floor was covered by a thin lavender carpet. A wrap-around counter stretched across the walls, its surface scattered with various note-taking supplies and instruments Analia didn't recognize, the wall hollowed out into crowded shelves.

In the center of the room, Deardryn sat behind a massive wooden desk, golden curls falling into her face as she scribbled in what Analia could have sworn was a diary.

At the quiet thunk of the door, her honey eyes flicked up.

"Honestly, Analia," she said, returning her gaze to her writing, "is this necessary?"

"Are you referring to my punctuality, or the fact I haven't bowed?"

Deardryn released a tiny sigh. Finally, she put down her pen and raised her head.

The Dragoness appeared more worn than Analia was expecting. She'd already noticed the shadows smudged beneath her eyes in the entryway, but her golden complexion was now pale and drawn. Yet, her gaze remained sharp as ever as Analia approached and took the seat across from her.

"It was a dress, Analia. Not ankle cuffs and a collar."

"I'm aware," Analia said. "But I thought it would be nice for us to finally face each other as we truly are. No schemes or secret chessboards."

"So, you've rebelled with your wardrobe."

"That would imply there's something to rebel against," Analia said. "But I'm not your subordinate anymore. I'm not your apprentice, and I'm not your pawn. I'm your prisoner. And I do not bow."

Analia kept her spine straight as Deardryn's gaze pierced into hers, then dragged down to her dark shirt and pants. She'd washed them in her tub the night before to get rid of the smell, but they were still recognizable as the clothes that had become her prison uniform.

Analia rested her hands on the desk, letting her damper cuffs thud against the wood. And Deardryn offered the ghost of a smile.

"You're learning," she murmured.

"I believe you said you wanted to see how much I've sharpened my fangs."

"I did. And I'm even more pleased to see you claim that work." Deardryn leaned forward. "Never let someone else take credit for your growth. They might have inspired you, even helped you, but you did that yourself."

Analia breathed through the ache in her chest. This was the woman that had left her uncle to die, tried to kill her brother, killed her sister, had used her relentlessly for her own gain. She should hate her—she *did* hate her.

So, why did a part of her long for the queen who had taken her under her wing? Who had given her the praise she had craved for so long? Even now, staring into her eyes, all she could see was an earnestness that had her heart breaking.

"I'm surprised you're not trying to claim some of the credit yourself," she said, tracing a groove in the desk.

"I like to think I fall under both the inspiration and help categories," said Deardryn. "After all, it was our training with my rings that finally stirred your magic awake."

Accalon's pin seemed to burn a hole through Analia's pocket.

"Is that why you've done your best to recreate the Ring Room?" Analia rose, wandering over to the nearest counter. "The endless books, the wrap-around feature. Although you've ordered Tavian to stay outside instead of inviting him in like Aaron."

"Aaron was permitted to enter because if he was in the Ring Room with you, he wasn't scheming somewhere else," Deardryn said, folding her hands on the desk. "I'm not worried about Tavian. Even if I were, the work we'll be conducting here is far more... delicate than sensing rings."

"You mean studying the Crystal," Analia said, lightly pressing down on a glass scale.

"I do."

"Then you would think actually having the Crystal with you would be beneficial." Deardryn tilted her head. "Who said I don't?"

"The fact that I only sense your magic network in this room," Analia said. Which also meant none of these objects were magical, either. "I'm assuming the inside of the rock the shard is kept in is a damper, but no damper on its own could contain that kind of power. It's been reinforced, and I *can* sense that magic."

She folded her arms, letting Deardryn read whatever she wanted in that statement. But Deardryn only toyed with her pen.

"So," she murmured, "you *can* still sense."

Analia's brows rose. Deardryn scribbled something down, then closed her diary and slid it aside.

"I do plan on researching the Crystal with you," she said. "That's the entire reason you and your abilities are here. But I believe we owe each other a discussion first. Particularly regarding how we left things."

The fact Deardryn could say that without so much as a tremble in her voice had heat flashing across Analia's skin.

"You mean after you killed my sister?" she asked.

She could have sworn Deardryn flinched. But she didn't hesitate to respond. "Yes. And you attempted to corner me into keeping you close in exchange for your help with the Crystal. A bargain *you* arranged—although I'm struggling to see how you've been upholding your end with how you've been digging your heels in."

"My helping you was under terms of you not harming my family," Analia spat. "Our agreement was voided the moment your dagger pierced my sister's throat. Right after you aimed for my brother, invaded my kingdom—"

"Your kingdom?" Deardryn cut in innocently. "I would have thought your loyalties lie elsewhere now, based on the ring line on your middle finger."

Analia's heart froze. She instinctively touched the spot where her ring had once sat, her mind searching for a response. But there was no point denying it. Not when Deardryn had had months to research everything she could on the Star Royals and their customs.

"We're betrothed," she said slowly.

"That's good," Deardryn said. "You've been well-trained to be queen."

Something about that statement bothered Analia.

Deardryn leaned back in her seat, her hooded eyes studying her closely. But thrown as she was, Analia still spotted the trap.

"Being queen requires having subjects to rule," she said. She folded her arms, waiting for the next mind game. But if anything, Deardryn looked pleased.

"Very good," she said. "You're thinking before blindly responding." She rose from her chair, her footsteps soft as she came to join Analia at the counter. "It's fair to assume I have no reason to know there's a hidden kingdom, so my question was an attempt to confirm. But both of my squads had trackers on them, and I know they made it into the Wild Lands before they disappeared. Just as I know Aaron must have been a little boy when the Shattering occurred, meaning since he's survived this long, he must have had at least one person who took care of him. And I doubt it was that nymph that rescued him."

Analia remained silent as Deardryn reached for a nearby pitcher, pouring herself a cup of pale green liquid. "For queen of a kingdom that prides itself on research," she finally said, "you build a lot of your conclusions on conjectures."

Deardryn let out a surprised laugh. "Fair enough." Taking an obvious sip from her drink, she slid Analia her own cup. "Perhaps I can start again with some concrete facts."

Not waiting for a response, she returned to her seat at the table, Analia warily trailing behind her.

"What would those be?" Analia asked.

Deardryn waited until she was seated across from her, then leaned forward. "I didn't want to kill Lucilla," she said. "I tried to heal her, but even if Cadmus hadn't gotten in my way, there are some injuries even magic cannot heal. For that, I am sorry."

To Analia's surprise, she believed her. Even as the grief sank its claws deep into her stomach. Because she could have sworn she saw the same lost, haunted look in Deardryn's eyes that she'd seen in her own after killing Pryanth.

"You still took her magic," Analia pointed out.

"Would you have preferred I killed Cadmus as well to get what I needed?"

All understanding Analia had curdled in her stomach. There was only Deardryn's voice calling him a "non-issue," Laness's silence as she waited for news of him from Ember. Gods, he had to be all right.

"Would you be apologizing right now if you had killed Cadmus?" Analia asked, choking out the words.

Deardryn gripped her bracelets, her features twisting into anguish. "Will you apologize for killing Pryanth?"

"You mean after he threatened to rape and kill me?"

Something in Deardryn's expression snapped. In a blink, a whip of sunlight slashed across Analia's face, blood trickling from her nose as Deardryn snatched at her life force.

But Analia refused to flinch. She kept her chin high as Deardryn's chest heaved, her magic winking out as quickly as it had come. Since when did she lose control like that?

"So," Deardryn said, her voice almost steady as she wiped the blood from Analia's face with a finger. "You no longer run from pain. I suppose you've felt far worse."

"Yes," Analia said, her own control beginning to fray. "At your hands as well."

"That's not the type of pain I was referring to."

Deardryn dropped her fingers to Analia's collarbone, Analia's weakened mind scrambling to figure out what she was up to.

"It's the pain in here that breaks a person. A pain that leaves no visible scar or trace, and sometimes, you don't even know its origin. Sometimes, it's the loss of that pain that hurts even more."

Deardryn brushed aside Analia's hair, touching the empty spot where her pin usually rested. "Tell me. Does your heart still ache for your uncle?"

Analia's lips parted, but no words came out. Because that pain *had* faded. She'd thought it was because she was healing, learning to live with his loss.

But had she simply become callous? Had she forgotten him, tossed him aside—no.

She would always miss him. He would have been proud she'd let that agony turn into an ache.

But there was something underneath that certainty. Something that felt like a needle dragging through her insides. The same feeling that had made her put her pin in her pocket that morning.

Analia reached for her glass, giving herself a moment as she took a sip of what she realized was pear juice. Replacing her cup on the desk, she asked, "Does your heart still ache for Pryanth?"

Deardryn's flinch was so small Analia almost missed it.

"That must be confusing," Analia murmured. "Still caring for the person who killed your son. On some level, it must feel like a betrayal of not just Pryanth, but yourself—"

Deardryn's eyes flashed. "Leave." She shoved Analia back, her expression hardening into something cold and empty.

Analia didn't wait to be told twice. She wordlessly rose from her seat, taking her cup with her as she exited the study.

Tavian waited for her outside. He lounged against the wall, only looking up once the door had shut behind her.

"That was fast," he commented.

"I was banished."

Tavian laughed. "I heard."

"How?" Analia asked.

"My Blessing." He tapped his ear. "My magic enhances all of my senses. I have something for you, by the way."

Analia's eyes widened as Tavian drew a dagger from his belt, offering it to her hilt first. "You found it!" She accepted the blade, fighting the urge to cradle it to her chest as she rubbed her fingers along the worn leather.

"I figured it would be best to wait until after your meeting," he explained. "It would be a shame if Deardryn spotted it and I had to track it down again. In that regard..."

Tavian's gaze flicked to the closed door. He pushed off the wall, gesturing for Analia to follow as he headed off down the hall.

"I appreciate you getting this," she said, falling into step beside him. "I assume Sylas didn't want to give it to me?"

"Maybe. I didn't ask. I just swiped it from that Sun guard dolt who was also on your prison rotation. So, actually, if someone does spot it, I would appreciate you leaving me out of it."

Analia smiled slightly, glancing at him from the corner of her eye. He reminded her of Aaron during his Sun guard phase: causing trouble, finding endless entertainment as he watched it unfold.

But where Aaron had been calculating, Tavian looked... restless. Like he would let the world burn just for the stimulation.

"Can I ask you something?" she asked.

"You can," he said. "I won't guarantee an answer, though."

Analia's smile grew. "Why did you disrespect your captain?"

To Analia's surprise, Tavian flushed. "It just popped out," he mumbled, rubbing the back of his neck. "I've been informed my mouth moves faster than my mind."

"Does that mean I should be worried about *you* being discreet?" she asked, tapping the dagger at her belt.

Tavian met her gaze. "Only if you give me a reason not to be."

Tingles ran along the back of her neck. Before she could respond, someone rounded the corner ahead of them.

The woman appeared to be a few years younger than Analia, a female guard with short blonde hair trailing behind her. Combined with the thrum of her magic network and her curly black hair, Analia was certain she was a Moon Royal. Analia dipped her chin to her, but the woman barely noticed.

"Tavian," she said, her casual tone ruined by the flush creeping across her cheekbones.

The corner of Tavian's mouth quirked, his brown eyes sparkling. "Good morning, Princess Marcella."

Marcella's flush deepened. Offering a greeting to Analia, she hurried forward, Tavian discretely trailing his fingers along her wrist as she passed. Marcella squeaked and quickly disappeared, leaving her guard to rush after her.

Tavian laughed under his breath.

Interesting. Filing away the information, Analia remained quiet on her walk back to her chambers.

And it was only once the door had shut behind her that she allowed her tiny smile to form.

Chapter 9

Dimitri paced before the book nook entrance, his ears straining for any sound of movement.

Ever since Rayner had claimed Analia was free, Dimitri had been doing everything he could to confirm the story—which wasn't much.

He'd gotten Sabi to promise to do some snooping. He'd reluctantly decided to pester Rayner when he came the next morning, but he'd woken up to find a tray already waiting on Sabi's desk. Which meant eavesdropping was his only option.

Early on in his work with Sabi, he'd learned that the glamor hiding the nook was like a door made from one-way glass. Regardless of whether it was open or closed, outsiders couldn't perceive any aspect of the nook. Yet, when it was open, anyone within the nook could see and hear everything going on in the library. Well, everything in range.

Sabi usually kept the door closed because she hated distractions, resulting in the entrance looking like the same blank wall outsiders always saw. But now, Dimitri had the door wide open, his eyes scanning the bookcase-lined aisle on the other side as he paced.

So far, only a few people had wandered close enough for him to overhear their conversations, no one mentioning anything about Analia. But he'd been a servant in the Sun Castle for twenty years. He knew how gossip spread. Either word hadn't gotten out yet, or Rayner was lying. And he was really getting tired of not knowing which.

Dimitri chewed on the edge of his thumbnail, his gaze wandering along the purple crescent moons across his forearm.

The smart decision was to stay put. Sylas hadn't gone through all the effort to free him undetected just for Dimitri to blow his cover. But the odds that someone would wander past this specific aisle saying exactly what he was hoping to hear was too unlikely. And every second he hoped otherwise was another second Analia was on her own.

Dimitri's eyes darted between the empty nook and the library. Sabi hadn't returned from her morning book deliveries. Most people living in the castle associated him with Rayner's disguise, not his actual appearance—although that disguise had already faded when he was dragged to the dungeon.

His entire being flinched as he tried to think back on that moment, but he was almost positive they had all been Sun guards, not Moon. He doubted there were many Sun soldiers loitering in the library. Even if there were, he had Sylas's vow to protect him.

Dimitri retreated to the corner where he kept his small pile of belongings, shrugging on a dark green cloak. The Old Hag didn't get to force him into hiding anymore. And heart pounding, he turned and marched through the book nook's glamor.

As soon as he was in the library, Dimitri fought the urge to turn and flee back into the nook. Every murmured voice felt like a spotlight trained directly on him, each pair of footsteps tingling across the back of his neck. He was completely exposed.

But that was the point.

Dimitri breathed in the comforting smell of wood and parchment. Then, he headed off through the aisles, keeping his chin high.

This was no different than his years of marching through the Sun Castle, blatantly avoiding his scrub work. He'd quickly learned no one gave someone moving with purpose a second look. It was when he tried to stay hidden, when he wandered aimlessly, that he was caught and punished. Still, he had to wipe his sweaty palms on his pants before reaching up to take a book at random as he passed.

He could do this. As far as he was aware, no one knew of his escape. Even if they did, the last person they would suspect was the random citizen browsing the stacks. He just had to stay calm.

Dimitri followed the yellow and green footprints on the carpet to the central reading area. A handful of people sat scattered around the various worktables, most taking notes on what they read. In the center of the space, two female Moon guards sat on a dark purple couch, speaking softly.

Dimitri started to skirt past them without pause. Just as the one on the left looked up, her blue eyes meeting his.

Dimitri's heart slammed to a stop. Crystal spare him, why did it have to be a guard? Yes, she wore Moon Kingdom colors, but did she have friends on the dungeon rotation? Did she recognize his eyes? Did she—

The guard flashed a polite smile, then turned back to her companion. Dimitri couldn't have kept the relief from his face if he'd tried. He quickly moved to an armchair tucked away in the corner, opening his book in front of him like a shield.

That was too close. And now, he was stuck in this spot, seeing as any movement would guarantee more attention. Well, he supposed he'd wanted to end up somewhere near here.

Dimitri didn't know how much time he spent in his armchair. He kept his gaze on his book, appearing completely engrossed as he listened in on the conversations around him.

Unfortunately, the two guards had nothing of use to him, just complaints about the Sun soldiers Deardryn had inserted into their patrols. Apparently, she was trying to help increase security after Patryclas's death.

Dimitri hunched his shoulders over his book, grief crackling down his spine. A grief that also had both soldiers take a moment before continuing—which was surprisingly comforting.

Patryclas wasn't just missed by Dimitri and Sylas. He'd left a mark on this castle, this kingdom. And Dimitri let that realization drag his mind back into focus, his hands tightening around his book.

She would *not* get away with this.

The soldiers left not long after that, but the reading area was never silent for long. People wandered in and out throughout the morning, Dimitri steadily making his way through his book. But he heard nothing of Analia.

Rayner must have been lying. He was just trying to worm his way back into Dimitri's good graces. Or maybe Sylas had told him to say so to get Dimitri to stop pestering him. And with every moment he remained in his chair, the chances of someone recognizing him grew higher.

What if he was in the wrong spot? This wasn't the only gossip hub in the castle. Could he risk wandering the halls when there were so many Sun people around?

"I swear," a female voice whispered, "Princess Marcella saw her this morning."

"Princess Marcella isn't exactly the most trustworthy source," a second voice replied.

"I thought the same. After all, red hair isn't exactly exclusive to Ash Royals. But apparently, Tavian has been assigned as her guard."

Dimitri's eyes shot up and over his book. Three young maids sat on the couch, their heads bowed together as they talked. Dimitri recognized the short brown hair of Alessi, one of Marcella's maids, in the center.

"You know how she gets when she sees him with another woman," Alessi said, her eyes sparkling. "I'm pretty sure she took note of every freckle Analia had."

It took every ounce of self-control Dimitri had to bring his gaze back to his book, his ears straining.

"I heard she was in the clothes she wore in the dungeon," the second maid said.

"Does that mean she was actually released this morning?" the third asked.

"No," said Alessi, the couch cushions squeaking as she leaned in conspiratorially. "I talked to Letta this morning. Apparently, she *chose* to wear that to provoke the queen."

A savage wave of satisfaction rolled through Dimitri's body.

"Are you sure?" the second asked, unconvinced. "That seems like a reckless move from someone who was just freed from the dungeon."

"Not as reckless as me making Princess Marcella wait for her book," Alessi joked, rising to her feet. "Apparently, the redhead had a dagger, and now Her Highness feels she must know everything about daggers to upstage her."

Dimitri's entire body buzzed as Alessi waved to her friends, then headed off into the stacks.

She was out. She was standing off against the Old Hag. She was *here*.

"I still can't believe Sylas let her out," the second maid muttered.

"I know," said the third. "At least we don't have to worry about him freeing the man that killed Patryclas."

The words hit Dimitri hard enough he was shocked they didn't cave in his chest.

And he didn't think. He couldn't think as he rose from his seat, his feet carrying him back through the aisles to return his book to the shelf, pivoting around and marching right out the library door.

He had to see her. Had to hear her voice. Had to do something about the black void that had been steadily expanding in his chest from the moment he pressed his glowing hands to Patryclas's chest.

Dimitri did a quick scan of the quiet corridor. Then, pulling up his hood, he headed off.

Knowing Sylas, he would have placed Analia in one of the guest chambers instead of in the Royal wing, both to irk her and appease Deardryn. The problem was, that was multiple floors away. But Dimitri knew a back way. If he could make it to the narrow staircase tucked away at the other end of this floor, he would be able to avoid most of the common paths.

Dimitri had barely finished the thought when someone coughed behind him. Crystal fuck him.

He sped up, struggling to keep his pace natural, knowing they couldn't recognize him from behind, the fork in the path approaching maddeningly slow. But if he could make it around the right corner, the staircase was there. Two flights, and it would just be a matter of figuring out which chamber was hers.

Dimitri's skin tingled as the footsteps gained on him. One pair. He could lose one pair.

Dimitri rounded the corner. And a horribly familiar laugh had him jumping back.

"I'm telling you," Dannel said, still laughing as he leaned against the wall with a fellow guard, "one tap to those nerves, and he was done."

Dimitri's magic pulsed in his stomach. He struggled to shove it down, trying to remain silent as he backed away.

"Hey." Dimitri nearly jumped out of his skin as Dannel turned to him. "Are you lost..."

Dannel's eyes met his. And unlike the guard from the couch, there was no mistaking the recognition. "You..."

"Apologies," Dimitri blurted, pitching his voice down, "wrong turn."

Then, he turned on his heel and fled. Continuing down the hall he'd come from, Dannel yelling after him, the person behind him asking what was going on. Crystal strike him down.

Dimitri raced around the first corner, footsteps pounding after him. He never should have left the library—he never should have left the nook in the first place. Gods, how did Deardryn have him terrified, running for his life, in every place he tried to make a home?

Dimitri stumbled around a second corner. Just for a hand to grab him and pin him to the wall.

Dimitri barely choked back what could have been a scream or a sob. He writhed in the person's grip, their touch flaring across his senses, Dimitri waiting for their warm fingers to tighten around his arm—why weren't they tightening?

"What are you doing out here?"

Gods, he couldn't handle this. Dimitri stared up into Rayner's face, emotions colliding inside him until he wanted to explode.

"Stop pinning me against things," he hissed.

Rayner started to reply. Then, his head snapped to the side at the pound of approaching footsteps. "Why am I not surprised?"

Dimitri tried to wriggle free, his clothes too rough against his skin, his lungs refusing to fill. But Rayner tightened his grip.

"I know you don't trust me," he said hurriedly. "But it's me or them."

Dimitri made to respond.

Rayner touched Dimitri's temple, the burst of magic sending him cringing back against the wall. "What did you—"

"I barely altered your features, now get off the wall."

Rayner took several steps back, Dimitri automatically obeying. Before he could make any sense of what was happening, Dannel and two other guards Dimitri didn't recognize rounded the corner.

"Easy mistake," Rayner said to Dimitri, clasping his hands behind his back. "His Majesty's chambers are two floors up. It'll be fastest if you—"

"Rayner," Dannel snapped, stepping toward him. "Who are you talking to?"

Rayner looked at him like he was worried he'd been hit in the head. "King Sylas's newest servant."

"Really." Dannel's hand landed on Dimitri's shoulder, Dimitri fighting back a flinch as Dannel turned him to face him. His golden-brown eyes dragged along his features, Dimitri not daring to breathe.

Who did he trust? The man who could have a knife to his back, or the one who was ready to stab him through the front?

"Why did you run away if you're a servant to Sylas?" Dannel asked softly.

Dimitri swallowed hard.

"Clearly you haven't been on the wrong end of His Majesty's temper," Rayner drawled.

Dannel's grip on Dimitri tightened. "I want to hear your response," he said, not taking his gaze from Dimitri.

Dimitri's magic expanded in his stomach, building the same way it had in Gritta's all those years ago.

He didn't know how he managed to force it back down. Didn't know how he managed to open his mouth. "His Majesty requested me ten minutes ago," he rasped, lowering his voice. "I ran because I'm late and have no idea where I'm going."

Dannel's eyes narrowed. Rayner pointedly cleared his throat.

"Apologies," Dannel said smoothly, finally retracting his hand. "For a moment, you looked like someone I know."

Dimitri gave him a shaky nod, not daring to speak.

"Come," Rayner said, ignoring the guards as he turned on his heel. "I'll show you to His Majesty's chambers."

Dimitri didn't remember telling his feet to move. But somehow, he turned around, following Rayner down the hall, around the corner, out of the guards' sight.

Rayner immediately wheeled on him. "What were you thinking?"

Dimitri wanted to cry as yet another wave of emotion slammed into him.

"Stop trying to help me," he spat, shoving past and continuing down the hall.

"I knew you would want to see her if I told you," Rayner said, hurrying after him. "But you couldn't have waited until I could change your appearance?"

"Because I could trust you to do that?" Dimitri demanded. "I could trust your disguise would actually hold up, that you wouldn't run straight to Sylas to have him stop me? Why, would you have given me your word this time? As if it means *anything*."

Dimitri fired off his accusations like arrows, waiting for Rayner to flinch as they struck home. But Rayner only dragged a hand down his face.

"My gods," he muttered. "You're like a little snapping turtle."

Dimitri's jaw dropped. "Excuse me?"

"You bite down on the first thing you see and refuse to let go."

Dimitri's ears burned. Especially as he saw the flash of amusement in Rayner's eyes.

Gods, how could he do that? How could he look at Dimitri like that when Dimitri didn't even want to hear his name. He didn't want to see his face, or hear his voice, or feel the nausea twisting in his gut whenever Rayner was around because Rayner was still fine. He had betrayed Dimitri, lied to him, and he remained the same.

At least if he'd punched Dimitri in the face, his knuckles would be scabbed over. But this?

He was completely unaffected. He had the audacity to be whole when Dimitri was in pieces.

And Rayner had dealt one of those shattering blows.

"When will you learn I want nothing to do with you?" Dimitri asked raggedly.

Finally, Rayner flinched. He didn't try to follow as Dimitri continued down the hall, his arms wrapped tightly around his middle. He only called, "She's in the guest wing. Third door on the left."

Dimitri didn't acknowledge the comment. He just focused on holding himself together.

Chapter 10

Analia sat at her desk, sketching a map of the Moon Kingdom. She barely registered the quick knock on her door, but her head snapped up as it immediately opened. "I didn't say you could enter."

"Tough shit. You're lucky I knocked in the first place."

Analia's heart leaped. She twisted in her seat, her response stuttering on her lips as she did a double take.

Same voice, slightly longer blond hair, same amber eyes and scrawny build. But everything was slightly off.

"Tell me that's glamor magic I sense," she said, rising to her feet, gripping the back of her chair.

"Masquerader, actually." The man wiped a hand down his face, his features momentarily blurring, then settling back into Dimitri's usual weaselly features.

Analia's eyes stung. She hurried forward, careful not to touch him as she breathed his name. But Dimitri grabbed her extended hand, pulling her into a hug.

Analia let out a startled laugh. "We hug now?"

"Sometimes." He shifted his arms around her, as if he wasn't quite sure he was doing it right.

Analia smiled, burying her face in his shoulder. And if she wasn't already convinced before, the way he momentarily stiffened had her absolutely certain.

This was Dimitri. He'd found her. Meaning the soft thrum of a magic network was also his.

It was just as faint as when she'd hugged him in the Ash Kingdom, to the point she'd started to wonder if she'd imagined it. But at that moment, she couldn't care less about his magic.

"Gods, I missed you," she said, resisting the urge to tighten her arms around him.

"I..." Dimitri's voice cracked. Analia froze.

For the first time, she realized she could feel his heart racing. She pulled back to look at him, something in her chest crumbling as she saw the tears in his eyes.

"Oh, Dima, no," she murmured. She steered him over to her bed, Dimitri not resisting as she guided him down beside her. "What happened?"

She expected him to shrug her off. But apparently, his feelings toward touch weren't the only things to have changed, for at her words, his expression crumpled. And out came the entire story of what had happened since he'd left Ash, his body curling in on itself as he slumped against her pillows.

Analia remained quiet as he talked, knowing all too well that this was a story that had to rip its way free. No interruptions. Even as he reached Rayner's betrayal and she could practically feel the heat of her flames through her damper cuffs. By the time he described Patryclas's death, all of his futile attempts, she was crying almost as hard as he was.

"I never wanted you to know this feeling," she said, wiping her eyes. "I am *so* sorry."

Dimitri shuddered, pressing his face into her pillow. And it was all Analia could do to keep her comforting touch to herself.

"I was in the dungeon for a while after that," he eventually went on, his voice muffled. "Sylas got me out, although he still hasn't told me why. But he's moved me to Sabi's book nook with Rayner—who's my personal servant—"

"He's still here?" Analia asked, sitting up straight.

"That's how I was able to get to you today," Dimitri said miserably.

Analia's fingers curled into the bedspread, but she kept her voice level. "Want me to take care of him?"

Dimitri let out something that could have been a laugh. *"You?"*

"You laugh now, but Aaron's brother has been training me. I can cause some damage now."

She wiggled her fingers as if summoning sparks, and Dimitri finally let out a true, tiny laugh.

"That's it," Analia said, softening once more. "I know it feels wrong, but laughing does help. And it *will* get easier to do so."

"I don't know how." Dimitri sat up, wiping his nose on his sleeve. "Every emotion is so fucking big. As soon as I think I've started to get my footing with the grief, the despair slams into me, and then out of nowhere I'm so angry I want to explode, and I can't *breathe*."

Analia rubbed her chest, feeling the residual ache of the same wound that had Dimitri fisting his hand in his hair. "Am I allowed to touch you?" she asked.

Dimitri's mouth pinched, but he nodded. Analia wrapped her arm around his shoulders, pulling him closer.

"I don't know how to do this," he mumbled. "I don't know how to survive."

"Believe it or not," Analia said, "you're doing it right now."

"That's fucking bullshit if this is surviving."

Analia laughed slightly. "You're telling me."

"How did you do it?" he asked, leaning his head against her shoulder. "How are you surviving better than I am?"

"Time, mainly."

Dimitri muttered another complaint.

"*You* asked," she said, poking his shoulder. "Yes, time helped the most. But beyond that, the best thing I've done is talk about him—Dimitri, I can feel you tensing up to argue, just let me finish."

Dimitri grumbled something, but settled back against her. Analia fought back her smile.

"I know it feels like talking about him is the most painful thing you can do," she said. "Just the idea sounds like ripping open a wound you've been trying to close. But I promise you, it feels a lot better to remember them than to deny that they're gone. Especially since this grief never completely leaves you. You just learn to cope with it when it comes. And eventually, it feels more like a reminder of what you had rather than something you lost."

Analia's hand drifted to her phoenix pin in her pocket, her mouth turning down slightly.

Dimitri didn't seem to notice. He tugged on a loose thread in his sleeve, obviously searching for a counter argument. Finally, he sagged against her. "I hate you."

"I love you, too," she said, leaning her head against his.

For a few long, aching minutes, the two remained like that. After all that, Analia was impressed Dimitri was still holding himself up. She was glad he was alive—although the fact that he was still in the castle, practically waiting for Deardryn to catch him, made her stomach turn.

She knew Sylas wouldn't have put him in the nook if he didn't think it was secure. But that solution felt temporary in the worst kind of way.

"So," Dimitri eventually said, drawing out the word. "Are you not going to ask about my magic?"

Analia hesitated. "Do you want me to?"

Dimitri went quiet, fidgeting with his sleeve. Clearly not wanting to speak, but not dissuading her either.

"Can I ask how I never sensed you until the Ash Kingdom?" she asked. "I know we were surrounded by Sun magic and I was only just tapping into my abilities, but even now, I can barely detect you."

"My magic isn't powerful," he mumbled. "It takes months for me to accumulate any kind of buildup, and in Sun I released it in the passageways. I was only just starting to reach my limit when I was caught, but by that point, I'd already used most of it when…" Dimitri choked off.

Analia tightened her arm around him, not forcing him to finish the thought. That at least explained why the passageways had been so difficult to block out.

"I almost burned Aaron alive when he provoked me into releasing my magic," she confided.

Dimitri let out a startled huff. "Figures." He paused. "Since you got to ask a question, does that mean I get to ask if you two are a thing yet?"

It was Analia's turn to laugh. "We are."

"Fucking finally."

Dimitri pulled out of Analia's grip, offering her the ghost of a grin. "I can't keep thinking about my sob story anymore," he said, settling back against her pillows. "What have you two been up to?"

Analia rubbed her face, not knowing where to begin with that one. But she told him the best she could, starting with her decision to leave the Ash Kingdom and going into her time in Starlight. Dimitri nodded along with the parts that Laness must have filled him in on, his body visibly relaxing when she told him Surce had discovered the Crystal had been split, meaning Deardryn only had one of three pieces. And he rested his booted feet against her thigh as she described their confrontation in Accalon's chambers, barely able to choke out her retelling of Lucilla's death.

"And that's how I got here," she finished, brushing away her fresh tears. "Sylas left me to rot in my cell for a week, just to summon me into a dream and tell me to plead my case."

"Typical," Dimitri muttered.

"Apparently I must have won him over, since he only made me wait a day before sending Letta, Tashia, and Leila to get me."

"He sent Leila?" Dimitri asked, sitting up.

"You know her?"

"She's one of Sylas's personal maids. The one he told me had been compromised by Deardryn."

Analia's mind buzzed.

Why would Sylas have sent a maid he knew was compromised? Especially when Leila wasn't even assigned to her. Unless...

"He wanted Deardryn to find out," Analia said slowly.

Dimitri's eyebrows shot up. "Why would he want that?"

"Because it makes perfect sense." Analia shoved off the bed, her mind racing as she started to pace. "Sylas knew as soon as Deardryn discovered both of us had been freed, she would suspect one person. But if he could find a way to let her *think* she'd caught him freeing me, then she might not suspect he could've freed you under her nose. And since Deardryn was supposedly planning on getting me out anyway, he could not only use me as bait, but if Deardryn caught him, she would hear what our oath was."

"He made you swear an oath?" Dimitri asked.

Analia nodded, raising her hand and pulling down her cuffs to show off her moon phases. "He planned it all."

"And knowing the Old Hag," Dimitri muttered, "she left it ambiguous as to whether she knew beforehand or stumbled upon you by accident?"

Analia nodded, her eyes widening. She knew Deardryn and Sylas had been playing this game decades longer than she had, but gods, their cunning was almost inspiring.

"Well," Dimitri said, arching his back in a stretch, "this just means you have to up your own scheming. And lucky for you, you have me."

Analia turned to him, about to speak.

"Would you look at this."

Analia's heart jolted as the shadows rippled beside her, Sylas emerging from the darkness with glower in place as he immediately spotted Dimitri.

"Who gave you permission to shadowjump into my chambers?" Analia demanded, stepping between him and Dimitri.

"The fact that *your chambers* are in *my castle*." Sylas's eyes barely flicked to her before returning to Dimitri, who slouched against the wall with his arms folded. "You're lucky it's me that stumbled upon you and no one else."

"And yet, you don't seem too surprised to find me," Dimitri drawled.

"Because Sabi came to me in a panic when she returned to the nook and found you gone."

Dimitri winced.

Analia started to speak, but Sylas stalked around her and toward the bed.

"Did you have a plan in case someone spotted you on your way over?" he asked, his disdain sharp enough to draw blood. "Or were you simply leaving it up to chance? Perhaps you wanted to test just how serious Deardryn is about keeping you locked away, despite all of my measures to prevent her from learning of your escape."

Shadows churned across Sylas's shoulders. But Dimitri didn't so much as blink.

"I was thinking I needed to see Analia," he said. "And that you vowed to protect me."

Sylas snarled. "Mangy little stray. Get up."

Analia stepped forward, acutely aware of her damper cuffs and Aaron's dagger in her boot as he reached for Dimitri.

"Oh no." Dimitri wriggled away from Sylas's hand and rose to his feet, jabbing a finger at Sylas. "This is not how this is going to go. *You* were the one who decided to pull me out of that dungeon. If you didn't want to deal with me, you should have left me in my cell instead of dropping me into another one."

"Ungrateful—"

"And if you're going to lock me in the book nook, I get bathing privileges." Without further comment, Dimitri turned on his heel and stalked into Analia's bathing chamber, kicking the door shut behind him.

For a few moments, Sylas stared at the closed door, shadows flickering around his shoulders. Analia watched him carefully, not sure if she was amused or uneasy as the sound of the faucet turning on drifted under the door. And slowly, Sylas's shoulders relaxed.

"Annoying little creature," he muttered, shadows winking out as he turned to Analia. "I should have tossed him out the day he arrived at my castle."

"Maybe," she said, leaning back against her desk. "Although, Dimitri's been here a long time. I can't imagine Sabi only just got back from her rounds."

Sylas's expression pinched. Before his shadows could flicker back to life, Analia caught his gaze.

"Thank you," she said softly. "Thank you for allowing him to see me."

"Patryclas would never forgive me if I hadn't," he said gruffly.

Just for a moment, Analia could have sworn she caught his composure crack.

"Dimitri told me what happened to him," she said, bowing her head. "I only spoke to Patryclas a few times at solstice ceremonies, but it was enough to know he was kind and honest. He didn't deserve to be turned into collateral damage."

Analia looked up as an icy shadow flicked past her ankle, catching something indescribable pass over Sylas's features. "I'm so sor—"

"Thank you." Sylas sharply turned away, the briskness in his tone having Analia's heart softening. "I'll be back in thirty minutes," he said, striding toward the door. "Dimitri likes to take his time. Inform him that I don't care if he still has soap bubbles in his hair, he'll be coming with me."

Reaching the door, he started to turn the knob.

"Wait!" Analia called, taking a few steps after him. "Give me access to the book nook. If he's there, I need…"

Analia trailed off.

She expected Sylas to shrug her off, at least put up a fight. But all he did was give a curt nod. Then, he disappeared through the door.

Analia's shoulders slumped. She moved to plop down on her bed, her head starting to ache as she turned over everything she'd learned.

Gods, there were so many pieces on this board. So many motives and reasons behind each move. And the worst part was, the more she thought about it, she didn't truly understand the motives of those who'd trained her to play this game.

Where did that leave her?

Analia sighed, leaning back against her pillows as the burble of running water cut off. She supposed there was only one option: figure it out.

Chapter 11

Analia was already awake the following morning when a knock sounded on her door. To her surprise, only Letta stepped inside, the door closing behind her.

"Tashia got stuck waiting for your breakfast," she explained, heading for Analia's armoire. "Are you going to be wearing your uniform again, or can I pick something else?"

"Well," Analia mused, "I think wearing the same outfit two days in a row might be a bit superfluous, don't you?"

Letta laughed. "Oh, most superfluous indeed."

Analia smiled slightly as she slid out of bed, heading for her vanity chair.

She wasn't surprised Deardryn was summoning her back so soon. She'd barely given Analia a day off from her training in the Sun Kingdom, so a pointed poke at her temper wasn't going to keep her away for long. Still, she had no idea what kind of impact that poke would have on their meeting today.

Analia grimaced as she took a seat, Letta emerging from the armoire behind her.

"You don't like it?" she asked, holding up a long-sleeved green shirt in the mirror.

"What?" Analia blinked, then shook her head. "I'm sorry, yes, it's perfect. Thank you."

A faint crease formed between Letta's brows. But she didn't push it as she pulled a comb from a drawer and got to work. For a few minutes, Analia let the quiet hang, absently toying with her phoenix pin on the vanity before her.

"You're awfully quiet this morning," Letta eventually commented.

Analia caught her golden-brown gaze in the mirror, her own expression having fallen back into a frown. "Yes, I'm fine. I just..."

Analia looked down at her hands, briefly biting her lip before glancing up once more. "Can I trust you?"

Letta started. "Of course you can. I've been assigned to take care of you, which means you're my top priority."

She tried to catch Analia's eye in the mirror, but Analia dropped her gaze. But she only let the silence stretch a few moments before admitting, "My stomach has been bothering me this morning. I think it's nerves. Being surrounded by all these Royals, never knowing what to expect from them, never knowing how they'll react...?"

"Of course," Letta said, her voice softening. "It can be unsettling trying to anticipate what the Royals want from you."

"I suppose I'm getting a tiny taste of what you and the others must deal with on the daily," Analia murmured.

"It gets easier. Once you learn their moods and particulars, it becomes instinctual more than anything."

"I hope you haven't needed to adjust to me," Analia said, twisting in her seat.

Letta tilted her head, the corner of her mouth lifting. "I've learned to expect fire from you. Even with these." She tapped one of Analia's damper cuffs, the protective outer layer shielding the spark of her network.

Analia laughed slightly. "I suppose that's accurate." She hesitated a moment, then asked, "Is it all right if we keep this between us? I've already got Deardryn focused on me. I rather not give her any reason to—"

"Your secret is safe with me," Letta promised, helping Analia to her feet.

Analia touched her arm in gratitude. Then, she accepted the bundle of clothes Letta passed her.

"**S**till no Crystal shard," Analia observed, letting the study door thunk shut behind her.

Once again, Deardryn sat behind her desk, not sparing Analia a glance as she scribbled in her diary. Knowing she wasn't one to be disturbed while working, Analia remained quiet as she crossed to her chair, craning her neck to see what she was writing—

"I've been thinking about our last meeting," Deardryn said abruptly, closing her diary.

Analia, expecting nothing less, asked, "Anything in particular?"

"What kind of teacher would I be if I told you first?"

Analia tilted her head. Deardryn rose, tucking her diary in a gown pocket and heading for the door. Poking her head out, she called, "You may enter."

Analia started to turn in her seat.

"No," Deardryn said, pulling her head back inside. "Keep facing forward. I swear to you on the Crystal and gods no harm will befall you."

Well, that was a serious oath. Slowly, reluctantly, Analia turned around, acutely aware of the queen at her back. But also, a second pair of footsteps, light and quick.

"You stay here," Deardryn said to the newcomer.

Analia tensed as she felt Deardryn come up behind her. But she circled around the desk without pause, settling in her seat to face Analia once more.

"Now," she said, "What do you sense?"

"Sense?" Analia repeated, her hands flexing around the edge of her seat.

"Yes, 'sense.' What magic is in this room?"

Deardryn pulled a dark blue book from a drawer in the desk and flipped it open, her pen poised. Analia studied her for a moment, completely at a loss. But seeing no obvious traps, she reluctantly settled back in her seat and reached out a mental hand.

"I sense your magic," she said after a moment. "Nothing else."

"Excellent." Deardryn made a note in her book. Analia twisted her head to see the silent person behind her.

"No turning, Analia," Deardryn chided. "We're not done. You," she said, looking over Analia's shoulder. "You may leave. Tell the next person to enter."

"Yes, Your Majesty," a soft, female voice murmured.

Analia struggled to remain still as the door creaked open, the quiet departing footsteps quickly replaced by a second pair. Once again, the door closed.

"What do you sense now?" Deardryn asked.

Knowing there was no point asking questions, Analia checked a second time, her eyebrows rising. "Your network, and another Blessed."

"Do you recognize the other network?" Deardryn asked.

Analia rubbed the cuff of her sleeve between her fingers, taking a moment to think. "Is that a Moon Royal?"

"Next," Deardryn called, eyes on her notes as her pen scratched furiously.

"What's the point of this?" Analia asked as the door opened and closed behind her. "We already established my sensory abilities a long time ago."

"Just three more tests," Deardryn said, brushing back a golden curl. "Now, again."

Analia bit back her response. She knew that smooth, analytical look on Deardryn's face. She wasn't going to get any answers until Deardryn was ready. Which meant all she could do was play along.

Person after person, Analia reported what she sensed: a strong Blessed network she didn't recognize. A far weaker network that was different from the first, but still unfamiliar. By the time she reached her fifth sensory test, Analia's patience was running out.

She did a cursory scan, her mouth opening to report no magic. Then, she paused.

"What is it?" Deardryn asked, her honey eyes bright.

"I thought there was nothing," Analia mused, absently stroking her phoenix pin through her pocket. "But there's something there. It's so faint, fainter than a whisper. But there's something."

Deardryn's face lit up. "Is it familiar?"

"I'll tell you if you tell me what all of this is about."

Deardryn smiled to herself. Gesturing for the person to leave, she said, "You are dampered."

Analia startled, looking down at her damper cuffs. "I am."

"And yet, you were able to accurately detect the magic networks of a Moon Royal, a Blessed, a Demiblessed with magic, and curiously, one of the rare Demiblessed with no magic, but the extended life span, heightened reflexes, and rapid healing of the Blessed. You also accurately detected my control in the magicless human I first sent in. All while dampered."

"What are you insinuating?" Analia asked slowly.

"A theory." Deardryn rose from her seat once more, pacing around the room. "I've been thinking about your adventure in my garden. It took us three days to summon you, and yet, your injuries from my thorn bush still hadn't healed, even though they normally would have in that time."

"Yes," Analia agreed. "Because the Devourist had drained whatever dormant magic I had."

"Exactly. It slowed down your healing, and I'm assuming your sensory abilities as well since you seemed to struggle for a time after that when hunting my ring."

Analia nodded slowly, the full picture starting to come into focus.

"Yet," Deardryn said, pacing back toward her, "you recognized my magic in your uncle's chambers when dampered. You further were able to correctly assess that the Crystal was not in this room yesterday, and as we just established, the magic networks of all varieties of Blessing."

"Are you saying dampers aren't able to completely block a person's magic?" Analia asked, leaning forward despite herself.

"I'm saying they can only block a certain aspect of magic." Deardryn returned to her seat, flipping through her notes. "We know that Gavare was the first to accidentally create a damper. An object that can block a person's magic is a highly coveted weapon, but due to how difficult it is to create them, access across Elefthia is extremely limited, making research even more so.

"But they were an integral piece to Star Royal life, specifically for the children who wore them while learning to use their magic. In that regard, it's unfortunate Aaron managed to escape. He could have provided so many answers…"

Deardryn paused to read one of her notes. Analia squirmed in her seat, trying to keep quiet as she waited. Then again, why bother?

"Do you think the Star Royals modified the dampers?" she asked. "Made it so their Star magic was blocked, but not the rest of their Blessing? If this happened while Talitha was still ruling, she would've had no trouble spreading the new technique—but then how did she know how to create that separation?"

"How she knew, I don't know," Deardryn said, surprisingly unbothered by Analia's interruption. "But you might have just unlocked *how* the magic was separated."

"You mean with the magicless Demiblessed?" Analia asked.

"And your sensory abilities still coming through your damper." Deardryn closed her notes once more, leaning forward in her seat. "What would you say if I told you we have two magic networks. One that the Crystal Blesses us with, resulting in magic we can wield. The other, passed down from our parents?"

"I would say that creates an entire list of new questions," Analia said.

Deardryn beamed. And despite all those questions forming a knot in Analia's stomach, she couldn't help her own curiosity.

Deardryn might have been a killer, a manipulator, and a traitor, but she was also a genius. And that combination had Analia's curiosity running a few degrees colder.

"So," she said, folding her arms. "Besides fulfilling your own curiosity, what was the point of this experiment?"

"Verification," Deardryn replied. "Now, I know I can keep you dampered."

The knot in Analia's stomach tightened a little more. Especially as Deardryn pulled a slender silver knife from yet another drawer.

"Shall we test our new theory?" she asked.

Before Analia could react, Deardryn reached for her hand. She flipped it palm up, her body freezing as she looked down at the thin, crescent scab running across Analia's palm.

"You got this from Sylas's scarsworn dagger?" she asked.

Analia nodded uneasily.

"Interesting." Without further comment, Deardryn released her hand, slicing a thin cut along the inside of her own forearm. Barely seeming to notice the blood trickling down her arm, she looked back to Analia. "May I?"

"Why?"

"So we can see if we heal at the same rate, regardless of your dampers."

Rising to her feet, she headed for the door, Tavian falling into step beside her.

"You know," she said, rubbing her temple, "most guards follow a few paces behind."

"But then I either have to be silent or talk to the back of your head."

"I suppose that simply won't do."

"Well, if Her Highness insists."

Analia let out a tired laugh. The two rounded a corner, and Analia winced, turning her head away from the bright morning light streaming in through the windows.

"You all right?" he asked.

"Headache," she muttered, keeping her eyes averted. "I've had it all day." She gave him a sidelong look, and he cocked his head. "I would appreciate you not sharing the information. I'd rather not give Deardryn another weakness to pounce on."

Tavian nodded, his eyes flicking up and down the deserted corridor.

The two remained quiet on the rest of their walk back to Analia's chambers. And it took all of Analia's self-control to wait thirty minutes before summoning Tashia.

Chapter 12

Dimitri sat at Sabi's desk, books and papers scattered around him as he took notes.

"You better clean all that up when you're done," Sabi said from the cushion where she read.

"I always do."

Sabi grumbled something, not bothering to look up as she flipped a page. Dimitri took the opportunity to swipe one of her fancy pens from the cup on her desk, drawing a path in shimmering gold through his map of the Moon Castle.

Ever since returning from Analia's chambers, he'd been gathering all potentially useful information for stealing the Crystal. After all, he'd been the Old Hag's servant for years. He knew her habits better than anyone. But that also meant he knew exactly how difficult it would be.

Dimitri was so distracted by his highlighting he didn't immediately register the ripple of magic behind him.

"This seems too complicated to be arts and crafts," Analia mused, leaning over his shoulder.

The constant, heavy fog weighing down Dimitri's being lifted an inch. He twisted to look at her, "How did you get in here?"

"I followed the magic. After Sylas caught you, I told him if he was going to keep you in here, I wanted access."

"I bet he *loved* that."

"Well," Analia said, "if Sylas refuses to tell us what his plans are, we can hardly be blamed for interfering with them."

Dimitri laughed, the sound noticeably rusty. Just as Analia's responding grin looked a little tight.

"I don't have much time," she said, turning to take in the space. "I asked Tashia to escort me here so I could find some books, but I don't know how long I can pretend to be checking these aisles."

Analia finally spotted Sabi tucked in the corner, staring at her owlishly over the edge of her book. "You must be Sabi. I'm Analia. I'm sorry to barge in like this."

"Friends are always welcome," Sabi said with a stretch. "I like your shirt. That dark green is flattering on you."

Analia looked momentarily taken aback. Then, she beamed. "Thank you. I like what you've done with your nook."

Sabi looked positively pleased. Rising to her feet, she asked, "I'm assuming it would be beneficial if your maid found herself horribly distracted?"

"Now I *really* like you."

Sabi grinned. "You have perfect timing. I was just thinking I need someone to talk at about the book on archway construction I've been reading." She breezed toward the exit, plucking the golden pen from Dimitri's hand as she passed. "Mine."

Dimitri looked down at his empty hand with a pout. Ignoring him, Sabi gave Analia a friendly wave, then disappeared into the library.

"Good news," Dimitri said. "You just bought yourself the rest of the afternoon."

Analia laughed, coming to take the seat across from him.

"I'm glad you came," Dimitri went on, turning back to his notes. "I've been compiling everything that could be useful in getting the Crystal. At first, I thought the Old Hag would keep it on her because she's paranoid, but then I remembered she used to hide all of her magical objects. I haven't managed to snoop through her chambers, but I've marked down how to reach them—"

"This is all incredibly helpful," Analia said, softening the interruption with a light touch to his hand. "You have no idea how much I appreciate this. And while I wish I only came here on a social call, there's something I have to tell you."

Something about her tone had Dimitri unable to look up. "What is it?"

Analia hesitated, barely a second. But that was all Dimitri needed to know the words about to come from her mouth.

"Deardryn knows you've escaped," she said gently.

Dimitri froze.

He'd known this moment was inevitable. Just like the moment she spotted him in Patryclas's family's bookshop. But this time, the moment didn't slam into him.

"Gods," Dimitri breathed, slumping back in his seat. "Everything about him bothers me."

"Because he betrayed you, or because he's trying to make himself the martyr?"

"Is that what it is?" Dimitri wrinkled his nose.

Yet, as Analia stole a green bean from his tray, he knew that wasn't quite it. Because Rayner had been telling the truth when he listed all the ways he'd helped Dimitri since leaving the dungeon. True, he didn't know what Rayner could have been doing behind the scenes, and changing his appearance once and keeping his mouth shut were almost laughably shallow lines in the sand.

But they were lines.

Dimitri looked up at Analia as she examined one of his many sheets of notes.

"Thanks for having my back," he mumbled, heat creeping over his ears.

Analia's expression softened. "Thank you for having mine. Speaking of which, I believe we have some notes to go through."

Analia returned to the seat across from him, nudging his tray of food closer to him. Dimitri rubbed his aching chest. Then, straightening in his seat, he turned his attention to his notes.

Dimitri gave the most abbreviated rundown he could. Analia paid close attention as he outlined all of Deardryn's favorite hiding places in the Sun Castle, the two converting the list as Analia described Deardryn's new study.

Seeing as this castle was not her own, Deardryn had three options when it came to hiding places for the Crystal. She either kept it on her person, locked it away in her chambers or study, or went through the extra effort to hide it somewhere that required shadowjumping—which clashed with Deardryn's paranoia and probable desire to keep an eye on it. And none of that included whatever security she'd put in place.

Analia was just folding up Dimitri's highlighted map of the castle when Sabi swept back into the nook.

"I saw Rayner leave a few minutes ago," she said. "I hope his harassed expression was because of one of you."

"Guilty," Analia said, raising a hand.

"Excellent." Sabi flopped down on her pillow. "The good news is I distracted Tashia for a while. The bad news is now she's *really* looking for you. I said I saw you across the library, so you have a little longer."

"Crystal spare me," Analia muttered, rising to her feet and rubbing the back of her neck. "I should go before she calls Tavian to start a hunting party. Speaking of which, is there something going on between him and Princess Marcella?"

"Oh, those two?" Sabi asked, perking up. "She's completely in love with him. I think he likes her, too, but it's hard to tell. They've been on and off for years because every time he seems genuinely interested, she convinces herself he's not and shoves him away. You would think he would be tired of the cycle, but he keeps coming back."

"I'm not surprised in the slightest," Analia said. "Although, how do you know so much about them?"

"Sabi is our local Marcella historian," Dimitri said, flipping through Deardryn's book orders.

"She's like a walking human experiment," Sabi enthused. "She's positively fascinating. I want to put her in a maze and see what she does."

"Good news," Dimitri snorted, "the hedge maze out back is ready whenever you are."

Analia's eyes gleamed. With laughter or something else, Dimitri couldn't tell as she turned away.

She took a few steps toward the exit. Then, she turned back, returning to Dimitri's chair and opening her arms.

Dimitri hesitated. But he rose from his seat, all the cracks in his chest he'd been trying to ignore smoothing a tiny bit as Analia pulled him into a hug.

"You will get your justice," she promised. "I'll make sure of it."

Dimitri nodded, not trusting himself to speak. Analia momentarily pressed her face to his shoulder. Then, she pulled away. Calling a thanks to Sabi, she stepped back into the library, Dimitri watching her go as the magic door remained open behind her.

"What was that all about?" Sabi asked.

Dimitri forced his heavy body to move toward the entrance. "I'm leaving."

He expected the decision to hurt. But it was only one more thing weighing him down, so much so he barely registered Sabi's thoughtful hum.

He reached for the magical door, Tashia's fussing as she and Analia reunited drifting through the opening.

"I'm sorry," Analia said, "I got caught up in the momentary freedom. I found my book a little while ago. I've been meaning to ask you, though. Can you have chamomile tea sent to my chambers? My throat's been bothering me all day."

Her throat hurt? Dimitri felt a little bad as he closed the door. He never would have suspected.

Chapter 13

Ember descended the dark stone staircase into the Ash Castle dungeon, her Sun guard escorts—a man named Joshel and the brutal guard from the walkway named Stanek—leading the way.

It had taken three days of healing Sun soldiers to earn enough trust from Othin to do so, Ember having to constantly remind herself she had vowed to heal any person in need as she worked. Even soldiers that might have harmed someone she loved. Even as every time she walked down a corridor to find an unfamiliar face, a Sun Kingdom banner where there should've been a phoenix, an Everflame sconce with no fire sprite in sight, another cut sliced through her heart.

But she kept it to herself. She healed without complaint alongside Tayla. And finally, it had paid off.

Now, Ember pulled her robes tighter around herself as she stepped into the dungeon, the chill from the stone walls seeping into her bones.

"You'll start on this end," Stanek said, gesturing with his Everflame torch. "It shouldn't take you long to make it through them all. You can inform His Highness of our kindness before we bring him up."

The purposeful demoting of Cadmus's title had Ember's nails digging into her palms. But, plastering a neutral look on her face, she nodded. She stepped aside, allowing Joshel to unlock the closest cell with one of the many jingling keys on the ring he pulled from his weapons belt. And when the door swung open, Ember barely choked back her sob.

The girl that sat huddled on a thin cot couldn't have been older than seven. She was all elbows and knees, her skin stretched too tight across her face, her red hair tangled around her shoulders. At the clang of the door opening, she shrank back with a squeak, her eyes darting between the soldiers.

Ember rounded on them. "What did you *do* to her?"

"We've left her alone," Stanek shot back.

"Oh, you certainly have. You couldn't have placed her with her parents?"

Joshel bit his lip and dropped his gaze. But Stanek folded his arms. "You're here to heal, not judge our orders."

Ember's heart pounded throughout her body as she looked back at the girl. And only the memory of a sharp, leafy smell kept her voice level as she said, "Stay out of the cell."

Then, not waiting for a response, she turned and stepped inside. The girl's blue eyes immediately darted to her, taking in her robes, flashing up to her eyes.

"I know you," she rasped. "I've seen you in the castle with Anna and Cadmus."

"That's right." Ember crouched before her, doing her best to block the guards from view with her body. "My name's Ember. You're Tenley, right?"

Tenley nodded cautiously, her eyes wide. "Why have you come *now?*"

"Because I've been granted permission to heal you." Ember extended her hand, letting it hover over Tenley's shoulder. "May I?"

Tenley murmured an affirmation, and Ember lightly rested her hand on her shoulder, practically feeling her thin tunic fray beneath her fingers. Shoving the burning thought aside, she sent a gentle wave of magic through Tenley's body. She checked her pulse, her breathing, her organs, bones, and everything in between. And to her relief, Stanek had been telling the truth: they'd left her alone.

So why have her come to this cell?

"The good news," Ember said, smoothing down Tenley's hair, "is on the inside, you look as good as I could have hoped. But that doesn't mean the outside is also fine." Ember ducked her head to catch her eye, not bothering to lower her voice. "Have any of them hurt you?"

Stanek coughed.

Ember gave an exaggerated eye roll, and Tenley's lips twitched.

"They haven't hurt me," she confirmed.

Thank the Crystal.

"Does *anything* hurt?" she asked.

Tenley took a quick breath, her eyes darting over Ember's shoulder. Ember squeezed her hand. Finally, Tenley hung her head, mumbling, "My wrists."

Ember looked down, spotting the heavy damper cuffs clamped around Tenley's wrists—how had she forgotten to check there herself? Sure enough, when Ember nudged the cuffs up her arm, all she saw was red skin rubbed raw, Tenley obviously having been pulling at her cuffs. Cuffs she never should have been put in.

"Good news," Ember said, forcing her hands to remain steady as she slung her healer bag from her shoulder. "This is an easy fix. Especially with my specialty."

Tenley watched silently as Ember pulled a small jar from her bag and popped off the lid. The thick green ointment inside was nothing special, just a concoction that helped conduct her magic across the skin. But as soon as she massaged it into Tenley's wrists, her shoulders relaxed.

"There," Ember said, "that should help. Give it some time to sink into your skin before you pull your cuffs back down. And try not to tug on them too hard anymore, all right?"

Tenley nodded, and Ember's hand lingered on her arm. Gods, she didn't want to leave her. But there was nothing left for her to do.

Ember looked back at the soldiers, back to Tenley, her voice sticking in her throat. "I... I have to go now."

She'd barely started to pull away when Tenley made a noise of alarm. She lurched forward, her eyes filling with tears. And the understanding that rolled through Ember's chest felt like a bruise of her own.

"Well, of course," she murmured, pulling Tenley into a hug. Tenley buried her face in the crook of Ember's neck, her chained hands tightening in the front of her robes.

"You're only here to heal," Stanek reminded her.

"She's a *child*," Ember said, her voice shaking almost as badly as Tenley. "She's been trapped, alone, in the cold and dark. Not all wounds are physical."

Ember expected Stanek to argue. Instead, the guards remained silent behind her, leaving Ember to murmur into Tenley's hair as she quietly cried. She didn't know what else to do.

After a few minutes that Ember was shocked she'd been given, she felt one of the soldiers come up behind her.

"Time's up," Joshel said, his voice flat. But the hand he rested on her shoulder was surprisingly gentle.

Tenley tried to tighten her grip. But, blinking hard, Ember carefully disentangled herself, Tenley hurriedly wiping the tears from her face.

"Hey." Ember caught her wrists with one hand, the other lifting her chin. "Remember what King Accalon always said."

"Rise again," Tenley whispered.

Rosala spare her, she didn't expect those words to hurt. She didn't expect her entire body to cry out for devinroot, for the chance to wash everything from this cell away.

Not trusting herself to speak, Ember nodded. Then, she rose and followed Joshel out of the cell, forcing her mind into something cold. Blank.

Ember lost track of time as she moved from cell to cell. The Royals immediately perked up when they spotted her, Ember having spent enough time in the castle to have interacted with all of them at some point or another. And that familiarity had each bruise, each broken rib and crushed finger she healed raking through her insides.

Rois had been right. The only hospitable thing about these conditions was the fact their heads remained attached to their bodies. And there was nothing fair about the guards behind her, keeping her answers brief as the Royals asked about their kingdom, their family, everything happening beyond their cells.

Ember stepped through the ninth door, finding Fayela, a Royal a few years older than herself, pacing the length of her cell. Her thick red hair and proud, regal features had always reminded Ember of a lioness, the look on her face as she twisted toward Ember solidifying the image. "My sister?"

"Tenley is all right," Ember breathed, taking in the blood crusted around Fayela's swollen mouth, the way she cradled her wrist against her chest. But there was no denying the blaze in her gray eyes as Ember got to work.

By the time she reached the tenth and final cell, it wasn't just the amount of magic she'd used that had Ember stumbling. She peered through the cell bars, and her hand drifted to her throat.

Cadmus sat cross-legged in the center of his cell. He didn't look up at the clang of the door opening, didn't so much as blink. He only rubbed his left wrist, his expression terrifyingly blank.

"Cadmus," Ember breathed.

It took a long, long moment for him to finally lift his head. Bruises decorated the left side of his face, most already yellow with age, some almost completely faded. His blue eyes reflected the firelight as they drifted up to hers, over to the guards on either side of her.

"Why?" he asked. Flat. Empty.

Ember didn't know if she was heartbroken or terrified. She jerked her head at the guards, waiting for them to retreat a few paces before coming to kneel before him.

"Othin has selected two healers to come work in the castle," she said, keeping her voice neutral. "I've been sent to heal all Royals to demonstrate his good faith. He chose me specifically because he thought our friendship would make you more likely to listen when I say he's requested you cooperate."

Ember stared into his face, searching for any sign he picked up on what little information she could give. Even as he nodded, she didn't like the faraway look in his eyes. Especially as his fingers continued to rub the inside of his wrist.

"Can I heal your injuries?" she asked, her own hands shaking as she reached for him.

Once again, all she got was a nod. Rosala spare her, what had happened to him in this cell?

Ember cradled the side of his face, sending her magic through his body. But all of the injuries she found were old and healing. She slid her hand down his arm to his wrist, her fingers covering his. "May I?"

Cadmus reluctantly let her guide his hand away and down to his lap, Ember making sure his wrist remained out of the guards' sight as she examined it. Nowhere near as red as Tenley's. But that wasn't her concern.

"Is the chafing bothering you?" she asked, tracing the black asymmetric star tattooed on the inside of his wrist.

Cadmus shook his head. Liar.

Gods, she had to help him. But how? She didn't even know if the creature from the volcano was merely whispering to him or invading his mind like it had Brenn.

Ember slid her hand down his wrist, tangling her fingers with his cold ones. "I've healed everything I can," she said, squeezing his hand. "But Othin has requested to speak to you."

Finally, the faintest reaction flickered across Cadmus's face as his lip slightly curled. "Then let's go."

Ember fidgeted with her robes as she, Cadmus, and their Sun guard escort stepped into the Throne Room. Most Ash Royals avoided the room all together, the dark stone walls and lack of windows making it feel worse than gloomy. But clearly, Othin didn't mind.

He sat on the obsidian glass throne in the center of the room, someone having brought in more Everflame torches and white Sun Kingdom banners to try and brighten up the space. But the deep lava flow lines carved into the stone swallowed the light regardless.

As soon as Cadmus spotted Othin on the throne, his entire body stiffened. Ember touched her fingertips to his back, not daring to do anything more as Stanek and Joshel eyed her from either side.

"You can leave, healer," Othin drawled, his amber eyes never leaving Cadmus's face.

Stanek reached for her, but Ember leaned away. "Your Majesty," she said, "I've healed King Cadmus's injuries, but he's still weak. It might be wise to keep me around in case something happens."

"To *King* Cadmus," Othin repeated, his eyes narrowing.

Ember clasped her hands before her. "I thought this discussion was to establish terms for a truce. Apologies if that doesn't mean both of you retaining your crowns."

Ember could only pray to Rosala that every shred of disdain remained wiped from her features.

"Do you think there would be any risk if she stayed?" Aeley asked, mildly interested as she stepped out from behind the throne.

Cadmus started. His eyes darted between Aeley and Othin, Ember waiting for the devastation to hit as he pieced it together. But he remained silent, his only reaction the slight flare of his nostrils.

Othin shifted in his seat to face her, his fingers lazily stroking along the sleek arm of the throne as he considered. "Fine," he decided. He jerked his chin at Ember. "You stay over there."

Ember bowed, trying to hide her relief as she scurried over to the narrow alcove Othin had gestured to.

And for a few long, agonizing moments, the chamber remained silent.

"So," Othin finally said, searching for a comfortable position. "This is the Ash King. A skinny little boy who got the crown by forfeit."

Cadmus raised a brow as if waiting for the punchline.

"A *silent* boy," Othin went on, shifting once more. "Who would have thought a week in a cell would be enough to break a king."

Ember bit down hard on the inside of her cheek. Cadmus remained silent. Waiting.

"Well?" Othin snapped. "Do you have nothing to say?"

"Where's my sister?" Cadmus asked, his voice hoarse from lack of use. But his eyes weren't on Othin. They'd shifted over to Aeley, who almost hid her flinch.

"Analia has been taken back to the Moon Kingdom with Deardryn," Othin said, settling back in his seat.

"I know," Cadmus said. "I watched Deardryn take her away after torturing her. Just as I watched as she plunged a dagger into Lucilla's throat and stole her magic. Where's *that* sister?"

Ember clapped a hand to her mouth, bile rising in her throat. Was *that* the full story of what happened in Accalon's chambers?

She looked at Cadmus, his icy tone still skittering through her bones. But that was nothing compared to the look that flashed across his face. There and gone, so quick she almost missed it. But that was an anger that could bring the world to its knees.

Across from him, Aeley took a small step back. But Othin only licked his lips.

"Her body," he said, "was stolen before we could retrieve it."

"Does that mean someone slipped through your security and heard what happened in my uncle's chambers? Or did you leave her body on the floor long enough for someone to stumble upon her and take her?"

His gaze flashed to Aeley, demanding a response. Aeley twisted her hands into her skirts, remaining silent.

Othin, meanwhile, offered a sneer. "I'll be happy to let you ask the thief yourself before we dispose of them."

Tingles ran across the back of Ember's neck. Gods, Rois better keep his head down. Her eyes darted around the chamber, checking no one had noticed her reaction. Just to spot a fire sprite hiding in the sconce flame across from her.

Ember's lips parted. The sprite clapped its little hands to its mouth and disappeared, Ember barely able to hear the tiny crackle over Cadmus's and Othin's voices.

"You've been making an awful lot of 'good faith' gestures," Cadmus said, stepping closer. "What's wrong, Othin? Are you learning the hard way that the Ash Kingdom burns too hot to be held on to?"

"Bold words for a dampered prisoner," Othin retorted. "I already conquered this kingdom—"

"Your *soldiers* conquered this kingdom," Cadmus corrected. "I have no doubt your wife outlined the plan, so she gets credit as well. But you?" His lip curled. "You sat in your cushy castle while you let everyone else fight your battle. You didn't saunter in until the blood was shed and someone else had claimed the throne for you."

Othin's face turned red beneath his beard. "I understand children have a hard time giving up their toys, but I've never seen one willfully break them out of spite."

"I don't see a broken crown."

"I'm not talking about your crown. I'm talking about your kingdom."

Othin leaned forward. "Do you really think your words hold no consequence? You might have been king a week ago, but now, you're trapped in a cell with no ability to back up your words. Meanwhile, I'm the man that dictates the fate of your people. Whether they live in peace. In fear. Whether their bodies lie broken across the streets.

"I'm offering you a chance to ensure that *doesn't* happen. And I would have thought as a Royal trained by Accalon, you would value the lives of your people over your pride."

Cadmus's jaw tightened. For a long moment, he studied Othin with the same considering look Ember had seen countless times on Accalon's face. But Accalon's gaze had never been so cold.

"This must be killing you," he finally said.

Othin startled.

"You're king of the Sun Kingdom, but constantly outranked by Deardryn—who, from everything I've seen, you don't particularly like. Now, she's given you a kingdom of your own. And you have to deal with the humiliation of not only being given a kingdom secondhand but also not being able to control it."

Othin started to spit a retort, but Cadmus spoke over him. "You already told me your proposal. My surrender in exchange for a promise of peace after your soldiers invaded my home, took one of my sisters captive, killed the other, and locked the rest of my family in our own dungeon. And I *know* my people haven't been treating you kindly while you wait on my answer. Otherwise, you wouldn't be desperate enough to manipulate my friend's healer oath to try and get me to cooperate."

Cadmus stalked to the foot of the dais, shaking off Stanek's hand as he tried to stop him. "You might have won over my mother, but she's in the same position as you are. She might have been queen, but she's no Royal. She doesn't command our people. *I* do. And there is *nothing* you can do to persuade me to stand peacefully beside you."

Ember huddled against the wall, pressing her fingertips to her lips as power rumbled across the chamber. But Cadmus, dampered as he was, didn't so much as flinch.

"The old Ash Kingdom is dead, little king," Othin said, struggling for calm. "Either you and your fellow Royals support my rule, or I make an example out of you."

Ember wanted to cry out, wave her arms over her head and call a time-out. But Cadmus remained perfectly still as Othin declared, "You have two weeks. It should honestly be two days, but consider this my final offer of good faith. You either stand with me in front of your people and declare my rule, or you stand with me in front of your people as you die."

Ember's heart pounded throughout her body. Please, Cadmus, *please*—

"I suppose I'll be seeing you in two weeks, then," Cadmus said. He gave Aeley a final glare, not seeming to notice how the blood had drained from her face. Then, not waiting for a dismissal, he turned on his heel and marched out of the chamber, only sparing Ember a nod as he passed.

For a moment, Stanek and Joshel remained frozen where they stood. Then, they hurried after him, the door thudding shut behind them.

Silence.

Othin sat back in the obsidian glass throne, his chest heaving. Ember realized she'd shoved her hands into her healer robe pockets, her fingers desperate for a shred of leftover leaves. But all she found was thread. And all she felt was terror as Othin finally noticed her and boomed a dismissal.

Ember scurried out the door, barely making it outside before she fell to her knees.

Cadmus was going to die.

Once, he might have considered Othin's proposal, used it to his advantage. But either from grief or rage or that mark, Cadmus wasn't himself.

Which meant this was all up to her.

Chapter 14

Analia was on high alert as she joined Deardryn in her study. Not because she didn't know what to expect—she was used to that by now—but because of the horribly familiar magic field that greeted her.

"I thought you didn't trust me with the Crystal," she said, easing into her seat across from Deardryn.

"I don't. But that doesn't mean I won't uphold our bargain. Especially now that you seem interested in cooperating."

Analia pursed her lips, and Deardryn laughed.

"Perhaps that was too extreme," she amended. She lifted the cracked gray stone from around her neck, the chain softly clinking against the table as she set it between them. "Think of it this way. Rather than assisting me with my research, you're satiating your own curiosity. You might even get to better understand your newfound abilities."

Analia didn't think Deardryn had intended her words to sting, but they did. Keeping her tone noncommittal, she asked, "Have you truly taken to wearing part of the most powerful magical object around your neck?"

"I thought about it," Deardryn admitted. "I was able to do so before you broke the seal. But now, even when it's shut, the power leaking through is unnerving. I have other ways of keeping it safe, though."

She ran a long, tanned finger down the crack, her silent threat clear: *Including from you.* Analia smiled faintly, the slight narrowing of Deardryn's eyes telling her she had no idea how much information she'd just revealed.

"So," Analia said, settling back in her seat. "What's the *real* reason you decided to pull this out today?"

Deardryn's eyes gleamed with approval. "The fact that we established yesterday I don't have to remove your cuffs."

"How fortunate for you."

Deardryn swatted her hand. "Fortunate for *you*," she said, "I intend to take my time. Today, all we're going to do is establish your tolerance for the Crystal's magic."

Analia's eyes shot to the rock. She could have sworn the magic stirred in response, sending a wave of nausea through her body. It didn't feel evil, per se. Just... wrong.

"My tolerance is nonexistent," she said flatly.

"That might be the case. But our baseline was unreliable. You received a direct blast of magic that had been stored up for millennia, yet you survived. Meaning there's no reason you shouldn't be able to handle partial exposure to magic built up over a week and a half."

She was so logical. Unconcerned. As if she'd forgotten what this magic had done. As if she wasn't reminded of that explosion every time she closed her eyes, the magic consuming, obliterating...

"Deardryn," Analia said shakily. "This is not a good idea."

"We'll take it slow," Deardryn said, reaching for the rock. "I'll stop it before anything goes wrong."

No, it *would* go wrong. Immediately. And she couldn't survive that twice.

"We're not doing this," Analia said, pushing back her chair.

"We'll start with a crack."

Analia started to retort, half-rising to her feet. But Deardryn had already cracked open the stone.

Pure white light beamed through the narrow opening. Analia fell back into her chair as the magic slammed into her, a thousand taloned hands trying to latch onto her mind.

"Breathe, Analia," Deardryn ordered.

Gods, she didn't know how. She didn't know how to think, how to move—only aware of the magic breaking off pieces of her for itself.

"Raise your mental shield," Deardryn demanded.

The word swam through Analia's mind, taking several seconds to find a place to settle. Shield, shield, shield—yes.

Slowly, painstakingly slowly, Analia reached for the mental shield she had forged back in the Sun Kingdom. Her senses screamed, completely overwhelmed. But somehow, she found the shield.

She dragged it up, imagining it forming a wall of stone around her mind. Hardening it to steel. To onyx.

The Crystal's magic scrabbled against the other side, searching for purchase. But the shield held.

Analia slumped back against her chair, her breathing ragged.

"Excellent, Analia," Deardryn said.

Analia struggled to blink the blur from her vision, barely registering the scratch of Deardryn's pen as she took notes. Completely unfazed, even as the stream of white light shone across her face.

"How are you fine?" Analia choked out. "How are you able to calmly take your notes when all that magic is right there?"

"This magic doesn't impact us the same, Analia," Deardryn said. "I'm able to faintly recognize my own magic, but the rest is a single stream of power. But with your abilities..."

Deardryn turned over her pen, something like sympathy in her eyes as she looked up. "I imagine you don't have one voice screaming for attention. You have countless individual voices yelling from all sides."

The magic hammered against Analia's mental shield. So many hands. Reaching for her. Clamping her arms to her sides, pressing against her heart, an arm to her throat—

"Analia," Deardryn said, snapping her fingers several times.

Analia dragged her gaze to Deardryn.

"Is this true?" Deardryn asked. "Is my description accurate?"

Analia nodded numbly. "Close it," she breathed. "You have to close it."

"Not yet. We need to see how much you can tolerate."

Deardryn opened the stone a little wider. The white light intensified, Analia gritting her teeth hard enough her jaw ached as the next wave hit.

She clung to her onyx shield, feeling it shudder with every blow, the aftershocks jolting through her body one after another. It had to hold. Even as cracks skittered across its surface—

"What do you feel, Analia?" Deardryn asked, her voice distorted in Analia's ears, barely distinguishable above the thrum of the magic.

"It's too much," she breathed.

"Your shield is holding, Analia. The rock is twenty percent open, and you're handling it."

Analia wanted to laugh. Or maybe sob as chunks of onyx rained down around her.

Her body was drenched in sweat. Her muscles were completely rigid. But this was "surviving"?

"Twenty-five percent, Analia. You can handle it."

Gods, Deardryn was going to kill her. Before Analia could voice the thought aloud, Deardryn opened the stone even more.

Analia screamed as the power slammed into her. It tore through the center of her shield like it was made of paper, Analia gripping the sides of her head as she tried to keep the rest in place.

Crystal spare her, there was so much magic. Screaming for her attention, thirsting for vengeance, wanting her for itself.

"Close it," she moaned. "Close it close it close it."

"Rebuild your shield, Analia. You can do it."

The onyx crumbled.

Magic barreled into her full force, launching her back to her uncle's chambers. The agony of the magic. Lucilla dead in front of her. Cadmus's scream. The heat that had raced through her body when she found her uncle's corpse.

Analia shoved out of her chair. She staggered across the room, away from the magic, just needing to get away. Even as the ground tilted beneath her feet. As her bones turned to liquid.

She didn't remember falling to her knees. She didn't remember emptying her stomach. All she knew was the burn of bile in her throat, the magic screaming through her head.

And abruptly, it was gone.

Analia gasped, tears streaming down her face. She didn't remember closing her eyes, but she kept them squeezed shut as footsteps hurriedly approached, warm hands catching her before she could slump forward.

"It's all right," Deardryn soothed, her voice shaking. "It's over. I promise, it's all over."

Deardryn guided her back and away from her mess, Analia not daring to open her eyes.

"I'm sorry," Deardryn whispered. "I thought you could... We won't be doing that again, I promise."

Analia barely registered her words. But as soon as she felt Deardryn's hand stroke her hair, she jolted away.

"Don't touch me," she spat, catching herself on her hands as she crumpled forward.

Analia could have sworn Deardryn sucked in a breath. But the Dragoness let her hand drop as she called for Tavian. Analia cringed at the increase in volume, her senses rubbed raw.

A few moments later, the door opened. Then, footsteps rushed toward her, Tavian's raised voice grating against Analia's ears, "What did you *do?*"

Analia felt Tavian drop down beside her, his hand gently turning her face to his. She finally opened her eyes, taking in his aghast expression.

"Fetch the nearest servant," Deardryn ordered, completely cool once more.

Tavian's gaze snapped over Analia's head. "And leave her alone with you?"

Analia should have been afraid of the deadly silence beside her. Instead, she was relieved as she finally got a chance to let her senses settle, only just realizing she was shaking.

"Are you defying a direct order?" Deardryn asked softly.

"My *order*," Tavian spat, "was to keep her safe. Given by *my king*. She doesn't look very safe to me."

Analia coughed, raising a hand to her throat. She expected Deardryn to argue. But she only responded with a curt, "Fine."

In a rustle of skirts, she rose to her feet, Analia not bothering to watch as she swept out the door. As soon as she was gone, Tavian turned back to her.

"I heard you scream," he whispered. "I tried to come, but the door wouldn't open until Deardryn called for me. What happened?"

Analia shook her head, not knowing what to say. Tavian pressed his lips into a line, but he didn't push it. He helped her sit up, leaning her back against his shoulder.

For a few minutes, the two didn't speak, Analia sagging in the silence. Eventually, the door opened once more. Deardryn swept inside, returning to kneel beside them.

"Drink this," she said, offering Analia a mug. "It will help with your throat."

Tavian's eyes darted to her. Analia ignored him as she reached for the mug, his arm curling around her to help.

"I'm all right," she rasped.

Tavian let his hand drop as Analia took a long drink of what was revealed to be chamomile tea. The same kind Tashia had brought to her the night before. She swished it around her mouth, only looking at Deardryn when she could no longer taste bile.

"We're done for today," she said.

Deardryn nodded mutely, her face pale.

Analia barely remembered Tavian helping her to her feet. He led her out of the chamber, his grip on her remaining tight even as her legs stabilized beneath her.

She expected him to leave her at her chambers without a word. Instead, he followed her inside, closing the door behind him and moving to perch on her desk.

"So," he said. "Sore throat, huh? Last I heard, you had a headache."

Analia knew this conversation was inevitable—she'd been hoping for it. But that didn't stop her from wishing it had come at any other time.

"I had to know who I could trust," she said, sinking down on her bed.

"And how do I know I can trust you?" Tavian countered.

"Fair enough."

Analia rubbed her temples, struggling to focus. All she wanted was to curl up beneath her covers, try and sleep the memories away. But there were destined to be more if she didn't get this right.

"Do you still want to know what Deardryn did to me?" she asked.

Tavian startled, but he nodded.

"She's hunting the Crystal. At some point, it was split into pieces, and today she exposed me to the shard she has."

"Why?" Tavian demanded, leaning forward.

"Apparently, she wants to unite the kingdoms—"

"No, why did she expose *you?*"

Analia hesitated, picking at a thread in her pants. She didn't like how many people were starting to know about her Blessing. Then again, what was the point in trying to hide it when the one person she would've liked to keep it from already knew?

"Because," she said, "my Blessing is... special."

"I'm going to need a little more context, Red."

The corner of Analia's mouth twitched at the nickname. "Somehow," she said, "I have access to all seven Royal Blessings, which means I'm more equipped to wield the Crystal and all its magic fields."

Tavian stared at her, his head cocked. Analia dredged up the last shreds of energy she had, waiting for his rebuttal. But all he said was, "Seems like you're not."

Analia breathed out a laugh. "You have no questions about my magic?" she asked.

"It sounds impossible," he said, rubbing his jaw. "But you're also dampered, so how should I know either way? It doesn't impact me regardless."

"Maybe not you," Analia said. "But it does the Moon Royals."

Tavian went still. Just as Analia had hoped.

"What do you mean?" he asked.

"Deardryn didn't just come to this kingdom to get a Crystal shard," Analia said. "You know all of the Royal deaths lately?"

"Don't tell me they were her."

"She's been collecting their magic in special rings so she can try to artificially control the Crystal. And she still doesn't have a Moon ring."

Tavian kept his gaze level on hers. "Why are you telling me all of this?" he asked slowly.

"I'm telling you because I understand if you don't trust me anymore. But someone you care about is in immediate danger."

Tavian looked like he was about to deny it.

"Tavian," she said, "we both know I saw what happened in the hallway."

Tavian opened his mouth, smiled slightly, then shrugged. Well, at least he wasn't one to lie when caught. Analia liked him even more for it.

"Do you love her?" she asked softly.

"Damn, Analia," Tavian protested, "how personal are you trying to get?" He ducked his head, but Analia still caught his blush. And if the deepening color meant anything, he knew it.

"You have to look out for her, Tavian," she said, leaning back against the wall. "Sylas has already warned all of them, but still…"

Tavian rubbed his temples, looking as though he were trying to solve a puzzle he hadn't intended to start. "So," he said, "you're here because Deardryn doesn't have all her rings yet, and she can use you in the meantime?"

"I'm here," Analia said flatly, "because she invaded my kingdom, almost killed me to get that shard, and then killed my sister in front of me to get a ring."

"Meaning you're out for blood."

"I have a plan," Analia hedged. "And I could greatly use your help."

Tavian cocked his head, a lethal glint in his eyes. "Does this plan involve getting Deardryn out of my kingdom?"

"If all goes well."

"In that case," Tavian said, pulling a dagger from his belt, "what do you need?"

Analia was too tired to feel triumphant. Shifting so she rested against her pillows, she said, "Tell Sylas I need to speak to him in our usual place. He'll know what that means."

Tavian nodded. He hopped off her desk, Analia's eyelids drooping as he approached.

"Good luck, Red," he said, adjusting one of her pillows. "You'll need it."

Analia didn't respond. But as he turned to go, Analia hoped he was wrong.

Chapter 15

Analia spent the rest of the day in bed.

As much as she wanted to prepare for her meeting with Sylas, the lingering effects of the Crystal left her unable to keep her eyes open, her mind alternating between nightmares and dreamless sleep. She only woke long enough to poke at the lunch and dinner trays left beside her bed, grateful either Tavian or her maids had decided to let her rest.

By the time she closed her eyes a final time that night, she was confident she felt as good as she was going to get. And as the sitting room materialized around her, Sylas looking as surly as ever where he sprawled in his usual armchair, she could only hope it would be enough.

"You summoned me?" he drawled.

"Technically, I think *you* summoned *me*."

Ignoring Sylas's scowl, Analia imagined one of the dark blue recliners from Aaron's library behind her. She sank back into the cushions, her heart aching as she breathed in metal and spice.

But this was no time to miss him. Especially since, if she played her cards right, she would be back with him all the sooner.

"I sincerely hope you didn't insist I bring you here so you could redecorate my sitting room," Sylas complained.

"Of course not," Analia said innocently. "I simply thought you'd like to know you have Deardryn sympathizers in your castle."

Sylas's expression didn't twitch. "I'm already aware."

"I'm not talking about Leila," she said, earning a quick flicker of surprise. "I've found more. But if my presence is too irritating for you to handle…"

"You need better bait than that if you're going to provoke me," Sylas said, picking at his nails.

Analia's eye twitched. "Fine," she said. "Maybe you'd also like to know Deardryn has discovered Dimitri escaped."

That got his attention. Barely. "She told you?"

"She threatened me. And since you rescued him from the dungeon, I'm assuming you were the one to take off his damper cuffs. Meaning we *both* know why we need to get him away from her as soon as possible."

"So, *that's* why you're baiting me with the sympathizers," Sylas murmured. "You need my help."

Analia shifted in her seat. "I have a plan."

"Which means you need my help."

Analia tightened her jaw. Sylas, in turn, looked as though she were asking him to pull off some impossible task.

Summoning a goblet to his hand, he took a long drink, half-grumbling into his wine. "Haven't I helped you two enough?"

"You say that," Analia replied. "Yet, you left our oath open-ended regarding your assistance. So, either you don't actually think so, or you were testing to see how closely I was paying attention."

Analia held his gaze. Completely unbothered, Sylas twirled his goblet between his fingers, his lack of retort telling her everything she needed to know. Even as he took his time before responding, letting the silence stretch uncomfortably long.

"Tell me the names and I'll consider helping you," he finally said, placing his goblet on the table beside him.

"Promise to help me and I won't tell Deardryn you were involved in releasing Dimitri," Analia countered.

"Oh, she already knows," he said dismissively. "She'd be a fool not to."

"In that case, you'll not only have to continue wondering who you can trust on your staff but also hope that my escape plan doesn't go horribly wrong."

Analia settled back in her chair, letting Sylas deliberate what she knew would be his deciding question: which scenario would inconvenience him more. Deardryn getting a hold of Dimitri, him assisting Analia's plan, or going through the effort to *stop* her plan. And the pained look on his face told her he'd realized no matter what, he was getting dragged in.

"Fine," he sighed, leaning his head back against his seat. "Tell me your names and I'll help you—*if* your plan shows any promise of succeeding."

Analia perked up, barely catching the flicker of curiosity in Sylas's eyes. Just as she'd hoped.

"Tavian is clear," she said, not wasting a moment. "Letta's questionable. She was rather entertained by my insolence toward Deardryn, but I wouldn't trust her completely until we determine how involved she is in the maid-servant gossip chain. Especially since news of my sore throat, which I asked Tashia to keep between us, somehow found its way to Deardryn's ears. Granted, she could have told one of her friends, who then told Deardryn. Either way, her entire group can't be trusted."

"Interesting," Sylas murmured, rubbing his jaw.

Analia waited for him to try to poke holes in her investigation methods, but he didn't inquire.

"It seems," he said, his voice perfectly level, "that in the wake of Patryclas's absence, some of my staff have tried to find solace in the next closest thing. Someone kind, thoughtful, some may say the light to my darkness. And with how long I've allowed her to stay here, I wouldn't doubt they've taken that as a sign she can be trusted."

Analia dropped her gaze to her lap, the shadows flickering around Sylas's shoulders the only tell of his temper. "I think," she said, "we tend to forget we can be just as blinded by the light as the darkness."

Crystal only knew how badly she'd fallen into that trap. Multiple times in fact.

Pryanth's chambers flashed through her mind. His voice in her ears, his bed frame digging into her back, her throat closing from the pressure of his forearm—

"All right then," Sylas sighed, dragging a hand through his hair. "Tell me about this plan of yours."

For a moment, Analia couldn't speak. She pinched her thigh, focusing on the pain, forcing those memories to sink down once more.

Gods, it had been so long since she'd thought about that. But as Sylas pulled his hand away from the chair beside him, Analia took a little comfort in knowing she wasn't the only one with ghosts in that room.

"Well," she said slowly, "my scheme depends on a few things. I hear you have a hedge maze behind your castle?"

"Yes."

"And I'm assuming that means you have exits leading out to it?"

"Are all of your questions observations about my castle?"

Analia had the strangest urge to laugh. She settled back into the cushions, into the familiarity that had her jittery pulse relaxing once more.

"That depends," she said. "Do you count me asking if there are any enka flowers in your hedge maze as an observation?"

For the first time throughout their entire conversation, Sylas gave her his full attention. "Enka flowers," he repeated, a chain of the white blooms appearing between his fingers with a gentle thrum. "What in the name of the five gods could you want with those?"

Analia smiled to herself. Then, she briefly explained her bracelet and Laness's enka flower transport abilities.

"I figured sneaking out of the back would be easier," she finished. "Especially with the hedge maze as an added protection. But if there are no enka flowers nearby, that might create some issues."

"I don't believe there are any in the maze," Sylas mused, turning the enka chain between his fingers. "But with how abundant they are in my kingdom, there have to be some close by."

"Would you bet on it?" Analia asked.

"Why must you question everything I say?" Sylas grumbled. "Yes, I would bet on it—although that might become irrelevant once I hear your plan."

Analia took the hint. Seeing no reason to draw things out any further, she filled him in on the plan she and Laness had pieced together. Sylas listened quietly as she spoke, absently arranging the enka chain on the seat beside him. It wasn't until she'd finished that he looked at her fully.

"That plan is astonishingly risky for how simple it is," he said.

Analia kept her chin high. "It's greatly improved through Rayner's help."

"You think I'll let you whisk away the one servant I can trust?"

"How much can you really trust him if his loyalty is grounded in a tattoo?"

Sylas snorted. Slumping back in his chair, he said, "I suppose you'll need me to rearrange the guard schedule, too. Although that still leaves Deardryn."

"I'll take care of her," Analia said firmly.

Sylas cocked his head at that. "So," he murmured, "you're not escaping after all."

"I never said I was. Not unless you can think of a way to steal the Crystal within the next two nights."

Sylas didn't respond, his bored mask slipping into something more akin to brooding.

"Will that be all?" he asked eventually.

Analia knew the smart response was yes, take the victory he was willing to give her and go. But while she cared about Dimitri's escape, it wasn't the only reason she'd requested this meeting.

"There's one more thing," she said, smoothing her hands down her thighs.

Sylas let out a dramatic sigh, his head falling back toward the ceiling. "She asks for so much, and yet gives so little in return."

"You'll get something out of this," Analia promised, her fingers curling into the soft velvet of her seat. "I want you to train me."

Sylas's head snapped upright once more. *"Train you?"*

An ancient part of her wanted to shrink away from that look. But Analia held his gaze, keeping her spine straight. "Yes," she said. "Train me."

"What in the name of the Crystal makes you think I would train you?"

"Everything about you." Analia leaned forward, ignoring the way Sylas's warning look sent her insides squirming. "The Moon Royals have been careful to keep their abilities hidden, to the point I never knew about your dreamwalking. Your abilities are your trump card in a world filled with enemy Royals. And now that Deardryn's not only in your castle, but trying to learn about my magic, your secret is under immediate threat."

"And it would be under an even bigger threat if I taught you how to tap into it," Sylas retorted. Once again not refuting her abilities. Not giving an inch, either.

Analia licked her lips. "That's true. But at least if you're teaching me, I won't be poking around in the dark with Deardryn. At some point, she's going to take my damper cuffs off, and if you train me, I'll know what to hide from her."

"Even if I were willing to teach you," Sylas said, folding his arms, "don't you think Deardryn would become suspicious if I not only started showing you any form of attention, but whisking you away for chunks of time?"

"She'll never have to know a thing because we can train in here."

Analia held her breath, waiting for Sylas's retort. But he only stared at her, a crease forming between his brows.

"What makes you think you can train in here?" he asked slowly.

Analia didn't know if that was a good sign or a terrible one. But she forged ahead anyway. "First, my lack of damper cuffs." She raised her hands for him to see. "I noticed they were gone in our first meeting, and after you explained how we're not in our bodies, but somewhere in between, I got curious."

Analia flexed her fingers. And ten tiny midnight flames flickered to life across her fingertips.

Sylas's eyes widened a fraction.

"This is my magic," she said, the heat surprisingly comforting as she let the flames spread down her fingers. "I'm not imagining them right now. I can feel my magic network. Just like I could when I lit the candle I *did* imagine last time. Which means we can train here at night, and Deardryn would never have to know."

Analia let her flames wink out, the magic settling back into her network like a key in a lock. Then, she waited.

All throughout this meeting, she'd had a good idea what to expect from Sylas. She knew his curiosity would entice him into asking about the spies, just as giving him pieces of her plan at a time would grab his attention. She knew he would put up a fuss when she asked for help, but he could be persuaded. More than anything, she knew Sylas was looking for someone to play his game.

But this? This wasn't just upending the board, but telling him she had figured out the rules he purposefully hadn't shared. And she had no idea if that was the best move she could have made, or the worst. All she could do was stay quiet as Sylas considered, running his fingers along the armrest of the chair beside his.

"You've thought all of this through, haven't you?" he finally murmured. "Why is this so important to you?"

Countless answers arose in Analia's mind. How she'd been afraid of her magic for too long. The danger she knew would arise if she *didn't* have it under control when the cuffs came off. The quiet, aching reasons she couldn't bring herself to name.

Knowing Sylas didn't care about any of that, she simply said, "Because I want to stop Deardryn. And I can't do that right now. And I don't know why you think I'm useful to you, but I know I am. And I would think if I'm going to be of use, you would want me as powerful as I can be."

Analia waited for Sylas to shrug her off. Instead, he nodded to himself.

"All right, then," he said, rising to his feet. "We'll train. *If* you manage to pull off your escape."

Analia fought to keep the triumph off her face. "Why the contingency?" she asked.

"Because I need to see if you're worth my time."

Fair enough. Before Analia could respond, Sylas flicked his wrist, and the sitting room started to dissolve.

Just before her vision faded to black, Analia caught Sylas's bored expression shift. It wasn't quite a smile. More like a smirk, as if she'd checked a box on a secret list.

And as Analia woke in her bed, she didn't know if she should be intrigued by that list, or positively terrified.

Chapter 16

"What do you mean she's planning an escape?" Aaron demanded. He stood in the center of his sitting room, barely registering Branten and Surce hurrying in as he faced Laness.

All that morning, he'd been struggling to focus on his various council reports, to the point he was faintly relieved when Laness burst through the door. As soon as she'd told him Analia got in contact, his mind had sharpened into a wicked clarity, unsure if he was hopeful or dismayed as she went on.

"That's what she said," Laness confirmed, pacing around him. "She said Deardryn found out that Dimitri escaped from the dungeon, so they have to get him out before she catches him."

"She certainly won't be kind to him after all the information he scavenged," Branten murmured.

Aaron winced. "Is Anna coming with him?"

"I don't know, she didn't say."

"You didn't ask?"

"There wasn't time," Laness shot back, momentarily pausing her pacing to glare at him. "We've only been able to talk in spurts because she's constantly surrounded by her maids. It's already a miracle no one has tried to take it from her."

That comment didn't sit well with Aaron. Especially since the same could have been said when Deardryn let Analia keep her phoenix pin, just to taunt her with it later.

"So, what's the plan?" Branten asked, perching on the couch's arm.

"Tomorrow night," Laness said. "Apparently, there's a hedge maze behind the castle that I'm to meet them at."

"Are there any enka patches nearby?" Surce asked from beside the fireplace.

"She said Sylas thinks it's likely," Laness said, fiddling with the bracelets on her arm. "Based on the climate, I would be shocked if there aren't any. Especially since Royals tend to have expansive gardens around their castles."

"So, what you're saying is you have a due date and tentative location," Branten summed up.

Aaron shot him a glare. "Anna doesn't make spur-of-the-moment plans," he said. "If she's gone so far as to set something up, that means she has other pieces in play. And she's confident enough to bet on them."

At least, he hoped that was true. That was one of the only things that had kept him sane from the moment he found out about her plan back in the Ash dungeon.

"Assuming there's no enka patch," Surce said, "what's your plan?"

"Roottravel to the closest one and keep her updated with our bracelets as I make my way there on foot."

Surce tapped her fingers on the fireplace as she considered, eventually giving a slow nod.

"If you're going to make it to the Moon Kingdom by tomorrow night," Branten said, "then you'll need to leave by this evening."

"And I'm coming with you," Aaron said firmly.

Laness froze midstep, the room going silent. Aaron didn't care. If there was even a chance to see her, whether she was escaping or not, he was taking it.

"Aaron," Laness said slowly, "I know you'd be useful, but bringing you is a big risk."

"I can control myself, Laness."

"I know *you* can, but what about Deardryn? As far as Analia can tell, she hasn't shared with anyone who you are. But if you show up? If she sees you?"

"She could expose you," Surce murmured.

"Or try to goad you into exposing yourself," Branten added.

Aaron knew they had a point. And that only irritated him more.

"Deardryn is going to suspect I had something to do with it regardless of if I'm there," he said, folding his arms. "Whether or not she exposes me is out of my hands now."

A fact that had his heart freezing over.

"So why tempt her?" Laness persisted.

"Because it's worth the risk!" he exclaimed. "You said it yourself: you don't know if Analia is coming, which means we might have to pull off another rescue. And if I come, I can not only shadowjump there at a moment's notice, but I can get us home again just as quickly."

"He has a point," Branten muttered, rubbing his face.

"I was able to jump to the Ash Kingdom in a little over three days no problem," Laness argued, jutting out her chin. "That's three times as far, I can handle this—"

"I'm not saying you can't," Aaron cut in, raking a hand through his hair. "I'm saying I can be an additional advantage—"

"You'll be a hindrance because you're so worried about Analia," Laness snapped.

Aaron's entire being went deadly still. Laness muttered a curse under her breath, but she didn't back down, her hands on her hips.

"Tell me that isn't true," she said. And the understanding in her eyes, the complete lack of accusation, had ice crackling through Aaron's veins.

He looked to Branten and Surce for support, the two sharing a reluctant look. One that had him momentarily unable to think through the flash of cold.

"Do you honestly think," he asked, terrifyingly calm, "that I would let my worry jeopardize not only Analia, but Dimitri? The rest of you? My *kingdom?*"

Aaron practically spat the word. Because the only thing more ridiculous than their assumptions was their inability to see forcing him to do nothing would cause more damage.

Is that what they wanted? For him to stay put and watch as his world slowly teetered inward? Did they think he could *survive* that? Or did they think locking him away, treating him like he was made of glass, would prevent him from shattering? As if their loss of faith in him didn't break him even more.

"Aaron," Surce said, "I know this is an unfathomable position for you."

Something in her tone had the ice in Aaron's veins running colder.

"*Especially* since it involves Analia. And I understand—"

"No!" Aaron exploded, twisting around to face her. "You *don't* understand. You can't. You've never even been interested in someone for over three months. You have no room to empathize me out of this choice."

As soon as the words were out, Aaron wanted to take them back. Especially as Surce's expression, always so unruffled, flinched. And that fury in his veins, urging him to lash out, to make someone else hurt for just a moment, turned on him with a vengeance.

"Surce," he rasped, "I shouldn't have—"

"No, you shouldn't have." Surce straightened beside the fireplace, her words sharp and precise as daggers. "You'll go with Laness, and you'll refrain from using your magic. I'll consult my tapestries."

"Surce, hold on..."

Surce stared at him, his voice trailing off, his half-extended hand falling back to his side. Then, without another word, she turned and swept from the room. And the ice in Aaron's veins frosted over in the sudden silence.

Keeping her head bowed, Laness mumbled something about gathering supplies. Then, she scurried after Surce.

Fine.

Aaron twisted on his heel, stalking away—he didn't know where. He didn't get a chance to find out as heavy boots thudded behind him, a hand clamping down on his shoulder.

"Hey." Branten spun him around to face him. "You're being a fucking asshole."

Aaron's magic surged. "I tried to apologize."

"Try harder."

Aaron glared, his magic flickering across his shoulders, ready for the fight.

Branten stared into his face, then shook his head. "Come with me."

"Branten—"

"You can either come walking, or you can come dragged."

In the end, it was a little bit of both. Branten hauled Aaron out the back door, the icy wind biting against his skin as they marched through the snow. A part of him was relieved as they reached the training hollow, the magic that protected it from the elements warming the air, the hollow still lush with moss and grass.

"Why?" he asked.

"Because," Branten said, "you've been riled up ever since Anna left. So, you can either take it out on me, or you can take it out on a dummy. Either way, this"—he gestured in between them—"stops now."

Surce's wounded expression flickered across Aaron's mind. And he didn't think twice.

His fist flashed out, connecting with Branten's jaw. Branten's head snapped back, something dangerous spreading across his features as he looked back with a grin.

"Thank the fucking Crystal," he said. Then, he lunged for Aaron.

The next several minutes were a blur. Aaron lost himself in the rush of fists and feet and elbows, not thinking through his movements, letting every impulse take over. And Branten matched him with every move.

He could tell from the force of each blow that Branten had been waiting for a moment to unload on him. But Aaron relished it. Every blow, every ache, every burst of pain. It was one new thing for him to focus on rather than the devastation rampaging through his insides.

"I get it," Branten panted, trying to grab him. "I get that Anna's gone, and you're stressed—"

"She's not 'gone,'" Aaron seethed, kicking him away. "She's been locked in a cell for a week. She's trapped with Deardryn and a Crystal shard that almost killed her. My only link to her is Laness, and do you really think either of them will tell me if something is wrong until it's too extreme to hide?"

Aaron's fist snapped out, but Branten caught it in his palm with a smack.

"Fine," he said, twisting Aaron's arm behind his back. "You're more than stressed. You're fucking pissed. You're terrified. You have every right to be. But you biting everyone's heads off isn't helping."

"Don't you think I know that?" Aaron twisted free, using his momentum to shove Branten to the ground. He landed on top of him a moment later, his fist spasming around Branten's jacket as he leaned in. "I can't think about anything other than those days in the Ash Kingdom. Turning over every move I made, trying to figure out if there was a way I could have fixed this or prevented it or done *something* other than come home and be trapped in this fucking house."

Each word sliced its way out of him. He stared into Branten's face, breathing hard, searching for anything in his expression that he could pounce on. But Branten only shook his head.

"You are so stuck in the past," he said. "You're fighting the wrong battle, brother."

Aaron made to argue, but Branten surged up, startling him enough to dislodge him. Within moments, their positions were reversed, Branten pinning him to the moss and leaning in close.

"Look," he said. "If you want to be miserable and angry at the world, fine. That's your prerogative. But you don't get to take it out on us. Not when all we're trying to do is help you."

"I'm not miserable and angry—"

"Oh please, you haven't been this much of an asshole since Elspeth died."

Branten's words hit Aaron like a blow to the chest. He immediately went still, the ice cracking, melting, everything draining out of him until he was completely limp. He stared up at Branten, his eyes wide, Branten softening as he realized what he'd said.

"Oh, Aaron," he said. "This isn't like that. This isn't your mom."

"I know," Aaron rasped, nevertheless struggling to fill his lungs.

"So, then what's your problem?"

Everything. *Everything* was his problem, and there was only so much he could do about it.

Aaron opened his mouth, then looked away. He waited for Branten to try and press him further. But Branten remained silent as he clambered off him, Aaron slowly dragging himself into a sitting position.

He looked down at his aching body, his knuckles split and bleeding. He deserved every bruise Branten had given him. Probably more.

Gods, how had he become that person again?

"I'm sorry," he breathed.

"Hey." Branten leaned forward, a bruise already blossoming along his jaw. Aaron winced. "Your last asshole phase lasted decades. You pulled yourself out of this one in less than two weeks." Branten clapped him on the shoulder. "We know who you are. Now, you just have to remember, too."

The sentiment made Aaron feel worse. But Branten was right: he'd given over to the self-pity for over a week now. He needed to focus on something else—he needed to *be* something else. But before all of that...

"I need to apologize to Surce," he said, rubbing the back of his neck.

"Yes, you do." Branten rose to his feet and offered Aaron a hand up. "Welcome back, brother."

Aaron didn't feel back. He felt fucking ashamed. And he should.

Aaron bowed his head, letting Branten pull him to his feet. Then, murmuring his thanks, he turned and headed for the house.

He knew he could have shadowjumped to Surce's studio, but he walked through the cold instead, letting himself feel every ache throughout his body.

A few months ago, this would have gone completely differently. He would have locked himself in his mother's room, icing everyone out until one of them—probably Branten—kicked the door in and demanded to talk to him. Even then, he doubted they would have reached the resolution that they had in the hollow. At least, not as quickly.

He just didn't know how to let himself rely on his family. Not in that way, at least.

But fortunately, there was one thing he knew how to do right.

Chapter 17

Aaron emerged from the curtain of beads, magic softly thrumming across his skin as he looked around Surce's studio. The seamstress sat behind her loom, her eyes fixed on her threads as she worked on a new tapestry.

A quiet, cowardly part of Aaron wanted to turn and flee while he still could. But admitting he'd fucked up wasn't supposed to be comfortable. Especially not this time.

"So," he said, stepping deeper into the room. "Apparently, there's a reason I hide in my mom's room. Turns out, I'm a moody asshole when I'm upset."

Surce's gaze briefly flicked to him.

Aaron decided to take that as a shred of encouragement as he stopped before her loom, ducking his head to meet her gaze. "May I sit?"

"You may," she hedged.

Gods, he really was a fucking asshole. Not trying to stifle his rush of shame, he retrieved a nearby stool and dragged it in front of the loom, determined to look her in the face even if she wouldn't look at his. Even as the soft whisper of weaving threads was worse than any silence.

"Surce," he said on an exhale, "I'm sorry. I had no right talking about your relationships—let alone judging them."

"No, you did not," she said, continuing to weave.

"Especially since you were nothing but patient when I was going through everything with Analia," he agreed. "Today, I was hurt and angry, and you just so happened to be the closest thing to lash out at. And that wasn't fair to you, nor everyone who had to watch. Branten made that sentiment loud and clear a little while ago when he kicked the shit out of me in the training hollow. I think I still have a few bruise-free spots if you'd like to make your feelings known as well."

Surce cocked her head as if she enjoyed the idea. Aaron's lips twitched, but he quickly sobered.

"I know I have to keep myself in check," he said. "The moodiness is back under control, and I'm paying extra attention to it now because that can't happen again."

"Well," Surce murmured, "you'll always be *a little* moody."

Aaron breathed a laugh. "Fair enough. How about I promise to keep the asshole part specifically under control?"

"I suppose that sounds acceptable," she said. But her gaze remained on her loom, not pointed exactly, but something else. Something that had Aaron reaching around the loom and lightly touching her hand.

"Surce," he said, finally catching her eye. "I'm sorry. I'm sorry for today, I'm sorry for the past week and a half, I'm sorry for it all. And I hope you know the things I said don't reflect what I think about you."

For a long, long time, Surce didn't respond. Aaron retracted his hand, wanting to squirm in the silence. But he remained quiet and still, taking on every shred of shame she deemed he deserved.

Because this was Surce. The woman who was so serene, so unruffled compared to his constant turmoil.

She was always put together. Steady. Unbreakable after everything she had been through.

Except she *was* breakable. That had been true hurt in her eyes back in his sitting room. Just as it was hurt that kept her shoulders curled as she wove.

And he had done that to her.

Aaron was just thinking he should start a whole new round of groveling when Surce sighed. She reached over to softly pat his hand, her eyes still downcast as she said, "It's not that I'm uninterested in anything beyond three months."

Aaron perked up, realizing this was never a topic they'd discussed before. "So what's stopping you?"

"What do you think?" Surce gestured halfheartedly to her loom, the tapestry only consisting of a dozen or so rows of what looked like golden-brown stone. "In so many ways, my glimpses of the future are a gift. They've protected my home, the people I care for. I like to think they've played a role in bringing the right people into our lives."

"Like Anna?"

"And the rest of you back when I was still in the Human Kingdom."

Aaron's mind flashed back to that night, practically able to hear the yells, smell the smoke from the torches. But Surce only continued her weaving, one of her balls of thread getting tangled around the frame of the loom.

"I sense a 'but' coming," Aaron said, slipping off his stool to fix the thread.

Surce's mouth curved in a tired smile. "I told the four of you long ago you're not allowed to help with my tapestries because of your propensities to obsess over what you all see. But that doesn't mean I'm immune to that myself."

Aaron looked up quickly from where he crouched.

"It's... difficult," Surce mused. "Not being able to control what I weave. It's inevitable a tapestry will be woven regarding whatever relationship I'm in. I can't help but turn over every possibility: every way it can work out, how it can tangle, how it can unravel. How no one I have met thus far is able to endure the future that has consumed my life."

Well, Aaron could understand a fraction of that. The conflict that came with being Blessed with a gift and a curse. The pain of feeling like that was a weight that could only be carried alone.

Surce turned on her stool to look at him. He tried to straighten his expression before she could see, but the faint smile that flickered across her lips told him it didn't matter.

"You need not pity me," she said, reaching down to ruffle his hair. "I've come to terms with my magic long ago."

"I wasn't pitying you," he said, eyes on the ball of thread. "I was thinking it seems like we're both trying to figure this out. You're just doing a more graceful job than me."

"Well, we must remain consistent."

Aaron let out something between a laugh and a sigh. He rose to his feet, his body surprisingly heavy as he returned to his stool.

"Why haven't you talked about this with any of us?" he asked.

"Because," Surce said, her gaze finally fully meeting his. "You're not the only one who prefers to mourn alone."

Those words hit him harder than he expected. Surce quickly dropped his gaze, her head bowing as she returned to her work.

Gods, how many times had he sat like that in his mom's room? Back when he thought the only thing he could do was submit to his magic, the future it carved for him. The possibilities it took from him.

But there *was* another way.

Aaron swiveled on his stool, his gaze wandering across the tapestries on the walls. Most of them he didn't recognize—probably because they had to do with Surce. But amongst them all he found an image of himself and Analia lying in the snow, a contented little smile on his woven lips as he watched her point up at the stars.

You're not the only one who prefers to mourn alone.

"I had her for eighteen hours, Surce" he murmured. "There were eighteen hours between when I brought her here and when Laness told us about Ember's and Dima's messages. Less than eighteen hours, because we fell asleep.

"It was one thing when I was pining and wondering, that was bearable. But the feeling of *finally* having her, just to immediately lose her?"

"That's a pain that will take everything down with it," Surce said softly.

Aaron hated that understanding flickered across her features. He ran a hand through his hair, blinking hard. "I'm sorry I tried to drag you down as well."

"I forgive you."

Aaron didn't know if he felt like the life had been sucked out of him, or if a little more had been breathed back in.

"You know," he said, trying for a smile as he rubbed his eyes, "today might have been a disaster, but at least I can now confirm the alternative to mourning alone is far better. You know, once you get the hang of not being a prick about it."

Surce let out a surprised laugh. "I'll keep that in mind."

"Enough so that you'll give group brooding a try?" Aaron asked. "I'll even volunteer myself as emotional training dummy."

"You've certainly always been a man of fairness," Surce replied, softening her words with a pat to his knee. One that had Aaron feeling a little more steady as he rose.

Surce returned her attention to her loom, presumably thinking their conversation was over. But Aaron circled around the loom, coming to tap her shoulder.

"You know," he said, "if you ever find someone you wouldn't mind sticking around, the family and I would be thrilled to vet them. We don't even need a tapestry to form our opinions. Sometimes, we're even accurate."

Surce's mouth twitched. "I'll keep that in mind, too."

"Good." Aaron kissed the side of her head. Then, he turned, quietly leaving Surce to her work. Just as he was about to step through the beads, she called after him.

"Dimitri is blond, yes?"

For a moment, Aaron was completely thrown. "He is." Aaron paused. "Should I ask?"

"It's probably best you refrain."

Aaron laughed under his breath. Then, waving goodbye over his shoulder, he stepped through the curtain, reappearing in one of his upstairs bedrooms.

As he headed off down the hall, the constant ache in his chest didn't ease, exactly. But there was some comfort in knowing he hadn't been completely alone. And he focused on that feeling as he went in search of Laness.

Chapter 18

Dimitri sat at Sabi's desk, trying not to squirm as Rayner changed his appearance.

The three days leading up to his escape had simultaneously blurred past and dragged excruciatingly slow. He'd spent most of that time compiling his notes on Deardryn, the idea of leaving becoming more palatable as he thought of all the ways he could help from the outside.

After all, he doubted Aaron was just sitting on his ass. Especially since according to Analia, he had a secret kingdom's-worth of resources hidden in the Wild Lands—because of course he did. Still, he couldn't fully shake his disappointment that she wasn't coming with him.

He understood why she had to stay. Not just for the sake of the plan she'd outlined to him, Sabi, and Rayner during the few visits she'd dared to the book nook, but because of the Crystal shard. The only thing more disappointing was the fact that Rayner played such an important role in said plan.

"Try to sit still," Rayner murmured, trailing his fingertips along Dimitri's jaw. "It's hard to match the sides of your face when it keeps moving."

Dimitri mumbled an apology, keeping his eyes squeezed shut as he forced himself to sit still. He waited for Rayner to continue, to use their moment alone as an opportunity to explain himself. But Rayner lapsed back into silence.

Now that he thought about it, Rayner had been unusually quiet the past three days. He hadn't tried to insert himself into their planning. He'd only offered advice or assistance when they hit a roadblock. Even when he dropped off Dimitri's meals, he didn't try to push conversation. Yet, Dimitri caught his look of wanting to say something every time their eyes met, just for Rayner to drop his gaze.

"I think I've got it," Rayner said, his hands falling from Dimitri's face. "Look at me?"

Dimitri didn't expect to be startled by the loss of Rayner's touch. He opened his eyes, his gaze flashing to Rayner's face, then immediately dropping to his lap. Gods, he could feel Rayner's eyes studying him, sending his insides squirming.

But their forced time together was almost at an end. They just had to make it out of the castle. Rayner would show him the way through the maze, and then he'd never have to see him again. And the twinge in his chest was so small he almost convinced himself it hadn't happened.

"You're all set," Rayner said, sitting back on his heels. "As usual, I couldn't change your eyes, but there's no resemblance to your previous disguise or your actual face."

"That's good," Dimitri mumbled.

He looked up, intending to ask if he knew where Sabi had stashed the servant uniform she'd stolen. But their eyes locked. And there was no denying the flinch as he remembered all the other times he'd seen that image.

Rayner kneeling before him. His gaze softened with something like consideration as he took in his handiwork. The way the left side of his mouth curled up before the right when he was satisfied, his smile remaining just a little bit crooked every time they had spiraled back into conversation.

Gods, how was all of that gone?

Rayner bit his lip, that same look of wanting to say something flickering in his eyes.

Dimitri opened his mouth, not sure if he wanted to snap at him or beg him to stop. But Rayner's head turned to the side.

"Sabi's coming," he rasped.

Dimitri's lungs squeezed. Before he could respond, Rayner rose, heading for the small mirror mounted on one of the bookshelves. And a moment later, Sabi swept inside.

"Everything looks good," she reported, coming to perch on her desk. "There are no Sun soldiers in the library, either, so you two should be able to slip out just fine."

"Thanks for checking," Dimitri said tightly.

Rayner mumbled his thanks as he changed his own appearance, but Dimitri refused to look at him. Sabi, either not noticing or not bothering to inquire, twisted on the table to prod Dimitri with her foot.

"Well, come on," she said, pulling him out of his chair. "You still have to get changed. And you better have packed your bag while I was gone because everything might be ready now, but—"

"Sabi!" Dimitri interrupted.

"What?" she shot back.

Dimitri turned in her grip, offering a faint smile. "I'll miss you, too."

Sabi's mouth trembled. "I hate you," she said. Then, she yanked him into a hug. "I better see you again."

Dimitri automatically started to assure her that she would, but the words stuck in his throat. Because he *didn't* know if he would see her again. Or the castle. Or the kingdom. Even once Deardryn was gone.

Dimitri cleared his throat, but Sabi didn't wait for his response. She shoved away, all business once more as she propelled him through the nook to where she'd stashed the servant uniform.

Just for a moment, Dimitri caught Rayner's eye in the mirror as he passed. And the softened look on his face had Dimitri wondering if he wasn't the only one thinking about everything he had lost.

"**C**ome on, Rois," Ember muttered, pacing back and forth before the abandoned castle stairwell.

In the days following Cadmus and Othin's confrontation, Ember had desperately tried to get in contact with Rois. While she had no problem spotting him throughout the castle, there was always someone around—and she doubted Othin would be pleased to hear she was hanging around a non-injured Ash soldier. She'd eventually resorted to slipping him a note as they'd passed in the hall, saying to meet her in the forgotten stairwell on the second floor while everyone had dinner.

And the bastard was late.

Ember rubbed her nose as she turned, the crackle of Everflame torches grating against her nerves.

She didn't have time for this. Every second she wasted was a second closer to watching Cadmus die. But she couldn't help him by herself. And her mind, her body, her entire being, *needed*—

Ember paused midstep as her eyes met a small black pair in the closest torch, her cravings momentarily forgotten.

"It's you again," she said.

The fire sprite squeaked in alarm. It shrank back against the wall, its body dissolving into the flames.

"Wait!" Ember yelped, reaching out her hand. "Don't go! I'm the only one here, I promise."

The fire sprite wavered. Slowly, its little body took shape once more, its fingers covering its mouth, its eyes wide. Just like the sprite in the Throne Room. But now that she got a good look at it...

"I thought I recognized you," Ember said, taking a slow, deliberate step toward the torch. "You're the fire sprite Lucilla sent to spy on me and Cadmus in the Council Chamber."

At the sound of Lucilla's name, the fire sprite ducked its head, its body curling in on itself. Ember couldn't blame it.

"So," she said, the word catching in her throat. "You know what happened, huh?"

The fire sprite nodded, not looking up.

"I... I'm sorry you lost your friend. I know she liked to play with you all."

Ember blinked hard, memories piercing through her mind like quick pricks of a blade. Lucilla laughing with a group of fire sprites in the entryway. This specific sprite perching on her shoulder to whisper in her ear. Her body crumbling to ash as she burned.

Ember squeezed the phoenix charms on her bracelet, her shoulders sagging. Part of her wanted to let the conversation end there, leave the fire sprite to its grief and herself to her own.

But there was a relief in talking about her. Not dancing around the subject, terrified to bring it up because Othin might be able to trace the story back to her. But Rosala spare her, she couldn't keep this grief, the memories, everything that was Lucilla, locked away inside her.

To Ember's surprise, the fire sprite seemed to agree. It lifted its head, reaching out a hand to her. Ember reached back, and the fire sprite hopped from the sconce to her fingers, its feet not quite hot enough to burn as it padded down to her palm.

"Are you willing to tell me your name?" she asked. She knew most sprites preferred to communicate through gestures, but she figured she'd ask since she'd seen this sprite speak to Lucilla.

"I'm Spark," the fire sprite said, the high crackle of their voice sounding neither male nor female.

"My name's Ember."

"Do you know what happened to Lucilla? We were trying to distract her in her chambers when you came for her help. We found her after that in the dungeon, but then..."

Spark wrapped their arms around themself, their body momentarily brightening to gold before fading back to orange. Ember barely noticed the burn of their feet as her heart cracked down the center.

"I don't know everything," she said, gently curling her fingers around them. "I know Deardryn used her and Cadmus as leverage against Anna. I know Lucilla died as a result. And... and I don't think there was anything we could have done to prevent that from happening."

At one point, Ember wouldn't have been able to speak those words aloud. For a long time, she'd wondered if she hadn't pulled Lucilla from her chambers, would she still have gotten caught? Would they have treated her any better if they found her in her chambers instead of in the apothecary?

But after seeing the conditions the Ash Royals were living in in the dungeon?

"Is that why I haven't seen any of you in the castle?" Ember asked. "Because you're all mourning?"

"Not just Lucilla. Our home, too." Spark curled up against Ember's fingers. "The Sun people are cruel. They swat us away from their candles like we're pests, or try to douse us along with the flames. Even the ones that leave us alone watch us from the corner of their eyes."

"They don't care they took your home, too," Ember murmured.

Spark nodded miserably.

"Well," Ember said, "Othin has decided to turn Anna's old chambers into mine. I know it's not much, but if you all need a place to hide, it's there. I can leave out extra candles."

Spark peeked up at her hopefully. Before they could respond, the stairwell door opened. Spark jumped.

"It's all right," Ember said quickly, glancing over her shoulder. "It's just Rois. You know, Ash Crystal Guard. Usually found moping after Anna, perhaps swinging a sword at someone."

Rois shot her an affronted look as he approached. "How many times do I need to tell you Anna and I are good?"

"I know that," Ember said innocently. "But what kind of friend would I be if I didn't constantly remind you how deep of a hole you had to drag yourself out of?"

Rois shoved her shoulder, and Spark tittered. Ember smiled down at them, hoping they couldn't see the tension around its edges.

"See?" she said. "He's a friend."

Spark nodded. But Ember wasn't surprised as they patted her hand, then disappeared with a quiet crackle.

"I've been wondering where all the fire sprites went," Rois murmured, moving to sit on a nearby windowsill.

"Turns out," Ember sighed, "we weren't the only ones who had our home invaded."

"Is that why you told me to meet you here?"

The momentary warmth in Ember's chest wavered, then flickered out.

"You don't even know the half of it," she said.

Ember quickly filled Rois in on everything that had happened. To her dismay, Rois only shrugged when she informed him they were officially searching for who stole Lucilla's body, telling her they would be stupid not to. She, in turn, told him he would be stupid if he didn't keep his head down, and while Rois assured her he would, she didn't believe him.

By the time she reached the end of her recount, she could barely think straight through the jumble of thoughts and emotions that had come to weigh down her mind. A problem she knew exactly how to solve...

"So," Rois said, "we have to get him out before the two weeks are up."

Ember blinked hard, realizing she'd been rubbing her fingertips together. "I don't know how," she said, shoving her hands into her robe pockets. "You didn't see him, Rois. There's nothing we can do to convince him to even *pretend* to work with Othin."

"I wasn't suggesting we reason with him."

"Well then what were you..." Ember trailed off, her eyes narrowing as Rois leaned back against the windowpane. "Are you suggesting we enact a prison break?"

"Yes," Rois said casually.

"You want us," Ember verified, "the people Othin is currently hunting, to enact a prison break."

"The fact that we got away with smuggling Lucilla's body out proves we're the people to do this."

Ember stared at him, nonplussed. "You've completely lost it," she informed him, slumping back against the wall.

"Maybe. But the fact that you summoned me here makes me think you want to do it, too."

Ember started to tell him there was a difference between wanting to do *something* and doing the riskiest option. But she paused.

Because that risky option also had the highest rewards. And every alternative her fuzzy mind struggled to summon always ended with a blade plunging toward Cadmus's chest, her own, Rois's, everyone's.

Rosala spare her, she couldn't think. She couldn't do nothing. But if every option could end in death, if only one promised safety for Cadmus and the Royals if pulled off...

"Even if we did this," she said, rubbing her face, "how are we supposed to get him and the rest of the Royals out? We can't exactly parade them out the front door."

"Of course not," Rois scoffed. "We get them out the same way I escape. Through the Royal vault."

"*That's* how you've been escaping?"

The only reason she knew about the vault connected to the dungeon was because she was friends with so many Royals. Still, she had no idea where the entrance was hidden within the dungeon, let alone that there was a door to the outside.

"It is," Rois said. He looked up from the sconce he'd been fiddling with, and Ember was taken aback by the blaze in his eyes. "This is my home, too. And there are some secrets Othin will *never* learn about, no matter how long he sits on the throne. So, we can either use them, or we can let our king die."

Rois's gaze pierced into hers, demanding an answer. As if he didn't realize he'd said the one thing she could never let happen.

Ember's shoulders sagged. "So," she sighed, "what do we do?"

"Overall," Rois said, rising from the windowsill, "we wait for the best time to break them free. Which means right now, we're going back to my chambers to plan."

How did his plans keep getting worse and worse?

"Do I really need to tell you," she asked, "why it would be a *terrible* idea for me to get caught in your chambers? As a healer apprentice sworn to celibacy? As the healer Othin chose *specifically* for neutrality?"

"If we can meet here, why can't we meet in my chambers?"

"Because I can pretend I ran into you on the stairs!"

Rois chuckled, sending Ember's blood fizzing through her veins.

"We can't plan in a stairwell," he said, stepping around her and heading for the door. "My chambers are only a couple halls away. We'll be fine."

Ember spluttered as she twisted to watch him, uselessly jabbing her finger at him.

Gods, why did she have to team up with a soldier? A man who was trained to charge into danger, who thought any problem could be solved with a blow, who learned risky plans could be the most advantageous.

Then again, perhaps she was the idiot. After all, she'd requested his help. She'd somehow agreed to his plan.

And her feet at some point had started moving after him.

"Stupid," she grumbled. "Stupid, reckless, 'I'll just cut my way out of any situation,' stupid little soldier."

"I thought I was mopey."

Ember poked him hard between the shoulder blades as they reached the stairwell door. Yet, as Rois pulled the door open, her response fizzled out.

Because on the other side, her brows arching in surprise, was Aeley.

Dimitri and Rayner walked through the quiet Moon Castle halls, both dressed in black servant uniforms. Even though Dimitri knew few people would be wandering around at such a late hour, even though he'd gotten used to roaming the halls with a disguise, he couldn't stop himself from constantly looking around.

"You're completely unrecognizable," Rayner whispered, eyeing Dimitri as he cringed at a far-off cough for the third time.

"I know," Dimitri snapped. But there was no bite to his words.

By the time they reached the hall leading to Deardryn's study, his nerves were positively frayed. He glanced around, taking in the closed study door, the empty hallway ahead of him. Had they gotten the timing wrong?

The thought had barely formed when Analia rounded the corner at the other end of the hall. She wore a gown of dark purple velvet, her hair loose around her shoulders, her sleeves pulled over her damper cuffs.

They'd planned on meeting in this spot to make sure their timing was synced, all the while knowing they couldn't risk acknowledging each other. Still, Dimitri's heart ached as they drew closer, knowing he had to stay silent with Deardryn's door mere feet away.

Analia looked at him, at the door, the empty hall. Just as they were about to pass, she mouthed something that looked a lot like, "Fuck it." Then, she reached for him.

Dimitri's lungs finally relaxed as Analia hugged him tight. He closed his eyes, knowing Rayner would keep watch, allowing himself to savor what would likely be his final good memory in this castle.

"Be safe," Analia whispered in his ear.

"You, too, Flashfire," he murmured.

Analia momentarily tightened her grip. Then, with a sigh, she pulled back. Glancing at Rayner, she mimed flicking a spark at him, Rayner's lips twitching even as he dropped his gaze.

And somehow, Dimitri let his arms fall back to his sides.

Analia stepped away, giving him a shooing gesture as she stationed herself beside the study door.

But as he and Rayner continued down the hall, he felt a little more solid. Not just in himself, but in their plan.

After all, he'd managed to stay undetected for over a week. He'd made it halfway across the castle *without* a disguise before getting caught, and even then, he'd wriggled free. And now, he had a disguise, he had a plan, and everything was going accordingly.

He just had to take it one step at a time. Down the stairs. Around a corner. The back door just a hallway away.

Dimitri rounded the final corner, Rayner a step behind. It took him a moment to register the voice echoing down the hall, another moment to process what he was hearing.

Because that was Tavian at the end of the hall, just as he expected. But next to him, completely oblivious to his surroundings as he talked and leaned against the door, was a Sun guard.

Chapter 19

"So," Aaron said. "That's the Moon Castle."

He stood at the top of a forested hill, staring up at the distant lights of the Moon Castle against the starry sky. He and Laness had set out first thing that morning, Aaron able to shadowjump them a good ways into the Wild Lands before Laness took over. Fortunately, the enka flowers they'd roottraveled to were able to withstand the winter chill thanks to their magic, but it was still slow going.

At least, compared to what Aaron was used to. Especially as the anticipation twisted into a knot in his stomach.

"I think this is the closest I can get us," Laness said, frost crunching beneath her boots as she came up beside him. "There are more flowers I can sense, but they're all beyond the maze. It'll be faster if we go on foot from here rather than trying to circle back."

Aaron nodded. "And we still have time?"

"We're right on schedule," she confirmed. "I told you I could handle this."

"I never doubted it," Aaron said, ruffling her short brown hair.

Still, he could see the exhaustion on her face in the moonlight as she drank from her canteen—understandably so. She'd made a lot of jumps in a short amount of time. And if they happened to run into trouble ahead...

"I can feel you worrying," she complained, sliding her canteen back into her pack. "You're such a fusser."

Aaron started to protest. But Laness marched off down the hill, calling over her shoulder, "Well, come on. We won't stay on schedule if you stop to brood."

Aaron laughed under his breath, his unease beginning to slacken.

Still, he couldn't help glancing up at the stars as he headed after her, silently hoping everything was going well.

Analia stepped into Deardryn's study, her fingers toying with her phoenix pin in her gown pocket. In the two days since Deardryn had tried to test her tolerance, she hadn't been summoned back—and she wasn't complaining. Not just because it allowed her to focus on her plan, but because the memory of that magic still sent a shudder down her spine.

But to her relief, there was no sign of the Crystal's magic field as the door closed behind her. All she could sense was Deardryn's network—and was that a pulse coming from her sun dragon pendant? Before Analia could be sure, Deardryn looked up from her notes.

"I wasn't expecting it to be you knocking on my door," she mused, brushing back her golden curls. "Especially not at this hour."

"I only just made up my mind and wanted to let you know, and the servants said you usually stay in here pretty late." Analia moved to the desk, easing into her usual seat across from Deardryn. "What are you working on?"

She expected Deardryn to wave the question aside. But she looked down, pulling her book closer to herself as she said, "I've been reading my notes. I find it helpful to go back through my thoughts, particularly when the big picture has become blurred."

"I see."

For a few heartbeats, the two lapsed into silence. Analia fidgeted with her fingers on the tabletop, Deardryn not seeming to notice as she closed her book, a thoughtful little frown playing across her lips.

As she slipped it into one of the desk drawers, Analia realized it wasn't the blue book she'd seen her take notes in before. It was the black-and-gold leather diary she'd been writing in the first day she summoned Analia. The same one she'd spotted Deardryn writing in during her only visit to her Sun Castle study.

Interesting.

"Well then," Deardryn said, primly folding her hands on the table. "You've made up your mind on something?"

"I have," Analia hedged.

She could feel Deardryn's expectant gaze on her, but she kept her eyes on her fingers, absently tracing a groove in the wood. Exactly where the Crystal had sat.

"Why haven't you summoned me the past two days?" she asked suddenly.

Deardryn's eyes widened a fraction. Her hand went to her golden bracelets, "Contrary to what you might think, my goal isn't to harm you."

"No," Analia muttered, "it's just a consequence of what you *do* want."

Deardryn opened her mouth as if to disagree. But she only looked away, her shoulders slumping with a sigh. "I suppose that's how it appears, doesn't it?"

Appears? Analia's hands curled around the edge of the table, her retort burning against her lips. But Deardryn beat her to it.

"I haven't summoned you because I thought you would benefit from some rest after you—after *I*—subjected you to the Crystal. In the meantime, I've been searching for a new approach for my research since that cannot happen again. I promised you that."

As if Deardryn's promises meant anything.

Deardryn leaned forward, her expression almost desperate. Pleading. As if she needed Analia to believe her, needed her to realize something.

But Analia had no idea what pieces Deardryn was trying to give her. And the fact that after everything she had done, she was coming to *her* of all people for a glimmer of redemption?

Analia bit her cheek, hard enough she tasted blood. She couldn't explode. Not yet. Not while Dimitri was still in Deardryn's reach.

Analia gave herself a moment to think of her friend. Then, she let her expression relax. She sat back in her chair, folding her arms.

"The good news," she said, remarkably level, "is you won't have to change your technique too much."

Deardryn's gaze dimmed. "Analia," she said, her hand half-extending across the table before sliding back. "You can't outlast the Crystal. Your Blessing might make you uniquely equipped to handle it, but it also makes you far more susceptible. I won't risk you."

"You won't have to," Analia said. "I've thought of another way."

"You have," Deardryn said slowly.

Analia nodded. "You weren't the only one thinking these past few days. And what I've decided is I want to help you research the Crystal."

Dimitri took one look at the Sun guard standing before the back door, still talking with Tavian. Then, he turned on his heel and fled back around the corner, Rayner cursing under his breath as he chased after him.

But Dimitri didn't go far. He sagged against the wall, his hand flexing around his wrist as his mind raced.

Gods, what was he supposed to do? It was only supposed to be Tavian at the door. Sylas had specifically assigned him because Analia had confirmed he could be trusted to let them out without question. And Sabi had confirmed on her way back to the nook that he was there.

Crystal spare him, had Deardryn already figured them out?

"Dimitri," Rayner whispered. "We have to keep going."

"I know," he ground out.

But how? There was no way that guard would let them pass without question. All of the other exits were too far from the maze, and even if this was the only door with a Sun guard, Tavian was the only Moon soldier who knew the plan. Which meant there was only one option.

Dimitri glanced at Rayner hanging back a few paces, giving him space. And he didn't have to ask to know they'd come to the same conclusion.

They had to lie. A lot.

Dimitri squeezed his wrist, hard enough he could feel his pulse. Then, he let his hand drop. He squared his shoulders. And, praying he wasn't about to make a massive mistake, he marched back around the corner, Rayner falling into step beside him.

Dimitri's heart pounded against his ribs as he walked down the hall, bracing himself for the moment the guard looked over at him. But the soldier seemed thoroughly engrossed in his conversation, Dimitri making out the words as he drew nearer.

"We're completely connected," he said, tapping the sun dragon clasp on his cloak. "The Moon military has nothing like that."

"I know," Tavian said, utterly disinterested. "It's such a shame. Oh look, servants."

Dimitri choked back a curse as the Sun soldier blinked, then twisted to look directly at him and Rayner. Crystal fuck him, it was the same soldier Dannel had been talking with when he'd caught Dimitri. Same square face, same olive skin, same chin-length black hair.

"You," the guard called, crooking his finger at Rayner. "What are you two doing here at this hour?"

"We have orders from His Majesty," Rayner said smoothly, his black hair falling into his eyes as he bowed his head.

"Is that so?" The Sun soldier's gaze flicked to Dimitri. "What could Sylas want at this hour?"

Dimitri swallowed hard, dragging his palms down his pants. But that was good. He was just another submissive servant, unnerved by a direct question from a guard. This was no different from any other tale he spun when avoiding his scrub work in the Sun Castle.

Dimitri looked up at the guard, the light from the full moon pouring through the door's window behind him.

"It's a full moon, sir," he said.

The soldier's brow furrowed. "What does that have to do with anything?"

"That's when the lunar hawks shed their feathers," he explained. "We're supposed to collect them in preparation for the next Full Moon Festival."

"Then why aren't you going out the front door to the woods? Or even out to the gardens. There's nothing this way except hedges."

Well fuck, that was a fair question.

Dimitri started to reply, not knowing what he would say, but Rayner cut in smoothly, "There's a nest just beyond the maze. We can usually find a good amount from the parents flying overhead."

"Huh." The Sun soldier scratched his face, Dimitri fighting to remain still.

There was no reason for this guard to question their story. Especially if he'd been to the last festival. But clearly, the boredom of being stationed somewhere instead of his usual patrol was getting to him. He opened his mouth, Dimitri bracing for the next round of questions.

"Let it go, Zan," Tavian drawled, slumping back against the door. "They're feather collecting. You do realize we're stationed here to prevent people from coming *in*, not from going out, don't you?"

Zan's face flushed, his hand going to the sword at his hip. "Our *job*," he said, "is to prevent any suspicious activity. I would say a request to leave the castle through the back door on the grounds of orders I'm not aware of is rather suspicious."

"You're not aware of them because Deardryn assigned you here, not Sylas," Tavian retorted.

"Are you saying you knew about it?"

"I know this happens once a month."

"So if Her Majesty has been here for so long, why wouldn't she have told me to expect this?"

"Because I would say Deardryn paying that close attention to everything happening in this castle would be suspicious in itself."

Dimitri's eyes bounced between the guards, his breathing fast and shallow. Gods, Tavian. They were supposed to slip out without making a scene, and yet, he was making thinly veiled accusations about Deardryn to one of her men. What was he thinking?

Beside him, Rayner shifted restlessly. Crystal spare him, the last thing he needed was Rayner trying something on top of it all. He had to defuse this. Fast.

"Apologies," he said, taking a half step forward. "I wish there was a way we could prove to you we're just trying to collect some feathers. You're welcome to search us for weapons. One of you could even accompany us outside."

The offer tasted foul in Dimitri's mouth, but he knew if he didn't make it, Zan would. And then, he would have no chance of Tavian taking that slot—although how would Tavian be able to keep his involvement hidden if he did accompany them?

Dimitri's questions turned into an ache behind his eyes. But he stayed quiet as Zan mulled it over, the guard momentarily looking up to meet his gaze. And Dimitri's stomach sank as Zan gave a slow, predatory nod.

"You two are servants, huh?" he asked, fingering his sword hilt.

Dimitri and Rayner exchanged a quick look. "We are," Rayner said warily.

"And you have orders from Sylas?"

The back of Dimitri's neck tingled. But he had no choice but to nod.

"I see."

Zan stepped closer, Dimitri's breath catching as he ducked his head to meet his gaze.

"Don't worry," he said, whisper soft. "I believe you. After all, you've been a servant for a long time. That's what happens when you have the Sun King's eyes."

A jolt ran down Dimitri's spine. He stumbled back, Rayner cursing under his breath as he moved closer, Tavian's chain mail clinking as he reached for something.

"There's no point denying it," Zan said, advancing on him. "Dannel told us how he recognized you in the hall. Everything changed except your eyes. Meaning you had that masquerader's help. And you walked right into the trap Deardryn set for you."

Dimitri's mind scrambled for a response, a plan, anything. But there was nothing. No way to deny, no time to flee, no way to fight back.

Dimitri's magic pulsed deep in his gut, building, building, building.

Zan reached for his sun dragon clasp.

Just for a sword tip to pierce through his throat. His body spasmed, words choking off, blood spilling down his skin.

Tavian withdrew his blade from the back of his neck. And Zan crumpled to the floor with a bloody hiss.

Dead.

Chapter 20

"What the fuck is the matter with you?" Dimitri demanded, whirling on Tavian.

"I just saved your ass, urchin," he retorted, sheathing his bloody sword. "That idiot has been bragging to me since the moment he got here that all of the Sun soldiers have been equipped with communication magic."

Rayner cursed. "He grabbed his cloak clasp right before you got him."

Dimitri shook his head, oddly dizzy as he watched the blood spread across the marble floor. How was their plan already falling apart?

"If he touched it," Tavian said, crouching beside the body, "we have to assume he got the message out. Which means you two need to go."

Right. Because the Sun guards were coming for him. They would be there any moment. And he and Rayner were completely defenseless in this hallway.

Dimitri hugged his stomach, forcing the flicker of magic in his gut back down. He couldn't fall apart. He had to focus, make a plan. *Think.*

"How are we going to explain that he was killed from behind?" he asked, his stomach heaving as he glanced back at the red-stained marble.

"I'll think of something," Tavian said. "As for me..."

Tavian pulled a dagger from Zan's weapon belt. Then, with an impossibly casual movement, he plunged it into the unprotected spot on his own shoulder, grunting a curse. Dimitri thought he was going to be sick.

"Again," he choked out. "What the fuck's the matter with you?"

"I'm keeping my cover. If I'm not going to chase after you, I have to have a reason."

He pulled the dagger free with a soft groan, Dimitri tasting bile as he looked away. Completely unfazed, Tavian shoved Zan's body away from the door, Rayner glancing at what had to be sheer nausea on Dimitri's face as he moved to help.

"You all right?" he asked.

"That's a lot of blood," Dimitri mumbled.

"You don't like the sight of blood?"

"Not *that much*. But Tavian doesn't have a sheath for that dagger, and he can't be found with a bloody weapon, so you have to take it."

Tavian hummed his agreement. Dimitri turned away as Rayner accepted the blade, a shudder running down his spine as he scanned the hallway.

There was no telling how close the Sun soldiers were. And if Deardryn had specifically stationed one here...

Dimitri squeezed his wrist, focusing on the black heart beneath his fingers as he took a deep breath. Let it out slow.

One step at a time.

"We can't waste any more time," he said, keeping his gaze on the door as he turned back. "There's nothing stopping us from still using the maze."

They'd just be pursued now.

"You're right," Rayner said, rising and reaching for the doorknob. "I can still lead you through the maze. But now that they know I'm helping you...'"

His gaze cut to Dimitri. He gave a quick nod, too focused on staying calm to register the surprise that flashed across his face.

"Then get out of here," Tavian said from where he knelt. "I'll stall as long as I can."

Dimitri nodded, the cool night air ruffling his hair as Rayner opened the door. Right before he stepped outside, he glanced back. Back at the closest thing he'd ever had to a home, its floors stained with blood, its halls haunted by ghosts and memories.

Well, that was how it usually panned out.

Dimitri blinked hard, then turned away. "Let's go."

Ember inched behind Rois, Aeley tilting her head as she looked them up and down. The former Ash Queen was mercifully alone on the other side of the door, a small potted peace lily cradled in the crook of her arm.

"I was wondering if anyone else remembered this stairwell," she said.

Rois clasped his hands behind his back, perfectly casual. Ember, meanwhile, could barely think over the pound of her pulse.

"Good evening, Your Majesty," he said politely. "Can I offer an escort wherever you're going?"

"I'm just going to my chambers. This stairwell is the fastest route from where I started. Ember, I can see you," she added dryly.

Ember fought the urge to duck behind Rois even more. Getting caught with him by any Sun person would have been bad enough, but Aeley? The woman who knew all of their history?

Doing her best to appear nonchalant, Ember stepped out from behind Rois, nevertheless unable to meet Aeley's gaze. "I like your peace lily," she mumbled.

She waited for Aeley to brush the comment aside, knowing the interrogation of what she and Rois were up to was inevitable. But Aeley only offered a small, polite smile.

"Thank you. I retrieved it from Galena this afternoon."

"Is that where you were coming from?" Rois asked.

"It was. I considered stopping at the dungeon to visit my son, but I didn't want to deal with the new increase in dungeon patrols."

Her deep blue eyes casually flicked to Rois.

Rois went perfectly still. Ember didn't think she was breathing.

This was it. Aeley not only had them cornered, but she'd figured out Rois's escape methods as well. She had everything she needed to nail them.

Ember tensed, waiting for the blow.

"May I enter my stairwell now?" Aeley asked after a beat.

Rois started. Recovering quickly, he stepped aside, only slightly flushed as he offered his apologies. Ember scurried back a few steps as Aeley entered, the clunk of the door shutting nearly sending her jumping out of her skin.

Gods, she couldn't make sense of this woman. First, she denounced the Ash Royals, but then helped get Ember of all healers inside, but then said *nothing* when Othin threatened to kill Cadmus—and agreed to work with him after his wife killed Lucilla. None of it made sense.

Ember's gaze bounced between Aeley and Rois as they continued their conversation, only able to read a cool indifference on the former queen's face.

"I'm surprised Othin hasn't assigned a Sun guard to you," Rois said.

"He tried, but I told him I would not be trailed by guards in my own home."

Aeley's gaze cut to Ember so fast she almost missed it. And all she could think about was the way Lucilla's eyes would dart to Cadmus the same exact way whenever she had an idea, always wanting to gauge his reaction but never wanting him to know.

Ember's hand went to her bracelet, the three phoenix charms digging into her palm.

Lucilla had sacrificed herself not just for her siblings, but this castle. This kingdom. The place Aeley just referred to as her home.

Rois started to reply, but Ember stepped forward. "Apologies," she said, her eyes on Aeley. "I only just realized I never gave you my report on my work in the dungeon."

Aeley turned toward her fully, her head tilting. Behind her, Rois vehemently shook his head, looking at Ember like she'd completely lost it. But she ignored him, Spark's Everflame torch flickering in the corner of her eye.

She had to know why the fire sprites had to lose their home. Why her friends were either imprisoned or dead. Why Aeley was doing what she was doing. And she could only pray to Rosala that the small nod Aeley gave her was one of confirmation.

"You're correct." She looked over at Rois, Ember not daring to breathe. "I believe *you* should be in your chambers?"

Rois winced. "Since I'm already out, I can escort you two to the Council Chamber," he offered.

He reached for the door, but Aeley stopped him with a touch to his arm.

"That won't be necessary," she said. "We'll be going to my chambers instead."

Ember straightened. She would have thought getting caught alone in Aeley's chambers would be even worse than Rois's.

"Your Majesty," she said carefully, "is that a good idea?"

"Are you questioning your queen?" Aeley asked softly.

No. She was questioning every decision she had made up until this point. Especially since the ones she'd told herself were made with a clear mind were seemingly worse than the ones that weren't.

"I can still escort you two," Rois offered, the stairwell having gone uncomfortably quiet.

"Your chambers are in the opposite direction," Aeley pointed out.

Rois started to protest, his gaze on Ember. Clearly not wanting to leave her alone to deal with the backlash.

Part of Ember was surprisingly touched. But there would be no getting the answers she needed if he was there.

"It's all right, Rois," she said, lifting her hand to scratch her healer markings. "We're just discussing information."

Her sleeve shifted down, the three metal phoenix charms on her enka bracelet flashing in the Everflame light. Rois's eyes moved to the charms, up to Ember's face, his jaw tight. But to Ember's relief, he gave a short nod. "Fair enough."

Aeley thoughtfully ran her finger down a peace lily leaf, but she remained quiet as Rois opened the door, giving Ember one last look before slipping out. And Ember could only hope Aeley's watchful eyes missed the way her hands started to shake as she turned and followed the former Ash Queen up the stairs.

"So," Deardryn said, her voice smooth as silk as she settled back in her chair. "You want to continue our research."

"I do," Analia confirmed, keeping her chin high.

"Interesting." Deardryn thoughtfully turned her sun dragon pendant between her fingers, the metal giving a quick magical pulse.

Analia's eyes narrowed. Before she could inquire, Deardryn smiled slightly, her fingers shifting to disentangle a golden curl from the chain.

"Tell me," she said conversationally. "What has triggered such a request?"

"You mean besides our bargain?"

Deardryn scoffed and swatted her hand. "We both know our bargain means nothing. You yourself informed me it was voided your first day in my study. So, why should I believe you have any interest now?"

From anyone else, the question would have been accusatory. But Deardryn only tilted her head, an expectant teacher waiting for her student's response.

"You should believe me," Analia said, "because my desire to continue working with the Crystal has nothing to do with wanting to help you."

Deardryn's eyes gleamed. "Go on."

Something about that look put Analia on edge. Still, she wouldn't hesitate and give Deardryn something to pounce on.

"I will never forget what the Crystal did to me in my uncle's chambers," she began, her hands fisting in her velvet skirts beneath the table. "But I also thought the same thing as you. That had been a release of magic stored up for centuries, maybe even millennia. It had to be more tolerable now that the buildup was gone. But after our experiment a few days ago?"

Analia shook her head. "I don't want to help your research. But I like the idea of you having a weapon that can completely incapacitate me even less."

All true statements. Judging by the thoughtful finger Deardryn rested against her chin, she knew it.

"So," she mused. "You want to continue our research to try and build up your tolerance."

"You get your research, and I get a dagger removed from my back," Analia confirmed.

"I would get research?" Deardryn asked innocently. "Does that mean you would cooperate with my tests?"

Analia pursed her lips.

"Come now, Analia," Deardryn chided. "You can't expect me to give you everything you want with nothing in return. Especially since your main motivation is to distract me while Dimitri escapes."

Dimitri hurried after Rayner through the hedge maze, the light from the full moon silvering the tops of the foliage that rose over a foot above their heads.

"How much further until we're out?" he asked.

"We still have a ways to go," Rayner said. "This maze is huge, but I've got us on the fastest path. At least, the fastest one I know of. I don't think Sylas even knows every route in here."

"What about the Sun guards?"

Rayner didn't reply. Dimitri's stomach twisted, his magic flickering through his network. But he shoved it down as he followed Rayner around a sharp left turn.

For someone who claimed to only know so much about the maze, Rayner seemed confident in where he was going. He chose paths without pause, one of which being a hidden opening in the hedge that left Dimitri's hands scraped and stinging from branches as he shoved through.

But he didn't complain. He just kept moving. That was all he could do, swearing he heard footsteps far behind them, slowly gaining, his ears pricking at every rustle of leaves from the wind.

"How close are we now?" he asked.

"About thirty seconds closer."

Dimitri grimaced. He knew he was being annoying—part of him wished Rayner would call him out already. But Rayner remained calm, focused, as he peered down the dark rows.

It was almost infuriating after everything that had happened in the hallway, with everything that could happen next. And even though Dimitri hated to admit it, it was also the smallest bit reassuring.

"Can I ask you something?" Rayner asked suddenly.

Dimitri jerked his gaze away from Rayner's face, his body tensing. But he supposed it was only fair at this point.

"Fine," he said.

"Why are we doing this?"

Dimitri started to tell him that was an obnoxiously vague question, but Rayner continued.

"I don't mean why are we escaping because I understand that. But why are we doing it this way specifically? Fleeing with nothing but hope that a friend you haven't seen or talked to for the majority of your friendship will show up to help you. Risking your life to keep another friend safe in the castle. I just..."

Rayner ran a hand through his hair, struggling for words. "How are you able to trust them like that? After growing up with nothing, only knowing people who betrayed you. How are you able to put so much trust in them?"

It was a genuine question. And that made it hurt all the more.

"Because," Dimitri said roughly, "they're everything to me."

"But *why?*"

"Because they proved themselves. Over and over again, no matter how hard I tried to push them away, they stayed. They cared about me.

"You think I'm the only one in danger with this escape, but they're risking so much as well. For me. So why wouldn't I do the same for them?"

"But it was only four months," Rayner pressed, taking the right turn at the fork in the path. "You said Analia was only in the Sun Kingdom for four months, and that was long enough for you to feel certain?"

"If you're trying to tell me," Dimitri said, his fists tightening, "that four months isn't enough to stop them from betraying me, don't bother. You already did."

Rayner's face twisted. Dimitri glared, ready for his retort. But Rayner only looked away, frost crunching beneath his boots as he rounded another corner. And that silent admission had Dimitri's nerves igniting.

"What's wrong?" he taunted, falling back into step beside him. "Are you realizing you can't deny it?"

"Forget I asked," Rayner muttered.

"Believe it or not, it's not fucking hard to be a decent person."

"Oh, get off your pedestal," Rayner snapped, whirling on him.

Dimitri took an automatic step back.

"I'm tired of you constantly snapping at me," Rayner went on, resetting the distance between them. "Not even letting me get a word out, as if you already know what I'm about to say. As if you have *any* idea what I've been through, what has made me act the way I do."

"Really?" Dimitri asked, craning his neck to glare at him. "The shitty childhood? *That's* the excuse you're going with? As if you're the only one who's been treated poorly?

Last I checked, *you* were the one who mentioned the misery I grew up in, and yet I never stabbed you in the back."

"Not yet, maybe."

"What's that supposed to mean?"

"If you'll recall," Rayner said dryly, "you weren't exactly warm and fuzzy when we first met."

"And you think that's the same as lying and spying on me?" Dimitri exclaimed, throwing up his hands.

"No," Rayner snapped, prowling closer, Dimitri's back hitting the hedges. "That's my point. You had twenty years of torment in a castle. I had…"

Rayner trailed off, his fists clenching and unclenching at his sides. Dimitri's heart hammered against his ribs, his chest heaving. And he fucking relished it.

Finally, an outlet. A reason to let everything explode. Not just the anxiety from the past hour, the grief and rage constantly warring inside him. But from the silence of the past three days: wondering what Rayner wanted to say, bracing himself for the moment he spoke, the way he wanted to curl into a ball and hide every fucking time Rayner walked in the room.

"What?" Dimitri asked, the word slicing between them. "You had *what?*"

Dimitri waited for Rayner to lash out, practically vibrating with anticipation.

But when Rayner looked back at him, there was no anger in his eyes. Not even regret. There was just an exhaustion that had Dimitri's temper stuttering.

"I've been on my own for almost a century," he said softly. "I've done what it takes to survive; I've pushed people away and betrayed those I couldn't, and I… I've come to terms with that. But with you?"

Rayner shook his head. Dimitri had no name for the emotion that sliced through him.

"You *should* feel bad," Dimitri said shakily. "Not just about me, but every person you've used and tossed aside for your own gain."

"I know."

"And yet, you're not sorry for doing what it takes to survive."

Rayner's lips parted, but no words came out. Dimitri looked away, dragging a hand down his face.

Gods, what were they doing? They were standing in a hedge maze, verbally eviscerating each other when they were supposed to be escaping. They were supposed to be fleeing from the Sun guards that could come at any moment.

He was supposed to be taking it one step at a time; he'd promised Analia he'd be safe. So how had he ended up so bloodied, and mangled, and ruined?

"What do you want, Rayner?" he asked, more tired than anything.

He expected Rayner to remain silent. But he didn't miss a beat as he said, "I want to make it right."

A dangerous question balanced on the tip of Dimitri's tongue: why? One little question that he somehow knew would completely destroy him.

He looked up at Rayner, his face cast in shadows by the moonlight. He hadn't realized how close they'd gotten.

Close enough he could smell his dark, earthy scent. Close enough he could feel the heat radiating off his skin.

Close enough he felt the wind against his cheek as the arrow whizzed between them.

Chapter 21

Ember shifted from foot to foot as Aeley shut her chamber door behind her. For as long as Ember had been roaming the Ash Castle corridors, this was one of the few chambers she'd never stepped foot inside.

It wasn't terribly different from Accalon's chambers, his massive bookcases replaced by a dark settee, Aeley's vanity stationed beside a messy desk. The large, central bed was covered by a charcoal-and-blue duvet, matching the minimalist landscape paintings framed on the walls.

Aeley stepped over to the window, making no attempt to disrupt the quiet. Ember scratched her nose, imagining a sharp, leafy smell on her fingers as she inhaled.

Gods, she would give *anything* for even a fragment of devinroot.

"Is this window all right?" Aeley asked.

Ember started. "What?"

"For the peace lily," Aeley said patiently, settling the dark blue pot on the windowsill. "You've already discovered I bring these to Arienne's and the child's graves once a month, so there's no point denying what it's for. But I won't be able to go for a few days. And since you specialize in herbology, I thought you might know if this window would provide the right amount of light in the meantime."

Ember stared at her blankly, her thoughts feeling fuzzy around the edges. She had brought her here... to talk about plants?

Aeley folded her arms, clearly losing patience.

"Yes," Ember said haltingly, stepping deeper into the room. "Peace lilies prefer indirect light, so this north-facing window works well."

"That's good to know." Aeley gave Ember a nod of thanks, then turned back to her plant.

Ember mouthed a "You're welcome," her stiff body easing down onto a nearby armchair. What was she supposed to do now? It felt too abrupt to go from plant care tips to motive interrogations—even for her.

Should she wait for Aeley to broach the subject herself? She clearly wanted to say something, seeing as she'd invited Ember to her chambers.

"You seem restless lately," Aeley observed, glancing over her shoulder.

Ember forced her fingers to stop fidgeting with her sleeve. "There's been a lot to stress about," she said carefully. "Like all the people I've had to heal."

"Yes," Aeley mused, coming to sit on the foot of her bed. "I can only imagine how uncomfortable it is to heal the soldiers who invaded your home."

"Nowhere near as uncomfortable as having to heal my Royals in their cells."

Aeley's lips parted. Ember leaned forward, ready to seize on any shred of redeemability Aeley could give her. But Aeley remained silent, lightly tugging on the ends of her golden hair. And Ember couldn't have stopped the words that burned past her lips if she tried.

"How could you do this? How could you stand there, *silent,* as that barbarian threatened to kill Cadmus? How could you side with him after his wife killed Lucilla? How do you have *nothing* to say for yourself—"

"That's enough," Aeley said softly.

But Ember couldn't stop. She'd spent the past two weeks bottling everything up inside, and now that the seal had been loosened, there was no going back.

"Lucilla died to protect this kingdom. Do you know that? She sacrificed herself trying to protect Analia and Cadmus, and now you've left them both to rot. I'm not surprised about Analia, you've never done anything for her. But Cadmus? What kind of queen are you? What kind of mother—"

"I *am* a mother," Aeley interrupted, her calm cracking as her magic chilled the chamber. "That's exactly it. I don't expect Othin or any of his headstrong, singularly male advisors to understand what that means. But I would have thought you would stop and think."

Her words hit Ember like a winter wind. She sat back hard in her seat, not daring to believe what Aeley was implying. Not when there were still pieces that didn't line up.

"So then why?" she asked raggedly.

Aeley dragged a hand down her face, not immediately responding. Ember waited silently, her nerves rubbed raw, just wanting this nightmare to come to an end.

Finally, Aeley rose to her feet. "This kingdom was turned into a battlefield nearly three weeks ago," she said, heading for a corner cart filled with liquor bottles. "In battle, there are certain rules. Expectations. You ask any military captain, and he will tell you that those battles are won by bloodshed."

"*'He will'* tell you?" Ember asked halfheartedly.

"Yes, 'he.'" Aeley uncorked a bottle of amber liquid and filled a glass. "He'll tell you battles are won by conquering land with swords and spears and arrows. All men's weapons, enacting men's strategies."

Ember didn't have the energy to indulge whatever excuse Aeley was weaving. But she felt obligated to point out, "There are plenty of female soldiers on those battlefields."

"There are," Aeley agreed. "But none of those weapons that supposedly win battles were designed for us."

Filling a second glass, Aeley turned. She offered Ember one of the glasses as she approached, Ember accepting it warily.

"What are you trying to say?" she asked.

"I'm not saying anything," Aeley said, reclaiming her spot at the foot of her bed. "I'm merely observing that those weapons are designed for brute strength. They require bravery—or perhaps idiocy—to charge into danger with no regard. And we can certainly reach that point. Some more easily than others."

Aeley gave Ember a pointed look. "But it's not as innate for us. So, we were given our own weapons. Tears, poison, smiles, and lies. And what a coincidence those weapons are the ones dismissed as weak, cowardly, and dishonorable."

Aeley took a long sip from her glass, almost managing to hide the way her face had twisted. But Ember didn't dare to hope. Not yet.

"Funny how those are the weapons anyone can wield," she said, twirling her glass between her fingers.

"Yes," Aeley agreed. "And funny how those are the weapons no one plans for."

Aeley's eyes met hers. And Ember sagged in relief as she saw the quiet blaze there.

Her instincts had been right back in the square: this was a facade. But something about the lingering chill of her magic had Ember unable to relax as Aeley placed her glass on the nearby side table, her fingers going to her diamond wedding ring.

"The night before Cadmus is to make his decision," she said, "Othin has scheduled a meeting with myself and his advisors to discuss all potential outcomes. He has also decided to increase dungeon security in the meantime. He seems determined to make sure nothing happens to the Royals. And if something *were* to happen, he would naturally ask me who I thought the most likely suspects were."

Ember's stomach sank. "You can't lie to your king, after all," she managed.

"No, I cannot. And I can only assume if I was that suspect, I would want someone to flee to."

"Someone?" Ember asked.

"Yes. After all, there would be no place in this kingdom safe for me after that."

Gods, she hadn't thought about that.

Ember brought her glass to her lips, barely tasting the woody notes of the whiskey as she downed it in one go. But even as it settled in a warm glow in her stomach, she knew that wasn't what she was wanting—what she was craving.

Aeley didn't pay Ember's spiral any attention as she wiggled her ring off her finger. "There we go. I've been trying to get this off for days now."

"Have you?" Ember croaked.

"Yes. Funny how the longer we wear something, the harder it is to erase." Aeley slipped the ring into a pocket in her gray gown. "Analia had a ring line on her middle finger when I last saw her. I suppose the struggle runs in the family."

Ember blinked hard, Aeley pulling her mind in several directions at once.

Was she suggesting Ember got Analia's help? But Othin told Cadmus in front of her she was with Deardryn.

"I would think," Ember said slowly, "that you wouldn't have many people available to help you."

She stared pleadingly into Aeley's face, needing a straight answer. Aeley thought for a moment, her eyes flicking to the chamber door. Undoubtedly aware of the lack of security—wait. Security, guard, Analia, ring line.

Was Aeley insinuating she should contact Aaron? But why bring up the ring line—unless she and Analia had more to catch up on than she realized.

Aeley gave her a small nod. "All you need is one person."

Rosala spare her, what had she gotten herself into? She needed a plan, needed to figure out how she could pull this off—she needed her devinroot. She needed it like roots needed water, like leaves needed sunlight.

To live. To survive.

"Well," Aeley eventually said, rising from the bed and heading for her vanity. "I believe that should cover your report?"

The abrupt dismissal smacked Ember between the eyes. Mumbling an affirmation, she rose unsteadily to her feet, her mind swirling. But at least she'd gotten what she'd come here for.

Aeley was on their side. But that didn't mean she wouldn't turn Ember in to maintain her cover.

Ember didn't even know if she could blame her as she stumbled to the door. Yet, as she reached for the doorknob, her farewell already on her lips, she spotted the phoenix charms dangling from her wrist.

"Your Majesty," she said, turning back.

Aeley briefly looked up as she unclasped her ruby pendant. "Yes?"

"I..." Ember swallowed hard.

She didn't have the tact to create careful phrasings. She didn't know if it was wise to blow her cover. But her mind, her heart, her gut, told her this was something she needed to do. She crossed to the vanity, unclasping one of the phoenix charms from her bracelet and offering it to Aeley.

"Rise again," she said, her voice cracking.

Aeley's eyes flashed to her face. Ember could have sworn her fingers shook slightly as she accepted the charm, something like hope and despair warring in her eyes as she found its groove.

She popped it open. Looked down at the contents. And there was no denying the tears in her eyes as she looked back at Ember.

"Rise again, Ember," she whispered.

Ember nodded, not trusting herself to speak. Then, she turned and quietly exited the chamber, just to slump against the wall outside.

Gods, how had she gotten here? She was supposed to be a healer—neutral, uninvolved in the Royals' political games.

Yet, the Ash King's life, her *friend's* life, now depended on her.

Ember rubbed her nose, her breath stuttering in her lungs.

She knew what she had to do.

Analia sat perfectly still, Deardryn's words hanging in the air between them. *Your main motivation is to distract me while Dimitri escapes.*

Across from her, Deardryn smiled slightly. Pushing back her chair, she rose and headed for one of the side counters, Analia's mind racing.

She'd always planned on Deardryn finding out about the escape—it was never wise to underestimate her. It was the precise reason she'd been trying to stall her by dragging out their conversation. But if Deardryn had already found out...

Keeping an eye on Deardryn, Analia gripped her wrist under the table, feeling her enka bracelet through her sleeve.

Dimitri needs help, she sent down the line, not daring to think more as Deardryn glanced back.

"You're awfully quiet," she commented, pulling a small jar of golden hair pins from the shelves set in the wall.

"I'm trying to figure out how you know."

Deardryn's eyebrows shot up, clearly not expecting the admission. Then, she gave a small nod.

"Wise move, little dragoness," she murmured. "Sometimes, there's benefit in revealing your plan when caught. I suppose it's only fair I return the gesture."

She turned to face Analia fully, her cobalt gown whispering across the floor. "One of the soldiers in my Crystal Guard is Blessed with mindspeaking abilities. As soon as I learned of Dimitri's dungeon escape, I requested he infuse some of his magic into the sun dragon clasps on all my soldiers' cloaks, as well as into my pendant. Just enough to enable a message or two. And a few minutes ago, one of my men sent a message saying he found Dimitri at the back exit. I believe you sensed the message coming through?"

Analia's mouth tightened as Deardryn slid her hand beneath her pendant, lifting it for her to see.

"I should actually thank Dimitri," she went on. "I got the idea after finding a torn enka flower bracelet in the entryway after he was taken to the dungeon. Unfortunate that the connection seemed to snap along with the stems."

Deardryn shrugged, and Analia's nails dug into her palms. She *had* felt that flash of magic a while ago. Meaning as much as she'd been playing Deardryn for time, Deardryn had been toying with her just as much. Not to mention Deardryn knew Dimitri had been in communication with someone on the outside.

Analia carefully kept her hands tucked beneath the table, hyperaware of her own bracelet against her skin. But she had also caught the way Deardryn's gaze had shifted at the end of her comment.

"You mean after you killed Patryclas?" she asked.

Deardryn's expression twitched. And Analia didn't give her time to recover.

"So," she said, rising from her seat. "You know Dimitri is escaping. You've known for some time now. Yet, you remain in here talking to me when we both know you have no qualms about doing what's necessary to get what you want. Why?"

"Because this has played out almost exactly as I expected." Ignoring Analia's glare, Deardryn turned, heading for a small, mounted mirror in the back corner. "I know after years of scuttling around my castle, Dimitri is adept at finding hiding places. Granted, it would only be a matter of time before I discovered his location. But why expend the effort when I knew the moment you found out I was aware of his escape, you would assemble an extraction plan. Meaning Dimitri would have to emerge eventually. And there are only so many places he can escape through. But what's really interesting is you aren't escaping with him."

Deardryn paused, giving Analia room to speak. But Analia only shifted around the table to watch in the mirror as Deardryn began to pin back her hair.

The image of unconcern. Only ruined by her honey eyes watching Analia in the mirror.

"I told you," Analia said stiffly. "I don't like you having such a powerful weapon against me."

"So, you come to my study, offering your assistance because you know it's something that will catch my attention. Clever, if rudimentary."

Deardryn's gaze dropped to her pins, missing Analia's jaw tighten. "Forgive me, Analia," she said, "but it's late and I anticipate having to deal with a report soon. I hope you don't mind me cutting to the point."

"That being?"

"Where I expect our arrangement to go." Deardryn twisted her hair into a bun, revealing the back of her smooth, tan neck. "First, you come to me with this proposal while you sneak Dimitri out—presumably with that masquerader's help. Since I doubt Aaron has come close enough to the Moon Castle to shadowjump here, you've more than likely stationed the nymph outside. If they're smart, both of them will be there so Aaron can retrieve *you* at a moment's notice. After all, we both know you aren't planning on staying with me forever. But the fact that you've chosen to stay for now intrigues me."

Gods, she really *had* anticipated everything. And she wouldn't even look Analia in the face as she proved it.

"I thought you'd already written me off as a distraction," she muttered.

"That's what's intriguing. I know you, Analia. I know the isolation and rejection you were raised in. I saw firsthand how that has made you cling to the connections you have. But you're also willing to do anything to fight for them. Even arrange your own truce marriage into an enemy kingdom.

"So, if your only friend in this castle is escaping with the man you love, and you're sitting here instead of joining them, you must have a strong reason for staying. Yes, neutralizing the threat of the Crystal against you is a worthy reason. But what happens if I agree?

"We spend a few days, or weeks, or perhaps even months working with the Crystal. All the while, you gain information, immunity, whatever else I'm not aware of. And what do I get? You certainly won't help me track down the other shards. I might even have to worry about you trying to steal my own."

"I suppose you'll have to hide it well," Analia deadpanned, perching on the edge of the table.

Deardryn laughed. She finally turned to face her, her hair neatly pinned back. "You've grown bolder," she said. "That's good. But it doesn't explain why I should take you up on your offer."

"It seems like you already have all the information you need," Analia said, hooking her foot around the leg of Deardryn's chair.

"You're not going to try to argue?" Deardryn asked.

"I don't think there's much point. You already know my scheme. We both know you wouldn't believe me if I told you I would help you find the other Crystal shards. But I'll still have to cooperate with your tests and research to get any of the information I want. And you'll be hard-pressed to get nearly as much information if you *don't* work with me."

"Careful, little dragoness," Deardryn cautioned, her footsteps as soft as her voice as she approached. "Overconfidence is dangerous in a strategist, as well as a ruler."

"I'm not overconfident," Analia said. "I'm pragmatic. I know no matter what, the final decision comes down to you."

Analia leaned forward, meeting Deardryn's eye over the back of her chair. "What will it be, Deardryn? Would you rather risk me escaping with crucial information, or send me away empty-handed and risk not being able to discover anything yourself?"

Deardryn's lips thinned. Analia pushed up her sleeve, raising her arm for Deardryn to see. And Deardryn's eyes gleamed with something like greed as she took in the smooth skin where her knife had sliced.

Chapter 22

Dimitri raced through the hedge maze, Rayner in the lead, the patrol of Sun soldiers shouting as they played chase.

Crystal spare him, why had he and Rayner needed to get into it in the middle of their escape? How had they allowed themselves to be distracted long enough for their pursuers to get close enough to shoot?

Dimitri dared a glance over his shoulder, cringing at the sight of small golden lights at the end of the row. Five of them. Fifty yards back.

"They're gaining on us," he gasped, forcing his legs to move faster. "And they have sunstone lights."

A small, quiet voice in his mind whispered that the stones responded to Sun magic; he could dim the lights. But Dimitri stomped down hard on his magic, stomped it out until not even a flicker remained.

He was no Sun Royal. He wouldn't use their magic. He would find another way. Even as the footsteps pounded closer, Dimitri stumbling as he tripped on a root.

"Keep moving," Rayner said, grabbing him by the collar and yanking him upright. "There are a series of quick turns coming up; we just have to make it there and lose them."

Dimitri staggered after him, his breath raking through his lungs.

Ten more paces and they'd be at the first turn. Five more and they could lose them. One step at a time. Three steps. Two. One—

Rayner sucked in a breath through his teeth as they rounded the corner. Dimitri's head snapped toward him. And his heart jolted at the sight of the arrow shaft sticking out between Rayner's fingers as he gripped his shoulder.

"Are you—"

"Keep moving," Rayner ground out. "I'm fine."

"But you're impaled!"

"If I take it out, I'll just bleed more." Rayner gripped the arrow shaft, only slowing his pace long enough to snap it in half with a crack. "It's fine, it was bound to happen with how narrow these rows are. Let's go."

Rayner shoved Dimitri forward, the blood on his fingers black in the moonlight. And somehow, Dimitri kept running, the voices sounding closer than before. Gaining fast. And Rayner was moving slower.

Gods, this plan was doomed. The Sun soldiers were bound to catch up. Rayner was injured. And if they finished him off, Dimitri would have no way of escaping the maze. And he was having a really hard time convincing himself that was the only reason he was afraid as Rayner cursed under his breath and gripped his shoulder.

Dimitri's fingers curled and uncurled uselessly as they reached a three-way fork in the path. He made to barrel down the right path, Rayner already angled toward it. But Rayner grabbed him by the back of his shirt.

"Wait," he hissed.

Dimitri couldn't comprehend the word. He whirled around to face him, the footsteps pounding closer. But Rayner cut off his response with a sharp jerk of his head.

"Listen."

Dimitri thought he was losing his mind. Yet, for a few agonizing moments, he remained still, struggling to hear as he and Rayner tried to catch their breath. Then, his heart sank.

"They're not just coming from behind anymore," he said. "They're also on the right."

"That's what I thought," Rayner said. Without another word, he turned and darted down the left path instead.

"Did they split up?" Dimitri asked, hurrying after him.

"They did. They know we're trying to escape, so they're herding us away from the exit."

Crystal spare him, there was no way out.

"What do we do?" Dimitri gasped, clutching the stitch in his side.

"There's another shortcut through the hedges. If we're lucky, they don't know about it. Then, we can circle back and still make it out."

Dimitri nodded, only able to focus on the footsteps. Just a row away.

He followed Rayner around another corner. Down another row. Pausing at a seemingly random spot as Rayner shoved the dense foliage aside and stepped through, letting out a hiss as the arrow shaft snagged on a branch. Dimitri followed close behind, desperately shoving leaves and branches out of his way, away from Rayner's shoulder, his hands sticky with blood.

Finally, they were through.

Dimitri let the hedge snap back into place with a rustle, his eyes darting along the row. But it was dark. Silent outside of their breathing.

For a few moments, neither of them moved, listening through the leaves as the footsteps approached on the other side. Dimitri held his breath—gods, don't let them know about the path, don't let them have seen.

The footsteps reached the other side.

And without pause, they continued on, still yelling for them to stop, to come quietly while they still could.

Slowly, disbelievingly, Dimitri's body relaxed. He looked over at Rayner, not immediately registering the way his face paled as his scattered mind searched for words.

And a hand landed on his shoulder. "Got you."

Dimitri's entire body cringed as he was spun around, coming nose-to-nose with Dannel. Standing ahead of him, rather than behind. Meaning...

"You weren't from the patrol sent out," he breathed.

"No," Dannel agreed, his tightening hand on Dimitri's shoulder making him want to jump out of his skin. "We were already stationed in the maze."

We?

Dimitri dragged his gaze over Dannel's shoulder, already knowing what he would see. But his insides still curdled at the sight of the four Sun soldiers behind him, one holding a knife to Rayner's throat.

They were done. Outnumbered. Wounded. And undoubtedly about to be surrounded as Dannel touched the sun dragon clasp on his cloak.

Gods, he'd really thought they'd planned for everything. But Deardryn remained a step ahead of them, just as she always did.

"I hope you enjoyed your stroll outside," Dannel said conversationally. "But you'll be coming back inside with us now. Her Majesty has been wanting to speak with you ever since I spotted you in the hallway."

So, Dannel *had* put it together. And after all the information Dimitri had gathered on Deardryn?

Dimitri squirmed, trying to break free. But Dannel held on easily, Dimitri's feet sliding as he started to pull him away.

He didn't stand a chance against a Crystal Guard. He would be dragged all the way back to the castle, dropped at Deardryn's feet like a misbehaving child for her to punish.

As if Deardryn had ever seen him as a child. Even with her family's magic destined for his network. And Sylas wondered why he wanted nothing to do with it.

But that didn't stop the magic from pulsing deep in his gut, sunlight expanding, flashing faster—not again.

Dimitri looked at Rayner, who'd backed up against the hedge, his eyes focused on something behind the Sun soldiers. Dimitri followed his gaze.

Just in time to spot the glint of a dagger soaring through the darkness like a shooting star, burying itself in Dannel's shoulder from behind.

Dannel swore. Dimitri wrenched free, staggering back several paces as Dannel and the other soldiers whipped around. And Dimitri barely choked back his sob as a figure stepped out of the darkness at the end of the row.

"You requested assistance?" Aaron asked.

"Fucking smartass," Dimitri breathed.

Aaron offered a one-finger salute, his silver eyes gleaming in the moonlight as the Sun soldiers drew their swords with a metallic rasp.

"You," Dannel hissed, stalking through the crowd toward him.

"Me," Aaron agreed delightedly.

"I knew I should have killed you back in Ash."

"But alas, you didn't. On the bright side, that means you get to see me again, since we established you can't stop thinking about me."

"Has anyone ever told you you talk too much?" a female voice grumbled, all eyes snapping to the short, muscular woman who stepped up beside him.

"Everyone has," Dannel griped. He paused a few paces away from Aaron, Aaron cocking his head as he studied the guard.

"Well, in that case," he said, "I suppose I better stop."

And before Dannel could take a step back, Aaron slammed his hand against his chest. A quick silver flash lit up the nearby hedges, Aaron pulling his hand back as fast as he'd extended it.

Dannel silently crumpled to the ground.

And chaos erupted.

Dimitri pressed himself back against the hedge as weapons clanged around him, Aaron and the nymph who had to be Laness moving so fast he could barely track them. By the time Rayner reached his side, the two stood in a ring of bodies, neither appearing seriously injured.

Five Sun soldiers. Dead in a matter of heartbeats.

"Is he who I think he is?" Rayner breathed, his wide eyes fixed on Aaron.

Dimitri could only shrug, the same awe in Rayner's voice settling in his bones.

He'd always known Aaron was deadly, but he'd never seen him in action before. And suddenly, he was fucking grateful they were on the same side.

"I can't believe you used your magic," Laness said to Aaron, hands on her hips. "The *one* thing you weren't supposed to do."

"I know, I'm sorry, I couldn't help it. He was right there. And he's always bothered me."

Aaron knelt beside Dannel's body, slitting his throat with a quick slash of his dagger. Covering his tracks, just as Tavian had done. But this time, it bothered Dimitri significantly less.

Removing his disguise with a quick swipe of his hand, he shoved off the hedge wall. "You just had to make a fucking entrance, didn't you, Bordello?" he called.

Aaron looked up, his expression brightening as he rose to his feet. "Dima! As foul-mouthed as usual."

Dimitri cracked a smile. "What are you two doing here?"

"Anna sent word that you needed help," Laness said. "We figured if we followed the noise, we'd find you sooner or later."

"Is she all right?"

"I haven't heard from her since, but nothing worrying has come through our bracelets."

Dimitri could have sworn Aaron's wry mask twitched.

"We should get going," Laness went on, adjusting her black fighting leathers, identical to Aaron's. "Pretty soon, those other patrols are going to catch up."

"Especially since Dannel notified them," Dimitri said.

Aaron's eyes snapped to him. "What do you mean?"

Dimitri quickly explained the communication magic, Aaron's expression having darkened by the time he finished.

"So, it's now or never," he murmured.

Laness touched his arm, Dimitri not understanding the shadow that passed over his face. But in a blink, his expression hardened.

"All right, then," he said. "Laness, I can jump us home. Dima, I'm assuming Anna already filled you in on how you can't tell anyone what you're about to see, but I figured I'd..." Aaron trailed off as he looked around, finally spotting Rayner lingering a few paces back. "Who are you?"

"I'm Rayner," he said warily, coming up to Dimitri's shoulder. "The masquerader."

"Ah." Aaron nodded. "You should get back to the castle before anyone spots you and your cover is blown."

"It's been blown for a while now."

"I see." Aaron twirled a dagger between his fingers, his voice sliding into an icy purr. "I suppose you're in quite the predicament, then."

"I think it means my only option is coming with you."

Dimitri's head snapped toward Rayner. Rayner didn't take his eyes off of Aaron, clearly the bigger threat as he rocked back on his heels.

For as long as Dimitri had known him, Aaron had reminded him of a cat about to pounce. It was something about his faint smirk, the way he'd moved so assuredly through the Sun Castle halls, not bothering to flash his claws because he was confident in his lethality. And he knew anyone who tried to test it wouldn't walk away unscathed.

But now, out of his Sun Kingdom disguise, all that predatory energy had distilled. Focused.

This was the King of Starlight. And the look in his eyes promised nothing good if he decided to pounce.

But Rayner held his ground.

"Aaron," Laness said in a low voice. "We haven't discussed bringing anyone else."

"My thoughts exactly."

Rayner started to speak, just to cut off as footsteps crunched down the neighboring pathway. Dimitri's eyes widened.

Aaron swore under his breath. "We have to go—"

"I know who you are," Rayner blurted. He stepped forward, into Aaron's reach, even as Aaron gave him a warning look. "I saw your magic. And if Dima has to keep your home a secret, everything is pointing to you *somehow* being a Star Royal."

Dimitri choked back a curse.

"I told you you shouldn't have used your magic," Laness grumbled.

Aaron pursed his lips. He ran a hand through his hair, his gaze cutting to Dimitri.

"He called you Dima," he said. "Is he a friend of yours? Because I could just kill him if not."

Dimitri shifted from foot to foot, the back of his neck tingling as the voices drew closer. One row away.

Rayner looked at him expectantly. But Dimitri's mouth went dry.

He felt like a coward. He felt like the worst person in the world.

I won't choose your life over mine.

"I don't think you want to kill me," Rayner said, clearly giving up on Dimitri as he folded his arms.

Dimitri's chest caved in. Aaron, meanwhile, raised a brow.

"Why's that?" he asked.

Rayner hesitated. He looked at Dimitri once more—was that regret in his eyes? Before he could be certain, Rayner squared his shoulders.

"Because," he said, focusing on Aaron once more. "You're going to want the only person who has ever escaped Scarsthain on your side."

Chapter 23

O f all the reasons Aaron was expecting to hear, that was not one of them.

"Last I heard," he said, "that title goes to Ren Inferita."

"Which is the exact reason why he couldn't be walking around with that name anymore," Rayner said, his voice, his face, the look in his eyes completely flat.

Well, that was an interesting point. Aaron looked at Dimitri, trying to confirm the story. But Dimitri looked as though he'd been slapped across the face. He twisted toward Rayner, Aaron bracing himself for what was clearly going to be an explosion.

But Dimitri didn't speak. He only stared, his expression morphing from shock, to realization, to disbelief, to rage as Rayner kept his gaze on his fidgeting fingers.

"No fucking way," he breathed.

Rayner winced.

"No fucking way," Dimitri repeated louder, jabbing a finger at Rayner. "So *that's* what you wouldn't say earlier?"

"Dima, I—"

Dimitri smacked aside the hand Rayner extended toward him, backing away several paces. Aaron could have sworn something like devastation flashed across his face, but before he could be certain, it hardened. Ignited as he turned his back on Rayner.

"He's telling the truth," he told Aaron, his hands shaking as he folded his arms. "Take him with us. He's the last person you have to worry about keeping his mouth shut."

Well, this was quite the scandal to walk in on. There was clearly history between the two that he was missing—and if the way Rayner bowed his head said anything, there was a lot.

"What do you think?" he asked, turning to Laness.

"I think we have no choice." She stepped between Dimitri and Rayner, offering them her hands. "I'm assuming it's best to keep you two separated during our jump?"

The two glowered, but they begrudgingly took her hands.

If Aaron was smart, he would leave it at that, take their hands, and go.

But he couldn't stop himself from looking up at the castle behind them.

She was in there somewhere. Alone. With Deardryn.

All he had to do was ask Laness to use her bracelet as an anchor. Just one jump, and he could see her, hold her, bring her home. They could figure out a different way to get the Crystal.

But Analia would be furious. She would call him a stupid, self-sacrificing idiot the moment he appeared, and she'd send him away just as empty-handed as he was now. Except in that scenario, he'd also have to see the hurt on her face when she realized he didn't trust her to pull off her plan. Didn't believe in her. And even though that wasn't true, he wouldn't be able to blame her for thinking so.

Gods, he couldn't do that to her. Not after the Ash Kingdom. Which meant...

"You're making the right choice," Laness said softly.

He knew that. But why did the right choice have to hurt so bad?

Aaron swallowed hard. Then, feeling his heart rip in two, he reached for Rayner's hand. And the last thing he saw was a flash of golden light coming around the corner as they disappeared.

Aaron blinked hard as he pulled his group through the shadows, an all-too-familiar cold brushing along his veins like a caress, offering to take it all away. But somehow, he shoved it down, focusing on deactivating the wards to let Dimitri and Rayner through. And a moment later, his sitting room solidified around them.

Mor and Surce immediately rose from the couch, Branten pausing his pacing around the room. All three looked from Dimitri, to Rayner, to Laness, to Aaron, clearly noticing the unexpected headcount. And all Aaron could think about was that castle as he filled them in.

Dimitri and Rayner kept quiet throughout Aaron's recount, Rayner grimacing as he shifted his injured shoulder. Branten tracked the movement from beside the fireplace, all restlessness gone as he kept watch. By the time Aaron finished, no one looked particularly comfortable.

Surce met his gaze across the room, her head tilted in a question. Aaron nodded.

Wordlessly, she gestured for Rayner to follow. Then, she turned, Rayner warily heading after her as she led the way up the stairs and to what Aaron knew would be a thorough interrogation. He'd check in with her later on whether Rayner could be trusted to see any more of the kingdom than he already had. For now, there was still Dimitri to deal with.

He stood between Aaron and Laness, his hands shoved in his pockets as he looked around the room. Branten and Mor shared a glance, but neither of them spoke. Aaron closed his eyes, searching for the energy to deal with what came next.

Dimitri turned to Laness. "So," he said. "You're the one who's been talking in my head."

Laness shrugged. "You think loud."

Branten shifted into a fighting stance. But Dimitri snorted.

"So," Laness said, "you like chocolate croissants?"

"Only if I don't have to make them."

"Those are the best kind." Laness stretched, then headed off toward the dining room door. "Come on. I have some in the kitchen. We can eat them while we watch Branten kick Aaron's ass during night training."

Dimitri let out a small, startled laugh. Then, with a quick glance at Aaron, he headed after Laness, the tension in the room loosening like a sigh of relief with every step. Still, Aaron didn't move as the door shut behind him, leaving him alone with Branten and Mor.

"You all right?" Branten asked.

Aaron shook his head, his body growing heavier as he sank down on the couch.

"What happened?" Mor asked, coming to join him.

"I left her," he said simply. "She was right there, and I left her. Again."

Aaron's heart crumbled a little more. He braced himself for the pep talk, the chorus of "You did the right thing."

"You need a second?" Branten asked, plopping down on his other side.

No, he needed a lifetime. But he nodded. Then, he let his head bow forward into his hands, Branten and Mor each putting a hand on his shoulder.

And somehow, that was all he needed. Not just to let the blow hit home, but to let the pain sink back down again. He'd made the right choice. *Somehow.*

Aaron released a long, shaky breath. Then, composing himself, he sat back against the couch, lifting his head to stare at the night sky through the glass back door.

She had to be all right. She had to come back to him. She just... had to.

Analia headed back through the quiet Moon Castle halls.

The moment she'd left Deardryn's study, she'd reached out to Laness. The nymph told her that not only had they successfully retrieved Dimitri, but Rayner as well.

She doubted Dimitri was thrilled about that, and the number of dead Sun soldiers was definitely going to cause some issues. But at least everything had worked out in the end. Including her end of the plan.

Analia rubbed her forehead as she stepped into her chambers. She'd known going into her conversation with Deardryn she would likely come out with an agreement, but that didn't stop all the maneuvering from the past week from forming an ache behind her eyes.

After all, Deardryn would have never believed her if she proposed this plan during their first meeting. Branten had told her as much all those weeks ago at their dining room table. *It's always easiest to show a man what he expects.*

So, she'd done exactly that. She'd let Deardryn see her resistance and hatred in their first meeting, her begrudging interest in their second, building up to the fear and supposed new scheme in the final two. She even let Deardryn see her scramble for control after the Dragoness surprised her with everything she knew.

Overconfidence is dangerous in a strategist, as well as a ruler.

Yes, she was aware. Which was why she'd allowed Deardryn to believe she'd influenced every move Analia had made from the moment she left her cell. Enough so that she thought she had an accurate assessment of how tactful Analia had become. Meaning she now felt comfortable keeping Analia around.

Analia looked at her pale reflection in her vanity mirror, her mouth set in a grim smile.

Deardryn might think she was moving all the pieces, but Analia had wound up exactly where she wanted.

And once, she would have attributed it all to Accalon.

Analia sighed, sinking down onto her vanity chair and pulling her phoenix pin from her pocket. She turned the familiar metal between her fingers, the smoky outer ring glinting in the light.

A piece of him, just as he'd promised she'd always have. A promise he'd fulfilled—in more ways than one. And somehow, that made it worse as she realized she didn't truly know what that piece looked like. What it was, what it meant, why it was hers.

At any other time, she wouldn't have second guessed. This was the man who had taught her, raised her, become a north star she could always refer back to. Even in creating her plan, she normally would have outlined it with him in mind, wondering what he would have done at every step and acting accordingly.

But that was the point: she could only wonder. Not just because he was gone, but because even when he was there, she only saw what he wanted her to see. Which was the exact same thing Deardryn had done to her in Sun.

Analia swallowed hard against the rising lump in her throat. Then, pulling open a drawer in her vanity, she placed Accalon's pin inside.

She had schemed her way into this castle, into an agreement with Deardryn. And now, she was going to get that shard. Alone.

Still, as Analia closed the drawer and rose to her feet, she couldn't stop her eyes from stinging as she turned away.

Ember stepped into the apothecary, something shuddering inside her as she breathed in the crisp, herbal smell of the plants lining the windowsills. A few customers browsed the nearby aisles, their voices far more subdued than Ember remembered.

But she couldn't bring herself to care. Not when every step toward the back room door had her body buzzing, aching, reaching out with desperate hands.

There was no part of her that wanted to second-guess as she wove through the aisles. As a herbologist, she had spent countless hours working with addicts, all of whom treated each day of sobriety like a gift.

But Ember didn't feel like she had a gift. She felt like she wanted to die. Like she was slowly withering away, second by second until none of herself remained.

Which meant she wasn't addicted. She had found what her body needed to function. And if she was going to get Cadmus out, she needed—

"Ember!"

Ember jumped hard enough her shoulder knocked into a shelf as Dane hurried out from around the central counter—since when did he come to work? Well, now that she was in the castle, she supposed he had no choice.

"Hi, Dane," she said, trying to edge around him. Just a few feet from the door.

Dane loosely gripped her shoulders, his blue-gray eyes darting over her face. "I haven't seen you since the attack. I was worried."

"I'm fine," Ember said, shifting from foot to foot. "I'm working in the castle now. Othin's orders."

"That's what I heard." Dane dropped his gaze. "It's just... it's good to see you."

Ember's entire being reached for the door, her nerves stretching thin. But she forced her friendly smile to stay in place.

After all, Dane being a little unusual was nothing new. As one of the few human herbologist healers, he'd given her a place to go early on in her healer training. Sure, he never seemed able to hold her gaze for long, and he tended to disappear during his shifts, but he'd always been kind enough. And he would definitely know far too much if he realized what she was doing there.

She didn't have time for his unnecessary concern. Not when she was mere feet away from everything she needed.

Ember didn't remember how she wrapped up her conversation with Dane. She didn't remember the breezy excuse she gave to duck into her back room, just that Dane only returned her wave before going back to work.

And after a few steps, she was inside. She crossed to her plant boxes, her hands shaking as she flipped open a lid.

Vivid orange and yellow leaves snaked around a bundle of moss, the plant having grown large enough in her time away to fill a medium-sized pot. Ember shuddered as she ran her fingers along the stem in a caress, the fuzzy leaves soft as a lie.

If there was any voice in her mind telling her to stop, reconsider, she couldn't hear it. Not over the wave of euphoria that washed over her.

It was instinct to pinch off a leaf.

It was exhilarating crushing it between her fingers and bringing it to her nose.

And it felt like safety as she breathed in the sharp, sour smell.

PART 2: RESISTANCE

Chapter 24

Analia sat at her desk, finishing her note to Sabi in the margin of her book when a knock sounded on her door. Her maids entered a moment later, both clearly startled to find her already awake and dressed.

"Would one of you be able to return this to Sabina for me?" Analia asked, closing her book and offering it to Letta. "I've heard she likes to inspect her books for any damage before replacing them on the shelves."

"Of course, Your Highness," Tashia said, sliding a breakfast tray in front of her.

"Analia," she corrected. "This castle is lonely enough. I don't need any more distance for formality's sake."

Analia speared a piece of melon with her fork and popped it in her mouth, catching Letta and Tashia exchange a tentative smile from the corner of her eye.

"Analia it is," Letta said softly.

The two maids busied themselves tidying the already pristine chambers, leaving Analia to her food. She'd just swallowed her last bite when another knock sounded on her door. Yet, when she called for them to enter, Tavian wasn't the only guard that stepped inside.

The man was noticeably taller and broader than Tavian. He wore gold-and-white fighting leathers, a spear poking over his shoulder, the planes of his face harsh and severe.

Analia didn't immediately recognize him. But as his indigo eyes met hers, her mind flashed back to her cell, pain radiating across her temple.

"Analia," Tavian drawled, "I'm assuming you remember Meryk?"

"Her Highness," Meryk corrected gruffly.

"No, I'm Tavian," Tavian said. "We've been over this."

A muscle jumped in Meryk's jaw. He snapped something at Tavian, and Analia looked to her maids, both of whom watched the bickering guards with wide eyes. This had to be Deardryn's doing, but why?

"Oh, shove it, sunshine," Tavian retorted. Then, not giving Meryk time to respond, he disappeared back through the door.

Meryk's nostrils flared at the dismissal. He wheeled on Analia, practically spitting, "Let's go."

Something sparked in Analia's chest. Ignoring the guard, she turned and offered her maids a farewell. Then, she headed for the door, making no attempt to hurry as she passed Meryk without so much as a glance.

She'd expected Tavian to already be halfway down the hall. But he waited for her just outside her door, falling into step beside her as they headed for Deardryn's study.

"So," Analia said, acutely aware of Meryk trailing behind them. "What's prompted this change?"

"One of Deardryn's prisoners tried to escape last night," Tavian explained.

"Tried?"

"Well, it wasn't exactly clean. He and his masquerader friend decided to use the back door—the one day I was on duty I should add—and they ended up killing a Sun soldier and stabbing me through the shoulder."

"What?" Analia's head whipped toward him. "Are you all right?"

Why would they have stabbed Tavian? Was it an accident when the fighting presumably broke out? Or had Tavian defected?

The thought had barely formed when Tavian flashed her a grin and winked, his face angled so Meryk couldn't see anything from behind them.

"I'm fine," he said. "But between the wound and trying to help Zan, I couldn't go after them. And from what I hear, he wasn't the only casualty."

"Her Majesty has subsequently assigned me to you as an additional guard," Meryk finished, bored.

Analia swallowed her retort. She'd known her plan was risky; she hadn't expected it to play out flawlessly. But between Deardryn figuring *everything* out, the bodies Dimitri left behind, and Deardryn now upping her security, this was not going to be a pleasant meeting.

Indeed, when Analia stepped through the study door a few minutes later, Deardryn's stare from behind the desk had her wanting to retreat back into the hall. Especially when she detected the nauseating pulse of the Crystal's magic field.

"Why the new guard?" Analia asked, striving for casual as she claimed her usual seat. "You've always known I would try to get Dimitri out. Why assign the extra security to me after the fact, not before to try and stop it?"

"Drop the arrogant act, Analia," Deardryn said, deadly quiet.

The blood seemed to drain from Analia's body. She knew how to handle Deardryn when she was irritated, enraged, even calculating. But as Deardryn dropped her gaze to the bracelets she twisted on her wrist, she was none of those things.

She was distraught. And it was unsettling how human it made her appear.

"What happened?" Analia asked, her lungs tightening.

"I had a rotating patrol waiting for Dimitri in the maze," Deardryn said, her voice far away. "I knew it was an optimal escape route; you'd be foolish to overlook it. Last night, it was Dannel's turn to patrol. And he was one of the five soldiers butchered and left for dead."

Deardryn's voice caught. Analia flinched, Pryanth's voice echoing through her mind. *Mother's personal guard.*

"Dannel was your guard," she said softly.

"For thirty-two years." Deardryn squeezed her eyes shut, Analia swallowing hard against the lump in her own throat.

Gods, she could never keep up with this woman. Every time she thought she drew close, Deardryn had to prove she was one step ahead, or flash a glimmer of humanity that had her heart softening.

After all, she knew exactly how it felt to lose someone special. Someone essential. Someone whose absence left her lost, grieving as she tried to reorient herself in a world that no longer felt like home.

"It never stops," Deardryn murmured, twisting her bracelets. "Pryanth, my nephew, Dannel, Lucilla, Accalon, Patryclas, all the other Royals. It never ends."

All sympathy Analia had evaporated into a puff of smoke. No, it was hotter than smoke. It was rage. Burning across her skin, sending her leaning forward in her seat, building and building and building until she was about to explode from the hypocrisy of it all.

Before she could speak, Deardryn shook her head and opened her eyes.

"I didn't assign a guard to you before," she said, "because I wanted to see how far you've come. But after seeing the cost of your schemes, my guard will be remaining with you at all times."

Analia started to retort, but Deardryn's expression had hardened. Sharpened. Slowly, Analia's response sizzled out, her fingers digging into the table as she struggled to push past her temper and think.

Finally, she asked, "Why were you willing to risk losing Dimitri?"

"Why were you willing to stay behind?" Deardryn countered.

Analia's eyebrows shot up. Why ask that question when she already suspected the answer? Before Analia could respond, Deardryn went on.

"Speaking of your presence, the only reason I'm dealing with you today is because you claim to have discovered a new way of researching the Crystal."

Analia had been so consumed by her tangle of emotions that she'd almost forgotten the magic slithering through the back of her mind. She eased back in her chair, her words slow and deliberate.

"I have. Part of the problem is it was too much magic, but it was also too close. Thousands of voices screaming at you will always be overwhelming, but it will be ten-times worse standing directly next to them."

"So," Deardryn said, "you're suggesting I slowly open the casing once more, but from farther away."

"*Much* slower. And I tell you when to open it more."

"That sounds agreeable," Deardryn said. Cool. Business-like as she pulled open a drawer, retrieving the Crystal casing in one hand, and her blue note-taking book in the other.

Analia's shoulders relaxed slightly. With a brief nod, the two rose to their feet, heading for opposite ends of the room.

Analia sank down on the carpet beside the door, expecting Deardryn to pull up a chair. But she settled on the floor without hesitation, taking a moment to arrange her golden skirts around herself.

Then, she reached for the Crystal's casing.

"Wait," Analia said, raising a hand. "Let me ready my mental shield first."

A part of her expected Deardryn to ignore her. All she had to do was open the casing, and she could subject Analia to every shred of pain Dannel's death had caused. But Deardryn sat back against the wall and folded her hands in her lap, perfectly patient. That had Analia even more on edge.

Tearing her gaze from the queen, she reached for her mental shield. Immediately, it slid into place around her mind like the stone walls of a fortress. As easy as a reflex. Still, Analia's stomach twisted as she gave Deardryn a nod.

The moment Deardryn cracked open the casing, the magic was out. Bright white light streamed through the narrow opening, refracting rainbows across the chamber as it slammed into Analia's mental shield. Analia tensed with the impact, feeling the magic scrabble against the stone, trying to wriggle through the cracks into her mind.

But her theory had been correct: the distance between herself and the magic quieted the screams, turned the hammering blows into more of a relentless tapping.

"Analia?" Deardryn asked.

"Give me a second."

Analia closed her eyes, only faintly aware of the scratch of Deardryn's pen. But she could hear it. Even with the magic screaming in her ears, her shield held.

Analia focused on the stone of her shield, imagining it darkening to onyx, the cracks curving into intricate carvings. Her mind wasn't just guarded. It was dampered. And nothing was getting in.

Seconds, minutes could have passed. But Analia remained silent and still, letting the magic hammer against her shield, just to be stopped in its tracks. And slowly, the magic settled into the background of her mind.

She opened her eyes, finding Deardryn watching her closely.

"Open it more," Analia said.

"Are you certain?"

Analia nodded. Deardryn set her pen aside, then opened the casing a little more.

The light intensified, Analia's hands curling into the lavender carpet as the magic slammed into her. Definitely stronger this time, each blow sending a wave of nausea through her body.

But she tightened her grip on the carpet. Focused on the soft fibers against her fingers.

She'd lost her uncle, been tormented by Pryanth, nearly killed by multiple Devourists, and almost consumed by this magic. She *refused* to let a fraction of ancient, vengeful magic take her down.

The magic hammered against her shield, but Analia hardened the onyx. And once again, the magic slowly settled into the back of her mind.

"More," she ground out.

Deardryn raised her brows as she scribbled in her book, golden curls falling into her face. But she didn't try to question Analia as she opened the casing even more.

The moment the light intensified, Analia knew she would regret her decision.

Magic slammed into her shield, sending her shoulders recoiling back against the wall. She couldn't focus. She couldn't think as wave after wave pounded against her shield, the impact shuddering through her body.

Gods, each hit was so hard. There were so many voices, screaming to be heard.

But she'd survived more than this. Not just in Accalon's chambers, but in this very room. She'd completely blocked it out without meaning to earlier that morning when talking with Deardryn—wait.

"Talk to me," Analia forced out.

"What?"

"Give me something else to focus on," Analia said, her lungs struggling to fill.

Deardryn looked up from her notes, and Analia wanted to scream as the silence remained intact. One second, two, three...

"What do you love most about Aaron?" Deardryn asked.

Analia's head jerked up. "I told you to distract me."

"And I'm posing you a question." Deardryn leaned forward, bracing her hands on the carpet. "If you are going to master this magic, Analia, you can't rely on other people to ground you. You have to do that yourself. So, I will ask you again: what do you love most about Aaron?"

Analia wanted to snap that this was her second attempt, this was when she needed the most amount of help. But Deardryn leveled her with the same look she'd given Analia when she'd asked for a hint on where the Ash ring was hidden. The Dragoness had made her decision, and she would not budge.

Analia swallowed her frustration, the magic having her wanting to duck her head and cover her ears.

But she at least had a question to consider. And to her surprise, even amongst the screaming, her answer pushed its way through the chaos.

"His compassion," she said, bracing herself against the wall.

Something flashed across Deardryn's face, too quick to read. "Very good. What's your favorite memory related to that?"

Analia's lungs tightened. The magic pounded against her shield. And memories flickered through it all like an underlying melody.

The look on his face as he told the council he would do anything to protect his kingdom. His faint smile as he taught Loliette, the orphan girl from Sun, to tie her hat to her head. Him, holding her together on her turret, in the Ash Castle Throne Room, at the lakeside. Even when he stepped back and let her find her footing, he always offered her something to hold on to.

"I can't choose a specific moment," she said, the magic quieting a fraction. "It's just... him. The way he cares so deeply for the people he loves."

The magic hammered on, but her shield held firm.

"I think it's scary for a lot of people to do that. After all, the more you care, the more it can hurt. But he's fearless. But I also think part of him craves that pain."

Analia relaxed back against the wall, her words coming easier. "Yes, he cares deeply. But that also lets him blame himself when something goes wrong. He's probably brooding over this entire situation right now."

Analia smiled slightly. Even without Laness's report, she could have guessed that. She just hoped he wasn't locked away in his mother's room—although she could see Branten bodily dragging him out of there all too clearly.

Analia blinked. Because she *could* see it. She could focus on that image in her mind. At some point, all that magic had once again been compartmentalized.

Analia looked up at Deardryn, just in time to spot something flicker across her expression. Something that looked a lot like a mix of regret and sorrow.

Catching Analia looking, she let her face smooth over once more.

"Well?" she asked.

"I've got it," Analia said on an exhale. "But I can't handle any more today."

"That's perfectly fine. The casing is open just as wide as it was a few days ago."

"Really?" Analia asked, disappointed. "I made *no* progress?"

"On the contrary. You couldn't stand to be in the same room as that power last time. But now, you're sitting up, conversing with me, and fully in control of yourself."

Deardryn closed the casing, and Analia sagged.

Deardryn smiled fondly. "You did it, Analia."

Something like hope stirred in Analia's chest. But she remained quiet where she sat as Deardryn gathered her things and rose. "You may go when you're ready."

Analia made a face, and Deardryn laughed. "There you are." Crossing the room, Deardryn offered Analia a hand up, which she begrudgingly accepted. "I'll see you tomorrow."

Analia mumbled an affirmation. Then, she turned toward the door, expecting Deardryn to follow. Instead, she returned to her desk, not sparing Analia a look as she tucked the Crystal back in the drawer.

Interesting.

Storing the observation away, Analia pulled open the door, finding her guards waiting outside. As soon as Tavian spotted her, he stepped forward, "Did she—"

"Nothing I can't handle," Analia said, glancing at Meryk as she shut the door.

Tavian frowned, but thankfully, he didn't push it. "Sabi brought this for you while you were in there," he said instead, grabbing a book from the nearby windowsill. "She said something about figuring you would like it and that I must guard it with my life until bestowing it to you."

"Such an odd woman," Meryk grumbled.

Analia smiled and accepted the book, recognizing the cover of an Ash Kingdom children's book. "I think she's charming."

And she was also the perfect excuse to start dealing with her next problem.

Analia sat on the couch in the quiet library, paying her guards no mind as she read her book.

That morning, she'd left a note in her book margins asking about Deardryn's request history and Dimitri's findings. She and Dimitri hadn't had time to go over it all, and with all of Analia's security, they'd decided it was best to leave his notes with Sabi. But now, Sabi had used her Blessing to copy all of Dimitri's notes onto the pages of her book. And there was *a lot* to go through.

It was honestly impressive. Not just how organized Dimitri was, but also how advanced some of the texts he'd been reading were. He had everything from Deardryn's book requests—organized chronologically—to his notes on each location he'd checked out, to expansive notes on Scarsthain. He also had notes on Deardryn's general routine both in Sun and Moon, and the people she interacted with most. Every page was invaluable, and Analia made a mental note to ask Laness to tell him so.

But the interesting thing was Deardryn hadn't requested any books from Sabi the last couple weeks. In fact, she hadn't requested anything starting the week before Analia arrived.

Well, that made sense: if Deardryn knew Dimitri was working with Sabi, it would no longer be safe to request books from her. But she only had one shard. She couldn't *stop* researching. Which meant she had to be looking elsewhere.

Analia remained on the couch for the next couple hours, making it to the end of Dimitri's notes. She closed the book and stretched, looking over to find Tavian fiddling with a balled-up piece of paper as he lounged beside her.

Analia's eyes narrowed. Meryk—stationed nearby—looked around the room, and Tavian threw the crumpled paper at him.

Meryk whipped around, "Stop that!"

"Just keeping you on your toes," Tavian said sweetly.

This guard was going to be the death of her. Telling Tavian to knock it off, Analia rose and headed through the stacks, eventually finding Sabi shelving books in the back.

"Hello," Analia said.

Sabi startled, then quickly turned. "Hello, Your Highness. Is that the book I gave you?"

"It is." Analia offered it to her. "You were right, I did enjoy it."

"I'm glad," she said. "I know the author put a lot of work into it."

"And clearly you did as well when creating this copy." Analia leaned against a shelf, her guards watching a few feet away. "I'm assuming you're the only person in this castle that people come to for books?"

"I am," Sabi said, drawing out her words uncertainly.

Analia looked over at her hovering guards, then pointedly back at Sabi. "Does that mean you're responsible for providing all the books for every person in this castle?" she asked.

She looked down at the book in Sabi's hands. Sabi followed her gaze, and Analia suppressed a wince at her obvious look of understanding.

"Oh, definitely not," she said. "People are welcome to request from me, but they're also free to look elsewhere. I have a list of other bookstores I usually send people to if things get too busy."

"And I'm assuming those who have been here a while know about that?"

"Your Highness," Meryk cut in, "we've already been here for hours. You should get back to your chambers."

Yes, he was certainly an impatient guard.

Analia nodded at Meryk, then offered Sabi a farewell. And as she left the library, she just had to hope Sabi had figured out what she'd been asking.

Chapter 25

In the days following their Moon Kingdom extraction, Aaron threw himself into work.

He blitzed through the reports from the council that had been piling up around him. He replenished the wards around his kingdom. He arranged meetings with his military captains, merchants, everyone he needed to speak to in order to ensure security remained top notch—even as he shrank away from the idea of an impending war. Thankfully, his mind never remained in one place long enough to dwell on it.

Whereas before, his thoughts had been sluggish, repetitive, they were now relentless. They flashed through his mind like a lightning storm, each so fast it felt more like an impression than actual words. It reached the point where he caught himself pacing around his sitting room in between meetings, just to stop and laugh to himself because he'd never been a pacer. But he'd lost track of how many times he'd watched Analia practically wear a hole in the carpet in the exact path he'd been following.

And all amusement drained away as those memories formed a cold, heavy weight in his stomach.

He knew he'd made the right choice in leaving her in Moon. But that didn't stop that choice from rotting inside him. It didn't stop him from spending most nights sitting on his mother's bed, replaying every choice leading up to that day in Accalon's chambers.

He just... He just wanted to feel useful.

The thought swirled through his mind as he sat at his dining room table, his family, Dimitri, and Rayner gathered around him as they traded updates over lunch.

Aaron had been quietly surprised when Surce had come to him only a few hours into her interrogation, giving an approving nod and passing him the dagger Rayner had offered unprompted. Apparently, her tapestries confirmed he was telling the truth about Scarsthain, and she believed him when he said his oath with Sylas would be no threat to the Starlight Kingdom.

Still, Aaron glanced at him from the corner of his eye as Laness ran through her report, his unease growing as Dimitri refused to look up from his plate.

"Ember's planning to free the Royals sometime next week," Laness finished, drawing Aaron's attention back to her.

"Good," he said. "Tell her to keep us updated on the timing and that we have plenty of room for her."

A quiet part of him wondered if just Ember would be coming, but he shoved the thought aside.

"Surce," he went on, "have you had any more luck with the scroll?"

Dimitri perked up. Laness had filled him in the night of his arrival on everything they'd discovered, and there was no mistaking his curiosity as Surce retrieved a stack of notes from beneath her chair.

"I haven't made as much progress as I would like," she said, sifting through the pages. "Not only are there countless sections to piece together, but my familiarity with the forgotten tongue is proving itself lacking. I did, however, find this."

Surce pulled a page from her stack and turned it to face the table.

"A map of Elefthia?" Branten asked.

"A *labeled* map," Mor said, leaning closer. "And there are words beside the Human and Starlight Kingdoms."

"Mt. Lanula has extra text, too," Laness said, pointing to the mountain. "Is that for the DovenU?"

"From what I can tell, yes," Surce said.

Aaron's mind raced. His eyes flicked over the page, some ancient part of him recognizing a few of the words. Kingdom. Mountain. Starlight. But that wasn't all.

"It's not just territory marked," he said slowly. "There are landmarks as well."

"How do *you* know?" Branten asked through a mouthful of bread.

"Ethelind had me learn the language before I went into the Underground. It's been even longer for me than Surce, so I'm honestly surprised I recognize any of this. But that"—he pointed to the top right corner of the map—"is some sort of garden in the Wind Kingdom. And down south it says 'Rosala,' so I'm assuming the second word is temple. There are more that look familiar, but I can't remember exactly."

"But why are they marked in the first place?" Laness asked, fidgeting with her fork.

"That's an excellent question," Aaron said grimly.

Gods, why couldn't Talitha give them a straight answer for once?

"Well," Surce said, turning the page back toward herself, "while that question remains a mystery, the fact that the Starlight Kingdom, Human Kingdom, and DovenU are labeled at the very least gives us a time frame."

"What do you mean?" asked Dimitri. Aaron held his breath as all eyes flicked to Dimitri.

He hadn't known what to expect when Dimitri arrived. The servant from the Sun Castle had an equal likelihood of indiscriminately ruffling feathers or sitting silently as far away from everyone as possible. And while Dimitri had certainly withdrawn, he remained... pleasant.

Even now, as he squirmed under everyone's attention, he didn't lash out. And Aaron didn't try to hide his satisfaction as he said, "I forgot I haven't filled you in on my kingdom's history."

"It's not like you've had three days to do so," Dimitri grumbled.

"Yes, and you've been so available all throughout that time. Honestly, Dima, your ability to disappear is downright impressive—although if you've discovered secret passageways throughout my house as well, I'd appreciate knowing about them."

"It's not my fault you haven't thoroughly explored your own house."

Aaron scoffed and made to whack his arm, letting his hand stop a few inches away. Dimitri looked down at Aaron's hand. And just for a moment, his expression crumpled into the same shattered look Aaron had seen in the hedge maze.

Aaron opened his mouth, not sure what to say. But Dimitri quickly turned away.

"So," he said, "why are the labels important?"

Aaron didn't have a name for the emotion that clogged his throat. But Mor stepped in smoothly.

"The Starlight and Human Kingdoms were established after the Blessed-Human Civil War," he explained. "And that was early in the Defiants' rule. The DovenU, on the other hand, was founded over half a millennia after that at the *end* of their rule."

"Which means," Laness said, "the scrolls had to have been created at the end of the Defiants' rule when all of these locations were founded."

"Huh." Dimitri scratched his head. "So, what does that mean?"

"It means," Aaron said, "we now know Talitha and whoever else used the forgotten tongue as an extra layer of security."

"Which means they *really* didn't want us looking at this," Branten finished.

Which meant whatever was hidden in there was getting worse and worse. Aaron rubbed the headache building in his temples, no one seeming too pleased by the realization. Especially not Surce, who toyed with one of the jewels on her goblet.

"There's more, isn't there," Aaron said, his stomach sinking.

"Possibly." Surce pulled another sheet from her stack, everyone watching her expectantly. "Most sections of the scroll are separated, like individual puzzle pieces. I was expecting this map to be its own piece. Yet, there was a connected block of text. I'm still trying to translate it, but the repetitive nature of the first line is bothering me."

"What does it say?" Laness asked.

"When three by three by three... And then there's a word after—"

"Align?" Dimitri asked sharply.

Surce startled, all attention redirecting to Dimitri. He gripped the edge of the table, his eyes a little too wide as he stared at Surce.

"It's possible," she said after a beat, returning to her notes. "What makes you ask?"

Dimitri didn't respond, instead turning to Aaron. "Can you try?"

Aaron raised a brow, but Dimitri didn't offer an explanation. He just watched as Aaron outstretched his hand, Surce passing him the page across the table.

For a moment, the room was silent as Aaron carefully scanned over the words. A few immediately jumped out at him: three, shadow, star, crown.

Dimitri's chair squeaked beside him as he shifted restlessly, and Aaron redirected his attention back to the first line. "When three by three by three... Yes. I think that's align. And then there's something about sleeping shadows—"

"The sleeping shadows will untwine?" Dimitri asked.

"Maybe." Aaron looked up from the page, finding Dimitri's face had drained of color. "I think you've got some explaining to do, Dima."

Dimitri nodded quickly, the story flying past his lips. The little girl's song from the boardwalk. The fact it was written on the door at Scarsthain. How Deardryn had gone there and found the Crystal shard after putting the two together.

"And now it's in the scroll that explained how the Crystal was separated into pieces," he finished. His eyes darted around the table, Aaron expecting him to look just as uneasy as everyone else. But if anything, he was excited.

"Do you know what the rest of the words are?" Surce asked.

Immediately, Dimitri deflated. Before he could respond...

"Their midnight stars may search for dreams," Rayner said quietly. "But keys are only born in threes."

Aaron started. Clearly, he hadn't been the only one to forget Rayner was there as everyone twisted to look at him, sending a flush creeping across Rayner's face.

"All right," Branten said, leaning his elbows on the table. "Now, how do *you* know that?"

"I saw the words when I was escorted into the prison," Rayner mumbled, unable to meet Branten's gaze. "At some point, I got in the habit of thinking them to myself whenever..."

Rayner's voice trailed off, his expression far away. Surce touched his hand on the table, everyone exchanging looks. Everyone but Dimitri, who had recoiled back in his seat the moment Rayner opened his mouth.

Aaron looked between the two: Dimitri's hands flexing around the table, Rayner nodding to Surce, his face still pale as he stole a look at Dimitri.

What had happened between those two?

"At any rate," Rayner said, shaking himself off, "those are the words."

"But not all of them," Surce said.

"That's right," Aaron said hurriedly, eyes back on the page. "That's four translated lines, but there are twelve total."

"And they're connected to the map somehow," Mor murmured, rubbing the spot where his golden hand met his wrist.

No one had a response to that.

The rest of lunch was noticeably quieter than before. Aaron smoothed out Surce's notes, his food forgotten as he turned everything over.

Clearly, the labels on the map were important. But why include those random locations? Why attach everything to those words?

Aaron still had no answers as lunch came to an end. Dimitri was the first to rise, his expression unreadable as he slipped out the door. The rest dispersed not long after that, Aaron rising to his feet as Surce came to collect her notes.

"I can help with your translations," he offered, passing her the page. "I'm far from fluent, but at least I'm another set of eyes."

"Yes, that would be helpful."

The word sent a soft buzz through Aaron's body. But that didn't stop his relief from catching in his chest as he spotted Rayner quietly slip from the room, clearly having waited until everyone else left. His mind flashed back to the vacant look on Rayner's face, Surce's hand atop his.

"Surce," he said, his voice low. "What exactly did Rayner go through in Scarsthain?"

"Nothing that would make him a danger to our kingdom."

"But he was still a danger to his friendship with Dima."

After all, Dimitri had been completely blindsided by Rayner's true identity. Something had clearly left him devastated. And if that had to do with Rayner's oath...

"Aaron." Surce placed her bronze hand on his shoulder, her voice firm. "You know my priority is this kingdom, yes?"

Aaron nodded.

"Then you must trust me when I say he's no threat. Even so, I won't be the one to tell you his story. But that doesn't mean there's no side you can learn."

Surce gave his shoulder a quick squeeze. Then, she turned and headed for the door, calling over her shoulder, "Talk to your friend. I think it will do both of you some good."

Aaron bowed his head, the door clicking shut behind her. It was almost unfair how often Surce was right. But what definitely wasn't fair was leaving Dimitri alone to deal with whatever had caused the broken look on his face.

Entrusting his kingdom's safety to Surce, Aaron headed off to find Dimitri's latest hiding spot.

Chapter 26

Dimitri slipped into Aaron's hidden side room, his body aching as he flopped down on Aaron's mound of extra pillows.

It wasn't the hidden passageways Aaron had alluded to, but that didn't stop Dimitri from spending the majority of his time tucked away inside. Not because he was avoiding Aaron's family—if anything, they had welcomed him with a startlingly natural ease. Between Laness plying him with pastries that first night and the general shit talking in the training hollow that followed, he'd almost managed to forget every calcified emotion weighing down his chest.

But then, he'd retired to the room Aaron had pointed out to him. Just to find a note on the bedside table.

I know you don't want to see me, so I thought this would be best. I'm sorry for what happened in the maze. You didn't deserve to find out like that. I have answers if you want them, but I'll leave you alone until then.

R.

Dimitri had read the note once, twice, three times, an ominous buzz building in his veins. And all of that buildup caved inward as he finally looked up, spotting the red knitted blanket folded at the foot of his bed. Almost identical to that of the only gift he'd been given as a child.

Dimitri squeezed his eyes shut at the memory, his hand digging through his nest of pillows until his fingers found soft, knitted threads.

Gods, every time he seemed to catch his breath, the next wave hit. The worst part was, he'd had all the evidence to anticipate this one.

Rayner's familiarity with wraiths. The way he'd turned away when they talked about Scarsthain. All his talk of loneliness, being untrustworthy—he knew what was on Scarsthain's door for the Crystal's sake.

But Dimitri hadn't put it together. And all he could think was he wanted Patryclas. He wanted to hear Patryclas tell him it would be all right. He wanted the closest thing he'd ever had to a parental figure to sit with him as each swell of emotion sent another chunk of his world crashing down.

But Patryclas was gone. The whole point of Dimitri being here was so he could do something about that, and the moment Surce had recited those lines, he'd felt a glimmer of hope.

He finally had something to contribute. But that also required dragging himself out of this room...

The thought had barely formed when the door creaked open.

"I should have known you'd be in here." Aaron shut the door behind him, his eyes scanning over the cluttered storage Dimitri had halfheartedly poked through, the hand-written notes falling off the wall, finally landing on Dimitri tucked away in the corner. "And now I see why you chose it."

"Sorry," Dimitri mumbled, toying with the edge of a pillow.

"Don't be. I'm jealous I didn't think of it first with how often my guests end up in here."

"Anna came in here, too?"

"Constantly," Aaron said, taking a seat at the long, narrow table across from him. "Although for a long time, there was a harp in here, so I can only blame myself for that one."

Dimitri cracked a smile, his gaze dropping to his lap. He knew he could let the conversation end there. The heavy, exhausted part of himself pleaded with him to do so. But the part of him desperate for Patryclas, the lifeline he'd unceasingly offered him, managed to pry his mouth open.

"So," he rasped. "Why *have* you tracked me down?"

"Because I've been a shitty friend, not checking on you sooner. Not just because you've seemingly been put through the wringer, but also because my kingdom can be... a lot."

"Sounds like you're speaking from experience," Dimitri commented.

"Well..." Aaron ducked his head, his hand going to the back of his neck. "Remember how I told you Analia spent a lot of time in here?"

"You didn't tell her beforehand, did you?"

Aaron winced. And somehow, Dimitri laughed. "She must have fucking loved that."

"She barely spoke to me for a week," Aaron confirmed.

Dimitri laughed again, the sound coming a little easier, some of that weight sliding away.

"So," he said, propping himself up on an elbow. "You and Anna?"

"She told you?"

"She and that stupid smile on your face."

Aaron's smile grew as Dimitri dragged himself free of the pillows, coming to claim the seat beside his.

"Is this the part where I ask for your approval?" he asked.

"Oh, fuck off, Bordello. As if I wanted to sit through any more of your pining."

"Don't be jealous, Dima," Aaron purred, "you know I'll always hold our drunken night fondly in my heart."

"You'd have more to remember if you didn't talk so much."

Aaron's wicked bravado shattered with a laugh. He offered a one-finger salute, Dimitri's own composure cracking. He leaned back in his seat, giving Aaron a once-over.

He and Analia made sense. Even back in Sun when he annoyed her more than anything, they fit. They were magnets, not having to think as they pulled each other in. And that ease had the small, lonely part of Dimitri ache a little bit more.

But that didn't stop him from being happy for them. Nor did it stop him from noticing Aaron's smile fade. He started to speak, but Aaron beat him to it.

"So," he said. "Since you got to pry into my life, does that mean I get to pry into yours?"

"You can try," Dimitri snorted. "But you won't find much."

"Even in the Rayner category?"

Dimitri's momentary contentment guttered. "The Rayner category," he said flatly, "consists of him fucking me over and only now feeling guilty about it."

Aaron stilled. His expression shifted into that of a cat that had just spotted its prey, his words slow and precise as he asked, "You mean by not telling you about Scarsthain?"

"I wish that was fucking all."

With that, the full story came out. Not just his investigation of Deardryn, but his time with Rayner. The hours they'd spent talking in Rayner's shop. The Full Moon Festival, their visit to Ferrin's statue, every little moment that had turned into chips of glass in the wound.

He'd barely made it through the story with Analia. But now, watching Aaron's expression grow darker and darker, something inside him began to harden. Not anger, but validation as he reached Rayner's betrayal and Aaron cursed.

"And then he clobbered you with his identity in the hedge maze?" he demanded.

"Pretty much."

Dimitri hesitated, the rest of his story clogging his throat. But Aaron shook his head. He rose from his seat, moving to a bench piled with various storage bins. Shifting them aside, he flipped open the top of the bench, Dimitri's eyebrows rising as he pulled out a bottle of amber liquid.

"You keep your liquor in a bench?" he asked.

"Just the good kinds. Branten and Laness have a habit of stealing them whenever I leave them out."

"That's annoying."

"Not at all," Aaron said with a faint laugh. "It's turned into a game. They would have stopped a long time ago if it bothered me."

Dimitri remained quiet as Aaron retrieved two chipped shot glasses from the bench, turning over the simple consideration of it all.

"I think Rayner's been trying to do that," he said, half to himself. "At least, I think that's what he'd like me to believe him not pestering me the past three days is. But he did the same thing in Moon: bringing me my poetry collection, telling me about Analia being freed, not telling Sylas about me leaving the library. And then he hit me with another secret."

"Well," Aaron said, bringing his bottle and glasses to the table, "as much as I'd like to call him out for his secrets, there's an entire house of people ready to call me a hypocrite."

Dimitri rolled his eyes.

"All I can say," Aaron went on, filling his glasses, "is that's fucking terrible. But Surce has also heard his side of the story, and she's adamant we keep him around."

Dimitri didn't know if that bothered him or was a relief. He accepted the shot glass Aaron passed him, bringing it to his lips. And as soon as he tasted the dry liquor, he wished he hadn't.

"That's fucking awful," he coughed, barely swallowing it down.

Aaron laughed, some of the darkness leaving his expression. "You don't drink it for the taste."

Dimitri made a disgusted noise and wiped his mouth with his hand. Still, he could feel the slow, warm path of the liquor through his body, loosening some of his tension in its wake.

"That's all you have to say, though?" he asked, slumping back in his seat. "You're not going to tell me to forgive him or go talk to him or whatever?"

"Gods no," Aaron said. "After all that, I don't think anyone could blame you for never speaking to him again."

He paused, turning his glass between his fingers.

"Why do I have a feeling there's a but," Dimitri grumbled.

The corner of Aaron's mouth quirked. "Do you remember our argument in the alleyway outside of Gritta's?"

Of all the responses Dimitri was expecting, that wasn't one of them. Still, he nodded slowly.

"I accused you of using Analia to learn how to read, and as an escape route."

"You also accused me of being ready to turn her in to the Royals the moment anything went sour."

"I did. And your look of guilt was the first sign that you'd started to care."

Dimitri dropped his gaze. "I don't think I could have gone through with that," he murmured, collecting the stray notes on the table.

"I've wondered about that," Aaron said. "Especially since you obviously didn't want to go to Gritta's, but you did anyway. Just as you tracked down Selbi's plant list without being asked, came with us to the Royal Garden, and even stayed behind to make sure Analia could escape the castle."

"What's your point?" Dimitri asked.

"My point is I knew you had some tangled motives in that alleyway. So, instead of making assumptions, I gave you a choice."

"And you're saying you trusted me immediately after that?"

"No. But we gave you a chance, and you stepped up. And look where we are now."

Aaron gestured to the tiny window, his kingdom lights sparkling in the snow. Dimitri, however, only glowered.

"I thought you said you *weren't* telling me to forgive him," he said.

"I'm not. If anything, you've already given Rayner a chance to step up, and leaving you alone after he fucked up is a laughably flimsy argument that he has. But I *do* trust Surce. And outside of that, I think it's a lot easier to make a decision based on answers, not assumptions."

"Which means I have to talk to him," Dimitri muttered, sinking down in his seat.

"Only if you want to." Aaron rose to his feet and stretched. "No matter what you decide, Anna and I will *always* have your back. As for this kingdom, it's open to you for as long as you like. I just need to know if I'll be making sleeping or burial arrangements for Rayner."

He offered a small, affectionate smile. One Dimitri believed. Immediately. And Dimitri didn't trust himself to respond as it hit him just how badly he'd needed that.

Aaron flashed him a knowing look. Then, collecting his bottle and glasses, he turned away. And the words were out of Dimitri's mouth before he could stop them.

"There's more after Scarsthain."

Aaron looked back.

"I went back to the Moon Castle. I saw Deardryn attack Patryclas. And I... I tried to heal him."

"You tried to heal him?" Aaron repeated slowly.

Dimitri could practically see him fitting the pieces together. He knew this was his moment to retreat, explain it away, hide. But Aaron had trusted him with his own identity back in the Sun Kingdom woods.

He took a deep breath. And somehow, he forced the words past the squeezing in his throat. "I tried to heal him with my Sun magic."

To Aaron's credit, he remained remarkably composed. Dimitri gripped his hands beneath the table, terrified to so much as twitch as Aaron stared at him from the doorway. Finally, Aaron returned to the table and offered Dimitri the bottle.

"Will you be drinking alone or with company?"

Dimitri's grip didn't relax. "You're not going to question me about my magic?"

"Is it under control?" Aaron asked.

"Yes."

"Do you know how to release the buildup?"

"Yes."

"Is it a threat to anyone in my kingdom?"

"No."

"Then it's none of my business." Aaron thunked the bottle on the table, then lightly touched Dimitri's shoulder. "I'll be around."

Dimitri nodded, and Aaron gave a quick squeeze. Then, he retreated, the door softly closing behind him.

Dimitri let out a long breath, his head bowing forward into his hands. He knew Aaron was right: he needed answers. Which meant, Crystal spare him, he had to talk to Rayner.

Chapter 27

"**Y**ou have got to be joking," Ember said.

She and Rois sat at Analia's vanity, Rois's hand-drawn map of the dungeon laid out before them. Othin had decided to assign Ember to the Ash Princess's chambers while she worked in the castle—which Ember couldn't decide was a gesture of good faith or a warning. What she *did* know was he certainly hadn't assumed her work would involve *this*.

"You were the one who agreed to plan a prison break," Rois said, smoothing out the wrinkles in his map.

"I also didn't want you sneaking into my chambers," she retorted. "Yet, here you are."

Rois scoffed, but Ember caught his self-satisfied smirk in the mirror. From the moment she'd returned from the apothecary, he'd launched a full-scale pestering campaign to let him help plan their rescue in her chambers, Ember finally caving a few days in just to make it stop. Even now, the memory had her twisting in her chair, giving the nearby fire sprites a long, suffering look.

There weren't many of them, maybe half a dozen huddled together on the candles she'd arranged along her windowsills. They'd slowly started showing up after her conversation with Spark, their posture always uncertain upon first arrival. Ember was careful to only offer a wave or smile before returning to whatever she was doing, hiding the soft glow in her chest every time the sprite wavered, then settled on a candle wick.

"What's your problem with my map?" Rois asked.

Ember blinked hard, then dragged her gaze back to the vanity. "First of all, I can't see all of it because your big head is in the way."

"We'd have more room if we could work at Analia's desk," Rois complained, leaning back in his chair.

"I already told you all of my healer gear is there; we're not moving it."

Especially since she didn't need Rois discovering the fuzzy orange plant now hidden in her jumble of supplies. She rubbed her nose, still able to faintly smell the sharp scent of the leaf she'd crushed before he arrived.

Gods, she'd almost forgotten how it felt to feel focused. Present, her eyes scanning over the neat, block-like dungeon.

"You do realize how big this is," she said, tracing one of the corridors with her finger. "Yes, it's a simple design, but *look* at it."

"It's not that bad. The Sun people are lazy and locked the Royals up right near the entrance."

Well, that was true. She'd only had to make a few turns when going to heal the Royals.

"But what about the others?" she pressed. "I went down that entire row of cells, and I didn't see any of the Royal spouses, and I *certainly* haven't seen them throughout the castle."

"They're being kept a few halls over. It seems like since they're only Blessed married to Royals, the Sun guard hasn't been paying them much attention."

"How comforting," Ember muttered.

"I was able to talk to one the last time I slipped out," Rois went on, playing with a discarded comb on the vanity. "She said when Sun breached the castle, many of the Royals grabbed their loved ones and shadowjumped them out before returning to secure the castle. The three that Sun captured are the ones who decided to stay and fight."

Gods, let that be the only reason there were so few. Ember rubbed her eyes, her mind starting to jumble as she turned over all the new information. Yet, one thing kept nagging at her.

"How have you been able to do all of this in the first place?" she asked, her knee bumping his as she turned toward him. "The dungeon door is locked."

"Yes, and all Royals have a key. Luckily for us, Anna left hers behind." Rois pulled a small key from his pocket, the gold flashing in the light as he spun it around his finger.

Ember sat up straight. "You rifled through Anna's things?"

"I knew exactly where she kept it," Rois said, passing her the key. "You forget, Anna hated me when I joined the guard, but we weren't always like that."

Ember grumbled under her breath, tucking the key back behind the vanity mirror where she *also* knew Analia kept it. He could ask for it back if he needed it. She turned back to Rois, about to speak. Just to cut off with a jolt as there came a thud outside her door.

"We're fine," Rois assured her, clearly noticing her flinch. "By the time anyone could get in here, you'd already be finished healing my hand."

"Your what?"

Rois dragged a finger across his palm like a slash mark, then wiggled his eyebrows. Ember scoffed and shoved his shoulder, her hands shaking.

She needed another hit. She needed to get this guard and his map out of her chambers.

Rois, either not noticing her irritation or simply ignoring it, lightly nudged her in return. "At any rate," he said, turning back to the map, "once we figure out how to get the cell keys, getting to the vault is easy. You just take two rights and a left from the family members' cells, then look for the door with a tiny phoenix carved next to the knob."

"Sounds easy enough," Ember said.

"It is. But then we reach the vault itself."

Rois slid the drawing of the dungeon aside, revealing the sheet underneath. Ember's eyes widened.

"Oh," she said faintly. "I see."

The vault was set up in the same rectangular format as the dungeon. Yet, where the dungeon consisted of straightforward, grid-like halls, the vault reminded Ember of a maze. Winding pathways, intersecting halls, dead end after dead end.

"It's not that bad," Rois said quickly.

One of the candle flames crackled as Spark hopped the short distance between the windowsill and the vanity. They padded over to examine the drawing, their little feet trailing wax. Then, they screwed up their face, gave Ember's thumb a consoling pat, and fled back to the candle.

"I think that means it's bad," Ember said, shifting restlessly in her seat. "Did you really draw all of this perfectly?"

"Every Crystal Guard has to memorize these paths upon initiation," Rois said. "The good news is, they're not as complicated as they look. You see all the sconces?"

No, she did not see the sconces. She could only see every way this plan would unravel, how it would end with herself, Cadmus, Rois, everyone, executed in front of the king-dom. But taking a steadying breath, she forced her attention back to the map.

"You mean these?" she asked, tapping the little doodles running along a hallway.

"Exactly. Those sconces are the key to navigating the vault."

A few fire sprites looked up from their candles.

"Well, don't stop there," Ember told him.

Rois flashed a crooked grin. "The dungeon is separated into three sections. The left side, the center, and the right side." Rois tapped each section of the map. "As you can see, many of these pathways converge on each other and, presumably, Azar and whoever built this castle didn't want to keep track of countless obnoxious directions. So, each pathway is marked by a different pattern of torches."

"Those being?" Ember asked.

"I was getting there," Rois said, swatting aside her fingers rapidly drumming on the map. "The left section has sconces that alternate between the left wall and the right wall. Torches on both sides is the middle. And sconces that are in groups of two are the right side. Granted, you still have to memorize the directions, but that's easy. To get out, you just follow the left path for three turns, turn left into the center section, take the fourth turn on that hall into the right path, and then follow that for four corridors until you can turn left and back onto the center section, and the door is right there."

Rois sat back in his seat like a performer at the end of his act. Ember, however, stared at him blankly. "Did you say turn left from the left section into the center section?"

"It's a maze, Ember," Rois said, rolling his eyes.

Ember couldn't even protest. She didn't remember enough of the instructions to do so. Well, hopefully that meant the Sun soldiers would be equally disoriented when hunting them down.

Or maybe they weren't functioning off of fading devinroot effects and they *could* keep it all straight. Rosala spare her, she needed to get Rois out of her chambers. They could figure out the rest later. Maybe she could tell Rois she had a patient—

Ember jerked out of her thoughts as Rois rose from his chair.

"We can go over it as many times as you need," he promised with a stretch. Then, he moved to flop horizontally across her bed. And Ember's horror intensified.

"Rosala spare me, do *not* lay on my bed."

"Why?" Rois whined. "My back hurts from Anna's tiny chair."

"It would be bad enough if anyone from Sun burst in and found you here. But to find you on *my bed?*"

"Fully clothed!" Rois protested.

"For now," Ember muttered, obsessively straightening the maps on the vanity.

Rois rolled his eyes, then paused. "Do you truly have people bursting into your chambers unannounced at any time?"

"Unannounced?" Ember asked. "No. At any time? Constantly."

Losing interest in the papers, Ember rose and crossed to her bed. She sat beside Rois, nudging him repeatedly until he finally groaned and rolled to his feet.

He returned to the vanity chair, Ember expecting him to sulk. Instead, his voice was thoughtful as he said, "That must be hard. Never being able to prioritize yourself because someone might need you."

Ember's agitation softened a fraction. "It's not much different from being a guard or a ruler."

"Maybe a ruler," Rois said. "But I'm only responsible for a handful of people. Not an entire kingdom." He hesitated, choosing his words carefully. "It must be difficult to feel like you're responsible for everyone else. That's a lot of pressure. I can only imagine what that might push someone to do."

Ember went perfectly still. "What are you insinuating, Rois?" she asked, her voice slipping into something low, dangerous.

Rois didn't flinch. Instead, he leaned toward her, something like concern on his face as he asked, "When did you start using again?"

His words hit her like an electric shock. Her spine straightened, her hands curling into fists at her sides. "I'm not."

"Em, you went from completely out of it to focused and fidgety. You've touched your nose thirteen times since I arrived, and I don't think you were aware of half those times."

"So, you've decided to jump to conclusions?" she demanded, a flush creeping across her skin.

"You telling me if I dug through your healer gear I wouldn't find even a leaf of devinroot?"

The fire sprites exchanged uncertain looks on the windowsills. And the heat across Ember's body turned into a blaze.

"You said it yourself," she said, shoving to her feet. "I have a lot of people I'm responsible for; I can't help them if I'm 'completely out of it.'"

"So, instead you're healing under the influence," Rois said, also rising and folding his arms.

Ember cringed. Even when using casually, she'd *never* healed while high. It was a part of her oath. An oath she'd broken over and over and over again.

"I don't use when I'm on duty," she said, heading for Analia's gilded harp in the corner. "I didn't even go back to it until Tayla and I had healed all of the injured from the invasion."

"I thought someone could knock on your door at any time."

Ember's fingers tightened around the harp's frame. "If I've used, I turn them away to Tayla."

"What if it's an emergency?" Rois pressed. "What if there's no time to find Tayla? Would you still turn them away? Or would you—"

"It's not like that!" Ember exclaimed, whirling around and covering her ears. "I'm a healer, Rois. I specialize in herbology. Maybe I took too much in the past and that was why it was taking me longer to recover. But I can't be recovering from devinroot if we're going to get Cadmus out. Once we get him out, I'm done. I'm weaning myself off. This is temporary."

"Ember—"

"Where do we end up when we exit the vault?" Ember asked over him.

Rois's jaw dropped. "Ember, we're not done—"

"How do we escape after exiting the vault?" she repeated, her body starting to shake.

Rois stared at her in disbelief, but Ember squared her shoulders. They were *not* going to discuss this. It was risky enough having him in her chambers. They were *not* going to waste that time arguing over a plant.

A muscle in Rois's jaw jumped, the silence stretching between them. Just when Ember thought he would refuse to speak...

"A little ways from the southeast wall," he said tightly. "The Royals created the vault exit as a last resort, so they made the exit within the walls to prevent anyone from using it to sneak in."

"All right then," Ember said, equally tight as she folded her arms. "So how do we get past the wall?"

"There's an opening. It's only activated by Royal blood or those given permission by the Royals, which only includes the Crystal Guard."

"Blood, not magic?"

"In case of dampers."

Ember nodded, her heart still pounding in her ears. Rois's eyes flicked to her collection of plants, jars, and other tools on Analia's desk, his mouth opening.

"How do we get the cell keys?" she asked.

Rois briefly pressed his lips into a line. "I'm still thinking about that. They're usually carried by the head guard of the dungeon patrol. They might be helpful with that."

Rois nodded to the fire sprites, who had gone completely still. As soon as Rois mentioned them, they let out a collective squeak and disappeared in a crackle. And something in Ember's chest snapped.

"All right," she said, marching toward him. "You're officially done here."

"Ember—"

"We'll figure out the rest later."

Ember ushered Rois to his feet, barely able to think over the buzzing in her ears. She opened the door, ignoring Rois's protest as she checked the coast was clear. Then, she shoved him back into the hall.

Right before she closed the door, she looked up, expecting to find the same tension on his face from before. Instead, there was something softer, Rois reaching back inside to lightly touch her hand.

And Ember had never hated herself more as she stepped away and closed the door.

Not wasting a second, she crossed to her desk, shoving plants aside until she found familiar fuzzy leaves. She crushed them between her fingers and brought them to her nose, her knees nearly giving out as she breathed in the sharp smell. Especially since she knew without a doubt that Rois remained on the other side of her door, completely aware of what she was doing.

If only that was enough to make her stop.

Chapter 28

Dimitri found Rayner on the roof. He sat with his feet hanging over the edge, his gloved thumb holding down the page of his book as the winter wind swirled around him. At the creak of the hatch opening, he looked over his shoulder, his tired gaze meeting Dimitri's.

"Have you come to talk?" he asked. "Or have you decided to take my brooding spot."

His tone wasn't accusatory, but Dimitri averted his gaze anyway.

"I'm not taking your spot," he mumbled, shoving his hands in his pockets.

"All right then."

Rayner watched him a few moments, clearly expectant. But Dimitri couldn't move. He couldn't so much as breathe. Not until Rayner bit his lip and returned his attention to his book.

Why was this so hard? He was the one who had decided to speak with Rayner; he *wanted* answers. So why couldn't he stop himself from curling inward just at the sound of his voice?

"You can sit," Rayner eventually offered, running his fingers over the green cover of his book. *Moss* green. The color he had once said was his favorite because it reminded him he was home.

For the longest time, Dimitri had considered it a throwaway fact. But now, standing on that roof, he finally realized that fact had an unspoken ending. Home, and not in a cell.

And somehow, Dimitri was stepping forward, brushing the snow aside with his foot, easing down beside Rayner on the roof's edge. Then, there was silence. Thick, smothering.

"How's your shoulder?" Dimitri finally asked.

"Fine." Rayner rubbed the spot where the arrow had skewered him. "Surce summoned a healer to tend to it after my interrogation. Sofika, I think. I still haven't gotten used to the fact that most of the healers here don't have any markings."

"They don't?"

"Sofika said it's because they can't travel to the Temple of Rosala without revealing the Starlight Kingdom, so they've decided to forgo that tradition. Only the healers trained before the Shattering have markings."

"That makes sense," Dimitri murmured.

The two lapsed back into silence. Rayner fidgeted with his book, his gaze focused on the snow-dusted kingdom below. But Dimitri could only stare at the side of his face.

He knew every part of that man. His voice, his gestures, his reactions. Even the way his hair started to curl from melting snowflakes was familiar.

He didn't know the precise moment a connection had been forged between them—he hadn't been aware of it in the first place. But now?

It wasn't like a wall had slammed between them. It was just... nothing. A complete, empty void. And there was no describing the unsettling wrongness of staring at a stranger whose every detail he knew as well as his own reflection.

But he *didn't* know Rayner. That was the point. That was why he was there.

"You said you would explain everything?" Dimitri asked.

Rayner looked at him quickly. But Dimitri had to give him credit, he'd always been good at rolling with it.

"I will." He hesitated, running a hand through his hair. "Do you want to go inside first?"

"I'm fine."

Rayner nodded. Then, with what Dimitri could have sworn was a quick, steadying breath, he slipped his book in a jacket pocket and began.

"The Moon Kingdom escape didn't go at all like I was expecting. I knew my job was to change your appearance and help you through the maze, and perhaps the mature thing to do was leave it at that. But I couldn't stand the thought of that being how we left things. Especially since you never informed me I wasn't coming with you."

"What does that have to do with anything?" Dimitri asked.

"I figured if you wanted nothing to do with me, that would be the first thing you did after hearing Analia's plan."

Huh. He had a point. So, why *hadn't* he said anything?

Dimitri wrapped his arms around himself, from the cold or irritation, he didn't know. But Rayner only cracked a faint smile and continued.

"Granted, I still knew you were furious with me. You made that perfectly clear. And I knew as long as we were in the Moon Kingdom, where I betrayed you, my oath with Sylas was still a factor, and your life was in danger, none of that would change. But I thought maybe if we got away from it all, we could... talk?

"You could finally catch your breath. You could think and do what you wanted without worrying about how it would impact your survival. And I was planning on explaining all of this and asking if I could come in the days leading up to the escape, but I couldn't do it. Not when leaving you alone had resulted in what felt like a fragile truce."

Dimitri's mind flashed back to those three days after Analia first came to the book nook. How Rayner had been unusually quiet. How his gaze had repeatedly flicked away from Dimitri's, leaving Dimitri to anxiously wonder what he was refusing to say.

"Is it because you didn't want to risk our 'truce,'" Dimitri said, "or because you knew I would say no?"

Dimitri waited for Rayner to bristle, his own temper sparking. But Rayner only rubbed the side of his face. "Honestly? Probably both."

Well, that wasn't fair. How was he supposed to snap back if Rayner agreed?

Dimitri's shoulders hunched, his temper sputtering out. "Keep going," he grumbled.

"There's not much more after that," Rayner said, drawing in the snow between them with his finger. "My last chance to ask was when we were in the maze. But then we spiraled out of control, and the Sun soldiers caught up, and I had an arrow through my shoulder, and I found out your rescuer was a gods-damned *Star Royal*. And telling him I figured out who he was didn't convince him to let me come. So, I just... panicked.

"I knew if you disappeared, I would never see you again. I would never be able to make it up to you. And I panicked."

Rayner trailed off. He bowed his head, his eyes on Dimitri's hands, still fisted in his jacket as he hugged himself.

Dimitri, in turn, took a moment to process. Thought about what he wanted. Then, he forced Rayner to meet his gaze.

"You do realize," he said slowly, "that all you've been talking about is what *you* wanted."

Rayner's lips parted, but Dimitri went on.

"*You* wanted to come because *you* wanted to make it up to me. *You* blindsided me because that's what *you* thought you needed to do to come."

Rayner didn't respond.

"Well?" Dimitri demanded, twisting on the roof to face him fully.

"You're right," he said simply. And that admission had Dimitri's temper burning hotter.

"Were you ever going to tell me about Scarsthain?" he asked, the wind picking up around him.

Rayner didn't flinch back from Dimitri's tone. "I like to think I would have. I certainly didn't want to clobber you with the information out of nowhere. You deserve to have been told first, individually. And I'm sorry that's not what happened."

He was sorry. He was fucking *sorry* for that, but nothing else.

"But you don't know if you would have told me."

"I don't exactly go around telling people," Rayner snapped.

"Holy Crystal above, which is it?" Dimitri asked, gripping the sides of his head. "Am I no one to you? Someone whose life you won't choose over your own, someone you won't tell your past to, someone you can bring yourself to betray? Or am I the person you're desperate to mend things with for reasons you *refuse* to tell me?"

"It's not either or, Dimitri!" Rayner protested. "The world isn't black and white; more than one thing can exist at a time. I would have thought you of all people would know that."

"Why me?"

"What about your magic?"

Dimitri recoiled. Rayner's eyes pierced into his, demanding an answer.

But Dimitri was the one who had come for answers. And all he'd gotten was the friend he'd thought he'd had was just one of the many masks Rayner wore. And he refused to show Dimitri anything of the man underneath.

Dimitri expected his temper to finally snap its leash. But the single word that managed to squeeze past his throat could barely be heard over the wind. "No."

Rayner opened his mouth. But Dimitri rose to his feet. He barely heard the snow crunch beneath his boots as he headed for the ladder back into the house, barely felt the cold against his hands as he started to descend. All there was was the black wave inside him, rising up, up, up.

But Rayner wasn't done.

"I know what I saw," he persisted, rising and heading after him. "You blasted me down the corridor with Sun magic. I saw you try to heal Patryclas—"

"Stop," Dimitri choked out, descending faster.

"I was the one who summoned the healers. I was the one who told Sylas what really happened. And I told him about your magic because I knew that was the only thing that would convince him you were worth getting out of that cell."

"You told him?" Dimitri stumbled off the ladder, feeling like he'd been kicked in the chest. Gods, that was why Sylas hadn't seemed surprised when Dimitri removed his cuffs—that was why he was so determined to remove them himself. He wanted to verify Rayner's story.

Dimitri turned to stare up at Rayner, at a loss for words as he stepped off the ladder. And though something seemed to crumple in Rayner's expression, he didn't retreat.

"I did," he said, softening a fraction. "And even though you don't want to hear it, I would do it again. Even if that means you feel like I've betrayed you twice. I'd rather have you alive and safe and hating me than rotting away or dead—and yes, I know that's another thing *I* wanted. We've established I'm a selfish asshole."

Rayner threw up his hands. But he didn't try to close the distance between them. And Dimitri didn't know what to do.

"You're a Sun Royal, Dimitri," Rayner said, his voice softening to a normal volume. "A bastard-born Sun Royal. Everyone in the Sun Castle knows you're Othin's bastard; rumors have undoubtedly spread outside the castle. But no one knows Othin's affair was with another Sun Royal."

"Rayner, stop," Dimitri whispered, his voice, everything, breaking.

"That kind of secret, especially since it's been kept for so long, could completely destroy the kingdom's trust in their Royals. Your mere *existence* could give you the justice you've always deserved, especially now that Patryclas—"

Dimitri stumbled back, cringing so hard he barely heard the following words. He'd already had this conversation with Sylas: this wasn't him—it *couldn't* be him. But Dimitri couldn't speak as Rayner finally took a step closer, his hand extending between them.

"You could have what you want," he repeated, almost imploringly. "But you relentlessly look for another way, even if it hurts you."

"You don't get to know why," Dimitri said shakily, his hand squeezing around his wrist.

"So then why am I obligated to explain myself to you?"

"Because last I checked, my back didn't fall on your knife."

Dimitri didn't know if there was a name for the emotion in his voice. But it had Rayner's lips parting, his eyes wide. And Dimitri didn't try to stop the broken, bloody pieces of himself from spilling past his lips.

"The thing about getting stabbed in the back is you don't just wonder why they did it. You wonder when they'll do it again. And you *did* do it again, Rayner. *Twice.* Maybe not in the back, but I'm ripped up and bloody because of you. And the worst part is, I don't know how many more daggers you have."

Dimitri brought a hand to his aching chest as he stared into Rayner's face, not knowing what he was looking for. Rayner shook his head slowly, seemingly struggling for words.

"Such a poet," he murmured. So quiet. But something in Dimitri's chest still broke.

"You know what?" he said, taking a step forward. "I *am* a poet. Do you know why all us poets describe betrayal with daggers and broken hearts and bloody cuts? It's because it fucking hurts. You hurt me, Rayner. You didn't just make me angry. You *hurt me*. And you don't even care enough to tell me why."

Rayner rocked back on his heels as if slapped. He braced his hand against the wall, absolutely stunned. And the fact that that was what it took for Rayner to get it had Dimitri's heart crumbling.

Without a word, he turned away. And Rayner didn't speak, didn't make a sound, as Dimitri dragged his heavy body down the hall.

Not angry. Not even resentful. Just completely devastated.

Chapter 29

Dimitri didn't have a destination in mind as he stumbled out Aaron's back door. All he knew was he couldn't breathe in that house. He couldn't afford to let his feet stop moving. Down the porch steps, across the yard, snow crunching beneath his boots as he entered the grove of birch trees.

Step after step after step.

He didn't immediately notice he'd found a path through the trees. But his pace slowed at the peal of laughter up ahead.

Gods, he was heading for the training hollow. And it was occupied by multiple people. Which was the *last* thing he wanted to deal with.

But he couldn't go back to the house.

Dimitri's shoulders slumped. Then, he forced his heavy body to speed up once more, following the laughter through the trees and to the training hollow's edge.

According to Laness, the hollow had been magically protected from the elements a long time ago, allowing the moss and grass to provide a lush pop of green against the snow. Branten and Laness stood in the center with their backs to Dimitri, gesturing to the training dummies set up in front of them: a blue one for Branten, and a red for Laness. Mor lounged on a patch of moss off to the side, his hazel eyes immediately spotting Dimitri.

"Oh, thank the gods," he said. "Someone else who's sober."

It took Dimitri a moment to remember how to respond. "Sober?" he asked.

At his response, Branten and Laness clumsily spun around. A row of daggers hung from their belts. They each clutched a heavy amber bottle, several more scattered around their feet, most of them empty. And all of them familiar.

"Dima!" Laness said brightly.

Dimitri began, "What are you—"

"We found Aaron's liquor stash!" Branten crowed, a wide, stupid smile on his face as he raised his bottle.

Dimitri kept his expression straight—although he doubted it mattered much. "You mean from the bar cart?"

"No!" Laness said. "From the hidden drawer at the base of the sitting room table."

Branten cackled and took a swig from his bottle. So, Aaron had more than one hiding spot.

"You can join us if you like," Mor offered. "I could use the additional sanity."

"Oh, come on, Mortie," Branten said, "you can drop the pained chaperone act."

Laness added, "We all know you enjoy our game as much as we do."

"Make sure you don't stand directly behind them, Dima," Mor called, eliciting near identical noises of indignation from Laness and Branten.

"*One* time!" Laness protested.

To Dimitri's surprise, his lips twitched. "What's your game?" he asked, taking a step forward, the temperature instantly warming to more comfortable levels.

"We call it Drunken Daggers," Branten said. "First, you find some of Aaron's good liquor. Then, you park your ass out here because he doesn't like dealing with you when you drink said liquor."

"And then," Laness said, "you grab some daggers and start throwing."

"And whoever's farther from their dummy has to take a drink," Branten finished.

They beamed up at Dimitri, positively pleased. Dimitri, in turn, eyed their half-empty bottles, the daggers at their belts, over to the daggers that lay scattered around the red and blue dummies.

"That sounds like a terrible idea," he said.

"What a fascinating way they pronounce fantastic in the Sun Kingdom." Branten turned, and in what Dimitri assumed was usually a smooth, lethal movement, he fumbled a dagger from his belt and threw. The dagger wobbled through the air, barely impaling itself on the edge of the blue dummy.

Laness groaned and took a swig from her bottle.

Dimitri looked at Mor, not sure if he was amused or afraid for his safety. Mor shrugged and flashed a half smile.

"What these two forgot to mention," he said, "is the loser has to pay for all of Aaron's replacement bottles."

"You replace them?" Dimitri asked, startled.

"Of course we do!" Laness exclaimed. "That's a part of the game. He hides them, we find them and steal them, and then we replace them so he doesn't notice."

"And when they disappear from that spot," Branten said, "that means he's on to us and we get to search once more."

That might have been the most ridiculous game Dimitri had ever heard. Mor caught Dimitri's eye, his lips twitching as he patted the moss beside him. And somehow, Dimitri's feet were moving, the bloody pieces of himself scabbing over just a little bit as Mor, Laness, and Branten beamed.

For the rest of the afternoon, Dimitri witnessed what could only be described as a drunken disaster. Branten and Laness seemed less interested in throwing the daggers than they did shit talking and drinking, regardless of if their dagger was farther from the target. Mor, in turn, provided a running commentary to Dimitri, the game devolving even further once Laness and Branten noticed.

Usually, the setup would have been Dimitri's worst nightmare: loud, chaotic activity, surrounded by people he didn't really know. But Laness and Branten left him alone. If anything, it felt like he was watching a horrifyingly enthralling performance with Mor, and he could handle one new person.

"How long does this usually last?" he eventually asked.

"Hard to say," Mor replied. "You know you're getting close when the taunting turns to sulking after each miss."

Branten threw a dagger, the two nearly collapsing in laughter as it flew directly between the dummies and thudded into the piled-up equipment beyond.

Dimitri snorted. "I'm assuming we have a ways to go."

Mor grinned. "Good thing we have a way to pass the time."

Dimitri sat up straight as Mor pulled a full, dark red bottle out from behind himself. "Where did you get that?" he asked.

"Branten and Laness's stolen stash." Mor placed the bottle between them, a cup appearing in each of his hands.

"Now, where did you get those?"

"My Blessing involves relocation," Mor explained, passing Dimitri a cup. "The house is just close enough for me to grab these from the kitchen."

"Can you put them back as well?"

"I could. But with the location being out of my sight, there might be a margin of error."

Dimitri snorted as Mor filled their glasses, his hazel eyes sparkling. Perhaps Mor wasn't as refined as he appeared. And Dimitri's curiosity piqued as he watched Mor's golden hand fumble with the cork, finally pulling it free with a pop.

"So," Dimitri said. "How'd you get your hand?"

Mor smiled slightly, seemingly unperturbed by Dimitri's bluntness. "You know about the Human Kingdom?"

Dimitri nodded.

"My mother and her family were from there, but her parents suspected my father was a Blessed from this kingdom. And since I showed no sign of magic until I was nine, my grandfather decided to cut off my hand to determine once and for all."

Mor sipped his wine, surprisingly unfazed.

"Well, fuck," Dimitri said after a moment.

Mor shrugged. "What about you?" he asked. "Sun King's bastard?"

"That's right," Dimitri hedged.

Mor took in Dimitri's tightened grip on his glass. Then, he raised his cup. "To terrible families."

Dimitri's grip relaxed. "Terrible *blood* families," he corrected.

Mor hummed in appreciation as they clinked their glasses. Dimitri took a long drink, finding the sweeter flavor far better than that from the side room bottle. Gods, *everything* was better than the wallowing that had happened in that room. Everything but his conversation with Rayner.

Dimitri's mouth pinched. Mor chose that moment to return his attention to the game, leaving Dimitri to turn over his conversation with Rayner.

He'd told himself he'd sought Rayner out for answers. Yet, he hadn't exactly been open to receiving them. If anything, he'd been looking for a reason to stay angry. Numb the wound beneath because it was hard enough having to wake up to the hole Patryclas's death had ripped through his being.

What was it Rayner had called him, a snapping turtle? Maybe that wasn't so far off after all.

All he knew was he couldn't keep turning this cycle. If this family could relentlessly harass each other while still respecting the other's boundaries, Dimitri could have a productive conversation.

"Wait," Branten said, staring down in puzzlement at the empty bottles he kicked. "Where's the last one?"

Dimitri and Mor shared a quick look, and Mor magicked their cups and bottle away.

"There's no other bottle," Laness said, "because you drank it all, you tree."

"Tree?" Branten pivoted toward Mor and Dimitri, both feigning nonchalance. "Mortie, the tiny screechy sapling called me a *tree.*"

"She's allowed to, since she won," Mor said with a stretch.

"What?" Branten exclaimed.

"Damn right!" Laness cheered.

Dimitri smiled slightly as Laness drunkenly danced around Branten, the warrior's pout lasting about three seconds before he dissolved into laughter. Mor shook his head as he rose, going to collect the empty bottles and scattered daggers. And Dimitri didn't try to resist as Laness came to drag him into her celebration.

By the time the four exited the hollow, Dimitri was flushed and stumbling with laughter. Yet, as Branten shoved the sliding door open, everyone piling inside, Dimitri's amusement caught in his throat.

Rayner sat on the sitting room couch, his back to the door as he spoke softly with Surce beside him. She passed him what appeared to be a small, folded tapestry, the two looking up at the sudden noise. And Rayner's gaze met Dimitri's.

Beside him, Branten and Laness went quiet. Dimitri struggled to relax his shoulders, reminding himself of his decision. But gods, he hadn't expected that conversation to happen *immediately*.

Rayner's eyes darted back and forth between Dimitri and Surce, clearly thinking something similar. She patted his hand, the silence stretching, stretching, stretching.

"Branten," Laness finally said in what was clearly supposed to be a whisper. "Do you think we should leave?"

"I think you're right," Branten whispered back. He turned to Mor, his empty bottles clunking together painfully loud. "Mortie, do you think we should go?"

Mor ran a hand down his face, looking as though he was wondering how he'd gotten himself in this situation. "I think we should all go."

He shot Dimitri a questioning look. Startled, Dimitri nodded, his hands curling into his jacket pockets.

"All right then," Mor said. "Let's get you two back to the big house."

Dipping his chin to Rayner, Mor shoved the stumbling warriors across the room toward the stairs. Surce murmured something to Rayner, then rose from the couch to help usher them along.

Dimitri remained by the door as the group somehow made it upstairs without incident, Mor's weary encouragements and Laness and Branten's laughter slowly fading away. Then, there was silence.

"Looks like those two had some fun," Rayner finally said, eyes on the folded tapestry in his lap.

"They were drunkenly knife throwing," Dimitri explained.

Rayner let out a small, startled laugh. "That sounds like a terrible idea."

"That's what I said."

The two glanced at each other, their eyes briefly locking before flicking away once more. Dimitri could feel the silence creep back in around them, just as it had on the roof. Just before things spiraled out of control.

But they weren't going to do that again. And the soft, lingering glow of his liquor made taking that first step a little easier as he finally came to sit on the couch perpendicular to Rayner's.

"Is it a coincidence you're down here?" he asked.

"Would you believe me if I said yes?"

Dimitri raised a brow, and he could have sworn the corner of Rayner's mouth twitched.

"I wanted to talk to you," he said, slipping his tapestry into a pocket. "Talk to you again, I mean, because our first conversation didn't go the way I intended."

"I know what you mean," Dimitri murmured. His eyes dropped to his hands, not sure what to say next. But Rayner stepped in without prompting.

"When I wrote you that note, I hoped you would come talk to me. I told myself I knew what I had to say, I could do it. But we both saw how well that went. And it wasn't until talking with Surce that I realized it's because none of what I was planning on saying was what I *wanted* to say."

"Why not?" Dimitri asked.

"Because all of that is a lot scarier."

Well, Dimitri knew that feeling. He finally lifted his gaze, acutely aware of how something fragile stretched between them like a thread of glass.

"Does that mean you've decided to tell me?" he asked.

Rayner nodded, slow and careful.

Dimitri took a long, steadying breath. "Then I'm listening."

Dimitri didn't have a name for the emotion that flashed across Rayner's face. His shoulders sagged, his hand drifting to the pocket he'd slid his tapestry in. But he didn't hesitate to begin.

"I've never been good at talking about my past, mainly because I had no one to talk to about it. From the moment I stepped foot in Scarsthain, I've been alone. Alone in the prison, alone as I healed, alone as I got my life together and opened my shop because I didn't know how to trust anything else. Not when trusting someone got me sentenced to torture.

"After a while, I became accustomed to the silence. I forgot what it was like to have anything else, even though I could feel something was missing. I just didn't realize what it was until I met you.

"I don't know when it happened exactly. But one day, I woke up and I was looking forward to seeing you. That feeling of missing something was gone. And the fact that I wasn't scared shitless by that was absolutely terrifying.

"So, I clung to my oath with Sylas because it was the only thing I could keep between us. Even though it hurt to do so. Even though it would hurt you, too." Rayner's voice cracked, but he continued. "I told myself there was no other option for someone like me. I'd done what I had to do. Even as you stared into my face from that windowsill and I thought I was dying as you told me you hated me.

"Yet, for weeks now, I've been watching you. A neglected, rejected bastard of the Sun King who has every reason to be just as broken and twisted as I am. But you're not. You love and are loved. You have friends that would do anything for you because they know you would do the same. And it's... It's been a long time since I've seen that. Since I've believed something like that is possible."

Dimitri could barely swallow the lump in his throat. Because he'd never realized how many people had come to care for him. Because one of those people was irrevocably, irreplaceably missing. Because Dimitri understood every emotion Rayner had described.

"What does all of this mean?" he rasped, his fingers digging into the couch cushions.

"It means I never wanted to hurt you," Rayner said. "But I did, because I was too afraid to let myself have you."

"So then why not push me away?"

"Because I'm lonely and self-destructive," Rayner said bluntly.

Dimitri huffed out a laugh. He couldn't criticize there. Rayner flashed a small, self-deprecating smile, but he quickly sobered.

"The point is," he said, "seeing you thrive in all your connections? That makes it a little less scary to admit I want that, too."

Gods, it was such a simple statement. A natural desire. And it was almost painful how much Dimitri understood the way Rayner had had to force out the words, his fingers anxiously twisting and untwisting in his lap.

"What does that mean?" Dimitri asked, sagging back into the couch.

"It means I want you to know I'm trying. I know my past few attempts have been a shitty demonstration of that because I'm still learning, but I *am* trying."

Gods, was this really the person he was furious with? Someone that very well could have been him if Analia and Aaron hadn't so steadfastly cared about him.

But understanding aside, did that excuse what Rayner had done to him? Did this confession make him any less likely to do it again? When he had been in this dark, miserable place, what had he needed to hear?

"Look," he said, leaning forward. "I get it. I know how fucking terrible it all feels. I appreciate you want to change, but you have to do more than *want*. Yes, you were in a horrific prison, I'm sorry. But at some point, you have to decide if you want to be the feral prisoner inside those walls, or if you want some fucking friends like you claim and then *act* like it."

"I know," Rayner said softly, bowing his head. "Dima, I'm sor—"

"No," Dimitri interrupted, raising his hand and cringing back. "Don't apologize to me unless you mean it. Don't say it unless you regret what you did, that if you could go back, you would do things differently."

Dimitri waited, not sure what he was hoping to hear. Rayner looked at him, then brought a hand to the purple tattoo peeking out from around his collar.

"What would you have done?" he finally asked.

Dimitri's voice cracked. "I wouldn't have betrayed you."

As soon as the words were out, he knew they were true. Just as he knew at one point, they wouldn't have been.

But Rayner waiting for him downstairs, telling him all of this… That was his equivalent of going after Aaron and Marcos.

"You say you hold yourself to your word?" Dimitri asked tiredly.

Rayner nodded.

"Then give me your word I can trust you."

It was the same choice Aaron had given him back in that alleyway. But Rayner answered a whole lot faster than he had. "You can."

The words didn't so much hurt as they did ache. He didn't know if it was a good ache or a bad ache, but it nevertheless had the tightness in his chest finally relaxing.

"Well, all right then," Dimitri said.

Slowly, Rayner sagged back against the couch. Dimitri hadn't realized how exhausted he looked: deep shadows smudged beneath his eyes, his light brown complexion noticeably pale. Dimitri doubted he looked much better.

Knowing there was nothing left to say, he hauled himself to his feet and headed for the dining room door. It was only when he had turned the knob, the door partially creaking open that he looked back.

"Sorry for being a snapping turtle," he mumbled.

Rayner turned his head toward him, his lips parting. But Dimitri slipped through the door, his ears burning as he let it shut behind him.

Chapter 30

Analia covered a yawn with her hand as she waited outside Deardryn's study, her guards quiet beside her. The two hadn't asked any questions when she'd summoned them that morning, Meryk because he didn't care, Tavian because he was too tired to care. Even now, he slumped on a windowsill, his cheek resting against the glass and eyes closed.

"I thought guards were used to waking up early," Analia said.

Tavian grumbled something that sounded like, "Leave me alone," his eyelids not so much as flickering.

Analia smiled to herself, her gaze drifting back to the study door. Normally, she would have tried to sneak inside while Deardryn was away, but the magic that faintly tingled around the door had put a stop to that plan.

She would love to know how Sylas felt about that defense measure, but that would require him being around. And in the three days since her successful escape plan, Sylas was nowhere to be seen. Not just in her dreams, but the castle as well.

"You're here early."

Analia shoved the thoughts aside as Deardryn swept down the hall, a few books tucked under her arm.

"I couldn't sleep," she said truthfully.

Deardryn nodded, her gaze flicking to the window. "I see you're hard at work, Tavian."

Tavian gave her a listless salute, slumping even more against the glass. Analia could have sworn Deardryn rolled her eyes the smallest bit.

Turning away from the guard, she pushed through the door, Analia surprised to note it hadn't been locked. And she didn't miss how the magic had quieted under Deardryn's touch.

Interesting. Definitely something to keep an eye on as Analia followed Deardryn inside, the door clicking shut behind them. But the safeguards on this study weren't the only reason Analia had arrived so early.

"Do you have any questions for me this morning?" she asked, settling on the floor beside the door.

"I always have questions, Analia. But I think they can wait."

Deardryn sat in her usual spot against the opposite wall, arranging what was revealed to be her blue book of notes and her black-and-gold journal on the floor beside her. And as she pulled the Crystal's casing from a gown pocket, Analia got all the information she needed.

The study might be magically guarded, but it wasn't her hiding spot. Which meant Analia had to find a way into Deardryn's chambers.

The rest of Analia's session was spent adjusting to the Crystal's magic. It was a slow process, even as her mental shield lasted a little longer than the session before. But there always came a point where the magic screamed so loud that she could taste the bile rising in her throat. And just like that first day, a distraction was the only lifeline she could grasp onto.

"Tell me about the dampers," Deardryn said, pen poised above her notes.

Analia wiped the cold sweat from her brow, Deardryn's voice little more than a haze through the hammering on her mental shield. "The what?"

"The dampers," Deardryn said patiently. "Aaron wore one the entire time he was in my kingdom. Did you ever sense him?"

Analia struggled to force her mind back to the Sun Kingdom. The gold marble floors. The sunstone chandeliers. Pryanth's lips across her cheekbone. *Don't make me have to kill you.*

Analia's shield faltered. The magic pressed in, white light shoving through the cracks in her mind—no. That was the wrong memory, the wrong man.

Analia took a deep breath, forcing the image of Pryanth away on her exhale. He was chaos. And she had chosen something to hold on to.

Analia closed her eyes, sinking into the memories of him. His voice. The safety of his arms around her. All his little habits that had become engraved in her memory: the way his smile turned crooked after a quip, how he ran his hand through his hair when he was worried, no longer having his damper chain to tug on.

Aaron. The damper. Keeping him completely concealed from her until she touched the chain back on her turret.

Then again, she hadn't been able to pick out Dimitri amongst all the Sun magic, and that flicker from the non-Blessed Demiblessed had been so faint. It was possible she hadn't been sensitive enough to notice.

Analia started to tell Deardryn what she was thinking. Then, she paused. Because Ethelind had recently been dampered in front of her. And still, there had been nothing.

"I could only sense him when in direct contact with the damper," she said, her voice surprisingly steady. "Somehow, the damper blocked me from sensing his second network, but you and I proved it doesn't stop that network from functioning."

"Very good, Analia."

Analia blinked. It wasn't until she registered Deardryn's pen scratching that she realized the magic had been compartmentalized once again. And she'd never seen that much light pouring from the casing in one of their sessions before.

"How open is it?" she asked.

"Almost three-quarters." Deardryn reached over, Analia's shoulders relaxing as the magic winked out. "Your tolerance is increasing with every lesson. Not only that, but your interactions are becoming increasingly complex. You are doing marvelously, my dear."

Analia mumbled her thanks, absently rubbing the ring line around her middle finger.

Gods, she missed him. Missed him in a way that had everything weighing on her feel ten times heavier.

But she couldn't fall apart until she was home. She couldn't go home until she got that shard. And as Deardryn came to give Analia a hand up, her free hand tenderly smoothing down Analia's hair, she knew she couldn't do it alone.

Which meant she needed a certain promise to come into play.

A nalia knocked on Sylas's chamber door for the third time, her patience rapidly draining.

"He might be asleep," Tavian said from behind her. "It's still early."

"Breakfast ended over an hour ago," Analia said. "And Letta confirmed he wasn't there. Again."

"Some might take that as a sign to leave him alone," Meryk commented.

Analia ignored him, knocking hard and fast on the door. She'd spent far too much time ducking her head whenever her father, her kingdom, deemed her not worth their time.

Sylas had made her a promise. And she intended on holding him to it.

"You might want to leave him alone, Red," Tavian said uneasily, stepping up beside her. "Sylas isn't someone you want to poke."

"Neither am I."

Analia started to knock once more. And the door flew open.

Shadows flooded the hallway, tendrils writhing across the carpet in a furious tirade of cold, depthless black.

Analia stumbled back with a yelp, but there was nowhere to go. Not as Sylas appeared in the small gap between the door and its frame, his network seething like a thunderstorm.

"What?" he snarled.

All of Analia's bravado recoiled inside her.

"I told you," Meryk muttered under his breath.

Analia ignored him, her attention caught by the blaze in Sylas's eyes. She'd become accustomed to his relentless boredom, the theatrical suffering at any inconvenience. But this?

This was raw. Feral. Almost desperate as he glared at her like she had tried to steal the breath from his lungs.

"I—I'm sorry." Analia looked to Tavian for help, but he'd retreated several steps—some guard.

"Is that it?" Sylas snapped. "You hammer on my door relentlessly, just to apologize for doing so? Are you trying to be the most incessant thorn in my side, or do I need to inform Deardryn she needs to do more to keep you occupied?"

Sylas spat out each word like they were poison. But Analia didn't retreat.

Deardryn. That was why she was here.

"I wanted to talk to you about my meals," she said, stepping forward.

Sylas's expression morphed into something thunderous. "*That's* why you're here?"

Analia opened her mouth, but Sylas was already swinging the door shut.

"Wait!" Analia stuck her foot in the opening, sucking in a breath as the door slammed into it. "You promised me! You said if I *proved myself,* you would let me eat my meals with the rest of you. You *promised.*"

For a long, agonizing moment, Sylas didn't respond. The pressure against Analia's foot didn't wane. She could feel Tavian and Meryk shift behind her, neither of them seeming to know what they should do.

But Analia kept her gaze on Sylas through the crack, silently urging him to remember the promise she couldn't bring up in front of her guards.

She could see the moment her words clicked in his mind. His lips pressed into a line, his knuckles turning white around the door.

"I don't have time to deal with you right now, Analia."

"I'm not asking for right now." Analia brushed a lock of hair behind her ear, letting Sylas see the moon phases tattooed around her wrist.

Sylas's eyes narrowed. He opened his mouth, Analia certain he was about to tell her to get out of his sight. But his voice cut off as the top of someone's head appeared behind him.

"Oh, apologies, Your Majesty. I didn't realize..."

"It's fine," Sylas said, his tone softening into something gruff. He opened the door fully and stepped aside, allowing the man to slip past.

He was old enough to have wrinkles etched into his ebony forehead. His short black hair was streaked with gray, the colors complimenting the green of his healer robes. He looked between Sylas, Analia, and the guards, his hand coming up to subconsciously rub the four purple rings around his eyes.

"Apologies for interrupting," he said.

Sylas flicked his hand, almost managing calm as he said, "You're fine."

The two exchanged a quick look. Then, briefly dipping his chin to Analia, the healer strode off down the hall, perfectly casual.

Huh. Analia watched him disappear around the corner, then turned back to a glowering Sylas. "Why was there a healer in your chambers?"

"I have a headache," Sylas said flatly. "And you're not helping."

His hand still gripped the door, Analia's foot ready to block it once more. But his posture had relaxed. Just enough to have Analia stepping forward through the lingering shadows, choosing her words carefully.

"I only want to know if you're intending on keeping your word."

Sylas released a long, deflating breath, dragging his hand through his blue-black curls. "I always do."

Analia spent the rest of the day in the library, much to Meryk's exasperation and Tavian's delight. It would only be a matter of days before Meryk started complaining to Deardryn, and if Analia remained perfectly compliant, she should hopefully have one less problem to deal with.

In the meantime, she continued the Crystal research she'd started back in Starlight, the Moon Kingdom providing plenty of new books on the topic—although their contents were proving to be much the same.

Eventually, Tavian and Meryk escorted her down to the Royals' private dining chamber for dinner. To Analia's surprise, Sylas had finally decided to join them. And she was equally startled when he announced to Deardryn and the dozen or so other Royals that Analia would be joining them for all meals going forward.

No one seemed particularly fazed by the news. But as Analia got ready for bed, she couldn't shake the fear that Sylas's proclamation was just another excuse to avoid dealing with her.

Crawling into bed, she closed her eyes, expecting another night of dreamless sleep. Yet, when she opened them once more, Sylas's sitting room had materialized around her.

"I do hope this is to your liking," Sylas said, looking more annoyed than usual in his armchair.

Gods, even his dream-self looked disheveled. There was an exhaustion that tightened the corners of his eyes, his face pale.

"Are you all right?" she asked.

"No. I have a persistent, red-haired princess who insists on holding me to the most literal interpretation of my word."

Sylas slouched back in his chair, a wine glass appearing in his hand. Well, that at least *sounded* like Sylas. If he didn't want to talk, she wouldn't try to force him.

"You said if I pulled off my escape, you would train me," Analia said, imagining Aaron's recliner behind her and sinking down into the soft blue velvet. "Well, I pulled it off."

"You also killed several of Deardryn's guards and unleashed the Dragoness on me and my 'questionable security.'"

"You never specified how clean of a job it had to be."

Sylas scoffed into his wine. "Annoying little girl."

"I only assumed the sooner you start training me," she said, "the sooner I can get the shard and leave, and you can be rid of Deardryn."

"I fail to see how you learning to use my magic in a dream while dampered in real life will enable all that."

"And yet, here we are."

To her surprise, Sylas's lips twitched. "You are too much like Accalon," he mumbled.

Something sharp lodged in Analia's throat.

Sylas, not seeming to notice, let out a dramatic sigh and placed his wine glass on the table beside him. "Well, we might as well get started. Summon some shadows."

Analia blinked hard, struggling to steady herself. "That's it?" she asked.

"What else were you expecting?" he retorted.

"I don't know, perhaps some instruction? Seeing as these are lessons?"

"Apologies, I didn't realize you needed someone to hold your hand."

Analia glared, Sylas unfazed as he went on.

"This is your magic, Analia. *You* have to summon it if we're going to get anywhere."

Sylas settled back in his seat, staring at her expectantly. Waiting for her to fail.

Analia's temper crackled. But refusing to waste her opportunity, she shoved it down and reached for her magic.

For a few long, uncomfortable moments, the sitting room remained silent. Analia didn't allow herself to consider what Sylas must have been thinking as her flames washed over her, begging for release.

She had to go deeper. Past the blazing heat, into the cavern beyond. She'd summoned the magic that dwelled there several times without meaning to; she'd called on it back in Accalon's chambers.

But Analia couldn't bring herself to part the flames.

"Why am I not surprised," Sylas muttered.

"Give me a second," Analia snapped.

"This should be instinctual for you."

"That's like saying since I know how to play the harp, I should be able to play the piano."

Analia opened her eyes and glared at Sylas. He, in turn, propped his chin in his hand, but the look on his face said he could concede that.

"Does that mean I must sit here staring at you indefinitely?" he asked.

"You could help me," Analia said pointedly.

"Analia, I've seen you summon a flame in this dream. If you're capable of that, I don't see what I can do to help you summon a different type."

"Summon your own magic," Analia suggested. "Let me get used to what it feels like."

"*Feels?*"

Analia briefly elaborated on how her sensory abilities had each magic feeling like its own melody to her, Sylas looking surprisingly thoughtful as he nodded along.

"All right, then." Sylas placed his hand palm up on his knees. Immediately, a ribbon of darkness wreathed between his fingers, the magic softly rumbling across Analia's mental shield.

It was the song of slow, muffled footsteps, the distant rumble of thunder. It was cozy, in a warning sort of way.

"I like your magic," she murmured. "It's dimensional."

Sylas muttered something Analia didn't catch, too focused on the melody. It was nothing to be afraid of. There was no promise of a fiery explosion, no pulse of memories across her mind.

Analia reached back into her flames, tunneling deeper, deeper, deeper, the heat fading around her fingertips.

And once again, she froze.

"I think we're done for tonight," Sylas said with a stretch.

"No," Analia snapped.

"No?"

"No. I can do this."

She squeezed her eyes shut tighter, forcing her hand to move, just a little deeper. But she couldn't. She was trapped within her flames. Her *uncle's* flames.

Just another secret. Just another question that he could never answer. And she knew finding the answer herself would rip that wound wide open.

"Analia."

Analia flinched as she felt Sylas's cool finger beneath her chin, not having heard him approach. She opened her eyes, Sylas lifting her face with a quick flick of his forefinger.

"We're done," he said firmly.

"I can do it," she insisted, her voice horribly small.

Something flickered across Sylas's face, but he didn't respond. He stepped back, starting to turn away.

"Wait!" Analia lunged forward and grabbed his wrist. "Promise me we can try again. *Soon.*"

Analia waited for Sylas to scoff. He had every right to shake her off and tell her this had been a waste of his time. But for a long, long time, he only stared at her, the faintest crease forming between his brows.

"You don't give up, do you?" he finally asked.

Analia shook her head.

"Which means you wouldn't give up harassing me until I brought you back here."

Analia shrugged.

Sylas sighed, clearly aiming for his usual petulance. But Analia caught the way his voice softened as he said, "We'll try again."

Analia started to respond.

Sylas snapped his fingers, the dream breaking apart around her. Just before Sylas disappeared into the darkness, Analia could have sworn she saw him look back at the empty armchair beside his usual one, something like resignation on his face as he shook his head. Then, he was gone.

Chapter 31

Aaron sat on his sitting room floor, an assortment of books and papers spread out around him.

After promising to help Surce with her scroll translations, he'd hunted down Ethelind's bins of his old school supplies and grabbed everything related to the forgotten tongue: worksheets, books, even a few notes written in his loopy seven-year-old handwriting. That, however, was proving to be part of the issue.

"You know," Dimitri said from the couch, "you have a table."

"The one in here isn't big enough," Aaron said, comparing one of Surce's translations to his notes.

"Then why not use the dining room table?"

"Why not read in the side room?"

Dimitri snorted. "Fair." Closing his book, he gave a long stretch, coming to prop himself up on the armrest. "Have you managed to decode anything?"

"Not really. The problem is I was sent to the Underground at such a young age that none of my study material goes beyond an elementary level. I think I've figured out the basic grammar, but my vocabulary isn't exactly robust."

"You mean to tell me," Dimitri said, "your kingdom has a tradition of rounding up troubled children, dumping them in an underground military camp for years at a time, and there's no education system?"

Something about Dimitri's tone had Aaron's eye twitch. "We have a system," he said, keeping his voice level. "There are literacy, history, mathematics, and various other tutors who work in the Underground. Just no forgotten tongue tutors. My grandmother had to track someone down to teach me, and I can't remember who she was at this point."

Aaron thoughtfully drummed his fingers on a practice sheet, then scribbled a note to himself to ask Ethelind who she was. Maybe she was still around.

"Well," Dimitri said, "shitty resources or not, you're at least getting somewhere. Meanwhile, none of your books on Scarsthain even *mention* those lines on the door."

Dimitri tossed his book on the table beside him with a huff. Aaron, however, remained unbothered. In fact, even with the constant knot in his stomach, he felt the calmest he'd been in the past three weeks.

Yes, he was making minimal progress with his translations, but it was something. Beyond that, the activity was surprisingly enjoyable. He'd forgotten how much he'd liked learning a new language as a child: finding the patterns, using the words he *did* know to figure out the rest. Even if it was just a distraction from the hole in his chest, the scream that had him jolting out of his nightmares every night—

"Maybe Rayner should be the one digging through all the Scarsthain information," Dimitri grumbled.

Aaron shoved the thoughts aside, his attention caught by the lack of venom in Dimitri's words.

"So," he said, casually leaning back against the couch. "Have you two made a breakthrough?"

Dimitri's eyes narrowed. "How much do you know?"

"Everything that Branten does."

"Really?" Dimitri asked. "Does that include that he found your liquor stash in the table drawer?"

Aaron's mouth curled in a slow, wicked grin. "Not at all."

"Huh." Dimitri flopped back against the couch, Aaron's grin growing as Dimitri struggled to maintain his indignation. Yes, Dimitri was fitting in with his family just fine. But becoming a part of the family had one specific consequence.

"Rayner, though?" he pressed, shifting to face him fully.

Dimitri took a breath, then looked away. "I got my answers."

"And?"

Dimitri squirmed, his ears turning pink. Before he could speak, the dining room door opened.

"Oh look!" he said, popping to his feet. "It's Mor. He probably has important news; I'll leave you to it."

Hopping over Aaron's papers, he skirted around Mor and scurried upstairs, leaving Aaron to smile and shake his head at the click of Dimitri's bedroom door closing.

"I'm assuming I just provided an escape route," Mor said wryly.

"I was asking him about Rayner."

"Are you meddling?"

"No!" Aaron protested. He started to collect his things, his voice dropping to a mumble. "It's just easier to deal with his problems than my own."

Mor's expression softened. Aaron tensed, bracing himself for the gentle check-in.

"So, what's all of this?" Mor asked, coming to help him clean up.

Aaron's shoulders relaxed. "My efforts to translate the scroll. I wasn't able to dig up much material, so I'll have to find time to go to the kingdom library."

"I can check the Human Castle library," Mor offered, passing him a book. "I don't know if they'd have anything, but it's worth a try."

"Especially since the scroll was hidden there," Aaron agreed.

Mor didn't respond. Aaron looked up from his stack, finding Mor rubbing the spot where his golden hand met his wrist. Now that he looked, Mor appeared unusually disheveled, from his golden-brown hair to the two incorrectly buttoned buttons on his blue jacket.

"I know Branten just pummeled me out of my asshole phase," Aaron said. "But risking being an even bigger one for calling you out... Are you doing all right?"

The corner of Mor's mouth quirked. "In what way?"

"Well, I know you've been busy with the humans. But it seems like whenever I see you, you're completely exhausted, and now you're rubbing your wrist, which either means it's bothering you or you're worried about something."

Mor opened his mouth to protest, then shook his head with a sigh. "It's the humans." Placing the stack of materials on the low table, he rose and went to flop on the couch. "They keep going through cycles of nonstop meetings, and then a few days of silence that put me on edge even more."

"Do you think they've realized we took the scroll?" Aaron asked, moving to sit beside him.

"If they have," he said, "they're not telling me. The meetings themselves feel odd. They go from obsessing over candle and oil lamp costs, to complaints about our heightened border patrols, to question after question about you and Analia."

"So, they're putting up a fuss," Aaron said.

"Yes, but they're usually overt with their reasons why. But now? There's something going on that they're not telling me."

Aaron's stomach did a slow roll. Problems with the Human Kingdom were the last thing he needed.

"What can I do?" he asked.

Mor flashed a tired smile. "I think when it comes to the humans, the best thing you can do is stay as far away as possible."

Aaron didn't know if he was relieved or guilty. He started to respond, just as the dining room door banged open.

"Gods, Laness," he said, "what's the..."

Aaron trailed off as he took in Laness's wide eyes, the hard set of her mouth as she fidgeted with the enka bracelets on her wrists. And his heart stumbled as she said, "We have a problem."

E mber paced the length of her chambers, practically vibrating with impatience.

In the three days since her argument with Rois, the two had barely spoken. They passed in the halls without so much as a glance, his presence having Ember's blood tingling with the memory of his accusations.

At any other time, she would have been content to let their petty war wage on, refusing to be the first one to crack. But every day that passed was another day closer to Cadmus's execution. And she couldn't rescue him alone.

So, that morning, she'd cornered him as he was leaving the Great Hall, only offering a terse, "Dinner time."

Rois nodded, something dangerously close to regret on his face. But Ember turned on her heel and marched away before he could speak.

And now, the bastard was late.

"I don't have time for this," Ember muttered, the fire sprites on her windowsill quietly watching her pace. "Dinner is going to end soon, and I have patients to check on."

Her eyes drifted to the middle drawer of her desk, a shudder traveling down her spine as she thought of the fuzzy orange and yellow leaves hidden inside.

She hadn't been lying to Rois when she said she never used when she was on duty. She was meticulous about it. She'd spent an hour after Rois left her chambers calculating how many leaves she could grow in a day, how long the high from one leaf lasted, how many she could afford to use in a day without depleting her stash. She'd even figured out how early she needed to wake up in order to relieve the ruthless cravings that assailed her each morning while still going to work with a clear head.

She had a system. And the longer she waited for Rois, the longer it would be before she could get to her patients, which meant the longer she had to wait to quell the longing gnawing through her bones.

"I can't wait any longer." Ember crossed to her table to retrieve her heavy healer's bag, slinging it over her shoulder. She would look out for Rois on her way to see her patients, maybe check out his usual haunts. She couldn't—

"Ember?"

It took Ember a moment to register the small, crackly voice. She turned toward the windowsill, her flexing hands relaxing at her sides as Spark straightened on their candle wick.

"We can help look for him if you like." They gestured to the candles on either side of them, Ember only just realizing how many fire sprites had gathered—at least fifteen. "It would be no trouble."

The sprites nodded their agreement, most noticeably less certain than Spark. But it was a collective offer all the same.

Ember swallowed hard against the sudden lump in her throat. "Yes," she managed. "That would be very helpful."

Spark beamed. Then, with a flurry of crackles, the fire sprites disappeared into the flames, leaving Ember blinking furiously in the center of her chambers.

Gods, what was the matter with her? One moment, she was ready to explode at Rois, the next, a kind gesture had her about to break down in tears.

Her eyes drifted to her desk once more, practically able to smell the sharp, sour scent. But she jerked her head to the side and headed for the door.

Just two patients. Quick patients with fevers that had almost broken that morning. Then, she would get to breathe again.

The words repeated in her mind as Ember headed through the castle halls, her eyes scanning for a familiar head of copper hair. But Rois was nowhere to be found on the three floors she scaled. As a matter of fact, she barely saw anyone outside of a few Sun guards whispering together in an alcove.

Something about that put Ember on edge. She pushed the feeling aside as she stepped into her first patient's chambers, a young female Sun soldier.

Just as she expected, her forehead no longer burned against the back of Ember's hand. A few spoonfuls of one of her herbal concoctions later, and Ember was out the door and heading for her second patient. Yet, the halls remained quiet.

By the time Ember finished with her last patient, it was long after the final stragglers usually wandered out of dinner. Normally, the castle would be abuzz with voices as people wound down for the night. But the corridors remained hushed. And there was still no sign of Rois.

Ember's stomach sank. She picked up her pace, her mind darting through every place Rois usually lingered. The foot of the second floor's main staircase, the alcove across from the library, the window seat on the fourth floor that looked out across the kingdom. Empty, empty, empty.

Ember hurried back to her chambers, her argument with Rois completely forgotten as she flung open her door.

Dozens upon dozens of fire sprites had gathered inside. They perched on everything from candle wicks, to Everflame torches, to the rims of empty apothecary jars on Ember's desk, their little fiery bodies subtly warming the chamber. But Ember barely noticed as her eyes swept the room, Rois nowhere to be seen.

And her blood turned to ice as the fire sprites all turned to her, their silent gestures coming to a halt.

"What happened," she breathed.

The sprites exchanged a look.

"We were able to find him," Spark finally said from their candle, their voice quiet.

"And?"

Spark bowed their head. Ember barely choked back a scream, knowing what they were going to say, just needing to hear it—to *not* hear it.

"He's in the dungeon," Spark whispered.

Ember released a long, shuddering breath. She stumbled over to her desk chair, her voice coming out a rasp as she asked, "What happened?"

"The Sun soldiers found him," Cinder—one of the first sprites to visit her chambers—said from a jar, wringing her hands. "Somehow, they figured out he stole Princess Lucilla's body."

"Did you talk to him?"

"I overheard a few soldiers whispering about it," Spark said. "I went to find his cell afterward. But he... he was unconscious. And his back..."

Spark curled into a ball and hid their face. Ember swallowed hard, all too familiar with what the sprite must have seen. Straight, bloody lines. Mangled flesh. She'd only healed a few victims of whippings before, but that had been enough to make her never want to see those injuries again. And the fact that it wasn't a stranger, it was Rois...

"I told him to be careful," Ember choked out, burying her face in her hands. "I *told* him they were looking for him. But he didn't listen. How did they even put it together?"

The sprites shrugged helplessly.

"We're sorry," Cinder whispered, hugging her knees to her chest.

A sob clawed its way up Ember's throat. Rosala spare her, how had all of this happened? The Royals were imprisoned, Cadmus was going to die in a week, Rois was being tortured, and now the fire sprites were *apologizing?* Apologizing for the Sun Kingdom's brutality?

"You do not apologize for this," Ember said fiercely, swiping a stray tear from her cheek. "*None* of this is any of your faults. These people invaded your home, killed your friends, forced you to flee. But not anymore."

The fire sprites glanced at each other, clearly puzzled. But Ember's despair had washed away, just as quickly as it had come. Now? Now, she was certain.

"What do you mean?" Cinder asked.

"I mean," Ember said, "we're beating the Sun Kingdom at their own game."

"How?" Spark asked.

"We're going to free our friends. Which means I'm going to need your help."

The fire sprites recoiled. Many launched into a flurry of hand gestures, a few disappearing with a crackle.

"Wait!" Ember said, lurching forward in her seat. "Don't go!"

"We can't free them!" Cinder exclaimed.

Spark said, "I thought you invited us here to protect us, not send us into battle!"

"I'm not sending you into battle!"

The fire sprites ignored her. They continued to wave their hands, the flickering light blurring before her eyes, the few crackling voices buzzing through her mind.

She'd known they wouldn't want to help—they'd disappeared when Rois even suggested it. But this?

"We're fire sprites," exclaimed Crackle, waving his arms frantically. "We're not fighters."

"Neither am I!" Ember exploded, throwing up her hands. The nearby sprites leaned away from the sudden whoosh of air, the words tumbling past Ember's lips. "I'm a healer. I'm not supposed to fight. I put people back together. That's my purpose, that's my *dream*. And for as long as I can remember, I've been told that if I just kept within the lines of being a healer, everything would be fine. I would be fine.

"But I can't heal my friends because they're locked in a cage. I can't follow the status quo anymore because there is no status quo. There is *nothing* normal about having your home invaded and having to disguise your allegiance to the people you love to survive. But we can't get back to normal when our king, our *friends*, are locked in a dungeon. And we will never forgive ourselves for doing nothing when we are the only ones who can get them out. So *please*. Help me."

Ember gripped the edge of her desk, her chest heaving. Her entire body felt like an emotional battleground, battered and bruised and not even sure which side was winning. Rosala spare her, she couldn't exist like this: swinging from one extreme to the next, her devinroot the only thing able to establish a temporary calm.

She. Needed. Normal.

She looked around at the group of fire sprites, desperate for even a hint of resolve. But while no more sprites disappeared, they all refused to meet her eye.

"I don't know what normal is anymore," Spark murmured.

"Then don't fight for normal," Ember said. "Fight for your home. Fight for your right to exist outside of these chambers."

"Even if we *did* fight," Cinder said, "there's not much we can do. We're small. We're easily extinguished."

"Your king also deemed you stronger than you appear."

Cinder dropped her gaze to her fingers. Spark hopped off their candle onto the table, padding along its edge until they could look up at Ember.

"Why us?" they asked. "Out of all the Ash soldiers and servants trapped in this castle, why ask for our help?"

They leaned forward on their toes, the same way they would when going to whisper something in Lucilla's ear. Ember's hand went to her enka bracelet, the two remaining phoenix charms resting against her fingers.

"Because," she said, "you all love Lucilla as much as I do."

The fire sprites looked up.

"Lucilla died protecting her brother," Ember said. "The Sun Kingdom killed her. And now, those very people have thrown the people she loved in the dungeon and are preparing to kill them, too. If we're going to honor her sacrifice, we can't let that happen. So, will you join me? Or will you turn your back on Lucilla's memory?"

Ember raised her chin. The sprites exchanged a long, quiet look.

Then, slowly, one by one, they climbed off their torches and jars and wicks. They lined up across the table. And together, they touched both hands to their hearts, then extended them out toward Ember palm up.

"We are with you," Spark said.

Ember could have collapsed under her wave of relief. Instead, she pushed back her shoulders.

"Good," she said, pulling open her desk drawer and reaching inside. "Now, let's get to work. We leave tonight."

Chapter 32

"And she's going to do it tonight," Laness finished, pacing around the kitchen.

Dimitri shifted on his stool at the island, Aaron's, Branten's, and Surce's expressions darkening around him. Mor had started off on the stool beside him when Aaron called the family meeting, but Laness had barely launched into Ember's report before he was heading for the stove, the sizzle of his pan underscoring Laness's words. Only Rayner remained quietly thoughtful where he perched on the counter across from Dimitri.

"She can't give us a little time?" Aaron asked, raking a hand through his hair.

"She was adamant it had to be tonight," said Laness. "There's no telling how long they'll keep Rois alive after what he's done."

"I don't like this plan," Surce murmured, tracing her finger through some spilled sugar on the island.

Dimitri didn't blame her. He wasn't exactly a wealth of knowledge on how to pull off a prison break, but doing it alone? Shepherding an injured group while trying to remain unseen?

"Could someone get in to help her?" he asked. "Bordello, you've been in the castle, can't you shadowjump in there?"

"Not with the wards," Aaron said. "The only time I've made it past them was when Analia was there. I can get us to the kingdom by nightfall no problem, but with no Ash Royal to control the wards?"

Aaron shook his head.

"I would offer to change your appearance," Rayner murmured. "Pretend to be a Sun guard, sneak through the gate. But that wouldn't do you much good without the uniform."

"There's no hope of getting through the front door," Branten agreed, leaning his elbows on the table. "But what if we used a different one?"

Surce gave Branten's elbows a disapproving look. But she only asked, "What are you proposing?"

Branten replied, "Ember said she's going to be escaping through the vault, right? So, that means there's an exit."

"And you're thinking we use that exit to go in and help her," Aaron mused, his eyes glinting.

From the stove, Mor asked, "Do we know where the vault exit is?"

"It's near the southeast wall," Laness said, plopping down next to Dimitri. "But it's on the inside. Apparently, the Ash Royals wanted it to be an escape route through the castle, but not a way in for invaders. Ember said there's also a secret opening in the wall that only Ash Royals and the Crystal Guard know about."

Aaron bit the inside of his cheek, his eyes darting as he thought. Spotting Surce's finger in the spilled sugar, something seemed to click for him.

"All right," he said, taking a spoonful of sugar and dumping it on the island. "If we're looking at the kingdom on a map, the castle is here"—he pushed a portion of the sugar into a pile—"and its wall is here." He traced his finger around the mound, forming a ring. "The Phoenix Gate is at the northern-most section of the wall, and the closest I've been to this secret exit is probably here." He touched his finger directly between the north and east points.

"You didn't walk all the way around the castle?" Surce asked.

Dimitri snorted. But Aaron was perfectly serious as he said, "I didn't have time."

"Why would you have..." Dimitri began, the look in Aaron's eyes having him trailing off. Crystal fuck him, Aaron really *was* always thinking ahead.

"You'll have a bit of a hike no matter what," Mor said, something spicy filling the air as he stirred the contents of his pan. "And since you don't know where the opening is, that will make things difficult."

"I can figure it out," Aaron said, resting his chin on his fist. "It's what happens when they're out that worries me."

Dimitri cocked his head, puzzled. Yet, everyone else, even Rayner, nodded in agreement.

"How come?" Dimitri whined.

"The problem," Surce said, "is if Ember pulls off her escape, she has been informed by Aeley that she would need to disappear, which is why Aaron will be bringing her back here. But that leaves however many Royals she's freed, plus their non-Royal partners, and Rois, all of whom will undoubtedly have injuries."

"They might be mild enough that they can handle the rest of their escape on their own," Aaron said. "Especially since I'll be able to remove their damper cuffs. But if their injuries are more severe..."

"It would be cruel to abandon them to their fate," Mor said softly.

Slowly, heavily, the meaning of their words clicked in Dimitri's mind. "Which means you might have to bring them here," he said. "Which means more people knowing about this kingdom."

"Royals at that," Branten muttered. He rose to his feet, hunting down the tea kettle Mor had stashed on the back of the stove.

"I'll have to make a judgment call," Aaron said, rubbing the side of his face. "Even then, we'll be losing our greatest advantage of having an insider in the castle."

Laness fiddled with her enka bracelets, but she didn't respond. No one did. Dimitri scowled down at the island, the sudden grimness in the air sending a low buzz through his veins.

Once again, Deardryn was regaining a step. She might lose the Ash Royals as leverage, but that was assuming Ember somehow got all of them out. Even if she did, they would lose their insider knowledge on Sun's movements and potentially risk Starlight's security. And no matter what, Deardryn still had control of the central Ash Kingdom.

Dimitri's hands tightened around the edge of the island, the buzz in his veins warming, pulsing. His reminder of why, even if Othin hadn't neglected him, Dimitri could never forgive him. No matter how much he fucking groveled—wait.

"Take me with you," Dimitri blurted.

Branten nearly dropped the mug he'd retrieved from a cupboard. *"What?"*

"Dima," Aaron said, "what are you—"

"You said you want eyes on the inside, right?" Dimitri asked, his plan rapidly unfolding in his mind. "Then send me in."

"Why you?" Branten asked, rifling through a basket of tea bags on the counter.

"Because," he said, magic tingling through his veins, "I'm Othin's bastard. And for some reason, he's obsessed with earning my forgiveness, even when ignoring me in favor of Deardryn and Pryanth."

A memory flashed across Dimitri's mind: one of tears in Othin's eyes, his voice telling him to go. Dimitri stomped it out even harder than his magic.

Across from him, Surce asked, "Do you truly believe his guilt will be enough to let you into the castle?"

"Oh, he won't be letting me in," Dimitri said. "There are Sun guards at the Phoenix Gate now. I'll be able to walk right in. And if I'm already inside, if it wasn't his choice to let me in? He won't be able to say no."

Dimitri's lip curled. Too much of a coward to make the decision himself, and too weak to resist the chance.

Aaron, however, didn't look convinced. "Dima," he said, "we barely got you out of Moon. If Othin decides to throw you in the Ash dungeon, or worse, hand you over to Deardryn? I don't know if we'd be able to get you out again."

Aaron's words formed a heavy knot in Dimitri's stomach. Because he was right. Dimitri would be a fool to ignore that.

He glanced around the room, the look of concern on every face having him wanting to take his words back, stay in this little hidden corner where he was cared about.

But he'd come to this corner in the first place to stop Deardryn. He'd helped by setting them on the right track with the scroll. Now, he had a chance to really *do* something. And the hole that had been ripped through his chest in the Moon Castle entryway had him straightening.

"I know it's a risk," Dimitri said, meeting Aaron's gaze. "But I also know Othin. The one thing that has always stopped him from reaching out to me is Deardryn, and she's not there anymore. This is a chance he won't be able to pass up. And I'll be able to get closer to him than Ember ever could. So, send me in."

Dimitri could feel everyone's eyes on him. But he kept his gaze on Aaron, watching the emotions warring across his face.

He'd seen the look Aaron had given Rayner back in the hedge maze. Aaron might have been a guard when they'd first met, but at his core, he was a king. His duty was to his kingdom. And as much as he loved his friends, his family, he respected them more. And Dimitri could see the moment Aaron realized all of this.

"You son of a bitch," he muttered, the corner of his mouth lifting. He turned to the rest of the group, Dimitri holding his breath as he asked, "Any objections?"

Mor shook himself as if from a dream, then pulled his pan off the heat. "Dima knows Othin better than any of us. If anyone should be making decisions involving the Sun King, it's him."

"This could work extremely well," Branten said, plopping a tea bag into his mug. "Especially if the Ash Royals hang around."

"They'll be able to shadowjump into the castle and retrieve you at any time," Laness murmured, nodding slowly.

Finally, all attention turned to Surce. Dimitri watched her hopefully, Surce twisting a ruby-encrusted bracelet around her wrist as she considered.

"I would feel better about this if I had a tapestry," she finally said, lifting her topaz gaze. "But I believe in you."

Her eyes met Dimitri's. Dimitri could have sworn she could see through every wall, every defense, straight to his soul. His mind flashed to the red blanket on his bed.

"All right, then," Branten said, pulling Dimitri from his thoughts. "Then it's settled. Dima, try not to get your ass kicked too hard while you're away."

Dimitri breathed out a laugh, completely overwhelmed. They had listened to him. They *believed* in him. And as Branten retrieved plates from the cupboard, Dimitri cradled that feeling close to his chest.

"Don't you need a plate?" Mor asked, eyeing the stack Branten passed him.

"Not today. I was supposed to be at Nova House twenty minutes ago—my orphan program," he added, clocking Dimitri's puzzled look. "Save some for me, would you?"

With that, Branten trudged toward the door, calling a farewell over his shoulder.

Leaving his mug of tea completely untouched on the counter.

Dimitri blinked. He looked at the mug, at the door, back to the mug, over to Aaron. "Did he just...?"

"Uh-huh." Aaron passed him a steaming plate of chicken.

Dimitri stared. "But he went through all that effort."

"He'll remember eventually," Surce sighed.

Dimitri looked around the room, Ember's escape, the implications, his own mission hanging over the room like a cloud of smoke. And it finally dissipated as he laughed. "That's fucking ridiculous."

Laness, Aaron, and Mor joined in, even Surce struggling to fight back her smile. Mor took Branten's vacated stool, gesturing for Rayner to join them.

Rayner startled, his gaze darting around as if he'd missed the last several minutes. Then, he slid off the counter, coming to sit beside Surce. And as his brown eyes met Dimitri's, he knew Rayner was still thinking about the mission.

Once, Dimitri's insides would have tightened at that. But now, he shrugged the thought aside and dug into his food.

Despite the impending mission that night, everyone still talked and laughed their way through lunch. Even Rayner spoke up a couple times. Yet, as the meal came to a close, that heavy weight in Dimitri's stomach slowly returned.

Eventually, Laness, Mor, and Rayner headed out. Aaron gave a long stretch and rose, telling Dimitri he was off to study Ash Kingdom maps. Dimitri made to follow him, but Surce reached across the island and lightly touched his hand.

Dimitri's eye twitched, but he stayed put, Aaron raising his brows before departing. Then, the kitchen was silent.

"Did you need something?" Dimitri finally asked, struggling for nonchalance.

"I thought you should know," Surce said, "that I've been speaking with Rayner. He expressed interest in both my tapestries and my shop during his interrogation, and I've since discovered he has a gift for colors and fabrics."

Dimitri nodded slowly, struggling to see where she was going with this.

"Between that and his masquerader abilities," she went on, rising and going to organize the tea bags Branten had rifled through, "he would be a great asset to this kingdom. I, personally, would be happy to help him set up a new shop, or perhaps bring him into my own."

"Why are you telling me this?" Dimitri asked, genuinely puzzled.

"Because you deserve to know Rayner is not your responsibility."

Dimitri's breath caught.

"He might have left his kingdom for you," she said, "he might not be able to return because he helped you, but he is not in danger. He has a place here. You're free to make whatever choice is best for *you*."

Surce's words pressed on a bruise Dimitri didn't know he had. Yet, instead of pain, there was a release. Slow, heady, undeniable as it rolled through his body, sending Dimitri's head bowing forward into his hands.

"Thank you," he breathed.

"Of course."

The two settled into silence, Surce returning her attention to the tea bags. Dimitri had the strangest certainty that he could either rise from his stool and slip out, or sit there indefinitely, and Surce wouldn't mind. And that lack of expectations somehow had the words rolling off his tongue.

"Did you weave a tapestry of me?"

He looked up, just in time to catch Surce's small smile as she turned to him.

"After Aaron and Laness made their plan to retrieve you," she said, "I went to my loom. I was expecting to weave an image of the hedge maze, perhaps something within the castle. Instead, I found myself looking at a cramped stone chamber with nothing but a cot on the floor. No decorations, no personal objects, nothing to suggest it was anything other than a cell. But huddled on the cot wasn't a man. It was a boy. A little boy with dark blond hair, clutching a red knitted blanket to his cheek.

"I was immediately struck by the color—such a violent shade matched the environment. But when I looked into that boy's face, I didn't see anger. Not even despair. I saw wonder. And I remembered there was more than one meaning behind the color red."

Dimitri didn't think he was breathing as the memory flashed through his mind. The small, cramped cell he'd lived in since he was three years old. The bang that woke him up every morning as Koz flung open his door, ordering him to get to work. Even on his birthday.

He'd spent the entire day with his head down and a lump in his throat, knowing even at five years old that he shouldn't mention what day it was. He'd returned to his chamber, expecting to fall asleep like any other day. But someone had left that blanket neatly folded on his bed, a note hidden inside that simply said, "Happy birthday." And Dimitri's entire being had lit up.

Now, Surce stared into his face, Dimitri unable to hide his wave of emotion as she nodded softly.

"For any person," she said, coming closer, "a life treated as a prisoner leads to anger. But looking at my tapestry, I saw a sweet soul that understands red can also mean love and passion."

Surce extended her hand. Dimitri nodded slightly, and Surce stroked his hair.

"It's all right to be angry, Dimitri. That was what you needed to survive. But that's not the only way anymore. And I hope that sweet soul knows it's safe to come out again."

Dimitri stared up at her, amazed he didn't start bawling right there. All he could think of was the Full Moon Festival, Patryclas's validations breaking him just as bad as Surce's.

Because he wanted them to be true. A part of him hoped they could be. But the rest of him didn't know how with the magic that ran through his veins.

"Good luck on your mission, Dimitri," Surce whispered. She kissed her fingertips, touching them to the top of his head. Then, she headed for the door, letting it softly click shut behind her.

And it was a long, long time before Dimitri felt like he could move again. He released a shaky breath, wiping the single tear from his cheek. Then, knowing he couldn't delay any longer, he rose from his stool and exited the kitchen.

Rayner was waiting for him in the dining room. He sat on the edge of the table, folding and unfolding what appeared to be the tapestry Surce had given him. As soon as he spotted Dimitri, he slipped it in his pocket and straightened.

"Can I come with you?" he asked.

Dimitri wasn't surprised. He dragged a hand down his face, then jerked his chin toward the door. "Follow me."

"Where?" Rayner asked.

"My room. I have to pack."

Rayner squinted at Dimitri, clearly suspicious. Finally, he slid off the table, the two remaining quiet as they exited the dining room and headed upstairs.

It wasn't until Dimitri had grabbed the pack he assumed Aaron had left on his bed and turned to his armoire that he finally spoke.

"Surce's offer is everything you want. Freedom from your oath with Sylas, protection from Scarsthain's wardens, safety."

"What I want is you."

Dimitri glanced at Rayner seated on his bed, eyebrows raised.

"I realized how dramatic that was the moment I said it," Rayner said sheepishly, ducking his head.

To Dimitri's surprise, he laughed. "You saying you want to take it back?" he asked.

"Perhaps the phrasing, but not the sentiment." Rayner tried for a smile, but he quickly sobered. "I know there's no repairing what we had before," he said. "But I was hoping we could start over. Even if that means you only let me come because I can be a helpful ally in Ash."

"Why's that?" Dimitri asked, shoving an armful of clothes into his pack.

"Because if Othin knows you're in the castle, it'll be a lot easier to sneak around with someone else's face."

True.

Rayner leaned forward, his expression the closest Dimitri had ever seen to vulnerable. "You can trust me," he said softly. "Let me help you."

Dimitri considered. Rayner was right that his skills would be useful in Ash. And ever since Dimitri had escaped the Moon dungeon, he'd been helpful. But Rayner had said it himself: he had to prove to Dimitri he could be trusted.

"Were you only my friend because of your oath with Sylas?" he asked suddenly.

Rayner startled, but his answer was fast and firm. "No. I found out Sylas was keeping an eye on you weeks after your first visit to my shop."

He stared into Dimitri's eyes, unflinching. And even though Dimitri knew he was telling the truth, all he felt was disappointment. Disappointment that all that potential had been squashed. But maybe this was their chance to see what remained.

"We leave in a couple hours," he said, turning back to his pack.

The bed squeaked as Rayner sat back, stunned. But seemingly choosing not to test his luck, he only gave a quiet affirmation, then rose and slipped out the door.

Dimitri looked over at his bed. Then, he grabbed the knitted blanket at its foot and stuffed it in his pack. He could only hope red wouldn't come to also symbolize regret.

Chapter 33

Dimitri descended the stairs into Aaron's sitting room, his pack over his shoulder. Aaron had stopped by his room a little while after Rayner had left, only staying long enough to tell him they were meeting at sunset and to pass him a small black satchel.

"Healer supplies," he explained. Then, he faded into the shadows, off to continue his own preparations. And Dimitri's stomach did a slow roll as he added the satchel to his pack.

He'd spent the rest of the afternoon restlessly pacing his room, the sitting room, the kitchen, the anticipation having time pass excruciatingly slow. But as soon as the sun touched the horizon, he was on the move.

Now, Dimitri looked around the quiet sitting room. He'd figured he'd be the first to arrive, his glimpses of Rayner and Aaron throughout the day suggesting they were far more relaxed than he was. But to his surprise, Laness sat on the couch facing him, fiddling with something in her hands.

"Are you waiting for Aaron?" Dimitri asked, pausing awkwardly at the foot of the stairs.

"Actually," she said, "I was waiting for you."

Dimitri's face twitched out of habit. But all trepidation vanished as Laness extended her hands, revealing the white flowers in her palm, their purple-and-black stems woven into a chain.

Dimitri began, "Is that..."

"You don't have to accept it," Laness said quickly. "I thought it was useful when you were spying in Moon. And now, not only could you use it to report back, but also let us know if we need to grab you and bring you home."

She looked up at him, her green eyes wide and hopeful. And Dimitri had no urge to hesitate at the sound of her final word. *Home.*

"What do I have to do?" he asked.

Laness beamed as he came to sit beside her on the couch. "It's simple magic," she said, looping the chain around his wrist and pinching it together. "All we need to do is share a truth."

"What kind of truth?"

Laness's expression dimmed. She looked down at the bracelet, her short brown hair falling into her eyes as she ran her free hand along the chain. Finally, she asked, "Do you remember how I told you about the war with the Human Kingdom?"

Dimitri nodded slowly, something telling him he should remain quiet. Indeed, after a few moments of thought, Laness began.

"During that war, I had an unfavorable encounter with one of the human commanders." Laness said the words as if they tasted foul. "I was then thrown into their prison camp where I met Aaron, and eventually, we escaped. And I thought I was all right. But as the war ended, as everyone's lives got back to normal, mine didn't.

"I couldn't eat. I couldn't sleep, even though that was all I wanted to do. I couldn't *stand* anything to do with nature, not even a glimpse of flowers through my window. Everything just... hurt.

"Eventually, Aaron suggested I go to the DovenU because he thought they could help me. Branten even volunteered to take me. At that point, I had nothing to lose, so I agreed. But Branten and I had barely taken two steps out the door before I was sobbing and begging to go back because I couldn't think of five things I liked about myself anymore, so how in the name of the Crystal would the DovenU be able to help me? Why would they *want* to?

"Branten then gave me a long—and quite frankly spectacular—speech, with the main point being that that commander had already taken so much from me. He didn't get to take who I was, too."

Laness smiled slightly as she twisted the chain around Dimitri's wrist, Dimitri not daring to move. "So, I went. I trained, I healed, and I came back here. Today, everyone teases me about how aggressive my garden out front is, and I relish it. Because that garden is a reminder of who I am. And who I am is too strong to be taken away."

Laness finally looked up at him, her jaw set, the blaze in her eyes gloriously unstoppable. And Dimitri had no words as he felt a tingle across his wrist, the stems weaving together to partially close the bracelet.

"I like your garden," he finally croaked.

Laness threw back her head and laughed, the blaze in her eyes shifting into something warm. "I like it, too. And now, we only have one truth to go."

Gods, how was she like this? She'd gone through so much darkness, but unlike Dimitri, she had reached the other side. And she was bright. Open. She knew who she was.

"I'm not *just* the Sun King's bastard," Dimitri blurted, the words popping out of his mouth before he could stop them. "I'm a Sun *Royal* bastard—although I'm assuming you already know that, seeing as you're Aaron's spy."

Laness shrugged apologetically. "I haven't told anyone."

There was no judgment in her expression. No questions, no demands for an explanation, no criticisms for the choices he'd made. And something about that look had the rest of his words spilling free.

"I have Sun magic. It's weak, and it took thirteen years to come in, but I have it. And I hate it. I hate that I share anything with Deardryn, anything that ties us together. But that's not why I refuse to use it."

Dimitri felt a rush of relief. A wonderful, terrifying relief that left his walls split wide open.

He stared into Laness's face, desperate for—gods, he didn't know what. But Laness only stroked the back of his hand with her fingertips, the enka chain giving a quick tingle as it finally sealed.

"It's done," she said, sitting back.

Dimitri's eyes darted, not sure what to do. "You're not going to ask me why?"

"No. You would have already offered that if you wanted to. And all we needed was one truth."

Laness smiled up at him, clasping her tan hands in her lap. It took Dimitri a couple seconds to shakily return the gesture, a part of him still not daring to believe it.

He'd said those words aloud. And everything was all right. *He* was all right.

Aaron and Rayner chose that moment to arrive. They shoved through the dining room door, packs over their shoulders, Aaron dressed in black fighting leathers with dark metal reinforcements.

"We ready to go?" he asked.

"Dima's *been* ready," Laness retorted, effortlessly shifting back into her usual brashness. Rising from the couch, she went to fuss with Aaron's pack, Aaron making a noise of protest and shooing her away.

It was such an easy, familiar exchange. But Dimitri caught the quick look they shared. And he knew Laness had used her bracelets to let him know when it was clear to come in.

Yes, Dimitri could definitely be content here. Especially as he looked up at the sound of his name, finding Branten, Mor, and Surce waving farewell at the top of the stairs before disappearing down the hall.

"All right, then," Aaron said, extending his hands. "Let's do this."

Dimitri looked to Laness. She gave him a quick nod, gesturing for him to rise from the couch. It was time to go. He needed to go.

But as Dimitri took Aaron's hand, Rayner claiming the other, he knew he would be back. And he held that certainty close to his chest as Aaron pulled them into the shadows.

The few times Dimitri had shadowjumped, he'd only spent a few moments in the cold, empty darkness. This time, it was almost a minute before the ground resolidified beneath his feet, his eyes blinking in the sudden return of light.

The three stood in a densely packed wood. Fading sunlight bled through the canopy above, casting the dusting of snow in a red glow. To Dimitri's right, he could just make out the black basalt wall surrounding the Ash Castle through the trees.

"We're actually here," he murmured.

"I'm insulted you sound so surprised." Aaron released Dimitri's hand, giving a long, feline stretch.

"So," Rayner said, his face oddly pale. "What do we do now?"

"Now," said Aaron, "we hike. And we pray Ember is able to pull this off."

Chapter 34

Ember sat on a stone bench in the entryway, taking stock of the healer supplies in her bag. The castle around her was noticeably quiet, most people already off to bed or their nightly duties. Still, Ember's hand shook every time she caught the soft murmur of voices passing by.

Did they suspect she wasn't checking her supplies after a long day? Did they know who she'd made all her salves and poultices for? Would Othin—

Ember startled as Spark shifted where they hid behind her hair. She'd become so accustomed to the spot of warmth against her neck that she'd almost forgotten the fire sprite was there, but their message was clear enough: *Stay calm.*

Ember closed her eyes, tightening her hands around a jar. She couldn't lose her nerve now. Laness had told her through her enka bracelet that Aaron was on his way. The sprites had already begun. But, Rosala spare her, the fact that she could still feel her fear through her devinroot was *not* an encouraging sign.

Ember jerked from her thoughts at the crackle of a sconce across from her. A fire sprite appeared in the golden flame, giving a quick gesture before disappearing once more.

"The dungeon is clear," Spark whispered.

A cold sweat broke out across Ember's skin. But she nodded a fraction. Then, with a casual look around the empty entryway, she repacked her supplies and rose to her feet.

Slowly. Unhurried as she headed off down the hall, her heart pounding against her ribs.

She'd known she wouldn't be able to descend into the dungeon whenever she pleased. Even with Rois's notes on the guards' rotation schedules, she would be asking to get caught. But the fire sprites had no problem keeping watch from the torches in the dungeon. And according to her messenger, all patrolling guards were away from the Royals' section.

Ember reached the dungeon door, the corridor silent and empty around her. And offering a prayer to Rosala, she fished Analia's golden key from her pocket, slipped it into the lock, and turned.

There came a click. Ember pushed inside. And the door shut behind her with a resounding thud.

Ember wrapped her arms around herself as she descended the cold, gloomy stairwell, reaching the bottom without incident.

Just as the fire sprite had promised, there was no sign of any patrolling Sun guards. There was just the crackle of torches, the distant whimper and rattle from the cells lining the branching hallways. Left, straight, or right.

Ember hurried down the left path, trying to quiet her footsteps, her breathing. The Royals were only two corridors away. Getting to them was the easy part.

Ember reached behind herself, trying to quiet the soft rattle of her supplies as she turned right. One more corridor. She could see the turn, about thirty feet ahead. Twenty.

Gods, she might actually—

"What are you doing down here?"

Ember's entire being froze.

"Move," Spark whispered, shrinking back behind her hair.

Ember didn't know how she managed to obey. But she turned, coming face-to-face with Stanek.

The Sun guard took his time as he approached from the end of the corridor, his hands shoved into the pockets of his gold military jacket. He must have just arrived in the dungeon. That was the only way he could have slipped past the sprites, who were busy tracking the already patrolling guards.

"Ember," he sighed. "Why am I not surprised it's you?"

Ember's lips parted wordlessly.

"I knew you were going to be a nuisance," he went on, still unnervingly slow as he prowled toward her. "From the moment you spotted that Royal runt in her cell."

Spark shrank back against Ember's neck. But the reminder of that day, of her reason for doing this, didn't so much as click in Ember's mind as it did ignite.

Ember straightened, her words burning past her lips. "I've been ordered to heal your latest prisoner."

"Really?" Stanek stopped about fifteen paces away, his head cocked. "By whom?"

"His Majesty."

"Is that right?"

Ember fought the urge to shift on her feet, the nearby sconces flickering. "How else do you think I got down here? Healers don't have keys to the dungeon—"

"So, where's your escort?"

Ember stiffened.

A slow, twisted grin spread across Stanek's face. He stepped forward, the sconce to his right crackling softly. "Yes, the only way for you to enter the dungeon is if you have a key, but the same goes for getting into your prisoner's cell. Unless you're insinuating His Majesty not only entrusted you with a key to the dungeon, but its cells as well."

He took another step forward, and Ember retreated. "You can't—"

"You're done, healer," Stanek said, velvet soft. "I can't wait to see your rings split when the healers find out you're nothing but a traitor."

Ember gasped, "I'm not—"

"Enough!"

Stanek lunged for her.

Ember stumbled back with a shriek.

And the torches erupted.

Golden flames flared from every torch lining the walls, trailing behind dozens of fire sprites as they leaped off the sconces where they'd been hiding. Within seconds, they'd joined together in front of Ember, coalescing into an impenetrable wall of flames that had Stanek staggering back with a yell.

"Ember, run!" Spark screeched, barely audible over the roar of the flames.

Ember's eyes stung. But she turned on her heel and ran, the heat from the flames burning her back.

From the very beginning, they'd agreed no one could know the fire sprites were involved. Not when Othin would make it his personal mission to destroy every sprite in the castle in retribution.

But the sprites had sacrificed that safety for her. Their mission. And as Stanek's voice boomed behind her, summoning reinforcements, she hoped that safety was the only thing lost.

Ember sprinted around the corner, grabbing the cell bars to her left to pull her around and to a stop.

"Spark," she panted, "can you—"

"On it." Spark pushed themselves off Ember's shoulder, coming to land on the lock. They pressed their hand to the metal—their body glowing yellow, gold, white—the lock starting to melt. Through the bars, Ember spotted Tenley sit up on her cot, the girl's blue eyes wide.

"It's all right," Ember said, struggling for calm. "We're here to help."

With a final flare, the lock melted away. Ember scooped up the tired sprite with one hand and slid open the cell with the other, her pulse pounding throughout her body.

"What's happening?" Tenley asked, shifting uncertainly.

"We're getting you out." Reaching Tenley's cot, Ember pulled the girl to her feet. "Are you injured?"

Tenley shook her head, her face pale.

"That's good. Spark here is going to melt your cuff chain, all right?"

Tenley had barely nodded before Spark hopped off Ember's shoulder and onto her wrist, shouts echoing around the dungeon. They were running out of time.

"You're going to have to be brave, Tenley," Ember said, propelling the girl toward the exit. "We don't have much time, and we have more people to free. And I need your help."

Tenley's entire body shook as she stumbled forward. Gods, why couldn't it have been any other Royal in the first cell?

But that was just it. She *was* a Royal. It was her duty to step up.

"Tenley." Ember spun her around, forcing Tenley to meet her gaze. "Remember what Accalon always said."

"Rise again," Tenley breathed.

With a metallic jingle, the chain connecting her cuffs snapped in the middle. Spark clung to one end as they swung free, Tenley's expression hardening as she caught the sprite. Good.

"Take this." Ember reached into her pack, pulling out two jars of thick green ointment. "It's the same ointment I used on your wrists to accelerate your healing. When the sprites open these locks, you're going to heal whoever isn't strong enough to move. Scrapes and bruises can be treated later. You understand?"

Tenley nodded, seemingly unable to speak as she passed Spark back to Ember. And all around, the yell of voices and pound of boots came nearer.

"Spark," Ember said, "can you melt the next lock?"

"I need a moment," they wheezed, huddling against Ember's neck once more. "Those locks have been magically reinforced. I don't know how many I can melt."

Ember's blood roared in her ears. Before she could completely panic, a torch crackled behind her, warm little feet landing on her shoulder a moment later.

"I can do this lock," Cinder said.

"Thank you," Ember breathed, her knees shaking. "How many more are coming?"

"I don't know."

The unspoken words hung between them.

"Do what you can," Ember said firmly.

Cinder nodded and hopped over to the cell. Ember gave Tenley's shoulders a quick squeeze, praying she could handle this. Then, she took off down the corridor.

She had to get to Rois. Even with her magic, he would need time to heal.

"Take this right," Spark instructed, sounding a little stronger. As the sprite who had found Rois, they'd agreed to stick with Ember to both interpret messages and direct her to his cell when the time came. Luckily, it was just a few halls away—although it was in the opposite direction of the Royal spouses.

Up ahead, a fire sprite appeared on a sconce, gesturing frantically before disappearing once more.

"The wall is holding," Spark reported. "We've set up a second blockade nearby, so the guards have to loop all the way around to get to us."

"But that also means fewer sprites to open the cells," Ember said.

Spark was quiet for several seconds. "We do what we can."

Ember nodded, a lump forming in her throat. She turned a final corner, Spark directing her to the cell on her right. They hopped off her shoulder and got to work melting the lock, the process going noticeably slower than before. Ember could practically feel the daggers at the back of her neck as the seconds ticked past, the shouts getting louder.

"Spark..." she croaked.

"Done." Spark staggered away from the lock, Ember catching them just in time. "I'm all right," they gasped, huddling beneath Ember's collar. "Go."

Ember didn't have to be told twice. She shoved the door open, a hoarse cry greeting her from the back of the cell.

Rois lay on his stomach on his cot, his head twisted toward the door. The moment he spotted Ember, he tried to prop himself up on his elbows, just to let out a hiss. And Ember's stomach heaved as she spotted why.

Rois's bare torso gleamed with sweat, the torchlight casting flickering shadows across his well-defined arms and shoulders. But there was no concealing the bloody whip marks etched into his back, his mangled skin red and inflamed. Gods, there had to be at least thirty lashes.

"Rois," Ember gasped, dropping to her knees beside him. "Rois, don't move, you're opening your wounds even wider."

"Tell me there's a poultice in that bag," he groaned, blood spilling down his sides and staining the gray blanket beneath him.

"Don't insult me." Ember tried for her usual arrogant grin, but the muscles in her face trembled. She quickly busied herself with her supplies, Rois's head dropping back to the cot. Time, time, they were running out of time.

Finally, Ember's fumbling fingers found the jar she was looking for. She wrenched off the top, pouring the green, oily paste across Rois's wounds.

Rois cried out, his back arching in pain.

"Stay still," Ember said, her voice shaking as she struggled to pin his shoulders. "I know it hurts, I'm sorry, there's just so much to heal. It's going to hurt a little more, but I promise—"

"Just do it," Rois snapped, his face flushed, his skin feverishly warm beneath Ember's hands. But he stiffly settled on the cot once more.

Ember whispered a final apology. Then, gripping his shoulders, she sent her magic through his body. Rois bit down on his blanket, stifling his yell. But he remained still as Ember's magic reached his back.

Gods, there was so much damage.

Ember shifted to get a better view of his back, just for a fresh wave of terror to roll down her spine. Because his wounds weren't healing.

But how? Was this magically inflicted? Was it impervious to her healing? Could she have made the paste wrong?

No, she couldn't have. Healing cuts was one of the first things she'd mastered, she'd barely had to think when mixing her ingredients that afternoon, especially with the help of her devinroot—Rosala spare her, had her devinroot messed it up?

She'd never created any supplies while high before—she'd never tried to heal. Was this her fault?

Her eyes landed on Rois's back once more. And pure, undiluted relief flooded over her as his bleeding slowed, Rois shaking beneath her hands as her magic and paste continued to heal, cleaning and disinfecting as they went.

Slowly, painstakingly slowly, a layer of delicate skin started to form across his lashes. Ember urged her magic along, knowing she'd already completed multiple weeks' worth of healing, she couldn't push Rois's body too hard too fast.

"Ember, we have to go."

Ember's sob finally broke free as she twisted around.

Cadmus stood in the cell entrance, the side of his face freshly bruised, his blue eyes blazing. A handful of exhausted fire sprites huddled on his shoulders, the exact shade of gold as his locked-away magic.

"What's going on?" Rois asked, brushing Ember's hands aside and dragging himself into a sitting position.

"Dace and Hallem are still imprisoned," Cadmus reported. "The fire sprites can't hold them back any longer; we have to go."

"We can't leave them!" Ember exclaimed. "What about their families?"

"Othin won't kill anyone immediately," Cadmus said. "He'll use them as leverage, and we can try to get them out before he gives up."

"But—"

"Ember, we have to go." Cadmus's voice was heartbreakingly firm. Grabbing a discarded tunic from the corner of the cell, he tossed it to Rois, a fire sprite hopping over to melt his cuff chain so he could pull it on. Then, Cadmus turned to Ember.

She didn't know when she'd started crying. She just knew that Cadmus pulled her to her feet, Rois gently nodding along as she fired off a list of instructions to keep his wounds from reopening as he stood. Then, they ushered her out of the cell, a group of disheveled Royals waiting outside.

And Ember's heart cracked down the center. Because she'd failed them. At least some of them.

She didn't even get a second to grieve as Cadmus led the way down the hall, everyone hurrying to keep up.

The vault, outside, the wall. That was all that was left as they made turn after turn, the voices getting louder, closer.

They rounded the final corner. Cadmus shoved open the door to the vault without pause, Ember ushering everyone inside before her. She was just stepping through the door when she glanced back. Just in time to see the first soldier round the corner before the door shut.

"They saw us," she breathed.

The Royals exchanged a single, terrified look. Ember's eyes darted, looking for an escape. But all she found was narrow, winding passageways, the dark stone lit by golden torchlight, the cells replaced by heavy metal doors with intricate carvings.

"Don't just stand there!" Rois barked. "Move!"

Everyone staggered back into movement. Clearly, no one was in condition for a prolonged run for their lives. But they managed to make it down two corridors before the door banged open behind them.

"Are they familiar with the vault?" Cadmus asked, falling back to the rear of the group with Ember and Rois, letting Fayela take the lead.

"Not as far as I'm aware," Rois ground out.

"Which means we keep out of sight and pray they get lost," Cadmus said grimly.

That sounded like a horrible plan to Ember. Especially as footsteps pounded closer, multiple pairs.

Faster, they had to go faster. But the Royals were dragging as Fayela led them onto the center path, the torches on either side of her turning her hair to flame.

"Two more turns," Rois breathed.

Ahead of them, Tenley stumbled. Rois reached for her, but Cadmus scooped her up first, Rois touching his back with a wince.

Rosala spare her, his wounds were reopening. Cadmus's pace was slowing as Tenley wrapped her arms around his neck, burying her face in his shoulder. And the shouts sounded only a few corridors behind.

They stumbled around the next corner. One more.

Ember clutched the stitch in her side, trying to move faster. They were so close.

They turned into the final corridor. Ember sobbed in relief as she spotted the thick iron door up ahead, carved with a phoenix in flight.

Freedom. They were almost there.

Fayela reached the door first. She slammed her hand on the phoenix's chest, and the corridor rumbled. Golden light raced along the carved lines, setting the phoenix alight even as Fayela's damper cuffs blocked her magic. But Rois had said the hidden entrance in the wall outside was activated by Royal blood, and this door must have been the same, for Fayela shoved the door open.

Ember gasped in the sudden rush of cold, fresh air.

Out, out, out.

Fayela held open the door as the Royals staggered through, Ember, Rois, and Cadmus hurrying forward. They were just about to step outside when the back of Ember's neck tingled.

She didn't think. She lunged forward, tackling Rois to the ground. Just as something sliced over their heads, slamming into the door frame with the shriek of metal-on-metal.

Ember waited for the clatter of a weapon falling to the stone, but it never came. She looked up, spotting a diagonal scratch running along the stone. The exact shape of the cut she'd healed on the recruit's face all those weeks ago.

And Ember didn't know if she wanted to scream or sob as she twisted her head, finding the patrol of Sun guards rounding the corner.

"Get up!" Fayela shrieked. She grabbed Ember with one hand and Rois with the other, yanking them to their feet. She pulled them through the door, letting it slam shut behind them.

Ember struggled to catch her breath, finding herself in a wide-open stretch of land, the black stone of the Ash Castle wall gleaming in the moonlight two hundred yards away.

"No," she breathed, starting to shake.

"Everyone scatter!" Rois ordered. "Meet up at the passage. No straight lines; if we're going to be targets, we won't make it easy."

Ember looked around the exhausted group, expecting to find her own sinking feeling. But all she saw was a grim determination as they nodded and took off, the crunch of their footsteps through the dusting of snow coming from all sides.

Rois grabbed Ember's hand. Then, they ran, only making it fifty yards before the door burst open.

"How are they already out?" Ember gasped.

Rois shook his head, clearly at a loss. Ember barely choked back her sob.

"You can't quit now, Em," Rois panted, half dragging her as they zigzagged through the snow.

"Rois, it's wide open! They'll see how we escape."

"Which is why we split up. There's more of us than there are them, it will take them some time to wrangle—"

Rois cut off with a curse as he jerked Ember to the side, magic tingling across Ember's skin as another whip sliced into the snow where they'd been standing. Ember twisted her head around, spotting Stanek forty yards back, gaining fast.

"Rois, he's gaining—"

"Get down."

Rois dragged Ember to the ground, another whip sailing over their heads and landing in the snow in front of them. Spark yelped against Ember's neck, the fall stirring them awake.

Ember twisted on her knees, staring up at Stanek bearing down on her, the air tingling with magic as he raised his hand.

There was nothing she or Rois could do.

Ember held her breath, bracing for the blow.

Stanek stumbled. He looked down, just in time to see a ribbon of fire loop around his ankle and yank, toppling him to the ground with a curse.

And behind him, his jaw set, was Cadmus.

"Well done, Crackle," he said, scooping the fire sprite out of the snow.

The fire sprite huddled against Cadmus's hand, his little body smoking. But his voice was satisfied as he said, "Just as we planned, Your Majesty."

With a jolt, Ember realized he was one of the many fire sprites that had been perched on Cadmus's shoulders, the rest now cradled in Tenley's hands as she watched a few paces back.

Cadmus nodded and settled Crackle back on his shoulder. Then, he stepped over to Stanek, who was struggling to rise.

"Tell your king, children should know better than to play with fire," he said. Then, he stomped down hard on Stanek's hand.

Stanek wailed as there came a snap, clutching his hand as he fell back in the snow. Cadmus didn't spare him a look.

"Are you two all right?" he asked, coming to offer Ember a hand up.

"Depends," Rois said. "How many of them are left?"

"Technically, all five. But between tripping hazards, sprite burns, and some stomped-on extremities, we've slowed them down. So, get moving."

Cadmus pulled them to their feet, Rois stifling a groan. Together, the four hurried toward the wall, Stanek cursing behind them.

This was it. Fayela had already opened the passage in the wall, the same golden light from the vault exit now shimmering in the shape of a tall, narrow door that Fayela held open. Staring at the stone, Ember had no idea how she'd found the specific spot, but that didn't stop the Royals from staggering through. And she, Rois, Cadmus, and Tenley were only fifteen yards away.

But that was when the yells began.

"They're back on their feet," Fayela called, her feline features pale.

Ember didn't dare look back. She ran faster, half choking on her sob.

Ten yards. Five.

Cadmus shoved Tenley toward Fayela, taking her place at the door as they staggered through. Rois followed, reaching behind him to grab Ember's hand.

She took a step forward.

And white-hot agony exploded across her back.

Chapter 35

Aaron raced through the trees, Dimitri and Rayner close behind as they aimed for the commotion up ahead.

"What's happening?" Dimitri gasped, his wide eyes cast in silver from the ball of magic Aaron held in one hand.

"I don't know," he said, "Laness hasn't reported anything."

"At least we picked a good spot to wait," Rayner panted.

The three had spent the evening hiking around the Ash Castle wall, careful to stay out of sight of any patrolling guards. Knowing it would be impossible to find the hidden exit, Aaron had tried to set them up in the optimal spot—which meant making a gut decision on which boulder they should sit and wait on.

Thankfully, it was close enough they'd been able to hear when the shouts began. But that kind of noise was never good when it came to an escape.

Aaron shoved the thought aside as the tree line came into view, Dimitri and Rayner nearly plowing into him as he came to a halt.

"They're coming," he said, letting his silver light wink out.

Indeed, within moments, the crunch of footsteps drew closer, the group of Ash Royals finally staggering through the trees up ahead. As soon as they saw Aaron and company, they recoiled.

"We're friends!" Aaron said quickly, raising his hands. "We're here to help."

He expected the Royals to sag in relief. Instead, they erupted into a flurry of voices, Dimitri recoiling from the noise.

Aaron struggled to untangle the individual words, his eyes flicking around the group. One little girl, a man and woman that looked to be a few years older than Analia, an older woman, and three men that could have been anywhere in between. Definitely not everyone. And where was—

"We have to go!" Cadmus pushed through the crowd, Aaron's heart stumbling as he recognized the robed figure he and Rois supported between them.

"Ember," he breathed. "What happened?"

"I'm fine," she ground out, her face unnervingly pale in the moonlight.

"You're *not* fine!" Rois snapped.

"Neither are you!"

"Ember," Cadmus said, "I saw his magic hit you—"

"Enough!" the younger Ash woman roared.

Everyone's mouths snapped shut. They twisted toward the woman who Aaron vaguely recalled was named Fayela, the sudden silence worse than the blare of voices.

Fayela dipped her chin to Cadmus. "Apologies, Your Majesty."

"No, you're right." Cadmus briefly looked away, composing himself. Then, he shifted to face his family, one arm still protectively around Ember's waist. "I understand we're all disoriented, but everyone yelling is going to lead the Sun soldiers to us, and all of this will be for nothing. So, we all need to take a breath, and let Aaron explain."

Aaron startled at the sound of his name. But that quick jolt was all he needed to snap to attention, his instincts taking over.

"Right," he said. "The quickest way out of here is to shadowjump. And lucky for you all, we've got these."

Aaron reached into a slit in the thigh of his fighting leathers, pulling out one of the damper daggers that had skewered him back on the ridge. The black blade glinted in the moonlight, some of the tension leaving Cadmus's face, the Royals murmuring behind him.

"Does anyone know a safe place we can go?" Aaron asked.

"The mining house," Rois said immediately.

Aaron had never heard of the place. But Cadmus gave a quick nod.

"That'll work." Making sure Rois had a grip on Ember, he offered his cuffed hands to Aaron, the snapped chain rattling. "I can take us."

Aaron wouldn't make him offer twice. He slid the dagger through the slits where each cuff met, Cadmus not hesitating to flick his hands free.

Immediately, the bright golden flash of Cadmus's released magic illuminated the forest, Dimitri letting out a muffled curse as he and the others cringed away. Aaron fought back his own wince as shouts started up in the distance once more—they were giving the Sun soldiers everything they needed to find them.

But Cadmus remained calm as his blue eyes, tight with pain, met Aaron's, then flicked to the rest of the group questioningly. Aaron shook his head a fraction. No one needed to know the specifics of his identity unless absolutely necessary.

Cadmus nodded, his body relaxing as the golden light faded, then winked out entirely.

"All right," he said, pocketing his cuffs, "everyone, huddle up."

The Royals scrambled to comply, Cadmus reaching for Aaron's hand before it could be claimed. Rayner took Aaron's other hand, Aaron's eyes darting around the group to make sure everyone was linked in. Then, he pulled them into the shadows.

Aaron's network churned as they moved along, not used to transporting so many people at once. But thankfully, the jump wasn't far. It only took a light nudge from Cadmus to get them on course, the ground resolidifying beneath Aaron's feet a moment later.

He glanced around, his senses on high alert. But they'd only appeared in a long-deserted sitting room.

Dust covered the collection of sagging, dark gray couches and armchairs. The Everflame sconces lining the room illuminated the rotting floorboards and peeling earthy-green paint on the walls, a large, rickety table shoved to the side like an afterthought. And all Aaron could smell was must.

As soon as they emerged from the shadows, Rayner released Aaron's hand and took several steps back, his face pale. Any other time, Aaron would have been intrigued by that. But now, he looked back at the Royals, discovering no one had moved.

They remained exactly where they'd appeared, their hands clasped, eyes wide, looking like they had no idea where to go.

Aaron's lips parted, but no words came out. Because he knew on an instinctual level this silence was not one to be broken.

It was a silence to be buried in, to survive. It was the silence of everything the Ash Royals had lost.

Aaron blinked hard, his mind flashing to a marble fountain, a silver castle, a refurbished Throne Room with a pile of rubble in its center.

This grief had history. And Aaron's entire being shuddered at the possibility that his home was the next page of its story.

Aaron didn't know how long they remained like that. Finally, a tiny voice broke the silence.

"Are we safe?"

Aaron looked down. And his composure nearly shattered as he spotted the little girl looking up at him, a group of exhausted fire sprites peeking out from beneath her collar.

Aaron nodded, and the girl's shoulders slumped. Releasing the hands she'd been holding, she stumbled across the room, pulled herself up onto a sagging armchair, and curled into a ball.

And somehow, that was enough. The Ash Royals finally released each other, their voices slowly coming back as they moved to collapse on the various couches and chairs.

Aaron took one last moment to shake his head at it all. Then, he got to work.

Sliding the three other damper blades from his leathers, he ordered Rayner to circulate them around, Dimitri already pulling the healer kit from his pack. He poked through its contents, clearly relieved when Fayela took it from him and assembled a makeshift healer station. Aaron slung off his own pack and started to pass around the provisions he'd procured. And slowly, the Royals came alive again.

Aaron turned to Cadmus, the flashes of released networks casting his unreadable mask in shades of gold, orange, and scarlet.

"How secure is this place?" he asked, his voice low.

"It's all we have."

Aaron pressed his lips into a line. Cadmus ran a tired hand down his face, asking what had happened on Aaron's end.

The two exchanged quick updates, Cadmus seeming torn between hope and something far heavier as Aaron filled him in on Analia's scheme.

"Don't forget," Aaron said, "she's already managed to smuggle Dimitri out, right under Deardryn's nose. And I learned a long time ago that when Analia sets her mind to something, the last thing you want to do is get in her way."

"That's true." Cadmus dropped his gaze, absently rubbing his wrist. "Dimitri's plan has promise as well, especially since we'll be around to assist."

"Does that mean you all will be staying?" Aaron asked, hating his flicker of hope.

Cadmus nodded. "Ember's the only one going with you."

"What?"

Aaron's head whipped around. She'd been so quiet, he'd almost forgotten her in the chaos. But now, Ember straightened where she'd been bracing her shoulder against the wall, the blaze in her blue-gray eyes disconcertingly stark against her pale face.

Cadmus wheeled on her, "Why haven't you been getting treated?"

"Because the Royals are worse than me," she snapped.

"Ember, I quite literally have your blood on my hands," Rois said from a nearby couch. He'd stripped off his tunic, allowing Fayela to smooth thick green paste over the rows of horrifically familiar lashes running down his back.

Aaron's stomach churned. He looked away, just catching the glare Ember shot Rois's back.

"I'm fine," she ground out.

"Then why aren't you ordering everyone around?" Aaron countered.

Ember looked as though she was deciding how she'd like to dispose of his body. Unfortunately for her, Aaron wasn't so easily discouraged. He crossed the room toward her, Cadmus close behind, Ember shrinking back as she protested, "I'm fine! And I'm not going with you."

"The sprites told me what my mother said," Cadmus argued. "It's not safe for you here."

"It's not safe for you either," Ember said, flinching away from Cadmus's hand. "I can't just abandon everyone."

"Ember, *please.*" Cadmus finally managed to grab her hand, his expression pleading as he tangled their fingers. "I've already had so much taken away from me. I need to know *one* person I care about is safe."

Ember stared up at him, her mouth trembling.

Cadmus took a step closer, his voice dropping to a whisper. "You already saved me. Now, let me save you."

Ember's lips parted. For several seconds, she stared at Cadmus, her eyes glassy, not seeming aware of the other Royals whispering around them.

She swayed on her feet.

A fiery little head popped up from beneath her collar. "Help her!" they shrieked.

And Ember crumpled.

Cadmus let out a hoarse cry. He tried to catch her, but clearly, Ember wasn't the only one who needed healing. Aaron had to grab the two before they could hit the floor, his heart thudding to a stop as his eyes landed on Ember's back.

"Oh gods," he breathed.

The entire back of Ember's robes was stained with blood. It spread out from the slashes cut through the fabric, the lines too clean to be from a blade.

Cadmus looked up at Aaron. And for the first time that night, Aaron didn't see the Ash King. He saw a nineteen-year-old boy, his face drained of color, his wide eyes staring, staring, staring.

And Aaron snapped into action.

"Get her on her front," he ordered, his hands flying as he eased her down across his knees, Ember gasping with the movement. "We have to get this bleeding under control if she's going to make it to one of my healers. Dima! I need gauze."

Aaron whipped a dagger from his sleeve and sliced down the length of Ember's robes, the shirt beneath. He was no healer, but he'd been around Branten long enough to understand the gist of how wounds were treated. But as he peeled the sticky fabric away from Ember's skin, he couldn't stop the bile from burning his throat.

Gashes as thick as his finger ran all the way down either side of her spine. Deep ones. Her lightly tanned skin stained red.

Aaron was faintly aware of Rois ushering everyone out of the room. Ember squirmed on his lap, letting out a whimper as she fumbled with something on her wrist.

"Ember, stop," he gasped, trying to hold her still, "you're making the bleeding worse—gods damn it all, Dima!"

"Here." Dimitri skidded to his knees beside him. He shoved a wad of gauze into Aaron's hands, his face turning green as he spotted Ember's back.

Aaron quickly spread the gauze across the closest wound, Cadmus mirroring him on the other side. But Aaron had barely pressed down, Ember crying out in pain, before the gauze was turning pink.

What kind of wounds were these?

"Cadmus," Ember gasped.

Cadmus looked up at Aaron, positively terrified, as Ember's hand fumbled for his. She pressed something into his palm, her voice so faint Aaron barely heard her. "Rise again."

Cadmus breathed her name.

Ember's head lolled.

And the room erupted into chaos.

Cadmus lunged for her, letting out something between a scream and a sob. Aaron shoved him back, "Cadmus, you can't—"

"Do something! Do something do something do something—"

"Dima!"

Dimitri leaned away as Aaron twisted toward him, his eyes impossibly wide.

"Heal her!"

Dimitri's jaw dropped. "Me? I'm not a healer, I can't—"

"You and I both know there's more than one type of healing," Aaron snapped. "We both know healers can't heal themselves. But you can stabilize her life force until we get to someone who can. Now *heal her!*"

Dimitri's eyes darted around the room, visibly recoiling as Cadmus rounded on him. *"Help her!"*

Aaron thought his heart would bust through his ribcage as Dimitri squirmed, his eyes finally landing on Rayner, who'd come to crouch on Aaron's other side.

"Do it," he ordered.

Dimitri squeezed his eyes shut. Then, hands shaking, he reached for Ember's back. And golden light flared from his hands.

Aaron flung up his arm against the light. Across from him, Cadmus's voice cut off, his lips parted as he took in the scene before him. But Dimitri kept his eyes shut, looking like his world was collapsing around him.

Seconds, minutes passed. Aaron forced himself to remain still, let Dimitri work, the frost crackling through his veins feeling like the only thing he had left.

But slowly, agonizingly slowly, Ember's breathing evened out. She settled against him. And the golden light winked out.

"She's stable," Dimitri breathed.

Aaron reached for him, not sure what to say. But Dimitri scrambled to his feet and backed away. And Aaron could have sworn his eyes shone as he fled through the closest door and into the hallway beyond.

Aaron looked between Ember and the door, not sure what to do.

"I got it." Rayner rose to his feet, looking like the only steady person left as he nodded to Aaron and Cadmus, then headed out the door.

Finally, there was silence.

Aaron glanced at Cadmus, the pulse in his throat just as fast as his own. But Cadmus almost managed calm as he asked, "Is Dimitri—"

"Dima doesn't like to be touched without warning, but you didn't hear that from me."

Cadmus stared at him for a heartbeat, then nodded slowly. Aaron pulled Ember closer, ready to shadowjump out of this nightmare and back to his kingdom. But something about the expression on Cadmus's face had him pause.

"Will you be all right?" he asked.

Cadmus looked at him as if he'd just asked the dumbest question in the world. "No."

Aaron opened his mouth, just for Ember to make a small, choked noise.

"Go!" Cadmus exclaimed.

Aaron didn't bother nodding. He faded into the shadows, using the dregs of his magic to race back through the darkness, through his wards, ignoring the magical exhaustion that plowed into him as his sitting room solidified beneath his knees.

"Someone get Sofika!" He yelled. *Now.*

Dimitri didn't know where he was going. He didn't know how he managed to tell Laness through their bracelets to fetch their healer.

All he knew was he couldn't think. He couldn't function. He couldn't exist in his body anymore as he staggered through a narrow hall, up a rickety staircase, higher and higher and higher until he pushed through the door at the top.

A distant part of him noted he'd found a tiny bathing room. But none of him cared as he collapsed on the floor and curled into a ball, the door shutting behind him and leaving him in darkness.

Crystal spare him, how had he found himself here again? His magic tingling through his veins, someone's life resting in his hands, their life force evaporating in front of him like rain in a desert. Again and again and again—

"Dima."

A sob ripped through Dimitri's gritted teeth as the door opened and shut, Rayner coming to sit close enough Dimitri could feel the heat from his skin.

"Dima, breathe," Rayner whispered.

No, he didn't want to breathe. He didn't want to do anything. He wanted everything to stop—

Dimitri yelped as something icy touched the back of his hand.

"Sorry," Rayner said. "It's my scarsworn dagger. I couldn't think of any other way to get your attention."

Several responses jumbled through Dimitri's head, none making their way to his mouth. He could only nod, needing several seconds to realize it was too dark for Rayner to see. All there was was a faint stream of light squeezing through the cracks around the door.

Seeming to take Dimitri's silence as a cue, Rayner started to pull his blade away. Dimitri made a noise of alarm, and Rayner quickly returned the blade to his skin.

Cold. Just like the icy metal of Ferrin's statue that had helped Dimitri focus all those months ago.

Inhale, exhale.

Slowly, Dimitri's pulse returned to normal. His thoughts straightened out. Finally, he eased back against the wall, the silence only interrupted by his and Rayner's breathing.

"Better?" Rayner eventually asked.

"Yes." Dimitri bit the inside of his cheek, his gaze dropping to his lap.

At any other time, his skin would have been burning from the fact that it was Rayner who had found him like this. But Dimitri couldn't bring himself to care.

"What happened out there?" Rayner asked, soft as a caress.

"Let it go, Rayner," Dimitri said heavily.

Rayner, unsurprisingly, pressed on. "I don't understand what's upset you. You just saved Ember's life. What's the problem?"

"The problem," Dimitri said shakily, "is I saved her life using my magic, and the last time I tried that was with Patryclas. And we both know how that ended."

Rayner went quiet. Dimitri wiped his nose with his sleeve, the hole in his chest yawning wider.

Don't turn it off.

"I don't want this magic," he said suddenly, his hand squeezing his wrist. "Everyone says it helps heal people, but all I've ever seen it do is harm. And I don't want to be like that. I don't want to be one of them. I don't want it."

"But you're one for two," Rayner pointed out. "And you're two for two trying to do good."

"Sometimes, trying isn't good enough."

The floorboards squeaked as Rayner shifted beside him. But Dimitri hauled himself to his feet, his body protesting with each movement as he pulled open the door.

Light from the hall spilled into the bathing room, revealing a cramped setup, complete with rusty faucets and a cracked, dusty mirror.

Dimitri glanced back as Rayner rose behind him, just in time to catch the relief flash across his face. Later, he would be intrigued by that. But now, he turned away.

"Hey." Rayner slipped in front of him, his hand brushing Dimitri's sleeve. "Today was a win. Regardless of everything else, you did good. You *saved* her. Let yourself feel that."

He stared into Dimitri's face, not stepping aside until Dimitri nodded faintly.

He had promised Patryclas he wouldn't turn anything off. He just didn't think this "win" would be enough.

Chapter 36

Dimitri paced up and down the rickety stairs, desperate for a distraction as he took stock of his surroundings.

There were three floors total. The first floor was completely taken up by the sitting room, plus a small pantry tucked in a corner. A narrow, dimly lit hall ran through the second floor, the four doors on either side leading to tiny bedrooms that had probably been cozy in their prime. And at the top of the stairs, there was a rundown bathing room on the left and right.

Between the paint peeling off the walls and the layer of dust coating every surface, it was clear the safehouse hadn't been used in a long time. Cadmus confirmed this when he eventually emerged from the sitting room, the color not quite having returned to his face as he gestured for Dimitri to follow him back upstairs.

Apparently, the safehouse had been created during Azar's rule, with the knowledge only passed down to the Royals and Crystal Guard. On the outside, it was glamored to look like an ordinary warehouse—which it technically was. If anyone managed to break in through the front door, all they would find was a giant storage area for mining supplies. What they wouldn't see was the second door, glamored to look like a back wall. And even if they did, it was further shielded to only let those who knew about the safehouse inside.

"That's how you, Aaron, and Rayner were able to get in," Cadmus explained, shoving open one of the bedroom doors. "Rois told you about it in the woods. That's also how he got Ember here when they…"

Cadmus's voice choked off. Dimitri glanced at him, Cadmus not seeming to notice as he rubbed his wrist.

"Aaron's nymph friend, Laness, told me she's unconscious but stable," he offered.

Cadmus's head drooped. Dimitri shifted from foot to foot, not sure what to say. But Cadmus quickly straightened and pushed back his shoulders.

"We'll talk more in the morning," he said, suddenly brisk as he turned to go. "You and Rayner will have to share the room. There's a bedroll beneath the bed."

Figured. Dimitri nodded and stepped into his room, barely having time to take in his narrow bed, the fraying red-and-orange carpet, and weathered chest of drawers in the corner before Cadmus closed the door behind him.

The following morning, Dimitri descended into the sitting room to find everyone already waiting—including Rayner, who had taken the bedroll without complaint. He'd been hoping the meeting would be quick, allowing him and Rayner to head out shortly after. Yet, the majority of that morning was spent ironing out their plans, the first thing agreed upon being Dimitri needed to wait.

As Cadmus put it, there was a fine balance between showing up too early and connecting himself to the escape and showing up too late to do anything. After much debating, Dimitri finally got the room to agree they could go the following morning—which barely appeased his twisting stomach. Fayela further asked the remaining fire sprites if they'd be willing to act as messengers, allowing Dimitri and Rayner to keep the Royals informed on what was happening, which the sprites amicably agreed to.

As a matter of fact, the sprites had already been fulfilling a version of this role. Using their ability to relocate to any nearby flame, they'd been spying on the Sun forces.

Apparently, Othin had been furious to find out the fire sprites had been involved, and had demanded all sconces, torches, and candles be removed from the castle. Aeley then informed him how the majority of the castle relied on those sources of light instead of electrical means, which resulted in Othin launching into an impressive fit before finally acquiescing to leave everything essential alone.

Spark was particularly smug when reporting this, only giving a dismissive wave of their fiery hand when Cadmus reminded them they had to be extra careful now. Thankfully, the three other sprites that had decided to stick around seemed to take it to heart. One of them, Cinder, reported Othin was still deliberating how to handle the Royals' escape, and what to do with the remaining prisoners, which left the room simultaneously satisfied and worried.

They went back and forth a little while longer, no one having a firm opinion on when the Royals should reveal they'd escaped to the kingdom. And eventually, their voices petered out.

Dimitri watched the Ash Royals wander off, trying to remember all of their names. One of them—a stocky man around Dimitri's age with a friendly smile—was kind enough to remind him his name was Tyce as he offered Dimitri a canteen.

Eventually, he stood from the couch, intending to head back to his room. But Rois pulled him aside.

"Are there any updates on Ember?" he asked.

Dimitri shook his head. Rois dragged a hand through his hair, clearly deliberating.

"Tell Aaron to keep an eye on her," he finally said.

"Why?" Dimitri asked.

"Just do it."

Dimitri wrinkled his nose, but he knew better than to argue with the tightened muscle in Rois's jaw. "How did Othin catch you?" he asked instead.

"I wasn't immediately found when Deardryn left the castle," he said flatly. "Apparently, the Sun Kingdom cares more about their convictions than confessions."

Dimitri's stomach did a slow roll. And Rois offered no reassurances as he slipped past him and headed up the stairs.

Dimitri sat on his bed the following morning, anxiously organizing his pack as Rayner examined his new appearance in the cracked corner mirror. He didn't think Rayner needed a disguise—Othin had no idea who he was. But Dimitri had learned a long time ago Rayner would take any excuse to use his magic, regardless of how small his tweaks were.

Even now, his changes were minimal. His full mouth a little thinner. His mahogany hair a shade darker, the wavy texture more defined.

"You still look like you," Dimitri said, half to himself.

"Do I?" Rayner ran his finger down his nose, the shape morphing into something hawkish and far too large for his face.

Dimitri snorted. "Now you just look like an amateur."

Rayner flashed a grin in the mirror, his nose shifting back to normal with a quick tap. "I used to have a whole ritual when doing this," he said, tilting his head this way and that. "I'd spend so much time trying to figure out who each appearance was. How they talked, how they walked, what they thought."

"How come?"

Rayner hesitated. Dimitri looked away, his shoulders hunching as he waited for their usual tension to crackle.

But Rayner surprised him.

"After everything that happened in Scarsthain," he said, his voice faraway, "I didn't know who I was anymore. I spent a lot of time trying out different names, different appearances, different mannerisms, searching for something that felt right. Eventually, I landed on the name and appearance you're used to."

Dimitri felt Rayner's eyes land on him, not needing to look to know Rayner was bracing himself for his reaction. For the snap.

Dimitri's fingers curled in his pack, finding soft, knitted threads. And his voice was perfectly level as he asked, "Is that why none of your changes are extreme?"

He looked over, just in time to spot Rayner's shoulders relax.

"It is." Catching Dimitri's eye in the mirror, he offered a faint smile, then returned his attention to his hair. "It can be disorienting to feel so... intangible. It's hard enough having such a fragile sense of self. But when it gets tied to your appearance, and then that changes?"

Rayner shook his head, his gaze momentarily going out of focus. "Before you came, I'd settled on a version of myself that I wasn't particularly fond of. But I liked who I was with you. Betrayal not included."

Rayner gave a sardonic eye roll. Dimitri's lips twitched, his gaze dropping back to his pack.

The more that he thought about it, he'd liked the version of himself in the Moon Kingdom, too. He was happier. Lighter. Safer—even with Deardryn lurking around every corner.

What do you want?

"That's the secret you've been trying to figure out about my shop," Rayner went on, perfectly casual once more.

Dimitri's head popped up, "I never said—"

"Oh please, Dima. Did you think I never noticed you eavesdropping on my consultations?" Rayner flashed a grin over his shoulder as he crossed to his pack on the floor. "Every time I offered a price you weren't expecting, your entire body would twist toward me on the couch with the most overt look of 'What the fuck are you doing' on your face. I had to start angling clients away from you."

Dimitri's ears burned. "I didn't realize," he mumbled.

"I know," Rayner laughed. "I didn't tell you because I didn't want it to stop."

Dimitri grumbled under his breath as Rayner laughed once more, but there was no bite to his words.

"At any rate," Rayner said, smile audible in his voice, "my starting price is high because I've learned the hard way you can't just change your appearance and expect everything to be fixed. A different nose isn't going to make the person you're pining after suddenly love you. Being a few inches taller isn't going to make you more respected. And if it does, that's going to cause more damage with how ephemeral my magic is—which is the *last* thing I want.

"The people I work with are the ones who understand themselves, what they want, and are comfortable with the risks and rewards involved. And they are the ones I charge far less, regardless of how big their changes are."

He looked over at Dimitri, his chin raised, eyes bright, looking like a ruler at the end of their speech. And that... That right there was Rayner.

"Come on," he said, pulling on his pack and rising to his feet. "Cadmus is waiting."

Dimitri gave a quick affirmation, his fingers fumbling with his pack zipper. And as Rayner pushed open the door, he didn't notice Dimitri's eyes linger on him, nor his faint nod as he rose to his feet and followed.

Getting into the Ash Castle was absurdly easy. Cadmus—now black haired and square jawed—shadowjumped them into an alleyway a few streets away from the castle, disappearing just as quickly as he'd come. At that point, it was just a matter of strolling up to the Phoenix Gate and giving Joshel—the guard on duty—a wave.

Now, Dimitri and Rayner followed a still wide-eyed Joshel through the busy Ash Castle corridors. The guard repeatedly tried to get Dimitri to explain his arrival, clearly refusing to believe the only response he was going to get was, "I've come to see my father."

After what felt like a barrage of questions, they finally turned onto the corridor leading to the Council Chamber. Just to be greeted by Othin's raised voice, loud enough to be heard through the thick stone door.

Joshel's pace slowed as they drew near, his blue eyes shifting uncertainly. They were still a few paces away when he finally turned to Dimitri, "His Majesty is busy at the moment—"

"No need," Dimitri interrupted, marching past. Then, he shoved through the door without so much as a knock, Rayner stifling a laugh as he followed.

Othin and Aeley stood on opposite ends of the otherwise empty council table. The former Ash Queen was dressed all in dark gray, her golden hair loose over her shoulders, the chamber noticeably cold as she studied the ranting man before her.

"How do I know you're telling the truth?" Othin demanded, a vein bulging in his temple. "This is your *family* that has escaped. Why should I believe you've given me an actual suspect? Why should I—"

"Hello," Dimitri cut in pleasantly.

Othin choked on the rest of his words. He twisted on his heel, his eyes flying wide as he spotted Dimitri lingering by the closed door. His mouth opened and closed several times, his face draining of color.

"Dimitri…"

"You remember me after all," Dimitri drawled. "I'm touched."

All the color rushed back into Othin's face. He jabbed a finger at Dimitri, his words coming fast and hard, "What are you doing here?"

"I'm here to see you, but you seem to be in the middle of something." Not waiting for permission, Dimitri crossed the room and plopped down on the closest seat. "Well, go on. Don't let me interrupt. This is Rayner, by the way," he added as Rayner took the seat beside him, looking thoroughly entertained.

Aeley raised a brow, looking as if this were an unexpected development she wasn't completely mad about. Ignoring Othin's spluttering, she turned to Dimitri and asked, "You're one of Analia's friends, yes?"

Dimitri nodded, surprised she remembered him.

"Yes," Othin said loudly, his amber eyes snapping back to Dimitri. "You *are* Analia's friend. You've spent some time in this kingdom. Tell me, who do *you* think would help free the imprisoned Ash Royals?"

"There was a prison break?" Dimitri asked, feigning surprise. "That's embarrassing."

"Dimitri," Othin hissed.

Rayner bumped Dimitri's knee under the table with his own, the warning clear enough. But Dimitri couldn't help himself when it came to Othin.

He wanted to humiliate him. Make him squirm. Make him feel even a fraction of the despair he'd subjected Dimitri to.

But in order to do that, he needed to stay in this castle. Which meant he needed to get this question right.

Dimitri threw up his hands, then slumped back in his seat as if begrudgingly considering the question. But lucky for him, Rois had told him everything he needed to know.

Keeping his gaze from Aeley, Dimitri finally shrugged. "I don't know, Ember?"

"Ember."

The sharpness in Othin's tone had Dimitri's face twitch. "Yes," he said. "She's some healer apprentice who's friends with Analia and Cadmus. Seems like she would hate you."

"Interesting." Othin turned to prowl about the room, Dimitri anxiously twisting his hands in his lap.

Had Aeley gone back on her word to Ember? Had she not—

"Your story checks out, Aeley," Othin said, stopping uncomfortably close to the queen. "That's either incredibly fortunate or *unfortunate,* seeing as you were the one who convinced me to bring her here."

"If you're trying to make a threat, Othin," Aeley said dryly, "you should know it lands far better if you're overt."

Dimitri cackled, Othin's knuckles turning white around the back of a nearby chair.

"So," Othin said, struggling for calm, "this is all because of you."

"Of course it is." Aeley stepped around him, perfectly cool as she headed for the painting of Mt. Vasolus on the wall. "Did you honestly believe I would turn my back on my son? Work with the kingdom responsible for killing my daughter?"

"And you think Cadmus will be able to stay hidden forever?"

"I think he knows this kingdom better than you do." Aeley turned back to face Othin, her gaze terrifyingly cold. "I might not be able to get my justice, *Lucilla's justice,* with Deardryn hiding in the Moon Kingdom. But I can get to her through you. And there is nothing you can do about it."

Othin's flush deepened, but Aeley didn't give him time to retort.

"There is nothing you can do to me, Othin. You already announced to the kingdom that I'm your endorser. If I end up dead around the time Cadmus has escaped, there's no way you'll be able to spin it as a coincidence. And my death will not only be fuel to the rebellion already brewing in the streets, but you'll have given Cadmus the ultimate reason to fight until your entire kingdom has burned to the ground."

"You silly girl," Othin said, his voice low, condescending. "You think death is the worst thing that can happen—"

Aeley's hand snapped out, her fingers latching onto his wrist.

"My kingdom may be fueled by fire," she said, horrifically soft, "but my magic is ice. Ice so cold I can make your hand unsalvageable from frostbite. I can freeze the blood in your veins until your extremities turn black. I can make your heart so cold, so slow, that it stops all together.

"That is what will happen to you or any of your men that try to lay a finger on me. *That* is a threat."

Aeley maintained her grip a moment longer, Othin's hand turning blue as he tried to yank free. Finally, she dropped his hand. Then, not sparing him a glance, she swept from the chamber, the door thudding shut behind her.

For a few moments, no one spoke. Dimitri and Rayner swapped a look, Dimitri suddenly grateful Aeley was on their side. Othin, meanwhile, shook out his hand, his chest heaving.

It wasn't the first time Dimitri had seen his father riled up before. If anything, that was his most familiar state. But there was something about the way his magic flickered across his skin, his fists coiling and uncoiling, that had Dimitri wondering if he wasn't *just* furious this time.

The thought had barely formed when Othin finally caught his breath. He slowly turned to face Dimitri, Dimitri feeling Rayner tense beside him. But it was with a re-markable calm that Othin asked, "What are you doing here?"

Dimitri's stomach rolled. Yes, he definitely had to play this delicately.

"I'm here," he said, resting his elbows on the table, "because I have nowhere left to go. I can't go home to Sun. Deardryn's captured Analia. The Moon Kingdom isn't safe for me anymore."

"So," Othin said, "you came here. An escaped prisoner of my wife."

"Did I mention I have nowhere else to go?"

Othin made a face as if tasting something unsavory. "And I'm supposed to believe it's a coincidence you show up two days after the Royals escaped?"

"I either have the shittiest timing, or the fewest fucks to give," Dimitri agreed.

Rayner coughed into his fist. But Othin snorted.

"So," he said, taking the seat across from Dimitri, "you came here, expecting me to trust you."

"Of course not," Dimitri scoffed. "And I don't exactly trust you either. But you're all I have left."

Othin looked momentarily taken aback, just as Dimitri had hoped.

"You say you've always been looking out for me," he said, meeting Othin's gaze. "That you've been trying to protect me. So, prove it. Don't let her hurt me. *Help* me."

Othin's face twisted. He stared down at the table as if its cracks held all the answers, Dimitri struggling to keep his breathing even.

He'd hoped that the opportunity alone would be enough—everything Othin had ever told him suggested it would be. But he'd forgotten how contrary his actions had been.

Beside him, Rayner shifted in his seat, his mouth pressed into a line. Something about that look had a warm pulse flutter deep in Dimitri's gut.

Not just his magic, but his trump card. There was nothing Othin could do if Dimitri threatened to reveal who he was. There would be no recovering from that kind of blow when his grip on the kingdom, his soldiers, was already so tenuous.

Dimitri looked down at his hands. Hands that had glowed as he pressed them to Patryclas's chest, to Ember's back.

"You saved me once," he said suddenly. "Back in Pryanth's chambers. You told me to run. One single time, you chose me over Pryanth. That's all I'm asking. *Choose* me."

Dimitri hadn't expected his voice to shake on the final words. Nor had he expected Othin's expression to crumble.

He rose to his feet, turning his back on Dimitri as he said, "I can't tell you anything. You're still a security risk."

A tiny, fragile part of Dimitri ached to make a scathing remark. Yet, all he could force out was, "Works for me."

Othin's shoulders shook, with a breath or a sob, Dimitri couldn't tell. But he was perfectly composed as he turned back to Dimitri and called for Joshel, telling him to take them to the guest wing.

With that, Dimitri was in. There were no questions as Joshel retrieved them and silently escorted them to their chambers. There was just Rayner's voice as he sat on one of the two beds.

"You didn't threaten him."

"No," Dimitri said, sitting on his own bed. "If we're going to take him down, we're not doing it their way. We're doing it my way."

Rayner nodded. But Dimitri caught that same look of wanting to say more as he turned away.

Chapter 37

All Ember felt was pain. Not the prick of a thorn. Not the ache of a bruise.

Pain. The kind of pain that snarled through her blood, stomped along her bones, radiated out from her spine until no part of her was spared.

She. Was. In. Pain.

"Sofika, what's going on?"

The voice faded in and out of the roaring in Ember's ears.

"Your Majesty, she's human. You're not used to seeing how slow and excruciating it is to heal without a Blessing. This is all to be expected."

Slow. Excruciating. Pain.

"What aren't you telling me?"

That she was in pain. And she was going to die.

Ember didn't expect the sudden relief that flooded over her. But it diluted the screaming, just enough to realize there was a hand holding hers.

But just as quickly, the pain was back, dragging her under once more with a long, agonized shriek.

Rosala spare her, she needed it to stop. Let it come to an end.

But how could it, when she no longer knew where she ended and the pain began? A pain that threw back its head and wailed as if mortally wounded, neglected. *If I suffer, you suffer.*

Gods, she needed devinroot. But she didn't have any. She didn't know when she would have any. There was nothing. Nothing, nothing, nothing, nothing.

Ember didn't register the burn in her throat. But there was no mistaking the acidic taste of bile as she lurched to the side, her stomach heaving. For a second. For eternity.

She didn't know when the cool rim of a basin materialized against her jaw. Nor the hands that pulled back her hair. The soft, murmured assurances as she eventually eased back, sending the pain burrowing into her chest.

She'd never had that. Not for long, anyway. There were just the images that flickered across the darkness in her mind.

Her mother's back as she walked away, leaving her at the Healer Temple. Accalon's chamber door, everyone screaming. Lucilla's body awkwardly draped over a funeral pyre. An open stretch of snow in the moonlight, trying to run, Cadmus waiting at a stone door, the pain—

Ember faintly registered a choked, whimpering noise. One that sent the pain shrinking back, curling into a ball and covering its ears.

Slowly, she registered the warmth trailing down her cheeks. The voice softly hushing her. The hand still gripping hers.

It was her. The sound was her as she turned her head, burying her face in what could have been a chest or a shoulder, breathing in something spicy and faintly metallic.

"Keep going," he whispered in her ear. "You're almost on the other side."

Ember didn't know what that meant. But the thought washed away as the darkness pulled her under once more.

Then, there was silence. A long, uninterrupted silence. A silence she wished could go on forever.

But eventually, she became aware of the pillow beneath her head. The cold, fresh air in her nose.

She flexed her muscles, a stiff ache moving from her toes to her neck. But everything seemed to be intact. And finally, Ember opened her eyes.

She lay in a modest bedroom. Dark wood paneling lined the walls, matching the furniture accented with silver detailing. Thick midnight-blue curtains blocked most of the light from the window to her right, the ends fluttering as a cool breeze moved through the room.

And the cravings struck.

They hit her like a long, drawn-out wail, Ember hunching forward as she gagged. She hurriedly reached for her pockets, fingers fumbling for fuzzy leaves. But she wasn't wearing her robes.

She pulled at the fabric against her torso, needing several seconds to realize she was dressed in an unfamiliar, lightweight shirt. Same with her pants.

She fumbled for her wrist, her breaths coming faster as she found her enka bracelet, a single charm pressing against her palm. Because she'd given the other to Cadmus. All of that night had been real. Which meant she was in Aaron's house.

And she had no devinroot.

Ember didn't think. She swung her legs out of bed, catching herself on the nearby wooden chair as her knees buckled. But she kept moving, coming to push back the curtains, her eyes darting across the view through the partially open window.

Snow. A wooden fence. Tall, sleek buildings in the distance. And a garden directly below.

Ember pressed her face to the glass, squinting against the afternoon light. Red roses, pink lotus flowers, too many more to count. All undoubtedly preserved by Aaron's nymph friend—and yes, those were enka flowers. Which meant she had plants that grew off magic. There didn't appear to be any fuzzy orange and yellow leaves, but if she could get a closer look...

Ember turned, gritting her teeth as the floor tilted and spun beneath her. But she made it to the door. Bracing her hand against the wall, she stumbled down the hallway beyond, toward the stairs, the house quiet around her as she eased her way down.

Reaching the bottom, she found herself in an intimate sitting room. Dark, comfortable couches. A black marble fireplace. Bookcases stuffed with books and various nicknacks. Where was the exit?

Ember's eyes landed on a glass sliding door. She headed straight for it, her bones grinding together. At the last minute, she shoved her feet into a pair of pink slippers left by the door that she vaguely noted were too small for her. Then, she yanked open the door. Just to stumble to a halt.

No, this wasn't what she'd been looking at. This was a porch, a snowy yard leading into a grove of birch trees.

Ember tasted bile. She collapsed on a porch swing—thankfully protected from the snow by an overhang—and struggled to piece her thoughts together.

Clearly, this wasn't the same view from her window. But it was the same house. Which meant she had to find her way around. There was still hope.

"You know, the more I get to know you, the more I realize how similar you and Anna are."

Ember nearly jumped out of her skin as Aaron stepped through the still-open door.

"What do you mean?" she asked, struggling for casual as she leaned back against the swing.

"Well, both of you have a gift for disappearing the moment my back is turned, although Analia never escaped her sick bed. Usually, that would give you bonus points, but you forgot a jacket."

Ember let out an uneasy laugh as Aaron lifted a light green jacket for her to see.

Rosala spare her, how could she explain this? She couldn't tell him what she'd been looking for. Then again, if she was so delirious she couldn't tell the difference between a front yard and backyard, maybe her best explanation was silence.

Indeed, Aaron didn't ask any questions as he came to sit beside her, only opening the jacket and helping her into it. To her surprise, it fit perfectly, the soft, thick fabric blocking out the chill she hadn't noticed until it was gone.

Aaron looked down, the corner of his mouth twitching. "Nice shoes."

Ember's face flushed. "I would have thought you'd be thrilled to see them, seeing as the more I get to know you, the more I realize what a fusser you are."

Aaron made an indignant noise, his hand dramatically going to his chest. Ember tried for a smile, but her withdrawal grabbed her insides and twisted.

She looked away, tugging on the sleeve of her jacket. "I assume this is borrowed, too?"

"Actually, it's yours. As soon as you were stable, Surce came to your room to get your measurements, and has been compiling a wardrobe for you ever since. She thought a green jacket would be comforting after the shock of my kingdom, and then your robes…"

Aaron trailed off, his gaze dropping to his hands. Ember's mind lagged behind, her reactions hitting her in quick succession. Touched by this woman's kindness; uneasy as to how long she'd had to compile; shock at the mention of a *kingdom*.

But none of that mattered as his final words registered.

"My robes?" Ember whipped toward him, her body buzzing. "Where are my robes?"

She'd stored the last of her devinroot in its pockets. It didn't matter what Aaron's nymph friend grew when she had those scraps, she could work with that.

Aaron leaned away, Ember only just realizing her intensity. And she was positively gutted as he said, "Ember, I'm sorry."

Ember barely heard Aaron explain how he'd had to cut her out of her robes. How they were already tattered and covered in blood. How Surce had tried to mend them, but there wasn't much left to do so. All she knew was the horrible, soul-crushing devastation that slammed into her.

"Ember, I'm sorry," Aaron repeated, looking genuinely remorseful as he touched her arm. "I know how important those robes are to you, what they mean."

"It's all right," she said tightly, her stomach heaving like she was going to be sick.

Aaron's expression fell. Ember looked away, anxiously rubbing her fingertips together in her lap.

She needed a new plan. If this was an entire Rosala-forsaken kingdom, then there had to be a devinroot plant somewhere. She just needed to figure out how to get rid of Aaron long enough to track it down—

"How are you feeling?" he asked tentatively.

All at once, Ember felt like the worst person in the world.

She dragged her gaze back to him, her withdrawal shrinking back as she rasped, "Like I've been slashed to pieces."

"Good news. That's how you're supposed to be feeling."

Aaron tried for a smile, but all Ember could see were the shadows smudged beneath his eyes, the pale pallor of his face. Only then did she realize it had been him. He was the one who had sat with her. Who had taken care of her for...

"How long was I out?" she asked, dreading the answer.

"Three days."

Ember's shoulders slumped, even her withdrawal crushed under her rush of shame. "And you stayed through it all. You held my hand, even though you didn't have to—"

"What do you mean, 'have to'?" Aaron asked, as if she'd suggested she could live without air. "You're my friend. I wasn't going to leave you like that. Beyond that..."

Aaron bit the inside of his cheek, clearly deliberating something. "Everyone in my family has died alone," he finally murmured. "And even though Sofika reassured me you would be fine, I was going to be there. Just in case."

Ember's heart ripped in half. Here was a man who had sat with her during her worst moments, had come to check on her afterward, and she was scheming to get rid of him. How had she become this person?

"That must have been a lot for you," she said, her voice small.

"Oh, you scared me shitless," Aaron agreed. "But Sofika was right. And now, here we are."

Aaron gestured to his surroundings as if displaying a grand treasure. But Ember didn't miss how his grin didn't reach his eyes.

The gnawing in her bones grew more insistent, but Ember did her best to tune it out.

"So," she said, easing back against the swing. "What do we do now that we're here?"

"Well," he said, "first, I'm going to harass you into going back inside because I am, as you say, a fusser."

Ember laughed slightly.

"Then," Aaron said, his own smile growing, "we're going to do what's become tradition around here whenever we have a guest. Family dinner."

"In that case," Ember said, "you better prepare me for what's to come. And what was that about a *kingdom?*"

Aaron finally flashed a genuine grin. As he started to fill her in, Ember pushed her withdrawal down as far as it would go.

And she hated how that wasn't far at all.

Ember wandered into the kitchen later that evening, her bones aching as she followed the smell of meat and spices. She'd expected to find Aaron inside. Instead, she jerked back at the sight of a lean man with golden-brown hair tending a pot on the stove.

"Sorry," he said, quickly turning to her. "You must have been expecting Aaron."

"Something like that." Ember braced herself against the counter with a shaky hand, her eyes moving over him.

He was handsome, in an ordinary kind of way: his nose straight, a scattering of freckles across his right cheekbone, his eyes shifting between shades of soft greens and golds in the light. There was something reassuring about his smile, as if he'd already read the situation and knew not to make any sudden moves.

The man's eyebrows twitched up. Realizing she'd been staring again, Ember introduced herself, the man thankfully not missing a beat as he told her his name was Mor.

"So," she said, inching closer. "Does Aaron know you've infiltrated his kitchen?"

"It's hardly an infiltration when he begged me to do so."

Ember's lips twitched. "Well, it smells like you know what you're doing."

"Here." Mor fished a spoon from a drawer and lifted the lid on his pot, revealing a chicken and vegetable soup. He dipped the spoon in the broth and passed it to her, Ember's magic perking up as his golden fingers brushed hers. And the rest of her lit up as she tasted the warm, seasoned broth.

She looked at Mor. Over to the pot. Back to Mor.

"So," she said, leaning against the counter beside him. "You cook here often?"

Mor laughed, his hand going to the back of his neck. "I take it you approve."

"Rosala spare me, he's humble, too."

Mor flushed and ducked his head, but Ember caught the sparkle in his eyes. "I see why you and Aaron get along."

"Guilty." Ember moved to take a stool at the island, quietly unsettled by her wave of relief as she sat. But she brushed the thought aside. "Your hand is beautiful, by the way."

Mor tossed a startled, yet delighted look over his shoulder. "That's not a usual first reaction I get."

"No," Ember agreed. "I assume you're used to people looking away."

"Or for too long." Mor's voice grew thoughtful as he retrieved a ladle from a nearby drawer. "I assume as a healer you see that quite often."

"More than you know," Ember muttered. Mor cast her a curious look over his shoulder, but Ember quickly went on. "The Ash Kingdom has created some stunning prosthetics thanks to our forges. But I've never sensed one so perfectly integrated with a person's magic network. Is the healer who made it still in this kingdom?"

"Actually," Mor said, "he was the exiled Moon healer Aaron and Analia met in Sun."

"Really?" Ember leaned forward. "How did *that* happen?"

"I'm not sure. I was in my early twenties when Aaron's grandmother brought him in. It's been so long at this point that all I really remember is how long it took."

"And despite all that time, it's still in excellent condition." Ember shook her head, thoroughly impressed. "I'd love to learn from someone like that."

Mor started to respond, but he broke off as the kitchen door swung open. Aaron and what had to be the rest of his family piled inside, Ember taking in the group.

An absurdly tall man with reddish-brown hair, his nose crooked as if broken and not properly reset. A woman with long, wavy dark hair and topaz eyes, perfectly matching the detailing on her dark green gown. And a nymph with short brown hair tucked behind her delicately pointed ears.

Aaron was midsentence, his eyes absently moving around the room. Then, he froze.

Whirling on Mor, he jabbed a finger at the stove, "Why would you make *that?*"

Mor innocently twirled his ladle as he said, "Because it's cold out, Ember's still recovering, and it makes enough that you and Branten won't starve while I'm with the humans."

"What's wrong with soup?" Ember asked.

"What's wrong," Aaron said, "is every time Mor makes it, we have to listen to Laness and Branten debate whether it's a food or a drink."

"It's a food!" Laness exclaimed, hands on her hips as she turned to Branten beside her.

"Then why can you drink it?" he retorted.

Laness looked like she was losing the last shreds of her sanity.

"The best part," Surce said to Ember, "is Branten knows it's a food. He just likes to see how far he can push her."

"And Mor's enabling him," Aaron said, coming to sit beside Ember with a huff.

Mor turned away, but Ember caught his smile as he reached for bowls.

Enabling or not, Ember quickly realized it was a perfect representation of what their meal would entail. Aaron, Branten, and Mor told her about how they met, featuring numerous tangents and playful jabs. Surce then told Ember about her tapestries, which gave Ember an opening to thank her for all the clothes. Surce smiled, her almond-shaped eyes crinkling.

Finally, Ember filled them in on everything that had happened in the Ash Kingdom, Aaron frowning as she mentioned the creature in the volcano and Cadmus's mark. Laness, however, jumped in to let her know everyone was fine, which eased some of the weight on Ember's shoulders.

"If I'm going to be staying here for a while," she said, "I'd love to speak with your healers. Find something to do."

"Of course," Aaron said. "As soon as you're healed."

"Fusser," Laness said under her breath.

Aaron flicked a piece of bread at her. But Ember had been expecting this.

"Aaron, I've already been up and about today. I'm fine."

Aaron started to respond, just to catch Branten and Laness grinning at him from the corner of his eye. He flicked pieces of bread at both of them, Branten catching his and popping it in his mouth.

Turning back to Ember, he said, "A week."

"Tomorrow," Ember deadpanned.

Branten chortled, "I like her."

Aaron reached for his bread, but Mor waved him off and thumped Branten on the head instead. Branten leaned away with a noise of protest, and Ember's lips twitched.

Fighting back his own smile, Aaron rested his chin in his hand as he considered. "Three mornings from now," he decided. "And you take it easy until then."

Ember sighed dramatically, her withdrawal roaring for her to do much more than that. But Aaron gave her a slow, feline smile that told her that was the best he was going to offer.

"Fine," Ember muttered, turning back to her soup with a pout.

She wasn't about to push her luck. Not when they'd had such a good dinner. Not when everyone seemed to have genuinely enjoyed her company as they eventually bid her farewell and headed off, leaving her with Aaron.

Because she had been pleasant. Normal. No one suspected what she was really after.

She'd confirmed through the entryway windows there were no fuzzy orange and yellow leaves in Laness's garden. But if anyone was going to have devinroot in this kingdom, it was the healers.

And as Ember followed Aaron up the stairs, she told herself she just needed to last three more mornings.

Chapter 38

Analia's days were starting to look disconcertingly familiar. Each morning, she ate breakfast with the Royals, Deardryn whisking her back to their research as soon as Analia's plate was empty. Their process was slow going, but Analia had gotten used to the magic enough that in addition to opening the casing, Deardryn had started inching closer to her with every session. It wasn't much, but it was progress—which was more than she could say about her training with Sylas.

To Analia's surprise, he brought her back to his sitting room almost every night to work on her magic. Yet, a handful of lessons in, and Analia still hadn't summoned even a wisp of a shadow. Sylas had ended their last dream with a snort as she thrust out her hand, just for a midnight flame to fill her palm.

Definitely not her finest moment.

But that morning, she finally managed to tolerate the Crystal fully open, even with Deardryn sitting halfway across the room. The Dragoness delightedly scribbled in her notes, leaving Analia to wipe the sweat from her brow.

Seeing her opportunity, she asked if this meant she could go back to just having Tavian as her guard, and Deardryn waved her permission as if she'd forgotten about Meryk entirely.

Something about that put Analia on edge. But that didn't stop her from heading straight for the library, Tavian covering for her outside as she slipped into the nook to talk with Sabi.

"It's about time you got rid of that page folder," Sabi said, shuffling through a massive stack of papers on her desk. "I don't think I could have been friends with you if you had to write in the margin of another book."

"I *am* sorry about that," Analia said from the chair across from her. "I would have never done that if you couldn't fix it."

"It's fine, I forgive you." Sabi shot her a look that clearly said, *This time.* "In fact," she went on, "I've forgiven you so much that I have a gift."

Analia perked up as Sabi pulled a sheet from her pile with a flourish. "Is that...?"

"All of Deardryn's book orders from the past three weeks," Sabi crowed.

Analia beamed. "I knew you were clever."

"The cleverest," Sabi agreed, passing her the page. "That was some good work back in the library. I understand why Dima likes you—especially since your face is much better at hiding things than his. I have to say, though, finding all of this wasn't exactly hard. All I had to do was track down the servant retrieving her books, ask what store they came from, and then go talk to the store owners."

Sabi shrugged, and Analia fought back a wince. Definitely not the subtlest method of going about it, but there was nothing she could do about that now.

"And this is Deardryn's order history from them?" she asked.

"Starting around the same time she stopped coming to me," Sabi confirmed. "Why do you want all of this, anyway? I thought Deardryn already got the Crystal and was tormenting you with it."

"The Crystal has been separated into pieces," Analia explained, scanning the list of titles. "She'd be a fool to stop searching for the rest."

She glanced up, catching Sabi make a face as if tasting something bitter. "What?" she asked.

"Well..." Sabi tugged on one of her dark brown curls.

Analia's stomach sank. "Sabi, what?" she insisted.

"It's just the shop specializes in ancient texts... But I don't think this is what you're looking for."

Analia quickly returned her attention to the list as Sabi continued, barely taking a breath as she rattled off the titles of each book from memory. Definitely ancient texts, and definitely a magical theme. But reaching the bottom of the list, Analia blinked. Turn the page over. But the other side was blank.

"There's nothing here about magical locations," she said. "There isn't even a landmark book. They're all books on magical oaths and bargains."

"With no other discernable theme," Sabi agreed uncomfortably.

Analia could have sworn the dampers against her wrists grew warmer.

"This doesn't make sense," she muttered, rising from her chair to pace. "There's no way Deardryn isn't searching for the other shards, especially since she's already betting on me escaping and trying to take hers with me."

"She is?" Sabi asked, aghast.

Analia waved a hand, "I always assumed she would find out. When dealing with Deardryn, it's best to plan for her already knowing everything. But she didn't know the Crystal was split. I know that was shock on her face when she first saw the shard. And in response to that, she requests *these* books?"

"Maybe the clues are in the *types* of bargains she's looking at," Sabi suggested.

Analia paused. Now that she thought about it, Deardryn *had* been interested in her scar from the scarsworn dagger.

"Go on," she said, resuming her pacing.

"Well, there's no specific style of oath that she's looking at. We have everything from the limitless bargains made with our scarsworn daggers, to the highly specific healer oath apprentices make when becoming master healers. I suppose there's some commonality with all the oaths having some physical aspect, like our tattoos and scars, and the healers'"—Sabi twirled her finger around her eye. "But beyond that?"

"We don't know how that connects to the Crystal," Analia finished.

Sabi shrugged helplessly, her green eyes tracking Analia's path back and forth across the nook.

How did Deardryn do it? How did she manage to so thoroughly cover her tracks that even when Analia found a lead, she had no idea what to do with it?

"I know she knows something," Analia said, coming to reclaim her chair. "She practically confirmed it to me."

Sabi cocked her head, and Analia filled her in on her session with Deardryn from a few days prior.

It had been the first time Deardryn tried to sit closer to Analia, and she had beamed when Analia quickly adjusted. Not wanting to waste an opening, Analia had blurted, "Where did you get the scroll?"

Deardryn looked up from her notes, startled. "Why do you ask?"

"Because retrieving that scroll was the reason Aaron came to your kingdom. I was just wondering why you had it."

For a few moments, Deardryn didn't respond. She softly drummed her fingers on her open book, clearly wanting to ask more. But Analia folded her arms as the Crystal's magic hammered against her shield.

Finally, Deardryn said, "I got it many years ago." She returned her attention to her notes, her voice softening into something faraway. "I've always had a fascination with magic. My sister says it's because of my unique situation as a healer, and she may have a point. But I believe it has more to do with my relentless desire to know. How does something work? How is this possible? How do I make something happen? In that, I think we are much alike."

Deardryn looked up, almost wistful as she opened the Crystal casing a little more. Analia winced, but she quickly adjusted to the fresh wave of magic. She nodded, and Deardryn returned her attention to her notes.

"Much of my research was dedicated to studying our three major mountains: Vasolus, Raegyr, and Lanula. Most of my study had to be done from afar once I was crowned queen during the Shattering War. But after the Star Kingdom became neutral ground, I was able to visit Mt. Raegyr a handful of times. And on one of those visits, about twenty years ago, I paid a great price to retrieve it."

Analia sat patiently, waiting for Deardryn to continue. But Deardryn only turned the golden bracelets on her wrist, her gaze lost in memories.

"So?" Analia finally prompted. "What was the price?"

"Entirely not worth it."

Analia made to speak, her mind buzzing with questions. But Deardryn opened the casing even more, and all those questions were lost under a wave of magic.

Yet, now, as she retold the story to Sabi, all those questions formed an ache behind her eyes.

"Clearly," Analia said, "she didn't want to talk about it anymore. But why pay a price for a scroll whose importance she didn't know? Or, if she does know its importance, why hasn't she been trying to get it back? Why tell me all of this in the first place?"

Sabi chewed on her thumbnail, not offering any explanations.

It just didn't make sense. Deardryn thought too many steps ahead, there was no way she was waiting until Analia escaped to start hunting again. So then why—

"I'm sorry I wasn't helpful," Sabi said, her voice small.

"What?" Analia blinked hard, just for her eyes to widen as Sabi's chin trembled. "Oh, Sabi, no, why would you think that?"

"Because your face got all scrunched up, and I thought you were mad at me because Dimitri's notes have been so helpful, and then the one thing you ask me to do only resulted in more questions."

Analia's heart ached. Was that the kind of message she was giving off?

"Sabi, I'm sorry." Analia rose to her feet and circled around the desk. "You've been incredibly helpful. You found all of this information, and I know it's important. I'm just frustrated because *I* can't put it all together."

She touched Sabi's arm, Sabi neither rejecting nor leaning into her touch. She dropped her gaze to her hands, her green eyes glassy as she said, "I just want to do something. I know this is between Royals, and Dimitri's involved because it's personal to him. But she killed my uncle. She's destroying my home. I know I'm only a bookkeeper, but I can't just sit here."

Analia's lips parted, but no words came out. Because she knew that feeling. It was the same feeling that had her infiltrating the Sun Kingdom all those months ago. And she knew there was nothing she could say to make it any better.

Analia's hand automatically went to her chest, the absence of her phoenix pin having her lungs squeezing. Gods, how did it never end? She'd already had to survive the pain of Accalon's death, the loss of a piece of herself. But watching Sabi furiously fight back tears for Patryclas, the uncle she clearly adored, had the hole in Analia's chest ripping wider.

Because Analia had mourned Accalon's death. But that was nothing compared to the pain of having to mourn the death of who she thought he was. The fact that, now, she would never get to know. And the pain of her uncertainty as to whether he would show her if he was still alive.

"You're making that face again," Sabi mumbled.

Analia bit the inside of her cheek, then shoved the thoughts aside. "Once again," she said, "it has nothing to do with you."

Analia reached for Sabi, intending to pull her into a hug. But Sabi leaned away, swiping at her eyes.

"I'm fine," she said, turning back toward her books. "I just needed a moment."

Analia slowly let her hand fall back to her side, Sabi refusing to look at her as she fussed over her books. Deciding not to press it, Analia returned to her seat, swallowing the part of her that wanted to say that hug wouldn't have been just for Sabi.

"**A**nalia, are you even paying attention?" Sylas whined.

Analia blinked hard, struggling to drag her attention back to the king seated on the floor across from her. He'd insisted a few meetings ago that being on the ground—and consequently in contact with the shadows—would help her become in tune with them. Yet, so far all it did was allow her to run her fingers through the soft carpet as her mind wandered elsewhere.

"Sorry," Analia mumbled.

Sylas rolled his eyes, then flicked his fingers in what had become his "do it again" gesture. Analia automatically raised her hand, reaching for her magic. A black flame flickered across her fingers, and Analia extinguished it with a scowl.

"I don't understand," Sylas complained. "I thought you said you've done this before."

"I have, but only by accident when I'm upset."

"You mean more than you are now?"

Analia glared. Sylas slumped back against the base of his armchair, his expectant gaze trained on the ground beside Analia.

It took her a moment to look down, to realize what he'd been doing. But still, the shadow of her recliner remained perfectly still. And the faint crackle of her temper fizzled back out.

"Well, that didn't work," Sylas said.

"I noticed," Analia muttered.

"Would you at least like to explain why I have to deal with your taciturn mood tonight?"

"You mean besides the lack of shadows?" Analia rubbed her eyes. "Sabi figured out Deardryn's new line of research, but it tells us nothing about where she thinks the next Crystal shard is. And while I've figured out she's more than likely keeping her own shard in her chambers, I have no way to get in."

Analia paused, but Sylas only grunted and folded his arms. "Do you know anything about the security around her chambers?" she asked. "Could you shadowjump inside and grab it?"

"Do you really think I would entertain you in my castle, my *dreams,* for this long if I could get rid of you that easily?"

Well, he had a point there.

"Her chamber has been guarded by detection magic," he went on, slumping even more. "Nothing unusual for a visiting Royal. But it notifies her any time someone steps through her door."

"And since you can't shadowjump inside," Analia murmured, "she's extended it into the chamber itself. Which means even if a pulsepearl found its way in there..."

"You think too much like Dimitri," Sylas grumbled.

Analia smiled faintly, Dimitri's recount of his scheme in the Wraithhouse having inspired that idea. Regardless, Deardryn had the upper hand once again. And Analia had a third, unpredictable player to contend with. She stole a glance at Sylas, who paid her no mind as he picked at his nails.

"Why is Deardryn still here?" she asked.

Sylas's eyebrows shot up. He finally looked at her fully, Analia expecting him to shrug her question off. But he only flicked his fingers at her.

Obediently, Analia raised her hand, feeling herself simultaneously reach for her magic and recoil away. And once again, a grape-sized ball of midnight flames flickered to life in her palm.

Analia curled her hand into a fist, waiting for Sylas to smirk and ignore her. But to her surprise, Sylas nodded to himself.

"Deardryn has been in my kingdom on and off for four months. She's integrated herself into the community of my castle, to the point any attempt to remove her would have to be done by force. And I'm not ready for the battle that will trigger."

"Huh." Analia shifted to sit on her knees, Sylas's eyes narrowing as he watched her. "Huh, what?"

"I was only thinking for someone so appalled by the slightest inconvenience, you do seem to like making things difficult for yourself—"

Sylas snapped his fingers in Analia's face.

Analia reared back, "What was that for?"

"I was trying to wake you up faster. Is it working?"

Analia rolled her eyes. Sylas smirked as he sat back, almost an actual smile.

"So," Analia said, "what are you waiting for?"

Sylas, evidently realizing what she was doing, flicked his fingers at her once more. And neither of them was surprised when all Analia summoned was a midnight spark.

Gods, what was blocking her? She wanted to summon the shadows, she knew they were there. But every time she got close to the cavern beneath her flames, it was like she hit a mental wall.

She looked up at Sylas, finding him absently running his fingers through the carpet, shadows swirling in his wake. Effortlessly.

"Well?" she asked, a bit sharper than she meant to.

Sylas remained completely unfazed. "What makes you think I'm waiting for something?" he asked.

"The fact that Deardryn *killed* Patryclas. I've known Aaron less than a year, and if she killed him, having a plan would be the only thing keeping me from burning her alive. And you were with Patryclas for *decades.* Not to mention you're not exactly the forgiving type."

Sylas shrugged, not denying any of it.

Analia made to speak, but Sylas flicked his fingers at her. "Oh no," she said, "that's not how this works. Answering a question with a question doesn't count."

To Analia's surprise, Sylas huffed out a laugh.

"Well," he said, "at least you have one thing going for you. You think before acting. You're skeptical. But that also makes you think too much."

"What do you—"

"Summon a flame," Sylas said. He rose to his feet with a stretch, waving off Analia's confusion as he sat on his armchair.

Seeing she wasn't going to get an explanation, Analia barely had to think before a peach-sized flame appeared in her palm.

"Good," Sylas said. "Now double the size."

The flame expanded.

"Now shrink it."

Analia complied, not batting an eye as Sylas's orders came faster. Hold, release, summon, shrink, release. By the end, his words were so fast Analia barely registered them before complying. But she'd already mastered this skill with Aaron. Indeed, when Sylas finally sat back in his seat, it was with a nod of approval.

"I see Adrian has trained you well," he said.

"Aaron," Analia corrected.

"Who?"

Analia scoffed. "What was the point of that?" she asked, rising and reclaiming her seat on her recliner.

"The point," Sylas said, "is you were able to do all of that on instinct alone. As easy as breathing. That's how it should be summoning my shadows. But you keep thinking."

A tendril of shadows flicked up from the carpet at Analia's feet and thumped her temple. Analia jerked away from the icy touch, "What are you—"

"Your thoughts are paralyzing, Analia," Sylas said, the shadows around the room beginning to churn. "Stop *thinking* about summoning my shadows and *do* it."

Analia opened her mouth to protest. But Sylas snapped his fingers, and the dream dissolved into darkness.

Analia's eyes shot open. She looked around her dark chamber, her damper cuff scraping against her cheek as she pushed the hair from her face.

That was it? That was all he had to say to help her: *stop thinking.*

And then he kicked her out of their dream, leaving her to do nothing *but* think about what he said. Was it another test?

Once, the thought would have had her fleeing for the turret roof. More recently, it would have had her flames seething. But now, her temper settled into a low, steady burn.

She knew how this worked. She was already playing Deardryn's game, Talitha's game, even her own game. Sylas was just one more player.

Analia rolled onto her side, determined not to let Sylas get the better of her. Still, she couldn't deny how her blaze briefly guttered as her eyes landed on her vanity drawer. Reminding her of the game she'd never realized she'd been playing.

Chapter 39

Ember didn't know how she survived the two days Aaron made her wait to see the healers. Her mind scattered in a thousand different directions, unable to focus on anything outside of the withdrawal twisting her insides, whispering plan after plan of how she could find devinroot on her own.

She wanted to cry. She wanted to scream.

But she forced herself to be good. Follow all of Aaron's rules.

She was tempted to point out her compliance as she hurried into the dining room on her third morning, Aaron already seated at the table. But she remained quiet, instead focusing on keeping down each spoonful of sticky, berry-sweetened porridge.

A part of her noted how Aaron merely moved his own food around his bowl, shadows smudged beneath his eyes. But the thought slipped away as he rose to his feet, his easy smile in place as he asked if she was ready. And Ember could have cried with relief as he pulled her into the darkness.

Within moments, the shadows peeled away, Ember expecting to find the familiar dark stone halls and archways of the Healer School. Instead, she stood in what appeared to be a sizable sitting room.

The floor was made from a light, polished wood, the majority covered by a colorful rug in shades of light blues, pinks, purples, and greens. Side tables filled with books and plants sat in between a cluster of couches, the long, low table before them covered in a half-completed puzzle. And surrounding it all were massive windows that looked out over a grassy hillside, a handful of stained-glass butterflies and mushrooms hanging from the curtain rods.

"Where are we?" Ember asked, her withdrawal grumbling through her blood.

Had Aaron lied to her? Was this not the Healer School? What was he up to?

"This is the Starlight Kingdom's Healer Center."

"Healer *Center?*"

Aaron chuckled at her obvious confusion.

"Come on," he said, releasing her hand and heading for the door at the back of the room. "Sofika should be around here somewhere. With anyone else, I would have jumped us straight to their study, but Sofika has informed me even kings must use the front door."

Aaron winked over his shoulder, and it took Ember half a beat to remember she should smile.

She couldn't raise his suspicions now. This Healer Center might *look* nothing like what she was expecting, but its nature was the same. Which meant there was still hope. And ignoring her withdrawal's impatient stretch, she hurried after Aaron.

Aaron led her down a long, brightly lit hallway, ajar doors on either side revealing unoccupied patient rooms. Ember's shoulders relaxed slightly as she breathed in the familiar, tangy scent of herbal disinfecting paste. But why were the walls painted to look like a sunny sky? And where was everyone else?

Back in the Ash Kingdom Healer School, the halls were always filled by apprentices heading to lessons, master healers checking on patients, family members of the unwell coming to visit. But this patient wing was almost deserted. Aaron ended up having to ask a random woman they passed where Sofika was, her long black hair falling over her shoulders in intricate braids.

"She's in room sixteen," the woman said, gesturing around the corner with a dark brown hand. "You actually have perfect timing. I have to attend to something, and I'm sure her patient will be thrilled to see you."

Aaron perked up. Thanking her, he continued down the hall, Ember hurrying to catch up.

"Who was that?" she whispered.

"That was Evena. She and Branten co-own the orphan program Branten mentioned at dinner."

Interesting. Ember started to respond, but they'd already reached the door marked "16." Aaron gave a quick knock, a clipped female voice calling for them to enter.

"Sorry to interrupt," he said, poking his head inside. "But Sofika, I brought—oh, it's you!"

Aaron pushed all the way inside as there came a small, delighted reply. Ember scurried after him, her hand reflexively going to her nose.

The patient room followed a similar motif to the rest of the building: a window looking out over the hillside, a large plant in the corner, the blue walls now including blossoming treetops. In the center of the room, two healers in emerald robes tended to a little boy with copper curls, his feet dangling over the edge of a lofted cot. As soon as the boy spotted Aaron, his face lit up.

"What are you doing here, Brookston?" Aaron asked, coming to sit beside him and ruffling his hair.

"I falled," he said, not seeming particularly perturbed by this.

"Oh really? Off of what?"

"A fountain."

"I see. Did you happen to be standing on said fountain's rim?"

Brookston giggled, trying to hide his grin with his hands. The healer on the left—a short, older woman with sharp features and light brown skin—gently pulled his hand back toward her, the scrapes along his palm only partially covered in green antiseptic paste.

"Your timing is impeccable as always, Your Majesty," she said dryly. The healer beside her, a man a few years older than Ember with warm, dark brown skin and eyes, stifled a laugh.

Aaron, meanwhile, flashed a dazzling smile. "I wouldn't be such a pain if you weren't the best healer in my kingdom, Sofika."

Ember straightened at the name.

"You should know by now flattery gets you nowhere," Sofika said, screwing the lid shut on her jar of paste.

"Ah, but what about a gift?"

Aaron gestured with a flourish toward the door where Ember lingered, both healers shifting in their chairs to see. And a jolt ran down Ember's spine.

"Sofika," Aaron said, "you remember Ember. Ember, this is Sofika, her apprentice Cenn, and *this*"—he playfully poked the little boy's side—"is one of Branten's little warriors, Brookston."

Brookston's blue eyes brightened as he noticed her. Pulling his hand free from Cenn's grip, he gave an enthusiastic wave, Cenn's lips twitching as he gently reclaimed Brookston's hand.

Ember struggled not to stare at the unmarred skin around his and Sofika's eyes.

"Yes, Ember." Sofika tasted her name like a foreign cuisine. "I was wondering when I'd be seeing you."

Before Ember could scramble for a response, she turned her attention back to Brookston.

"All right, Brookston. Now that we've cleaned all of your cuts, it's time for me to heal them. It will sting for a couple moments, but then you'll be good as new. Would you prefer we start with the deeper cuts on your knees or the scrapes on your palms?"

Brookston looked at Aaron, who gave an encouraging nod. "Knees, please."

"Excellent. Now, I'll touch your left knee, right below the gash, and here comes the sting…"

Brookston screwed up his face as Sofika started to mend his skin, his eyes growing wider, wider, wider. Aaron reached for him, but Cenn had already placed a hand on Brookston's thigh, giving a squeeze.

"All right, little warrior," he said. "You're doing so well. It will be over in three, two, one…"

Brookston relaxed as Sofika pulled her hand back, the green paste on his knee wiped away to reveal new, pink skin.

"Well done," Sofika enthused, smiling up at Brookston. "What do you think, Cenn? Have we ever had a patient hold so still before?"

"Definitely not."

Brookston puffed out his chest, Aaron leaning in to whisper something in his ear that had him dissolving into giggles. But as Sofika dipped her chin to Cenn, Ember knew that initial compliment had been for him, too—and rightfully so.

Ember had lost track of how many apprentices she'd seen excel with adult patients, just to fall to shambles when dealing with children. But Cenn handled it perfectly. Impressive.

"All right, Brookston," Sofika said, "same story for your other knee. Are you ready?"

Brookston nodded, nestling into Aaron's side. Sofika reached for him, her eyes flicking to Ember at the door. "You wished to speak with me?"

Ember startled, having momentarily forgotten why she was there. Shoving down the whine of her withdrawal, she only missed a beat as she dredged up the speech she'd prepared.

"I did," she said. "And since you said you've been wondering when you'd see me, that means you've figured out I'm a healer apprentice."

"The tattered robes and rings around your eyes were strong indicators," Sofika said vaguely.

So, they knew about healer markings here.

"Exactly. And my markings are proof that I'm an advanced apprentice. I've mastered herbology, external healing, and medical mysteries, and I'm confident in my internal healing abilities. Yet, I know there's still so much to learn. Aaron says if I want to excel as a healer, *you're* the person to go to. So, I would be honored if you allowed me to prove I'm not just worthy of your time, but that I can also be an asset to the people in this kingdom."

Ember clasped her hands before her, thinking she'd done pretty well. Sofika, however, didn't respond immediately. She kept her attention on Brookston's knee, finally wiping away the excess paste to reveal another flawless healing. Brookston's face had gone pale, but he bounced back quickly as Aaron and Cenn consoled him. And no one paid Ember any mind.

But she knew this game. Sofika was testing her patience, her interpersonal skills. She might be talented at healing, but as Cenn had proven, that wasn't all there was to being a healer.

So, Ember remained silent. Patient. Kept her body language relaxed and open.

Finally, Sofika turned back to her, giving her a long, scrutinizing look.

"Cenn will show you around our center," she decided. "You two can make poultices for the rest of the day. Depending on what you present me, I'll decide if you'll come back tomorrow."

Aaron flashed Ember a congratulatory grin. Her withdrawal roared its delight. But something about Sofika's phrasing had her skin prickle as Cenn rose from his seat, bidding the room farewell as he came to join her at the door.

Cenn led the way through the quiet Healer Center, Ember vaguely aware of his running commentary as she scanned for devinroot.

Apparently, the reason everything was so unfamiliar was Sofika. She had been wholly unimpressed by the dreary stone temple the healers had been thrust into after the Shattering. She'd also noticed a decline in patient recovery.

"Sofika then started her own studies," Cenn explained, Ember's eye twitching at the informality. "She found that a patient's environment plays a critical role in recovery. Everything from colors, to plants in patient rooms, to the view through their windows proved to impact morale, which then improved their healing experience. Even the way we talk to patients can have an impact."

Cenn beamed as he pushed through a door, the bright patient wing replaced by a warmly lit hallway, the carpet speckled with shades of gray and green. He looked over at her, clearly expecting her to join in his enthusiasm—which she normally would have. But all she could focus on was the concurrent familiarity and differences grating against her nerves.

Cenn's expression dimmed. Ember rushed to assure him his story was fascinating, his answering smile not quite convincing. Before Ember could panic that he knew something was off, Cenn pushed through the door at the end of the hall. And every fiber of Ember's being lit up.

The door led to a massive greenhouse. The first floor had been turned into a workspace, featuring tall shelves of various gardening and healer supplies, long worktables arranged in front of them. And above was row after row of lush green foliage.

Ember took a deep breath through her nose, the warm, humid air smelling of soil and growing things. This was home. And those were fuzzy orange and yellow leaves on the second floor to the left.

"Welcome to the greenhouse." Cenn descended the few steps to the first floor and turned to Ember, spreading his arms wide.

"It's beautiful," she breathed, completely genuine for the first time in she couldn't remember how long.

Cenn beamed. "This is my favorite spot in the center," he said, heading for one of the shelves. "We not only grow everything needed to make our supplies, but also the plants for our patient rooms. Laness, one of His Majesty's friends, helped us put it together, and she and a group of nymphs help us maintain it all."

"We have a similar setup back in the Ash Kingdom," Ember said, reaching up to stroke a trailing leaf as she stepped inside. "Although ours isn't usually so quiet."

"The internal, external, and mystery apprentices all have their own preferred areas to study. I don't mind, though. I'd rather have a quiet place to work, even if it means only having Sofika to help me."

"Are you saying you're the only herbology apprentice in the kingdom?"

"I am." Cenn grabbed a mortar and pestle from the shelf. "I think that's partially why Sofika assigned me to you today. She's not just testing your abilities, but also, if there's anything you can teach *me*. Speaking of which..." Cenn plopped his supplies down at one of the tables and sat, folding his large hands as he looked up at her. "Where shall we begin, master apprentice?"

Ember laughed slightly as she rubbed her nose, her mind racing. Having an apprentice lingering around her was not ideal. But if helping him was how she could get in with Sofika...

"All right," she said, forcing herself not to stare at the devinroot as she approached his table. "I won't insult you by starting off with the basics. Have you learned how to make a blood clotting enhancer?"

"Not officially."

Something about the twinkle in his eyes had Ember wondering if he was more like her than she'd realized.

"In that case," she said, grabbing a few indigo stalks from the pot nearby, "you slice these stems, I'll collect everything else."

Passing Cenn the stalks, she headed for the stairs, barely hearing Cenn calling directions to each plant over the buzz in her veins. It was time. Her devinroot was here.

Finally, she would be able to focus. Feel emotionally stable. She could *finally* like who she was again.

Ember collected her supplies, slowly circling closer to the cluster of devinroots.

Four rows away. Three. Two...

Ember's withdrawal screamed for life as she inched toward the final row.

Yet, as she adjusted her bundle of plants, devinroot within reach, she hesitated.

Cenn was still here. And he was too sharp not to notice her shift.

Ember bit her lip, her withdrawal screaming for her to take the risk, it was worth it. But getting caught now meant never being able to come back for more. It meant everyone finding out. It meant within hours, she would be dying.

Ember tightened her grip on her plants. Then, feeling as though she was ripping in half, she turned. And she didn't know how she resisted the long, drawn-out wail of her withdrawal as she headed back downstairs.

Ember spent the rest of the afternoon walking Cenn through various poultices. He proved to be an attentive student, watching every move she made, a tiny line forming between his brows as he carefully copied her techniques. Most of it he seemed familiar with. Yet, even when Ember made corrections, he adapted impressively fast.

By the time Sofika wandered through the greenhouse door, the sun had started to set, and Ember could barely think around the fuzzy leaves nearby.

"Well then," Sofika said, twisting her shiny black hair into a knot atop her head. "Let's see what you two have produced."

Ember and Cenn watched expectantly as Sofika reached for one of their many jars and vials. Screwing off the lid, she sniffed its contents, the thin green oil sloshing as she tilted the jar this way and that. Then, without even a flicker of acknowledgement, she replaced the jar on the table and reached for the next.

With every concoction she studied, Cenn's grip on the edge of the table grew tighter, his body practically vibrating with anticipation. But Ember sat quietly and waited.

Finally, Sofika put down the last jar of deep blue paste, giving the two a nod. "Excellent work."

Cenn's entire body straightened at the praise. Even Ember perked up.

Sofika rattled off a list of instructions for Cenn to take care of the following day, Cenn thanking her again and mouthing "We did it!" to Ember before exiting the greenhouse. Then, Ember was left alone with Sofika.

"So," Sofika said, perching on a nearby table. "How's your withdrawal?"

Ember felt as though she'd been smacked between the eyes. She recoiled in her seat, stammering, "My *what?*"

"Your withdrawal," Sofika said patiently. "You must be what, seven days clean? I'm impressed you're already on your feet, let alone concocting such advanced—"

"I'm sorry," Ember interrupted, "I don't know how we reached that conclusion."

"Because I was the one who healed you." Sofika crossed her legs, the casualness sending heat flashing across Ember's skin. "I already had my suspicions based on how raw your nose is and how depleted your body's resources were when recovering. But based on how frequently your eyes wandered to my devinroots while I examined your creations, it seems to have dug its nasty little claws into you deeper than I thought."

Ember couldn't breathe. She wanted to hide, she wanted to snap back, she wanted to *explode.*

Sofika leveled her with the same steady, open look Ember had given countless addicts throughout her career. And she could barely hear Sofika's words over the screaming in her ears.

"I didn't tell His Majesty anything I saw. Fortunately, he's unfamiliar with what human healing and withdrawal look like, so your anonymity should be intact. I would highly recommend telling him, though."

"There's nothing to tell," Ember ground out, gripping her hands beneath the table painfully tight.

"I see." Sofika nodded to herself. Then, she straightened her posture, brisk once more as she said, "Based on your work today, you're one of the brightest apprentices that has walked into my center. It would be my honor to continue your training. But I require all of my apprentices to be sober."

The word hit her like a blow to the chest. A word that had once meant nothing to her, but now—no, it still meant nothing. It couldn't mean something. She was too careful for it to mean something.

Ember forced her muscles to relax, breathing in the earthy air. And her voice was almost calm as she said, "That won't be a problem."

"Good. Because your career depends on it." Rising to her feet, Sofika headed for the door, calling over her shoulder, "We start tomorrow."

Then, with a nod of farewell, she exited the greenhouse, leaving Ember alone. With the devinroots.

Ember's withdrawal screamed for her to run, fast as she could. But the final intact piece of herself recognized Sofika's move for what it was. A challenge. The same challenge she'd been given the moment she discovered her specialty: *Prove yourself.*

Ember stomped down hard on her withdrawal. Then, she rose to her feet and marched toward the door, determined to prove Sofika wrong. Even as her withdrawal seethed it was only a matter of time.

Chapter 40

Aaron walked through his snowy kingdom streets, having just shadowjumped Brookston and a newly arrived Evena back to Nova House. He'd been reluctant to leave Ember on her own, Sofika clearly noticing as she finished Brookston's healing.

"Don't worry, Your Majesty," she said briskly. "She'll do great."

He didn't doubt that. But that wasn't what he was worried about.

He hadn't needed Rois's passed-along request to keep an eye on Ember to know something was off.

It went beyond the faint waxy hue of her skin, the way she subtly braced herself against counters and chairs. It was the way her once endearingly brazen nature had sharpened. Not overtly. Just enough that he felt like he needed to watch his step with every interaction. Hopefully, being with the healers would help with whatever was going on—especially since he was certain Sofika knew something.

Aaron rubbed his face as he turned the corner, the wind ruffling his hair. He knew he could have shadowjumped to the library in the heart of the Pulse and spared himself from the cold. But there had always been something comforting to him about walking through his kingdom: seeing the flourishing businesses, his people talking and laughing, all of their statues and fountains and creations.

Somehow, after everything his people had been through with the Shattering and the Starlight War with the humans, they hadn't crumbled. They'd thrived. They'd found a way to still look to the future and hope.

It was a magic he'd sworn to himself to protect the day Ethelind gave him his crown, and until recently, he'd felt good about the decisions he'd made to do so. But lately, he'd found himself not only dwelling on Analia during his nightly visits to his mother's room, but the imminent future of his kingdom. Wondering how his people would continue to hope if they knew the potential war that loomed over them. A war that left Aaron feeling cornered.

Aaron dragged a hand through his hair, banishing the thoughts as he stepped through the library's glass double doors.

For a library atrium, he'd always found it surprisingly grandiose. It was all high ceilings, carved arches, and crystal chandeliers, the floor made from a gray-and-white marble that matched the elegant silver pillars, most twined with chains of blue iris flowers. Yet, his shoulders relaxed as he breathed in lavender and chamomile, the hushed murmur of voices drifting down from the second floor.

Despite the tables and benches spread out across the wide-open space, most preferred to read on the upper levels. And as Aaron headed for the central spiral staircase, he secretly hoped it was because of the painting taking up the back wall.

The seven Defiants fighting their way up Mt. Raegyr. An army of Devourists flooding down to stop them, their dark gray bones poking out through patches of black, scaly skin. Three pillars of swirling darkness waiting at the peak, the five gods hovering in the air as they cheered the Defiants on.

"You always get such a look on your face after seeing that painting."

Aaron struggled to straighten his expression, looking up to find Zella waiting for him at the top of the stairs.

The head librarian was composed of gentle lines, from her round face, to her soft curves, to her chestnut curls haphazardly coiled in a knot on the top of her head. She wore her usual pastel pink, blue, and purple jacket, the sleeves partially obscuring her hands just as she liked.

"You would think we've discussed its meaning so many times I would know to let it go," he said, stepping onto the second floor.

Zella tutted, her tiny stature having her barely able to reach high enough to ruffle his hair, even though he was the shortest of his brothers. "I would have thought being king would make you a little less cheeky."

"We've already established I'm reluctant to change."

Zella laughed. A warm, affectionate laugh that had Aaron wondering why it had been so long since he'd visited.

"In that case," she said, "you can regale me with all of your artistic complaints while you help me organize my returns."

"Why must there always be an ulterior motive?" Aaron asked, feigning a pout.

"Because I *refuse* to change."

With a wink, Zella gestured for Aaron to follow her, looking comically small beside the towering stacks as she headed for a large, cluttered desk off to the side. Aaron laughed to himself, relaxing into something softer than muscle memory as he came to sit in one of the desk's empty chairs.

"Check outs and check ins?" he asked.

"And I'm on sorting the books themselves," she confirmed. She nudged two stacks of papers toward him, then turned to her collection of precariously piled books.

Aaron grabbed one of the many pens scattered across the desk, ready to start cross-checking. Just to look down and scoff.

"Really?" he asked.

Zella tried and failed to smother her cackle as Aaron brandished the page-sized rendition of the painting on the wall, her tawny eyes sparkling.

"Apologies," she said. "I thought you might appreciate it more in a smaller form."

"Uh-huh." Aaron tossed the rendition on the desk between them, intending to shake his head and leave it at that. Yet, he'd only made it through three entries on his lists before the familiar words were popping out of his mouth. "It just seems so wrong. I understand the gods and Ancient Ones are level with each other because it's symbolizing the equality of good and evil. But then why are there five gods and only three ancient ones?"

"Because," Zella said, perfectly patient, "while good and evil might be equal concepts, there is more goodness in the world than not."

"So then, why were they just *watching?*" Aaron asked. "If the gods are the good ones, why did they leave seven humans to take care of the Ancient Ones?"

"I don't know," Zella said simply. "Maybe they didn't. Maybe there are things we don't know—aren't *meant* to know. But that uncertainty is part of believing in something."

Zella smiled over at him as she sorted her books, Aaron propping his chin in his hand. When he was younger, the analysis had felt like knives in a wound he didn't have the courage to examine. While the ghost of the prickle still remained, he couldn't stop his gaze from lingering on the gods.

Because he *did* believe they were the good ones. But he'd believed in the goodness of the Crystal, too, just to watch it nearly kill Analia. Just to be left alone in his kingdom, terrified it would finally destroy her as she tried to retrieve it.

"It all comes back to perspective," he murmured, dropping his gaze to his stacks. "We say the painting symbolizes good and evil, but I don't think any of the beings in that painting would consider themselves the villains. Which means if the Ancient Ones were to look at this painting, they would see the exact *opposite* interpretation as ours."

Zella hummed, quietly encouraging him to go on.

"I'm just... Why is it that we're the good ones? Who decides what makes someone moral or immoral? What's the difference between a well-intended choice with poor consequences, and a bad choice?"

Aaron wasn't expecting that last question. Nor was he expecting how badly he needed an answer as he stared at Zella.

She remained quiet for several seconds as she organized her books, her tongue pushing against her cheek in the same way it always did when she was thinking.

"You've always had a gift for finding the heart of the matter," she finally said, lifting her large eyes to his. "Unfortunately, I don't think your question has a singular answer. But I can say the fact that you're so intent on such questions is a good sign you're on the right path."

Gods, he hoped that was true. But he couldn't shake the part of himself that wasn't sure.

"Would you like to talk about why you're dwelling on this?" Zella asked, nudging his foot beneath the table with her own.

A part of Aaron was tempted to speak. But he knew he couldn't tell her. Not about the Crystal, Deardryn's threat, Analia's mission. He loved her too much to put that burden on her. So, he wordlessly shook his head.

And Zella, wonderful, intuitive Zella, didn't try to push it.

"All right, then." She turned back to her books, perfectly conversational once more as she said, "So, how are those brothers of yours?"

"Good," Aaron said on an exhale, returning his gaze to his lists. "Mor's discovered he has a talent for cooking, and sometimes, I think he's a better king than I am. Branten's running around all day between Nova House and military duties, and he's even managed to retain all of his fingers and toes."

"Oh, sweet Branten," Zella laughed. "It's a shame he could never sit still long enough to visit my stacks. I did see you managed to keep him out of the fountains at our last Ruhari Releasing, though."

"I can't take any credit for that."

"You know what I also saw at the Ruhari Releasing?" Zella asked, elbowing him repeatedly in the side. "You, on the Council Building roof, with your arm around a pretty redhead."

Aaron didn't know why he bothered being surprised by Zella's maneuvering abilities. He ducked his head, Zella letting out a squeal as she caught his flush.

"Oh, tell me everything! I hear her name is Analia, and she's an *Ash Royal*—how intriguing! I've only seen her from afar, but everyone who passes through says she's lovely. And I do love the way she looks at you."

"How does she look at me?" Aaron asked, not quite managing nonchalance. But his failure only had Zella beaming brighter.

"Like you are her moon and stars. The same look you have right now." Zella squirmed in her seat like a child promised sweets. "Oh, this is wonderful! I knew you wouldn't have brought her here unless you loved her—why haven't you told me everything?"

The obvious answer was because she hadn't given him the chance to do so. But Aaron was too overwhelmed to care, in the best possible way. He tipped back his chair, staring up at the ceiling as he searched for words.

"Analia is... everything. She's fiery and clever and too perceptive for her own good."

"You mean yours."

Aaron grinned, not trying to deny it. "She is everything this kingdom stands for. And she gets my ass in line whenever I go astray."

"Good," Zella said. "You need someone who can go toe-to-toe with your moods."

Aaron laughed. "Fair enough."

"I will say," Zella said, a little more tentative than before, "I haven't seen her through my windows lately."

The tiny spark that had flickered to life in Aaron's chest dimmed.

He meant what he'd said about her. He knew she could handle herself. But that didn't stop the twinge of something he couldn't quite name as he said, "She's taking care of something."

"I see." Zella hesitated, bending down to retrieve more books from beneath her desk. "Does this have anything to do with why you've come to visit me?"

Gods, Aaron loved that woman.

"Actually," he said, letting his chair thump back down, "I was wondering if you could help me with something."

Zella perked up. Aaron briefly explained how he'd been trying to learn the forgotten tongue, framing it as needing something to do.

"Firstly," he said, rising to place his completed records with the rest on the shelf behind him, "I was wondering if you have any reference books I could use. But I was also hoping you remembered who my tutor was when I was a child. I asked Ethelind, but she hasn't had time to get back to me yet."

"It was Taya," Zella said immediately.

"Really?" Taya had been one of the many who had died during the Starlight War. "I wish I had remembered that," he murmured.

"That war took too many lives," Zella agreed, setting one completed pile of books aside. "The only other person I know of in the kingdom who's fluent is Councilwoman Marion."

Aaron twisted around, feeling as though he'd been smacked upside the head. "Are you certain?"

Zella gave him an affronted look. "When have I ever been wrong about shared information?"

Gods, she was right. Sometimes, Aaron wondered if Zella knew more of the happenings in his kingdom than he did. Which meant if he wanted to get any further with his and Surce's decoding, he needed to tell the council. *Everything.*

"Oh, don't pout," Zella said, grabbing his sleeve and tugging him back into his seat. "There are far worse people to deal with than Marion. And she has always been an excellent teacher."

"Maybe," Aaron mumbled.

Zella scoffed and swatted his hand. "You know," she said, her voice softening as she shifted in her seat to face him, "I've missed having you in my library."

Something uncomfortably close to guilt squirmed in Aaron's stomach. "Have you?"

"You were always a delight when Ethelind would bring you here as a little boy. But after the war, I would hazard to guess you spent more time in here than not. You'd spend hours hidden away in the legends section reading every book you could. And it was such a joy when you started to let me into your world, telling me about what you'd been reading, asking for recommendations."

She looked over at him, something wistful in her eyes. Something that had Aaron's heart breaking, just a little bit. Because those times she mentioned were the worst moments of his life.

The years when everything had become dark and silent and numb, where he spent so much time hiding in the library because he couldn't handle being around other people. It was the time of his life he was most ashamed of. And this woman who had seen him, extended so much compassion toward him, somehow remembered that time without judgment.

"This place was my refuge," he rasped.

"It still can be." Zella slid her arm around his shoulders, resting her head against his. "I know the crown has a busy schedule. But don't forget to take care of the man beneath. Nor that your friendly librarian is around to do more than harass you with a certain painting."

"That fucking painting," Aaron muttered.

Zella snorted and patted his shoulder. Aaron closed his eyes, giving himself a few more moments to savor the contact.

He hadn't realized how much he'd been missing her. If he was being honest, he'd been avoiding the library and all its memories for a while now, each visit he made quick and efficient. Yet, there was no denying how just sitting with her, talking like they used to, left him feeling a little more grounded than he'd been before.

Don't forget to take care of the man beneath. He wouldn't. Coming to visit more often would be a crucial part of that.

And as he finally pulled away, Zella giving him directions to the forgotten tongue section, he just hoped he would be able to take care of his kingdom, too.

Chapter 41

Dimitri strolled through the Ash Castle corridors, hands in his pockets, fighting the urge to whistle as the passing Sun soldiers stole obvious looks at him. Clearly, four days had been enough for news of his arrival to spread, but not for everyone to believe it. After all, what kind of king replaced his nine escaped prisoners and traitor healer with his bastard son? Certainly not one making wise decisions.

Dimitri smothered his sneer, heading down a wide stone staircase. He'd been prepared for all that emotional turmoil to get expelled toward him, just as it had back in the Sun Castle. But perhaps it was the change in scenery, the overall tension in the air, that had the majority of looks he received being bafflement. Well, a bit sharper than that. But that didn't stop Dimitri from being endlessly entertained by it all.

Dimitri turned into the hall leading to the Council Chamber, pleased to find the dark stone corridor quiet and empty. Not only had he been harassing the Sun people with his presence the past few days, but he'd been mapping out the castle: finding the hidden stairwells and passageways, the common paths versus those avoided. And most importantly, learning Othin's council schedule.

Now, Dimitri shoved through the council door, giving any watching eyes no reason to doubt he was supposed to be inside. Even though the chamber beyond was completely empty. And as the door thunked shut behind him, he got to work.

Dimitri headed straight for the map set up at the end of the table. Just as he'd hoped, it was the Sun forces military map, various gold and gray figurines marking Sun and Ash positions. Based on the scattered nature of the gray pieces, Dimitri felt safe to assume Sun wasn't certain about how Ash's forces were distributed. But the careful organization of the gold pieces was a different story.

Dimitri pulled a pen and folded piece of paper from his pocket. Then, he plopped onto the closest chair and got to work on his sketch. He'd barely finished his general outline when a sconce behind him crackled.

"Othin is on his way," Spark called.

"Is Rayner ready to distract him?"

"Yes, sir."

Dimitri smiled slightly, even as his stomach lurched. Thanking Spark, he returned his attention to his map, his hand moving faster.

He'd thought he would have more time. According to some gossiping servants, Othin spent an hour in his chambers at this time every three days, giving Dimitri a solid window. But if he was already coming...

Dimitri drew faster, his lines getting sloppier. He had to get all of this down. Especially since, the longer he looked at Sun's setup, the more he knew Cadmus needed to see it.

The majority of the gold pieces formed a ring around the central kingdom, with smaller patrols moving within. Yet, there were no forces spread out across the rest of the kingdom. But there was an unusually large group placed at Mt. Vasolus.

"He's two minutes out!" Spark reported, crackling onto the sconce across from Dimitri.

Dimitri cursed, his grip painfully tight on his pen. "What happened to Rayner?"

"He slowed him down for a second, but Othin shook him off. He seems mad."

"When isn't he," Dimitri muttered.

Spark made a flurry of quick gestures that could have been agreement or fret. "Hurry!"

With a crackle, they disappeared once more. But Dimitri was already done with his map. Quickly folding the page, he shoved it and his pen back in his pocket, spinning on his heel to go. But something caught his attention.

He'd barely registered all the paintings on the walls when he first walked in. Analia had told him they were depictions of Elefthia's history, her uncle apparently spearheading the project during the early years of his kingship. But as his gaze slid across the paintings, something nagged at him.

Yes, the paintings showed important moments from their history: the Defiants holding the Crystal aloft, the Ancient Ones getting sealed away, even the destroyed Star Castle. But why include a painting of Analia's phoenix pin beside the Phoenix Gate? What was the hollow filled with identical red, pink, white, and yellow flowers on the gate's other side? And what was that black spot on the center-most flower?

Dimitri stepped closer, acutely aware of his time running out. Was it a smudge? No, there was no other black in that painting. Besides, it was too perfectly centered.

Dimitri leaned closer, close enough to feel the cold radiating off the wall. Was that mark a stone?

Dimitri raised his hand.

And Othin's muffled voice boomed on the other side of the door.

Dimitri jumped. Gods, he'd run out of time. He fled to the nearest chair, plopping down and struggling to straighten his face into something bored as the door flew open.

"I don't care if you'd advise against it!" Othin bellowed, nearly slamming the door on the man beside him, dressed in black-and-gray robes. "Those Ash Royals have been skulking around my kingdom for a week. It's only a matter of time before someone spots them, or they decide to reveal themselves, and you want me to say *nothing?*"

"What I'm advising," the man said, his flat voice insultingly slow, "is you have two options. Keep your hunt for the Royals quiet and bring them back without anyone needing to know, or announce to the kingdom that you *lost* nine prisoners."

A vein bulged in Othin's temple. He jabbed a finger at the man, his face almost purple as he started to retort. Just to spot Dimitri from the corner of his eye.

"Dima!"

Dimitri stomped down hard on his temper as Othin twisted toward him, the familiar conflicted look back on his face.

"What are you doing in here?"

"Waiting for you. We're hunting Royals?"

Othin opened his mouth, undoubtedly to tell him off. But the man beside him said, "His Majesty is deciding how far he's willing to go to retrieve his escaped prisoners."

Dimitri's stomach lurched.

Othin whipped around, "I didn't tell you you could speak."

"Apologies," the man said, examining his nails. "This is your child, yes? I assumed you brought him in to be an advisor."

Othin hissed out a breath between his teeth. But the man only turned to study Dimitri.

His weathered face was definitely not one Dimitri recognized. His nose was long and sharp, the gray peppering his light brown hair matching his deep-set eyes. He adjusted the neck of his robes with a heavily scarred hand, then extended it palm out to Dimitri.

"Ronun Akir," he said. "I am the Ash Kingdom interrogator. And you are Dimitri."

Dimitri nodded, hesitantly pressing his palm to Ronun's in the Sun Kingdom's traditional greeting. Othin, meanwhile, looked as though he was gearing up for an eruption that could rival Mt. Vasolus.

"I'm not waiting any longer, Ronun," he hissed, stepping back into the interrogator's line of sight. "Out of courtesy, I tried it your way. But those fucking *matchsticks* have refused to tell me anything freely, and they haven't revealed anything under duress. So, I'm *done.* There is no reason to be patient when their pleas for their lives before the kingdom will have the Ash King brat come running. That's what happens when a kingdom is forged by noble fools."

Othin's lip curled. And the breath whooshed from Dimitri's lungs.

He couldn't kill the Ash prisoners. No one had recovered enough to shadowjump in and retrieve them—Cadmus had barely been able to transport Dimitri and Rayner a few streets over. They weren't ready. And while they'd been trying to recuperate, Othin was *torturing* the ones left behind.

Othin and Ronun continued to go back and forth, the contrast between Othin's raised voice and Ronun's level tone overstimulating Dimitri's senses. Gods, he had to do something.

"This kingdom has run free long enough!" Othin declared, banging his fist on the table. "I tried to rule through peace like Deardryn ordered. Now, I'll rule through fear. *Respect.*"

"You're making a mistake!" Dimitri blurted.

Othin swung around toward him, the back of Dimitri's chair digging into his spine as he recoiled. "This has nothing to do with you," he hissed. "You shouldn't even be here—"

"But you need me." Dimitri didn't have time to think through his words as he gripped the sides of his chair, his plan rapidly unfolding in his mind. "You want control of the people, right?"

Othin clenched his jaw, but he nodded.

"Then you need to think like the people. And you can't do that. You've been king too long. But I've been a servant my entire life. I not only *was* the people, but I spent every day listening to what the rest of the people thought."

"Interesting," Ronun mused, leaning against the wall.

Othin's face twitched. But Dimitri held his gaze, his eyes wide with what Othin would hopefully interpret as pleading and not terror.

Finally, Othin softened a fraction.

He yanked out the chair across from Dimitri, Dimitri shuddering at the scrape of wood on stone. But Othin sat. Fixed Dimitri with a look. "What would you suggest?" he asked.

Dimitri forced himself to pause. Pretend to consider. Finally, he said, "I doubt you'll be able to get the entire kingdom on your side. But that doesn't mean you can't get some. Offering the Royals mercy is the best way to create a divide between those who want to fight and the people who are exhausted and want peace. But if you kill them? You'll give every single Ash citizen a reason to rally against you, which is all Cadmus will need to swoop in and start a rebellion—and you don't have the resources to handle that."

Othin's eyes flicked to the map, and Dimitri winced. Definitely not the smartest move to tell Othin he'd been snooping. But as Othin let out a tiny sigh, Dimitri realized he wasn't surprised. Dimitri's insides twisted tighter.

Across the room, Ronun wisely kept his mouth shut, his expression unreadable. Finally, Othin squared his shoulders.

"The Royals have three days to tell me what they know," he said. "Then, we send a message to the Royal brat."

The insinuation had Dimitri tasting bile. But Othin didn't wait for a response.

He rose to his feet, shooting Ronun a venomous look and stalking out of the chamber. Ronun's lips pressed into a line, but he followed.

Then, Dimitri was alone. And he could barely give them a minute head start before he shoved out of his chair and darted for the door.

He had to tell Cadmus. He had to find a fire sprite. He had to warn the prisoners—Crystal spare him, he couldn't let them die.

Dimitri raced around the corner, just to slam into something warm and solid on the other side—oh gods, no—

"Dima." Rayner grabbed Dimitri before he could lose his footing. "What are you—what happened?"

"Othin's torturing the Royals. He's going to kill them in three days. We have to tell Cadmus—we have to *do* something—"

"Come with me."

"What?"

"Come with me."

Rayner gripped Dimitri by the sleeve and dragged him down the hall, Dimitri's feet stumbling beneath him. Before he could process what was happening, Rayner yanked him into a dimly lit side room and shut the door behind them.

Rayner turned to Dimitri, his voice, his dark brown eyes, feeling like the only stable ground left as he said, "Dima. I need you to slow down."

Dimitri wrapped his arms around himself, the request unfathomable. He couldn't slow down. How was he supposed to slow down when their time was running out? He should be speeding up—

"Dima." Rayner stepped closer, his voice softening into a whispered, drawn-out caress. "Slow."

Dimitri squeezed his eyes shut, focusing on the word. Slow. Slow as he inhaled through his nose, smelling something dark and earthy as Rayner took another step closer. Close enough he could feel the heat of his skin.

Focus. Breathe.

Slowly, Dimitri's body relaxed, his pulse mostly evening out.

"Good," Rayner murmured. "Now, tell me what happened."

Dimitri opened his eyes, finding Rayner impossibly close. Close enough he could make out his heavy, intent gaze in the dark room. But he didn't recoil. Instead, he explained everything that had happened in the council chamber.

Rayner listened quietly, the calm, attentive look on his face never shifting. Even as Dimitri reached Othin's threat, his hands beginning to shake, Rayner remained perfectly steady.

"We will fix it," he promised.

And against all odds, Dimitri believed him. He tightened his arms around himself, wanting to close his eyes, wake up to find everything had been fixed. Instead, he felt his mouth open, his words so soft he barely heard them. "I can't have any more people dead because of me."

Rayner seemed genuinely taken aback. "Dima," he said, "what happened to Patryclas was *not* your fault."

Those words hurt. A lot. But it was nowhere near the pain of Dimitri's silent response: *Not just him.*

A warm, flickering pulse expanded in his stomach, but he stomped it out.

"Hey." Rayner reached out, his hands hovering over Dimitri's shoulders. "You did good today. You gave them, gave *us,* time. That is everything."

Gods, Dimitri hoped that was true. He looked down at Rayner's hands, still carefully avoiding contact with his shoulders.

As if he'd noticed Dimitri flinch with every touch in the beginning. As if he'd noticed that reaction slowly fade away. As if he recognized that was a privilege he might have lost.

A dull, heavy ache rolled through Dimitri's chest. But he nodded. And he didn't shift out of reach as he asked, "Can we find a fire sprite now?"

Rayner nodded, Dimitri having no name for the depthless look on his face. But Rayner didn't offer any explanations as he turned and pulled open the door, light from the corridor beyond spilling into the sitting room.

And as they stepped outside, Dimitri caught the tension he hadn't previously noticed ease from Rayner's shoulders. The same way his muscles always tightened and relaxed after shadowjumping.

"It's the dark," Dimitri said without thinking. "You don't like the dark."

Rayner looked back at him quickly, Dimitri bracing for the rebuke. But Rayner remained perfectly calm as he said, "I've spent enough time in the darkness of that cell."

His gaze pierced into Dimitri's, not looking away until Dimitri nodded. And as they headed off down the corridor, Dimitri couldn't help but wonder if that was the only type of darkness Rayner had been referring to.

Chapter 42

Analia's days passed with an infuriating lack of progress. Sabi continued to monitor Deardryn's book requests, and despite her persistent interest in magical oaths, they were no closer to figuring out why. Analia was also making little progress during her training with Sylas. Yet, worst of all was the fact that her nightmares had officially returned.

Every night Sylas didn't pull her into his sitting room, she found herself back in Pryanth's chambers: his bed frame digging into her back, her magic ripping free, his scream echoing in her ears. Each morning, she woke gasping for breath, her hands tightening around her dagger—*Aaron's* dagger.

Gods, she didn't want his dagger. She wanted *him.* But that required retrieving the Crystal—which was the only area she was making progress in.

With every session, Deardryn was able to sit a little closer to her, Analia barely needing to spare a thought to keep the magic at bay anymore. She'd finally managed to make it through the Crystal's entire release, allowing her to confirm even the Crystal's resting state was nauseatingly powerful.

But she was handling it.

"Put out your hand," Deardryn said one morning. She sat in front of Analia within arm's reach, the Crystal in her palm flickering with lingering magic.

"I thought we were talking about my childhood music lessons," Analia said, running her fingers through the carpet.

"Analia, do you think I can't recognize when someone isn't paying attention? I raised a boy. I've spent *years* getting talked over by councilmen who have forgotten their place. I can spot that faraway look from halfway across the kingdom."

The gentle chiding had Analia's fingers digging into the carpet. "Does that mean I'm to be punished?"

"Of course not," Deardryn scoffed. "When you first came in this room, you couldn't handle a sliver of the Crystal's magic. Now, you're not only blocking it out, but you're maintaining a full conversation with me while clearly dwelling on something else. What you've earned is a victory. Now look."

Analia realized Deardryn's plan a second before she acted. She shrank back against the wall, acutely aware of the magic, the screams. But Deardryn caught her hand. And gently, she placed the Crystal in her palm.

Analia sucked in a breath.

And nothing happened.

Her shield remained intact. No magic tore through her being. Everything remained perfectly still.

"Analia," Deardryn whispered. "Look down."

Analia's hands shook in her lap. She knew what she would see when she looked. She didn't know why she didn't want to check anyway. But slowly, she dragged her gaze down.

The Crystal shard sat in the palm of her hand, its translucent face sparkling with a rainbow of colors in the light. She could feel its weight, its polished surface as she curled her fingers.

She was holding the Crystal. She'd officially built up the tolerance needed to smuggle it away. And the radiant look on Deardryn's face had her chest hollowing out.

"Analia, you did it," Deardryn said, snatching up her discarded pen and scribbling furiously in her notes. "This is excellent! Your first stage of training is a success, and we've already collected so much information."

She'd finally won against the Crystal. And in doing so, she put Deardryn another step ahead.

"This is an impressive feat, my dear. Even with my limited sensory abilities, I could hardly stand to hold the Crystal for long. That type of power..." Deardryn shook her head, her eyes bright. "This is a truly wonderful victory, Analia."

A victory that had her clock ticking faster. And she was no closer to figuring out how to steal the shard.

"I must assume this is because of your Blessing," Deardryn went on. "We know it came from Accalon, but with how unusual of a Blessing it is, we'll undoubtedly learn more if we can figure out how it came to be."

Analia's breath caught. Deardryn didn't seem to notice as she flipped to a new page, her pen poised.

"Was Accalon's magic always so powerful?"

"I don't know," Analia managed, the words cracking down her chest.

"That's understandable, you only knew him for twenty-two years."

The crack dug a little deeper.

"Did he have access to other magics as well?"

"I don't know," Analia repeated, her hands starting to shake. She couldn't do this. Not now, not ever. But Deardryn kept going.

"Do you think he knew his magic would get passed down in his death? Did you notice any odd habits? Was he unusually sensitive to magical objects? Was there ever a shift in his perceived abilities—"

"I don't know!" Analia exploded. "I don't know, I don't know, I don't know! He never *told me* anything. I know *nothing.*"

Her words cracked off the walls, bouncing back and impaling her like a volley of arrows. She. Didn't. Know.

Deardryn slowly looked up from her notes, her lips parted. But all she did was stare. And Analia couldn't bring herself to care as a flush spread across her skin, her fingers tightening around the Crystal, her entire body shaking, shaking, shaking.

"I'll be away on business the next three days," Deardryn finally said, her words slow, precise. "After such a *victory,* you deserve a break. We'll be back to our studies soon enough."

She gave Analia's knee a single pat. And that touch shattered the last of Analia's control.

Thrusting the Crystal back into Deardryn's hands, she wordlessly rose to her feet. Then, she headed for the door, trying not to rush, trying to drag what little dignity she had left out of that room.

She didn't remember if Deardryn called after her. She didn't remember closing the door behind her. She didn't remember Tavian jerking upright as he spotted her, his hand reaching for her, his words fuzzing out in her ears.

All she knew was she ran. Down the hall, around the corner, needing to get as far away from that room as possible.

She. Didn't. Know.

A distant part of her heard Tavian calling her name as he chased after her. But she couldn't stop. She had to move. Faster and faster, finding the stairs, stumbling down to the entryway.

She needed out. Out of this castle, out of this kingdom, out of this prison whose air couldn't fill her lungs—she needed *out.*

Analia reached the central fountain, a sob squeezing past her throat as she spotted the guards at the door. They wouldn't let her out. She didn't know. She didn't know, she didn't know, she didn't—

"What in the name of the five gods is going on?"

Analia hadn't heard Sylas approach. But suddenly, there was a hand on her arm, wrenching her around, Sylas's horrified expression blurred through her tears.

"Analia," he said, his hand tightening, "What—"

"I need *out*," she sobbed. "I haven't been outside in a *month*. I haven't had any privacy for a *month*. I have been trapped in this castle for a *month* and I can't *breathe*."

She'd barely gotten out her words before Sylas pulled her closer, the hazy purple light of the entryway's lanterns mercifully fading into darkness. Empty, stagnant, gone far too soon as Sylas pulled them out of the shadows.

The first thing that hit Analia was the cold. She lifted her face, a shudder running down her spine as she stared up at the cloudy sky, the wind softly blowing over her face. Fresh, open air. But that wasn't dirt beneath her feet.

Analia looked around, finding herself on a massive balcony. To her left, a few cushioned armchairs sat pressed up against the castle wall, an ornate overhang extending above. The right-most quarter had been turned into a raised section hosting a circular glass table, a chessboard placed atop it. And arranged throughout it all was row after row of massive potted plants.

"What is this?" Analia asked, struggling to catch her breath.

"My private balcony." Sylas released her, stepping over to the railing that overlooked the snow-crusted hedge maze far below. "Patryclas had this made for me a century back. Said I needed a 'happy place.'"

"Your happy place is plants?"

"It's anywhere I don't have to deal with people. Patryclas added the plants because he claimed they're soothing, whatever that means. Nevertheless, here we are."

Sylas spread his arms mockingly. Analia, in turn, needed several tries to swallow the lump rising in her throat. Still, her voice was unbearably small as she asked, "Why?"

"Because you said you needed out. And this is the closest you're going to get, if you don't want to deal with security and eavesdroppers." Sylas turned a knob on the balcony railing, the temperature warming to more tolerable levels with a quick thrum of magic. Then, he headed for the raised section, not looking back as he said, "Touch the plants. They're far more receptive to a meltdown than my entryway."

Analia scowled. Sylas paid her no mind as he sat at the glass table and started to assemble his chessboard—he better not expect her to play with him. Not after that jab. Still, Analia couldn't deny that jab ignited the tiny spark she needed to wipe her tears and step into the aisles of plants.

Clearly, Patryclas had tried to maintain a semblance of organization. But either the plants had grown too big, or he'd amassed too many, for Analia quickly found herself weaving through a tangle of greenery.

Leaves of all shapes and sizes brushed against her face, her arms, her thighs. Most were varying shades of green, but she trailed her fingers over the bright splashes of pink, white, and yellow, that crack in her chest smoothing a little bit. That, however, only made room for the thoughts from that morning to swirl.

"I hope you know I'm not going to start babbling to you," she called, picking at a long, drooping leaf.

"I appreciate that."

Analia glanced over her shoulder. Sylas moved a piece on his newly set up board, then turned the glass tabletop like a wheel until the other side of the board was facing him. He studied the situation, then moved another piece.

Analia wasn't surprised in the slightest. She fully expected that to be the end of their interaction. Yet, as the silence settled around them once more, Analia couldn't help the words that spilled past her lips.

"Deardryn started asking me about him today. Question after question after question, and I couldn't answer any of them."

"Who?" Sylas asked, bored.

"Accalon," Analia said. "I thought you weren't listening."

"Apologies, it was reflexive."

Sylas moved another piece. Analia pulled at another leaf, not trying to stop her words.

"He was my one person. The one certainty I had amid my father turning on me, my kingdom's hatred, the absence of my magic. The one person who knew me inside and out. I thought I could say the same about him. But it seems like with every day since his death, I'm learning just how little I knew him.

"Not tiny details, like his favorite color was actually gold, or he had a friend from the forges I never heard about. *Massive* secrets. World-altering secrets. And saying it out loud, I feel *ridiculous* for whining about why he didn't share any of it with me. I just..." Analia squeezed her eyes shut, trying to steady her voice. "All I can think is how could someone who claimed to love me unconditionally leave me questioning everything?"

Analia's voice cracked. She peeled off another section of leaf, not sure if she wanted Sylas to say something, or pretend she'd never opened her mouth. Gods, she wished she could pretend none of that morning had happened.

"Come here," Sylas said suddenly.

Analia started. "Why?"

"Because you're terrorizing my plants, and I removed you from my entryway to minimize your destruction."

Analia looked down, only just noticing the small pile of leaves collecting at her feet.

Sylas snapped his fingers. "Hurry up."

Analia was tempted to ignore him. But knowing there was no point, she turned, her shoulders slumping as she came to stand beside the table.

Sylas pointed at the seat across from him. "Sit."

Analia scowled, but she complied.

"Now, move a piece."

"Why?"

"Because I'm tired of playing alone. And if I'm going to indulge your 'babbling,' I better get something out of it."

Sylas stared at her expectantly. And Analia, realizing she had no fight left in her, shifted one of her dark purple pawns on the board.

"All right," Sylas said, propping his chin in his hand. "You were saying?"

Analia's cheeks flushed. But there was no judgment on Sylas's face as he moved a white piece, just a resigned sort of prompting.

"I just want to know why he didn't trust me," she mumbled.

She expected Sylas to merely grunt in acknowledgement. Instead, he shook his head at her like a chastising parent.

"Analia, how old were you when he died? Twenty-two? He didn't tell you because you were a child. To all of us over one hundred and fifty, you're *still* a child, just slightly older and marginally wiser."

"Marginally?"

"I know, I was trying to be generous. The point is, of course he wasn't telling you everything, but that doesn't mean he wouldn't have told you at the right time."

Analia opened her mouth.

"What, are you going to argue?" Sylas taunted. "Are you going to say you were entitled to every piece of information about him whenever you pleased?"

"Not when you phrase it like that," Analia muttered.

"That's the only way to phrase it." Sylas moved a piece, and Analia dropped her gaze. "This doesn't come back to trust, Analia. It's the simple fact that you were the child, and he was the adult. It wasn't your job to know everything, and at that time, it wasn't your place either."

Analia bit the inside of her cheek, knowing he had a point. But that didn't stop the knot in her chest from wanting to argue anyway.

"You know," she said, "you talk a lot about the parent-child relationship for someone so disinterested in children."

Sylas started to protest. Then, rolling his eyes, he settled on a scoff and stole one of her pieces.

"Hey."

"You deserved it."

Analia shrugged halfheartedly. "I know everything you're saying," she said, her eyes back on the board. "But it's hard to remember all of this when I still don't know how *much* I don't know. As far as I'm aware, he could have been hiding two percent of who he was or one hundred percent. And when the gap is that big..."

Analia trailed off.

"You are quite the extremist," Sylas commented.

Analia's face scrunched as Sylas hopped his piece across the board, coming dangerously close to her queen. "I grew up with an entire kingdom who hated me and one person who loved me unconditionally," she said. "Forgive me for not automatically remembering there's a middle ground." She claimed one of Sylas's knights, Sylas remaining amicably silent as she went on. "It's just... he shaped so much of who I am. And even with the middle ground, I don't feel like I really know who he is anymore. So how am I supposed to know who I am anymore?"

Sylas released a long, heavy breath, running his hand through his blue-black curls. "There are a lot of bad people in this world, Analia," he finally said. "Some even evil. For the most part, it's easy for them to blend in with the crowd. But when you get to know them? I don't care who they are, no one can keep their shit together for more than six weeks."

Analia let out a small, startled laugh. "Why six weeks?"

"How should I know? I just observe it."

Well, that was certainly true about Pryanth. Even Deardryn, although her signs were so subtle Analia still wasn't completely sure what they meant.

"How old did we say you were when Accalon died?" Sylas asked.

"Twenty-two," Analia mumbled.

"And in any of those twenty-two years, did you see a mask slip?"

"No," Analia said, bowing her head.

"Exactly." Sylas leaned toward her. "Accalon wasn't an evil man. He wasn't even a bad one. He was one of the good ones—annoyingly so." Sylas rolled his eyes, but there was no bite to his voice as he said, "Don't dismiss the things he taught you when, secrets or not, all he ever did was try to keep you safe."

A fresh ache rolled through Analia's chest. Because she knew he was right. But the secrets still hurt anyway. Now, there was the added pain of questioning him on top of it.

Sylas stared into her face, clearly deliberating. Finally, he pushed back his chair. "Go to bed early tonight," he said.

"Why?" Analia asked, rubbing her eyes.

"Must you question everything?" Sylas circled around the table, coming to rest his hand on Analia's shoulder. "You go to bed early tonight because I told you to."

Analia made to respond. But Sylas pulled them into the shadows, reappearing a moment later in Analia's chambers.

"Right after dinner," he said, releasing her and stepping away. "Don't make me wait."

Analia rolled her eyes, unfazed by the abrupt exit as he started to fade into the shadows. Leaving her alone. Exhausted, rubbed raw, and left to replay the display she had put on that morning.

"Sylas," she said, her voice catching.

To her surprise, Sylas paused midjump.

"How bad was it?"

For a moment, she didn't think he would respond. Finally, he said, "Your outburst, while unpleasant, had fortunate timing. Most of my staff was preparing for lunch in the Great Hall. And the few who witnessed understand everyone deserves a second to breathe."

Sylas gave her a significant look. And before Analia could thank him, he faded into the shadows.

Chapter 43

"Stop looking at it."

Dimitri blinked hard as Rayner whispered in his ear, only just realizing his gaze had drifted back to the clock tower across the square. "I know; I'm sorry."

He and Rayner sat on a curved bench on the Council Building's balcony, Othin's small group of advisors softly conversing on the opposite end. Originally, they were all supposed to wait inside while the clock tower's chimes gathered the Ash citizens. Yet, after ten minutes of Dimitri alternating between prowling around the space and pressing his face to the balcony door's window, Othin had had enough. He'd ordered Dimitri outside, clearly trying to make it look purposeful to the gathering citizens as he sent Rayner and the advisors to join him.

Rayner knocked his boot against the leg of the bench, the thud having Dimitri jerking his gaze from the clock tower once more.

"Are you all right?" Rayner murmured, angling his head away from the advisors. "Because your face is saying—"

"That I'm panicking and I need to move but I'm not allowed and I'm nauseous and everything hurts behind my collarbones, but I don't want to talk about it."

Dimitri wrapped his arms around himself, his voice thankfully coming out a whisper. Even as the growing crowd below hummed with a hatred that was terrifyingly familiar. Even as each slow boom of the clock tower had him wanting to jump out of his skin. Even as Dimitri's eyes darted over every soldier stationed around the square, up to the roofs where the three sun dragons crouched, waiting.

To Rayner's credit, he didn't lean away. He remained quiet for a few beats, his eyes trained on Dimitri's face, close enough Dimitri could feel his breath on his temple. "All right."

Dimitri's gaze shot to Rayner as he settled back against the bench, leaving him alone. And he had the strangest prick of disappointment.

But this was good. His panic wasn't going to go away until this meeting was over, and he couldn't keep relying on Rayner to drag him back to sanity. He had to sit with this feeling. Learn to work around it.

Even as the clock tower finally fell quiet, and the pain behind his collarbones flared.

Dimitri expected the crowd to settle into an uneasy silence. Yet, the voices barely quieted, most folding their arms as they waited. And they had no idea what was in store for them as the balcony door finally slid open.

A ring of brilliant blue magic crackled out across the floor, forming a shield around the balcony. Othin followed a moment later, surrounded by a unit of Sun soldiers. But that wasn't all.

"He's not wasting any fucking time," Rayner hissed, barely audible over the cries of outrage below as Othin shoved the five cuffed, bloodied prisoners into full view. Dimitri could only shake his head, his stomach roiling at the open gashes across their skin, the way the woman on the left had to be supported by the pale, red-haired man beside her.

Clearly, Othin had no desire to hide his interrogation methods from the crowd.

"Citizens of the Ash Kingdom," Othin bellowed, his voice magically raised by the circular amplifier on his jacket. "Today, I come to you with a choice. A final chance to decide what future you wish to see for your kingdom. And my offer to you remains the same as it has always been.

"Peace. A harmonious, bloodless peace that would keep this kingdom intact. A peace some of you have decided to claim. To those of you who have remained quiet, admirably trying to maintain order throughout this transition, I see you, and I thank you."

The crowd twisted into movement. Voices raising, fingers jabbing, accusations flying as people tried to defend themselves and uncover the traitors. Everyone turning on each other, just as Othin wanted.

Dimitri bit down hard on his lip, Rayner stiff as marble beside him.

"This is a path I offered to your Royals as well," Othin continued, spreading his arms above the chaos. "I gave them every comfort as we negotiated our new kingdom. Food, beds to sleep on, healers to tend to them, opportunities to speak their concerns. They knew the paths ahead of them, even more intimately than you all. And instead of choosing your safety, they've chosen violence. They chose themselves over you."

Othin paused, letting the voices surge. Dimitri's eyes flashed to the clock tower, his stomach twisting, the five prisoners visibly struggling to keep quiet and still.

"A week ago," Othin called, gripping the railing, "eight Ash Royals decided their freedom was their top priority. They left behind members of their family to deal with the consequences of their actions. All for the *potential* of a crown. And they can't even face you to explain what they did."

Dimitri wanted to scream that wasn't true as the crowd roiled like boiling water, voices clashing, weapons unsheathing. But were they angry with each other, the Royals, or Othin? Even if it was the latter, Othin was still getting everything he wanted: a kingdom too fractured to unite.

"Unfortunately," Othin said, not sounding particularly remorseful, "this selfishness cannot go unpunished. Peace is fragile. It needs protection. And it demands respect."

Othin gestured, and the Sun soldiers shoved the Ash prisoners forward. "The Royals need to understand there's a price to defying peace. So, I'm offering them a choice." Othin's amber gaze swept the crowd, his jaw set, nostrils flared. "You hear that, Cadmus Valarus? I'm giving you one more chance to choose peace. Either you can reveal yourself now and return to the castle to resume our negotiations, or you can watch your traitorous family die."

Dimitri wanted to cover his ears as the voices turned into a roar. But Othin remained horrifically calm, turning from the crowd to take in the prisoners struggling against their guards. He crooked his finger at the man on the right, the shorter of the two Ash Royals whose mouth was swollen as if recently bashed.

His blue eyes widened as his guard pushed him forward, his feet tangling beneath him. The guard grabbed him by the back of his tunic, yanking him upright and shoving him forward.

Dimitri's heart pounded in his ears. He looked to the clock tower, back to the Ash man now shoved to his knees, the voices screaming, screaming, screaming.

"What is your name?" Othin asked, towering over the Ash Royal.

The man looked up at him, his hands cuffed behind his back. Then, he spat, Othin jerking away from the blood that now stained his boots, his patronizing mask twisting into wrath.

"Stanek!" he roared.

One of the Sun soldiers stepped forward, Dimitri nearly jumping off the bench as fingertips brushed his knuckles. He flipped his hand to grip Rayner's, Rayner squeezing back hard enough Dimitri's bones ground together. Gods, *please*—

"This," Othin boomed, "is what happens to those who threaten the peace of this kingdom."

He gripped the man by the hair and yanked his head back, exposing his throat. Stanek raised his hand, a thin, almost translucent whip shimmering into existence between his fingers.

Dimitri squeezed Rayner's hand.

The crowd screamed.

Stanek brought his hand back. And just as he was slicing down—

"Ash Kingdom citizens!"

Stanek's whip went wide, slicing through the railing with a metallic crash. Othin twisted around, the crowd following suit. And Dimitri nearly sobbed with relief as he looked to the clock tower.

Cadmus stood on the roof of the tower, dressed in the gray and orange of his kingdom, his feet planted, golden flames flickering across his shoulders. The Ash King reborn. Risen again.

And the crowd barely had time to gasp before the dragons dove toward him, Othin bellowing over the noise. "Seize him!"

All around the square, Sun soldiers drew their weapons, the air buzzing with magic. But Cadmus had already disappeared into the shadows, his disembodied voice echoing around the square from his stolen amplifier.

"You know in your hearts that Othin is *lying* to you." He reappeared on an elevated walkway on the opposite side of the square. "This *invader* stands on our balcony, blustering to you about peace, about all of his charitable generosity because he knows words are all he has left."

Incinerating a volley of arrows, he disappeared once more, reappearing on a nearby rooftop. "Othin can say whatever he wants about the 'peaceful' efforts he's made that you can't see. But look at everything the Sun people have done that you *can see*."

He disappeared, the crowd, the Sun soldiers, the dragons all twisting back and forth as he shadowjumped around the square, his voice echoing around them.

"They've killed your friends and families to seize a castle. They've stationed guards in your streets to bloody you into submission. They use fear now to divide you, which only makes their rule grow stronger. They tried to shatter your trust in *me*."

Cadmus appeared on a fountain rim in the center of the square. The crowd surged toward him, hands touching his boots, his legs, his torso, Cadmus reaching down to grasp their hands in his. Dimitri's grip on Rayner tightened—this wasn't part of the route they'd meticulously planned the past three days.

But something settled over the crowd as he stood with them. Something reflected in the hardened look on Cadmus's face. Even as his eyes widened and he shoved people away, the crowd letting out a collective shriek as a wave of indigo magic tore through the open air where Cadmus had stood a moment before.

Othin roared in frustration. But Cadmus kept going, raising his voice over the noise, walkways and balconies shattering in his wake.

"Othin isn't a king. He's Deardryn's puppet. The queen who has been killing Royals for her own gain. The queen who stabbed Princess Lucilla in the throat and left her to die on the cold stone floor."

The crowd exploded into noise, practically drowning out Cadmus's words as he appeared on the Council Building roof. "Deardryn thinks she can turn our kingdom into a step in her plan. But fire isn't something to be tamed. It's something to ignite—"

"Enough!"

Dimitri jumped as Othin bellowed loud enough his bones vibrated, the crowd recoiling. Othin turned to Cadmus, his chest heaving, his eyes wild. "Either you come quietly, or I slit his throat."

The entire square followed Dimitri's gaze as he looked down, spotting the dagger Othin pressed to the Ash man's throat. He struggled, trying to break free, but Othin pressed the blade even harder, a trickle of blood running down his skin.

Cadmus reappeared on the balcony railing, battered and smoking, looking like an avenging god staring down at a heretic. Othin grabbed his thigh, his hand starting to glow. But Cadmus pulled a dagger from his sleeve and sliced it through the air, Othin's shield flaring blue as the damper blade cut through.

Othin's face contorted. He shoved Cadmus away, sending him toppling off the balcony. Cadmus twisted and faded into the shadows.

And white flames engulfed the balcony from behind as Fayela finally made her move, no longer blocked by Othin's shield.

Dimitri shrank back from the heat, Sun people shrieking around him. They retreated to the edges of the balcony, the flames forming a ring around the prisoners.

In a blink, Fayela appeared in the flames, grabbed three of the prisoners, and disappeared once more. Cadmus took her spot a moment later, gripping the two remaining prisoners by the shoulders and pulling them into the darkness.

Just before he vanished, Stanek whipped around and snapped out his wrist. His magic sliced through the flames, raking down the side of Cadmus's face.

Dimitri's heart jolted. Before he could panic, the Ash King disappeared, his voice echoing through the crackling flames. "Rise again."

And chaos erupted.

Dimitri barely registered the cheers of the crowd below. Barely registered the Sun people's outrage, the hands shoving him to his feet, back into the Council Building, up the stairs to the roof where the sun carriage waited.

All he knew was the wave of relief. It rolled down from his head to his toes, Rayner having to tug his shaking body down into his seat.

Dimitri automatically looked over at him, their eyes locking. And just for a moment, Rayner gave him a radiant, triumphant look. One that could have rivaled the sun.

And as the carriage took off, Dimitri decided he wouldn't mind if he was associated with that sun.

Tyce waited for them in their chambers. The Ash Royal paced around the room, a fire sprite perched on his shoulder, his brown eyes darting to them as Dimitri opened the door. "We need your help."

Dimitri didn't think twice. He took Tyce's offered hand, Rayner accepting the other, and Tyce dragged them into the shadows. They reappeared a moment later in the safehouse, which had once again been transformed into a healer station.

Fayela weaved through the crowd of Royals, barking orders and shoving jars into people's hands as they tended to the wounded spread out across the couches. Fire sprites flitted throughout the chaos, offering assistance where they could.

Dimitri's stomach heaved at the memory of his magic, bloody skin beneath his fingers, the lingering smell of herbal paste.

"What do we do?" he croaked.

"We're on Cadmus duty." Not releasing Dimitri's hand, Tyce led him through the crowd, Dimitri's magic flickering through his veins. "He got a nasty cut on his temple from that Sun guard. Nothing serious, but he keeps insisting on helping."

"So, you need someone to bicker him into submission?"

Tyce looked over at him with a tired smile. "From what I've seen, you're best for the job."

Dimitri snorted, practically dizzy with relief as he shoved his magic back down. Before he could respond, Tyce's smile faded.

He pulled Dimitri to a stop at the edge of the crowd, suddenly serious as he asked, "Othin doesn't suspect you, right? You're safe?"

Dimitri startled. He stared into Tyce's face, expecting something strategic as he calculated the cost of losing a spy. But all he found was genuine, unconcealed concern. One that had him only able to nod.

Tyce nodded back. Then, he nudged Dimitri back into movement, leading him over to the couch where Cadmus sat.

True to Tyce's word, Cadmus was not only bleeding heavily through his gauze but also having none of his family's attempts to help. Dimitri had no problem shoving back against his arguments that he was king, he had to help. He put up an admirable fight. But clearly realizing he was no match for Dimitri, Cadmus finally slumped back against the couch with a glower, Tyce struggling to maintain a straight face.

Thoroughly pleased with himself, Dimitri perched on the couch's armrest, his eyes wandering over the crowd. It didn't take long for him to spot Rayner off to the side, his hands on Rois's shoulders as he changed the guard's appearance.

Even from the side, Dimitri could tell from Rayner's pinched mouth that he wasn't pleased. But he barely finished changing Rois's appearance before he pulled away, his posture noticeably stiff as he slipped out the door.

"What was that?" Dimitri called as Rayner turned and headed for him.

"Rois harassed me into changing his appearance so he could scope out the kingdom." Rayner plopped down on the couch between Dimitri and Cadmus with a scowl. "He said we need to know how everyone is reacting."

"That's true," Cadmus murmured.

"It's also true his back isn't completely healed. You can see it just from his posture."

"No one is in one piece around here."

Something about the dull tinge to Cadmus's voice had Dimitri shifting uneasily. He looked over at Tyce on the other arm of the couch, his forehead wrinkled. But neither of them spoke as Fayela and the other Royals finally pulled the newcomers into the shadows, presumably bringing them to rest in their rooms.

They might be free, but they were far from safe. And there was definitely something off in Cadmus's eyes as he rubbed his wrist.

For a long, long time, they sat quietly on the couch, no one having the energy to move. Eventually, a handful of Royals came back downstairs, including the little girl who, thankfully, had been kept away from the carnage. But no one truly stirred until the front door opened, a blond Rois slipping inside.

"Good news and bad news," he said, wiping Rayner's magic away with a heavy hand. "The Ash citizens seem reinvigorated. Even the ones who have retreated from the chaos in the square. But Othin has unleashed the Sun forces."

Dimitri swallowed, the looks on everyone's faces telling him they, too, didn't need any more details.

"I don't understand," he said. "Tyce was able to shadowjump into the castle to get us. Why can't you all appear in Othin's chambers and get rid of him?"

If anyone was surprised by his callousness toward his father, they didn't show it.

"Because," Cadmus said, turning something small and metallic between his fingers, "Tyce was able to grab you because only Ash Royals can change the wards around the castle. And since Othin knows this, he'll be prepared. Magic, soldiers, who knows what else."

"Besides that," Rois said, coming to claim the empty spot on Cadmus's other side, "Othin is only Deardryn's pawn. All killing him will do is prompt Deardryn to send in a new figurehead. And knowing her, this one will be able to shadowjump."

"Which is the only advantage we currently have," Fayela said from the opposite couch.

"Which means," Cadmus said, "we need an army."

The word tingled across the back of Dimitri's neck. And no one had a response to offer.

Dimitri didn't know how long he remained seated in that dark, heavy silence. Eventually, Tyce rose from the armrest, coming to offer Dimitri and Rayner his hands. He pulled them into the shadows, promising to keep them updated before dropping them off in their chambers and disappearing. Then, they were alone.

Dimitri looked around, the Everflame sconces barely lighting the chamber as they automatically dimmed for the night. But he didn't need to see Rayner to know his face had paled as he sank down on his bed.

Dimitri hesitated, feeling the ghost of a hand squeezing his. Then, he crossed to the closest torch.

"Let's keep these burning," he said, the flame brightening as he touched the sconce. "For the fire sprites."

Rayner remained quiet as Dimitri followed the wall, brightening each sconce until the room was cast in a soft, orange glow. Just enough for him to see Rayner mouth, "Good idea," before he turned away.

Dimitri moved to plop down on his own bed, the memory of Cadmus's voice settling across his shoulders.

Army. They were going to need an army.

Chapter 44

"I still don't know why we had to start so early," Analia said. She sat on Sylas's sitting room floor, the lingering exhaustion from her outburst that morning having her head resting back against her recliner.

"Because," Sylas said, seated across from her, "you've shown no aptitude for summoning shadows for weeks now. And since I refuse to waste my time, we're trying something new. Which means you'll need all the time you can get."

Sylas peered at her over the rim of his wine glass, clearly waiting for her retort. But Analia only rolled her eyes, not having it in her to fuel his usual theatrics.

"So, what do I do?" she asked.

Sylas cocked his head, his thick brows contracting as he studied her. Yet, all he said was, "Cup your hands and summon a flame. It doesn't have to be big, just enough to fill your palms. And don't ask me why."

Analia scoffed, the question already balancing on the tip of her tongue. Knowing there was no point trying to push it, she silently cupped her hands, a ball of midnight flames crackling to life in her palms.

"Good," Sylas said. "Now, close your eyes and think of someone familiar. Someone you like, someone you know as well as yourself. And don't extinguish your magic."

"Let me guess," Analia said. "I shouldn't ask why?"

"She's slow, but she learns."

Analia flicked a spark at him, Sylas's mouth twitching as he brushed it aside. And something about that look had the dark, heavy knot in her chest relaxing a fraction. She closed her eyes, resting her hands in her lap, not having to think twice before settling on her person.

The precise lines and angles of his face. His dark, tousled hair, made worse by how frequently he ran his hand through it when he was worried. His starlight eyes. Combined with his full mouth and smooth slope of his nose, he was undeniably handsome.

Not in a rugged way like Branten. He was more... elegant. He was beautiful—and she could see his smirk if he ever heard her say that. Just as she could hear his laugh as she rolled her eyes in response, his own eyes sparkling.

"Your flame, Analia," Sylas prompted.

A cool, shadowy hand tapped her wrist, Analia realizing her flames had dwindled. She quickly replenished them, Sylas's words drifting through the quiet between them.

"Don't just think about what they look like. Think about how they feel, how they smell. How you feel when you're around them."

Analia barely processed his words before it was there. The slick glide of his network. The weight of his arm as he slid it around her waist, always nudging her closer before pulling her into the shadows. His whispered warning warm against her temple, metal and spice filling her nose as she relaxed into him.

It was the same routine every time, always ending with one of them pulling away. But now, Analia froze the moment, let herself sink into everything that was him. His moods, his wit, his secrets, his consistency, his safety. *Aaron.*

"Focus, Analia," Sylas said softly. "How would it feel to have him right here."

Like she was complete. Like she could relax without fearing her world would come crashing down. Like everything would be all right. Gods, the ghost of his presence was so strong, she could practically feel it.

"Analia."

Analia's face twitched as she felt Sylas kneel before her, the magic in her palms tingling.

"When you open your eyes," he said carefully, "you're going to be startled. But I need you to hold on to the feeling you have right now. All right?"

Analia nodded, her hands starting to shake. But she focused on Aaron. Focused on the peace his presence brought her as she opened her eyes. And a sob lodged in her throat.

The flames cupped in her hands had transformed. Veins of black, midnight blue, and deepest purple flickered around the edges, forming the frame of a miniature window. And through its center...

"How?" Analia asked, her voice breaking as she stared at Aaron on the starlit bridge, looking out across the quiet lakeside.

"It's your magic." Sylas slid his hands under her shaking ones, helping to support the weightless window. "I told you you were thinking too much to summon my shadows. But shadows aren't the only aspect of my magic."

"And you taught me how to summon it without letting me know that's what I was doing," Analia finished faintly. "And you had me maintain my flames so once I was distracted, I wouldn't notice when a new magic got pulled up."

Sylas shrugged, not trying to hide his self-satisfied smirk. Yet, as Analia returned her attention to the window, she didn't feel victorious.

Because now, it was official: she had multiple Blessings she could use consciously. And the likelihood Accalon hadn't been aware of this aspect of his magic withered into something impossibly small.

Analia closed her eyes, giving herself three seconds to process the ache of the final puzzle piece sliding into place. Then, she looked up at Sylas, her voice shaking as she asked, "Can I see him?"

Sylas's expression softened a fraction. "You can. You just have to make it wide enough to step through."

"What if I can't hold it?"

"I can do that."

Sylas rose to his feet, careful not to bump the window as he pulled her up by her wrists. She didn't resist as he guided her hands up, the window stretching with the movement, Sylas maneuvering her hands through the air until the window had shimmered into something closer to a doorway. Then, blinking hard, Analia stepped inside.

Magic softly tingled across her skin. She could feel Sylas step through behind her, the tightness in her lungs easing as she let him take control of their dreamwalking. And finally, she was there.

The dream was warmer than she expected. A gentle breeze moved across the bridge, sending a quiet current rippling through the lake below. Thankfully, a thick bank of fog had formed around the perimeter of the shore, blocking the Starlight Kingdom and all surrounding details from Sylas's view. But all Analia could focus on was him.

He stood at the peak of the bridge about fifty paces away, his elbows on the railing, his gaze fixed on the starlit water. Aaron.

Something in Analia's chest cracked. She took a few steps closer, her hand already extending to touch him as she breathed his name.

It was really him. Everything from his embroidered black-and-blue jacket, to the dagger hilt peeking out of his boot, to the way his spine straightened as he realized he was no longer alone. He pivoted toward her, his silver eyes locking on hers.

Analia's lips parted.

And Aaron recoiled. He screwed up his face, turning away once more.

Analia stumbled back, his reaction piercing through her chest like a blade. "Aaron..."

"I can't do this," he mumbled, pressing his face into his hands. "I'm barely holding it together while I'm awake. You can't haunt me here, too."

That blade pushed in deeper, finding her heart and twisting until it shattered. She turned to Sylas, desperate for help. But he only gave her a look of *This is your problem; you deal with it.* Then, he summoned his dark red armchair and sat, a wine glass appearing in one hand and a book in the other.

Analia gritted her teeth. But that tiny spark was what she needed to drag her gaze back to Aaron, the length of their dining room table stretching between them as he refused to look at her.

Gods, this was worse than she'd been expecting. She'd known he would struggle with her mission, her quick updates from Laness confirming this. But leaning against that railing, he looked exhausted. Lost in a way he had only allowed her to see.

"Aaron," she said, taking a few cautious steps closer. "You're right, this is a dream. But it's real."

"Please, don't," Aaron whispered, his fingers tightening around his face.

Analia's eyes stung, but she pressed on. "Turns out, Moon Royals can not only manipulate shadows, but they can form connections between people's dreams."

Behind her, Sylas made a noise of protest.

"Oh, knock it off, Sylas, you knew I would have to tell him."

"Sylas?" Aaron finally looked up, his brow furrowing as he focused on Sylas over Analia's shoulder. "Why in the name of the five gods am I dreaming about *you?*"

Sylas's network rumbled.

"You didn't dream Sylas or me up," Analia said, quickly intervening. "You're asleep, but this dream is a middle ground I've brought all of us to."

Slowly, agonizingly slowly, Aaron dragged his gaze down to hers. "How do I know?" he asked. "How do I know you're real and this isn't just me torturing myself?"

Well, that was a fair question. Analia cocked her head, her mind going back to her first night in the sitting room. How Sylas had summoned wine glasses, side tables, and Dimitri's letters from thin air, just to vanish them again. All things that weren't impossible in a regular dream. Except...

"Imagine something," she said.

Aaron's eyebrows flicked up. "Like what?"

"You know I can't be the one to tell you that."

The corner of Aaron's mouth quirked the smallest bit, sending Analia's heart stumbling. He looked over her shoulder once more, Analia not having to turn to know Sylas remained slumped in his armchair, the picture of apathy.

But Aaron perked up. Twisting to his left, he focused on the bridge, his dark blue recliner materializing beside him a moment later. And Analia could have sworn a tiny spark brightened his eyes.

"So," he said, running his finger along the velvet armrest. "I'm definitely dreaming. But how does this prove anything?"

He looked over his shoulder, Analia struggling to remain composed as his gaze hesitantly met hers. She couldn't spook him. She had to remain calm. Even as her body hummed with how close he stood.

"It will prove everything after you imagine me doing something," she promised.

She expected him to argue. But Crystal Bless that man, he only nodded and rocked back on his heels. Then, there was silence.

Aaron's eyes roved over her face, down the length of her body, clearly waiting for a reaction. But Analia remained perfectly still.

Even as his eyes narrowed. Even as the silence stretched, Analia not daring to breathe, not daring to name the look that slowly spread across his face.

"Nothing's happening," he finally said, his voice soft with wonder as he took a step closer.

Analia stared at him, her body starting to shake.

"You can move," he murmured, taking another step closer, finally within reach. "I'm not imagining anymore. Just tell me how."

"It's because I'm not a part of your dream." Analia's lungs stuttered as his fingers grazed her neck, drifting down to brush over the pulse in her throat. "Dreamwalking creates a bridge between our minds, allowing us to meet in the middle. But since we're independent of our mutual environment, we can't control each other."

"Which is why you didn't move," Aaron murmured.

Truthfully, Analia hadn't been certain it worked like that. Sylas had never explicitly told her, but she figured since he'd never sealed her mouth shut, it was because he couldn't. And she had never been more grateful to be correct as Aaron's fingers skimmed down her arm, the denial in his eyes giving way to a hope so pure, so undiluted it had her knees shaking.

"You're real?" he asked, his fingertips finding her wrist.

Analia flipped her hand, interlacing their fingers. "I'm real."

Aaron released a long, shuddering breath. Then, he pulled her closer, his hand releasing hers to fold her into his arms. And Analia would never understand how such a simple movement could release her from all the armor she had.

She buried her face in his chest, her hand tightening around the back of his jacket as he whispered something into her hair. And Analia needed that moment to last for a lifetime.

It didn't matter this was a dream, that they were separated by all of the Wild Lands. After a month of scheming, worrying, being exposed to the Crystal's magic, she was finally home. She was safe. And she was so, so tired of always having to be strong.

Analia didn't know how long they stayed like that, Aaron's lips pressed to the top of her head. Eventually, he pulled back, chuckling as she whined in protest and tried to press closer once more. He lifted her chin, his eyes taking her in with a thoroughness that had her knees shaking.

"You're in one piece?" he asked.

Analia nodded, not trusting herself to speak.

"You're as safe as you can be?"

Another nod.

Aaron leaned in, his broken whisper warm against her mouth. "You're coming back to me?"

"My constellation, I'm always searching."

Aaron blinked hard, his eyes shining. And finally, his mouth found hers.

Aaron kissed her like she was the air in his lungs. Slow, deliberate, every move as essential as an inhale as his tongue caressed hers, his fingers skimming along her jaw, her neck, the curve of her shoulders. Analia slid her hand beneath his jacket, following the raised lines of the scars that stretched across his back.

It. Was. Him.

The sweet taste of him. His moan against her mouth as she softly nipped his lower lip. The way his network harmonized with her own.

Aaron kissed her cheek, her chin, the tip of her nose, Analia whispering against his mouth as he brought it back to hers. "I miss you."

Aaron shuddered. He pulled her closer, his fingers curling into her hair, guiding her head back, giving himself better access. And there was no beginning, no middle, no end as she kissed him. Only them.

"Normally," Sylas drawled, obnoxiously loud, "I would be gone by now. But that would mean this little moment would have to end, too."

Analia broke away with a wince, finally remembering they weren't alone. But Aaron wasn't so much as fazed. He ran his lips along her jaw, his nose coming to brush the shell of her ear.

"Your dream," he said, "has the most annoying echo."

Analia laughed, Sylas grumbling something from his armchair behind her. Aaron didn't give him a shred of attention as he leaned in once more, his kiss deep and lingering and over far too soon.

"Well then, my shooting star," he said, leading her over to his recliner, his arm sliding around her waist and pulling her down beside him. "It seems as though we have much to discuss."

His tone was light enough. But that didn't stop the soft glow in Analia's chest from flickering out, her head coming to rest on his shoulder with a sigh. "More than you know."

For the next several minutes, she and Aaron took turns filling each other in. Aaron insisted she go first, Analia assuming he wanted time to craft a response that wouldn't reveal anything to an eavesdropping Sylas. Yet, the more she talked, the more he relaxed into her, his thumb moving back and forth along her arm as if reassuring himself she wasn't going anywhere.

Analia couldn't blame him. Not when the same worry had her snuggling into him, her hand playing with his free one, trying to preserve every sensation like raindrops in the desert.

By the time she made it through her recount, Aaron's face had noticeably paled. Yet, all he did was press a kiss to her temple, murmuring, "My clever shooting star."

Somehow, all of her questions about Deardryn's research, the blockade of her guarded chamber door, every other obstacle in her path, seemed a little more surmountable. She turned her head, her lips brushing his jaw. "Your turn."

Unsurprisingly, Aaron's updates were quick and discreet. Analia nodded along as he outlined their findings with the scroll, Aaron chuckling at her obvious shock at Dimitri and Ember trading places. Thankfully, he also clarified that everyone in Ash was doing all right—although the news that Cadmus had a mark had her stomach twisting.

"I've started helping Surce with translations," he said, toying with a lock of her hair. "But my skills are about as good as hers are. And the only other person familiar with the forgotten tongue is Marion."

Aaron made a face. And his initial lost, exhausted look made a lot more sense. After all, Analia knew firsthand how exasperating councilmen could be. But she also knew how essential they were.

"Have you decided what you're going to do?" she asked.

"Well, originally I was planning on pouting in my mom's room, but with these new dream abilities, I might try imagining a new language expert."

"I'm sure your creation will know more than you do," Analia said, patting his knee consolingly.

Aaron brought a dramatic hand to his chest, "Analia, how you hurt me."

Analia scoffed and tapped his nose. "Smartass."

Aaron grinned, catching her wrist and pressing a kiss to her palm, but Analia spotted the lingering brooding on his face.

"You know," she said, "this might not be as bad as you think."

"How so?" he asked warily.

"Well, we both know this isn't something you'd be able to keep from her forever. Asking for her help now lets her feel like you're inviting her in, which she'll be far more receptive to than your usual interactions."

Aaron winced, clearly remembering how rocky their council meeting had been when trying to get into the Star Royal vault. "Nothing ever goes well when I involve them," he muttered, running his hand through his hair.

"Does it not go well," Analia asked, "or does it not go how you want?"

Aaron scowled. Analia laughed and kissed the corner of his mouth.

"I know they don't approach things the same way you do," she said. "But you all have the same goal. And sometimes, you need to hear the differing opinions to figure out the best thing to do."

She stroked his cheek, Aaron closing his eyes and leaning into her touch.

"I suppose it's a tomorrow problem," he murmured.

Something about that phrase snagged Analia's attention. Her mind flickered back through the events of that day: talking on Sylas's balcony, her meltdown at the fountain, training with Deardryn. *I'll be away on business the next three days.*

"Deardryn's going away on business tomorrow," Analia said slowly.

It was such a small detail, swept away by her turmoil over Accalon. But looking up at Aaron, she could see the same sinking realization across his face. Because the last time Deardryn had gone away on "business," she had killed a Sand Royal for her rings.

Aaron began, "Has she found—"

"No, she can't have." Analia shook her head, her eyes darting between Aaron and the bridge, wanting to pace, not wanting to move.

But Aaron nudged her up. And her feet took care of the rest.

"There's no way she's found the next shard," she said, pacing back and forth in front of him. "Sabi and I have all of her research, and there is *nothing* that hints at a location."

"Unless we're missing something," Aaron muttered.

The comment stung behind Analia's sternum. She tugged on her jacket sleeve, her mind rapidly shoving details together, pulling them apart again.

"She's researching magical oaths," she said. "The only way they could be connected was if the shard was sealed away with one. But even then, how would she have found out where it was?"

"I don't know," Aaron said. "Regardless, you need to get that shard and escape before you find out."

Analia nodded, her stomach sinking further and further.

"And how are *you* helping with this?" Aaron asked pointedly.

Analia startled, pivoting around to find Aaron's gaze had latched onto Sylas farther down the bridge. At some point, he'd switched from his book to a chessboard, his black eyes barely flicking up from the table.

"I'm training her," he drawled, just far enough away he had to raise his voice.

"Which is irrelevant until her cuffs are off and she's escaped. Meaning you either are an extremely cocky king, or a complacent one."

Shadows rippled around Sylas's feet. "This might be a dream, boy," he said, "but you should still watch who you provoke—"

Sylas cut off as the bridge rumbled. Cracks skittered out around his chair, the stone letting out an ominous groan, the fissures burrowing deeper, deeper.

"I don't care if you have all the faith in the world in Analia," Aaron said, the ice in his voice sending a chill down her spine. "She is *not* a pawn for you to use and discard. And if you even consider sacrificing her for your own gain, I will be there with my damper blade. And you will learn why Deardryn has to keep Analia cuffed to keep her in line."

The bridge gave a menacing rumble. Sylas pressed his foot down on the closest crack, his black, considering eyes never leaving Aaron as the stone resolidified around him.

Analia quickly returned to her spot on the recliner, ready to reel Aaron in, for Sylas to shatter the dream with a dismissive flick of his hand. But Sylas only turned his attention to her.

"I can't tell you what my plans are," he said slowly. "But everything is almost in place. And if I can pull it off, you'll be safely back with *him* and Deardryn will be out of my kingdom for good."

Analia blinked. That might have been the most straightforward answer Sylas had ever given her.

Nodding cautiously, she turned to Aaron, knowing he would be less than pleased. But she recoiled.

"Aaron," she gasped, "you're fading."

Aaron startled. He looked down, taking in the blur around the edges of his hands, his eyes widening. He whipped toward Sylas, all ice melting away, "What's happening?"

"You're waking up," Sylas said, picking at his nails.

"No! I'm not ready, I can't—dammit." Aaron turned back to Analia, his image fading as he pulled her closer, pressing his forehead to hers. "Listen to me," he said, his eyes blazing. "I don't care if you have all the power of the Crystal or not a drop. You are the spark that can light up the world. Don't be afraid to burn."

Analia's eyes stung as he leaned in, the brush of his mouth against hers fading with every word. "Do what you have to do to come back to me."

"Aaron..." Analia reached for him, a sob lodging in her throat as her hand passed through his chest. And before he could respond, he was gone. And Analia's entire being shut down.

She sagged forward, her head falling into her hands, her muscles going rigid as they locked her into place.

She couldn't move. She couldn't break. She couldn't—

Footsteps echoed off the stone. Analia held her breath as she felt Sylas pause before her, his gaze weighing on her for several seconds.

"Analia," he finally said, "look at me."

Analia shook her head.

Sylas let out an exasperated sigh. "Why must you make everything so difficult?"

He knelt before her, Analia trying to resist as he pulled her hands down. But he forced her to meet his gaze.

"My gods you're an extremist," he muttered, shaking his head. "You're not with Deardryn. You're not in my castle. You're not on your mission. You're in a dream. You're allowed to feel a pinch of this without shattering completely. Just *feel it.*"

With that, Sylas released her wrists. Rising to his feet, he retreated to lean against the railing. And somehow, Analia moved.

She curled into the recliner, pressing her face to the back, still warm from where he'd sat. And finally, her silent tears slipped free.

Not just for Aaron. But for Accalon, Lucilla, the Ash Kingdom, everything that had happened the past month. *Just a pinch.*

Analia gave herself ten more seconds. Just ten more seconds to drown in it all. Ten seconds that would never be enough.

But somehow, when that time was up, she straightened. Wipe her eyes. And as she looked over at Sylas leaning against the railing, she could have sworn she saw a flicker of approval.

"Don't lose this side of you, Analia," he said, surprisingly soft. "It might not always be safe to show it, but don't become so hardened by your schemes that you have nothing to come back to."

Analia nodded mutely. And as the dream faded around her, she could have sworn the constant ache in her chest became a little less acute. Even as she woke to find tear stains on her pillow.

Chapter 45

Aaron's eyes snapped open. He sat up in bed, pressing his face into his hands, the cold sweat across his forehead slick beneath his fingers.

It was a dream. It had to have been a dream. But when had his dreams become so vivid?

He hadn't just seen her, heard her voice. He'd smelled the floral scent of her hair. He'd tasted her. Gods, he'd felt the tiny sigh she always released the moment he kissed her against his mouth.

It had to be real. But if he let himself believe it, just to find out it wasn't true?

Aaron fumbled for his enka bracelet, struggling for words. *Laness, have you—*

She already got in contact, came Laness's breathless reply. *She says the dream was real.*

Laness's giddiness pulsed against his wrist. And her words seemed to strip him of every bone in his body.

He slumped back against his pillows, hoping he'd sent his thanks across before his hand fell from his wrist.

It was real. It was her.

And the realization had the shadows in the back of his mind swirling into a rampage.

They shoved to the forefront, pushing his thoughts aside, pressing him down, down, down, until only darkness remained.

He couldn't remember how to move. He couldn't separate his thoughts into words. He didn't know how to exist.

Aaron squeezed his eyes shut, wishing, fearing, he could stay like that indefinitely. Then, he forced himself upright. He stumbled out of bed, the darkness clinging to every movement like cobwebs. But he was moving. And within minutes, he was dressed, not bothering with the hallway and stairs as he faded into the shadows.

A moment later, his sitting room solidified around him. Branten and Mor looked up from the couch, far too accustomed to his shadowjumping to be fazed by his sudden appearance. Yet, as they took in the look on his face, they straightened.

"Are you two busy?" Aaron asked, the words sticking in his throat.

Branten and Mor swapped a look. Then, Branten rose to his feet with a stretch. "Looks like you two are coming with me today."

"And all of it was real," Aaron finished. He stood in the center of Nova House, a row of red training dummies newly arranged in front of him as he and Mor helped Branten set up his training equipment.

The moment Branten had come to him with his idea for the orphan program, Aaron had given him the riverside manor. It was one of the original buildings from when the kingdom was only a hidden base, Aaron surmising it was meant to be a secondary house for any visiting Star Royals.

Thankfully, that had made it easy enough to convert the upstairs into living quarters. But Branten had decided to open up the first floor, turning it into a single, massive training area, the floor covered in brightly colored mats, training equipment scattered around its edges.

"That's good," Branten said, slapping down a thick, circular mat at the end of what resembled a stepping stone path. "She's close to getting the Crystal, and you verified she's all right."

"I guess," Aaron mumbled.

Mor looked up from the tangle of ropes that would eventually become a climbing net, his head cocked. "Why is it *not* good?"

"I don't know," Aaron sighed, running a hand through his hair as he crossed to a nearby pile of equipment. "Sylas being there was annoying, but nothing I couldn't work around. And seeing Anna—gods, I would have given anything to have even a minute longer with her. Although she did tell me I should talk with Marion."

Aaron glanced at Branten, expecting him to make a face. Yet, he only chuckled as Aaron pulled free a long, wooden balance beam.

"Brother," he said, "if you didn't want to hear common sense, you *never* should have told her."

"What do you mean?" Aaron protested. "You hate the council."

"Oh, I do. But I also know Marion is the fastest, most reliable way to decode the scroll. And if it comes between fighting alone out of spite, or recruiting a disliked, but trustworthy teammate?"

Aaron scowled, dropping the balance beam at the end of Branten's stepping stones with a thud. He turned to Mor, desperate for an ally. But Mor avoided his gaze as he tied the net to its metal frame.

"Not you, too," Aaron groaned, his head falling back.

"The council already knows about the Crystal and Deardryn's plans," Mor said apologetically. "And they must have noticed Analia is gone."

Aaron nodded, not offering the vague excuses he'd spun for the council during their meetings.

"Well, then, this moment is less of a choice than an inevitability."

"Unless you disband the council," Branten said, hopping up on the balance beam and starting to pace.

Aaron scoffed. It was far from the first time Branten had made the suggestion, just for him to say the council was helpful with the small scale. If he was honest, he knew they were better for even more than that. Still, going to Marion felt like forfeiting a control he couldn't bear to let go of.

Aaron sighed, his eyes wandering back to Mor on the ground. He'd managed to tie three corners of the net to the frame, but Aaron could have sworn his golden fingers were stiffer than usual as he struggled with the final knots. He twisted his wrist, just for his face to pinch in irritation as the rope slipped between his fingers.

Aaron dropped his gaze back to the beam, careful not to look up as he said, "If you're going to make me see reason, Mor, the least you can do is help me straighten this."

He shoved Branten off the beam as he paced within reach, only then looking back at Mor. Just for a moment, he could have sworn something like knowing flickered across his face. But Mor made no comment as he rose, his shoulders relaxing as he came to kneel at the opposite end of the beam.

"So," he said, "is *that* what's bothering you?"

"No, that's been bothering me for days now. This is..." Aaron bit his cheek, searching for words. "Seeing her, knowing it was real, was like learning how to breathe again. But the longer I was with her, the more it felt like I was shriveling from the inside out."

Gods, even the words were heavy. They weighed down his chest, just like the feeling that had urged him to pull Analia closer, even as it whispered he didn't deserve to so much as touch her.

"Is it grief?" Mor asked, shifting the opposite end of the beam. "Because you knew you would wake up and she wouldn't be there?"

Aaron shook his head—although that thought hadn't helped.

"Guilt?" Branten suggested, having returned to the pile of equipment.

"No, it's sharper than that. It's more like shame than…"

Aaron trailed off, the word clicking in his mind like a key in a lock. And he wanted nothing to do with the tidal wave that flooded out of that opened door.

He rose to his feet, backing away from his words, the looks of understanding on Branten's and Mor's faces.

It was shame sending him to his mother's room at night. It was shame having him turn over that day in Accalon's chambers, searching for what he could have done to prevent this. It was shame that had him cracking apart, piece by piece. But *why?*

"I don't understand," Aaron blurted, twisting on his heel and prowling back toward his brothers. "I've survived the Underground, torture, war. I watched Analia almost lose herself to her magic. I watched Ember nearly bleed out and fight for her life for three days. And I stayed composed. I'm *excellent* in a crisis. But I was *worthless* back in Accalon's chambers."

Aaron slammed his fist into a nearby dummy, the sting across his knuckles nowhere near strong enough.

"Aaron," Mor said, surprisingly firm as he approached, "do you not remember all of the injuries Sofika healed when you came back?" He ticked them off on his fingers. "Broken ribs. Dislocated shoulder. Broken nose. Countless bruises. That's not even everything and already it's unbelievable you did as much as you did."

"But it still wasn't enough."

"Enough for what?" Branten asked, his boots squeaking on the mats as he joined them. "Enough to rescue Anna from the plan she'd already decided on? Does Anna strike you as someone who would appreciate being rescued without being asked?"

Aaron pressed his lips into a line, knowing he was right, the writhing shadows in his mind not caring in the slightest.

"Aaron," Mor said, "Analia didn't make that plan because she didn't believe in you. She made it because it was the only way she wouldn't have to choose between you and the Crystal." He squeezed Aaron's shoulder. "You didn't let her down."

It was such a simple sentiment. And it had Aaron wondering how relief could feel so much like a physical blow. It radiated out from his chest, aching and releasing at the same time, sending his knees shaking.

"So then, why?" he rasped. "If there was nothing I could have done differently, if I didn't let her down, why am I barely holding it together?"

"Because this has nothing to do with *shame*," Branten said as if it were obvious. "It's because you only do well with crises that are right in front of you."

For a moment, the shadows in Aaron's mind paused. He looked at Branten on his right. Stared a couple seconds. Then, he looked to Mor.

"You don't do well with being powerless," Mor said apologetically.

"And you're shit at asking for help," Branten added.

Well, that sounded about right. Aaron breathed a curse, his forehead coming to rest against the cold, sleek material of the training dummy.

It all came back to wanting to do something. And he had no idea how to cope with the fact that there was nothing he could do. Especially since with Dimitri gone, Ember with the healers, and his translations at a standstill, he was fresh out of distractions.

"Well, Branten," he said, rubbing his eyes, "who would have expected you would put it all together?"

"Excuse me," Branten huffed, "I am quite the philosopher."

"More like full-of-shitter," Mor murmured.

Branten threw back his head with a laugh, the sound echoing around the room. "Oh, I like that one."

The two went back and forth a little while longer, eventually wandering back to the equipment and giving Aaron some space. He absently straightened the line of training dummies, feeling like he'd been given a crucial piece to a puzzle that he had no idea where to place.

He didn't know how much time had passed when he registered the quick patter of little feet behind him. He turned, spotting the group of twenty or so children flooding down the closest staircase, the oldest looking no older than twelve. And in front—

"Aaron!"

Aaron braced himself as Brookston barreled into him, flinging his arms around his legs. "Hi!"

Aaron breathed something between a chuckle and a sigh, his hand smoothing down Brookston's mess of curls. "Hello, Brookston."

Brookston caught his hand and tugged, not letting up until he'd pulled Aaron down to kneel at his level. "Why are you sad?" he asked.

Aaron started. "What makes you think I'm sad?"

"Your face looks like this." Brookston let his expression fall, his mouth drooping into a frown, his gaze theatrically downcast.

Well, that wasn't a reassuring look. And knowing Brookston, he wouldn't let it go until he got an answer. But how was he supposed to explain any of what was swirling through his mind to a five-year-old?

Aaron looked over Brookston's head, but Branten and Mor had busied themselves with the rest of the group, Branten conveniently not calling Brookston over as he explained the obstacle course. Fine, he got the hint. No retreating to dark, quiet corners to fester.

Taking a moment to think, Aaron returned his attention to an unusually patient Brookston. "I'm sad because Analia is gone."

Brookston's eyes widened. "Where did she go?"

"Not too far," Aaron said quickly. "She's just not in the kingdom right now."

"Why?"

"Because," Aaron said. "She... She had to take care of something."

"Will she be back soon?"

Before that morning, Aaron would have said something reassuring, even as he was afraid to cling to it himself. But now, he let himself fully believe it as he nodded. "She'll be back as soon as she's finished what she's started."

Brookston seemed to consider this. He braced his hands on Aaron's thighs, clearly thinking hard as he squinted up at him. Then, he threw his arms around Aaron's middle.

Aaron made a startled noise. He automatically hugged Brookston back, "What's this for?"

"Whenever I'm sad, Branten or Evena give me a hug and say, 'I hope it gets better soon.'" Brookston patted Aaron's back, his voice muffled against Aaron's shoulder. "I hope it gets better soon."

Aaron took a breath, but he couldn't speak. Not as those words loosened his grip on his control. And instead of breaking into pieces like he'd feared, he finally settled back into himself.

Aaron sighed, Brookston's curls soft against his cheek. "Thank you."

Brookston beamed up at him. And Aaron could only shake his head as he nestled him closer.

"You're too cute for your own good, you know that?" he asked.

"That's what Branten says whenever I ask for an extra snack."

"Really? And how often do you get said snack?"

"Branten says we're not supposed to talk about it."

Aaron laughed, those final shadows in his mind settling once more. He started to speak, but Brookston's eyes latched onto something over his shoulder.

"The climbing net!" he squealed. Wriggling free from Aaron's grip, he charged off toward the rest of the group, not seeming to hear Aaron as he called a farewell.

Aaron smiled to himself, not even offended.

For the next several minutes, he quietly watched the children navigate Branten's obstacle course: climbing the net, hopping across the stepping stones, testing their balance on the beam, their yells and laughter echoing off the walls. One of them, a little girl with shiny, straight black hair, scurried across the balance beam as if it was normal ground, her dark eyes lighting up as Aaron gave her a nod of approval.

"It makes me tired just watching them," Branten said at one point, coming to hook his arm over a dummy.

"They're certainly relentless." Aaron watched Brookston try to race across the balance beam, just to immediately wobble off the side. "And they're all orphans?"

"That or their parents didn't feel capable of taking care of them," Branten's eyes drifted over to Brookston as he wobbled off the balance beam once again, Mor coming to offer him a hand up. "You'd think after running this place for over a decade I wouldn't be fazed by them anymore. But there's something special about how the children who have experienced grief, loss, pain they should never have to know, are the ones who refuse to give up."

"It's incredible how resilient they are."

Aaron turned at the sound of Evena's voice, Branten's co-owner brushing back her intricate braids as she joined them.

"Your Majesty," she said, dipping her chin to him.

"Evena, how many times must I tell you to call me Aaron?"

"As many as you like," she said. "In fact, the more you say it, the more amusement I get out of ignoring you."

Aaron snorted, Evena's jade-green eyes sparkling as she turned to Branten.

"I've gone through all of our clothes," she said. "We definitely have enough to make it through the end of winter, but with spring on the horizon, we should really stock up on some lighter layers."

"I completely agree," Branten said. He turned to Aaron. "We need to stock up on lighter layers."

"Oh, so that's why you brought me here," Aaron griped.

Branten clasped his hands, his eyes wide and pleading.

Aaron shoved him. "You know the gold is already yours. Besides, Evena is far better at that look."

Evena smirked.

"Fair enough," Branten said. "Ev, I'd offer to unleash Surce's love of shopping, but I'm assuming you've already got everything covered?"

Aaron could have sworn Evena straightened slightly. Yet, she remained perfectly composed as she pulled a list from her pocket, her elegant dark brown fingers unfolding it with a flourish. "Of course. I've already cataloged everything we should need and separated it by priority, which is then broken down by price."

"Get whatever you need, and I'll give you the gold," Aaron said.

Evena beamed. Thanking him, she bustled off, Aaron's attention lingering on the confident set of her shoulders, the logical, organized list in her hand.

"Evena prefers women, yes?" he asked.

"As far as I'm aware," Branten said. "Why, what are you up to?"

"Nothing at the moment."

Branten's eyes narrowed. Aaron shoved his arm, Branten seemingly deciding it wasn't worth pushing as Aaron turned back to the children on the balance beam.

The dark-haired girl had skipped back to where Brookston still struggled to make it across the beam. Pointing a finger at him, she hopped up on the beam, demonstrating her careful walk with arms outstretched.

Brookston clambered up behind her, needing several attempts to find his balance. But finally, something seemed to stabilize. And the little girl clapped with delight as he slowly crossed the beam, reaching the other side with a victorious whoop.

Aaron smiled to himself. And he focused on that image as he eventually exited the manor, heading for the Council Building.

Chapter 46

T he day after Cadmus's reveal, Dimitri kept a low profile. And by low profile, he meant coincidentally ending up in Othin's line of sight all throughout the day. Thankfully, it wasn't hard to follow his path.

The Sun King stormed through the Ash Castle halls like a hurricane, roaring at his advisers, demanding reports from his soldiers, slamming doors in his wake. Numerous times, Dimitri had to console a fire sprite nearly overtaken by Othin's tirade, to the point he told a trembling Spark to spread the word that they could hide in the safehouse for the day. But all of this was good.

Now, Dimitri sat on the entryway floor, his back resting against a pillar as he flipped through his poetry collection. Othin had stormed past a few minutes prior on his way to the Council Chamber, Dimitri not faking his jump as he felt Othin's amber eyes sear into him. But at least he had proof Dimitri wasn't off scheming somewhere. He was completely unconnected to Cadmus's reveal.

Dimitri turned the page, the words so familiar he barely had to read. Still, he didn't look up as the castle door swung open.

"I informed him last time," came Joshel's agitated voice. "It's your turn."

"Fuck no," Stanek retorted. "He's already throwing a fit. I'm not putting myself in his war path to tell him we *still* have no sign of them."

"He likes you more."

"He likes what I can do for him. And right now, what I *can't* do is find those Crystal-forsaken Royals."

Dimitri peeked at the guards as they bickered on, the two having paused at the foot of the stairs. Well, this could be interesting.

Returning his gaze to his book, Dimitri drawled, "You don't have to worry about Othin."

The guards cut off. They pivoted toward him, Dimitri's shoulders tensing under their familiar contemptuous stares.

"What do you mean, runt?" Stanek demanded.

"Call me by my name and I might tell you," Dimitri shot back.

"Dimitri." Joshel stepped toward him, his hands extended in what Dimitri could have sworn was a genuine peace offering. "What do you know?"

Dimitri glowered a moment longer, especially as he caught Stanek's eye roll behind Joshel's back. Finally, he turned away with a sniff. "I overheard some maids talking about how Othin is considering doing nothing about the Royals."

"What?" Joshel demanded.

"Bullshit," Stanek spat.

Dimitri shrugged as they took a few steps closer. "That's what they said. Apparently, he's tired of taking the fall for Deardryn's scheme. She's limited his resources, and hasn't shown him an ounce of gratitude. Then there was something about if Deardryn wanted this kingdom, she could come and hold it herself." Dimitri flipped a page. "I think his pride is wounded."

Stanek spat a vicious curse. After all, this wouldn't be the first time Othin slunk away in shame. Meaning everything these soldiers had been through—fighting, bleeding for this castle, being removed from their homes—was all for nothing.

Dimitri struggled to keep a straight face as the guards stormed up the stairs, their rants echoing off the stone. Going in the opposite direction of Othin and the Council Chamber.

Oh, this was going to be fun.

Grinning to himself, Dimitri rose to his feet and stretched. Might as well get a final check-in on Othin before he made himself scarce.

Tucking his book in a pocket, Dimitri headed off down the hall, his gaze absently moving over people's faces as they passed. He didn't realize he was looking for someone until he spotted wavy mahogany hair down the hall, and all of his senses perked up. Yet, as he drew closer, he realized it was just an Ash servant heading for the stairs that led down to the kitchen.

Dimitri looked away, mentally chiding himself. *I won't choose your life over mine.*

The sentiment had always grounded him in his moments of doubt. Yet, it didn't stop him from speeding up as he turned into the Council Chamber's deserted hall, Rayner's voice softly echoing up ahead.

What was he doing in the Council Chamber? Had Othin left? Was he collecting information?

Dimitri reached for the knob on the ajar door, a greeting on his lips.

"You don't have to lie to me," said Othin from within. "I know who you are."

Dimitri's heart jolted. He dove behind the door, his fingers spasming around the knob. Crystal spare him, he'd almost walked in on Rayner and Othin talking—why were Rayner and Othin talking?

Dimitri peeked around the door, certain he had to be mistaken. But that was Othin standing at the head of the table, arms folded. And that definitely was Rayner seated in a nearby chair, one hand casually resting on the back as he sat sideways to face him.

"Who am I, exactly?" he asked, drawing out the words.

"You're Sylas's masquerader. Deardryn told me how you reported on Dimitri's movements, just to disappear the same night he did."

"Does that mean she knows he's here?" Rayner asked.

"Do you honestly believe she wouldn't?"

Rayner shrugged. Dimitri barely caught himself before he could slump against the door. What in the name of the five gods was happening?

"What are you doing here, Rayner?" Othin asked, his question the smooth, lethal slide of a blade.

But Rayner didn't flinch. He crossed his ankle over his knee, his dark eyes giving Othin a long, considering look. "Are you asking as a father, a king, or a conqueror?"

"What do you think?"

Dimitri had no idea. But Rayner's lips flickered in a secretive smile that had Dimitri's insides twisting until it hurt.

"Sylas sent me here to keep an eye on Dimitri," he said. "He's not thrilled having Deardryn in his kingdom, but he likes the idea of Dimitri roaming free, spreading nonsense he'll eventually have to deal with, even less. So, what I'm doing is going where my king needs me most."

The breath whispered from Dimitri's lungs. He didn't hear Othin's response. He didn't feel the doorknob slide from his grip.

All he knew was his feet had started moving. Away from the door, away from the voices, farther and farther until his back hit the opposing wall at the end of the corridor. He shuffled to the side, barely making it out of view of the door. Then, his entire being collapsed inward.

Dimitri slumped against the wall, not sure if he was breathing, part of him hoping he was no longer existing.

Because Rayner hadn't changed. He hadn't been trying. He'd donned the perfect mask to whittle down Dimitri's resolve, wriggle back into his good graces. And he'd fallen for it. *Again.*

Gods, how had he gotten here? Back in Sun, he'd perfected the art of burning bridges. He'd numbed himself to the fact there were few people who *tried* to know him in the first place.

So, how did he keep getting betrayed? How did he end up falling apart in an empty corridor when the servant from Sun would have shoved through that door, verbally eviscerating them until all of his pain had become their own?

Then again, there was still time to do so.

Dimitri pressed his forehead into his palms, his eyes landing on the black heart on the inside of his wrist. And he could practically see the disappointment on Patryclas's face at the idea.

Gods, he couldn't do this. He couldn't go back to that sad, broken little boy. He couldn't let down the man who, at every opportunity, had given him the benefit of the doubt. Even when he didn't deserve it.

Dimitri's gaze shifted to the pane of shattered glass on his other wrist. His first oath with Rayner.

Dimitri's shoulders slumped. Then, he dragged himself off the wall, each step cracking in his chest as he headed down the corridor.

Dimitri pulled himself onto the turret's flat roof. It had taken him a bit of wandering to find the right turret, but as soon as he'd spotted the worn cracks and dents in its side, perfect for handholds, he knew he'd found Analia's spot.

Now, he brushed away the snow on the lone metal bench, barely registering the cold as he sank down and pulled his knees to his chest.

He wished Patryclas was there. Even if he didn't know what to believe, he would know how to slow Dimitri down, help him figure out how to proceed.

But Patryclas was gone. Reduced to memories and tattoos and the unpredictable tides of grief. Even Analia and Aaron were kingdoms away.

He was alone. Alone in a way he hadn't felt in a long, long time.

"There you are."

Dimitri's head snapped up at the scuff of boots on stone, Rayner pulling himself onto the roof a moment later. No, he couldn't—

"I was wondering how you so thoroughly disappeared," Rayner went on, adjusting his jacket with a gloved hand. "But then I remembered you telling me about this place."

Dimitri gave a jerky nod, his arms tightening around his knees.

What was he supposed to say? He'd come up here to figure out what to do. But now Rayner was here, standing on Analia's turret, displacing the ghost of her in a way that felt like sacrilege. And Dimitri couldn't bring himself to tell him to leave as he came closer.

"So," he said. "This is the place Analia would come to train."

"And talk with her uncle," Dimitri blurted.

Rayner nodded to himself. He turned in a slow circle, taking in the view of the snowy kingdom far below. "This is a good spot."

"Uh-huh."

Should he pretend like nothing had happened? No, based on the faint crease between Rayner's brows, his expression had already removed that option. Should he accuse him? Startle him into a response? Crystal spare him, what was he supposed to do?

"I had an interesting conversation with Othin today," Rayner commented.

Dimitri nearly fell off the bench. "You *what?*"

"It wasn't planned," he said, coming to sit beside Dimitri. "He spotted me leaving the library and practically dragged me after him as he bellowed at his advisors. I tried to catch your eye for help when we passed you in the entryway, but you didn't look up from your book."

Well, that last part was true; he'd purposefully avoided looking at Othin out of fear of becoming his next target. But was this the beginning of an excuse? Had he spotted Dimitri outside the Council Chamber and was trying to cover his trail?

"What did he want?" Dimitri asked, watching him closely.

"Well, apparently he and Deardryn have been talking, and not only did Othin tell Deardryn you're here, but she told him I would be with you. Seems like my 'unpredictable loyalty' got their attention."

Rayner rolled his eyes, not seeming to notice Dimitri's hands begin to shake as he pulled his knees closer to his chest.

"What did you tell him?" he rasped.

"That he was right, and Sylas sent me to keep an eye on you."

Dimitri couldn't help his tiny gasp. Rayner looked over at him, his eyebrows shooting up at Dimitri's expression.

"You don't honestly believe that?" He sat up straight, Dimitri having nowhere to go as Rayner's hand came to hover beside his ankle. "Dima, do you think Sylas could care less about what you're up to outside of his kingdom? He's probably thrilled you're gone and that he no longer has to deal with you."

Rayner flashed a grin, his eyes dancing with amusement. The warm, playful amusement of a private joke. And Dimitri wanted to be on the inside, wanted it more than he ever would have imagined. But there were still holes in Rayner's story.

"Why would you say it, then?" he asked, easing his feet back to the roof.

"Because it felt like the perfect opening." Rayner shifted to face him fully, his knees carefully avoiding bumping Dimitri's. "We already knew Othin would start suspecting us after Cadmus's display. I figured if he thought I was just another Royal puppet and an extra pair of eyes on you, he might let down his guard a fraction. It seemed to work, but that man is so volatile I never know what to expect."

"Oh."

Dimitri dropped his gaze, his fingers tracing the spiraling lines carved into the bench's cold metal leg.

It all made sense. It made more sense than any of the alternatives. And Rayner hadn't even hesitated before answering his questions—he'd volunteered the information in the first place.

"You weren't expecting me to tell you," Rayner said slowly.

Dimitri's shoulders curled inward, his mouth automatically opening. But Rayner waved a dismissive hand.

"It's fine, I deserve that. It's why I came to tell you in the first place."

"Because you thought I don't trust you?"

"Because this was something you needed to hear from me. Immediately."

Something in Dimitri's chest shuddered as Rayner met his gaze. Unflinching. The flecks of gold surrounding his pupils catching the sunlight, highlighting so many ghosts and mistakes and broken dreams.

But all Dimitri saw was the promise Rayner had made to him back in Aaron's spare bedroom. *You can trust me.* And Dimitri had no doubt in his mind that promise remained intact.

"I'm glad you told me," he said, his words feeling like an offering he didn't know how to extend. Because he *was* glad. No, he was fucking relieved.

Relieved Rayner had told the truth. Relieved he'd taken a breath before reacting. Relieved that finally, for the first time since leaving his cell, he was certain he'd made Patryclas proud.

He slumped back against the bench, his words flooding free, "I saw you talking to him."

Rayner's tentative smile had barely formed before his head snapped up. He stared at Dimitri, then cursed under his breath. "No wonder you looked like that when I arrived," he muttered.

"Like what?" Dimitri asked.

"Like I'd slapped you across the face and you were waiting for me to do it again."

"I forgive you," Dimitri offered.

"Good. That means I can finally give you these." Rayner pulled a pair of gloves from his jacket pocket and tossed them to Dimitri.

Dimitri caught them reflexively, then cocked his head. "Why do you have these?"

"Because I first went to our chambers when looking for you, and once I saw them, I realized where you were. Now, put them on, your hands are turning red."

Dimitri had the strangest urge to grin. A huge, face-aching grin. Not wanting to give Rayner the satisfaction, he kept his face straight as he pulled on his gloves with numb fingers, muttering, "Bossy."

Rayner scoffed. "Whiny."

"Am not," Dimitri whined, Rayner's laugh feeling like a victory he hadn't known he was aiming for.

"Come now, Dima," he said, lightly elbowing him. "You can do better than that."

"Oh, fuck off, Royal puppet."

"I can't do that. You would have nothing left to complain about, and Othin would see through you for sure."

Dimitri barely stifled his laugh. He twisted away, hiding his face, "I changed my mind, I don't forgive you."

"Is it because you're blond now?" Rayner asked, leaning in conspiratorially. "You were so much more scathing with dark hair. I could fix that for you, you know—"

Dimitri covered his mouth as his laugh finally broke free. Rayner quickly joined in, only laughing harder as Dimitri kicked him in the shin. He turned his head to look at him, taken aback by how close Rayner had come: his laugh warm against his cheek, his shoulder brushing Dimitri's.

But Dimitri didn't mind. He inched a little closer, savoring the heat radiating off Rayner's skin, his eyes following Rayner's smile as he turned back to the view.

It really was a great spot.

Chapter 47

When Ember had said she wanted things to be back to normal, this wasn't it.

Every morning, Aaron shadowjumped her to the greenhouse where Cenn usually waited, Sofika having left them a list of poultices to prepare. Around midafternoon, Sofika came to investigate their work, Cenn bustling off to his other assignments while Sofika tested Ember on everything from plant revitalization to her magical stitching skills, demonstrated on orange peels. And that was it. That was her day.

The rational part of her brain knew Sofika was determining her skill level before assigning her anything. It further noted that based on the complexity of some of the poultices, ointments, and pastes, she was trusting Ember to teach Cenn. But it also noted that based on the population size, Sofika didn't need nearly as many supplies as she was requesting.

From what Ember could tell, the Starlight Kingdom was a little smaller than the central Ash Kingdom. Yet, there were no surrounding towns, no apprentices deciding to travel to the central Healer School to learn. Meaning not only was the kingdom smaller than she was used to, but so was the number of healers.

She got glimpses of them as she wandered through the center on her breaks, the majority too young to bear rings from training before the Shattering. The only thing more unsettling than not knowing who was an apprentice and who was a master was their friendliness as they greeted her, even as she reluctantly told them her specialty.

It was just... wrong. The kind of wrong that had her pacing around the greenhouse during her chunks of alone time, knowing she should be working, but unable to force herself to sit back down.

She should be relieved she was surrounded by kind, supportive healers that wanted to get to know her. She should be honored she was working under such a talented healer. Gods, she even got to spend time with the group of nymphs—often led by Laness—that stopped by every other evening to tend to the plants.

But Ember wasn't in the mood to be grateful. In fact, each "improvement" to the system she was raised to respect had her resentment growing sharper. But worst of all was the devinroot.

Staring at her. Calling to her from the second floor. Riling up her withdrawal until she couldn't focus for more than a few minutes at a time.

"You should come to training with me," Branten said one morning. He sat at the dining room table, blearily watching Ember pace as she waited for Aaron to bring her to the Healer Center.

Ember's withdrawal snapped that he should mind his business.

"Excuse me?" she asked instead, still a bit harsh. But Branten remained unfazed.

"You're pacing so fast it's stressing even me out," he said. "Training can help with that, get out all the pent-up energy. I have some free time now that I'm not training Anna; we can go out to the hollow tonight."

Ember paused at the opposite end of the table, positive she was mishearing. "You," she said slowly, "want *me,* to train. As in warrior training."

"You say that like it's absurd."

"You say that like it's not."

"Why, because you're a healer?" Branten pushed his plate aside, resting his elbows on the table. "Training isn't just about learning how to punch someone in the face—although that's not a bad skill to have."

"Not happening," Ember replied.

"Then at least come running with me."

Ember's withdrawal recoiled. She folded her arms, her tone shifting into something grave. "I do not *run.*"

"Sure you do," Branten said. "What if there's an emergency?"

"Well, if you feel faint during your run, I'll be sure to get there as soon as possible."

Branten threw back his head in a laugh. "Oh, challenge accepted, healer girl."

Ember rolled her eyes, Aaron thankfully choosing that moment to push through the dining room door. Yet, as they faded into the shadows not long later, she couldn't shake Branten's words.

She didn't have pent-up energy. She was bored because she had nothing challenging to do. And she didn't have her devinroot to stop her mind from scattering in a thousand different directions as she concocted even more poultices.

Ember's eyes drifted up to the vivid orange and yellow leaves on the second floor, half-listening to Cenn's recount of how Sofika had let him heal a patient's fractured ribs.

She couldn't shake the feeling she'd been left with the devinroots as a test. Then again, it didn't matter because she was passing. She'd looked at those plants countless times and not once had she tried to steal a leaf. Even as the desire had the humid air feeling too thick in her lungs.

She. Was. Not. Addicted.

The words played on an endless loop in her mind, getting louder and louder as her days passed with little change. It reached the point she was relieved when Aaron knocked on her door one evening, asking if she wanted to go on an adventure.

"What kind?" she asked, shrugging off the healer robes Cenn had surprised her with on her first day working in the greenhouse.

"Something for Anna," he said vaguely. "I'll tell you when we get there."

That might have been the one thing he could have said to distract her from the headache arcing across her forehead. So, she agreed.

To Ember's surprise, Aaron opted to walk to their destination instead of shadowjump. She kept her hands in her jacket pockets against the cold, Aaron taking the opportunity to fill her in on Analia's updates as he led her through the busy streets.

According to Laness, she was investigating the magic around Deardryn's study and chamber doors while Deardryn was away, trying to find a way inside. Every now and again, he paused his recount as someone called a greeting, Ember startled each time they waved to her as well. Yet, she never minded when he stopped to talk for a few moments, her eyes absently wandering over the streetlights and lit-up store fronts. Just for her attention to be caught by a familiar laugh.

Ember twisted around. Cenn sat at an outdoor table nearby, a woman with chestnut curls and delicate features seated beside him. With a smirk, she swiped his water glass and took a sip, her own wine forgotten in front of her.

Cenn said something Ember didn't catch over the general chatter. But there was no mistaking the dimple in his cheek as he smiled, poking her repeatedly in the ribs until she was laughing and he could steal his glass back. The woman didn't seem to mind, the streetlights casting a soft glow over her light brown skin as she laced her fingers with his.

Ember's jaw dropped. She took a few steps closer, barely noticing the people that moved around her.

Cenn was a healer. And he was holding hands with someone? In public? Judging by the way he ran his thumb along her knuckles, this wasn't new either.

Ember stared, something disturbingly close to envy stirring in her chest.

"What are you looking at?" Aaron asked suddenly.

Ember's heart jolted. She hastily pointed to a nearby tavern, "Someone absurdly tall stumbled out of the door. I thought it was Branten, but I couldn't get a good look."

"Really?" Aaron looked around, Ember casually shifting to block Cenn from sight. "I think Branten is staying over at Nova House tonight. You'll be dismayed to know there are numerous tall, muscular warrior men wandering about my kingdom."

"'Warrior men?'" Ember repeated.

"That's what Anna calls us," Aaron said, heading for a shop whose display window sparkled with jewelry. "Speaking of Analia, we've arrived."

Aaron climbed the front steps, a cheerful bell tinkling overhead as he held the door open for her. And while Ember was quickly distracted by Aaron's surprise, even as she genuinely enjoyed herself, she didn't forget what she'd seen outside. And she didn't waste any time the following morning.

"I saw you last night with that woman," she blurted. She sat at her usual table in the greenhouse, the words popping out of her mouth the moment the door creaked open.

Cenn paused in the entrance, his arched eyebrows flicking up. "You did?"

"I won't tell Sofika," she added quickly. "Trust me, with how much flirting I did back in Ash, I understand how fun it is. But you can't cross that line, Cenn. You're too talented to risk your healer status."

Ember leaned forward imploringly, needing him to understand. Cenn stared at her like she'd switched into a foreign language.

"What are you talking about?" he asked.

Ember thought her head was going to explode. "I'm talking about you clearly being in a relationship with that woman despite your healer's oath!"

She gripped the edge of the table, expecting Cenn's face to pale. But Cenn only blinked. Once. Twice. Then, he dissolved into laughter.

Ember bristled, her chair scraping across the floor as she shoved to her feet. Cenn raised his hands.

"I'm sorry," he said, struggling to compose himself as he came toward her. "I'm not laughing at you. I just forget sometimes that you're not from here and don't know all the ways we've changed."

As placating words went, those were pretty good. Still, Ember folded her arms as she eased back into her seat, her tone clipped. "Enlighten me, then."

Cenn smiled, taking the seat beside her. "Marisa and I have been together for five years."

Ember's jaw dropped. She started to respond—more likely screech—but Cenn gestured for her to let him finish.

"Her mother owns a pottery studio in the Mirage, and I found that sculpting is a good activity for me when I need to feel... grounded. Marisa was actually the one who taught me how to work with clay. And after a few months, I realized I was disappointed on the days I walked in to find she wasn't there. Even then, she had to make the first move—and by that, I mean she threw a rag at me and called me an idiot because how many hints did she have to drop before I realized she was interested?"

Cenn grinned at the memory. And that fond, adoring sparkle in his eyes was the same one Ember had seen in Aaron's every time he looked at Analia during his brief stay in Ash.

"That's a lovely story," she said, struggling for calm. "But Cenn, your oath."

"That's what I'm getting to." Cenn sat back in his seat, tracing a circle around his eye. "Based on my reading, your rings don't just represent your stage of mastery, but also the oath you swear, first when joining the healers, then when becoming a master. That includes having no relations, no children, even how much wine you can drink with a meal. But that's not how we do things here.

"It's understandable why you all maintain those values," he went on, seeming to take Ember's stunned silence as encouragement. "If you're going to be a healer for a kingdom's-worth of people, it's perfectly reasonable to not want any distractions. Our healers felt the same while in the Star Kingdom. But when we separated from everyone else, the younger healers like Sofika started to question those rules.

"After all, loving someone, being loved, doesn't stop you from caring about others. If anything, it makes you care more. And what we realized is the old way of doing things was trying to keep us detached. Give us distance to spare us from the difficult cases. But here, we feel those highs and lows are what helps us preserve our humanity, and seeing as Rosala has continued choosing us, I don't think she minds. At any rate, that's why you don't have to worry about me and Marisa."

Cenn shrugged. And Ember had to turn away in her seat, hiding her face so he couldn't see the vitriol blazing through her blood.

She wanted to call him a heretic. She wanted to snap that she didn't care less about her patients because she kept her distance. She wanted to scream that this entire kingdom had lost sight of what it meant to be a healer.

Ember pulled at the neck of her robes, the greenhouse too hot as her withdrawal demanded she let those words free. She was sorely tempted to listen.

But Cenn didn't deserve her tirade. Not when, looking back, all she could see was a genuine concern on his face that left her feeling like a monster.

Ember took a deep breath. Focused on the smell of growing things.

"She's very pretty," she forced out.

"She's beautiful," Cenn corrected. "And she's unreasonably good at puzzles."

Once, a sentiment like that would have had Ember squealing. She would have demanded he tell her everything, thrilled to see her friend so happily in love. But now, she could only swallow the bitter taste in her mouth as she nodded.

"All right, then," she said on an exhale, reaching for the folded paper in the center of the table. "Let's get to work."

Cenn cocked his head, his dark eyes studying her face. Seemingly deciding to let it go, he busied himself organizing his supplies. But even as they fell back into their usual rhythm, Ember couldn't shake the blaze in her blood.

Because these people might wear the robes and have the magic, but they weren't healers. That was probably why Sofika thought she was an addict. She couldn't wrap her head around the idea that Ember could have simply had a slipup.

The word settled in Ember's mind like the answer to an impossible question, keeping her calm until Cenn offered a farewell and got up to leave.

It had only been a slipup. After all, she'd used devinroot for years to help her focus, and she'd been fine. People used devinroot all the time and didn't become addicted.

Ember rose from her seat, her eyes on the devinroots as she climbed the stairs.

She wasn't an addict. She'd accidentally taken too much. But she was in control.

Ember reached the second floor, her hand already extending as she turned into the devinroots' aisle. She just had to be careful.

Her withdrawal perked up, obviously onboard with this plan. It guided her hand forward, every muscle in her body relaxing as her fingertips brushed over fuzzy leaves.

Gods, it would be so easy. But she couldn't. She had to prove she had control.

So, heart sinking, she dropped her hand and headed back toward the stairs. Proving her problem wasn't as bad as Sofika believed.

But as Ember returned to her table, waiting for Sofika to arrive, she couldn't stop her fingertips from rubbing together. Just as she couldn't stop herself from fantasizing about the fuzzy texture, the sharp, sour smell as she went home later that night.

And she couldn't shake the feeling of how wonderful it would have been to breathe it in as Sofika summoned her to her study the next day. She sat in a cushioned chair at Sofika's desk, only half paying attention.

"You have excellent scores in all areas," Sofika said, flipping through a pile of notes across from her. "At this point, there's little left for me to teach. I presume you're still sober?"

Ember struggled not to stiffen, her attention finally caught. "I haven't used any devinroot if that's what you're implying."

"And you haven't told anyone either?"

Ember pressed her lips into a line, Sofika's almond-shaped eyes narrowing in response. Yet, her tone remained brisk as she rose to her feet.

"I feel you are more than capable of tending to patients," she said, crossing to a massive snake plant in the corner of the room. "But seeing as I've already put you through rigorous testing, I'll give you the next three days off. Then, you may return and start your official work."

Sofika poked at her plant, missing the horror Ember knew was plastered across her face. Because poultices were easy, but at least they were a distraction. But being home? Alone? For three days?

Sofika finally looked back, Ember's response coming in a rush. "Thank you, Master Sofika."

"Sofika," she corrected.

Ember's stomach churned. Not just at the informality. But because backward or not, she needed to have a place as a healer. And Ember had no idea how she was going to make it through the next three days.

Chapter 48

Aaron drummed his fingers on the back of his dining room chair, oddly reluctant to sit as he waited for Marion to arrive. She'd been surprisingly open to his request to meet at the big house, Aaron figuring it was a neutral enough spot. The Council Building always put him on edge, and he didn't want to meet in his actual home.

The big house, though, had the right combination of familiar, but not emotionally significant. And as a knock sounded on his front door, Aaron knew he was going to need all the reassurances he could get.

Passing through his entryway, he pulled open the door, forcing his expression into something pleasant as he spotted Marion on the other side. Her dark hair sat coiled in a knot atop her head, her black council jacket replaced with a deep green one that complimented her hazel eyes.

"Good afternoon, Your Majesty," she said, perfectly polite as she bowed her head.

"Councilwoman." Aaron dipped his chin, his gaze drifting up to her face. And for a long, excruciating moment, that was where their conversation ended.

Marion shifted, a wrinkle forming across her dark brown forehead as the silence stretched. One heartbeat. Two.

She opened her mouth, just as Aaron blurted, "Come in."

Aaron barely stifled his cringe. Marion, however, didn't miss a beat as she thanked him and stepped inside, leaving Aaron to stare longingly at the lake just beyond his lawn's stone wall. Then, with a sigh, he closed the door.

"It's an honor being invited into your home," Marion said, following him back into the dining room. "Believe it or not, this is my first time inside."

Aaron choked back his quip just in time. "I'm not surprised," he said instead, gesturing for her to take a seat. "My grandmother kept work and home strictly separate."

"Your father was the same way. I presume since you don't live here full time, we aren't disturbing the tradition?"

"Exactly."

Aaron searched for something else to say, knowing he shouldn't leave it at that. But Marion seemed content to peer around the room, making a soft hum of approval at the arched doorways, the ornate crystal chandelier. And Aaron didn't bother asking before heading for his liquor cabinet.

Gods, what had he been thinking? He wasn't a diplomat. He was an antagonist. He was trained in the Underground to observe, provoke, and pounce. Analia was the one who knew how to turn a conversation into a chess game—and gods, was she good at it.

In a matter of one conversation, she'd captivated the council enough that even Samuel and Jasper had allowed them into the vault. She could have won Marion over in seconds. Actually, she wouldn't have needed to because she would have realized they were simply having a conversation.

Aaron didn't think the word was supposed to send a bead of sweat trickling between his shoulder blades as he selected a bottle and glasses. Especially since talking was a talent of his.

He just had to be pleasant. Polite. Say *anything* to fill the silence creeping back in.

"I appreciate you meeting me here," he said, heading back toward the table. Even his smile felt stiff.

He was supposed to be working with her, not shutting her out. But the thought alone had his magic stirring, his face desperate to smooth into a blank, unreadable mask as he passed her a glass of amber liquor.

"Your Majesty," she said, dragging him from his thoughts. "Might I be frank?"

"Please," he said, slumping into his seat.

"We're not in the Council Room. You're not wearing your crown, and I'm not in my uniform. We're sitting in your childhood home. I think we can abandon formalities, don't you?"

Aaron hadn't noticed he'd shifted into them in the first place. But at her words, the rigid filter around his mind slackened, his words coming easier to his lips.

"I think we can do that," he said. "As long as you call me Aaron."

"And you call me Marion."

Aaron nodded cautiously, Marion's weathered face softening into a smile.

"In that case," she said, rising with glass in hand, "I would appreciate a tour of your house."

"Really?"

"I think you underestimate how long I've been wondering what Ethelind has been hiding in here." She circled around the table, coming to pause beside him. "Shall we begin?"

Aaron didn't think there was much question in her words. But having nothing else to lose, he pushed back his chair and retrieved his drink. "I suppose we shall."

Aaron led Marion through the closest arched doorway, his mind wandering elsewhere as he narrated the short, carpeted hall.

He'd worked with Marion long enough to know she didn't make requests without reason. Yet, all he could see was genuine delight on her face as they stepped into the kitchen.

"Oh, this is beautiful." Marion ran her fingers along a dark marble countertop, the sunlight streaming through a row of windows flashing off her golden rings. "I spend so much time in my kitchen. It must be wonderful having so much space to cook and bake, and you have that lovely table for company as you work."

"I'm usually at the table," Aaron said, half to himself. "Mor says I'm not allowed to touch the stove."

Marion laughed. Aaron started, his eyes darting to her as she moved to examine the small corner table.

He'd never heard her laugh before. It was a nice sound, warm and inviting, matching the look she gave him as she rejoined him at the entrance.

"Let's go this way," she said, stepping back into the hall. "We can discuss why you've brought me here as we go."

Aaron's throat tightened. But if he'd already made it this far...

Not giving himself time to second-guess, Aaron knocked back the last of his woody liquor. Then, setting the empty glass on the counter, he took a steadying breath and forced his feet to head after Marion.

"I wish I had a better topic to offer," he said, taking the lead as they headed down another hall. "We got confirmation that Deardryn was hunting the Crystal, as you know. And the 'business' I told you Analia was taking care of..."

"Is retrieving said Crystal," Marion said promptly.

Aaron shot her an incredulous look. "Is it that obvious?"

"Only to me," she said, taking a sip from her glass. "The other council members were paying attention to Analia as she told her story, but I was watching you. Fifteen years of meetings, not including the decades when Ethelind was still queen, and that was the first time I saw your unreadable mask slip. And I've seen that look on your father's face enough times to know it must be an extraordinarily special mission for you to have stayed behind."

Something about the approval in her tone had Aaron's spine straightening. It was the second time someone in his kingdom had commented on the way he looked at Analia. The foreign princess who was the biggest threat to their security. And they both had been pleased.

"That's definitely true," he said.

They turned the corner, Marion making a noise of delight. "I recognize these," she said, trailing her finger along the gilded frame of one of the countless paintings covering the walls. "These were part of Elspeth's art collection."

"That's right," Aaron said, perking up at the change in topic. "My grandmother told me in the decades she lived in the Star Castle, she'd amassed enough paintings to cover every hallway. Yet, these water-themed ones were her favorite. And when my father was evacuating everyone to Starlight, he made sure they ended up here, too."

Aaron straightened a painting of a waterfall tumbling into a lake filled with water lilies, the knot in his chest softening. Ethelind had told him countless stories of his father throughout his life, his hazy early memories of him having faded long ago. But that one had always been his favorite.

It was his window into who his father had been, not as a king, but as a person. A husband. A man.

"That sounds like him," Marion murmured. She paused beside a painting of a starlit lakeside, her fingernail lightly tapping against the frame. "Did you know Elspeth painted this?"

"She *did?*" Aaron quickly crossed to the opposite wall, pressing his fingers against the frame as if seeing it for the first time.

The painting had always been one of his favorites, the lake not only shimmering with starlight, but reflecting its ripples back up into the sky. The technique was masterful. Yet, he'd never seen his mother even hold a brush.

Could Marion have been mistaken? Or was this one more thing Elspeth's grief had taken from her?

As soon as the thought had formed, he knew it was true. He swallowed hard, needing a moment before he could ask, "How did I never know she made this?"

"Elspeth was protective of the things she cared about," Marion explained. "She preferred to keep things private until absolutely necessary. You two are alike in that sense."

Aaron kept his gaze on the painting, the comment smoothing a few jagged pieces of himself he'd never realized he had.

For a few moments, Marion watched him quietly, his fingers shifting to rest against the cool glass above the lake. Finally, she stepped around him, that thoughtful tinge still in her voice as she said, "I'm assuming that's why we're here."

Aaron gave himself one more moment to remain where he was, the family history in that hallway settling around him like the reassurance he'd so desperately needed. Then, he turned, following Marion down the hall.

"Unfortunately," he sighed, "it is. The good news is we managed to open the scrolls, and apparently Talitha decided to split the Crystal into thirds. So, even though Deardryn has a shard, she still has a ways to go. Especially once Analia smuggles it back here. But the bad news is the scroll is written in the forgotten tongue."

"Clever," Marion murmured.

"Between Surce and I, we've started to piece it together. But we don't have anywhere near the fluency needed to translate it completely."

"Which means you need my help." Marion paused in the entryway to the sitting room, then snorted. "Oh, I do hope this is Ethelind's doing."

Aaron followed her through the door, Marion practically glowing with glee as she spread her arms, taking in the explosion of stripes, florals, and other patterns covering the room.

"Trust me," Aaron laughed, "we nearly went to war over this room when she returned to the DovenU. The only reason it's still like this is because she told me if I so much as removed a throw pillow, she will disown me, take my crown, and give it to Branten. I thought I'd be able to hide it all once she left, but she keeps returning unexpectedly to make sure everything is still here."

"Ethelind always had a wicked sense of humor."

"More like decor taste," Aaron griped, sitting on a purple couch, a scratchy orange pillow tumbling onto his lap.

"Aaron, when was the last time you saw Ethelind wear stripes? Or orange for that matter?"

Aaron frowned, images of Ethelind throughout his life flashing through his mind. Outfits ranging from black, to blue, to purple, several of her gowns featuring floral detailing. And yet...

"Don't tell me," he said.

"I believe Ethelind has been messing with you."

Aaron flopped back against the couch with a groan, Marion laughing as she adjusted a green-striped lampshade. "Branten and Surce have been mocking me over this room for *decades*," he complained. "This room was normal for so long, it only started deteriorating during the last years of her queenship. I thought she was taking out her frustration on the color scheme."

"In actuality," Marion said, "she was preparing an heirloom."

Aaron buried his face in his hands. "Stop knowing things about my family."

Marion chuckled. "Fortunately, I also know the forgotten tongue."

Aaron looked up as the couch dipped, the corners of Marion's eyes crinkling as she sat beside him. "Does that mean you're willing to help with translations?" he asked.

"Of course."

Aaron paused, bracing himself for the caveat. But Marion only sipped from her glass, clearly having nothing to add.

"What?" she asked, noticing his stare. "Did you expect me to refuse?"

"I…"

Now that he thought about it, he didn't know what he'd been expecting. All there had been was the feeling that sharing with her was a bad idea, so all-encompassing that it didn't leave room for the reasons why.

Yet, he hadn't thought twice when actually telling her. There wasn't even a flicker of frost in his veins.

"How did you do that?" he asked, almost a whine.

"I gave you a distraction," she said simply. "I knew if you were willing to come to me of your own volition, it must be important. But I wasn't lying when I said you're like your mother. And whenever she came to me, clearly knowing she needed to talk despite not wanting to, we would paint until the words came. That's why I'm the only one who knows that painting in the hallway is hers."

Aaron's lips parted, but he only shook his head. He'd been completely played by this woman. Yet, instead of icing her out, he found himself asking, "Why?"

"Because just like Elspeth, I wanted you to know you're safe to trust me." Marion placed her half-empty glass on the low table before them, her hand coming to touch his knee. "This is a dangerous time for our kingdom. Our future queen is behind enemy lines, your identity could be revealed at any time, and this kingdom is on the brink of becoming a battlefield. If we're going to make it through this, we're going to need our king. But no king can survive constantly carrying that burden alone."

"You mean me," Aaron said bluntly.

Marion took a breath, obviously choosing her words carefully. And that tiny action ached far more than it should have.

After all, it was his choices that had gotten them into this situation. He was the Royal. He was the one with the final say, the one who was supposed to be protecting this kingdom.

It was the oath he'd made the day he accepted his crown. The same oath he'd made to Analia when he slid the ring on her finger that now sat buried in a box in his dresser drawer.

Marion squeezed his knee, his heavy gaze lifting to hers.

"I've served on three generations of Star Royal councils," she said. "While you, Ethelind, and Hester have been distinctly unique rulers, the one thing you have in common is a tendency to take your rule... personally. The state of the kingdom, its climate, every decision and its success or fallout, you all put on yourselves. And while it has created passionate, driven rulers, it has also created lonely ones."

Aaron started to protest, but Marion lightly tapped his knee.

"I have watched you not only fight your way out of the darkness, but prove yourself worthy of your crown. You should be proud of everything you've accomplished. But that doesn't change the fact that no Royal can singlehandedly carry the weight of a kingdom. That's why you have a council. And it makes you no less a king to let us share that load."

Her words struck a direct blow to Aaron's pride. A blow he needed to feel. But one that also had him muttering, "Even Iphen?"

Marion scoffed and swatted his arm. "Don't be territorial. He might have had his eye on Analia, but he's taken your side in more matters than I can count."

"Which only irritates me more," Aaron grumbled. But there was no bite to his words. Not as he finally registered the full extent of the weight that had been pressing on his shoulders. The glimmer of relief at the thought of Marion's offer.

He opened his mouth, not sure what he was about to say. But he cut off as the air in front of him shimmered, his enka bracelet tingling as Laness appeared in front of him.

"Laness," he began, "what are you..."

Aaron's words lodged in his throat as Laness's eyes, wide with panic, met his.

"Apologies, Councilwoman," she said, her voice high and fast.

"Laness, what's wrong," Marion asked, sitting up straight.

But Aaron couldn't move. Not as Laness came to grip his hands, giving him something to hold on to as she said, "It's Anna."

Chapter 49

After three days of failing to break into Deardryn's chambers, Analia wasn't in the mood to deal with the Dragoness's schemes. Yet, the morning Deardryn returned to the castle, Tavian was at her door, having been ordered to retrieve her and bring her to the study.

By the time they reached the study, Tavian had thoroughly convinced himself it was a trap. Analia, however, didn't see the point.

The door only tingled with the same detection magic around Deardryn's chambers. She didn't sense the Crystal's casing inside—which was agitating, since she hadn't been able to detect it in Deardryn's chambers either. Meaning wherever Deardryn had gone, she'd taken the shard with her.

Analia's stomach rolled. Seeing no reason to delay, she stepped up to the door, Tavian hovering behind her as she reached for the shiny brass knob. Yet, as she pushed inside, nothing happened.

No alarm. No flare of magic. Just the soft tingle of the detection wards across her skin as she stepped forward, the magic not even attempting to stop her.

"This is strange," she murmured, wandering through the silent, empty study. "Why would Deardryn allow me in here unsupervised?"

"There's a note," Tavian called from the desk.

Analia hurried over. He passed her a folded sheet of paper with her name written on the front, then plopped down on the nearby chair to watch as she opened it.

"Dear Analia," she read, perching on the edge of the desk. "Now that you've successfully grown accustomed to the Crystal's magic, it's time we develop your tracking abilities. I've stationed myself somewhere within the castle, and as soon as my wards notify me of your presence in my study, I will open the casing. You will have ten minutes to locate me without leaving the room. If you try, my wards will notify me. Deardryn."

Tavian grumbled something about queens and their schemes, Analia not paying attention as her mind raced.

It had already been thirty seconds since they'd walked inside. She knew from her time in the Human Kingdom she could expand her sensory abilities, but that had involved releasing a massive amount of magic. Even without knowing this, Deardryn had clearly given her so much time because she expected the dampers to interfere. But if she could figure it out fast enough...

Raising a hand to quiet Tavian, she closed her eyes, reaching for her magic. Not down to the empty well where her flames usually slumbered. But up. Up to her mind where the wards tingled across her senses and she summoned her mental shield from.

Immediately, stone walls closed around her mind, as easy as a reflex. But this time, Analia imagined the stone softening. She allowed it to condense into itself, folding and collapsing into a thin, flexible ring. Then, gritting her teeth, she shoved it outward.

The ring moved like a band already pulled taut. Tension crackled along its edges as it expanded beyond her mind, the study, stretching into the rest of the castle from all directions. With every inch, a new magic field joined the clamor across her senses, sending a bead of sweat rolling down her temple.

But she'd endured the Crystal's magic. She could handle a few Blessed, wraiths, magical light sources—yes. There.

At the opposite end of the floor beside the library, the Crystal shard's magic field slithered through the noise, its buildup having already been released to draw as little attention as possible.

Analia gave herself one second to verify. Then, she released her hold.

The band snapped back into place, Tavian grabbing her as the relief sent her pitching to the side.

"Analia," he said, "what—"

"I found it," she wheezed, blinking the spots out of her vision. "I'm all right, just give me a second."

Tavian looked like he might explode with questions. But he kept his mouth shut, his grip not loosening on her as she pressed her forehead into her palms.

That had taken more out of her than she'd been expecting. But she couldn't afford to waste any more time.

"Go close the door," she said, her legs thankfully steady beneath her as she slid off the desk.

"Why?"

"Because we have eight minutes to search this room for anything to do with the Crystal, magical locations, or a way to deactivate the wards on Deardryn's chambers."

With any other person, she would have anticipated a follow-up question. But Tavian—destructive, pot-stirring Tavian—only ran a hand through his bronze hair, a slow, maniacal smile curving his mouth. "I knew I liked you for a reason, Red."

With that, the two split up. Tavian headed for the door, Analia circling around to Deardryn's side of the desk as the door thudded shut.

She pulled open drawer after drawer, her eyes scanning over pens, spare paper, empty folders, all typical study supplies. Come on, where was it.

"No relevant titles on the bookshelves," Tavian called.

Analia cursed under her breath. She'd watched Deardryn pull all of her essential supplies from these drawers. Always on the right side—yes.

Analia pulled out Deardryn's damper box. Dropping it on the desk, she flipped open the latch, acutely aware of her time ticking out. But thankfully, the box's contents were a disorganized mess. Meaning, Analia didn't have to worry about leaving a trail as she plunged her hand into the jumble of smooth, polished jewelry and textured stones.

She knew there had to be something that would help her get into Deardryn's chambers. But she didn't have time to investigate as her fingers closed around a cold, metal chain.

Analia pulled out Aaron's damper, her heart aching at the faint flicker of his magic contained in the chunk of onyx. Part of her squirmed at the idea of Deardryn realizing it was gone. But she was tired of playing on the defensive.

"Good luck getting Star magic now," she muttered, sliding the damper into her pocket. Closing the box, she returned it to the drawer. Just to spot Deardryn's blue book of notes tucked away in the corner.

Analia's blood tingled. She fished out the flimsy book, the cover unadorned outside of the royal blue background, but undeniably the same book of notes.

"I hope that's something good," Tavian called. "We're down to five minutes."

Gods, that was nowhere near enough time. Analia flipped open the book to a random section, her eyes darting. But the page was blank.

She quickly turned the book to the first page, but Deardryn's neat handwriting was upside down. Flipping the book right side up, she expected to find the true first page blank, Deardryn presumably working backward for whatever reason. But no, there were Deardryn's notes from Analia's first exposure to the Crystal.

But if there were blank pages in the middle...

Analia flipped to the back of the book, her eyes scanning.

Healer markings. Practice first established by Helia Oshar when negotiating healer-Royal separation. Ink said to uphold healer oath, but no specific Blessing mentioned.

Crystal strike her down, she'd found Deardryn's research notes. And if she was keeping those notes in the same book as her notes on the Crystal...

Tavian continued to clatter around the room, but Analia didn't notice as she hunched over the book.

Page after page, she read through Deardryn's careful cataloging of the healers: their ceremonies, the stipulations of their oath, the consequences if that oath was broken. Analia had thought she had a good understanding of the healers thanks to her friendship with Ember. But Deardryn had assembled a story that had even her surprised, especially as she skimmed Deardryn's questions in the margins.

Why must apprentices travel to the Temple of Rosala to seal their oaths? Why would a Defiant request the ceremony? Why reinforce the oath with ink?

Analia's mind scrambled to piece everything together.

If Deardryn was writing these notes in her book dedicated to her Crystal research, it had to be connected. Then again, Deardryn had been chosen by Rosala. It was natural for her to be curious about the group she'd had to turn her back on.

Could it be the subject of the book wasn't the Crystal, but rather her current research?

Analia started as there came a clatter and a curse from Tavian behind her. And the Crystal's magic field flickered to life in the center of the room.

"I see you've been rummaging through my things," Deardryn commented, completely unfazed as she emerged from the shadows.

Analia's blood tingled through her veins. But she kept her gaze on the book. "If you didn't want me to see it, you wouldn't have left it behind."

Deardryn hummed softly. Analia chanced a peek as she felt Tavian come up behind her, Deardryn's gaze fixed on the Crystal's casing she turned between her fingers. Gods, what was the Dragoness thinking?

"Tavian," she finally said, "you may go."

Tavian made a noise that sounded a lot like, "As if." He turned to Analia, looking all too ready to reach for the sword hanging from his hip. But Analia shook her head.

"It's fine."

Tavian opened his mouth to protest. Analia touched his arm, giving him a meaningful look. Finally, he relented.

Fixing Deardryn with a venomous glare, he stalked toward the door, Analia knowing he would be waiting outside as he yanked the door shut behind him. Then, she and Deardryn were alone.

"I'm assuming this was a test," Analia finally said, her voice surprisingly level.

"Among other things." Deardryn slipped the Crystal's casing in a pocket of her deep green gown, then came to pluck the book from Analia's hand. "I presume you located the Crystal before enacting your search?"

"You were beside the library."

Deardryn nodded to herself, satisfied. But Analia didn't relax. She remained perfectly straight in her chair, waiting for the rebuke, practically craving it.

But Deardryn only pulled out Analia's usual chair and sat. "Excellent."

Analia stared. One, two, three seconds. Deardryn retrieved a pen from the cup on the desk, golden curls falling into her face as she made a note in her book.

And Analia's control snapped.

"Why are we doing this?" she demanded, gripping the edge of the table. "Why are we pretending to be civil when you should hate me? You told me as much back in my uncle's chambers. Why do you uphold this facade?"

"Because," Deardryn said, infuriatingly calm, "I see myself in you."

"What does that even *mean?*" Analia asked, throwing up her hands.

She knew she was letting Deardryn see she was getting to her. But she was tired of scheming and hiding and staying perfectly composed. Especially as Deardryn went quiet for a long, long time, her fingers absently rubbing the golden bracelets on her wrist.

Just when Analia thought she might explode, Deardryn finally spoke.

"During the Shattering War, I was on the battlefield like most Royals. Yet, I wasn't engaging in the conflict. I was part of a first response healer squadron that would heal our injured on the battlefield and relocate them to safety. Even though I had chosen my duties long before this point, the healers welcomed me without hesitation. Especially since I had my dragon."

Deardryn rose from her seat, Analia keeping her narrowed gaze trained on her as she drifted toward the counter. "Her name was Ina. I presume, since you met Pryanth's dragon, you understand the nature of our connection?"

"Each Royal in your kingdom bonds with a sun dragon at a young age," Analia said slowly.

"Indeed. And have you ever wondered why you've never seen me with mine?"

Deardryn turned back to her, the grief twisting her face taking Analia's breath away.

"It's because on one of my missions, we were trying to rescue a group of injured soldiers Elspeth had captured. The others had told me not to, it was too dangerous for a healer. But Ina and I knew we could do it, we had the aerial advantage.

"Indeed, we were able to swoop down and grab them. But not before Elspeth somehow got a poison-dipped dagger through Ina's scales. I did everything I could to heal her, and even bleeding out, she got us back to the command center. But then..."

Deardryn clenched her fists in her skirts, struggling to hold back the tears shimmering in her eyes. "Elspeth took something from me that day," she finally said, her voice shaking. "Not a pet, not a friend. A part of me. A part I could never get back. And so, I…"

Deardryn looked down, her shoulders curling inward. Analia's heart ached. But as she pieced the rest of the story together, it wasn't for Deardryn.

"You kidnapped and killed Elspeth's children," she finished.

Deardryn pressed her lips into a line, looking like she wanted to speak. But she remained silent. And the last of Analia's control ignited.

"Say it," Analia said, pushing to her feet. "Say that you put them behind a shield and killed them. You *killed* them, just like you killed Lucilla. You probably don't even remember their names, their faces, because you only viewed them as disposable—"

"Their names were Kir and Hali."

Analia's mouth snapped shut. Deardryn went on, sounding like she was reciting a long-memorized script.

"They were fourteen and eight respectively. Kir was a quiet boy, surprisingly solemn knowing his parents, but there was an intensity to him. It was something about the way he looked at you, like he was taking in your every word, every move, trying to understand exactly who you were.

"Hali, on the other hand, was barely walking when the war broke out. I only got glimpses of her over the years, but she seemed like a handful, always ending up where she shouldn't. Both of them favored Hester in looks, with their sandy-brown hair and deep-set eyes. But Kir, Hali, and Aaron all have the same smile. The one that makes you think they're up to something, and they're unreasonably entertained by it. And they are dead because of me."

Analia wrapped her arms around herself, at a loss for words. These were Aaron's siblings. A brother and sister he never got to know, didn't even remember anymore. All because of Deardryn. And she couldn't show so much as a flicker of remorse as she stood beside the counter, her voice, her face, completely empty.

Finally, Analia understood what Sylas had been trying to steer her away from on the bridge. *Don't let your schemes harden you to the point you have nothing to come back to.*

"You don't even feel it, do you?" she asked, almost pitying as she stepped closer. "The grief and guilt over what you've done. Even as you remember all that to punish yourself."

"I told you," Deardryn said, "I see myself in you. And contrary to what you might believe, I'm *telling you* this to prepare you for the cost of the crown you'll soon receive."

"Murder isn't a mandate of being queen."

"But impossible decisions are." Deardryn turned, her gown hissing across the carpet as she started to pace. "When you become queen, you're no longer responsible for just yourself. You have an entire kingdom's-worth of people depending on you. It is your duty to put their best interest above everything else. Even your humanity."

"Then why bother being kind to me?" Analia demanded. "If I'm doomed to lose myself to the crown, why spend so much time trying to build me up?"

"Why do you no longer wear your uncle's pin?"

Analia recoiled as if doused by ice water. "What does that have to do with anything?"

"Everything. Just like the magic in your veins." Deardryn turned, fixing Analia with her honey stare. "You may sit here and judge my decisions, but even Accalon compromised himself for the crown.

"He *lied* about his magic, even to you, the person who would inherit it. He was the master of maneuvering people in conversations to get what he wanted. He was infamous for making plans and not telling his allies about them until they were completed."

"And you think that's on the same level as killing innocent people and invading kingdoms?" Analia asked, dumbfounded.

"Do you truly believe Accalon has no blood on his hands?" Deardryn countered.

Analia took a breath, just to let it out wordlessly. And Deardryn's eyes gleamed with a hunger that had her insides twisting.

"Face it, Analia," she said. "Accalon knew just as well as I do that the crown is a Royal's greatest source of power. But it is also our greatest detriment. And it is an armor we cannot afford to take off."

Deardryn paced toward her, close enough Analia could smell the honey-sweet scent of her skin.

But Analia didn't flinch. Not from her words, not from the memories, not from the slow, languid pulse of Deardryn's magic.

Because she'd spent months watching Aaron's demeanor shift based on whether he was with his family, the council, or his people. She could tell if he was the Starlight King or Aaron just by the set of his jaw.

Deardryn would say it was part of his strategy. But he had stripped himself bare in Surce's studio, offering her every secret, every weapon that could be used against him. He proved to her that armor could be removed. And Crystal spare her, it was nothing Accalon hadn't already shown her.

He'd shown her every time he emerged from the Council Chamber, his entire de-meanor relaxing the moment the councilmen were gone. He'd shown her when she was small and he'd bring her to his chambers after a difficult day, pulling her onto his lap and asking about her day until the worry lines around his mouth had softened. He'd shown her every time he joined her on her turret.

Meanwhile, Analia had never seen Deardryn's mask slip for more than a second.

"Accalon not only knew how to remove his armor," she said shakily, "but he knew how to take off his crown."

Deardryn sneered, but Analia's voice grew stronger.

"Yes, he kept his magic a secret. But it wasn't to manipulate anyone. It was because he knew this magic put a target on his back—which you have so aptly demonstrated this past month. He wasn't trying to harm anyone. He was protecting himself. He was protecting *me*. But you?

"You can't even see the line anymore. You've murdered and tortured and manipulated people for your own gain without a second thought, and you can't show me a flicker of remorse. My uncle might have made decisions I'm not aware of, but at least I could see they weighed on him. At least he gave me reasons to believe he had good intentions. You might both be rulers, but comparing his actions, his secrets, to yours?" Analia shook her head. "You're not a queen. You're a monster."

With those final words, the last of the puzzle pieces clicked into place in Analia's mind.

Sylas was right, she did see things in extremes. And when comparing Accalon to Deardryn? The difference couldn't be more stark. And Analia's heart broke just a little bit that she hadn't realized that until now.

Analia folded her arms, waiting for Deardryn's retaliation. What she wasn't expecting was for Deardryn to flinch, her face crumpling with something that looked a lot like devastation. Before Analia could be certain that was what she'd seen, Deardryn's expression hardened.

"Give me your bracelet," she said, deadly quiet.

A chill ran down Analia's spine. "What bracelet?" she asked.

"The enka bracelet my guards found on your ankle back in the Ash Kingdom. The one I told them to let you keep because I wanted to see what you could do with it. But if you insist I drop my 'facade,' I'm happy to oblige."

Deardryn's hand snapped out, Analia's mind scrambling as she retreated back into the desk.

She always knew this moment would come. But Crystal spare her, she had no time to talk her way out of it, nowhere to go as Deardryn shoved up her left sleeve.

"Not on this wrist," Deardryn mused.

Analia cringed away, trying to hide her arm behind her back.

Laness, she thought, *She's found my bracelet, I'm—*

"There." Deardryn snatched Analia's arm and yanked up her sleeve, revealing the woven purple-and-black stems resting above her damper cuff.

"This changes nothing," Analia spat, trying and failing to pull away.

"Oh," Deardryn said, untying the stems with a quick flick of her fingers, "I think it changes everything."

With an infuriatingly casual movement, she pocketed the bracelet. And Analia prayed Deardryn couldn't see just how right she was.

Chapter 50

Aaron sat on his sitting room couch, numbly watching Laness pace as she recounted what she'd sensed from Analia's bracelet. At first, he'd been grateful she hadn't waited for everyone else to arrive, Branten and Surce hurrying through the door midway through her recount. But now, hearing the full story, watching Branten and Surce struggle to piece together what they'd missed, all he could do was focus on staying present in his body.

The one comfort he had was Laness had only sensed anger, then shock before the connection went dead. There was no fear. No pain.

But that didn't stop him from ordering her to Moon, Laness disappearing before he could finish his sentence. It didn't stop him from having to chip away a layer of ice before he could accept Branten's offer to train. And it nearly crushed him as Surce told him she'd start a tapestry immediately.

He just had to make it through the day. There was no way Analia wouldn't find him in his dreams and explain. He just had to stay busy until then.

But even with his plan, the rest of the afternoon passed like a waking nightmare. Thoughts and what ifs haunted him through every task, Branten and eventually Mor hovering nearby to help drown them out. But those worries always lingered in the shadows in his mind, whispering to him one after another.

What if, what if, what if, what if, what if.

Ember returned from the Healer Center around dinner time, finding him organizing the clutter that had piled up in his side room.

"Laness filled me in," she said, pressing a tea bag into his hands. "Drink this after dinner. It will help you sleep."

Thank the gods. Aaron squeezed her hand, his thanks stuttering on his tongue as he took in the dull look in her blue-gray eyes.

But he didn't have enough room in his body to worry about her, too. He didn't have enough room in his mind to remember the rest of his evening, the fuzzy sound of his family's voices during dinner blurring with the light, floral tea he gulped down soon after.

To his relief, it didn't take long to feel the effects. He fell into bed, his eyes closing of their own accord.

He had to dream of the bridge. Everything would be all right if he dreamed of the bridge.

The words swirled through his mind, whispering over and over again until they faded into darkness. And when he opened his eyes, Aaron breathed something between a curse and a sigh of relief.

He was back on the bridge. It was warm enough to be a summer night, just like before. But when he looked out across the railing, there was no fog obscuring his kingdom. And he was completely alone.

He must have still been in his own dream, not the middle ground Analia had pulled him into.

Aaron ran a hand through his hair, coming to grip the back of his neck as he started to pace. He couldn't remember how long it had been before she appeared last time. Gods, he couldn't even remember if his dream had started with her appearance.

Aaron pulled off his blue-and-black jacket, tossing it onto the railing as he moved back and forth. Come on. Come on, come on, come on, come on—

Aaron pivoted. And where the bridge had been empty a moment before, she was there. Standing with Sylas about thirty paces away, Sylas not sparing him a look as he turned to retreat farther down the bridge, a bank of fog swirling to life along the lakeside.

Aaron's lips parted. And he barely had time to breathe her name before she ran into his arms.

"There you are," he sighed, pulling her closer, cocooning her in his arms.

He didn't need to imagine her doing something to know this was her. He knew from the way she fit against him, the heat of her skin, the electricity that crackled down his spine as her fingertips brushed the back of his neck.

It was her. She was with him. And fuck if that wasn't the only thing he cared about in that moment.

"Thank the gods," Analia said, her voice muffled against his chest.

"It's all right," Aaron soothed, running his hand down her hair. "I've got you. You're safe."

"I was so worried."

"We'll figure it—you *what?*"

"I've been worrying about you all day," she said, tightening her arms around his neck. "I knew as soon as you found out I lost my bracelet you would panic or brood—or both." She lifted her head, her eyes narrowing as she studied him. "You did both, didn't you?"

Aaron blinked. Once. Twice. Then, a slow, stupid smile spread across his face as he shook his head. "My shooting star."

"Oh gods," she muttered, "you *did* do both."

Aaron chuckled, the entire situation leaving him feeling fuzzy and lightheaded. He leaned down, brushing his nose against hers as he said, "As a matter of fact, I remained busy all day."

"Oh, did you?"

"You've left me unsupervised for a month, and I've learned how to panic, brood, and multitask all at once."

"Is that so?" Analia asked, her eyebrows lifting in mock astonishment. "That's quite the accomplishment, Your Majesty."

"I know. The parade is scheduled for next week."

Analia laughed. And that was all Aaron needed to settle his nerves as she said, "I'll have to see if I can make it."

She tilted her head. And Aaron forgot every quip he could have possibly made as she fit her mouth to his.

He pulled her closer, her kiss deep and drugging and something he never wanted to break away from. But they didn't have much time.

Reluctantly, Aaron turned his head, skimming his lips along her cheekbone until he found her ear. "Tell me what happened," he whispered.

He didn't know what kind of reaction he was expecting. But it wasn't for Analia to roll her eyes.

"I poked Deardryn's temper a little too hard," she explained.

Aaron listened quietly as she filled him in on her search of Deardryn's study, Analia seeming more annoyed than anything—which was reassuring. Yet, that didn't stop the buzz from her kiss from fading in his veins, dwindling down to a spark once she reached the end.

"I don't like that she's always known about your bracelet," he said, playing with a lock of her hair.

"Me neither. But it's been a possibility ever since her guards searched me in my Ash Castle cell. I was hoping they didn't know what it was and didn't care to report it, but as it turns out?" Analia shrugged. "What's bothering me is the fact that she left her notes for me to find."

"Could she have gotten cocky?" Aaron asked.

"Never," Analia said immediately. "Leaving her notes was a test at best, and her wanting me to find them at worst."

"What would she gain by letting you see them?"

"Confusing me," Analia suggested, tracing a silver embroidered thread in his collar. "Throwing me off her trail. But Aaron, it wasn't a few notes she could have scribbled in thirty seconds. This was pages upon pages of organized, detailed notes. I can't see her wasting that kind of time just to throw me off."

"So, then," Aaron mused, "the question is, what do the healers have to do with the Crystal?"

Analia pinched the bridge of her nose, clearly having already dwelled on that question far too long. She started to pull out of his grip, sending a tiny jolt down his spine.

"Where do you think you're going?" he asked, tightening his arms around her.

"Not far." Analia gently pried his hand from her hip and interlaced their fingers. "You're coming with me."

Aaron's grip relaxed. "Well, as long as I'm coming with you..."

Analia flashed a small, tired smile. She led him over to the railing, coming to lean against it as she stared out into the fog. Aaron watched her quietly, knowing by the tightness of her mouth he should leave her be.

Part of him was surprised he didn't sink into his own brooding. Then again, he didn't think he could worry about Deardryn and her schemes more than he already was.

"Could you ask Ember if she knows anything that might be helpful?" Analia asked, pulling Aaron from his thoughts.

"I was already planning on it."

He squeezed her hand, Analia running her thumb across his knuckles in response. Yet, the line between her brows didn't smooth.

"I can't believe the only thing in my way is a *door*," she said, picking at a crumbling section of the railing. "I've lost track of how many times I've considered forcing my way inside, magic or not. But you wouldn't be able to shadowjump inside to get me, and even if Laness used my bracelet as an anchor, she's too far away for one jump."

"I sent her to Moon this morning," Aaron said. "She should be there by tomorrow."

"Of course you did." Analia leaned into him, Aaron breathing in smoke and jasmine as he nuzzled the top of her head.

He knew she would figure it out. He might worry what Deardryn was doing to her every day she was gone, but whether or not Analia would succeed? Never. With her, it was only a matter of when.

Still, Analia's distracted gaze remained fixed on the fog.

"You know," he said, lightly tugging on her hair, "what *I* can't believe is Deardryn turned my damper into one of her rings. I can only pray Surce weaves a tapestry of her face the moment she finds out it's gone."

"She definitely won't be pleased," Analia agreed. "I already tried unlocking my cuffs with it, but it's too thick to fit between the cuff ends. It would be nice if it could…"

Analia trailed off, something sparking to life in her eyes. Something that had Aaron's blood rushing a little faster through his veins.

"Aaron," she said, turning to face him fully, "can a damper only block one person's magic network at a time?"

Aaron cocked his head, intrigued. "No. A damper is going to suck up as much magic as it can contain, regardless of how many networks it draws from. So, even though I was wearing my damper in Sun, if you had come in direct contact with it, it would have trapped as much of your magic as it could until you broke away. It's why damper cuffs have a protective outer layer."

"Just like Deardryn's jewelry box," Analia said, something glorious unfolding across her face. "So, even though your damper has been sealed to maintain your flicker of magic, it should still absorb whatever magic it comes in contact with?"

Aaron looked down at her. And his mouth curled into a grin as he finally caught up.

"My clever shooting star," he said, ruffling her hair, "That should work perfectly."

Analia's entire being lit up. No, she blazed. And Aaron had never been happier to burn as she made a noise of success and stretched up on her toes, crushing her mouth to his.

Analia's kiss was hot and demanding. Aaron immediately pressed her back against the railing, Analia momentarily breaking away as she gasped. But she pulled him back in, her tongue curling around his, moaning against him as his hand slid up her leggings, his fingers digging into her ass. And Aaron was hard, and addicted, and couldn't think beyond the pleasure rushing through his veins.

This was what he'd been craving. From the moment he saw her on the bridge that first night, the moment he realized she was all right, the moment his lips found hers once again.

He wanted a release. The blaze in his blood as she scraped her teeth up his neck. He wanted something to remember when he ravaged himself later.

Aaron dragged his lips down her throat, coming to suck on her pounding pulse. Analia made a small, breathy sound. And Aaron couldn't understand why there was fabric beneath his hands.

Why was she not bent over the railing, his lips exploring the arch of her spine, feeling her writhe against him as he buried himself in her—

There came a loud, pointed cough from down the bridge.

Analia winced. And Aaron was going to disintegrate the stone beneath the Moon King's feet.

Before he could, Analia gently extracted herself, her mouth swollen, her face flushed—Aaron was going to murder him.

"Don't start, Sylas," she called, recovering far faster than Aaron. "You were the one who decided to not turn away."

Sylas grumbled something, Aaron not bothering to listen. He braced his hand against the cold stone railing, his chest still heaving as he tried to refocus on the matter at hand.

Analia. His damper. Deardryn—oh, that did it.

"If you already have my damper," he said unsteadily, "you can't afford to wait much longer."

"I know. At this point, there's no reason to continue dragging things out."

"What does that mean?" he asked, craving, fearing her response.

Analia squared her shoulders, bold and beautiful and fearless as she said, "Tell Laness to be ready tomorrow morning."

Aaron swallowed hard.

It all came down to this. Tomorrow, either Analia would come back to him, or Deardryn would capture her and make her pay. Tomorrow, Deardryn would decide if she turned her sights on Aaron's kingdom. It was the culmination of every fear he had.

He looked down at Analia, not sure what to say.

But Analia wasn't afraid. She stood with her arms folded, her eyes blazing with triumph, the fog swirling behind her like a plume of ghostly smoke. And Aaron might have gone back to the tapestry of her wedding night for decades, but he could have stared at that image for a lifetime.

"Analia Valarus." Aaron slid his arms around her waist, his voice dropping to a murmur as he guided her to him once more. "Rise again."

He pressed his lips to her forehead, his eyes closing. Analia rested her hand against his chest. And while Aaron didn't know how long they stood like that before he started to fade, it didn't stop the reality of their situation from settling in his chest.

This was Analia's mission. She had to finish what she started. And all he could do was keep it together long enough to be there when she returned.

Analia watched Aaron fade away, feeling like she had solid footing for the first time in a month.

She knew how to get into Deardryn's chambers. There was nothing left that she could learn or uncover. It was time.

Analia looked back at the sound of approaching footsteps, not sure what to expect from Sylas. She'd been ready to bicker him into submission when she'd cornered him after dinner that night, saying they had to meet in the sitting room. Yet, he'd only trailed his hand along the back of the chair beside him. The one seat he never allowed anyone to take at any meal.

Then, he nodded. And he'd barely made any snide remarks as he guided her through starting their dreamwalking, eventually taking control once again.

Now, he paused beside her, his black eyes considering.

"Summon a shadow," he said.

Analia blinked. But she raised her hand, hesitantly reaching for her magic.

Beyond the well of crackling flames, the soft rumble of Sylas's magic rising up to meet her. And a cold ribbon of shadows laced between her fingers.

Sylas gave a satisfied nod. "I presume you'll be needing my assistance tomorrow?"

"All I need from you is to go through with whatever plan you've been plotting."

"What makes you think it's ready?" he deadpanned.

"The fact that you haven't outright told me no."

Analia let her shadows wink out, barely catching the corner of Sylas's mouth quirk. For a moment, she thought he would finally let his bored mask slip, give her a glimpse of the man behind the crown.

"Don't get yourself killed," he drawled.

Analia scoffed. "Just admit that you like me."

Sylas snapped his fingers, Analia unsurprised as the bridge started to fade around her. But just before everything went black, she caught him murmur, "Good luck."

She was going to need it.

Chapter 51

When Analia was eight, she'd snuck into the gravel training arena behind the Ash Castle to watch Cadmus train. At five years old, he'd already attained an impressive control over his magic, his trainer applauding as he slowly expanded and shrank the ball of golden flames in his hands. But Analia didn't have time to dwell on her envy before two of her older cousins strolled into the arena.

"Would you look at that," Dace said, his blue eyes latching onto her huddled in the shadows. "It's the Princess of *Ash.*"

Analia didn't remember what she said in response. She just knew no one was surprised when she turned and fled. Just as she wasn't surprised when her uncle found her on her turret not long later.

"Why are we the Ash Kingdom?" she asked, rubbing her stinging eyes as she leaned against him. "Fire is able to create and cleanse and warm and attack. Ashes are the useless remains when the fire dies out."

"If you think that," Accalon murmured, "I must be doing a terrible job teaching you."

Analia looked away with a frown.

"Come now, little fledgling," he said, sliding his arm around her to poke her ribs. "Does that mean you would say something else? Perhaps that I've been an excellent teacher? Grand? Superb? I might go so far as to say you're thinking spectacular."

He poked her ribs with each suggestion, Analia's frown crumbling into a tiny laugh.

"You're 'spectacular' at complimenting yourself."

"Ah, but at least I know how to make you smile." He ruffled her hair with his free hand, offering a soft smile of his own as she finally peeked at him. "We are the Ash Kingdom," he said, "because yes, we create, we burn. But most of all, we're not defeated by our failures. We rise from them."

Accalon pulled her close, whispering into her hair. "They can douse your flames, but they can't steal your ashes. So, rise again."

Rise again. Her uncle's favorite saying, the memory swirling through Analia's mind as she paced around her chambers, the sun slowly rising beyond her window.

Deardryn might have claimed she was trained to be queen, but this was her birthright. Rising from every lost battle to conquer the war.

Analia rubbed her chest, feeling the ghost of warm metal against her skin. Her gaze drifted to the top drawer in her vanity. And a knock sounded on her door.

"Come in," she called.

Letta stepped inside a moment later, her black hair hastily braided back, her golden-brown eyes groggy.

"You summoned me?" she asked.

"I did." Analia crossed to her, Letta hesitantly taking her extended hands. "I need you to intercept Deardryn on her way to breakfast. Tell her I'm not feeling well and won't be coming to the study this morning. If anyone asks, I didn't want a tray sent to my chambers either. Most importantly, I need you to keep Deardryn out of her chambers as long as possible."

"Why?" Letta breathed, all sleepiness gone.

"I can't tell you. I just need you to stall her. And you can't tell Tashia."

Analia squeezed Letta's hands, letting the cool, unruffled mask she'd worn like armor throughout the castle finally fall. And it wasn't an Ash Royal, but Analia who said, "I'm trusting you. Can you do this?"

She stared into Letta's face, knowing her methods of testing her loyalties hadn't been foolproof. But her gut had told her to request Letta's help. And as Letta nodded, her eyes wide but focused, Analia knew she'd been correct.

"I'll do what I can," Letta vowed. She squeezed Analia's hands. Then, she released her and turned for the door.

Just before she exited, she looked back. "Thank you for protecting my home."

Then, she left, her words echoing in Analia's mind.

Protecting. She liked that. And as her eyes returned to her vanity drawer, she knew Accalon would have, too.

Analia sighed, sinking down on her chair. She pulled open the drawer, finding her uncle's pin exactly where she'd left it, her fingers caressing the metal ring for the first time in weeks.

All throughout her time in the Moon Kingdom, she'd been trying to separate herself, not just from him, but his shadow. Yes, he had raised her, trained her. But she needed to figure out who she was without him. She needed to establish herself as worthy of the spot at the Royal chessboard he'd left her, prove that she didn't need him to be formidable.

She just hadn't realized she didn't need to reject him to do so. Just as she didn't need to lose him because she'd been hurt by him.

Analia closed her eyes, a few silent tears finally slipping free.

For her uncle. The side of him she never got to know. All the sides of him that she missed. All the scars that had her questioning him. And all the questions she would never get answered.

Analia took a steadying breath. Then, fastening his pin to her tunic, she knew she had the one answer that mattered: Accalon had loved her enough to take off his crown for her.

You have been well-trained to be queen.

That was true. Now, as she retrieved Aaron's dagger and damper from under her pillow, it was time to figure out what she wanted to do with all those lessons.

Analia pulled open her door, coming face-to-face with Tavian and Sabi on the other side.

"Sylas told us what's happening," Tavian explained.

"We're helping," Sabi added.

Analia took both of them in, Tavian quietly fuming, Sabi waiting impatiently. And she didn't think twice. "Then let's go."

Ember sat on Aaron's porch swing, anxiously rubbing her fingertips together. She was barely fourteen hours into her mandatory time off, and she felt like she was about to jump out of her skin.

Just an hour before, she'd accidentally snapped at Branten that, like every other morning, she wasn't going running with him. And riddled with guilt, she slunk outside to watch the snow melt across the backyard. Definitely not fantasizing about how wonderful it would feel to inhale a sharp, sour smell.

"Hey, this is my brooding spot, get your own."

Ember hissed softly. Gods-damned Starlight King, popping up everywhere, talking at her relentlessly, all while studying her as if he could see into her soul. Shouldn't that mean he could see she wanted him to leave her alone?

The thoughts spit through her mind. But Ember stomped them out, forcing her face into something she hoped was neutral.

"You have a designated brooding spot?" she asked.

"Technically," Aaron said, coming to join her on the swing, "mine is my mom's room in the big house. That was just something Anna said to me when she found me brooding on the Sun Castle roof."

"That sounds like her."

Ember shifted, angling herself ever so slightly away from him. Gods, take the hint.

"You look... pensive," Aaron finally said.

Ember released a small breath through her nose. Then, submitting to the fact she wasn't getting rid of him anytime soon, she said, "You're allowed to say awful."

"I am?"

"Yes, because then I can say you look the same."

Her withdrawal begged her to deliver it like an insult. But Ember said it like a fact—which it was. His face was pale, his hair disheveled, his eyes red and irritated as if he'd been rubbing them too much. But Aaron offered a half smile.

"If I tell you why I look awful, will you tell me why you do?"

Sofika would have *loved* that arrangement. Ember shrugged, hoping she kept the sneer off her face. And that seemed enough for Aaron.

"Analia should be starting her plan any minute," he said, tracing the edge of the swing with a finger. "She still doesn't have her bracelet, and Laness isn't there yet. And I've lost enough of my mind sitting around waiting that I'm considering going to translate the scroll with Marion for the distraction."

Aaron rubbed the back of his neck, not quite meeting her gaze.

Once, Ember would have known exactly what to do in that moment. She would have found the proper combination of validating words and reassuring touches that would have him settling back against the swing. Because if nothing else, she was a good friend. She was proud of that. And Ember had never missed that part of herself more as she searched for a sentiment not coated in withdrawal.

"Analia is the last person you have to worry about," she finally said, placing her hand atop his icy one. "If she can survive the Ash Kingdom for twenty-two years, there's nothing Deardryn can do to break her. Nothing we can't help her put back together, at least."

She tightened her fingers around the back of his hand, wishing she'd found something better to say. But some of the tension left Aaron's shoulders as he bowed his head.

"I know."

Ember's fingers lingered on his hand, something telling her there was more to come. But Aaron only sighed, running his free hand through his hair.

"Do you know if the healers have any connections with the Crystal?" he asked.

Well, that wasn't the response she was expecting. She shook her head, "Nothing overt enough for me to think of off the top of my head. Why?"

"Last night, Anna told me Deardryn was poking around the healers. I just..." Aaron shook his head. "We can discuss it later. For now"—he bumped Ember's knee with his own—"what's going on with you?"

"It's... a healer thing."

Aaron deflated slightly, sending her withdrawal bristling. Before she could say something she'd regret, Ember added, "I think you should go see Marion. Anna wouldn't want you sitting and stewing, and you'll be able to shadowjump back here the moment she and Laness return."

There. That was some decent advice. Still, that didn't stop her from squirming as Aaron studied her for a few moments, a faint line appearing between his brows. Finally, he nodded.

"You're right." He rose to his feet, offering her a hand. "Would you like to come?"

Ember shook her head. Thankfully, Aaron didn't try to push it, only offering a farewell before his image faded into the shadow of the house.

Just before he disappeared, he looked back at her and said, "I hope whatever it is gets better soon."

Ember's lips parted. And thank the Crystal, Aaron disappeared before he could see her resolve shatter.

She hunched forward, her head falling into her hands as tears welled up in her eyes. Because it *wasn't* going to get better. This was her second time going off of devinroot, and somehow, it was worse than the first. Who knew when her symptoms would subside—*if* they would subside.

But Aaron was barely holding it together. She could only imagine what condition Analia would come back in. Which meant she couldn't afford to fall apart as well. She had to be whole. She *deserved* to be whole.

Ember rubbed the tears from her face. Then, rising to her feet, she didn't care what anyone thought anymore as she headed back inside and toward the front door.

Chapter 52

"What do you mean you're not going after the Ash Royals?" Dimitri demanded, kicking open Othin's chamber door.

The room was surprisingly sparse, mainly taken up by a few armchairs and the central bed covered in a gold duvet. Clearly, Othin hadn't tried to make the place feel homey. And, based on the fact that he sat behind a carved wooden desk, the Ash Royals didn't believe in attached private sitting rooms.

At the commotion, Othin's head snapped up from the papers he'd been reading. His amber eyes flashed to Dimitri, over to a spluttering Joshel behind him, then back to Dimitri. "Don't you knock, boy?"

"Sorry," Dimitri drawled, sauntering deeper into the chamber. "I was never raised with manners."

Othin's face twisted. Joshel stepped forward, "Apologies, Your Majesty, I tried to tell him you were busy, but he shoved past—"

"It's fine," Othin interrupted, his tone suggesting the opposite. Folding up his papers, he grabbed an envelope from the desk and shoved them inside. "Go deliver this."

"Yes, Your Majesty." Joshel came to grab the proffered envelope, his bow a little stiff as he turned away.

Dimitri looked down as he passed, just catching the letter S on the front of the envelope. Interesting.

"You wanted something, Dimitri?" Othin asked, reclaiming Dimitri's attention.

Joshel paused by the door, looking like he'd like to hear the answer to Dimitri's question. But after a sharp gesture from Othin, he departed, the door clicking shut behind him. And Dimitri didn't make Othin ask twice.

"Why aren't you planning on doing anything about the Royals?" he asked, plopping down on the edge of the bed.

Othin's eyebrows shot up. "Who said I wasn't?"

"I overheard some of your maids whispering about it in the halls."

Granted, Dimitri had started the rumor in the first place, but Othin didn't need to know that. Especially as his face reddened beneath his beard.

"I never said I wouldn't—why do *you* care if I'm leaving the Ash Royals alone?" He leaned forward, his chair creaking as he stared into Dimitri's face. "I thought you were friends with Analia. Why would you be upset that I'm not hunting her family?"

"Because I'm friends with *Analia,* not her family," Dimitri said as though it were obvious. "If Deardryn finds out you're letting them have free rein of the kingdom, that means she's coming back here. And if it's a choice between my friend's family—most of whom were assholes to her—or me?"

Dimitri shook his head, leaning back on his elbows. The insolent, self-serving servant Othin knew and ignored.

Indeed, Othin didn't question this statement. He turned his pen between his fingers, his voice dropping to a murmur. "You truly are my son."

Othin couldn't have said something that would hurt Dimitri more. He curled his fingers into the plush bedspread, not trying to stop his mouth from twisting.

"What are you doing then?" he asked tersely.

Othin didn't respond immediately. Rising to his feet, he moved to the nearby window, resting his broad hands atop the sill.

Dimitri tapped his feet, rapidly losing patience. Just when he thought their conversation was a bust, Othin turned back to him.

"You told me in the Council Chamber you think like the people," he said, his voice slow and smooth as honey. "I followed your suggestion, and it ended with Cadmus stealing my captives and a riot in my streets."

"You're really going to blame me for your lack of security?" Dimitri asked.

Othin shook his head. "The execution went wrong, but your theory was correct. So, I'm asking for your opinion again."

He returned to the desk and pulled a smaller version of the Council Chamber's war map toward himself, the gold and gray figurines shifting slightly. "What would you advise if I told you one of them had been spotted by my men?"

Dimitri cocked his head. Othin folded his hands on the desk, his eyes narrowing the slightest bit as he studied him.

Waiting for him to hesitate. To squirm as he desperately searched for a way to protect the Royals.

But Dimitri didn't pause.

"I would follow him, see where he goes and what he's up to, and then attack when his guard is down."

"No mercy?" Othin asked.

"If they're smart enough to capture your prisoners, they're smart enough to know you're going to retaliate. But since they got away with their scheme, they'll be underestimating you. So, strike while you can."

Othin rubbed his jaw, Dimitri paying him no mind as he investigated a rip in the duvet with his fingers. And all he offered was a shrug as Othin nodded his approval.

For the next several minutes, Othin peppered Dimitri with questions. He indulged a few of them, but he eventually whined for Othin to let him go, he hadn't come here to be his new strategist, he thought he wasn't supposed to be trusted with such information.

Finally, Othin showed him out, the ghost of his hand between Dimitri's shoulder blades buzzing across his nerves the entire walk back to his chambers. But as he slipped inside, spotting Rayner waiting on his bed with what appeared to be Surce's small tapestry spread across his knees, some of that tension relaxed.

"Did he fall for it?" Rayner asked.

"Every last bit," Dimitri confirmed.

Rayner grinned. And Dimitri relaxed a little bit more. He crossed the room, coming to perch on the edge of Rayner's bed.

Rayner shifted to give him space. And Dimitri slumped back against his pillows with a sigh.

"We should let Cadmus know," Rayner said, folding up his tapestry and slipping it into his jacket pocket.

Dimitri nodded, his mind circling back to the day before. Tyce had appeared in the center of their chambers, bringing them back to the safehouse to iron out their next moves.

Cadmus hadn't been lying when he'd said they needed an army, and relying on the citizens under Othin's control could get dicey. But according to the map Dimitri had sketched, Othin's forces didn't go beyond the central kingdom. Meaning they had all of the neighboring towns to draw from—if Cadmus could convince them to rise up.

Thus, their plan was born: send out decoys to keep Othin distracted while Cadmus, Fayela, and a few others readied their forces.

It seemed like a solid enough plan. Yet, Dimitri hadn't missed the way Cadmus had drifted into thought for minutes at a time, his hand rubbing his wrist.

At first, he'd assumed it was exhaustion—which was understandable. Yet, he'd also been uncharacteristically short with Dimitri when he'd asked about the forces assigned to Mt. Vasolus.

"Our mines are nearby," he said, barely looking up from the table. "He's probably stealing our resources."

Maybe. But something felt off. And not just with Othin.

"Something's going on with Cadmus," Dimitri murmured, kicking off his boots and curling into a ball. "He's not the same person I met last summer."

"Last summer," Rayner said, "he hadn't watched Deardryn kill one of his sisters, torture the other, and then get locked in his own dungeon. That's going to change a person."

"Maybe. But he also didn't have that mark Ember told Laness about."

Rayner didn't reply. Dimitri turned his head into Rayner's pillow, breathing in something dark and earthy.

Once, he'd associated that smell with something like security. More recently, even a whiff made his stomach churn. But now, curled in his bed, Rayner not trying to disturb their quiet, it felt like the opening to a question.

I won't choose your life over mine.

"Why did you apologize to Sabi but not me?" Dimitri asked. He propped himself up on his elbows, expecting Rayner's expression to close off.

Instead, he sighed as if he'd been waiting for the question. He shifted toward Dimitri, Dimitri's toes lightly pressing against his thigh in a way that had his nerves lighting up. But it wasn't in a bad way as Rayner began.

"After you disappeared in the Wraithhouse, I knew there was no way you wouldn't find out I betrayed you. And I think I knew that if I had to face up to how much I hurt you, I wouldn't be able to recover from that. So, I apologized to Sabi, hoping it would assuage even a fraction of that guilt. But it only made me feel worse."

"So," Dimitri said, inching his feet a little closer, "you doubled down to try and convince yourself you'd done what you had to."

Rayner's lips quirked. "Sounds like you're speaking from experience."

"I may have a track record of pushing people away."

"Really?" Rayner lightly ran his finger around the top of Dimitri's sock, sending the hairs on his arms standing up. "What have you learned?"

"That it's better to let them stay."

Rayner hummed. And Dimitri found it far easier to accept his explanation than he expected.

He settled back against Rayner's pillows, his eyes closing as Rayner played with his sock, the hem of his pants.

He didn't know when he drifted off. He just knew he jerked awake as Rayner's hand clamped down on his ankle, the smell of smoke filling his nose.

Tyce emerged from the shadows in the center of the room, his brown eyes wild. "We need your help."

Chapter 53

Ember stepped into the greenhouse, the balmy air sticking in her lungs.

She knew Cenn wouldn't be inside—he had patients to check on. But her eyes still did a quick sweep of the first floor, finding no one, her withdrawal roaring for her to hurry.

No, not her withdrawal. Her sanity. It was the promise of sanity that had her feet marching forward, the vivid orange and yellow leaves already visible as she ascended the stairs.

There was no choice anymore. She'd proven she had the control needed to do this. So, why continue to suffer when her friends needed her? When *she* needed her.

Ember stepped onto the second floor, her heart pounding hard enough to have her hands shaking.

She could practically feel the fuzzy leaves, a row away, between her fingers. She could smell the sharp, leafy scent, feel the cold rush of clarity finally coat her mind.

So. Close.

Ember extended her hand, euphoria tingling through her blood as her fingertips made contact—

"I figured you would end up here today."

Ember jumped. She whipped around, the roaring in her veins reaching a crescendo.

Because sitting on a stool amongst the plants nearby, looking completely unsurprised, was Sofika.

Dimitri blinked the last of the darkness from his vision, Tyce's grip on his hand painfully tight as he looked around.

Wisps of smoke squeezed through the cracks between the safehouse's windows, stinging Dimitri's nose. Thankfully, most of the Royals appeared unharmed where they crowded around the central couch, their voices an anxious tangle as they passed around healer supplies and canteens of water.

"What happened?" Dimitri asked, craning his neck to see who the three people on the couch were.

"Sun soldiers," Tyce ground out. "They found us."

Tyce continued talking, but his words fuzzed out in Dimitri's ears. All he could hear was his own voice, telling Othin to follow the Royals. Telling him to strike while he could. Othin's voice, hissing down his spine. *You truly are my son.*

And as the crowd shifted, his entire being went numb.

"Dimitri?" Tyce asked uncertainly.

Dimitri didn't respond. He stared at the three Royals slumped on the couch, their red hair as dark as the blood that stained their skin, expressions tight with pain—

"Dima."

Dimitri blinked hard as Rayner stepped in front of him, blocking Dimitri's view. But Dimitri could still see them.

The older man he thought was named Barden, a bloody cloth pressed to his forehead. Fayela in the middle, her jaw clenched as one of her siblings splinted her fingers, blood crusting around her broken nose. Cadmus slumped against the couch's armrest, his eyes closed, a group of fire sprites clustered around his head as he clutched a bloody cloth to his side.

"What's wrong?" Tyce asked, his voice swimming through Dimitri's ears.

"Go help your family," Rayner ordered, surprisingly firm.

"What? I can't just—"

"Go!"

Rayner yanked Dimitri's hand away from Tyce's, Dimitri's hand falling limply to his side. Tyce started to protest as Rayner spun him around, clearly not one to be shrugged off. But his words died off as Tenley emerged from the crowd before him. The little girl wordlessly reached for his hand, struggling to keep her mouth from trembling.

Tyce's shoulders slumped. Casting Dimitri a final look, he led Tenley over to a nearby couch, Tenley sitting beside him and pressing her face to his shoulder—gods, how much bloodshed did she have to witness? How much because of him?

"Dima, focus on me."

Dimitri dragged his gaze back to Rayner, voices ringing in his ears, smoke stinging his eyes. Rayner guided him back into the corner, his dark eyes demanding Dimitri's attention.

"You can't shut down," he said. "Not right now."

"It's my fault," Dimitri breathed, his lips barely moving. "All of this is my fault."

Rayner's brows scrunched. But he was clearly just as good at following Dimitri's thought process as rolling with his bluntness.

"We won't know that for sure until everyone is healed. And we're going to need your help."

Dimitri flinched, but Rayner didn't pause.

"You and I both know there's only so much our healer supplies can do when none of us are healers. But you can stabilize their life forces. You can give them the time and strength they need to recover."

No, no he couldn't do it. He couldn't let the magic pulsing in his stomach free. Not with everyone watching. But more than that...

"I can't have anyone else dead because of me," he whispered.

Something like heartache twisted Rayner's features. "Dima," he said, unbearably gentle. "What happened to Patryclas was not your fault."

He wasn't talking about Patryclas. Patryclas was an extra couple inches in the hole that had been burrowing into his chest from the moment he was born.

Dimitri opened his mouth, not sure what he was going to say. But Rayner took his hand and guided it to his chest, pressing Dimitri's palm over his heart.

"You feel that?" he asked, his heart beating beneath Dimitri's hand. Slow. Steady. "Focus on that. We're going to take ten breaths, and then you're going to push through the shock and help them."

Dimitri wanted to protest, wanted it with every fiber of his being. But he knew Rayner was right. So, he nodded. And not missing a beat, Rayner took a slow, deep breath.

His chest rose under Dimitri's hand, Dimitri's lungs screaming as they struggled to expand. Rayner stroked the back of his hand with his thumb. Then, he let his breath out slow, Dimitri sagging against the wall as he followed.

Inhale, exhale. Dimitri's fingers dug into the soft fabric of Rayner's shirt, each breath feeling like a lifeline he couldn't quite grasp. But Rayner didn't falter. And Dimitri continued to follow his lead.

Eight breaths. Nine breaths.

Dimitri released his final breath, the reality of his situation settling over his shoulders. He looked up at Rayner, something dark and earthy filling his nose.

"Are you ready?" Rayner whispered.

Not in the slightest. But Dimitri nodded.

Rayner gently pulled Dimitri's hand from his chest and interlaced their fingers. And swallowing the bile burning in his throat, Dimitri let Rayner lead him over to the cluster of Royals.

The one thing Analia had going for her was everyone was preoccupied with breakfast. She, Tavian, and Sabi passed through the quiet halls without problem, Analia hoping they could be in and out of Deardryn's chambers just as quickly. But before that could happen, she had to deal with the magic thrumming along her senses.

"There are definitely two separate detection wards," she said, studying Deardryn's chamber door before her. "One on the door, one on the floor inside."

"So, how do we get past them?" Sabi asked.

"With this." Analia pulled Aaron's damper from her pocket, the chunk of onyx dangling by its chain as she lifted it for them to see.

Sabi's face lit up. She clasped her hands, Tavian's eyes glinting diabolically as he stepped closer.

"Where'd you get this, Red?" he asked, running his fingers along the chain.

"Stole it from Deardryn's damper box."

Tavian grinned. "I thought I saw you pull something out of there. Better get to it before she realizes it's gone."

Sabi made a choked noise as if she hadn't considered that. She turned to Analia, Analia offering a reassuring smile even as her stomach rolled. And not wasting another second, she pressed the damper to the door.

For a few moments, no one moved. Analia could feel Sabi's and Tavian's attention trained on her, her own anticipation tingling down her spine.

She had to be correct. This damper had been made for a Royal; it was designed to contain a massive amount of magic. Deardryn sealing away a flicker of Aaron's network couldn't impede that. She couldn't have changed the nature of the damper.

The thought had barely formed when the onyx tingled beneath her fingers. The faint crackle of Aaron's magic shifted within the stone, pressing back as if making room. And a cool, lethal satisfaction rushed through Analia's veins as the damper sucked up the magic across the door.

"Well?" Sabi demanded.

"We're in."

Sabi cheered, Tavian shushing her as Analia twisted the doorknob. She gently cracked open the door, Tavian starting to march forward. But Analia put out her foot to stop him.

"The magic is still inside the chamber," she explained, sinking into a crouch as she slid the damper down the door to the floor. "Which means we have to do this."

Tavian cocked his head. Beside him, Sabi practically vibrated with questions, but she somehow kept them to herself. And hoping she wasn't making a massive mistake, Analia nudged open the door.

She shifted her grip, ensuring the damper came before her fingers as it slid along the floor with the door. Once again, the damper tingled beneath Analia's fingers as it drew the magic across the chamber to itself. All while keeping its hold on the door's magic.

"Just as I thought." Analia looked up at them, a warm, steady blaze building in her chest. "Dampers don't care about how many sources they're pulling from. If they have the room, they'll attract the magic. So, as long as we maintain both points of contact, the magic will remain in the onyx."

Just as Aaron had promised. And the genuinely impressed look on Tavian's face had Analia pushing back her shoulders.

"This *does* mean one of us will have to stay outside to hold it in place," Sabi pointed out, tapping her fingers against her lips. "Which means we're losing a searcher."

"But gaining a lookout," Analia said.

"That should probably be you, Sabi," Tavian said, casually adjusting his weapons belt. "You should get the chance to run. Especially since you're not dressed for combat."

He gestured vaguely to Sabi's midnight-blue gown. Sabi's eyes narrowed.

"Excuse you," she said, hands on her hips, "since when does liking dresses mean I'm ineffectual? *You* do it."

Tavian started to respond. Sabi shoved him toward the door, hiked up her skirts, and marched into the chamber beyond, not catching Analia's grin.

Tavian made a noise of protest. He turned to Analia for help, but she only beckoned him closer.

"You'll have to hold the damper in place with your boot to avoid direct contact," she explained. "I'd hate for the one person whose heightened hearing can inform us of approaching people in advance to lose that ability."

"I can do that inside, too," Tavian whined. But he obediently pressed the damper to the door with his boot. And Analia prayed a sulky guard would be the least of her troubles as she thanked him, rose to her feet, and followed Sabi inside.

Analia found herself in a sitting room similar to Sylas's. Various armchairs and couches sat arranged around a central low table, the balcony door replaced with a small marble fireplace. Lush green plants decorated the handful of windowsills, the walls taken up by bookshelves, drawers, and an ornate wooden desk.

Definitely a lot of hiding places. And that wasn't including the bedchamber through the door on the left and its attached bathing chamber. But that wasn't the problem.

"What's wrong?" Sabi asked, already poking through desk drawers.

"I can't sense the Crystal *or* its casing," Analia said. "Which means she either brought it to breakfast, even though Letta told her I wouldn't be working with her today, or she's put it in her jewelry box."

Meaning no matter what, they were blocked. And Deardryn could shadowjump back to her chambers at any moment.

Sabi's face paled. And Analia snapped into action.

"Start searching this room," she said, heading for Deardryn's bedchamber. "Drawers, bookcases, beneath cushions. All the spots Deardryn would deem too obvious. We can't mess this up because she anticipated us overestimating her."

Sabi didn't need to be told twice. She immediately got to work, Tavian offering suggestions over her minor ruckus as Analia pushed open the second door.

Her eyes did a quick scan: bed in the center, small bookshelf beside it, a few nicknacks arranged across the windowsill and vanity, the door to the bathing chamber on the right. Still, no whisper of magic outside of Sabi's and Tavian's networks. But was it because the jewelry box wasn't there, or because the protective casing blocked her from sensing the damper within?

She assumed she'd found it in the study's desk drawer because Deardryn had been planning on implementing its contents into their research. But if she was wrong—no, she'd confirmed Deardryn brought the Crystal with her each day. She had no reason to hide the Crystal in the study that morning. Meaning it was dampered in the box, and that box was here.

"How's it going out there?" Analia called, checking beneath Deardryn's pillows.

"I mainly see books," Sabi replied. "None of the ones she checked out for her research."

"Those are in here," Analia said, skimming over the titles on Deardryn's small shelf as she pulled them out, nothing hidden behind them.

"You two need to be quieter," Tavian ordered in a low voice. "The door is wide open."

Analia cursed. She pulled open the drawers in Deardryn's vanity, looked behind the curtains, even checked behind the painting of Mt. Raegyr on the wall for hidden compartments. Nothing, nothing, nothing.

"What color book did you say Deardryn wrote her research in?" Sabi asked, only marginally quieter.

"Blue, why?"

"I think I found it."

Analia perked up. She hurried back into the sitting room, finding Sabi perched on the couch's arm and flipping through Deardryn's little blue book. "Where did you find that?"

"There was a false backing on one of her shelves," Sabi explained. She started to go into a full description of how she figured it out, but Analia raised a hand. "Right, sorry. Anyway, if this is her research, and you didn't get a chance to read all of it..."

Sabi wiggled her fingers, her replication Blessing tingling across Analia's senses. Analia's mind raced.

Having a copy of Deardryn's notes would be invaluable. But she'd be losing her last search partner. And breakfast would be ending shortly.

Analia looked at Tavian.

"No one's coming," he reported.

Analia didn't second-guess. "Do it."

Sabi beamed. She slid down the arm to sit on the couch, snatching a small book from the nearby table and flipping it open on her lap beside the blue book. And feeling their time rapidly ticking out, Analia rushed back into the bedchamber.

This was up to her. Months of training with Deardryn in the Ring Room, countless hours thinking through her potential moves, day after day studying her in the Moon Castle. She knew Deardryn. She could figure this out.

Yet, as Analia tore apart the chamber, not caring about leaving a trail, she found nothing. No hidden compartments, no false backings. She even pulled up the carpet, stomping on the stone and listening for anything hollow. Nothing.

Analia tugged on a lock of hair that had come free from her braid, trying to take a steadying breath. But all she smelled was the honey-sweet scent of Deardryn's skin. Reminding her of the Sun Castle, the nightmares of Pryanth that had invaded her sleep once again—she had to focus.

Analia forced herself back into movement. She headed into the bathing chamber, identical to her own.

Would Deardryn risk the box getting wet? Did that even matter? She didn't know.

But that didn't stop her from flinging open the drawers beneath the sink, shoving towels and bottles aside as she turned to the shelves built into the wall. She had just poked through Deardryn's small trash can with her foot when Tavian's voice hissed through the chambers.

"Someone's coming."

Analia's heart jolted. She hurried out of the bathing chamber, her voice hushed as she ordered him to close the door. But Tavian was one step ahead of her.

He slid the damper along the door with his boot, around the corner, coming to the back side. Sabi replaced his foot with her own, keeping the damper in contact with the door as she shut it. Then, she slid to the ground, her foot on the damper as she went back to her copying, her hands shaking.

Analia's heart pounded in her ears. Mouthing an encouragement, she turned and raced back into the bedchamber.

Their time was almost up. And at the sound of the familiar voice drifting under the door, she knew Tavian would have to put on the performance of a lifetime.

"Why are you outside Her Majesty's chambers?" Meryk asked, Analia practically able to hear his eyes narrow.

"Two weeks working together and I don't even get a hello?"

Analia shifted the wardrobe aside as quietly as she could, her entire body cringing at the scrape. But all she found was dust.

"You know Her Majesty is at breakfast," Meryk said, his voice coming closer. "Why would you wait here to get your assignment from her instead of going to the Royal dining room?"

"Do you really think Deardryn wants a soldier interrupting her meal?" Tavian asked. "Especially when the reason I have to inquire what to do is because my charge is trying to ignore her summons."

Analia returned to the small bookshelf, her mind racing.

Deardryn didn't make decisions on a whim. She had no reason to bring the Crystal with her to breakfast... Unless she'd noticed Aaron's damper was missing. But then why not try to take the damper back?

"If it means *that much* to you," Tavian sighed dramatically, "you can escort me down to the dining room and watch me ask her."

The only reason she wouldn't be able to sense the Crystal was if it was in the box. Which meant Deardryn had to know the damper was missing... unless she hadn't checked thoroughly?

But Deardryn thrived on details. Her notes—her book orders for that matter—were proof of that.

Analia ran her fingers over book spines, Tavian's and Meryk's arguing voices tingling across the back of her neck. Gods, most of Deardryn's books were huge. How had she had time to make it through all of them?

"I've been in this castle long enough to know when you're up to something," Meryk said. "What are you hiding?"

"Currently, I'm trying to hide my exasperation, but I don't think I'm doing too well."

Analia thumbed through the books, her palms starting to sweat as she read each title. *The Oath of a Healer. The Magic of Blood Oaths. Scars and Markings with Magical Vows. Healers Through the Ages*—that wasn't on Sabi's list of titles.

"Step away from the door, Tavian," Meryk said, so quiet Analia almost missed it.

"Mind your business, Meryk."

Analia pulled the book off the shelf, needing both hands to support its weight.

Sabi knew every book Deardryn had requested. And Deardryn was too organized to include a separate book with her research.

Analia flipped open the cover. And she could have cried with relief as she looked down at the damper box, the book having been hollowed out so it could fit inside.

Tavian's and Meryk's raised voices echoed beyond the door, underscored by the metallic rasp of weapons being drawn.

Yanking open the box, Analia dug around with her free hand, finding the slithering magic field in seconds. She pulled out the Crystal, her eyes searching the jumble of trinkets for her enka bracelet.

Just as the door banged open. And the detection magic flooded back into the chamber as Sabi shrieked.

Analia gasped. She slammed the lid closed on the jewelry box, closed the book, voices and cries and magic clamoring in her ears. She shoved the book back on the shelf, barely having time to drop the Crystal in her pocket and turn before Meryk stormed through the door.

"You," he began.

Analia drew her dagger from her boot and threw. It wobbled through the air, Meryk easily batting it aside.

"Of course you're here." He raised his hands. Chains of vivid purple light rattled forth, whipping across the open space toward her.

Analia yelped. She dove out of the way just in time, Meryk cursing as she rolled under the bed. He came deeper into the room, angling himself to send his magic after her. But Analia popped up on the other side, her discarded dagger now in reach as she lunged for it.

Her fingers brushed the hilt. Just as Meryk rounded the bed. And Analia screamed as he brought his boot down on her hand with a crunch.

Analia collapsed onto her elbows, pain exploding across her senses.

"I'll take that." Meryk swiped the dagger from her limp fingers and shoved it into his belt. Analia tried to squirm away, but Meryk grabbed her arm, yanking her to her feet.

His chains rattled around her, pinning her arms to her torso, forming shackles between her ankles within seconds.

"I told you, Princess," he whispered in her ear, "I like to see Royals get what they deserve."

Analia swallowed. Meryk shoved her forward, Analia stumbling as each step sent pain flaring across her hand.

She had to find a way out. But all plans crumbled as Meryk pushed her into the sitting room where Sabi and Tavian were similarly shackled, the former hyperventilating through her tears, the latter bruised and spitting curses as he tried to wrench free. But the magic held.

"I'm sure Her Majesty will have countless questions for you," Meryk drawled, infuriatingly smug. Keeping a grip on Analia, he raised his free hand, the chains on Tavian and Sabi extending like leashes for him to grab.

And as he dragged them out the door, Analia's only hope was that she couldn't sense Sabi's network.

Chapter 54

Ember braced herself against the devinroots' wooden rack, watching Sofika rise from a rickety stool a few aisles away.

The woman who had relentlessly accused her of being an addict. The one who was in control of her future. The one who had just seen her reaching for a devinroot leaf.

"You're not in trouble, Ember," Sofika said, weaving through shelves and tables as she approached. "As a matter of fact, you're right on time."

Should she go on the offensive? Stop her accusations before they could come? No, then Sofika would say she was defensive, which would only prove her point.

Could she play dumb? No, that would be insulting. Rosala spare her, silence was all Ember had left as Sofika stepped into her aisle, her emerald robes blending in with the foliage.

"Usually," Sofika said, "I see people break far earlier than this. The fact that you've made it this long is something to be proud of."

"What do you mean, 'usually,'" Ember ground out.

Sofika ignored the question, twisting her straight black hair into a knot. "Your work ethic combined with your determination to prove me wrong is a powerful poultice. But unfortunately, addiction isn't something you can cure. It's something you must stay on top of, and if this past week is any indicator, you have more than enough will power to stay clean."

Ember's spine dug into the rack, Sofika's words hitting her one after the other. *Addiction. Cure. Clean.*

"Why are you so insistent on labeling me as an addict?" she demanded. "You've said it yourself, I haven't touched devinroot for two weeks, and I'm *fine*. I'm *excelling*. No addict could go this long, achieve this much, without their drug."

"Don't be crass," Sofika snapped, stopping before her. "You and I both know that a sober addict is still an addict. It's their respect for that very fact that not only keeps them sober despite immense psychological strain but also excelling. It's a respect you would do well to develop."

"You mean like the respect you've shown me?" Ember shot back. "Deciding I'm an addict. Dangling my career over my head. Sitting here, waiting for me to fail your test."

Ember took a sharp inhale, her realization igniting the last of her control. "This was all a setup," she said, jabbing a finger at Sofika. "You purposefully gave me these days off because you were hoping I would be bored enough to use, and then you could catch me and prove your point."

Ember waited, practically dared, Sofika to disagree.

Sofika folded her arms. "I did."

Ember thought her body would erupt into flames.

"How dare you?" she seethed, pushing off the rack. "What do you think your king would say if he knew you were manipulating his friend?"

"That depends. How do you think he would react to first finding out that said friend is suffering from addiction and didn't want to confide in him?"

"I'm not addicted!" Ember screamed, stomping her foot. She felt like a child, felt out of control, felt like she didn't know how to care anymore.

Gods, why was she crying? She turned away, furiously wiping her eyes.

But Sofika didn't give her the dignity of privacy. She came closer, Ember stifling something between a scream and a sob as Sofika's hands landed on her shoulders.

"Look at yourself, Ember," she said, her voice as firm as her grip. "Would someone who only used devinroot recreationally be screaming at me in a greenhouse? Would the words sober, addict, and clean feel like an attack to someone those words didn't apply to?"

"Leave me alone," Ember begged, something breaking inside her as her eyes landed on the cluster of devinroots.

"This doesn't mean you're broken," Sofika said, coming to stand in front of her. "It's not your fault that something tragic has led you here. But it *is* your choice whether you remain here or not."

Ember turned away, her breaths coming in ragged gasps. She wanted to disappear, to not hear the words coming out of Sofika's mouth. Saying she needed to be clean, implying she wasn't.

She was dirty. Worthless. Weak. Everything her fellow healer apprentices had ever said about her.

"I can't force you to believe you're an addict," Sofika said, something scraping across the floor. "Just as I can't force you to remain sober. These are things you must come to terms with yourself. So, we're going to stay here until you decide."

Ember's withdrawal howled. Sofika returned to her side, pulling her over to the first of two chairs she had set facing each other in the center of the aisle.

And Ember knew she was going to die as Sofika took a seat and placed one of the potted devinroots on the floor in between them.

Analia awkwardly cradled her broken hand against her chest, Meryk pulling her, Sabi, and Tavian down the stairs toward the entryway by their chains. She hadn't asked any questions on their walk through the castle, knowing Deardryn well enough to assume where things were headed.

Indeed, she wasn't surprised to spot the Dragoness waiting below.

She stood beside the fountain, her hair pulled back in an elegant twist, her violet gown belted with chains of small, clear crystals. Sylas slumped beside her, unmistakably bored as he listened to whatever she was telling him. Yet, what *was* surprising was the crowd.

They lingered on the outskirts of the entryway, their numbers quietly growing, their tattoos and uniforms marking them all as Moon people.

Their presence wasn't unusual—Deardryn had picked a public spot. But why did she want an audience?

Before Analia could dwell on the question, Meryk called a greeting. Deardryn's hushed voice drifted off, her honey gaze flicking up. And in unison, the crowd turned.

Analia kept her chin high as the stares landed on her. She carefully stepped off the stairs, Sabi yelping as her own ankle chains sent her stumbling, Tavian barely able to extend his hand enough to grab her. And Meryk only maneuvered behind them, trapping them between himself and the crowd.

"Deardryn," Sylas finally said, his voice painfully dry in the silence, "would you like to explain why you have restrained my guard and my bookkeeper?"

"For security's sake." Deardryn dragged her gaze from Analia, unnervingly composed. "My magic alerted me that all three broke into my private chambers, just as I presumed they would."

In the crowd, Letta caught Analia's eye, her face pale as she mouthed, "I'm so sorry."

Analia gave a fraction of a nod as Deardryn turned to Meryk, inviting him to deliver his report.

She had to find a way out of this. But she couldn't think over Tavian's protests, the thud of Meryk's fist slamming into the back of his head, Sabi inching close enough to Analia she could feel her shaking.

They were cornered. Shackled, their weapons hanging from Meryk's belt, Analia's magic dampered. All advantages neutralized.

"They seemed to be after this," Meryk said. Shifting his chains to one hand, he pulled something from his cloak and raised it over Analia's head for Deardryn to see.

"My notes?" Deardryn cocked her head, seeming genuinely puzzled. "What would you want with that, Analia?"

"I didn't have time to finish reading when you caught me yesterday," she said coolly.

"I see." Deardryn crossed the twenty paces between them, reaching over Analia's head to accept the book. And a jolt ran down Analia's spine.

Her enka bracelet sat on Deardryn's left wrist, positioned right above the stacks of thick golden bracelets she always wore. But why?

Deardryn caught Analia looking, her eyebrow lifting ever so slightly. Daring her to ask.

But Analia only said, "That is a bold move."

"Would you say as bold as breaking into my chambers?" Deardryn asked. "Especially the morning after I confiscated your one connection to your love, and you stole his damper. I must say, I was wondering if you'd be clever enough to block my chambers' magic with it. But I'm curious. Meryk, have you searched her?"

Analia's blood went cold.

"No, Your Majesty," he said.

She couldn't have made it this far, couldn't have found the Crystal, just to lose it now. Her eyes darted over the whispering crowd, looking for a way out, Sylas watching with arms folded.

"Do it," Deardryn ordered.

Meryk reached for Analia. And Analia lunged forward.

Deardryn flinched back, Meryk snarling a curse as Tavian rammed him with his shoulder. The two toppled to the ground, the chain around Analia's arms and torso pulling painfully tight. She strained forward, the crowd buzzing around her, no one trying to intervene, Sabi's network still undetectable as she scurried away from the thrashing guards.

"My dagger," Analia breathed. She took another step toward Sylas, a dozen paces away—he had to help her. She couldn't breathe.

Sylas's eyes widened, his hand starting to reach—

"Enough!" Deardryn exclaimed, flinging out her arms. Golden light erupted from her hands, the crowd letting out a collective gasp as the magic slammed into Analia, Tavian, Meryk, and Sabi.

Analia flew back, her head colliding with a moonstone pillar with a crack. She crumpled to her knees, her hand shrieking as she instinctively tried to catch herself—gods, this was not going well. Blinking the spots from her vision, she looked around, Tavian and Meryk having crashed into the stairs, Sabi seemingly unharmed as she sat up nearby.

Analia squeezed her eyes shut, struggling to reorient her senses as the floor tilted and spun beneath her. It took her a few moments to focus on the crowd's hushed murmurs. But it was Sylas's voice, colder than she'd ever heard before, that had her peeking beneath her lashes.

"This is *my* castle," he seethed, shadows writhing at his feet. "You dare shackle my people and *attack* them in front of me?"

"After they invaded my private space and attacked my soldier?" Deardryn challenged. "That is for me to punish."

Analia dug her fingers into the cold marble floor, bracing for Deardryn's retaliation.

But Deardryn's response seemed to fizzle out on her lips. And if Analia hadn't known better, she would have thought her remorse was genuine as she bowed her head. "Apologies, Your Majesty. You're correct."

She turned back to the stairs. "Meryk, you can release Tavian and Sabina; we have overstepped with them. But Analia is *my* prisoner. And I will search her."

Analia's stomach lurched. She desperately struggled to rise, her tightening chains keeping her in place. Sabi and Tavian tried to protest as they were finally freed, but Sylas beckoned them to his side. And Analia thought she was going to be sick as Deardryn came to kneel in front of her.

"Don't make this difficult, Analia," she said softly.

Analia didn't listen. She thrashed, trying to push Deardryn away as she reached for her pocket, the honey-sweet scent of her skin filling her nose, the languid thrum of her network skittering across her senses—no, no, no.

Analia tried to claw her enka bracelet off of Deardryn's wrist, but Deardryn easily dodged. And as she retrieved the Crystal from Analia's pocket, something horrifically close to pride in her eyes, Analia could only sag against the pillar.

"Very good, little dragoness," Deardryn murmured.

"Crystal strike you down," Analia spat.

Deardryn's mouth tightened. She looked down at the Crystal in its casing, that same blank expression from when she'd killed Lucilla passing over her features.

She slipped the rock in a gown pocket. Then, she lifted Analia's chin with a stiff finger.

"I wear your bracelet," she said, soft enough only Analia could hear, "so your nymph friend can inform Aaron of every way I make you scream. So far, she hasn't said anything. I wonder how long it will take."

Analia's breath caught. That didn't sound like Deardryn's typical style at all. But as Deardryn trailed her finger down Analia's throat, the ghost of pressure pressing against her lungs, she supposed there was no room for "typical" anymore.

Before Analia could speak, Deardryn let her finger drop. She gracefully rose to her feet, turning to face the stunned crowd.

"I apologize to you all," she said, her queenly mask back in place. "I'm sure that must have been upsetting to witness. Especially since, in the months your king has graciously allowed me to pursue my research in your halls, I've tried to be nothing but respectful. I've tried to show you all the utmost appreciation for welcoming me into your home. And as a result of that, I feel I owe it to you all to explain why this has happened."

The crowd exchanged a variety of looks, no one daring to interrupt. Sylas folded his arms. Analia flexed each of her muscles, testing her restraints and checking for injuries.

"Analia and I have a long history," Deardryn began, drifting over to the stairs. "It started when she advocated for a truce marriage with my son after her uncle was found dead in his chambers. Today, we know that he was killed by his own brother, who has since been punished. But at the time, she assumed my family was at fault. And she used her arrangement to infiltrate my home, collect blackmail against my family, and murder my son on their wedding bed, only to abscond with her guard whom she's now betrothed to."

Deardryn paused, letting the murmurs echo. Analia clenched her jaw, the familiarity of it all prickling across her skin. But she remained quiet.

"After our kingdoms went to war, Analia offered herself once again as a show of peace. She said she would come with me as my prisoner in exchange for me leaving her kingdom and not harming her loved ones, and I complied. Yet, I fear I haven't adequately kept her in check. For after being freed from the dungeon, she has poisoned two of your own. She persuaded them to disobey His Majesty's orders, infiltrate my private space, and steal from me. They undoubtedly thought their assistance was in the name of justice, although, forgive me, I don't understand how enabling the man who killed Patryclas to escape the kingdom is justice."

Several sharp exclamations echoed around the room, some people actually shoving forward into the entryway. Deardryn raised her voice.

"I've already made the mistake of overstepping my authority in capturing them, and for that, I once again apologize. I understand it's up to His Majesty to decide what to do with his people. And seeing as this is his castle and I am but a guest, I won't try to insert myself into his decision regarding Analia either."

Deardryn bowed her head, letting the voices swell. Across from her, Sylas's nostrils flared, undoubtedly recognizing the corner she'd put him in.

Either he could punish Analia, or leave himself open to ridicule and suspicion. And Analia?

"She's lying!" Tavian yelled.

"She's trying to manipulate you!" Sabi exclaimed, her head whipping back and forth as she took in the restless crowd.

The two made to go on, but Analia raised her hand as much as her chains would allow. Begrudgingly, they fell quiet, the crowd needing a few moments before they noticed. But slowly, their voices faded, replaced with an anticipation that crackled across Analia's skin. Finally, there was silence.

"Tavian," Analia said quietly. "Can you help me up?"

Tavian looked at Sylas, who gave a short nod. He quickly crossed the entryway, her dagger glinting in his belt as he helped her rise.

Analia swayed as the ground tilted beneath her feet. Tavian shot a hovering Meryk a vicious glare, his grip tightening on her elbow. But Meryk didn't loosen her chains. And Analia didn't care as she spotted the tilt of Deardryn's head.

The polite, pacifying look of someone expecting nonsense, but deciding to indulge it anyway. Analia's temper crackled, begging to explode.

But that would be playing into Deardryn's hands. It would be allowing Deardryn to shove her into yet another mold she'd designed for her. Apprentice, adversary, research partner, villain.

Analia turned, taking in the sea of faces around the entryway, piling up in the branching hallways. And she kept her chin high as she said, "What Deardryn says is true."

The crowd sucked in a breath.

"Deardryn said you deserve to know how we got here, and I agree. Which means you deserve to know the parts of the story that she left out.

"She told you I suspected her family of killing my uncle. What she didn't include is that I thought this because Sun had come to my kingdom the day before to discuss how my cousin, Baylen, was found dead on our border. She told you my father killed Accalon, but she didn't tell you how she killed Baylen to collect his magic for her research. Just as she didn't tell you how the research she's conducting here is how to kill one of your Royals to steal their magic as well. And when Patryclas got in her way, she killed him and framed Dimitri."

Analia raised her voice over the growing noise from the crowd, her confidence building. "She told you Ash and Sun went to war. But she didn't tell you she started that war to try and kill my brother, killed my twelve-year-old sister instead, and stole her magic to replace the Ash magic sample I destroyed. She didn't *tell you* that I killed Pryanth after he pinned me against his bed, pressed his arm against my throat, and told me he'd either consummate our marriage against my will, or he'd kill me."

Analia barely finished before the crowd erupted. Words flew across the entryway like arrows, some calling her a liar, some aghast, some demanding justice. But Analia didn't hear any of them.

She turned to Deardryn, taking in her pale face, the hand she braced against the railing. And Analia could practically taste the ashes she rose from as she said, "I understand why you hate me. I used Pryanth to infiltrate your castle, and I killed him. You have every right to hate me for that. But you also have to know I wanted things to work with him.

"I thought your castle could be my home. I wanted to find a way to give my uncle justice, but also stay in a kingdom that actually seemed to care about me. I *wanted* to love Pryanth. But while your kingdom, your castle, our relationship, provided solace, they were also riddled with deception and betrayal. And I experienced worse than that with Pryanth.

"Most days, I don't know if I understand him, pity him, or hate him. All I know is I am who I am because of him, and in spite of him. And you should be appeased and gods-damned repentant for that."

Analia spat out the final words like they were poison. Not to attack. But to cleanse, finally ridding herself of the toxins that had been flowing through her veins.

And staring into Deardryn's eyes, Sylas calling for order, she could see it. The moment Deardryn finally processed what had happened between her and Pryanth. Her lips parted, no words coming out.

And standing there, in a foreign castle, shackled, dampered, and weaponless, Analia had never felt more free. She had won.

But Deardryn was never one to give up.

Sylas finally got the crowd to quiet, Analia watching Deardryn tuck her realization away for later.

"Do you see, Sylas?" she asked, perfectly cool once more as she stepped toward the fountain. "This is the person I tried to warn you of. The princess who has been so neglected and broken by her people that she would use her own grief as a weapon. A woman who has admitted to murder, deception, and betrayal."

Analia didn't recoil at the accusations. Sylas dragged a hand through his blue-black curls, unusually serious as he considered.

"I believe," he finally said, "there's someone who should be here for this decision. If I'm gone for five seconds, will you all tear each other apart?"

"Of course not," said Deardryn smoothly.

Analia shook her head, the crowd murmuring their agreement.

"Good," Sylas grunted. Then, he faded into the shadows, leaving Sabi to shift awkwardly from foot to foot beside the fountain.

Analia looked over at Deardryn, phantom flames crackling through her blood as their eyes met. But neither of them moved. No one broke the silence across the entryway.

One, two, three, four, five seconds. Right on time, Analia sensed a flicker of magic, her eyebrows rising as the shadows rippled at the top of the stairs.

Two figures appeared in the darkness, one slightly taller than the other. Deardryn turned. And there was no denying the alarm on her face as she took a step back.

Sabi made a choked noise and hurried forward, the crowd sucking in a breath. Tavian's hand tightened on Analia's elbow.

But Analia barely felt it. She could only stare as the figures fully emerged. First at Sylas on the left, his expression tight. Then, over to the right.

Uncomprehending as her eyes met the brilliant green gaze of Patryclas.

Chapter 55

All Dimitri knew was blood. The metallic scent, its rusty color, the way it stuck to his fingers as he pressed his hand to Cadmus's side.

A distant part of him registered Rois telling everyone to back up, Rayner's fingertips resting on his back as he kneeled behind him.

"You can do this," he murmured, his breath warm against Dimitri's ear.

He knew he could. He could feel it in the flicker of magic in his stomach, ready to be released. That was the problem.

"We know what happened with Ember," Fayela rasped, catching his shifting gaze.

Dimitri jumped. "You do?"

"It's a small place," Cadmus ground out. "No one cares. Just *do it.*"

The fire sprites around his head on the armrest flinched back. But the order was surprisingly helpful. It had Dimitri ducking his head, closing his eyes. And it left no room for second-guessing as he finally let his magic loose.

To his relief, there came no gasps, no surprised exclamations as golden light flooded the room. Instead, the Royals softly conversed with one another, their voices the middle ground Dimitri needed to ease into his magic.

In his limited experience, he'd discovered a person's life force was reminiscent of a lake in the center of their chest, spilling into arteries and veins like an intricate river system. Thankfully, Cadmus's lake was fuller than he'd anticipated.

Dimitri tried to decrease his magic output, having summoned far more than necessary, just for the golden light to dwindle to a flicker. He cursed, trying to build it up again.

He had to save some of his magic for Fayela and Barden. But he didn't have anywhere near the amount of control needed to make this go smoothly. And if he messed this up...

Rayner's fingertips skimmed down his back, Dimitri realizing his breathing had become shallow. He took a deep breath through his nose, forcing himself to focus.

He imagined his magic flooding into the lake in Cadmus's chest, filling it with gold, sending it throughout the rest of his body. He directed some of his sunlight to replenish Cadmus's magic as well, hoping that would help with his healing. Yet, the moment his magic came in contact with Cadmus's network, something dark and slick as oil recoiled.

Dimitri's eyes popped open, staring at Cadmus through the golden light. "What was—"

"You can stop," Cadmus said, pulling away from Dimitri's hands. "I'm stable."

Dimitri wasn't going to argue with that. He let his magic wink out, wiping the sweat from his brow with shaky hands. But even though the color had returned to Cadmus's face, Dimitri caught the tension in his jaw as he turned his face away.

Dimitri started to speak. But Cadmus beat him to it.

"You and Rayner should know what happened."

With that, he launched into his story. And knowing better than to push it, Dimitri remained quiet as he stabilized Fayela and Barden.

Apparently, Othin's men hadn't found Tyce like they'd planned. They'd spotted Rois, who had slipped out to smuggle more healer supplies from an apprentice friend of his. They didn't know if the soldiers had tracked him back to the safehouse or if they made a lucky guess. Regardless, it wasn't long before they'd set fire to the warehouse.

Thankfully, being a kingdom built near a volcano and with fire-wielding Royals, most structures were magically reinforced against flames. They weren't fireproof, but it would take a lot more than a few torches to burn them down. Which meant it all came down to strategy.

Cadmus, Fayela, and Barden had pretended to be smoked out of the warehouse, coming face-to-face with Othin and a squadron of soldiers. Othin had already summoned a shield around the warehouse to prevent them from shadowjumping away, and clearly having learned from the square, he was ready to replenish his magic the moment Cadmus sliced through with his damper blade.

Eventually, they'd created a large enough gap to fade into the shadows. But seeing as they had to fight off a squadron of soldiers in the meantime?

"Fortunately," Fayela said, picking up the story, "this works to our advantage."

"How?" Dimitri demanded, his mind reeling.

"Think about it," Cadmus said, the fire sprites now asleep on his shoulders. "Othin only saw three Royals leave the safehouse, and since the glamor on the door remains intact, his men found nothing in their ensuing search. So, now, he's going to scour the kingdom for wherever the rest of the Royals are—which is logically where the three of us have fled to."

"But instead, you're all here," Rayner mused, still beside Dimitri on the floor. "The one place he's already checked and won't think you'll return to."

"Yet, here we are." Cadmus spread his arm mockingly, the other still holding pressure on the wound in his side.

Dimitri only had the energy to shake his head. He looked over at Rois, the guard unusually quiet where he lingered in the corner, his head bowed. Because even though everything had worked out, it was still his fault. Just as it was Dimitri's.

Gods, Dimitri wanted to crawl into bed and pretend this day, this month, had never happened. Yet, as Cadmus looked up, his blue eyes locking on him, he knew his day was about to get a whole lot worse.

Indeed, it wasn't long before Cadmus requested the room clear out. The Royals murmured to each other as they shuffled toward the door, Fayela and Barden having recovered enough to fade into the shadows. Rayner remained where he sat, but Cadmus didn't give him a second glance.

"When are you going to embrace the power you have?" he asked Dimitri the moment they were alone.

Dimitri didn't know why he bothered recoiling. "I just healed you. You really want to start questioning me?"

"I want to question why you had to be forced to do so." Cadmus shoved himself upright on the couch, his blue eyes blazing. "You have every reason to hate Deardryn, and your very *existence* is the best way to get back at her. You are a twenty-year-old lie that not only threatens the Sun Royal succession, but could completely shatter her people's trust."

"I'm not a Sun Royal," Dimitri ground out.

"That's the point! You're not a Royal. You're a Royal *bastard*. You have their magic. Why don't you use it?"

"Because then it's real!" Dimitri exploded. He shoved to his feet, the fire sprites on Cadmus's shoulders startling awake. "The moment I let everyone know, it becomes real. Everyone will know I have their magic, they'll think I'm a Royal, and I don't want to *be* that."

"This isn't just about you!" Cadmus exclaimed. "Do you think you're the only one who's been impacted by Deardryn? I've lost *everything* because of her. Do you have any idea what I would do to have the advantage over her that you have?"

Cadmus bit off the rest of his words, his jaw clenching tight. Dimitri's heart pounded in his ears. He and Cadmus started to speak at the same time, the air crackling between them, but Rayner abruptly rose to his feet.

"This isn't going anywhere good," he said, thrusting out his arms. "You two need to take a breather."

"No," Cadmus spat. "Dimitri needs to realize the situation we're in." He turned away on the couch, his words burning hotter than his flames. "Come to me when you're ready to train your magic."

Dimitri's temper pulsed in time with the dregs of his magic. Not giving Cadmus the satisfaction of a response, he spun on his heel, shoving through the door and marching up the stairs.

He didn't have a destination in mind. He didn't know where he was going in the first place. All he knew was the ache of his fingers as he squeezed them into fists, his nails biting into his palms.

Everything wasn't about him? Well, it wasn't about fucking *Cadmus,* either.

"Hey."

Every nerve in Dimitri's body jolted as hands landed on his shoulders, spinning him around on the top step. Rayner stood a few stairs below, the remnants of his patient mask cracking along its edges.

"Don't fucking start," Dimitri spat, trying to wriggle free.

"Don't be a gods-damned child," Rayner shot back.

Dimitri stiffened, but Rayner went on.

"I've kept my mouth shut for over a month. I haven't asked questions; I haven't harassed you into using your magic. But I just had to convince you to save your friends' lives, which means this isn't some petty stance you have. So *talk to me.*"

Dimitri's blood burned. His clothing felt too rough against his skin. His entire body itched to spit every word he knew would send Rayner recoiling.

Rayner shifted, his shirt collar falling to the side to reveal intricate purple lines. Curving toward his shoulder where Dimitri's blood had formed a key. The matching pair to the lock on Dimitri's.

He looked down at his hands, at the black heart on the inside of his wrist. And a small, broken part of himself had his shoulders sagging.

"Do you know how they decided to keep my identity a secret?" he asked.

Rayner blinked. Then, he shook his head.

"They chose an innocent woman at random, said she was my mother, and killed her. They claimed it was to send a message, whatever the fuck that might be. All that matters is an innocent woman is *dead.* Because of me."

The words burned in the back of Dimitri's throat. He stared into Rayner's face, craving the look of disgust that coated his entire body. And while Rayner's face paled, he didn't push Dimitri away. Instead, he stepped closer, Dimitri shaking in his grip.

"That woman," he said, annunciating each word clearly, staring into his eyes, "is dead because of Othin. She's dead because of his choices—"

"Which resulted in me!" Dimitri ripped out of Rayner's grip, his words sharp as shards of glass. "Don't you get it? She died to protect me. A miserable, lowlife little servant. I'm the furthest thing from being worthy of—it wasn't even a sacrifice. It was an exchange of lives. And by embracing my magic, I'm embracing the fact that I am the person that got an innocent woman killed, and I can't *be* that."

Dimitri buried his face in his hands as his voice broke. Those words had been haunting him for almost twenty-one years. And now that they were finally out, he didn't feel cleansed. He felt like he was decaying from the inside out.

But Rayner didn't let him rot in peace. He gripped Dimitri's wrists, his fingers gentle but firm as he pulled Dimitri's hands away.

"I'm not going to pretend like I have any idea what you're feeling," he said. "All I can tell you is you are who you are, no matter how much you try to deny it. You. Are. A. Royal. Bastard. You have their magic. And while they have used it for evil, you don't have to choose that path.

"You just healed three people. You can help even more. And if you have this magic and refuse to help those you can? That's what would make you no better than the Royals. *That's* what would make you unworthy of her sacrifice. So, be worthy."

Dimitri's lips parted. Rayner squeezed his wrists. Then, he let go. And backing down the stairs, he gave Dimitri space to shatter.

E mber hoped she would never remember that afternoon. She hoped she wouldn't remember how she started off frozen and petulant, refusing to look at the devinroot placed in front of her until her withdrawal wailed so loud she almost vomited. She hoped she would forget how she unleashed all of that built-up pressure at Sofika, alternating between insults and calling her insane for thinking she was an addict.

In those moments, Ember didn't care about Sofika's feelings. She didn't care about *anything*. Not when there was devinroot right there, and Sofika was watching her, and she was a monster, beaten and broken and staring at salvation that would kill her if she indulged, and would kill her if she denied.

She. Couldn't. Do. This.

"Would you like to break something?" Sofika asked, perfectly composed in her seat across from her. "It can help."

"Don't fucking patronize me."

"I'm not. We're three hours in, and you haven't made a single move to grab a leaf. When I was at this stage, I was so delirious and shaken that I would have caved hours ago."

Ember barely registered the implications of Sofika's words. Screwing up her face, she turned away, the thick, earthy air having her trying not to gag.

Rosala spare her, she needed this to be over. She needed to get away from those plants, or she needed to inhale every leaf until she didn't know her name anymore. But she couldn't cave.

So, Ember sat. She seethed. She felt her withdrawal stomp across her bones, breaking her with claws and fangs and every vicious word it could think of.

Coward. Failure. Worthless. Broken. Dirty. Stupid human herbologist healer.

Ember hugged her knees to her chest, the afternoon light streaming through the glass windows stinging her eyes.

There was no point arguing with her withdrawal. Why torture herself when there was nothing left to redeem? Why say no when at least if she had a leaf, she could feel alive in her misery.

"It's pulling you under," Sofika said, sounding horribly far away. "Don't let it win."

Gods, why not? If she was only resisting to prove Sofika wrong, it was pointless. She'd seen everything she needed to see.

She just wanted it to stop. Please, make it stop. Make it stop, make it stop, make it stop—

"I can't make it stop, Ember," Sofika said, her hands cool against Ember's sweaty skin as she brushed back her hair. Ember hadn't heard her approach, let alone realize she was speaking aloud. "This is something you will have to deal with for the rest of your life. But it will get easier. You just have to acknowledge it for what it is, and then I can help you."

Ember took a breath, tasting salt on her lips. But she couldn't make a sound. Not when saying it out loud made it real.

As real as the plant sitting in front of her that completely and utterly ruled her life. And that... that wasn't supposed to be the case.

Ember squeezed her eyes shut, the realization so simple, yet so indescribable all the same. But it finally allowed those words to slip free.

"I'm addicted," she whispered. And her world collapsed.

Sofika shifted to kneel beside her, wrapping her arms around Ember as she sobbed those words over and over again.

She was an addict. She hadn't been careful enough. She couldn't take it back. And now, she had to grieve a part of herself she could never get back. And she cried, and she cried, and she cried.

After what felt like an eternity, Ember's tears slowed. She swallowed hard, her muscles cramped, her head fuzzy and aching.

Finally, she opened her eyes. Looked at Sofika, waiting for the final blow.

But Sofika stroked her hair and murmured, "You did it."

Ember sniffed, feeling like the only thing she'd done was break herself apart.

"What now?" she asked, her voice scratching through her throat.

"Now," Sofika said, "you go somewhere you feel safe to recover from the war you just won."

"I used to feel safest with plants," Ember mumbled.

Sofika sighed, that statement seeming to hit closer to home than Ember expected. "We can go to my study," she offered. "There are only good plants in there."

Ember nodded. And she hated with every fiber of her being how Sofika had to lead her a roundabout way out of the greenhouse to avoid her seeing any orange and yellow leaves.

Chapter 56

Analia didn't know how long the entryway remained frozen. No noise, no movement, no one seeming to breathe. They simply stared at the ghost of their king at the top of the stairs, Sylas's arm around his waist supporting his weight.

He was dead... But he was also very much alive.

"Your Majesty," Tavian breathed. Releasing Analia's elbow, he dropped to one knee, his head bowed in respect. One by one, the crowd followed suit, their knees hitting the ground, their voices rising up like a symphony.

"Your Majesty."

Analia shifted, trying to figure out how she could kneel or bow in Meryk's chains. But Patryclas caught her eye with a faint smile, Analia struck by the almost translucent appearance of his skin. The exhausted lines that had been carved into his face.

But most of all, she noticed how Deardryn remained frozen at the foot of the stairs as he took in the crowd.

"Thank you," he said, his soft voice drifting across the entryway.

And those two words broke the spell. The crowd rose to their feet, their voices growing, whatever invisible line they'd refused to cross swept away as they surged forward.

"How?"

"What happened?"

"Are you all right?"

Analia's mind swirled, struggling to process it all.

She never would have guessed this was Sylas's secret plan. But it explained how he'd held it together long enough to make his move. And with a jolt, she realized it was also why she'd spotted the healer coming out of his chambers.

Analia allowed the crowd to jostle her to the side as they reached her, only able to shake her head. Meryk stepped closer, now standing beside a stunned Tavian. And before the crowd could completely overtake the entryway, Patryclas raised a hand.

"I appreciate your concern," he said, clearly struggling to raise his voice. "I promise, I'll answer your questions. But first, I need you all to back up. Let's not overwhelm our guests."

Analia expected it to take several seconds for the request to register. But immediately, they reversed direction, their voices dying down as they retreated back to the fountain.

Analia, Tavian, and Meryk remained where they were, Sabi lingering nearby, silent tears streaming down her face as she looked at her uncle. And still, Deardryn remained at the foot of the stairs.

"You look surprised, Deardryn," Sylas drawled.

"That's because I am." Deardryn shook her head as if waking from a dream, her eyes casually marking the spots of gold in the crowd. "We've been under the impression that Patryclas is dead for over a month. I never would have foreseen this."

"No," Sylas agreed. "It's rather jarring when things don't go as you expect, isn't it?"

Patryclas touched Sylas's chest, Sylas's face twisting in a sneer as he went quiet.

"Don't mind him," Patryclas said to Deardryn. "He's been worrying about me for over a month. There's only so much an emotion can build up before it starts to leak out. Just like the panic I sense from you."

Deardryn's started to speak, but Patryclas looked over her shoulder.

"I missed you, Sabina."

Sabi made a choked sound that could have been "I missed you, too." She reached her hand toward him, Patryclas mirroring the movement despite the distance between them.

Shifting his tired green gaze to the side, he dipped his chin to Analia. "Your Highness."

"Hello," Analia mouthed, having no name for the emotion clogging her throat. But there was no denying the crackle of tension as Patryclas finally turned back to Deardryn.

"It's good to see you, Your Majesty," he said. Stepping out of Sylas's grip, he carefully descended the stairs, Sylas's shadows extending to flicker around his feet. "I regret that we left off on such a contentious note. But out of the peace that we both preach, I thought it fair to offer you the opportunity to explain to my people what transpired between us. Perhaps then, we can have a civil resolution."

Analia shifted in her shackles, waiting for Deardryn's move. But Deardryn merely took a breath, the silence only interrupted by the slow descent of Patryclas's footsteps.

"I won't pretend to understand your flicker of relief," Patryclas said. "But I'll take your silence as a sign you would prefer I explain."

He paused in the center of the staircase, lifting his gaze to his people. And leaning against the railing for support, his voice weak, Patryclas claimed every fragment of attention in the room.

"Sylas told you all I was dead to protect me. He wanted to give me time to heal without worrying about another attempt on my life. For if I were to survive, I would be able to tell you that Deardryn poisoned me at our last Solstice Meeting so she could heal me and gain our trust. I would be able to say that she has been hunting the Crystal to help her conquer the six kingdoms. And I would be able to tell you that, after I confronted her about this, she attempted to kill me, and blamed it on Dimitri."

Analia inched closer to Tavian as magic thrummed across the entryway, the shock of the crowd sparking into rage. But no one spoke, allowing Patryclas's voice to echo around them.

"Deardryn came to us as an ally. She may have integrated herself and her soldiers into our castle life, but she has proven herself to be a deceiver, a traitor, and an immediate threat to our home. And we cannot let this stand."

Deardryn didn't move.

"Guards!" Sylas barked.

Analia's eyes widened at the rasp of weapons being drawn, Moon guards having quietly positioned themselves between the citizens and the Sun guards. As if it had been planned. And as Deardryn twisted, eyes wide, Analia knew she had no cards left to play.

"Round them up," Sylas ordered.

And the entryway descended into chaos.

The majority of the crowd rushed toward the halls, all quiet shattered as they tried to get out of the way. A few Moon soldiers broke off to help direct them. But the majority closed ranks around the scattered Sun soldiers, voices colliding, magic thrumming, weapons clashing as the Sun soldiers shook off their shock. But Analia only had eyes for Deardryn.

She stumbled away from the stairs, her magic flaring as Sylas's shadows whipped toward her. And Analia's heart jolted as her image started to fade.

"Sabi!" she yelled.

But Sabi was already moving. She charged forward, her released network flaring a near translucent blue as she pulled Aaron's damper out from under her dress. With a shriek, she barreled into Deardryn from behind, wrapping her arms around her and pressing the damper to her throat.

Deardryn made a noise of outrage. She tried to shake Sabi off, but she clung on tight.

Analia grabbed her dagger from Tavian's belt—right in reach, just as she'd positioned. Freeing Tavian to twist and slam his fist into Meryk's jaw.

Meryk crumpled, unconscious. Taking his chains with him.

Analia lunged for Deardryn, Deardryn's eyes widening as she spotted the dagger aimed for her throat. She threw up a protective hand. And Analia's own broken hand screeched as she snatched at her enka bracelet. *Please be close.*

Analia tried to shift her position, reaching for Deardryn's pocket. But Deardryn recovered fast. Grabbing Analia's broken hand, she snapped it back, Analia crying out as the flash of pain sent her to her knees.

Shadows rippled around Deardryn's feet, trying to restrain her. But Deardryn slammed back her elbow, her released magic illuminating the entryway in gold as she finally shoved Sabi away. And before Analia could retreat, Deardryn's hand clamped down on her shoulder.

Pain exploded across Analia's skin, racing down her arm, her collarbone, a pop reverberating through her body as Deardryn's magic wrenched her shoulder out of its socket. Analia gasped. She tried to pull away, a tendril of shadows wrapping around Deardryn's wrist.

Magic tingled beside Analia. And finally, Laness appeared, dressed in her black fighting leathers.

She took one look around. Then, she punched Deardryn in the stomach.

Deardryn stumbled back, releasing Analia and gasping for breath. Sylas took the opportunity to wrap his shadows around her as he hurried downstairs, forming his own shackles. Just in time for Analia to lunge, sending her dagger through Deardryn's dress and into her thigh.

Deardryn shrieked. She whipped her head from side to side, her golden curls coming free from their twist and falling into her face.

Just for a moment, her eyes met Analia's. And Analia would never forget her look of shock as she finally managed to fade into the shadows.

"Are you all right?" Laness gasped, the crowd roiling behind her as she dropped to her knees beside Analia.

"Nothing I can't handle," she ground out. "How's Sabi?"

"She's fine," Tavian called, having gone to help her at some point. Deardryn had evidently pushed her back into a pillar, but she only appeared dazed as Tavian helped her to her feet.

Analia swallowed, almost afraid to ask. "Did you...?"

"Of course I did." Sabi limped over to them, Sylas reaching the foot of the stairs as she raised her hands. In the left, she held Aaron's damper chain. And in the right...

"She was so distracted by you she didn't even notice," Sabi said, offering Analia the Crystal. "Also"—she reached into her gown pocket, the full skirts having obscured the lump of her book as she pulled it out. "I didn't have time to copy all of Deardryn's notes, but it should still be helpful."

"More than you know." Analia accepted all three items, lightheaded with disbelief as she pocketed them. Her plan had actually... worked?

"This is no time to relax," Sylas snapped, hauling her to her feet. "You might have slowed her down with that injury, but she'll be back for her soldiers. And she will notice the Crystal is gone soon enough. *Go.*"

Laness didn't need to be told twice. She gripped Analia's uninjured hand, her magic tingling across her skin.

"Wait." Analia reached out her hand, looking between Sabi and Tavian. "Thank you."

Tavian nodded, his jaw tight. Sabi touched Analia's fingertips with her own. Finally, Analia looked at Sylas.

"Tell Dimitri."

Sylas nodded, taking Patryclas's hand as he finally made it down the stairs. With that, Laness tightened her grip, the entryway starting to fade.

And Analia could have sworn she spotted a flicker of approval in Sylas's eyes as she disappeared. Taking the Crystal with her.

Chapter 57

The rest of Dimitri's day passed in silence. He and Rayner didn't speak as they helped the Royals in the safehouse, Tyce eventually jumping them back to their chamber. Right before he disappeared, he looked over at Dimitri, something like concern in his light brown eyes.

Yet, he shadowjumped away without a word. Leaving Dimitri to avoid Rayner's eye as he slipped out the door, going to spend the rest of the afternoon on Analia's turret.

That's what would make you unworthy of her sacrifice.

He'd never considered that angle of not using his magic, and honestly? It was because he'd been too afraid to. But where did that leave him?

Dimitri had no answers by the time the sun set. He had no answers after he finished a silent dinner with Rayner, unable to stomach even a glance at Othin across the Great Hall. And all he wanted as he burrowed under his covers was dreamless sleep. A small reprieve from the dark, heavy knot weighing down his chest.

Yet, when he opened his eyes, he knew that wish wouldn't be granted.

He stood in the center of Sylas's sitting room, thick gray carpet beneath his boots, his attention flicking over the red armchairs and bookcases.

"What do you want, Sylas?" he sighed, barely glancing at the Moon King standing before him.

Sylas's thick brows lifted. "How do you know this is real?"

"Analia told me about your dreamwalking. Even if she hadn't, there's no way I would dream of you on my own."

Sylas glowered. He grumbled something about gods-damned princesses and their schemes, Dimitri not paying attention as he picked at a thread in his sleeve.

He didn't have the energy to deal with Sylas. He didn't even have a scathing remark to offer.

"Why do *you* look wounded?" Sylas demanded. "I'm the one who should be pouting after hearing Analia shared confidential information."

Dimitri could have sworn he heard the whisper of a sigh, but he was too busy rolling his eyes to be sure. "If you're so distraught," he said, "then tell me why you brought me here or let the connection die."

Dimitri folded his arms, waiting for Sylas's retort. Yet, Sylas only gave him a haughty look. "Fine."

Then, he stepped aside. And the image of what lay behind him hit Dimitri like a punch to the gut.

Patryclas sat on one of the armchairs. His usual perfect posture was slightly slouched, his brilliant green eyes dull. But it was unmistakably him.

"What the fuck, Sylas," Dimitri choked out, something ripping in his chest as his eyes darted away.

Sylas stood up straight. "*Excuse* me?"

"I haven't been in your kingdom for weeks. I haven't so much as pestered you since I left. Why are you torturing me now?"

The words flew past his lips, hot and stinging as the tears behind his eyes. He'd already been dragged through the wringer that day. Why of all nights did Sylas decide to subject him to a blow he could never come back from?

"Dima..."

Dimitri cringed away from Patryclas's voice—he'd already started to forget the sound. But as soon as he heard it, the memory was back, sliding into place as if it had never been gone.

But it was. Dimitri kept his eyes firmly fixed on Sylas, shadows rippling around his feet.

"You insolent little creature," he said, taking a step closer. "Do you have any idea—"

"Sylas," Patryclas cut in, rising from the armchair. "I told you this would happen."

"You told me he would be reluctant to believe it. The one time I try to do something nice, and this urchin throws it back in my face."

Dimitri's hands flexed at his sides, his retort burning against his lips. Patryclas looked over at him, sending Dimitri's words fizzing out as he recoiled.

Because Patryclas. Was. Dead.

Patryclas's eyes lingered on him, Dimitri's shoulders curling. Then, he turned back to Sylas. "Go sit on the balcony."

"No!" Sylas protested. "This is *my* dream, I won't allow him to—"

"Sylas. Balcony." Patryclas pointed to the glass door behind them, Dimitri only just noticing the moonlit area outside. "Go be soothed."

Sylas made a hissing noise between his teeth. Patryclas cocked a challenging brow. And Sylas's face sagged into his usual petulant look.

Glancing back at Dimitri, he muttered, "Creature," as if addressing a particularly nasty bug on his wall.

Dimitri flipped him a rude hand gesture. Sylas ignored him, lightly touching Patryclas's cheek before heading for the balcony. With one last dark look over his shoulder, he pulled open the door and slipped outside.

Then, Dimitri and Patryclas were alone.

Dimitri turned to sit on a nearby armchair, curling up against the back like a cat. He could feel Patryclas watching him, thankfully not coming any closer.

"You don't have to be here," he finally mumbled, refusing to look up. "You can go. I don't need closure or comfort or whatever else. I already know you're dead."

Dimitri choked on the word. He pressed his face against the back of the armchair, futilely trying to brace himself for the sound of Patryclas's voice.

"Dima, I can feel how this is destroying you. You have to believe I would never do that to you on purpose. I'm only here because I'm alive."

Dimitri didn't know how to describe the agony of the word, let alone the hope that it stirred. "You're part of Sylas's dream," he said, curling in on himself even more.

"I am," Patryclas agreed. "Do you think Sylas could bring someone who is deceased into his dream?"

"How should I know?"

Patryclas chuckled. He took a few steps closer, his voice softening as he said, "Has Analia told you about how you can manipulate these dreams with your imagination?"

Dimitri nodded.

"So then, wouldn't it make sense that, if I'm part of the dream Sylas conjured, you should be able to manipulate me as well?"

"I guess."

"All right, then. Imagine me doing something."

Patryclas came to kneel beside the armchair, close enough Dimitri's senses prickled.

He could see the logic in Patryclas's words. Yet, he still had to gather his courage before looking over at him.

Gods, every detail was the same. Not just his dark brown hair, the black and purple tattoos peeking out from beneath his sleeves and his collar. It was the tilt of his head. The faint line between his brows as he studied Dimitri. The look in his green eyes that he finally realized was tenderness.

Dimitri swallowed hard. And a fresh crack ran down his heart as he imagined Patryclas disappearing.

Seconds passed. But Patryclas didn't move. Dimitri kept a careful hand over the hope in his chest, funneling all of his concentration into that single image: the sitting room empty in front of him. Still, Patryclas remained.

"You're safe to believe it, Dima," Patryclas murmured. "I'm alive."

"But how?" Dimitri asked, his voice impossibly small.

"You." Patryclas reached out, waiting for Dimitri's cautious nod before stroking his hair. "You replenished just enough of my life force for me to hold on until the healers arrived. Granted, there was so much damage that even with my Blessed healing, it took a long time to recover. But I wouldn't have gotten the chance if not for you."

Dimitri blinked hard, Patryclas's words circling around him, unable to land.

Patryclas lifted Dimitri's chin, their eyes meeting. "You saved me," he whispered.

And Dimitri's heart didn't so much as shatter as it did relax.

He reached for Patryclas, Patryclas leaning forward and wrapping his arms around him as his tears spilled free. Because Patryclas was warm, and solid, and alive. And that? That was a gift he never thought he would receive.

"Don't take this relief away," he said, his voice muffled against Patryclas's shoulder. "It aches, but it's a good ache."

"I won't," Patryclas promised, running his hand up and down Dimitri's back. "I'm sorry Sylas didn't tell you sooner. Sometimes, his paranoia overcomes his empathy."

"I've noticed."

Patryclas scoffed and tapped the back of his head. "I'm proud of you for not turning it off," he said, softening once more.

Dimitri let out something that could have been a laugh. "I promised I wouldn't."

He closed his eyes, giving himself a few more moments to soak it all in. Then, he pulled away, wriggling out of Patryclas's grip and onto the floor so he could lean against him. "There's so much I have to tell you."

"And I want to hear it all."

At his words, a light that had been snuffed out inside Dimitri finally flickered back to life.

For the next several minutes, he told Patryclas what had happened the past month, Patryclas listening intently as he nodded along.

"I think we've managed to redirect Othin for now," he finished, running his fingers through the carpet. "But Cadmus and the others still have to build an army, and I don't know if our chances are good or not."

"Don't underestimate the power of a common enemy," Patryclas replied. "As soon as my people had evidence of Deardryn's nature that she couldn't refute, the tide turned quickly. We're still flushing the last of the Sun people out, which is why Sylas was reluctant to fall asleep now, but I harassed him into it."

Patryclas squeezed Dimitri's shoulder, Dimitri knowing the calm that washed over him had nothing to do with his magic.

"What about Anna?" he asked.

"She escaped with the Crystal."

Dimitri grinned. "I knew she would."

"Yes, she's a clever one. Based on how much Sylas has been grumbling about her, he's rather fond of her, too."

Dimitri made a face, unable to stop himself from mumbling, "Uh-huh."

Patryclas laughed. Dimitri's lips twitched. But looking around the sitting room, the night-darkened balcony, that light in his chest dimmed.

"How much longer do we have until one of us wakes up?" he asked.

Patryclas sighed, running a hand down his face. "Hard to say."

Dimitri bit his lip. He looked down at his hands, suddenly unable to meet Patryclas's eyes as he asked, "Will I ever see you again?"

He didn't think he wanted to hear Patryclas's answer. After all, they were going into a war, he was all the way across Elefthia, Patryclas had responsibilities to attend to. Who knew what would happen?

Patryclas reached over, flipping over Dimitri's hand in his lap. "You see this?" he asked, tracing the black heart on the inside of Dimitri's wrist. "This was my oath to you that you would have a place in my kingdom. And the ink is still black."

Dimitri swallowed hard. Patryclas ducked his head, meeting Dimitri's gaze.

"You will always have a home here," he said. "Whether in my castle or somewhere else. No matter what, I will always be a place you can come back to. And we *will* see each other again."

He pressed a kiss to Dimitri's forehead. "I love you," he whispered.

Dimitri wrapped his arms around himself, savoring those words. "Love you, too," he mouthed.

And a few minutes later when the sitting room started to fade around him, Dimitri didn't panic. He didn't try to resist. He closed his eyes as Patryclas hugged him goodbye, knowing this wasn't the end.

When Dimitri opened his eyes, he was back in his chambers. He sat up in bed, feeling the ghost of Patryclas's arms around him, his voice freshly echoing through his mind. And there was no stopping his grin as he buried his face in his hands.

He was alive. Patryclas. Was. Alive.

Dimitri didn't know when he'd started laughing. Or maybe crying. He rocked back and forth, the words repeating over and over again in his mind.

"Dima?" Rayner asked, his voice thick with sleep. Then again, sharper this time, "Dima?"

Dimitri continued laughing as Rayner's duvet rustled, his own bed dipping a moment later as Rayner sat beside him.

"Dima," he said, "What's wrong—"

Dimitri twisted and threw his arms around Rayner. Rayner froze, his arms half-lifted as if not sure what to do.

"Hug me back," Dimitri said, still laughing as he pressed his face to Rayner's bare shoulder. "These are good tears, so hug me back."

It took a moment, but Rayner complied. His arms gingerly wrapped around Dimitri's back, Dimitri shifting into a more comfortable position.

Rayner relaxed. And Dimitri finally understood why people did this.

It was because of the sigh that escaped his lips as his head fit against Rayner's shoulder. The calm that settled over him as Rayner pulled him closer. The security as Rayner's hand came up, cradling the back of his head.

And for the first time in over a month, Dimitri was content exactly where he was.

"Dima," Rayner said, starting to laugh as well, "what's going on?"

"Patryclas is alive."

"He *what?*"

Dimitri could tell just from the jerk of Rayner's head that he wasn't in on Sylas's plan. He quickly filled Rayner in on his dream, lifting his head to watch the emotions flash across his face. By the time he was done, Rayner's jaw had dropped, his warm, dark brown eyes wide.

"And you're positive this dream was real?" he asked.

Dimitri nodded, disentangling one of his arms to wipe the stray tears from his face.

"But how did he survive that?" Rayner asked.

Dimitri took a breath, the words hesitating on his tongue. But Rayner didn't need to hear them.

"It was because of you," he said softly.

Dimitri's fingers flexed into Rayner's back, realizing what he'd walked into. But the words that rushed out of Rayner's mouth were the furthest thing from what he was expecting.

"Dimitri, I'm sorry."

Dimitri thought his eyes might pop out of his head. But Rayner only tightened his grip, looking like the words couldn't escape his mouth fast enough.

"I'm sorry for everything that happened in the Moon Kingdom. I should have told you about Sylas's orders, or refused to work with him, or gods, I could have asked Patryclas for help. I had so many options outside of lying to you and betraying you, and I was too much of a coward to take them. I didn't think I was worthy of taking them. Especially since my punishing myself came at the price of hurting you.

"I know I will never be able to understand how badly I hurt you, but I'll try every second the Crystal gives me. Because I was supposed to be in your corner, and instead, I was yet another person who burned you. I'm still trying to find new ways to make that up to you. But you told me I shouldn't apologize until I meant it and understood what I did wrong. And so, I'm telling you. I'm sorry."

Dimitri stared, lost for words. Rayner held his gaze, his face wide open and earnest. No, it was more than that. It was *him.*

This was Rayner. Earnest, grieving, remorseful, hopeful. Human.

"Thank you," Dimitri whispered.

Dimitri didn't have a name for the emotion that lit up Rayner's face. He just knew he liked it, liked that he was the one who ignited it.

Rayner pulled him closer, Dimitri having no urge to resist.

"You know what this means, right?" Rayner asked, his breath warm against Dimitri's temple.

Dimitri shook his head.

"You have a perfect record. Patryclas is alive because of *you.*" He ran his fingers up Dimitri's spine, his voice dropping to a whisper. "That's what you could do. That's what you could *be.*"

Dimitri swallowed hard. He looked up at Rayner, only just noticing how entangled they'd become. How the faint torchlight sent shadows flickering across his lightly muscled shoulders and arms, something about the sight having Dimitri's mouth going dry.

His gaze drifted down, skimming along smooth, light brown skin, down to his chest. And Dimitri's breath caught as he took in the full, unobstructed view of Rayner's oath tattoo with Sylas for the first time.

Dark purple lines took up the majority of his chest. In the center of his sternum, the ink paled into a lavender full moon, a scattering of stars sparkling around its perimeter. Dark, wispy clouds swirled behind it all like a hazy night sky, their tendrils curling up and around his collarbones, continuing over his shoulders, around to the back of his neck.

This was the tattoo that had subjected not just Dimitri but Rayner to so much misery. So much destruction. He'd expected it to be crude, maybe even ugly.

But it was beautiful. Elegant, in a heartbreaking kind of way.

Dimitri looked back up at Rayner, finding him watching him closely. Maybe even nervously, the chamber having gone quiet around them. And all at once, Dimitri realized this was the closest he had ever been to another person before.

Yet, there was no trace of panic through his veins as he murmured, "I like your tattoo."

Rayner went perfectly still, not seeming to breathe. Dimitri sighed, his fingers absently going to the black heart on the inside of his wrist.

"I guess I have to take Cadmus up on his offer to train," he finally murmured.

Slowly, the unease that had crept into Rayner's expression drifted away. No, it dwindled, reigniting into a light that seemed to spark in Dimitri's own chest.

"I suppose so," Rayner replied. He gave Dimitri a quick squeeze. And Dimitri knew the pride in his eyes would have been mirrored in Patryclas's.

PART 3: ACCESSION

Chapter 58

The sun rose and fell in the sky as Analia and Laness made their way through the Wild Lands' forests, back to the Starlight Kingdom. Most of their time was spent in the earthy darkness of Laness's roottravel, Analia only just realizing how much magic it required. Each time they reappeared for a break, the shadows beneath Laness's dappled green eyes appeared darker, her face tight with effort.

Yet, whenever Analia asked if she was all right, Laness shrugged her off. Analia, in turn, rejected the various provisions Laness offered her, her appetite nonexistent as she restlessly scanned their surroundings. Even as Laness popped her dislocated shoulder back into place, easing some of her constant pain, she couldn't relax.

By the time the sun touched the horizon, Analia was seriously worried about Laness. Ignoring her concerns, Laness reclaimed her hand, her fingers icy as she drew them back into the thick, earthy air.

Analia bit her cheek, the darkness stretching longer, longer, longer than any of their previous jumps. She squeezed Laness's hand, about to tell her to stop.

Just as there came a sharp jerk in her gut. And a moment later, the darkness faded away, revealing the dimly lit sitting room.

Mor slumped half asleep against the couch's armrest, Branten restlessly pacing in front of him. The moment Analia and Laness appeared in the center of the room, the two jerked to attention, their mouths opening to speak.

Laness's grip slackened. Analia's gaze shot to her, Laness swaying on her feet, her green eyes going out of focus. And her knees buckled.

Branten cursed. Analia staggered as Laness slumped into her, her broken hand shrieking in protest as she tried to catch her, the ground tilting beneath her feet—

"I've got you." Mor steadied her before she and Laness could hit the ground, Analia's shoulder twinging. She struggled to shift Laness into a less painful spot, Branten sparing her the effort as he came forward and easily lifted Laness into his arms.

"Is she all right?" Analia gasped.

"She's fine," Branten said breezily, resting his fingers against her throat. He shifted his hand to hover over her mouth, then shook his head. "Typical Laness. She pushed it too far and used up all her magic. Nothing a good night's sleep won't fix."

Analia sagged into Mor, her blood still buzzing. Branten trudged toward the stairs, Laness's tiny frame looking doll-like against his broad chest and shoulders.

"Find Ember when you're done," Mor called.

"Ember?" Analia repeated, almost missing Branten's confirmation as she twisted to look at Mor. "I thought you said she was all right."

"I meant for you."

"Me?"

"Anna, I'm pretty sure I'm the only thing keeping you on your feet right now."

Analia scowled, realizing how much she was leaning into him. "I'm fine," she said, struggling upright. "We need to get Aaron and Surce here so we can go over everything that happened; Deardryn won't be slowed down for long."

"Aaron will be here any minute," Mor soothed, sending Analia's impatience flaring. "I promise we'll talk about everything, but we have to heal you first."

Gods, he didn't get it. She'd barely gotten a step ahead by stealing the Crystal; they didn't have time to take a break.

Analia squirmed in Mor's grip, starting to protest.

"Why am I not surprised you're being difficult?"

Analia's head whipped to the side. The shadows rippled beside her, something shuddering in Analia's chest as Aaron emerged from the darkness.

No, there wasn't time for that. Even as the slick glide of his network brushed along her senses. As his starlight eyes immediately found her, scanning over her face, down her body, taking her in as if memorizing every detail.

Something in his expression flinched as he spotted her broken hand. He reached for her, Analia's fingers curling into the front of his shirt as Mor transferred her into his arms.

"I have so much to tell you," she said.

"I don't doubt it," he murmured. He skimmed his fingers along her jaw, lowering his face to hers. "We can start with what happened to you being careful."

The sharp focus across Analia's mind hazed over slightly. She allowed him to nudge her closer, his breath hot against her mouth.

"I *was* careful," she insisted.

Aaron made a soft, unconvinced noise. He slid the band free from her braid, his fingers weaving into her hair, Analia's focus fading, fading, fading. She closed her eyes, his lips brushing hers.

In a flash, his hands shifted. And Analia yelped as her feet were no longer beneath her. "What are you—"

"Would you look at that," Aaron said, utterly pleased with himself as he carried her over to the couch and settled her on his lap. "I knew you had it in you to be cooperative."

He turned her face to his, claiming her mouth in a kiss that was deep enough to have her head spinning. But Analia pushed him back against the couch.

"That was dirty, Stelingente," she complained.

"My shooting star, you haven't been home long enough for me to show you what 'dirty' is."

"Maybe *I* should get Ember," Mor mumbled, having retreated to the perpendicular couch.

Aaron chuckled, nestling his face against Analia's neck. "Sorry, brother."

Analia rolled her eyes. But she couldn't deny how his voice, the soft kiss he left below her ear, had her relaxing into him. Not completely. Especially not as he pulled away, and his smile didn't reach his eyes.

"When did they get back?" he asked, redirecting his gaze to Mor.

"A few minutes ago. I'm guessing Laness didn't tell you?"

"No," Aaron griped. "She's been pacifying me with vague updates all day. I only came because she stopped responding to my questions."

Analia perked up, starting to ask what he'd been doing.

"Uh uh uh," Aaron said, resting a finger against her lips. "You're taking a break and having quiet time."

Analia screwed up her face. "What if I don't want quiet time?"

"Then you can regale me with your list of injuries."

Aaron brushed his fingers over her red and swollen hand, a barely-there touch. Before Analia could protest, the door opened.

"Don't bother asking her that," Ember said, sweeping inside. "She's been downplaying her injuries since we were children."

"Well, hello to you, too," Analia grumbled.

Ember smiled. But Analia's attention went straight to the faint puffiness of her red-rimmed eyes.

"Did Laness summon you?" Mor asked, rising to help her clear off the table.

Ember nodded, Aaron muttering something that sounded like, "Figures."

"I'm sorry I'm late," she said, coming to kneel before the couch. "I had to take care of something. May I?"

Ember extended her hand, her usual flourish replaced with a dull sort of resignation. One that had Analia wondering what had happened while she was away.

Knowing it wasn't the time to ask, she nodded and interlaced their fingers. Then, with a gentle thrum, Ember's magic spread across her skin, seeping into her body like rain into soil. And, to Analia's surprise, she still couldn't sense Ember's network.

"Good news," Ember said, drawing Analia from her thoughts. "Nothing too bad. You've got a decent knot on the back of your head, but I can heal it and the bones in your hand. Beyond that, there's just some inflammation around your shoulder, and your wrists are irritated from your cuffs—"

"You can't take them off," Analia yelped, shrinking back against Aaron's chest. "My magic has been sealed for a month; we can't release it now."

"We won't remove your cuffs," Aaron soothed, his face pale as he cradled her against him. "We'll just take care of everything else, all right?"

Analia nodded, her pulse still jittering. Gods, she couldn't relax. Even as Mor offered Ember his assistance, Ember passing him her bag and turning back to Analia, her entire body buzzed.

But she nodded her approval. Just for a moment, she could have sworn apprehension flashed in Ember's eyes. But she didn't hesitate to begin.

To Analia's relief, Ember worked fast. Her head, shoulder, and wrists were fixed with a few different pastes and a quick flurry of magic. But the deep, rolling ache across her hand as Ember mended her bones had her biting down on her tongue, Aaron murmuring into her hair as his thumb rubbed soothing lines along her hip.

Finally, they were done. Analia slumped back against Aaron, Ember looking equally spent as she wiped the sweat from her forehead.

"Your hand and shoulder will be a little sore," she said. "Since you're Blessed, it will probably be gone by the morning, but I'll make a list of stretches you can do to help stabilize everything."

Analia thanked her, giving her hand a squeeze. Ember squeezed back, harder than Analia expected. Before Analia could say anything, Ember nodded and released her hand.

Analia frowned. But knowing Ember would come to her when she was ready, she looked up at Aaron. "Can we discuss now?"

Aaron considered, absently rubbing the last of the green paste from her wrist with his thumb. "Tomorrow morning," he decided.

"Aaron—"

"Breakfast. First thing, everyone in the dining room. Can you two pass that along?"

Ember and Mor nodded.

Analia started to protest—she couldn't wait that long. But Aaron offered a "Good night" to the room, and a "Fair warning" in her ear. Then, he pulled her into the shadows.

The moment their bathing room reappeared around them, Analia was talking.

Aaron nodded along as he turned on the tub's faucet, all too familiar with the high she was working her way down from. He knew she would settle soon enough. But that didn't stop his heart from aching as he remembered how she hadn't fully relaxed into him, her eyes constantly moving, her list of injuries.

"I didn't have time to check if there was a second shard in the box," she said, not seeming to notice as Aaron untied her tunic. "I don't think I sensed anything, but Aaron, she was gone for three days."

"I know, we'll figure it out. Arms up, please—thank you."

Aaron pulled off her tunic and camisole and tossed them on the counter, Analia still talking at top speed. His eyes did a quick scan over her stomach, her arms, the small curves of her breasts, only finding smooth, unmarred skin.

But she hadn't been like that a few minutes ago. She had been beaten and broken, trying not to moan in pain as Ember healed her. And Aaron had been powerless. Powerless to prevent it from happening, powerless to help, only able to murmur useless words as he held her, terrified to move and accidentally hurt her more.

But he couldn't fall apart yet. She needed him to be steady, and fuck if he wouldn't be anything and everything she needed.

Aaron knelt to pull off her boots, his hand brushing a lump in her pocket as he pulled her dagger from her belt. He reached inside, pulling out the Crystal's casing, his damper, and a small black book.

"My clever shooting star," he murmured.

Analia didn't seem to notice as he placed everything on the counter. Then, stripping off the last of her clothes, he rose to his feet and nudged her toward the tub.

Analia stepped in with little prodding. She turned in the steam to face him, her sentence half completed. Just for her words to drift off.

She stared at him, finally seeming to focus. And Aaron could see the moment the fight drained from her body.

"Is it sinking in?" he asked.

Analia nodded.

Aaron stepped closer, rubbing her cheek with his thumb. "Are you all right?"

"I will be," Analia sighed.

She sank down into the tub, Aaron coming to kneel on the other side. Reaching into the warm water, he found her hand and interlaced their fingers, Analia resting her temple against the tub's ledge.

Aaron shifted, the ledge digging into his side.

"Fuck this," he muttered.

"What?" Analia lifted her head, the alarm in her eyes turning to confusion as he pulled off his shirt. "What are you doing?"

"If you think a gods-damned tub is getting in my way when you've been gone for a month..."

Aaron rose, kicking off his boots and pants. Then, turning off the faucet, he climbed in behind her. He guided her back against his chest, Analia sighing as she *finally* relaxed into him.

And Aaron didn't know if it was the quiet, the warm water, or having her safe in his arms, but for the first time in a month, he felt like he could take a breath.

Aaron brushed her hair over her shoulder, his lips finding the back of her neck. "Hi."

"Hello," she murmured. She lightly traced the muscles in his arm with a finger, droplets running off her skin and down his own.

Aaron closed his eyes, breathing in the sweet scent of her skin as he skimmed his nose up her neck. But her hair smelled like pine.

Aaron frowned. He reached for the jasmine-scented soap on the inset shelf.

"I can do that," Analia said, trying to take the bottle from his hand.

"You are awfully full of protests today." Aaron placed the bottle on the ledge behind him, then nudged her back against his chest. "I know you can do it, but I *want* to do it."

Analia started to respond, but Aaron softly nipped her ear.

"You've been with Deardryn, constantly on guard, for a month. You deserve a minute to catch your breath. And I deserve a chance to savor you." He brushed a kiss behind her ear, whispering against her skin. "Let me take care of you."

He expected Analia to argue. Instead, she melted into him, her only response a nod.

Aaron kissed her shoulder. Then, he reached for a different bottle and folded cloth on the shelf.

True to his word, Aaron savored every moment he washed the Moon Kingdom from her skin. He savored her sigh as he ran his damp cloth along her temples. He relished the way her shoulders relaxed beneath his hands. He loved every point of contact: his knuckle grazing the curve of her breast, his fingertips running along her arm, the way her fingers laced through his as he reached her hands.

"What's this?" he asked, lifting her hand from the water to examine the moon phases tattooed around her wrist.

"That was my bargain with Sylas," she mumbled. "I hadn't realized it turned black."

She twisted to look at him, checking his reaction. Aaron brought her wrist to his lips, smiling against the full moon in its center. "I think I'm going to enjoy this too much."

Analia breathed a laugh. And Aaron didn't have words to describe the feeling in his chest as she closed her eyes and settled against him once more.

He quietly returned to his work, the steam brushing his face now tinged with vanilla from his soap.

If Analia noticed he took more time than necessary as he ran his cloth along her hips, her thighs, she didn't comment. She simply allowed him to scoot her forward, the corners of her mouth flickering as he guided her head back into the water.

Aaron kissed her closed eyelids. He reached for the jasmine soap behind him, just starting to think she wouldn't speak at all.

"Patryclas is alive," she murmured.

Aaron started. "I thought Sylas said he was dead."

"He did. It was part of his strategy to get rid of Deardryn."

"Does Dima know?"

"He'd better," Analia muttered. She hesitated, letting Aaron help her back into a sitting position. "Is it bad I resent him? Just a little bit?"

Aaron sighed, his eyes dropping to the soap he dispensed into his hand. "We can be happy for Dimitri tomorrow," he finally said.

Analia sniffed. Swallowing hard, Aaron kept his attention on his hands as he massaged the soap into her hair, doing his best to block out the grief rolling through his chest.

Because he was happy for Dimitri. But he was also painfully aware that he had received a gift Aaron never would. And he hated that Analia knew that turmoil well enough that they didn't have to speak it aloud.

"So much is gone because of her," Analia murmured, resting her head back in Aaron's hands. "Lucilla, Accalon, your mom, your siblings, the Star Kingdom..."

"I know," Aaron rasped. "And we can wallow in all of that tonight, too. But Anna..." Aaron turned her to face him, careful not to let any soap drip into her eyes. "You got the Crystal. You got her only source of Star magic. Deardryn might have won in the past, but this round is yours."

Aaron couldn't tell if the concept steadied her or had her deflating. She leaned back in the tub, Aaron reaching around her to rinse the soap from her hair. He took more time than he needed to, his fingertips massaging along the backs of her ears, sliding down until they met at the back of her head. And when Analia eventually sat up, her smoky gaze was level as it met his.

"We keep going," she said simply.

Aaron nodded, not trusting himself to speak. She slid her arms around his neck, his hand on her back pulling her closer. And her kiss tasted like a vow he wished they didn't have to make.

Aaron gently parted her lips with his own, a shudder running down his spine as his tongue curled around hers. Circumstances or not, this was her. It was real as his mouth trailed down to her neck, Analia sighing as his hand curved around her breast, her nipple pebbling under the caress of his thumb.

Maybe they didn't have to wallow. Maybe, they could spend the night remembering what they *did* have.

He pulled her closer, a quiet invitation, Analia not hesitating to accept as she wrapped her legs around him—fuck, he loved his spacious tub. Almost as much as he loved Analia's whimper as he licked away the droplets that had collected along her collarbone, the sound shooting straight to his cock. She rocked against him, water sloshing, Aaron gasping at the rush of pleasure through his veins.

Gods, she was so close to where he wanted her. He just had to lift her, and she'd be sliding down onto his cock, taking him in, his entire body tightening as she rocked her hips.

Aaron ran his hands up the smooth skin of her thighs.

And Analia pulled away. "Aaron, I can't."

Those three words jolted down Aaron's spine. He jerked back, his hands falling away—gods, what had he done to make the color drain from her face?

"What's wrong?" he asked, his heart pounding.

"I..." Analia bit her lip, her gaze growing distant. "There were so many reminders of him. And I know you're not him, you would never, but I can't. Not tonight."

Aaron didn't immediately respond. Every ounce of control he had was focused on keeping his expression composed as the arousal in his veins crackled into frost. Because Aaron fucking hated Pryanth. He hated what he'd done to Analia, hated that she still had to deal with it, hated that he was dead and Aaron couldn't kill him himself.

But that hatred would only make things worse.

Aaron released a slow breath, forcing his hands to unclench at his sides. "We don't have to do anything," he promised.

Analia blinked hard. And the ice started to thaw as she nestled against him once more. Aaron slid his arms around her, ignoring his aching cock as he rested his cheek against her damp hair.

"What do you need?" he murmured.

"Just this," Analia sighed. She paused, her fingertips brushing the back of his neck. "And maybe dinner."

Aaron had the strangest urge to laugh. He pulled back, just enough to press a kiss to her forehead. "Done."

He nestled her back against him, letting her decide when she was ready to pull away. And even though the color had returned to her face when she finally did so a few minutes later, Aaron couldn't wipe that faraway look from his mind.

Chapter 59

As it turned out, they didn't end up meeting in the dining room. After spotting the circles beneath Laness's eyes and Mor's barely concealed yawn, Aaron redirected them and their retrieved box of pastries to the sitting room. Surce valiantly hid her dismay as she and Branten arrived, carefully cradling her chocolate croissant in a napkin and glaring at Branten until he did the same.

By the time Ember descended the stairs, her hair disheveled, everyone had settled across the couches with their food. Analia passed Aaron her muffin, rising to her feet and going to meet her halfway.

"Since we didn't get to yesterday," she said. Then, she pulled Ember into a hug.

The two stayed like that for a long moment. Analia eventually whispered something in Ember's ear, and Ember gave a quick nod. Extracting herself, she moved to sit beside Branten, not quite hiding her wince as he passed her a muffin. And clearly deciding not to push it, Analia returned to the couch, Aaron sliding his arm around her shoulders.

Then, the updates began.

Aaron went first, his words coming far easier now that he didn't have to worry about Sylas listening in. Every now and again, his family chimed in, Aaron not sure how he felt about Analia's delighted surprise as he reached his conversation with Marion.

"We spent all of yesterday translating the scroll—which I'm sure you're thrilled to hear," he added with a pointed look at Laness.

Laness scoffed and kicked his shin. "You needed time to practice working with her. Besides, we were fine."

"You would have gotten home a lot faster if I shadowjumped you."

"But then we wouldn't have all of your fascinating translations to go over today." Laness fluttered her eyelashes, Analia covering her laugh with a hand. And the irritation prickling across Aaron's skin softened as he rolled his eyes.

"Believe it or not," he said, reaching for another sticky cinnamon roll, "there's not much to report. We're still trying to arrange all of our pieces into a story, but it's looking like Talitha didn't split the Crystal."

Branten accidentally kicked the table as he startled upright. "What does *that* mean?"

"We're not sure how or why, but it seems like the Crystal was already broken when the pieces were hidden."

"I've been wondering if that was the case," Surce mused, wiping her fingers on the napkin in her lap.

Mor asked, "Could one of the other Defiants have broken it?"

Aaron shrugged. "We're still looking for the beginning of the story."

"Well," Analia said, "maybe this can help." She reached into her pocket, pulling out the small black book Aaron had discovered the night before. "This is a copy of Deardryn's research on the Crystal—well, most of it. And interestingly, she decided to put her notes on the healers in the same book."

Surce looked up from the croissant she was splitting, her eyes gleaming as she passed the other half to Laness. "Perhaps the Defiants had nothing to do with the separation."

Aaron paused midchew, everyone else perking up. That would be an unexpected twist.

"If anyone can figure that out," Analia said, "it's Ember."

At the sound of her name, Ember's wandering gaze snapped to Analia. "Me?"

"I know you said you couldn't think of any connections," Analia said, leaning forward to offer her the book. "But as a healer, there are bound to be important details in here that only you'll pick up on. And if you can decode my uncle's book of symbols, I know you can figure out what Deardryn's aiming for."

"I can try," Ember said uncertainly, accepting the book. "Maybe I can covertly ask Sofika if she can think of anything."

Aaron's stomach shifted at the idea of his people finding out about Deardryn. But he didn't interject as Analia nodded. In fact, he was quietly pleased she was taking charge.

"The good news," Analia said, popping the last of her muffin in her mouth, "is even if that book is a bust, that's not the only advantage we have."

With that, Analia launched into her recount of her time in Moon. Even though Aaron had already heard the majority of it, the details of Deardryn's "research" still had frost crackling through his veins, only growing colder as she reached her escape. Based on the looks Analia stole at him, him reacting wouldn't be helpful. So, he pulled her closer, letting everyone else's frequent—and loud—reactions speak for him as he rubbed his thumb along her shoulder.

"I didn't manage to get my bracelet back," she finished, reaching into her pocket. "But I did get these." She tossed Aaron's damper and the Crystal's casing on the table, the stones landing beside the empty pastry box with synchronized thumps.

But no one spared the stones a look. Even as the Crystal's magic leaked through the crack, the whisper of power slithering against Aaron's nerves. They stared at Analia, even Surce's usual placidity cracking.

"I wish you could have stabbed her in the throat," Branten spat, his muffin crushed in his fist.

"And Sylas did *nothing* to help you while you were awake?" Mor demanded on Aaron's other side.

"Why can't she leave you alone?" Laness asked, thudding her head back against the couch.

Analia raised a hand, looking slightly overwhelmed. Aaron, meanwhile, hoped they would go on. Not just for his own catharsis, but he wanted her to see how many people were enraged on her behalf.

Analia turned to him, searching for an explanation.

"You didn't deserve it," he said simply.

Analia looked as though she hadn't considered that angle.

"Wait," Ember said, scratching the three white rings around her eye. "You said Deardryn *magically* dislocated your shoulder?"

Analia shifted, obviously grateful for the distraction. "Yes, why?"

"It might be nothing," Ember murmured. "It's just with a normal dislocation, you're at risk of damaging everything from muscles to tendons. Deardryn could have destroyed your entire shoulder with her healer magic. But you had a perfect dislocation."

Ember's words formed a cold, heavy weight in Aaron's stomach. He glanced at Analia, finding the same distant look she always had when thinking fast.

"Could she not have had enough time?" Surce asked.

"Maybe," Ember said, sounding doubtful.

The weight in Aaron's stomach grew heavier. Before his mind could spiral, Analia piped up.

"Laness," she said, "did Deardryn use my bracelet to contact you?"

"She did," Laness said slowly. "She was taunting me with updates, mainly that she'd captured you and I was running out of time."

Silver light flashed across Aaron's knuckles. He quickly reeled in his magic, focusing on the warmth of Analia's fingers as she squeezed his hand. But there was no stopping the frost from freezing his veins as she said, "Deardryn wanted me to escape."

The couch squeaked as Branten whipped toward her. "Why would she want to lose you *and* her shard?" he demanded.

"I don't know," Analia said. "But everything points to that."

She looked to Aaron, her smoky-gray eyes assessing. Not the situation, but him. And that realization had him able to chip away enough ice to force his body, his mind, back into movement.

"What are you thinking?" he asked, remarkably steady.

"I'm thinking she enabled my escape." Seemingly satisfied with his reaction, Analia rose from the couch, Aaron reluctantly letting her go as she started to pace. "Deardryn knew I stole your damper, but she didn't try to take it back. She left the Crystal shard in her damper box when she knew I had a way into her chambers. She wore my enka bracelet to inform Laness of her timeline. And she didn't injure me as badly as she could have. She *wanted* me to escape."

Unsurprisingly, no one was happy by how neatly the pieces clicked into place. They all launched into a flurry of questions, Aaron barely listening as he struggled to shove down the churning shadows in his mind.

It was bad enough knowing that Deardryn would be hunting her, his kingdom. But to think she let Analia go on purpose, and they had no idea why? When she'd already been put through enough?

Gods, the future kept getting darker and darker. But it had also been a long, long time since he was in a position where he could crumble under such matters.

Aaron closed his eyes, running his hand through his hair and giving a quick tug. Then, he straightened.

"There's nothing we can do about Deardryn's motives," he said, voices dying off as all eyes flicked to him. "Knowing Deardryn, she wants us to waste time trying to prevent every possible move. What we *do* know is she's hunting the Crystal, which means we keep our wards strong, run patrols at all times, and do everything we can to find the other shards first."

Aaron looked around the room, everyone relaxing as he gave them something solid. Something to hold on to. Because he was fucking king.

"Surce," he said, "do I even need to ask you to consult your tapestries?"

"I believe I already have a few that could be illuminating," she said, composure solidifying as she spoke.

"Good. As for you." Aaron turned to a still-pacing Analia, leaning forward to catch her hand as she passed. "Come here, you're making me nervous."

Analia blinked, clearly struggling to slow the wheels turning in her mind. "Because of the pacing?"

"No, from you being so far away." He pulled her onto his lap, savoring his own "something to hold on to" as he nestled her against him.

Branten, always quick to bounce back, flashed a taunting grin. "Separation anxiety starting to chafe, brother?"

"Yes," Aaron sighed, pressing his face to the top of Analia's head. "Thank you for noticing."

Branten snickered, the rest of the room joining in as Analia gave Aaron's shoulder a consoling pat. Aaron smiled, breathing in the floral scent of her hair.

Jokes aside, his nerves did settle at the contact. Not entirely. Just enough that he didn't have to force his calm anymore as he looked up, taking in his family.

"So," he said. "Looks like we've got work to do."

"And our first order of business," Analia said, playing with his fingers, "is taking off my cuffs."

Analia and Aaron walked through the sleepy kingdom streets, Aaron thankfully not trying to disturb their quiet as Analia's mind wandered.

She wasn't necessarily worried about Deardryn letting her escape—she would have no sanity left if she dwelled on Deardryn's motives. Rather, it was everything else.

The way Aaron's expression remained a little too controlled. The uncertainty that had replaced Ember's usual bravado. And the echo of Deardryn's words that had been nagging at her the moment she and Aaron left the house.

You've been well-trained to be queen.

Once, the sentiment would have felt like a confirmation. Validation, even. But there was something about being back in her kingdom, having learned everything she had in Moon, that had the mantle of queen feeling heavier than before.

Not to the point where she was rethinking things. If anything, watching the milling citizens' faces light up as they noticed her, immediately coming over to welcome her home, had her more certain than ever that this was where she wanted to be. Especially as Aaron squeezed her hand after every interaction, looking more pleased by it all than she was.

She just didn't know what to make of everything yet. That, however, gave her time to consider the task at hand.

"Analia," Aaron said in a singsong voice. "Do you need a smoke signal to find your way out of your thoughts?"

Analia blinked. Then, she shoved his shoulder. "You're far too fond of the sound of your own voice."

"I enjoy the sound of yours more, but I won't deny getting to respond is a perk."

Analia laughed, letting the feeling brush away all thoughts of the Moon Kingdom.

"I was thinking about my cuffs," she said, one of the few remaining snow patches crunching beneath her boots. "I know I was the one to say we had to get them off today, but the longer it takes to actually do it...?"

"Would you like to shadowjump to the lake so we can get it over with?"

"No, that would make it worse," Analia said as if it was obvious.

Aaron's mouth twitched, the two looking up as someone called a greeting from farther down the street.

"I know a month's worth of buildup is unnerving," Aaron said once the woman had passed. "But don't forget you've made it through far larger releases."

"I guess," Analia mumbled, turning the heavy cuff hidden beneath her jacket sleeve.

"Hey." Aaron gently tugged her to a stop, Analia tilting her head as she looked up at him. Aaron smiled, dropping his voice so only she could hear. "One more thing, and you're free."

Gods, that sounded like a wonderful concept.

Analia started to respond.

"Anna!"

The two turned. Brookston barreled down the street toward them, Evena releasing an obvious sigh as she watched from Nova House's doorway nearby.

Analia braced herself for impact. But at the last moment, Brookston seemed to remember something. He skidded to a halt, then took a few quick steps back, clasping his hands before him.

"What's wrong?" Analia asked.

Brookston grinned sheepishly. "Branten says I have to ask permission before hugging people."

Analia shared a fond look with Aaron. Then, releasing his hand, she opened her arms. "Permission granted."

Brookston beamed. He threw his arms around her, Analia surprised by how easily he snuggled into her.

"I missed you," he said.

"I missed you, too," Analia laughed.

"Aaron missed you the most. He was really sad when you were gone."

"Was he?"

"I find the fact that you questioned that concerning," Aaron chimed in.

Analia flicked his arm. Returning her attention to Brookston, she lowered her voice confidentially. "Was he broody?"

Brookston nodded sagely. "He looks better now, though."

"He's also wondering when he gets his hug," Aaron said.

Brookston perked up as if he'd forgotten. Wriggling out of Analia's grip, he reached for Aaron, Aaron leaning down. And at the last moment, he scooped Brookston up and over his shoulder.

Brookston squawked, his little hands slapping Aaron's back. "What are you doing?"

"Sorry," Aaron said, grin audible in his voice as he headed off. "I'm broody and unpredictable. And you have training to get to."

Brookston dissolved into giggles, Aaron reaching back for Analia's hand. He led her down the street toward an obviously amused Evena, Analia's own face hurting from her smile.

Gods, she'd almost forgotten how good it felt to enjoy herself. She released Aaron's hand as they reached the house, letting him meet Evena at the top of the stairs.

"Delivery," he said, settling a still-giggling Brookston on his feet.

"I'm sorry," Evena said, her full lips twitching. "He saw Analia through the window and got excited."

"I don't blame him." Aaron ruffled Brookston's hair, then shooed him back inside, Brookston calling a goodbye over his shoulder.

Aaron and Evena swapped a few more remarks, Evena eventually waving to Analia before heading inside. And when Aaron turned back to her, for the first time since she'd been home, his smile met his eyes.

"What?" he laughed, returning to her side.

"I'm just enjoying everything I've been missing." She touched his chest, stretching up on her toes. "Like your smile"—she kissed the corner of his mouth—"and your laugh"—she kissed the other corner—"and you."

She fit her mouth to his. Aaron's hand curled around her hip, even as he pulled back a moment later.

"Analia," he said, dramatically hushed. "There could be *children* watching."

"I know. And think of all the questions they'll have for Branten."

Aaron's eyes sparkled. "In that case," he said, "we should make sure they know what they saw."

He leaned in once more, his kiss soft and sweet and everything she needed. Sighing, she turned her head, looking around at Nova House, the kingdom, the people going about their days.

"Come on," she said, reclaiming his hand. "We have cuffs to remove."

It was the second time she'd said it. But this time, as she led Aaron back to the street, she meant it.

Chapter 60

Dimitri was starting to think training with Cadmus was a bad idea. He sat on the safehouse floor, Tyce and Rayner watching from the couch to his right as Cadmus eased down across from him.

"Before I can teach you to wield your magic," he said, noticeably cool, "I have to know what control you already have. I'm assuming since you've made it this long without being detected, you know how to release the buildup?"

Dimitri winced as Gritta's inn flashed across his mind. The explosion of golden light, the men shrieking as they staggered away, the wall pressing against his back. But he nodded.

"Show me, then," Cadmus said.

Dimitri's head snapped up. "In here?"

"Would you rather go outside where everyone can see?"

"Cadmus," Tyce said softly.

A muscle in Cadmus's jaw jumped. With a crackle, Spark hopped off a nearby sconce and landed on his shoulder, whispering something in his ear.

Dimitri's nails dug into his palms, struggling to hold back his own words as the seconds ticked past. But finally, Cadmus let out an audible breath through his nose.

"I need you to release your magic," he said, "so I can assess your technique." He sounded like a schoolboy being forced to make friends with his desk partner.

Dimitri glanced at Rayner, his pursed lips suggesting he, too, was having doubts. But catching Dimitri looking, he straightened his expression and offered an encouraging nod.

Dimitri sighed, then turned back to Cadmus. "Fine."

Folding his arms, he closed his eyes, reaching a mental hand toward his magic. A wave of sunlight flashed up to meet him, Dimitri instinctually trying to shove it back down. But Rayner's words whispered through the warm, languid thrum. *That's what would make you unworthy.*

Dimitri braced himself. Then, he set his magic free.

Immediately, the darkness behind his lids flared crimson. He screwed up his face, forcing his eyes to open, forcing himself to stare at Cadmus's unreadable expression through the golden light. One second, two, three.

"Shut it off," Cadmus said abruptly.

Dimitri didn't need to be told twice. He let his magic wink out, his shoulders slumping. But he was far from relaxed as Cadmus nodded to himself.

"You're afraid of your magic," he said.

Dimitri's face spasmed. "I'm not 'afraid' of it."

"Whatever you are, your magic has more power over you than vice versa—fine, I'm sorry, that was rude, stop giving me that look, Tyce."

Cadmus threw up his hands, then winced and rubbed his injured side. Tyce murmured something from the couch, Dimitri not catching it as he took in the tension across Cadmus's face.

He might have had a point about Dimitri's magic, but his delivery wasn't... him. Yes, Rayner was right that he'd been through a lot; it made sense he was different from the quiet Ash Prince Dimitri had first met. But whatever was going on with him was clearly getting worse. And something told him the darkness he'd sensed in Cadmus's magic network had something to do with it.

Regardless, if they were going to get anywhere, he would have to be the one to play nice. Unfortunately, that was not his specialty.

"All right," Dimitri said, dragging a hand down his face. "We've established I can release my magic, turn it off, and I'm scared of it. What now?"

Spark curled up against Cadmus's neck, clearly coaxing. And while the ice in Cadmus's eyes didn't thaw, his voice returned to something akin to calm as he said, "Now, we start working with small amounts of your magic at a time."

"How do we do that?"

"We use the salt pinching exercise." Cadmus leaned back against the base of the couch, the squeak of the floorboards making Dimitri wince. "I'm assuming you've seen how cooks pour salt into their palm before pinching off what they need. That's what you want to do with your magic. Reach in, and take a pinch."

Cadmus flexed his hand, golden sparks crackling to life on his fingertips. Dimitri bit his cheek, genuinely trying to keep his thoughts to himself. His attention flicked to his magic, Cadmus, back to his magic.

"That makes no fucking sense," he blurted. Cadmus's eyes flashed, but Dimitri went on. "My magic isn't *salt*. It's light. How do you take a pinch of light? Even if you could, what are you supposed to do with it—"

"Cadmus," Tyce cut in, "I can take over training if you'd rather help Fayela plan her negotiations upstairs."

Dimitri snapped his mouth shut, only just realizing how warm the room had become. He stole a look at Cadmus, the Ash King horrifically still and quiet, his blue eyes narrowed into slits. Crystal fuck him, he should have kept his mouth shut.

Dimitri squirmed. Just when he was starting to think he should apologize, Cadmus's jaw relaxed.

"Don't let him leave without making any progress," he said.

Dimitri made a noise of protest. Tyce ignored him, giving Cadmus a nod. Then, with a clipped farewell, Cadmus faded into the shadows, taking Spark with him.

The moment he was gone, Dimitri turned to Tyce and Rayner. "That was not my fault."

"I know," Tyce said, flashing an easy smile as he rose from the couch. "Cadmus is on edge. His injury is taking longer to heal than he'd like, so now he has to rely on Fayela to meet with the soldiers from Flickerwood, all while hoping Hallem's distraction goes well."

"He's been on edge longer than just today," Dimitri muttered.

Tyce's brown eyes flickered away. He settled on the floor across from Dimitri, Dimitri swapping a quick, knowing look with Rayner.

"I think for your training," Tyce said, clearly trying to change the subject, "we have to take it back a few steps."

As if a backstory could make Dimitri's magic any more like salt. But knowing he had to be good, he only folded his hands in his lap.

"For many Blessed," Tyce began, "we imagine our magic being stored in a well deep inside us." He cupped his hands, a ball of white flames flickering to life in his palms. "When we use our magic, we're drawing it up from that well. So, when releasing buildup for example, it rises up inside us, then spills out." The flames in Tyce's hand shot up like a miniature geyser, sparks descending back into his hands as they reached the top.

"The majority of the time, though, we customize the amount of magic we draw forth. To do that, we reach into the magic instead of letting it explode out, taking what we want and then drawing it up and out."

Tyce shifted his flames to one hand, using the other to reach in, pinch a spark, and then lift it for Dimitri to see. Dimitri nodded slowly, the concept starting to click in his mind.

"That being said," Tyce said, his magic winking out, "not everyone views their magic this way. So, ignoring everything I just said, I want you to sit with your magic for a moment. Feel how it moves, how it rests inside you. Then, tell me if you have a well, or something else."

"That's it?" Dimitri asked.

"For now," Tyce said teasingly.

Well, Dimitri couldn't argue with that. Even as the prospect of sitting with his magic made his stomach twist.

But he had to do this. So, he closed his eyes.

His magic flared, rushing to greet him after being blocked out for so long. Dimitri's muscles tensed, his shoulders curling as if expecting a blow. But he forced his body to relax. Let himself become accustomed to the magic.

And to his surprise, the sunlight calmed in response. It sank down once more, settling in his stomach.

But not in a well. It was just light, softly pulsing under his attention.

"It feels like the sun," he murmured.

"Good," said Tyce. "How does it move?"

"Like the sun." Dimitri opened his eyes, trying to illustrate with his hands. "It doesn't rise up in a column like yours. It expands out from all sides."

He spread his arms in a wide arc, feeling like an idiot. But if anything, Tyce looked fascinated.

"That's exactly how it looked when you released your magic," he said. "That makes sense."

Dimitri didn't expect those words to be as comforting as they were. He wrapped his arms around his middle, grateful that, if nothing else, he and his magic weren't broken. This was doable. Although...

"I don't know how to direct magic that explodes everywhere at once," he mumbled.

Tyce put a finger to his chin, considering.

"Well, hold on," Rayner said, leaning forward on the couch. "When you heal people, the magic *only* comes from your hands. Based on the brightness of the light, you seem to summon more than you need at first, and then you adjust until you find the right level."

Dimitri startled. That was exactly what happened when he healed. Was Rayner really watching him that closely?

"Is that true?" Tyce asked, drawing Dimitri's attention back to him. "Dima, you don't give yourself enough credit."

Rayner's lips pressed into a line. Dimitri didn't have time to wonder why as his ears burned. He mumbled a thanks, Tyce laughing and scooting closer.

"All right," he said, offering his hand. "Pretend you're healing my magic network."

Dimitri's eyebrows shot up. "Really?"

"Don't overthink it. Just follow your instincts and see what happens."

Dimitri eyed Tyce's hand, his magic shifting uncertainly. Tyce wiggled his fingers. And sighing, Dimitri placed his hand atop his, not pausing to think as he summoned his magic.

Golden light flared in between their hands. Tyce's calloused fingers curled around his hand, giving a quick squeeze.

Dimitri jumped, but that was actually helpful. It freed his attention from the rush of magic, allowing him to focus on his body, how that magic moved.

"My magic isn't in a well," he realized. "It's in a chamber, and there are windows with curtains on all sides. And when I direct my magic through my hands, I only open those curtains. I also open them too wide at first," he added in a mumble.

He let the light wink out, that curtain falling shut once more. And even though figuring that out should have felt like a victory, he couldn't help his stomach sinking as Tyce beamed. And their true training began.

For the next hour or so, Tyce led him through what he dubbed, "The curtain opening exercise." Since Dimitri already had practice keeping his curtains closed tight, and had no problem opening them all the way, Tyce wanted to get him used to inching them open. One curtain at a time.

By the end of the lesson, Dimitri had managed to send his magic full force through his index finger instead of his entire hand, but that was about it. Tyce, however, seemed pleased by this.

"I'm going to go check on Cadmus and Fayela," he said, rising to his feet. "After that, I can bring you back to the castle." He headed for the door, smiling down at Dimitri as he passed. "Well done."

Gods, that was not supposed to leave Dimitri wanting to hide. He dropped his gaze to his lap as the door opened and shut, the only sound the muffled thud of Tyce's boots as he climbed the stairs. Then, he and Rayner were alone.

Dimitri looked over at him, not sure what he was expecting. But it wasn't to find Rayner's expression had pinched.

"What's that look for?" he asked.

"Tyce is very... friendly," Rayner said dryly.

Dimitri cocked his head, but Rayner only patted the couch beside him.

"What's *your* look for?"

Dimitri sighed, his body heavy as he pushed himself to his feet. "It feels wrong," he said, coming to sit beside Rayner. "I know you're right, this is how I can be worthy, how I can help instead of harm like the other Sun Royals. It's just... If I've built my entire identity around *not* having this magic, who does that make me now?"

"You're Dimitri," Rayner said simply.

Dimitri huffed a laugh, rubbing his eyes. "That simple, huh?"

"If you let it." Rayner rested his fingertips against Dimitri's knee, something like smugness flashing across his face as Dimitri relaxed. "Working in my shop, I've had a lot of people request minor changes. New noses mainly. Sometimes, it's out of curiosity. But most of the time, they're trying to get a new reaction, whether that be how they feel about themselves, or how people respond to them. But the nose doesn't do that on its own. The value we place in that nose, what we believe about it, is what gives the nose power."

"Noses have power?" Dimitri asked, smirking.

Rayner swatted his hand. "Yes, and mine has the power to make you shush until I'm done."

Dimitri snickered. Now that he looked, though, Rayner did have a nice nose. It was proportional to the rest of his features, with a small bump in the bridge. It made him interesting to look at.

"Anyway," Rayner said, Dimitri's eyes darting away, "the same can be said about the Royals. It's not that they were chosen by the Crystal, or descended from the Defiants, or even their magic that makes them Royals. It's the people deciding to believe that. Yes, those factors might contribute to that belief. But when you take the people, their beliefs, away? The Royals are no different from the rest of us. Look at what happened to Analia when her people decided she wasn't good enough."

Dimitri scowled. That was certainly true.

"What's your point?" he asked.

"My point is everyone knows what to make of a Sun Royal. But the biggest reason you're a threat is because no one knows how the people will react to the king having a child with the wrong Royal. Which means right now, you have a clean slate."

"You realize once they figure out I exist, they'll have opinions," Dimitri pointed out.

"True." Rayner paused, his fingers idly circling Dimitri's knee. "What are three things you enjoy?" he asked. "And no, I won't explain until you answer."

Dimitri scoffed, his questions reluctantly bubbling back down. "I like books, and dessert, and talking to you," he said, not giving himself time to think. It wasn't until he spotted Rayner's smirk that he realized what he'd said. "I take it back," he sighed. "You're annoying."

"Oh, sweet Dima, you're only making it worse."

Dimitri elbowed him, but he couldn't fight his smile as Rayner laughed.

"At any rate," Rayner said, "all of those things are still true about you. Now, you're learning to wield your magic, too."

He made it sound so simple. And it was almost off-putting how his words had the puzzle piece Dimitri had been trying to jam into place rotating, finally sliding into place. Not comfortably. But it was there.

Dimitri rubbed his face, his eyes wandering back to Rayner. Taking in the appearance he'd attached his identity to. The pep talk that had come so easily to him, as if it wasn't the first time he'd considered it all.

"You're Rayner," he said, half to himself.

Rayner cocked his head. "I am?"

"When you were convincing Aaron to take you with us, you told him he would want help from the only person who has escaped Scarsthain. But you're not Ren Inferita. You're Rayner.

"You like mossy boardwalks, and clothes, and those abstract paintings you had all over your shop. You were an escaped prisoner once, but now, you're Rayner. No matter what face you wear."

Dimitri twisted his hands in his lap, his words nowhere near as eloquent as Rayner's. But Rayner looked at him like he'd offered him all the stars in the sky.

"Rayner and Dimitri," he rasped.

The weight in Dimitri's chest eased. "I like that," he murmured.

Rayner offered a half smile. And when Tyce eventually returned, asking Dimitri if he wanted to train again the following day, Dimitri hesitantly agreed.

Chapter 61

Aaron offered Analia a hand down the slope to the deserted lakeside. The clear water reflected the cold gray sky above, the sun hidden behind a bank of clouds.

Even though Analia had solidified her plan, Aaron couldn't help making a face as he knelt at the shore, the icy water brushing against his fingers.

"Anna, are you sure you want to do this?" he asked, rising to his feet. "The winter has made it even colder than I anticipated."

"It's almost spring," Analia said dismissively, bending to untie her boots.

"That 'almost' is doing a lot of heavy lifting."

"It can handle it."

Analia pulled off her boots, her confidence marginally settling Aaron's insides. She offered him her cuffed wrists, and he shook his head.

"I suppose there's no point in asking you to be careful," he said dryly.

"That part depends on you." Analia turned her cuffs, exposing the slit where the ends came together. "Do it fast before I lose my nerve?"

Part of Aaron wouldn't have minded that happening. But with how much magic she had, and with how long it had been building up?

Aaron sighed. Then, unsheathing his damper dagger, he ran the blade through the crack in each cuff.

"Good luck," he murmured, touching her hair. Then, he retreated several feet, his magic stirring in anticipation as Analia closed her eyes.

And only hesitating a moment, she flipped her wrists.

The moment the cuffs fell from her skin, black fire erupted from the onyx. Aaron threw up an arm against the heat, the thud of the cuffs hitting the ground drowned out by the roaring flames. They flared toward the sky, Analia completely concealed, her magic reaching higher, higher, higher—gods, this was worse than the first time.

Aaron's magic rose inside him in an icy wave. Gods, he hated this. But turning his face away, he set his magic free.

A wave of starlight slammed into the flames, the collision reverberating in Aaron's bones. The column of flames flew back from the force, Aaron unable to see Analia as she splashed into the water, far enough out he was confident she didn't land directly on the rocks. He hurried to the edge of the shore, steam hissing up from the lake as it extinguished her magic.

Slower than he expected. Regardless, the cold should have been enough to snap her back into her body. She should emerge any second, back in control.

Aaron scanned the lake. And Analia didn't surface.

Seconds ticked by.

Aaron's nails dug into his palms. Had he miscalculated? Could there have been a rock, or was the cold too much, or—fuck, he didn't know what.

As the tenth second passed with no sign of her, Aaron decided he didn't care. He kicked off his boots, the frigid water a few degrees warmer as he splashed into the lake.

Aaron headed for the cloud of black sparks a dozen feet ahead, rapidly winking out. A few more moments, and he'd be able to see her, pull her back to air.

The water reached his chest, Aaron barely registering the cold, his eyes searching. And his knees shook as a foot in front of him, the surface rippled.

Analia's head popped out of the water, hair plastered to her face and coughing.

"Thank the gods," Aaron breathed, the water slowing him down as he waded toward her.

Analia pushed the hair from her face as he reached her, and her eyes widened. She shoved his chest, "What are you doing?"

Aaron nearly fell back in surprise. "You didn't come up!"

"I was letting the lake extinguish my magic, and now you're cold, too—"

"Anna." Aaron drew her closer, her skin icy as he pressed his forehead against hers. "You. Didn't. Come. Up."

It took her a few seconds to process his words. Then, she sagged in his grip, mouthing a silent, "Oh."

Aaron rubbed his thumb along her spine, her reaction oddly soothing. Until he noticed her lips turning blue.

Aaron murmured a warning. Then, he pulled her into the shadows.

As soon as they reemerged, the true cold set in.

Aaron's muscles seized. He sucked in a breath through his teeth, his fingers fumbling as he went to retrieve their discarded boots.

"Bad idea," he mumbled, pivoting to grab the fallen damper cuffs.

Analia's teeth chattered too hard for her to respond, her hands shaking as she squeezed the water from her hair. But her wrists were bare.

"Let's get you home and warm," he said, returning to her side and sliding an arm around her waist.

Analia hummed an affirmation, burying her face in his shoulder. And Aaron drew them into the shadows. They reemerged a moment later in the empty sitting room, kindling thankfully already waiting in the black marble fireplace.

Before Aaron could consider grabbing matches, Analia pointed, sending a midnight flame zipping over to the wood and setting it alight. So, she hadn't released *all* of her magic.

"Clever girl." Aaron kissed the side of her head, then nudged her toward the flickering heat. "Clothes off."

With that, he tossed their boots beside the fireplace and headed for the side room.

"No one's home, right?" Analia called, still shivering.

"They're all gone for the day. And we can be gone the moment we hear the door open."

Aaron pulled free a bundle of spare blankets, his fingers finally cooperating as the warmth of his house started to register. He dragged everything back into the sitting room, just as Analia pulled off her shirt and hung it on the mantel with the rest of her clothes.

Aaron slowed, his gaze dipping to admire the curve of her ass, the dimples above, her pale skin covered in goosebumps—he needed to get her clothes off when he *wasn't* worrying about her. Then again, after what had happened the night before, it might be best he kept his hands to himself.

Tearing his gaze away, he plopped his bundle on the floor beside the fireplace, stripping off his wet clothes and tossing them beside Analia's. And Aaron's plans of keeping his hands to himself became a little less solid as he caught Analia's eyes trail down the muscles in his chest, his stomach. Lower.

"Come here," he said, finding the edge of the top layer in his nest. He wrapped it around his shoulders and laid back, Analia coming to curl up in front of him. He pulled the duvet over her, stifling a wince at her icy skin.

"Let's not do that again," she said, hiding her face under the duvet.

Aaron released a shaky laugh. "Agreed."

He ran his hand up and down her arm, angling his face toward the flickering heat. From Analia's flames.

"Do you remember the radiating magic technique I taught you?" he asked. "The one that just so happens to increase your body temperature?"

"Already on it," Analia mumbled.

Of course she was. He pulled her closer, her shaking starting to subside. Still, it took a few minutes before her body returned to a normal temperature, thawing Aaron in the process.

Aaron sighed, his muscles loosening as he traced her ribs with a finger. "How was the release?" he finally asked.

"Unpleasant but tolerable. Not having to worry about hurting anyone definitely helped."

She turned her head, stealing a quick look at him. The same way she'd looked at him when recounting her month with Deardryn that morning.

"Why do I get the feeling you're checking on me?" he asked, tapping her nose before she could turn away.

"Because I am."

Well, Aaron wasn't expecting to get that confirmation so easily. Analia turned in his arms, her fingers pleasantly warm against his chest.

"I've been thinking something feels off with you ever since I got back," she said. "You seem... careful. I thought you were trying to hide your reactions because you didn't want to upset me. But now, I keep thinking about how Brookston said you were having a hard time while I was gone."

"How do I keep getting exposed by a five-year-old?" he muttered.

He waited for Analia to smile. But her expression remained thoughtful as she stroked his chest, some of his careful composure starting to melt. But the shadows in his mind still stirred.

"You're doing it again," Analia said softly. "Talk to me. I've missed you too much to only have part of you."

Well fuck if that didn't hit him in the chest. He tightened his arms around her, wanting to hide his face from her perceptive gaze. Because she'd partially been right: he hadn't wanted to overwhelm her after everything she'd been through. But more than that?

Analia traced a curved scar along his shoulder, giving him time to deliberate. And something about that patience had his mouth tentatively opening.

"Brookston's right. I *did* struggle with you gone. I wasn't lying when I told you I learned how to multitask while I missed you, but I also spent so many hours turning over what happened in that chamber, looking for what I could have done differently."

"Why?" Analia asked.

"Besides the fact that you ended up trapped for a month with a queen who tortured you and would do gods know what if she caught you stealing her shard?"

His words came out harsher than he intended. He rubbed her back, trying to soften the blow. But Analia didn't look upset. She pressed closer, her hand curling around his arm.

"That was my plan, Aaron. You can't fault yourself for it being a success."

"But I can for failing you."

Aaron wasn't expecting those words. But as soon as they were out, there was no stopping the ones that tumbled free in their wake.

"I wasn't enabling your plan. I was failing you—failing my promise to you. I don't care we were only pretending you were my betrothed to the humans, I meant it when I put that ring on your finger and promised to protect you. And then you came home broken and buzzing from the danger you'd been in. And I..."

Aaron's voice cracked. He dragged his gaze from the crackling flames, the tears shimmering in Analia's eyes stomping out what little composure he had left. Before he could—gods, he didn't know what—Analia whispered his name and wrapped her arms around him.

Aaron's lungs tightened. He wanted to draw her closer, lose himself in her until the cracks in his heart had been stitched back together. But a cold, ancient part of him whispered he didn't deserve her comfort.

Analia kissed his chest, right above his heart. Sending that whisper drifting away as he closed his eyes, burying his face in her hair.

"You can't blame yourself for this," she said. "You didn't fail me. You respected my plan. And that plan was the only way we could have gotten the shard and saved as many lives as possible."

Aaron wanted to argue that point, but he knew he couldn't. "I just wish—"

"Uh-uh." Analia pulled back and pressed a finger to his lips. "No wishing. It's over, there's nothing you can do about it. And if I don't blame you, you can't blame you. So, think forward, not back."

Aaron swallowed hard, Branten's voice whispering through his mind. *You're fighting the wrong battle.*

Gods, he felt like he was fighting *every* battle. But staring into Analia's eyes, feeling the heat of her skin, had surrender feeling a little more tenable.

Analia sighed. She skimmed her lips along his jaw, sliding her calf over his. "What do you need?" she whispered.

You.

Aaron swallowed the word, not wanting to pressure her after seeing that faraway look on her face in their tub.

But unlike the night before, Analia didn't freeze. She trailed her lips down his neck, finding the spot below his ear that had him sucking in a breath.

She lingered there, her mouth warm and deliberate. "What do you need?"

Aaron's hand tightened around her hip as she flicked her tongue against his skin. Gods, she wasn't going to stop. And Aaron's thoughts were growing hazy at the soft sound of each kiss, a buzz starting in his veins.

"Analia," he breathed, her name a warning kind of melody. "Why are you asking me to be coherent when your mouth is on my neck?"

"Would you prefer it somewhere else?"

Fuck. Him. Fuck him straight to the Hell Realm as Analia's fingers followed the muscles in his stomach, heating the blood in his veins, sending it rushing to his cock, her hand drifting lower. Lower—

Analia dragged her palm up his cock, Aaron moaning at the flash of pleasure. Analia smiled against his neck, her fingers curling around him. But Aaron covered her hand with his.

"I don't need—you don't need to do this. Only if you want..."

Aaron struggled to string his words together, the anticipation, the need, sending his mind spinning. Analia lifted her head, her gaze present. Smoldering.

"You're wonderful." She stole a quick kiss, Aaron's cock twitching in their hands. "I'm all right now. I *want* this." She lowered her lashes, her voice dropping to a whisper. "So, what do you need?"

The surrender from before finally brushed his fingertips. And Aaron breathed a single word. "You."

Analia's answering smile was going to be the death of him. Before he could pull her back to him, she was gone. Pressing him onto his back, sliding down his body, pushing the duvet aside. And the rasp of her tongue dragging up his length had him seeing stars.

He gripped the back of her neck, her lips agonizingly close to his swollen head. "You are cruel," he ground out.

"Cruel?" Analia repeated, tasting the word. She ran her hand up his cock in a long, slow pump, Aaron's breath hissing between his teeth. "And here I was anticipating everything I've been imagining the past month."

She was going to destroy him. Either from the images she conjured in his mind, or the softness of her lips as they finally sealed around his head, her tongue swirling—gods, definitely her mouth.

Aaron's head fell back, moaning a curse. But she took her time drawing him in, her hands running up from the base of his shaft. Testing. Learning him. Finding the sinful pressure of her lips and twist of her hands that had him writhing, just to back off once more.

And Aaron couldn't think, couldn't function, beyond the silken heat of her mouth. He didn't know when his hips started moving, just that Analia moaned as she took him in deeper, the sound tingling along his nerves, having him move faster, harder, her cheeks hollowing as she sucked him down, release barreling closer, closer, closer—no, not like this.

Aaron ripped away. He flipped her onto her back, his elbows digging into the soft mound of blankets as he landed on top of her.

"You," he said, chest heaving, "have a wicked little mouth."

Analia's fingers curled into the back of his neck, her eyes dark, voice smoky. "Then why do I still have to imagine how you taste?"

She tried to pull him down, but he turned his head, dragging his lips along her cheek.

"You didn't think," he said, finding her ear, "that after a month of craving you, I would be content fucking your mouth and calling it a day? You didn't think I would want to savor every inch of you?"

He ran his teeth down her earlobe, her response breaking off in a whimper.

Aaron's blood fizzed. He ran his hands up her sides, needing to relearn every angle, every curve, every sound he could draw from her lips. But first...

"My turn?" he whispered.

Analia shifted against him, her voice thick with need. "Please."

Aaron's cock throbbed. And the last of the barrier he'd built between them shattered as he kissed her.

It was far from their first kiss since she'd returned. But this? This was a culmination, his tongue sweeping into her mouth, tangling with hers.

Gods, it had been a *month*. A month without exploring her mouth, her taste, her moan as his hand found her breast. He pinched her nipple, the scrape of her nails down his back sending lightning sparking across his nerves.

But he wanted more. So much fucking more.

Aaron ducked his head, flicking his tongue around her nipple. Analia gasped, Aaron's breath hitching as she ground against him. He drew her nipple into his mouth, licking and sucking, soaking in every breathless plea that fell from her lips as he moved to the other side.

He needed to feel her fall apart. On his fingers. On his face. On his cock. Now.

"Gods, Analia," he panted, running his fingers down her stomach. "How are you even more perfect than I remember?"

He traced the V of her hipbone, Analia's back arching with a whine. He let her drive his fingers lower, breathing out a curse as he found her soft and wet and ready for him.

"Perfect," he repeated. He pushed two fingers inside, and Analia gasped his name.

Aaron captured her lips with his own, swallowing the sound, Analia grinding against his hand. Fast. Relentless. Taking what she wanted from him. And her whimper as he crooked his fingers had all thoughts leaving his mind.

Aaron pushed her thighs apart, kissing down her torso until he reached her clit. He sucked, long and soft, his fingers still pumping in and out. Finding his rhythm. Drinking in her taste, her moans, his tongue flicking against her.

And Analia came undone.

She cried out, her back arching, muscles tightening around him. Aaron guided her through, so turned on it was fucking painful. Finally, she slumped back against the blankets, breathing hard. And Aaron was nowhere near done with her.

"My shooting star." He moved back up her body, his cock dragging up the smooth skin of her thigh as he kissed her once more. But before his thoughts could spiral, Analia broke away.

"Aaron."

Aaron jolted back. His eyes darted over her face, struggling to think straight—gods, what was wrong?

Analia smiled, brushing her fingertips along his cheek. "Slow down."

It took Aaron a few seconds to register her words. His chest heaved, the heat from the dying fire fueling the flush across his skin. "What?"

"Slow. Down." Analia took his hand, bringing his fingertips to her lips. "I'm here."

Something in Aaron's chest cracked.

Analia kissed his fingertips, then brought his hand to rest over her heart. "I'm here."

Aaron blinked hard, his spinning mind struggling to still. But that was her unsteady pulse beneath his fingers. Her chest rising and falling with each breath, mingling with his.

"Anna," he said, his voice a broken whisper.

"I'm not going anywhere," she said, running her fingers through his hair. "I came back to you. So don't fuck me. Love me."

Aaron hadn't known the edge to his desperation was fear until her words brushed it away. She guided his face back to hers. And his dark, spinning mind finally tilted back onto its axis as she kissed him.

Aaron melted into her, her kiss soft. Welcoming. Claiming control with every stroke of her tongue.

He didn't know how long it was before her hand moved down between them, guiding him to her entrance. Aaron opened his eyes, a shudder running down his spine as he took in the flush across her cheekbones. And Analia sighed against him as he slid in, and in, and in.

Aaron dropped his head to her shoulder with a groan. "You are everything."

Analia's only response was to shift her hips, letting out a soft moan. And Aaron complied. He gripped her hip, moving in slow, steady strokes.

Gods, he wasn't going to last long. Especially as Analia met him with every movement, his cock throbbing inside her. But he let her determine the pace, the two building into something faster, deeper, Analia's nails digging into his shoulder as she dragged him down. His mouth clumsily slid over hers, registering nothing outside of the taste of her, her heat, the pleasure building at the base of his spine.

"Let go for me," he breathed. He brought his hand between them, his fingers circling her clit.

Analia gasped. His balls tightened. And Aaron didn't know which one of them came first as he buried himself inside her. There was just the release that had his head kicking back with a shout, tearing through his body, breaking him down into dust, into seconds—that exact moment.

Aaron didn't know how long it took for his senses to fade back in, both of them breathing hard. He rolled off of her, Analia still shaking as he gathered her to his chest. He kissed her shoulder, her neck, her ear, Analia's fingers curling around his arm.

"I love you," he whispered against her temple.

Analia melted into him, murmuring the words back. And that moment felt better than any of the ones before.

For a long time, the two remained like that. Analia drifted off within minutes of Aaron pulling the duvet back over them, allowing him to settle into the slow, steady rhythm of her breathing.

Quiet. Peaceful. And Aaron didn't so much as lose himself in her as he was found. He existed in the space between each of her heartbeats, smoke and jasmine filling his nose and melting his ice away.

Think forward, not back.

Aaron sighed, smoothing a lock of hair behind Analia's ear. The problem was, the future was just as torturous as the past. Waiting for Deardryn's next move. Fearing for the future of his kingdom.

Logically, all he could do was something. Not in the future, but now.

Aaron lifted his head at the distant sound of the front door opening, Branten's voice barely distinguishable. Checking the fire was out, he shifted Analia against him, then pulled both her and their blankets into the shadows.

Do something. It always came back to doing something. And as Aaron pulled them out of the shadows in their bed, he knew one thing he could do. As much as he dreaded it.

Chapter 62

Ember stepped over the knee-high stone wall into the garden, her arms wrapped tightly around herself.

Even though she was only on day two of her break, she'd headed straight for the Healer Center once everyone had left the house, her anxiety from the past fifteen hours intensifying as she searched in vain for Sofika. Eventually, she bumped into Cenn rounding on Sofika's patients, and he told her she was tending her garden in the Pulse.

He'd offered to show her the way, but Ember didn't want to pull him from his work. So, she'd asked for directions and thanked him before heading off.

Now, dead foliage crunched under Ember's boots as she looked around. The rectangular lot was surprisingly large for such a central location, taking up half the space of Aaron's house. The numerous wooden benches throughout undoubtedly provided a nice place to rest when moving between the surrounding restaurants and shops, especially when the central birdbath was filled.

But now, there was only debris from the winter months and neat rows of dormant shrubs. And kneeling in the center of it all, a small wheelbarrow beside her, was Sofika.

Ember hurried toward her, choking out her name. Sofika looked up, her face flushed from the lingering chill.

"Ember," she said, "I wasn't expecting to see you—"

"I had to heal Analia last night," Ember blurted, coming to a stop beside her.

Sofika cocked her head. "Analia's home?"

"Yes, and she was injured. Laness told me through our bracelets when I was walking home from the Healer Center, but then she didn't respond to any of my questions, and since I didn't know how bad it was, I didn't want to waste time returning to the center to get someone else, so I had to heal her."

The words rambled over Ember's tongue, practically blurring into each other in her haste to get them out. The situation had been playing on an endless loop in her mind from the moment it happened, to the point she spent most of the night pacing around her room in a panic. Even now, the list of everything that could have gone wrong had her trembling.

Sofika studied her, her small, hazel eyes thoughtful. Then, she patted the ground beside her. "I'm assessing the winter damage to my bushes. Help me finish this section."

Ember nodded, grateful for something to do as she sank to her knees on the cold, hard earth.

"So," Sofika said, returning her attention to her shrub, "is Analia healed?"

"Yes," Ember said on an exhale, her hands sifting through branches. "My healer bag was by the front door, so I was able to reduce the swelling and irritation. Her hand had clearly been crushed, and she had a decent head injury, but I mended her bones and accelerated blood absorption from the contusion. The rest was minor."

"It sounds like you knew what you were doing," Sofika commented.

"I did. But what if I hadn't? What if there were complications I wasn't expecting? What if her injuries had been far worse?"

"Why are you worrying about hypotheticals?" Sofika asked, infuriatingly calm.

"Because I'm terrified!" Ember exploded. Her voice echoed around them, no one thankfully nearby to hear. "I've spent the past fourteen years working myself to the bone to prove myself as a healer, convincing myself I was better than I was because that was the only way to survive the prejudice. But then I got suspended. My kingdom was invaded. One of my friends was tortured, the other locked in his own dungeon, and a third was *killed,* and I was the only one that could help. And I got addicted to a gods-damned *plant.*

"A plant that was supposed to help me focus. But now I wake up every morning with a splitting headache and sick to my stomach and I've gone from loving spending time with people to wanting to jump out of my skin if they look at me too long. And I never saw it coming. So, what else could I be blindsided by?"

"Ember," Sofika said, sitting back on her heels. "You're spiraling."

Ember thought she would erupt into flames. "I know! That's why I'm here because you told me you could help me, so *help me!*"

It took Ember a few seconds to register Sofika's face pinch. A few more to realize her chest was heaving, her lungs desperate for air. And her shoulders slumped as she realized the tirade she'd just unleashed.

"I'm sorry," she whispered.

"I forgive you."

Sofika reached over, her skin rough with dirt as she gave Ember's hand a squeeze. Ember felt worse.

"You can't lose faith in yourself, Ember," she said, rubbing her thumb along Ember's knuckles.

"You mean lose faith in a person who got addicted?" Ember asked bitterly. She hadn't intended on saying the words aloud, but then again, what was the point of keeping them in?

"Don't go down that road," Sofika warned. "Shame is toxic to us. Especially since it is undeserved."

Ember didn't mean to make a face at that. But judging by Sofika's narrowed eyes, she'd noticed. She released Ember's hand, twisting to scoop up a handful of wet leaves and toss them in her wheelbarrow.

"It seems like," she finally said, "when you tell your story, all you see is failure. You failed to prove yourself as a healer when you got suspended. You failed to prove your competence when you became addicted. You failed yourself and your friends. Am I close?"

Horrifically so. Ember kept her eyes on the hedge, pretending it was her examination that had her shuffling away from Sofika as she nodded.

"That's interesting. Because when I hear that story, I don't see someone who woefully put herself in this situation. I see someone who was trying to survive impossible circumstances. I see someone who realized she was in trouble and came looking for help. I see someone who is trying to not just survive, but live again."

Ember bit her lip, Sofika's words hitting her one after the other. But this didn't feel like the physical blows from the greenhouse. This felt like shifting logs in a dam, allowing some of the built-up pressure to flow free.

Gods, she wanted to believe her. But Ember's eyes still stung as she whispered, "How?"

Sofika smiled like she'd passed the final question on her exam. Rising to her feet, she stepped around Ember to assess a neighboring bush, the early spring breeze rustling the branches.

"What was the predominant feeling you had when you first saw Analia?" she asked.

Rosala spare her, she didn't want to think about that. She started to ask why that mattered, but Sofika wagged a finger at her.

Ember pressed her lips into a line. But knowing Sofika wouldn't explain until she was ready, she tentatively let her mind drift back to the night before.

"I was apprehensive," she finally said, branches scratching her hands.

"How come?"

"Because I hadn't healed anyone for weeks."

"And?"

Ember shot Sofika a look, but the master healer ignored her as she shuffled down her row. "Because I wasn't sure if I could."

"And?"

Ember's fingers tightened around a branch, images flashing across her mind. The way Analia had been fidgeting on Aaron's lap when she'd come in, just to go still at the sight of her. The look of faith in Aaron's eyes when she'd hesitated before starting her healing.

"I was worried they would realize something was wrong." Ember's throat closed around the words. She pulled out a dead section of branches with a rip, something dangerous bubbling up inside her.

Sofika started to speak.

"What's the point of this?" Ember demanded over her.

To Ember's surprise, Sofika smiled to herself.

"When people come to me asking how they can stay sober, what they're really asking is 'How can I do it without feeling the pain?' And the answer is, you can't. You have to sit with it, understand it, and then you can start to manage it."

Rosala spare her, Sofika's answers were getting worse and worse. Ember hunched over her shrub, not thinking she had the wherewithal to go much longer. But Sofika went on without prompting.

"Instead of judging what you find, *shaming*"—she shot Ember a look, Ember giving a tired eye roll in response—"what you do is be curious."

"Curious," Ember repeated flatly.

"Curious," Sofika agreed.

Ember reached the end of her row, knowing she should bite her tongue. But the thought had barely formed when the words were popping out of her mouth.

"I'm sorry, that makes no sense. When you have a broken bone, you don't prod at it. You leave it alone to let it heal."

"But we're not dealing with a bone," Sofika said, rising and stepping over to a tangle of fallen branches to Ember's right. "We're dealing with your mind. And when you 'leave it alone,' it builds up until there's nowhere left to go."

"I assume you're speaking from experience," Ember muttered.

"I am."

Ember froze. She glanced at Sofika, perfectly composed as she collected her branches. And finally, her words from the past twenty-four hours registered in her mind.

When I was at this stage. Shame is toxic to us.

Ember didn't know if she felt like the worst person in the world, or the most foolish.

"I'm sorry," she said, bowing her head.

"That's all right." Sofika circled around Ember to drop her branches in the wheelbarrow, a small, cleared-off section starting to form. "It has been seventy-six years since I had a sip of liquor."

Sofika returned to her branches, missing Ember mouth, "Wow." She couldn't imagine seventy-six days, let alone years. Just the thought had her cravings giving a long, aching stretch in her chest.

No wonder Sofika had spotted her addiction so easily: she'd had a lifetime of dealing with it. But that was also why she cared so much.

"Can I ask what happened?" Ember asked tentatively.

Sofika nodded as if she'd been wondering when Ember would do so.

"When the Starlight War broke out with the Human Kingdom," she said, voice distant in memories as she collected her branches, "I was a young master healer. Up until that point, I dealt with the typical injured soldiers, sick children, adults that had made some questionable decisions. There had certainly been difficult cases in the mix, some that even left me rattled. But I always had time afterward to recover. But the same could not be said when the fighting began.

"Suddenly, I was dealing with bloody, mangled soldiers, listening to their wails, their last words, only having so much I could do. Even with magic, there were so many fatalities. People whose final breaths I felt under my hands. And the moment they were gone, I was shoved along to the next person who needed me. No time to process, no time to grieve. Just death after death after death."

Sofika paused, cradling her armful of branches against her chest. Ember swallowed against the lump in her throat. Before she could say anything, Sofika shook herself off.

"Eventually, she said, going to drop her branches in the wheelbarrow, "I started having a goblet of liquor with dinner every night to take the edge off. On the extra hard days, I had a second because I deserved it. But then all of my days were hard, so I always had two. And then three, then four... I presume you understand where this is going.

"By the time the war ended, I couldn't make it until lunchtime without a drink. Naturally, my old master healer noticed. At that point, our journeys are rather similar. But I think the defining moment for me was when I returned to work after being sober for a month.

"I was already nervous, but the longer I remained in that gloomy gray-stone temple, devoid of color or decorations, I could feel myself slipping. I started taking my lunch breaks out on the nearby hill to escape the place. And that was when I started to wonder if that dreadful environment was negatively impacting my recovery, how was it not doing the same to our patients?"

"So, you started your research," Ember murmured, eyes on the space Sofika was clearing off. "Cenn told me about how you discovered all these influences on healing, and then created the Healer Center to incorporate them."

"Indeed, and with great success. Not just for the patients, but me. Because in that time, I realized I feel my most stable when I'm busy, when I'm doing something I'm passionate about, and when I have a routine."

"And you're seventy-six years sober as a result," Ember said.

Sofika nodded, tossing the last of the branches in her wheelbarrow. "You know what the most helpful thing has been?"

Ember shook her head.

"Having someone to talk to." Sofika returned to sit beside Ember, forcing her to meet her gaze. "You coming to talk to me today instead of stewing alone is a victory. Today, you won. And I'm letting you know I will always be someone you can talk to. I've been given permission to say you can also talk to Cenn."

"Cenn?" Ember repeated, falling back on her heels. But Cenn was so fastidious, so friendly and relaxed—the complete opposite of how she'd been feeling. "Is he really?"

"It's his story to tell. But he noticed your preoccupation with the devinroot, and asked me to pass the message along if he was correct."

"Is that why you paired us together?" she asked.

"I 'paired you' because you're both herbologist apprentices, and I thought you could learn from each other."

Fair enough. Ember rubbed her forehead, not caring as she scrubbed dirt across her skin. This conversation was taking one turn after another. But to her surprise, as Sofika rose and dusted the dirt from her hands, she felt more grounded than she had in a long, long time.

"Unfortunately," Sofika said, "I have patients I must attend to now. Will I be seeing you in the center the day after next?"

Ember looked down at her shrub, a lump rising in her throat.

"You will." She rose as well, clasping her hands before her. "Thank you."

"Of course."

With that, Ember turned to go, unable to bring herself to look back as she called, "There are new buds at the end of my bush. Make sure you cover them with a sheet before you go."

Sofika's confirmation was soft and fond. And Ember turned over everything she had said as she started the walk home.

It was almost overwhelming how many tools Sofika had given her. Helpful tools. But just because she had them didn't mean she automatically knew how to use them. She didn't know if she was *ready* to use them.

Ember sighed, reaching up to open Aaron's wooden gate.

It was funny, really. She'd started using devinroot all those years ago because she was desperate to lengthen her attention span. She'd told herself she was medicating her mind. But if she was being honest, she was also medicating her loneliness.

She used because she was lonely. She just hadn't expected her using to leave her feeling even more alone. But now...

Ember turned on the porch steps at the clomp of heavy boots behind her. Branten headed up the front path, fighting leathers on and face gleaming with sweat.

"Is someone after you?" she asked.

"Constantly," Branten panted. "But this run was recreational."

He reached the steps, Ember reflexively shifting out of his way. Yet, as she watched him climb, she couldn't help but remember their conversation in the dining room.

Him telling her she needed to get her pent-up energy out. The way he invited her to join him every morning.

"Do you run *every* morning?" she asked.

Branten looked back at the top of the stairs. "Unless there's an emergency. Why?"

Ember bit her lip, Sofika's voice softly echoing in her mind. *Routine.*

"Can I come next time?" she asked. She braced herself, waiting for Branten to taunt her about finally coming to her senses.

Instead, he flashed a genuine grin. "Of course." He turned and opened the door, calling over his shoulder. "I hope you like waking up early, healer girl."

Ember groaned. But following Branten inside, she reminded herself this was her chance. A chance to start living again.

She just hoped she wouldn't regret the tool she'd chosen the following morning.

Chapter 63

Ember was distraught to learn what Branten considered early. The sun had barely peeked over the horizon through her window the following morning when he knocked on her door, calling she had ten minutes before meeting him downstairs.

Ember groaned, pressing her face into her pillow. She was tempted to tell him she would start tomorrow. But that had been her mantra when considering weaning off devinroot. And more importantly, Branten was still banging on her door.

Calling an affirmation, she dragged herself out of bed, her muscles stiff and head aching. But at least the knocking stopped as Branten, seemingly trusting her word, trudged back downstairs. And Ember used all ten minutes braiding back her hair and dressing in a charcoal-colored shirt and dark pants.

She stumbled downstairs, Branten giving her a nod of approval where he waited by the back door.

"Ready to go?" he asked.

"Don't ask me that," she grumbled, rubbing her eyes.

Branten laughed and slid open the back door, Ember jumping at the sudden rush of cold.

"Why are we going that way?" she asked.

"Because now that the snow is gone, we can use the trails back here."

It took Ember a few seconds to process his words, her cravings clamoring for attention. But Branten only winked at her over his shoulder.

"Ready, set, go!" he yelled. Then, he charged out the door.

Ember yelped. Her legs started moving of their own accord, chasing after him down the porch steps, across the muddy yard, Branten waiting for her at the edge of the birch tree grove.

"Why are we starting immediately?" she complained, staggering to a halt beside him.

"It's running, healer girl. You can start any time." Turning, he jogged off into the trees, calling over his shoulder. "We'll go slow today to account for the mud. Make sure you watch your step."

Rosala spare her, what had she gotten herself into?

Knowing Branten wouldn't wait for her to catch up again, she hurried after him, the ground hardening beneath her feet as she reached the path. And to Ember's dismay, they did, in fact, run.

The grove stretched farther back than she anticipated, Branten taking her on a curving route about the size of the Pulse's square. Numerous times, another beaten-down trail intersected their own, Ember vaguely wondering where they led to. But the majority of her attention was fixed on the various ruts and protruding roots in her path, her lungs spasming every time she stumbled.

Branten did his best to steer them away from the worst of it, the grove quiet around them outside of their pounding feet and Branten's occasional warnings. But even with that, even though he kept them at a steady pace that was obviously slow for him, Ember was clearly not made for this.

By the time they finished their first lap, she was clutching the stitch in her side, gasping for breath. Branten passed her one of the two canteens hanging from his belt, Ember gratefully gulping the water down. She handed it back to him, hoping that meant they were done.

But calling a "Let's go!" over his shoulder, he jogged off once more. Leaving Ember to look up at the sky in betrayal as she staggered back into movement.

Gods, how did Branten *enjoy* this? She'd heard stories from her soldier patients about how after running long enough, there came a rush. But as Ember followed Branten around a bend, all she felt was the sweat coating her skin and the cold air doing nothing in her lungs.

Maybe she hadn't hit the time quota yet. Maybe it was right around the corner.

Yet, as they finished their second lap, not only did Ember's legs tremble, but she was at peace with the fact that she wasn't meant to experience that high. She could stop now and live a fulfilled life not knowing the wonders of running. Her life would probably be better if she did.

"One more lap," Branten said, passing her the canteen.

"*You* do one more lap," Ember grumbled childishly.

Branten grinned and patted her head. "One more lap and I'll buy you breakfast."

Crystal strike him down, he was barely winded. Meanwhile, Ember was discovering the unsettling experience of overheating while standing out in the cold.

"Come on," Branten said, wiggling his eyebrows. "Don't tell me you're a quitter."

Ember shot Branten a glare. Just to realize that was exactly what he'd been aiming for.

"I don't like you," she muttered.

Branten laughed, heading back into the trees. "I'll earn back your love with napkin swans."

Well, she did enjoy those. And it would be nice to get out of the house—without running. So, with a sigh, Ember staggered after Branten, her legs whining in protest.

Clearly noticing Ember dying beside him, Branten decided this would be his chatty lap. Thankfully, he didn't offer any encouragements, instead prattling on about how when he and his brothers had first emerged from the Underground, Ethelind made them run this route when she grew sick of their antics.

Ember didn't have the breath to reply, instead imagining how satisfying the thud would be if she shoved him into that tree. Or if he tripped over that rock. Or if one of the branches above fell and whacked him on the head.

Not hard. Not to the point she couldn't heal him. Just a little smack.

Ember grinned to herself, a hysterical grin that almost distracted her from her pounding pulse. Branten looked over at her. And fine, his genuine delight was enough that she wouldn't shove him. This time. But that didn't stop her from wanting to cry with relief as the backyard came into view once more.

She slowed to a jog, then a walk, finally slumping against a tree trunk.

"If you tell me one more lap," she managed between gasps, "I will hurt you."

Branten laughed as he paused beside her, wiping the sheen of sweat from his brow. "No more laps," he promised. "We can go inside now."

Thank the gods. Ember dug her nails into the soft bark, bracing herself to stand upright once more. Just to notice Branten shifting beside her, his eyes lingering on the path.

"You want to keep going," she said slowly.

Branten started to disagree. Ember didn't know why that touched her as much as it did. She raised a hand, still noticeably out of breath.

"You keep going. I have to wash the sweat off me."

Branten ran a hand through his reddish-brown hair, clearly hesitant. "Are you sure?"

"As long as I don't have to join you, you can run as many laps as you like."

Branten's dark eyes gleamed. With that, he passed her her canteen and headed off once more, the thud of his boots noticeably faster than before. And as Ember slumped against her tree, her face hot and sweaty, she was grateful Branten hadn't taken her on his usual route through the kingdom.

Now that she looked around, it was actually rather peaceful. The occasional chirp of waking birds, the rising sun peeking through the gaps in the tangled branches above. The crisp air in her lungs. She'd gone out to the porch several times when trying to distract herself from her withdrawal, and yet, she hadn't fully taken it in.

In fact, as she finally pushed off her trunk, she felt more settled in her body than she had in a long time. Even under her attention, her cravings felt more like an annoyance than an all-consuming need.

As Ember entered the house, going up to the guest bathing room and starting the bath, she wondered if this was what those soldiers had been talking about. Not an actual high like she was used to. But the focus in her mind that she didn't have to consciously force. The motivation to get to work that she didn't have to build her way up to.

Ember stepped into the tub, sighing as the hot water warmed her wind-chilled skin. It was unfortunate that it came at the price of running—not to mention she didn't know how long the high would last. But scrubbing the sweat from her hair and skin, her mind went back to Sofika recommending a routine.

She'd never been good at those. But if she continued running with Branten, she would have someone to hold her accountable. And if that could disrupt her spiral?

Ember tipped her head back into the water, giving herself a few more minutes to enjoy the calm. Then, she climbed out of the tub, inhaling the citrus steam from her soap as her eyes lifted to the mirror.

She hadn't stopped to really look at herself since before Sun's invasion. Now, all she could see was how stark her healer marks looked against the shadows under her eyes, how dull her skin had become, how all of her soft curves had noticeably shrunk.

She didn't look like herself. She didn't feel like herself. But, wrapping herself in a towel and heading back to her room, she finally had the smallest glimmer of hope that she could find her way back.

Ember pulled on a soft pink shirt and pants, then grabbed the black book off her bedside table and headed downstairs. She flopped on the couch, faintly registering voices behind the closed dining room door as she flipped through Deardryn's notes.

She might have been a conniving queen, but Ember would have killed to have her penmanship. Even the notes she scribbled in the margins were elegant. Although, the more she skimmed, the more Deardryn's questions had her insides squirming.

Why must healer apprentices uphold celibacy, wine limitations, and all other stipulations of the healer vow when they haven't been magically bound yet? Why make a healer's successes and failures permanently tattooed across their faces for all to see? How did we come to believe our traditions were Rosala's wishes? Are they Rosala's wishes?

Based on the Starlight healers, they weren't. So then, why had such a rigid system been created? Why had Ember been trained to fear stepping out of those lines? And why did indulging those questions have Ember's heart squeezing?

Ember ran her fingers through her damp hair, flipping to the beginning of Deardryn's notes to start reading in earnest. And the dining room door opened.

"There you are," Aaron said, shutting the door behind him.

"Isn't Anna with you?"

"She is. I asked Laness to come distract her so I could show you this." He came closer, practically giddy as he tapped the small lump in his jacket pocket.

Ember's eyes widened. She sat up straight, tossing her book aside, "It's ready?"

"This part is. I snuck out this morning to grab it while Analia was still asleep."

Ember made a silent squeal, turmoil momentarily forgotten. "Let me see."

Aaron grinned, reaching into his pocket.

The door opened.

Aaron yanked his hand away, Analia already talking as she entered.

"Laness says I need to convince you to expand her garden radius in the front yard because there are now two plant lovers in the house—Oh, hi."

Analia gave Ember a little wave as she spotted her, Ember returning the gesture.

"How was your run with Branten?" she asked, coming to perch on the arm of Ember's couch.

"I sent him to do extra laps to pay for what he's done."

Analia laughed, Aaron's eyes sparkling as he looked down at her.

"I was just telling Ember she'll have the house to herself this afternoon," he said.

"Yes, but you haven't told me why," Ember said, catching his drift.

"Aaron has decided to call a council meeting today," Analia explained, leaning back on her hands. "Seems like it's time to fill them in on everything going on."

Aaron made a face that Ember wasn't sure was feigned or not. Analia, clearly assuming the latter, reached for his hand.

"Come on," she said, pulling herself to her feet. "The faster we get ready, the faster you can get it over with."

"I thought you were the one who said that makes it worse," Aaron complained, letting her tow him toward the stairs. Analia chided him, then called a farewell to Ember over her shoulder.

Just before they reached the top of the stairs, Aaron looked back and caught her eye. Ember gave him two thumbs up.

It was about time something good happened. Especially since she still had one charm left on her enka bracelet that she had no idea how Analia would receive. But that was an issue for another time.

Ember retrieved her book, only making it a few pages before the back door slid open.

"How many laps did you do?" she asked, marking her page.

"Twenty, plus some training in the hollow," Branten said, his face flushed, eyes bright. "Why?"

"I just wanted to know how many laps I need to do to meet you."

"You mean beat me."

That hope in Ember's chest glimmered a little brighter.

"That's tomorrow's business," she said, tucking her book under her arm and rising from the couch. "Right now, you owe me breakfast."

Branten sighed dramatically, Ember shooing him toward the stairs.

Yes, this might be a routine she could stick to.

Chapter 64

Analia stood in her bathing room, sliding the final pins into her hair.

"Marion won't be a problem," Aaron said from their room. "Jeneva is the only one who consistently sees things from my perspective, so that's good. But that still leaves Samuel, Jasper, and *Iphen* to deal with."

"Iphen will behave," Analia promised, not missing Aaron's disdain as she smoothed down her hair, the front pieces braided around her head like a crown.

Aaron huffed. Analia rolled her eyes, although after how she'd reacted to Vivienne in the Star Royal vault, she had no room to judge. She was honestly surprised this meeting was happening in the first place, Aaron only mentioning it to her once he'd gotten confirmation the night before.

"I hope you know you're doing the right thing," she said, stepping back into their room.

Aaron sat at the foot of their bed tying his boots. He looked up, about to respond. Then, his eyes widened.

He turned to face her fully, taking in the floor-length skirts of her midnight-blue gown, moving up to the sleeves that flared below her elbows, pausing to admire the curve of her collarbones before finally reaching her eyes.

"If you're trying to distract me with your beauty," he said, his voice shifting into something smoky, "you're doing an excellent job."

Analia's face warmed. "You can flip from brooding to flirting impressively fast," she said, coming to join him.

"It's not hard when you look lovely in blue."

He drew her down beside him, his mouth warm and luxurious against hers. She closed her eyes, more than happy to enable this kind of distraction. But it wouldn't help their case if they were late.

"Does this mean I can persuade you to tie my dress?" she murmured against his mouth.

"Only if I can untie it later."

Analia shoved his chest. "You're incorrigible."

"And yet, you keep me around."

Aaron stole a final kiss. Then, he twirled his finger, Analia letting out a huff as she turned her back to him. But there was no irritation in the sound. And there was something softer in her chest as he brushed her hair aside, careful not to mess it up as he tied her gown shut.

"You know," he said, his fingers grazing the back of her neck, "if you're in the mood to indulge me a little longer, I have something for you."

Something in his tone had Analia glance over her shoulder. He shifted on the bed, somewhere between eager and nervous, even as he lightly bit the inside of his cheek.

"Is it something *good?*" she asked.

"*I* think it is." His eyes flicked up to hers, their sparkle settling the slight twist in Analia's stomach.

"All right."

Aaron offered his Phoenix Gate smile. Patting her hair back into place, he rose from the bed.

"As we've already discussed," he said, heading for his desk, "I had a hard time with you being gone for so long. Eventually, I realized having a distraction helped. But what really helped was making plans for when you returned."

Analia cocked her head as he reached into the pocket of the jacket he'd been wearing that morning, now draped across his chair.

"Granted, I really only had one plan I was working on. But the thought of giving this to you was the only thing that kept me sane while waiting to hear news of your escape."

Gods, her heart would never get used to hearing that. The way he'd tormented himself, blamed himself, all while fearing for her safety. But when Aaron turned back to her, a small smile played across his lips.

"I'm glad you found a distraction," she said, her voice small.

Aaron's smile grew. "Well," he said, returning to sit beside her, "you can make it even better by opening it."

He offered his hand. And Analia's own hand drifted to her mouth.

A small, black velvet box rested in Aaron's palm. The same box he'd shown her the morning they went to the Human Kingdom. The same box that held her gray moonstone ring. But he said he'd been working on something.

Analia's eyes bounced between Aaron, watching her closely, and the box, struggling to name the feeling settling in her stomach. "What did you do?" she breathed.

"This." Clearly losing patience, Aaron flipped open the box. And all Analia could do was stare at the sparkling ring inside.

The same oval gray moonstone sat in the center, its face reflecting a milky blue sheen in the morning light. But now, a ring of tiny diamonds sparkled around its edges, continuing partway down the band, which was now black and dainty.

Analia rested her fingers against the box's soft velvet edge, the first thought in her mind popping out of her mouth. "That's my moonstone."

"It is." Aaron plucked the ring from the box, turning it between his fingers so she could see all sides. "I told you the ring I gave you felt tainted, but Ember said you wouldn't want to abandon it completely. So, we thought this would be a good compromise. I still have the original band if you prefer it," he added, stealing a quick look at her. "We can make any changes you want, what's most important is you love it. That's why I brought Ember along. I figured she's known you all your life, she was bound to have good insights on what you'd prefer—and she certainly had opinions, thank the gods, because I—"

"Aaron," Analia said quietly. "You're rambling."

Aaron breathed a laugh. "I know," he said, returning the ring to the box so he could run a hand through his hair. "You're not giving me much of a reaction to go off of."

Analia winced, knowing he was right. And that only made her stomach sink further.

"You don't need to be nervous," she told him, tracing the moonstone with a finger. "The ring is perfect. And we already established back in Surce's studio that I choose you."

"I know. But I didn't get the chance to wax on about how I catch my breath when you walk in a room, and how my heart is yours in this lifetime and the next, and that I'll destroy anyone that tries to harm you."

Analia let out a small, startled laugh.

"There it is," Aaron said, his voice softening.

"What?"

"The smile I fell in love with." Aaron rested his fingertips against the corners of her mouth, gently nudging them higher. "What's making me have to cajole this out of you?"

Analia swallowed hard, her words clogging her throat. She rested her hand over the one he now curved around her face, her eyes inexorably dropping to the ring.

She hadn't been lying when she said it was perfect. She'd loved the moonstone from the moment she saw it, and the fact that he'd gone through so much effort to ensure she would like her ring meant more to her than she could say. Gods, she'd told Deardryn they were betrothed, even though they hadn't explicitly agreed to anything. They didn't have to.

Except looking at the ring made not for their scheme, but her?

"Hey."

Analia startled at the snap of the box closing, Aaron tossing it behind him on the bed and out of her sight.

"Eyes on me," he murmured, turning her face to his. "What are you thinking?"

"Probably too much," she mumbled.

Aaron's lips quirked. "Care to share?"

Not really. But Aaron deserved an explanation.

"I love the ring," she said, fingers fidgeting in her lap. "I want the ring. But I don't think I'm ready for what it entails."

She braced herself for his flash of hurt, even disappointment.

But Aaron nodded slowly. "Are we talking in general, or something specific?"

Crystal Bless that man, he was completely calm. Not even a flicker of his network to betray him. And maybe it was her month of questioning motives, her lifetime of fragile tempers, but Analia was dizzy under her wave of relief.

She leaned her cheek into his hand, her response still halting, but no longer sticking in her throat. "Deardryn told me I've been well-trained to be queen, and I don't think that's entirely wrong. But growing up watching my uncle, I only saw the nobility in ruling. It was taxing, but being king let him put so much good out in the world. Watching you rule reminds me of that in a lot of ways."

The comment had been half to herself, but Aaron's lips still parted, something like amazement passing over his features. He ran his thumb along her cheekbone, making no move to interrupt her as she went on.

"When viewing being queen through that lens, I felt like it was something I could handle. But I spent the last month entangled with a queen who sought out power to create peace, just to be corrupted by it, and a king who devastated his people to use his husband's death to his advantage, and I... I don't want to turn into that.

"And yet, when my uncle resisted the game, he was killed by the closest person to him. I watch you walk that line, and while you've held on to your humanity, Marion's right. You *do* take on burdens you don't deserve. And now, when I look at that ring, I don't *just* see a life with you. I see a kingdom I love, and a crown I've been trained to wear by so many contradictory lessons that I'm still sifting through. And I just want to make sure I have my footing before we do anything."

As soon as the words were out, the knot in Analia's chest unraveled, leaving a dull, heavy ache in its place.

Analia sighed, her gaze finally lifting to meet Aaron's thoughtful one. "Any comments?" she asked weakly.

Aaron considered, his fingers trailing down her neck to toy with her phoenix pin. "I think the fact that you're thinking about this means you're more ready than most."

Well, that was a little comforting. But she still had no answers.

"I want to show you something," Aaron said after a moment.

Analia's attention flashed back to him, "We can't be late for the meeting."

"We'll be perfectly on time," he promised. He nudged her to her feet, Analia starting to protest as he rose and slid his arm around her waist. But Aaron whispered, "Fair warning." Then, he pulled them into the shadows.

Within moments, the darkness peeled back, Analia ready to let her protests loose anyway. Then, she looked around.

They'd reappeared in the council room she'd visited a few months prior. The councilmen's chairs sat empty around the thick wooden table, its surface painted black, the central carving of the Crystal made up of stars highlighted in silver.

"I thought you said you wanted to show me something," she said.

"I do." Aaron led her over to the side wall, the thick maroon carpet muffling their footsteps. He reached over the counter to tap the wood panel wall, Analia only just noticing the rows of thin, finger-length scratches.

"Who did this?" she asked.

"Jasper." Aaron tapped his finger along the markings, his mouth twisting in a grimace. "After my mom died, Ethelind gave me a year off of being prince so I could grieve. No responsibilities, no expectations. And as she later realized, nothing stopping my spiral from getting out of hand. So, once my time was up, she demanded I started attending council meetings with her. And Jasper, the prick, started a tally a few months in."

"Of what?" Analia asked.

"Any time I acted unprincely in a meeting. I think he was aiming for something more specific, but I gave him too many categories. Coming to meetings late, hungover, smelling of a woman's perfume, meetings where I refused to acknowledge anyone—I was quite the petulant brat if you couldn't tell."

Analia shook her head, hardly able to believe it. "Aaron," she said, running her nail along a scratch, "there are so many."

"I know. Once Jasper realized it pissed me off, he really committed to it. And at some point, I decided I wanted to see what would happen first: Jasper giving up, or me filling the entire wall."

Aaron rolled his eyes, sliding some book stacks on the counter aside to reveal even more scratches. Gods, there had to be hundreds.

"I knew you were difficult when dealing with the council," Analia said, trailing her fingers along the scratches as she moved farther down the counter. "But I can't picture you earning all of these."

"That's because you know me fifteen years into being king. Before that?" Aaron winced. "Thankfully, I mostly got my act together, and Jasper stopped making his scratches about forty years ago."

"So why not cover them up."

"Because they're my reminder." Aaron smoothed a hand down her hair, offering a soft, adoring smile. "I don't think becoming a ruler is something anyone is ever ready for. Even the most prepared person will have to learn as they go, and in that regard, you're more than qualified."

Analia let her hand fall from the wall, finally starting to see his angle. "Is there such thing as being overly qualified?" she asked.

"Maybe. But I don't think that's you. Yes, you had a handful of rulers teaching you different things, but you've also had the benefit of seeing how each lesson played out. You have a house full of people looking out for you, and ready to call you out and help you back up when you inevitably fail. And you have me."

Aaron winked, and Analia's lips quirked.

"That being said, he continued, softening once more, "we have no timeline. You could be crowned queen tomorrow or in fifty years for all I care. You could wear my ring for a hundred years before making anything official if that's what you want. All *I want* is you."

He rested his hand over her heart, Analia's eyes stinging.

"Even if that means I can't agree to marry you yet?" she asked.

"My shooting star, I fear we're on vastly different pages if you think a ring and some vows can encompass all we are."

Analia had the strangest urge to laugh. Or maybe cry.

"Tell you what," he said. "You tell me when you're ready, and I'll ask again. All right?"

Analia nodded, not trusting herself to speak.

"Good." Aaron brought her left hand to his lips, kissing the empty space at the base of her middle finger. And Analia didn't realize how much weight had been pressing on her shoulders until that tiny gesture lifted it away.

She slid her arms around his neck, letting metal and spice brush away the last of her emotional debris. "I love you," she said, staring into his eyes, needing him to know how much she meant it.

Aaron looked as though she'd said everything he needed to hear. "I love you, too."

He kissed her temple, nestling her against him. Analia closed her eyes, his heartbeat steady beneath her ear. Once again giving her something to hold on to.

"Thank you," she murmured.

"Of course." Aaron paused. "Do you feel up to this meeting? Because I could cancel it if not."

"Nice try."

Aaron heaved a sigh, and Analia laughed. Pulling away, she led him over to their seats, feeling like the ground had become a little more stable beneath her feet.

Someday soon, that ring would be on her finger. But for now, they had a far more pressing issue at hand.

Would Aaron be able to control himself once their meeting began?

Chapter 65

All things considered, Aaron thought he was handling the councilmen incredibly well.

He made no snide remarks when Jasper and Samuel arrived, both shocked to find him early to their meeting. He kept his glare to himself as Iphen entered with Marion and Jeneva, immediately greeting Analia—although based on Marion's warning look, he didn't conceal his smugness as Analia smoothly offered Jeneva the seat beside her.

But he couldn't poke any tempers today. The council was bound to be miffed when they found out he'd not only been sitting on crucial information, but he'd asked Marion for help before informing the rest of them.

He needed to win them over. Because as much as he hated to admit it, strong wards and constant border patrols would only do so much if things went south and the council wasn't on his side.

"Now that we're all here," Marion said, settling in the open seat on Aaron's left, "shall we begin?"

Aaron brushed the thoughts aside. He sat up straight as all eyes flicked to him, a quip pressing against his lips. But he let it sink back down, focusing on the soft pressure of Analia's hand on his knee.

"We shall." Aaron let his gaze move from face to face, carefully keeping his tone level. "The last time Analia was in this room, we discussed how Queen Deardryn Oshar is hunting the Crystal and the threat she's already posed to the other five kingdoms. Thanks to your generosity in letting us into the vault, we've been able to locate the remaining scroll and open all three, which is partially why I've gathered us today. But first, Analia has news after spending a month with Deardryn."

"*That's* where you were?" Jeneva exclaimed, the other councilmen bristling as she turned to Analia.

Analia's eyebrows shot up. "Where did you tell them I was?" she asked Aaron.

"Taking care of business," he said innocently.

Analia shook her head, not even surprised. Turning back to Jeneva, she said, "I think he forgot the only person we had to worry about charging into the Moon Kingdom and destroying our cover was himself."

Jeneva snorted. Aaron made a vaguely offended noise, Jeneva's amusement slowly moving around the table, even Jasper's lips twitching.

Gods, Analia was good at this. She didn't need a crown to accurately read a room, finding the perfect response to have tempers subsiding once more. Even he felt more at ease as the initial tension slackened.

"Now that we've cleared up my location," Analia said, amused, "I can show you what I brought back with me."

She pulled the Crystal's casing from a pocket in her gown, setting it on the table before her. Marion's and Samuel's expressions tightened, undoubtedly sensing the same whisper of power that had Aaron's insides shifting. And everyone recoiled with an exclamation as Analia opened the casing.

Bright white light erupted forth, refracting rainbows across the room. Aaron gripped the edge of the table, every instinct screaming for him to flee. But he remained where he was, focusing on the creak of chairs as everyone leaned away.

Because this release was minuscule compared to the one back in Accalon's chambers. And it was nothing compared to the ice in his veins at the thought of how many times Analia had had to endure it.

Sooner than he expected, the light started to fade. It dwindled down, lingering in a final glimmer across the Crystal's face before finally winking out.

Aaron released a tiny breath. He looked around the table, expressions ranging from discomfort to dismay. Only Analia remained unfazed.

"What in the name of the five gods was that?" Samuel spat, wiping the sweat from his wrinkled brow.

"That," Analia said, pulling the shard free from its casing, "was the Crystal."

The table exchanged shocked looks.

"Wait a moment," Iphen said, squinting at the shard in Analia's hand, "that doesn't look like the Crystal. That looks like a piece."

"Because it is." Analia passed the shard to Jeneva, Jeneva's azure eyes wide. "At some point in history, the Crystal was separated into three pieces. And this is the shard that Deardryn found. But that's at the end of the story."

With that, Analia settled back in her seat and began. The Crystal slowly made its way around the table, Analia starting with Deardryn's invasion of Ash. But as Aaron watched her, he didn't hear her words.

He saw the way she subtly emphasized her story with her hands. The way she looked at each person around the table to engage them. The way she didn't try to conceal the emotions across her face as she spoke.

Gods, how had the Ash Kingdom not wanted her? Aaron had only spent half a day in Accalon's presence, and even he could see she was the spitting image of the king they adored. She was more than that.

Aaron touched the enka bracelet on his wrist under the table. *At the council meeting. Can you tell Anna when she's done speaking that she's a goddess and should trust her uncle's storytelling lessons forever?*

Laness's response tingled across his wrist a moment later. *Of course. You'll do great, too.*

Aaron blinked, not expecting the reassurance. Just as he hadn't noticed the knot coiling in his stomach that Laness had obviously sensed down their line.

"It's possible Deardryn found her second shard," Analia said, turning the casing between her fingers. "But even if she has, there's one already out of her grasp. And I stole back her only access to Star magic, which should help. But that leaves the question of what her next move will be."

Shrugging, she settled back in her chair. And Aaron loved the silence as the council took in everything she'd said.

"That's... a lot," Iphen finally said.

"And much good intel as a result," Marion mused, turning the crystal shard between her rich brown fingers. "Especially if Ember is able to find anything in Deardryn's notes."

"It also means," Jasper said, rubbing the scar that curved down from his temple to his jaw, "the potential target Her Highness first brought to this kingdom has become a definite."

"And Deardryn has already gotten close to discovering our location with her patrols," Samuel added.

"Would you rather we leave the shard with her?" Jeneva retorted, tossing her auburn braid over her shoulder.

Samuel fired back a retort, Aaron not paying attention as Analia's fingers found his under the table. He looked at her, her smile telling him Laness had delivered his message. And he didn't need to hear her thoughts to know her own message as she squeezed his hand.

"I think," he said, not giving himself time to second-guess, "we should have the context from the scroll before deciding anything."

Jasper's mouth snapped shut. He and the other council members twisted toward him, Aaron's walls rising up in response.

But he couldn't shut them out. Analia had proven how effective letting them in could be. And Marion was right: he couldn't keep carrying this burden alone, no matter how desperate he was to do so.

So, Aaron took a deep breath. Then, he began.

He started with retrieving the scroll from the humans, his voice tight. But the further he got, the easier the words came, Aaron eventually not having to constantly monitor his expression.

As expected, the council swapped irritated looks when they discovered he'd been working with Marion, but Marion brushed their grumbled comments off with a wave of her hand. And Aaron never would have suspected how freeing it would feel to have a council member on his side.

"Unfortunately," he said, accepting the shard Marion passed him, "we still don't have a full picture of what's going on. But we have more information than Deardryn. And Marion, Surce, and I are all translating as fast as we can."

He ran his thumb along the crystal's smooth face, his eyes scanning around the table. Iphen propped his chin in his hand, exchanging a considering look with Jeneva across from him. Jasper sat with his arms folded, Aaron knowing it was only a matter of time before the thoughts that had his nose wrinkling burst free. But Samuel was the first to break the quiet.

"Why are you telling us this?" he asked, his gray-green eyes narrowed. "You've made it abundantly clear you detest us—or perhaps I should say our propensity to question your decisions. So, why come to us voluntarily?"

Aaron took a moment to consider his words. "I'm telling you," he finally said, "because keeping this kingdom safe has been my top priority from the moment I received my crown. And you're right, I don't enjoy these meetings. I don't enjoy having to fight to do what I think is best for the kingdom. Especially since I don't have a good history with half of you—and I know that's in part my fault.

"But I also know there's only so much I can do on my own." Aaron paused, his throat squeezing at the confession. "This kingdom is in immediate danger, and the last thing I want is for that danger to come to fruition. But if it does, I'm going to need your help. So, I tell you this so you all can understand our situation. And I'm saying I'll let my hostility drop if you do, too."

Aaron shot Samuel and Jasper a pointed look. Samuel frowned, but Jasper met Aaron's gaze.

"Are you asking us to forget the four strangers you brought to our home, which catalyzed this danger?" he asked, surprisingly calm.

Frost whispered through Aaron's veins. But he kept his voice level as he said, "I'm asking you to remember Deardryn hunting the Crystal would threaten us regardless of if I brought any outsiders here. And now, two of those people are in Ash working as spies for us, one is analyzing Deardryn's notes, and the fourth not only retrieved the one shard we do have, but is your future queen."

Aaron stole a quick look at Analia, not sure how she would react to that last comment. But she kept her assessing gaze on Jasper.

Jasper pressed his lips into a line, his brown eyes shifting to Marion. "Were you planning on telling us that you were working with His Majesty?"

"For the three days before this meeting?" she asked, arching a thin brow. "No. His Majesty assembled a meeting so he could tell you himself."

Jasper's chair creaked as he sat back, annoyed. Aaron's hands flexed around the edge of his seat, braced for the next rebuke.

"I'll work with you," Jeneva piped up.

Aaron blinked. She stretched her hand toward him across the table, the silver star-shaped buttons on her black council jacket flashing in the light.

"I don't want to go into whatever's waiting for us divided," she said. "So, I'll work with you—as long as I can still disagree with you."

"You can," Aaron said, his throat tight. He took her hand, her fingers warm as they shook.

"I'll continue working with you as well," Marion said, taking his newly freed hand.

"As will I," said Iphen.

Some of Aaron's wonder curdled at that, but he shook Iphen's hand anyway. Which left Samuel and Jasper.

The two had a quick, silent conversation. Then, Jasper turned to Marion.

"You trust his word?" he asked.

Aaron made a face, but Marion replied without hesitation. "I do."

"Then we agree."

Jasper offered his hand to Aaron, followed by Samuel, the firmness in their grips letting Aaron know they were yet to be convinced. But with that, the council had officially been won over. And Aaron was left to sit with the fact that it had been far easier than he'd anticipated.

Because Marion was right: they *had* been looking for an opportunity to work with him, not against him. And he'd been the one denying them.

Aaron's gaze drifted to the wall of scratches as they wrapped up the meeting, Marion reminding everyone of their meeting the following afternoon. Then, it was over.

Samuel and Jasper were first out the door, neither sparing a backward glance.

"I'd love to hear more about the research you did with the Crystal," Jeneva said to Analia, hooking her arm over the back of her chair. "I've always been interested in magical objects, so I might be of use figuring out how to track down the rest."

"That would be incredibly helpful," Analia replied.

"I would love to join you two," Iphen chimed in.

Aaron's eye twitched. But Analia offered Iphen a smile.

"Of course." She turned to Aaron, "See you at home?"

Aaron nodded, struggling not to glare at Iphen as he rounded the table. But his attention was quickly caught as Analia leaned toward him, turning his face to hers with a hand on his cheek. And Aaron couldn't have stopped his wicked satisfaction at her slow, lingering kiss if he tried.

"You were incredible," she whispered.

"Just following in your footsteps." He fixed a pin that had started to come loose in her hair, reveling in the eyes he could feel on them. "If he bothers you," he went on, low enough only she could hear, "feel free to scorch him. We can find a new council member."

"I'd offer you the honors, but that would suggest you have competition."

She kissed his jaw, and Aaron didn't know how he let her pull away. She dipped her chin to Marion still seated beside him. Then, returning the Crystal to her pocket, she rose, she and Jeneva already deep in discussion as they exited. Iphen trailed behind them, visibly deflated.

Once the door clicked shut behind them, Aaron turned to Marion. "I love that woman," he informed her.

Marion's eyes twinkled. "I see why."

Gods, he would never stop loving that sentiment.

"While we're both here," she went on, rising from her chair, "I thought I could share with you my latest translation."

Aaron perked up as she crossed to the corner wooden cabinet, pulling out a thick burgundy folder. "Did you figure out the rest of Dimitri's poem?"

"I did." Marion returned to her seat, pages rustling as she searched for the right one. "It took me a while to figure out the last line, but—ah, yes here it is." Pulling free a page, she settled back in her seat and cleared her throat.

> When three by three by three align,
> The sleeping shadows will untwine,

Their midnight stars may search for dreams,
But keys are only born in threes.
The crown that's Blessed with mortal veins,
Can break the cracks,
Can mend the whole,
And bars may snap,
Then shackles hold.
With blood that's cursed with ancient rage,
These sketched-out tombs may be refined,
If three by three by three align.

"Huh." Aaron rubbed his face, turning over the words. "I have no idea what that means."

Marion laughed. "Hopefully, once we uncover the surrounding context, things will become clearer. I was thinking, though. Your friend said that the first four lines were written on the location of where the Crystal shard was hidden, correct?"

"Yes," Aaron said slowly. "And Dimitri couldn't find it documented anywhere."

"Perhaps because Talitha didn't want it to be common knowledge."

Aaron sat up straight. "Can I see your translation?"

Marion nodded, clearly a few steps ahead of him as she offered the page. While Aaron didn't know much about poetry, he could recognize patterns. And skimming through...

"This poem is written in three sections," he said.

"And there are three Crystal shards," Marion agreed.

Aaron's mind raced. "Can I make a copy of this to see if Ember recognizes anything?"

"I've got one right here." Marion passed him a second piece of paper, Aaron folding it up and sticking it in his jacket pocket.

He had no idea if their theory would lead anywhere—especially if Talitha was covering her trail. But if they were on to something?

Aaron exchanged a few more thoughts with Marion, eventually rising to his feet to go. Just before he faded into the shadows, Marion called his name. He paused, his head cocked.

"You proved yourself an excellent king today," she said.

Aaron blinked hard. He nodded his thanks, fading into the darkness once more.

He just hoped his precautionary measures wouldn't need to come into play.

Chapter 66

Ember stepped through the Healer Center's front doors, rubbing the cuff of her robes' sleeve between her fingers.

She hadn't been this nervous to go to work since her first day as an apprentice fourteen years ago, but she was ready for this. She'd gone on another mildly torturous run with Branten that morning; she'd had breakfast with everyone else; she had Deardryn's notes in her pocket as backup if she ever hit a lull. She was as prepared as she could be.

"You're right on time."

Ember looked up as Sofika pushed through the door across the colorful welcome area, Cenn close behind. The two wore their emerald robes, Sofika's black hair twisted in its usual knot at the top of her head.

"My old master healer would say punctuality was the only acceptable timing," Ember replied, coming forward to meet them.

"One less thing I have to teach you." Sofika smiled, her small, hazel eyes taking Ember in as she paused before her. "Are you ready?"

Ember wished such a casual question didn't have so many undertones. But she nodded. And clearly seeing something she liked in her expression, Sofika hummed in approval.

"In that case," she said, "we have patients to see."

With that, she turned on her heel and headed back through the door through which she'd arrived. Ember started, then hurried after her, Cenn falling into step beside her.

"You've been freed from the plant prison," he whispered, miming a cheer.

Ember snorted and shoved his shoulder. She had to admit, though, stepping into the sky-blue halls, a handful of healers bustling about, did feel like a kind of freedom. Dauntingly so.

"I presume you've been here long enough to realize we have a system," Sofika said, drawing Ember from her thoughts as she strode down the hall. "You'll be pleased to know it's not far off from the Ash Kingdom school. Yet, instead of organizing patients by healer specialty, we go by patient severity. Cenn?"

"Blue wing is minor," Cenn said promptly. "These are the patients we can heal in one session, like cuts and common colds. The lavender wing is for the moderate patients who need multiple treatments, but we're confident in their recovery. And the emerald wing—"

"Is the extreme cases," Ember guessed. "Those who require constant treatment and monitoring."

"Precisely." Sofika waved to a few young healers as they rounded the corner ahead of her, Ember surprised to note she recognized all three girls. "In the blue wing, apprentices at your and Cenn's level are permitted to tend to patients by yourself. But for today, I'll be monitoring your work to assess your skills."

"Makes sense," Ember replied.

"I'm glad," Sofika said, something a bit too knowing in her eyes as she glanced over her shoulder. "Because your first patient is waiting."

Without further comment, Sofika knocked on the closest door, then pushed inside.

Gods, Sofika really had her diving in headfirst. No time to prepare, collect herself, the soft promise of her devinroot brushing along her sudden rush of nerves.

Cenn elbowed her in the ribs. Ember's eyes darted up, but he only gave her an easy, encouraging smile.

She could do this. It was no different from any other shift in Ash.

Ember took a steadying breath. Then, focusing on the familiar sharp, leafy smell of antiseptic paste, she pushed back her shoulders and followed Sofika inside. And she immediately brightened.

Evena stood at the window overlooking the hillside. She wore a casual, plum-purple dress that complimented her dark brown skin, her fingers lightly drumming on the sill. At Sofika's greeting, she turned, offering a hello. And recognition flashed in her jade eyes as she spotted Ember.

"I know you," she said. "You're His Majesty's friend."

"I am," Ember said, pleasantly surprised Evena also remembered their brief interaction in the hall. "I know the room is full, but I'll be the one examining you today if that's all right."

"Of course." Evena plopped down on the patient bed and beckoned her over, Cenn stifling a laugh as he and Sofika stationed themselves at the back wall. Ember's lips twitched, her nerves settling more and more.

"What's brought you in today?" she asked, taking the seat beside the bed.

"It's nothing," Evena said dismissively. "It was my turn to make breakfast, and you can imagine feeding twenty children means a lot of pans.

"And even more opportunities to burn yourself," Ember agreed. "May I see?"

Evena proffered her hand. Ember angled it toward the light, nodding to herself as she took in the thick red burn running down the edge of Evena's thumb.

"That pan got you good," Ember mused. "I hope one of the children you were cooking for wasn't Branten; Aaron already fed him this morning."

The words popped out of her mouth before she could stop them. Her eyes darted to Evena's face in horror, every part of her recoiling as her master healers' voices flashed through her mind. Telling her healers needed to be professional, give their patients confidence in their skills.

But before Ember could apologize, Evena snorted. "He *wishes* I would feed him. That man would live off of stale bread and water if not for his family's pity."

"He's a warrior," Sofika said dryly. "He's learned to live off of worse."

"That's the problem!"

Evena's head fell back dramatically, and Ember found herself joining in as Cenn laughed. Gods, the Starlight healers really did operate differently. But as she twisted in her seat, asking Cenn to pass her the jar of burn salve off the corner cart, she was surprised to note this difference had her shoulders relaxing.

"The good news," she said, still smiling as she turned back to Evena, "is your burn hasn't blistered, which means this is an even quicker fix than I expected."

She accepted the jar from Cenn, Evena releasing a sigh of relief. Unscrewing the lid, Ember poured some of the thick, dark green paste onto her fingers, placing the jar on the chair beside her and offering her hand to Evena. "May I?"

Evena nodded, and Ember smoothed the salve along her thumb.

"This will itch for a few moments," she said, "but it will be over in a few seconds."

With that, Ember took a moment to steady herself. Then, she summoned her magic. She didn't need much, just enough to stimulate the salve to repair the top layer of Evena's skin.

Simple. Easy, even.

And as Evena's hand relaxed in hers, something inside her stabilized. For when she wiped the remaining paste away, Evena's skin was perfectly healed.

Ember looked back at Sofika. And a single nod had never felt so good.

For the rest of the morning, Ember made her way through the patients in the blue wing. She and Cenn took turns leading or assisting on each case, every door they walked out of leaving Ember feeling a little more settled into her routine.

Yes, this center was different from the school she knew. But the injuries and illnesses she healed were the same. The skills she used were the same. This was her.

By the time they reached Ember's lunch break, she was pleasantly tired. Politely declining Sofika's and Cenn's invitations to join them, she took her food to the greenhouse, wanting a little quiet.

Now, she sat on a wooden bench amongst the fragrant lavender plants on the second floor, an apple in one hand and Deardryn's notes in the other.

Even though Analia said it wasn't all of Deardryn's research, there was still a good amount to get through. Thus far, all she could tell was Deardryn had a fascination with the origin of their traditions, from their vows to their markings. She supposed it was related to the Crystal because the Crystal Blessed each healer with healer magic, but that felt like too flimsy of a connection.

What was interesting, though, was most would agree the healers' current manifestation came about after the healer-Royal separation. But she never knew that their markings were one of Helia's stipulations in that separation. And the more she read, the more it seemed like the Royals were the ones who wanted the divide. But why?

Ember turned her apple between her fingers, lost in thought. Eventually, the door softly slid open below, Ember peering over the nearby railing as Cenn called her name.

"Up here," she said.

Cenn craned his neck, taking a moment to find her among the lavender plants. "There you are." He ascended the stairs, weaving around rows of plants to join her. "I hope that apple isn't your lunch."

"It's what remains," Ember said, pocketing her book. "What's going on?"

"Sofika says we're on plant duty for the rest of the afternoon. Apparently, the nymphs aren't able to make it today, which means it's up to us to check on everything."

Ember winced, looking around the massive greenhouse. "Any chance the plants will be nice and *not* require a lot of magical managing?" she asked.

"We can only hope," Cenn said gravely.

Ember snorted. Rising from the bench, she stepped over to the railing and tossed her apple into the large composting bin below with a thud.

"Good aim," Cenn said from the bench.

"Why, thank you." Ember flashed a grin, slightly taken aback by the ghost of her old bravado. In a good way.

Smile softening, she turned to the closest plant.

For a few minutes, she and Cenn made idle small talk as they examined the lavender plants. Thankfully, they didn't require any assistance, allowing them to quickly move on to the next block of plants. Yet, as Ember examined her violets, her gaze kept wandering back to Cenn at the end of the row.

Where most people would have skimmed through, knowing there were countless more to go, he took his time. Nothing to prove as he carefully assessed each plant.

She'd known for two days that he was an addict, and she still couldn't wrap her mind around it. He was just so... stable. Comfortable in who he was. Meanwhile, Ember had needed to double check with Sofika that the devinroots had been removed from the greenhouse before she'd felt safe to enter. Even now, she caught her thoughts wandering to the empty racks, painfully aware of how cutting off her use as abruptly as she had felt like trying to stop halfway through slipping on a sheet of ice.

"Ember," Cenn said, catching her eye with a smile. "You're staring at me."

Ember blinked, then stifled a curse. She'd gotten distracted again. Ember quickly apologized, Cenn's dark eyes twinkling as he waved a hand.

He turned back to his work, Ember about to do the same. But she hesitated.

Cenn was only a few years older than her, meaning he couldn't have decades of sobriety under his belt like Sofika. And if he had managed to attain such stability already, maybe he could help her.

Sofika would love that idea. But it would also require Ember revealing what she was.

Rosala spare her, why did all of Sofika's tools have to be all the things she didn't want to do? She chewed on her thumbnail, tempted to brush the possibility aside. But Sofika had been right about having a routine. And since the idea of being "curious" had her making a face, that only left talking.

Ember steeled herself. But her voice still came out a little tight. "Hey, Cenn?"

Cenn looked up, almost at the end of his row. "Yes?"

Ember swallowed, her mouth dry. "Do you remember the observation you made about me to Sofika? The one you didn't know if you were right about or not?"

"I do," he said slowly, turning to face her fully.

Ember squirmed, her fingers flexing around her plant pot. How was it just as hard to say it this time as it was the first? She looked away from Cenn, her words stumbling out on an exhale.

"Well, you were right. I used devinroot—I'm addicted to devinroot." The word felt awkward in her mouth. But as soon as it was out, the rest came rushing free. "And Sofika said I should talk to you, and you don't have to tell me anything you don't want to, but I—"

"Ember," Cenn said.

Ember deflated. "Yes?"

"What do you want to know?"

Ember dropped her head into her hand, her face not knowing which expression to fall into. Because she'd told another person. And he didn't look at her any differently. If anything, he seemed amused—and she'd take that any day.

She looked up at him, Cenn's full mouth twitching as he fought back his smile. "I guess..." She pulled at the neck of her robes, not knowing where to begin. "I guess I'm just wondering how did you get to this point? How are you so steady and easygoing and settled in yourself?"

Cenn looked taken aback. Before Ember could worry she'd said something wrong, his smile finally formed.

"I'm glad that's how I appear," he said, moving on to a block of aloes. "Because it definitely wasn't easy to reach this point."

Ember trailed after him, not daring to break his thoughtful silence.

"When I was younger," he finally said, "I was particularly accomplished academically. I didn't have to work to understand most concepts, the answer popping into my head without me knowing how I got there. Naturally, my parents and teachers were impressed, constantly telling me how smart I was, how talented, how proud of me they were. And when I was chosen by Rosala at twelve, that 'gift' followed me into my apprenticeship."

Cenn paused, eyes on his aloe. Ember watched him from the end of the row, something about the set of his shoulders having her biting the inside of her cheek.

"Eventually," he said, "I turned seventeen. The healer work I'd been doing had been steadily getting harder, more complicated. And slowly, the answers stopped popping into my head. I had to think through each problem, just to realize I had no clue what I was doing. It was like all my life, I'd been able to jump from point A to point E, and consequently never learned how to get to point B. Gods, I never learned to create a true work ethic.

"At that point, everyone started to notice I was slipping. And even though they never criticized me for it, I felt... untethered. Worse than that. All my life, I'd only been praised for my intelligence. And now that I was losing that?"

Cenn bit his lip, Ember's heart softening.

"You lost who you were," she said quietly.

Cenn nodded, the brown spots on his aloe fading under his touch. "I didn't so much spiral into a dark place as I did plummet. I don't like looking back at that time, who I became. All that matters is one day, a friend at the time crushed a fuzzy yellow leaf and stuck it under my nose, telling me to just see if it helped."

Ember gasped. "It's devinroot for you, too?"

Cenn nodded, still lost in thought. "For most people, it helps organize thoughts, increase focus and concentration. But for me, it was like I'd been looking through a rain-streaked window, and the devinroot finally wiped it clean. I wanted to learn again. I wanted to see my friends, learn how to study, resecure my spot in the Healer Center that I was close to losing. I wanted to live again. And at some point, my living became dependent on that plant. Even though the longer I was on it, the more questionable my actions became. I'm sure you're familiar with the rash decisions, irritability, lack of sleep, everything else?"

Ember nodded, her eyes wide.

"That was me for about three years. I won't get into my interventions, but I will say I will always be grateful to Sofika and Marisa. Not just for helping me, but for giving me reasons to want to be better. For reminding me I want to help people, not hurt them. And having those goals is how I got to where I am today."

Ember shook her head slowly, at a loss for words. She expected Cenn to sag as he came to the end of such a story, but instead, he looked peaceful. Like he'd told it countless times before.

"You're doing an incredible job," she told him.

"So are you."

Ember blinked, the compliment feeling like a cooling stove she didn't know if she wanted to touch or not. "Thank you."

"It's the truth." Cenn came toward her, his fingers skimming over plants. "You were excellent today with our patients. Sofika had her 'I'm going to brag about my apprentice to the other master healers' look all day."

Ember let out a startled laugh. "Really?"

"Undeniably so. I'll show you where they usually gather so we can eavesdrop when she does it; it's quite the performance."

Ember smiled, Cenn returning the gesture as he stopped before her.

"You asked how I reached this point," he said, softening once more. "I'm assuming Sofika told you shame is toxic to us, but for me, I also need to remember to be kind to myself." He touched her shoulder, Ember blinking hard. "You're worth being kind to. Also, have lunch with me and the other apprentices; the mysterious loner angle only works so long."

Ember laughed, her eyes stinging. "Is that what I'm doing?"

"That's what everyone thinks." Cenn flicked her arm, then turned and headed back down the row. "Come on, master apprentice. If I'm going to tell you my dark and tragic past, you better help me heal these plants."

Ember rolled her eyes, not immediately noticing her smile had grown. He really was impressive. Not just in his recovery, but the way he so effortlessly reestablished their usual rapport.

Ember followed him down the row, turning over his words as they moved to a new block.

Having a goal felt like the first tool she'd been given that she knew how to use. She'd spent the past fourteen years working to prove herself, become the best healer she could. After Ash was invaded, all she'd wanted was for things to get back to normal. But there had also been her other goal.

Ember looked down at her enka bracelet, the last phoenix charm dangling from her wrist. She swallowed hard, knowing the moment to hand it over had finally come.

But for now, she had her goal of making it through her first day with full apprentice privileges. And she had a feeling that that goal, at the very least, was going to be met.

Chapter 67

Dimitri had to admit: he really loved being a pain in the ass.

While he spent most mornings training his magic with Tyce in the safehouse, the rest of his time was open for whatever fuckery he could come up with—which was a lot.

Encouraging Othin to increase patrols to keep an eye on the Ash Royals, just to rile up the soldiers as they complained about their schedules. Waltzing into the Council Chamber to shift the gray pieces marking the Ash Royals known locations on their war map. Casually dropping details around Ash servants and soldiers that would spark some hope.

The best thing he did, though, was discover that when Othin locked himself in his chambers for an hour every three days, he was writing a letter. He'd figured that was the case after barging in to confront Othin over the "rumors," but he had to be certain. So, he arranged to have one of his increasingly frequent consultations with Othin at the same time three days later. And sure enough, he passed Joshel a letter marked "S" as he escorted Dimitri inside. Meaning Dimitri had some plotting to do.

Three days after Dimitri got his letter confirmation, he arrived at Othin's chambers fifteen minutes early.

"Here to see His Majesty?" Joshel asked, straightening from where he'd been slumped against the wall.

"As always," Dimitri sighed.

Joshel's lips twitched. Turning, he knocked on the door, Dimitri reaching back to shift the spot of warmth pressed between his neck and flipped-up collar. Before he could start to second guess his plan, Othin's muffled voice called for them to enter.

"Dimitri's here to see you, Your Majesty," Joshel said, partially opening the door.

Othin grunted. "He's early."

Dimitri edged around Joshel to peek inside. Sure enough, Othin sat at his desk, pen in hand and amber eyes narrowed as he spotted Dimitri.

"I'm bored," he whined.

"I'm too busy to entertain you."

"I can entertain myself."

With that, Dimitri slipped past Joshel and into the chamber. He took a few quick steps forward, Othin's mouth half open to protest. But clearly deciding he couldn't be bothered, he turned back to his letter, grumbling for Joshel to shut the door.

"If you bother me," he said, not looking up, "I'll kick you out."

Dimitri paused beside the bed, surprised by his own flinch. Even when he was an asset to Othin, he was disposable.

Othin cleared his throat, and Dimitri blurted an affirmation. It was just another reason to dismantle his operations.

Keeping his back to Othin, Dimitri wandered around the chamber, Othin's pen scratching through the silence. He didn't bother trying to be inconspicuous—that would implicate him more. Especially since Othin was bound to catch him. That, however, didn't stop his stomach from shifting at the thought of Othin discovering Dimitri wasn't the only one who'd entered his chambers.

Dimitri checked Othin remained distracted. Then, he nudged the spot of warmth against his neck with a finger, Spark wriggling to the front of his collar so they could see—although there wasn't much to look at.

The chamber remained as sparse as when Dimitri first visited: large central bed, some armchairs scattered around the perimeter, a wardrobe of clothes in each back corner. He doubted Othin kept anything in the attached bathing chamber—although the messy stack of papers on the bedside table seemed promising.

Keeping Spark angled away from Othin, Dimitri plopped down on the bed, pulling the papers toward himself. He did his best to keep the rustle of the pages to a minimum, Othin thankfully too engrossed in his letter to look up. But as Dimitri skimmed through, his lips pursed.

They were all reports, ranging from the patrols sent to track the Royals, to border patrols, to assessments on citizen cooperation. He knew all of this already. He flipped to the next page, the scratch of Othin's pen pausing.

Dimitri tensed, Spark diving back behind his collar. But with a sigh, Othin's pen started up once more.

Crystal fuck him, he had to wrap this up.

Dimitri flipped through pages, quick and quiet as he could. Border patrol. Food stores report. An old speech. Mt. Vasolus patrol—what was that at the bottom?

Dimitri squinted at a small table marked "Extractions," the various quantities and percentages below arranged by date. So, Cadmus was right: they were stealing Ash Kingdom resources from the mines. A good amount, from the looks of it.

Dimitri caught Spark's eye, then tapped the numbers. Spark nodded, leaning forward to memorize the table.

Othin's page rustled behind them. He was going to be done any minute. And Dimitri still hadn't found anything particularly useful.

His eyes darted around the room, his hands starting to sweat. Logically, the most crucial information would be hidden inside Othin's desk, but Othin was right there. So where?

Spark tapped Dimitri's neck. Dimitri started, then twisted his head to see where Spark was pointing. The extra wardrobe?

Dimitri raised a brow, but Spark pointed more insistently. Shooting Othin a look over his shoulder, Dimitri rose and crossed to the wardrobe, wincing at the creak as he pulled it open. Just to discover a haphazard array of clothing.

Everything from tunics, to jackets, to shirts hung from tangled hangers, piles of tossed-in pants and shoes littering the bottom shelves. Clearly, Othin didn't let his maids in this wardrobe—which was unusual.

Dimitri shifted a pile of pants, uncovering a single black boot. Come on, there had to be something hidden in here. He reached for the sagging pile in the back corner. Just for something to tingle across his fingertips.

Dimitri's heart leaped. He pushed Spark back behind his collar, his other hand resetting the mess as he stumbled away. And his back hit something solid.

"What are you doing in my wardrobe?" Othin asked, spinning Dimitri around to face him.

Dimitri's heart pounded against his ribs. "I told you, I was entertaining myself."

"In my wardrobe?"

Dimitri shrugged, praying he kept his racing thoughts off his face. "I already knew everything in the papers on your bedside table. Why do you have so many clothes?"

"I'm a king, Dimitri." Othin shook his head, Dimitri's face twitching as his hands flexed on Dimitri's shoulders.

Did Othin believe he was just snooping? Had he spotted Spark's faint light before Dimitri had hidden them away? Had he taken it too far?

Dimitri stared into Othin's face, watching him consider. Finally, Othin scoffed. "Don't go through my things, boy."

Dimitri's hands shook, but he kept his nod nonchalant. Othin, clearly unimpressed, turned away, jerking his thumb at Dimitri to follow.

"We have reports to go over."

Dimitri obediently followed, Spark pressing against the back of his neck as he took his usual seat at the foot of Othin's bed. Othin returned to his desk chair, Dimitri's eyes dropping to the large hands he rested on the table. He might not have discovered what was hidden in Othin's wardrobe. But it was important enough for Othin to put a shield around it.

The rest of Dimitri's time in Othin's chambers was uneventful. Apparently, Othin's patrols had noticed the Royals had a tendency of slipping through the central kingdom instead of shadowjumping to their locations, which included the homes of notable military captains. Yet, they always shadowjumped away when done, preventing any Sun soldiers from tracking them back to their hideout.

Dimitri, feigning ignorance, asked why Othin thought they would risk walking *to* their locations. Othin suggested they were trying to rally the people with their appearances, to which Dimitri shrugged and told him he had to provide his own reminder. After all, they couldn't afford to have Cadmus successfully organize an army. And the glint in Othin's eyes as he reassured Dimitri he was already on it had Dimitri's stomach sinking.

Eventually, Othin decided he'd milked Dimitri for all the opinions he had. Settling back in his chair, he dismissed Dimitri with a flick of his hand, Dimitri's jaw tightening in response. But this was where his true performance began.

He rose from the bed with a stretch, not sparing Othin a look as he headed for the door. Only when he passed the desk did his gaze flick up.

"Want me to give this to Joshel?" he asked, tapping the sealed letter on the desk.

"What?" Othin dragged his attention from the report he was consulting. "Oh, yes, do that."

Dimitri's nerves tingled. Offering a sarcastic salute, he retrieved the letter and sauntered toward the door, struggling not to run out before Othin could change his mind.

"Joshel," he drawled, opening the door, "Othin wants you to deliver this."

Othin grunted something about impertinence, but Dimitri closed the door on him. He turned to the guard, who rubbed his pale blue eyes.

"I forgot that was today." He reached for the letter, Dimitri forcing his fingers to release the envelope.

"He said it's urgent and needs to be delivered immediately," he added, lowering his voice so Othin couldn't hear through the door.

Joshel started to retort, but quickly bit off his words. He dragged a hand through his thick, light brown hair, clearly struggling to straighten his expression. "That's... difficult."

"Why?" Dimitri asked, shifting away from the door.

"If I deliver this immediately, there will be no one guarding the chamber."

"How do you usually do it?"

"I wait until my shift is over to drop it off—although with our new patrol schedule?" Joshel bit his lip.

"Give him a day or so," Dimitri said, picking his nails. "He's bound to change his mind."

Joshel snorted. Clearly, he was one of the many soldiers exhausted and resentful of Othin's new patrol system—especially since days before it was implemented, Othin was considering doing nothing. But Dimitri could respect Joshel's look of guilt.

"I shouldn't have said that," he murmured, mirroring Dimitri as he shifted even farther from the door. "His Majesty is trying to rule a rebelling kingdom with little assistance. He's allowed to have second thoughts."

"That's a polite way of saying he's talking out of his ass," Dimitri commented.

Joshel pressed his lips together, smothering his laugh. "Do you really want to say that, as the king's son?"

"You mean his bastard that he only acknowledges when it benefits him?" Dimitri wrinkled his nose. "Don't be mistaken. I'm only here because it's my one sanctuary from Deardryn. And if giving Othin my opinion every couple days is what I have to do to survive, then who cares?"

Joshel cocked his head, not responding immediately. Dimitri's gaze flicked around the quiet corridor, wondering if he'd been a bit too honest. But finally, Joshel nodded slowly.

"Fair enough."

Dimitri startled. Since when did anyone from Sun validate him?

But Joshel made no move to take it back as he sighed, dropping his gaze to the letter he turned between his fingers. And Dimitri's back straightened a little bit.

"What are you going to do about that?" he asked, gesturing to the letter.

Joshel winced. "Any ideas?"

"Pass it off to a servant?" Dimitri suggested.

"Do you trust an Ash servant to not go through Othin's mail?"

"True."

Dimitri tugged on his collar, Spark's warm little body shifting restlessly against the back of his neck. He let a few moments go by in silence, Joshel frowning as he deliberated.

"Well," Dimitri finally said, "good luck with that."

Then, he turned and headed off down the hall.

Not too fast. Leaving room to consider before he reached the corner, the hall silent behind him.

Had he read Joshel correctly? Or had he gambled too much on the fear of Othin's temper?

Dimitri approached the corner, fighting the urge to look back as the silence stretched, stretched, stretched—

"Wait."

Dimitri held his breath as he turned.

Joshel took a few quick steps after him, offering him the letter. "Can you deliver this to Othin's mailers? They'll know where to send it."

Every nerve in Dimitri's body screamed for him to grab it. Instead, he wrinkled his nose. "You think Othin wants me delivering his mail?"

"What he doesn't know can't hurt him." Joshel took another step closer, his eyes darting back to his empty station. "Just this once."

Dimitri pretended to consider. Finally, he sighed. "Fine." He accepted the letter, Joshel's expression sagging in relief. "Don't mention the letter at all to Othin, all right? Don't give him an opening to pry."

"Of course not," Joshel said as if it were obvious. Then, thanking Dimitri, he turned and headed back to his post. And Dimitri somehow managed not to run all the way back to his chambers, the letter safely hidden in his pocket.

By the time he pushed through his door, he couldn't suppress his cackle. He flopped down on his bed, grinning into his pillow. "We did it, Spark."

Spark gave a little cheer, wriggling their way out of Dimitri's collar.

"How did you know about the wardrobe, anyway?" Dimitri asked, shifting onto his side.

"Lucky guess. Originally, that chamber only had the left one." Grinning, Spark hopped onto a nearby sconce, the flame crackling. "Should I find Rayner?"

"No," Dimitri decided. "I can fill him in when he gets back."

Sitting up, he pulled out his letter, practically lightheaded from the rush in his veins. He brought the letter over to Spark's sconce, the sprite watching intently as Dimitri softened the wax seal with the heat. Then, retrieving a knife from the bedside table, he carefully slid it beneath the golden seal.

"This better be good," Spark murmured as Dimitri opened the envelope and pulled out the letter.

Dimitri murmured his agreement, already reading Othin's cramped handwriting.

My love—Crystal fuck him. He knew exactly who S was.

Spark cast him a quizzical look from their flame. And shoving down the pulsing magic in his gut, Dimitri cleared his throat and read.

"My love." He made a face. "I wish I had more answers for you regarding Deardryn's brief visit home, but I don't think anyone knows what goes on in that woman's mind. She's an utter contradiction, fueled by spite and hiding behind peaceful words. It helps to remind yourself that it's only to be expected. After all, you and I both know that your sex is ruled by emotions. Such lapses in judgment can only be criticized so harshly when it's nature. Then again, we've been undeservingly subjected to such irrationality, so why bother giving any grace?"

Dimitri rolled his eyes. "You can pop his pride just looking at it too long."

Spark snickered, and Dimitri returned his attention to the letter.

"She shows no consideration for our position. Yes, she's back in Sun now that the Ash mouse has escaped, but what about the month before that when both the Sun King and Queen were out of the kingdom? What about her demands that we try to rule peacefully over a kingdom she invaded? Not to mention she's left me to clean up her mess, and refuses to tell me why we bother holding this kingdom."

Well, that was interesting; even Othin didn't know why Deardryn wanted Ash. Dimitri continued reading, but it was much of the same complaining. By the end, both he and Spark had had more than enough.

Promising to deliver the information to the others, Spark disappeared with a crackle, leaving Dimitri alone in the quiet chamber.

He tossed the pages on his bed, restlessly drumming his fingers on his thigh as he paced around the chamber. When would Rayner return? He wanted to see the look on his face when he read that disaster of a letter.

His gaze drifted around the room, snagging on a corner of dark fabric peeking out from beneath Rayner's pillow. He moved to get a better look, the lingering rush having him not thinking before pulling the fabric free.

Just as he thought, it was the small tapestry Surce had woven for Rayner. Yet, as he unfolded the image, something heavy settled in his chest.

The tapestry depicted a cell. The outer wall was made up of bones, the inside only consisting of dirt and dark, crumbling rock. Identical to every cell Dimitri had stumbled past on his run through Scarsthain, the memory having his lungs constricting.

But this cell had a pair of broken shackles on the ground. And the door was halfway open.

Dimitri blinked hard, rubbing the rolling ache in his chest.

This was Rayner's cell. This was where he'd been imprisoned for Crystal knew how long, tormented and brutalized and he didn't want to know what else. Because somehow, looking at that tapestry, everything Rayner had told him finally felt... real. Heartbreakingly so.

Dimitri might have been trapped in his own kind of cell, but at least he had a bed, food, a castle. He had Analia and Aaron to guide him out of that darkness. But Rayner had had none of that. And yet, he was still... human.

Yes, he'd betrayed Dimitri. He was confident any prisoner who had escaped that prison would have done the same. But how many of them would have felt ashamed? How many of them would have tried to make it right? How many of them would have been kind, and thoughtful, and passionate?

"The door being half open has always felt appropriate to me."

Dimitri jumped. He whipped around, Rayner having somehow approached without him hearing. His eyes darted between the tapestry and Rayner's face, bracing himself for the rebuke. But Rayner remained perfectly serene as he went on.

"I know I've escaped the prison, but it doesn't always feel that way. But for some reason, seeing that open door always grounds me in the present. I would have shown it to you if I knew you were interested."

Dimitri hung his head, the sincerity so much worse than any outrage. "I'm sorry for snooping," he mumbled, offering Rayner the tapestry.

"Remember to ask me next time, and we can call it even." Rayner accepted the tapestry, folding it up and tucking it back under his pillow. As if he'd done it countless times.

"You deserve to be out," Dimitri blurted.

Rayner looked back at him, eyebrows raised.

"In case that was ever something you questioned, I mean," he mumbled.

Rayner stared for a moment. Dimitri flushed, starting to back away. But Rayner smiled to himself, his fingertips coming to graze Dimitri's arm.

"Come on," he said, heading for Dimitri's bed. "I see you successfully stole the letter, and I want to read it before we deliver it."

For a moment, Dimitri remained rooted to the spot. Finally, he came to sit on the bed beside Rayner, Rayner flashing a smile as he settled back to read. And Dimitri had no idea how much strength it required to have that smile reach his eyes.

Chapter 68

When Analia fell asleep that night, she was expecting her usual nightmares. What she wasn't expecting was to open her eyes in Sylas's sitting room, the Moon King tapping his foot as he waited on his red armchair.

"Finally," he said, the picture of suffering as his head fell back. "I've been trying to reach you for a week." Rising to his feet, he crossed the room, giving her a surprisingly thorough once-over. "Why must you fall asleep so late?"

He stopped before her, Analia staring up at the harsh planes of his face. And her temper erupted.

"How dare you?" she spat, shoving his chest.

Sylas took a step back, his thick brows shooting up. "Excuse me?"

"How dare you not tell Dimitri Patryclas was alive? How *dare you* put him through that kind of grief—"

"I did tell him," Sylas said indignantly.

Analia's flames sputtered. "You did?"

"Yes. The night Patryclas was revealed, I met him in his dreams—"

Analia shoved him again. A shadow lashed up from the floor to catch her wrist, but Analia knocked it aside with her own shadowy whip.

Sylas cocked his head, studying her more closely.

"So," he mused, an icy shadow thoughtfully brushing her ankle, "you're getting better at summoning my magic."

Analia scoffed. "That was my temper more than me. I haven't even tried to touch your magic while awake."

"How come?"

Honestly? She hadn't had the time. And the flames seething through her blood couldn't care less.

"Don't change the subject, Sylas," she said, folding her arms. "Why didn't you tell him? You trusted the information to your healer and the handful of servants undoubtedly taking care of Patryclas in your absence. Why did I have to ask Laness to make sure he knew?"

"Because I still needed him."

Analia made to argue, just to pause. Since when did Sylas give up answers so easily? She narrowed her eyes, Sylas paying her no mind as he turned to prowl around the room.

"When Dimitri arrived in my kingdom," he said, surprisingly agitated, "I had already agreed to enable Deardryn's research. Granted, that didn't include her easing into a constant occupancy in my castle, nor the guards she slowly brought in, but I didn't know how insidious her plans could be. What I *did* know was going back on my promise could have disastrous consequences for not just me, but my kingdom. I couldn't risk that on the word of a Sun bastard that had every reason to hate her.

"Yet, that bastard also gave me an answer as to who poisoned Patryclas. And I was relieved. Because while she had already infiltrated my kingdom, at least I knew who to keep an eye on. But that also made me even more afraid of what Deardryn might do if I crossed her."

"What does this have to do with anything?" Analia asked, her fingers digging into the plush arm of a nearby armchair.

"Everything." Sylas twisted back to face her, raking a hand through his blue-black curls. "My relief was paralyzing, Analia. I couldn't afford for Dimitri to find out Patryclas was alive back in his cell and risk him slipping into that complacency."

"So you subjected him to the worst pain you could think of?"

"Do you think he would have fought so hard to get you out of the dungeon, escape Deardryn himself, and now spy on her operations if not for that grief?"

Analia's jaw flexed, her body uncomfortably warm. Because her retort was neither immediate nor definite. All she knew was if Accalon was alive, and no one told her?

"You should have told him," she repeated. But her conviction had noticeably waned. She imagined Aaron's blue recliner behind her, her body slumping back into the velvet.

"Are you saying if this had been your Star Prince, you wouldn't have done the same?"

Sylas's words jolted down Analia's spine. She sat up straight, Sylas pausing his pacing and eyeing her curiously.

"I don't know how to answer that question," she told him, her tone noticeably defensive.

"You don't have to worry about revealing him," Sylas drawled, moving to claim his seat across from her. "I already know. Your tattoo manifesting as a constellation was interesting, but he gave himself away on the bridge. That boy didn't speak to me like an arrogant guard like you and Dimitri claim he is. He threatened me as an equal. That and I've never been in a dream where the environment was so heavily obscured."

Sylas settled back in his seat, positively pleased with himself. Analia flicked a spark at him, but she didn't try to deny his claims as he whined and batted it away. There was no point.

"Is that why you summoned me here?" she asked instead. "To share your theories?"

"I was actually planning on updating you on Deardryn until you steered us off topic."

"You didn't seem to mind a couple seconds ago," Analia muttered.

In a blink, a shadowy tendril flicked out from Sylas's feet, Analia wincing at the icy smack to the back of her hand. She shot Sylas a look, Sylas smugly summoning a wine glass and taking a long sip.

"As I was trying to say," he drawled, "Deardryn is officially out of my kingdom. Unfortunately, we weren't able to damper her in time, and she shadowjumped to her chambers, collected all her belongings, and fled. I don't know where she went, and neither do the soldiers we managed to take in for questioning. They did, however, confirm that on one of the three days Deardryn was on 'business,' she returned to the Sun Castle."

Analia perked up. "So, that's what the brief visit home was referring to in Dimitri's letter," she mused.

"The rabble found a letter?"

Analia flicked another spark at him, but she nodded and explained Dimitri's stolen letter. "It's no surprise she's back in Sun," she finished, rising from her chair to pace. "But why did her guards only know where she was one of the three days she was gone?"

"And why return to the Sun Kingdom?" Sylas murmured into his glass. "She invaded my kingdom because she wanted the Crystal shard hidden within. So, presumably she would go to Ash—"

"Because it has something she wants," Analia finished, her stomach sinking.

Sylas made a face. "You need to learn to wait your turn."

"I only interrupt you because I know it bothers you."

Sylas muttered something under his breath. Analia continued pacing, running her fingers along smooth wooden counters and bookshelves as she thought.

Deardryn had claimed she invaded Ash to lure Analia out of hiding, but Analia had always assumed there had to be more if she bothered holding on to it. But if it was something she refused to even tell Othin?

For several minutes, she and Sylas went back and forth, none of their possible explanations promising. Eventually, the sitting room started to fade. Analia pivoted to face Sylas, still in his chair.

"Stay in contact," she told him.

She expected Sylas to glower, never one to enjoy being told what to do. But Sylas simply nodded. Then, her dream faded to black.

Analia opened her eyes, finding herself back in her bedroom. Morning light squeezed through the cracks in the closed black-and-silver curtains, Aaron's arm draped over her waist as he slept beside her.

Analia sighed, wanting nothing more than to settle into his warmth, the slow, even rhythm of his breathing. But she couldn't stop thinking about her conversation with Sylas.

Careful not to disturb him, she slid out of bed, moving to her armoire and pulling out clothes at random. She was no closer to figuring out Deardryn's scheme, but what really bothered her was Sylas asking her what she would have done in his situation.

The truth was, she didn't know. Yes, she had schemed while in the Moon Kingdom, but none of those lies hurt anyone. She could respect that Sylas had an entire kingdom's safety to consider when making his plans. But even though she'd told Aaron she wasn't ready to take on that level of responsibility, she couldn't help but wonder if there could have been another way.

Analia bit her cheek as she pulled on a long-sleeved violet shirt, then headed for the bathing room. She braced her hands on the cool countertop, staring into her face in the mirror.

Someday, that type of decision would be hers to make. And while she viewed her relationships in extremes, she had too many perspectives when it came to ruling.

But maybe Aaron was right. Maybe, instead of treating those lessons as contradictory facts, she should view them as options. And while Sylas's plan had worked out, it came at the cost of his morality. And the one thing Analia knew for certain was that wasn't something she was willing to sacrifice.

Analia nodded, her gaze clearing in the mirror. She would have told Dimitri.

Analia finished up in the bathing room, feeling a little more grounded as she returned to her room and quietly slipped out the door. Just to spot Ember emerging from her room at the end of the hall, her hair damp from the bath.

"How was your run?" Analia called, padding across the thick, midnight-blue carpet toward her.

Ember winced. "I'm telling myself at least it's not your night training."

Analia grinned. Branten had given her two days to recover before dragging her back to the training hollow, Ember visibly horrified when she came back with bruised knuckles.

"I'm glad I bumped into you, though," Ember went on, sobering disconcertingly fast. "I've been meaning to give you something."

Analia cocked her head, the two meeting at the top of the stairs. "What is it?"

Ember sighed, pushing back her sleeve. "Your sister's ashes."

Analia and Ember stood on the big house's roof, the kingdom spread out below them as Analia opened the phoenix charm. Aaron had offered to join them, Analia finding him awake when she'd gone to leave him a note as to where she was going. But something told her it should just be her and Ember.

Apparently, Ember had been wanting to give her the charm for a few days, but hadn't been able to work up the courage until that morning. And as the gentle breeze carried the pinch of ash away, Analia couldn't blame her.

"Rise again, Lucilla," she murmured, her heart giving a long, aching squeeze.

Ember sniffed, the silent tears staining her cheeks matching Analia's. But this was good. This was the goodbye Lucilla deserved—maybe not in her home, but somewhere safe. Somewhere she probably would have loved.

"Thank you," she said, her voice thick as she turned to Ember. "Thank you for rescuing her body, for upholding our tradition, for everything."

"It was the least I could do," Ember said, rubbing her eyes. "She deserved to be sent off by her family."

Analia swallowed hard, her tears cooling against her cheeks. "I wish we felt more like family." She sat on the edge of the roof, Ember looking at her curiously as Analia pulled her knees to her chest. "Don't get me wrong, she's my sister, I love her. But I was already eleven years older than her. And then Brenn did everything he could to keep her away from me."

"Asshole," Ember muttered, settling beside her.

Analia shrugged, not having it in her to do much else. "I feel like I only got to know her from afar."

Gods, that was a whole new layer of grief to unpack.

Analia bit her lip, remaining quiet for several moments. "Do you remember her sixth birthday, when she snuck down to the kitchen and charmed our baker into giving her all of the desserts made for that evening for breakfast?"

Ember laughed. "I remember Brenn's tirade when he found out."

"Meanwhile," Analia said, starting to smile, "Aeley and Cadmus sat on the entryway floor with her and enjoyed the chocolate cake she'd smuggled. She even snuck me a piece when no one was looking."

Analia's smile faltered; the fact that even at six, Lucilla knew she had to stay away was a special kind of ache. Ember clocked the look on her face.

"She only got worse as she got older," she said. "Cadmus originally tried to keep her out of our research, so she sent a fire sprite to spy on us and then used it as leverage until we let her in."

Analia let out a surprised laugh. "Accalon would have loved that."

"Cadmus was appalled," Ember agreed, settling back on her elbows.

For a few minutes, the two traded stories about Lucilla, each one having the ache in Analia's chest softening a little more. She turned the metal phoenix charm between her fingers, finally slipping it in her pocket as their voices drifted off. She looked over at Ember, who had tipped her face back to enjoy the warmth from the rising sun.

It had been a few days since she'd noticed the distant, uncertain look on her face from the night she returned home. Yet, there was a heaviness to her presence that she'd never had before.

"Speaking of the Ash Kingdom," Analia said tentatively, letting her feet hang over the edge, "you've given us plenty of updates on the kingdom before you left. But how have *you* been?"

Ember's lips pursed. She dropped her gaze to the roof, rolling a stray pebble beneath her finger with a quiet scrape.

"I'm worried about Cadmus," she finally said. "I know he's stronger than Brenn, but I also don't know what that mark entails. And all I can assume is the longer he has it, the worse whatever he's dealing with will become."

Gods, it was hard to find fault in that logic. Analia wrapped her arms around herself, the wind feeling colder.

"We can ask Surce to consult her tapestries," she said, trying to reassure herself as much as Ember. "According to Aaron, Zella has been anxiously waiting to meet me, so maybe I can go to the library and see if I can find anything on ancient oaths."

Which, oddly enough, was what Deardryn had been researching as well. Analia frowned, Ember not seeming to notice as she played with her pebble.

"Did Accalon have the mark?" she asked.

"No," Analia said immediately. Confidently. Which only gave them more questions. And Ember hadn't fully answered her original one.

"Are you sure that's all that's bothering you?" Analia asked.

Ember took a breath. Hesitated. Then, she looked away, rubbing her nose. "Can I ask you something?"

Analia nodded.

"Why didn't you accept Aaron's ring? I know you're not ready for the crown, but he said you could have as long of a betrothal as you like. So, why'd you say no?"

Analia released a long, heavy breath. She'd been expecting the question ever since returning from the council, Ember visibly restraining her words as Analia told her everything. But to her surprise, her answer easily came to her lips.

"It didn't feel right. It happened right before going to the council to ask for their help dealing with Deardryn, and agreeing to be queen felt like another step in that plan. And I love Aaron too much to let that become all we are."

"Well," Ember mused, "from what I've heard, he's never been great with timing."

"No," Analia agreed. "And we're both prone to overthinking. But it will happen. We trust that we'll come to each other when we're ready."

Analia gave Ember a significant look. One that had Ember's mouth opening. Then, she nodded slightly.

"I should get to the Healer Center," she said, half to herself. "I promise, I'm all right."

Analia was tempted to point out being all right and having nothing wrong were two different things. But trusting Ember would come to her eventually, she nodded and rose to her feet. Ember followed her lead, Analia heading for the hatch back into the house.

She just hoped whatever was going on with Ember wasn't getting worse as time went on.

Chapter 69

E mber arrived at the Healer Center lost in thought.

Branten had been kind enough to stop by on his way to Nova House to let Sofika know why she'd be late, which Ember had hoped would spare her from a chiding—tardiness was rarely tolerated at the Ash Kingdom Healer School. After all, there were only so many healers, and her patients needed her.

Yet, when she found Cenn and Sofika in the lavender wing, she was only met with compassion as Cenn pulled her into a hug. She leaned her head against his shoulder, taken aback by how strong her rush of relief was. Sofika quietly stood beside them, waiting until Ember disentangled herself to wave her and Cenn into a nearby empty patient room.

"Are you all right?" she asked, closing the door behind them.

Ember wished that question didn't have as many layers as it did. Just as she wished her cravings hadn't been getting worse from the moment she spotted Analia in the hallway that morning.

But unlike on the roof, when Ember opened her mouth, her words spilled out without hesitation.

She told them everything: how she'd been carrying around Lucilla's ashes for weeks, how Analia had given her the perfect opening to talk about her addiction, but she froze.

"And I don't know why," she finished, plopping down on the patient bed.

She expected Sofika's and Cenn's brows to furrow, perhaps for the two to exchange a troubled look. But Sofika merely cocked her head as she examined the corner fern, Cenn nodding from the windowsill as if she'd said their robes were green.

"That's usually how it goes," he said.

"What do you mean?" Ember whined.

"It's always hardest to tell the people you're closest to," he said. "Those are the people who know you best. They're the ones that will be the most surprised, the ones you stand to lose the most with."

Rosala spare her, that was exactly it. But why?

"It's not like I expect her to take it poorly," Ember said, rubbing her forehead with her knuckles. "She's not the type to judge—I don't think she'd even say 'I told you so.' So, why can't I do it?"

"How long have you two been friends?" Sofika asked, prodding a browning leaf.

"Sixteen years."

"Which means you have sixteen years of history weighing on you."

Ember bit her lip. To her, at least, it was sixteen years. She always suspected it took Analia a lot longer to believe in their friendship, but she didn't hold that against her. If anything, earning that trust weighed on her more than the years themselves.

She just... she couldn't lose Analia. Not after everything that had already been taken from her.

"What are you doing after work today?" Cenn asked suddenly.

Ember blinked, struggling to shove her thoughts aside. "Probably reading or tagging along with whatever plans Anna has."

Despite being in the Starlight Kingdom for a month, she hadn't exactly created a life outside of healing and Aaron's house. Just another thing that had slipped away.

"Not anymore," said Cenn. "You're coming out with me instead."

"Where?" Ember asked.

Cenn winked, his short hair inky black in the sunlight. "You'll see."

Ember should have known Cenn's plans would involve Marisa.

The large pottery shop sat tucked in the corner of the Mirage, the front windows displaying everything from bowls glazed with celestial patterns, to delicate mugs, to animal figurines. A cheerful bell tinkled overhead as Cenn pushed open the door, but Ember barely caught the sound over the flood of voices from within.

"Busy night?" she asked, taking in the twenty or so children spread out across the studio. Most sat talking and laughing at the long, central tables, a few investigating the pottery wheels off to the side. All of them, however, eagerly reached for the plate-sized slabs of clay that Marisa, Branten, and Evena circulated around the room.

"I promised to rescue you from a quiet night at home, didn't I?" Cenn shrugged off his healer robe and hung it on a cluttered coat rack by the door, revealing the earthy-green tunic he wore beneath. "I hope this meets your expectations."

His tone was casual enough. But Ember spotted his fingers fidgeting with his tunic buttons. Was he... *nervous?*

She turned back to the noisy studio, Branten and Evena calling for a group of boys not to use their wooden tools as swords.

Truthfully, she wasn't that experienced working with clay, nor did she think she would learn much with this group. But Cenn had brought her as a distraction. And in that regard?

Ember offered Cenn a tiny smile. "I don't think you could have chosen a better place."

Cenn beamed. Taking Ember's shrugged-off robe, he hung it beside his own, Ember about to ask what her night would entail. Just to cut off as a high, female voice called across the studio.

"You made it!" Marisa hurried toward them, her chestnut curls braided over her shoulder, teal sleeves pushed up to her elbows.

Cenn's entire body turned toward her voice, a light Ember had never seen before kindling to life in his eyes.

"You say that like you expected me to be late," he said, reaching for her as she approached.

"You say that like it's never happened before."

Cenn made a delicate, offended noise. Marisa grinned, stretching up on her toes to kiss him, Cenn's hand curling around her hip.

It was such a quick, casual exchange. Like they'd done it a thousand times before and expected to do it a thousand times again. And Ember didn't anticipate the ache behind her sternum.

"You must be Ember," Marisa said, pulling Ember from her thoughts as she twisted in Cenn's grip. "I'm Marisa, it's so nice to finally meet you!"

"Likewise. Cenn has told me a lot about you."

"And he's told me even more about you." Marisa stepped out of Cenn's grip and looped her arm through Ember's. "Come, we can compare notes while I show you around."

"Do you think I've been lying about you two?" Cenn interjected.

Marisa flapped a hand at him to shush. Then, she pulled Ember deeper into the studio, Cenn chuckling as he trailed behind them.

For how large of a space Marisa had, she didn't waste time lingering in any specific spot. She led Ember past display cases filled with everything from mugs to intricate figurines, over to a counter with countless bottles of glazes with names like "Starlight Silver" and "Lake Water Blue." All the while, she talked about the programs she'd implemented since taking over the studio and the different painting techniques Ember could try, Ember keeping up with about half of what she said.

But she didn't mind. Comprehension or not, the sheer enthusiasm on Marisa's face was infectious, reminding her of how she used to prattle on about herbology at any given chance.

"I keep most of my equipment in the back room," Marisa explained, "just to avoid any accidents. But we've reached the clay station!"

Marisa paused at the back corner, gesturing with a flourish to a large, rolling cart. Bags of grayish-brown clay covered its three levels, some still sealed, others obviously missing chunks.

"Feel free to take as much as you like."

"Are you sure?" Ember asked, her hand resting on a bag. "I can pay you; now that I'm officially working for Sofika I have the gold—"

"Don't be silly," Marisa said. "Tonight is already funded by His Majesty."

"It is?"

Marisa's eyes widened. She wheeled on Cenn quietly leaning against a nearby counter, hands on her hips. "Did you not tell Ember what tonight is?"

Cenn winced. "We were getting there."

"You mean when you told me tonight was a surprise?" Ember asked, unable to help herself.

Cenn ducked his head, clearly anticipating Marisa's huff.

"You are too humble." Grabbing a bag of clay, she tossed it to Cenn, gesturing for Ember to take the bag her hand lingered on. "Cenn put all of this together," she explained, almost a brag. "Once a month, all of the children from Nova House come here to play with the clay."

"Really?" Ember turned to Cenn, who struggled to hide his pleased look as he fiddled with a floral mug on the counter. "Why didn't you tell me?"

"I was going to," he promised. "I just wanted you to enjoy the night before learning its meaning."

Ember cocked a brow. Smiling, Cenn gestured for her to follow him back toward the central tables, Marisa practically buzzing beside her.

"I told you that I first met Marisa because I discovered pottery helped quiet my thoughts," he began. "What I didn't mention was that was in the early days of my going off of devinroot and I thought I was losing my mind. I couldn't concentrate; I couldn't exist around every emotion I'd buried erupting at once. But the clay didn't care. It could take whatever I threw at it. And as I started to get my life together and realize I wanted to help people, I thought why stop at healing?"

"He arranged everything himself," Marisa said, seemingly unable to help herself. "Scheduling with me, introducing the idea to Branten and Evena, getting the funding from His Majesty. And now, here we are."

Marisa paused at the head of one of the tables, beaming at the chattering group of orphans. Cenn mumbled something Ember didn't catch as she looked around.

All of this was born from his addiction. Children who had lost everything, who had every right to be angry at the world, laughing as they played with their clay.

Ember looked down at her own bag, then up at Cenn, who watched her curiously. "I think everyone needs an outlet like this."

Cenn's expression softened. Marisa slid an arm around his waist, pride shining in her eyes as he stroked her temple.

That ache behind Ember's sternum started up again. Before she could consider why, someone called her name. She glanced around, spotting a boy with copper curls and large, impossibly blue eyes waving at her from the opposite end of her table.

"Brookston?" she asked, needing a moment to remember his name.

Brookston's face lit up. He hopped off his stool, calling over the noise as he scampered toward her, "Are you staying? You have clay! Come sit with me!"

Ember barely had time to open her mouth before he reached her, his little hand grasping for hers.

"Careful, Brookston," Branten said, ambling over from a nearby table. "Don't get clay on her." Turning, he winked at Ember. "I didn't know you were coming tonight, healer girl."

"I'm a last-minute guest—although I still don't know what I'm doing."

"That's part of the fun," he said as if it were obvious.

Ember whacked his arm.

"All you have to do," Cenn said, stifling a laugh, "is think about your day and see what your hands create."

Ember was certain there had to be more than that. But before she could ask, Brookston grabbed her hand, his skin dried out from clay as he tugged her over to his end of the table.

For the rest of the night, Ember found herself squished between Brookston and his friend Isla, a girl around seven with long, straight black hair and deep brown eyes. The two took turns explaining what each of their tools did, neither of them seeming to mind as her attention faded in and out.

Think about your day and see what your hands create.

She thought the whole point of Cenn bringing her was so she *wouldn't* think about her day.

Ember prodded at her cold, stiff clay, no design in mind.

Maybe she was doing it wrong. Cenn said he worked with clay to turn off his thoughts. But the longer Ember was off her devinroot, the more her thoughts raced, splitting off into tangents and forming new thoughts before the originals could conclude. Her desperation to slow them down was what got her hooked on devinroot in the first place. So, how did Cenn's addiction turn into such an incredible event, while Ember's was—whatever her clay lump was.

Ember smoothed her palms down the sides, the clay slowly becoming more malleable from the heat of her hands.

She shouldn't be surprised by their different reactions. Cenn was trained in a system that believed in forging connections. He had a master healer who cared about him beyond their roles as master and apprentice. Gods, Ember had barely been a part of their ranks for a month, and look how much the two had helped her.

She was sober. Excelling at her healing—Sofika let her take the lead on their moderate patients that day. And all of the Ash healers would have been horrified.

Ember pressed down on the top of her clay, forming a flattened cone.

To them, her addiction wasn't something to be managed and forgiven. It was a violation of her oath. It was her, taking her ability to heal and compromising it.

Ember's mind flashed to Rois's cell, her wave of panic as she thought she'd concocted her healing paste incorrectly because of her devinroot.

Her nails dragged through the clay.

If it was up to the Ash Healers, she wouldn't have been consoled that morning and rewarded with clay. She would be exiled, her markings split at the corners of her eyes just like the drug lord Analia had met in the Sun Kingdom. Honestly, with how many times she'd tested her oath, she couldn't fathom why her markings remained intact. Although the Starlight healers had proven one experiment at a time that they didn't even need those rings to be considered healers to Rosala.

Ember's gaze drifted over the crowd, finding Cenn at a pottery wheel with his back to her. His fingers moved along his clay, graceful as a dancer as he formed a perfect cylinder. Marisa stepped up behind him, sliding her arms around his waist and resting her chin on his shoulder to watch. And the ache behind Ember's sternum dug a little deeper.

Just one more thing she had sworn off for the healers when she was too young to know what she was losing. And she couldn't even say it was for Rosala anymore.

"It's a tree stump!" Brookston squealed.

Ember tore her gaze from Cenn and Marisa. She looked around, needing several seconds to realize Brookston was pointing to the clay in front of her, which now resembled a tree stump the size of a dinner plate. She didn't remember deciding to make that. But the resemblance was undeniable, from its shape to the rings she'd carved with her nails.

"I guess it is," she murmured.

"Where are its roots?" Isla asked. She squinted at the base of the stump, the back of Ember's throat burning as she only found smooth clay.

"I don't think it has any," she managed.

Isla frowned, clearly dissatisfied. But Brookston shrugged.

"That's all right," he said, kicking Ember repeatedly under the table. "They'll grow later."

Ember hunched over the table as if struck. Brookston, not seeming to notice, returned to his own clay, which resembled a lopsided bunny. And Ember would never understand how hope and devastation could feel so similar.

The rest of the night passed in a blur. Eventually, Branten and Evena called for cleanup time, most of the children whining that they wanted to keep playing. But they all rose to help, Cenn coming over to look at the tree stump Ember had quietly completed. He nodded to himself, his eyes lingering on the rootless base.

"Want to come back with me tomorrow?" he asked.

Ember's response came on a tired exhale. "Yes, please."

Twenty minutes later, the studio was clean once more, and Ember's tree stump sat drying on a shelf. They all headed for the door, Branten, Cenn, and Marisa all offering to walk Ember home, but she gently declined.

She sat on the bench outside the studio, voices fading as the group continued down the star-painted street.

She missed her devinroot. She missed not questioning her oath. She missed normal.

But at least she knew that when she rose from that bench, her feet wouldn't carry her to the greenhouse. And at that point, that was all she could ask for.

Chapter 70

Dimitri paced back and forth along the edge of the ridge made from black, hardened lava, summoning and banishing his magic to his fingertips.

"Please be careful," Rayner called, seated on a small boulder a few feet away.

"He's fine," Rois said from the boulder beside him, casually sharpening his sword. "It's not that steep of a decline. If he slips, he'll learn his lesson."

Rayner shot him a disgusted look, the sun catching the golden flecks around his pupils. "Soldiers," he muttered.

"You sound like a healer," Rois retorted.

"Enough," Cadmus said. He sat on the ground in front of the bickering men, not bothering to look up as he traced his fingers along the cracks and swirls in the rock before him. Dimitri, meanwhile, continued to pace.

He hadn't been expecting to spend his morning in the eastern outskirts of the kingdom, the faint scent of smoke stinging his nose, lava ridges and ravines as far as he could see. But Cadmus had appeared in his and Rayner's chambers after breakfast with Rois in tow, the Ash King telling them to clear their schedules, they were coming with him.

Apparently, the captain of the nearby town's military was reluctant to join Cadmus's efforts due to the rumors coming out of the central kingdom. Cadmus had tried to reassure her everything was going according to plan, but she wanted to hear from Cadmus's spies directly.

"Do we really have to meet her all the way out here?" Dimitri asked, the ridge crumbling beneath his boots as he paced.

"The longer we're in her town, the greater the chance word gets back to Othin," said Cadmus absently.

"Dima, the ridge," Rayner said.

Dimitri paced on. "Othin's soldiers don't go beyond the central kingdom. How paranoid is she—"

Dimitri broke off with a yelp as the hardened lava beneath his foot crumbled away. He flailed his arms, unable to regain his balance as he tumbled down the slope in a shower of clattering pebbles, his hands scraping uselessly along the rocks until he landed awkwardly in the black sand ten feet below.

Dimitri sat up with a wince, his hands stinging as he spat out gravel.

"You all right?" Rayner called.

Dimitri sighed, examining the torn skin along his palms. "Fine."

He looked up at the fresh clatter of pebbles, finding Rayner picking his way down the slope, Rois coming to peer down at him from the ridge's edge. He met Dimitri's eye. Then, he offered a salute, Dimitri's rude hand gesture having him laughing as he turned away.

"I hate him," Dimitri muttered.

"I tried to warn you," Rayner said, making it to the bottom of the slope. He came to kneel before Dimitri, reaching for his hands. "Let me see."

"Why?" Dimitri asked, pulling his bloody hands to his chest. "I already told you I'm fine."

His tone wasn't harsh. If anything, it matched the puzzlement on Rayner's face as he sat back on his heels, his head cocked.

"What?" Dimitri asked, starting to squirm under Rayner's gaze.

"I was just thinking about how when I was growing up, my sister and I would always run to our mom whenever we got hurt."

"You have a sister?" Dimitri asked, perking up. For all the talking they'd done back in Rayner's shop, Rayner had divulged few details about his personal life.

Now, he nodded. "Katia, four years younger. She was such a pain, always kicked my ass at everything."

"Was?"

"I lost track of her after I was imprisoned," he explained, trailing his fingers through the sand. "I was only in there for a year, but that was long enough for her to disappear."

Gods, he said only as if a year of relentless torment was nothing. Dimitri bit his lip, Rayner not seeming to notice as he went on.

"It took some time, but I was able to track her down in the Mist Kingdom. She has a jewelry shop. Completely innocent, as far from the usual masquerader path as you can get."

Rayner's lips lifted in a small, proud smile, Dimitri's mind spiraling back to his first day in Rayner's shop. *Many of my fellow masqueraders put their Blessing to nefarious purposes. Assassins, spies, con men.*

Dimitri's swallowed hard. But before he could ask just what had gotten Rayner thrown in Scarsthain, his faraway look cleared.

"At any rate," he said, "I was just thinking about how I grew up having someone who took care of me. I always knew if I was hurt, I could go to my mom and she would clean me up, kiss my wound, and I would walk away feeling better. But you never had that, did you?"

All thoughts of Rayner's past were abruptly swallowed by the lump in Dimitri's throat. One he hadn't anticipated. After all, taking care of himself was one of the pillars he built his life upon. But something about the softened look in Rayner's eyes had him realizing just how ugly and sad that pillar was.

Dimitri nodded, not trusting himself to speak.

"Well," Rayner said, scooting closer, "even though you said you're fine, I asked to see because you have an alternative now."

"You taking care of me?" Dimitri asked wryly. Even as his heart skipped a beat.

"Your hands at least. I might not have my mom's touch, but I think I can be an adequate substitute." He extended his hands once more, his faint, crooked smile rolling through Dimitri's veins, thick and warm as honey. "Would you like help?"

Dimitri looked down at Rayner's proffered hands. Over to his own scraped ones, still held close to his chest. Then, he silently rested his hands palm up in Rayner's. And the warmth of Rayner's fingers curling around his hand had some of the cracks he'd discovered smoothing over.

"Oh, Dima," Rayner said, shaking his head. "What am I going to do with you?"

He brushed away the black sand clinging to the scrapes along Dimitri's palms, Dimitri wincing at the sting.

"It's not *that* bad," he mumbled, his ears burning.

"I've seen worse," Rayner agreed. Placing Dimitri's hands in his lap, he pulled the canteen from his belt.

"That's your water," Dimitri protested, starting to retract his hands.

"I think I'll survive with a little less." Catching Dimitri's hands, Rayner gently pulled them back to his lap. He opened his canteen, then moved Dimitri's right hand so it was over the sand. And Dimitri's lips parted as the cool water trickled over his palm, Rayner brushing away the remaining sand clinging to his bloody skin.

He watched, transfixed, as Rayner repeated the process on his other hand, the light brush of his fingers sending tingles racing down his spine. Seemingly satisfied he'd cleaned the wounds, Rayner placed Dimitri's hands back on his thighs.

"Now what?" Dimitri asked tentatively.

"Now," Rayner said, "we cover everything up." Drawing the dagger from his belt, he pushed up his jacket sleeve, not hesitating to slice through the shirt cuff beneath.

"What are you doing?" Dimitri yelped.

"Creating wrappings." He sliced off the cuff on his other sleeve. "Not the most sanitary option, but we'll get you properly cleaned up back at the castle."

He smoothed the deep red fabric over Dimitri's palms, lifting his hands one after the other to wrap the fabric around and tuck the corner in to secure it. And Dimitri had the strangest urge to cry.

This was a different kind of care he felt being with Analia, Aaron, and Sabi. It wasn't even the comfort he got from Patryclas. This was different. Tender in a way that left him feeling cracked wide open.

"What's that look for?" Rayner asked softly.

"I just..." Dimitri swallowed hard. "I know you say I'm a snapping turtle, but I think for a long time, I was a wet, stray cat."

Alone. Unwanted. Left to survive. But Rayner's eyes sparkled.

"I bet you were a sweet cat," he said.

"I was feral."

Rayner laughed, "But you're so domesticated now." As if to prove it, he released Dimitri's right hand, running his fingers through Dimitri's hair.

Dimitri's nose scrunched. "Why are you petting me?"

"Because I like your hair. It's soft, and such a nice shade of gold in the sunlight."

He stroked Dimitri's hair again, his touch longer. Softer. Loosening the aching knot in Dimitri's chest.

"You really are a cat," Rayner said delightedly. "Even your eyelids go all heavy like a sleepy kitten when pet."

Dimitri rolled his eyes. "Don't forget," he said, "even kittens have claws."

"I know," Rayner said, smoothing his hand along Dimitri's hair a third time. "But even kittens know how to put them away." He ran his thumb along the back of Dimitri's ear, Dimitri's head automatically leaning into his touch.

Just for a moment, their eyes met. Dimitri became acutely aware of every place they touched: his hand in Rayner's, Rayner's fingers curled around his head, something dark and earthy in his nose.

Rayner's lips parted.

And a jolt raced down Dimitri's spine at the clatter of footsteps above, Cadmus and Rois calling greetings.

"Looks like the captain is here," Rayner said, jerking his gaze to the side. He let his hands fall away, Dimitri realizing he'd been holding his breath.

"We"—Dimitri cleared his throat—"we should probably get up there."

Rayner nodded. Rising to his feet, he offered Dimitri a hand up, the two dusting the black sand from their clothes before ascending the jagged slope.

By the time they reached the top, Rayner's expression was perfectly composed. But Dimitri's attention lingered on him as his dark eyes swept over the three newcomers standing at attention a dozen feet away, their horses obediently waiting nearby with reins dangling.

The soldiers wore orange-and-gray military jackets, the short, black-haired woman on the left and lean, square-jawed man on the right standing a pace behind the central woman. Her golden hair was braided over her shoulder, her large, light brown eyes almost childlike. But the crescent-shaped scar along her right cheekbone was anything but.

Rayner came forward to greet the group, Rois deep in conversation with the woman on the left. Dimitri made to follow, but Cadmus stopped him with a hand on his shoulder a few feet back.

"Be careful with Rayner," he said, his voice low enough the rest couldn't hear.

Dimitri's eyebrows shot up. "What do you mean?"

"The fire sprites overheard you two talking after your first training session about Rayner's identity—don't protest, they were right to inform me. Because people like him? They don't change."

The sentiment slithered through Dimitri's insides. Cadmus, clearly not expecting him to have a response, reached into his jacket pocket.

"See this?" He lifted a small phoenix charm for Dimitri to see, the copper flashing in the light. "This charm holds my twelve-year-old sister's ashes. My closest friend gave it to me when she was bleeding out on the safehouse floor after she was attacked by Sun soldiers. All because Deardryn invaded my kingdom so she could lure Analia out of hiding and *torture* her. *That's* what people like Rayner do. And you'd be a fool to forget it."

Dimitri couldn't force himself to breathe. He stared into Cadmus's hard blue eyes, his mind frozen and spinning all at once.

"Rayner is on our side," he managed.

Cadmus's lip curled. "For now."

The words hit Dimitri like a kick to the gut.

Pocketing his charm once more, Cadmus turned to go. "Everyone's waiting."

Dimitri didn't remember telling his legs to move. But he followed Cadmus over to the rest of the group in a daze, unable to pay attention as Cadmus introduced everyone and immediately launched into discussion. All he knew was the horror that tingled through his veins.

He didn't know when he'd started letting Rayner back in—he hadn't made the conscious decision to do so. But somehow, in between letting his anger go back at Aaron's house and their moment back in the sand, those walls he had constructed had opened up, as natural as flower petals under the sun.

And the worst part was, Dimitri liked it.

But was he wrong for feeling that way? He'd thought it was a sign of growth from both him and Rayner, but could it have been the opposite? Could he be falling back into the same cycle as before?

No, Rayner had changed, he was trying. But was Dimitri not supposed to forgive him regardless? Crystal spare him, he didn't know how any of this worked. And the more he tried to figure it out, the faster his thoughts spun, his hands starting to shake as he stuffed them in his jacket pockets. Still wrapped in Rayner's shirt cuffs—Crystal strike it all.

"Dimitri?" Cadmus asked.

Dimitri jolted from his thoughts, his eyes darting around the group. He had no idea what they'd been talking about, let alone for how long. He hadn't even noticed when they'd all moved to sit on the nearby cluster of boulders.

"Yes?" he asked tentatively.

Cadmus looked at him as if wondering if he'd hit his head during his fall. "Would you like to tell Captain Lynne and her guards what you've been up to?"

Yes, he was there to vouch for Cadmus. And based on the look on Lynne's face, his credibility was rapidly slipping. He ran his tongue along his dry mouth, his stomach twisting tighter, tighter, tighter.

But he wasn't in the position where he could spiral. If he couldn't pull himself out of it, he would have to work around it.

"Right." Dimitri tried to straighten on his boulder, his hands still shaking where they hid in his pockets. "I've been fucking with Othin's plans for a little over a month now. Everything from stealing information, to redirecting his attention, to stalling his efforts."

Dimitri's fists clenched at how halting his words were. But across from him, Lynne nodded, drawing a knee to her chest.

"Are there specifics you can share?" she asked.

Yes, there certainly were. And not giving the spiral time to take over, he began.

The longer he talked, the smoother his words became, his attention slowly dragging away from the knot in his stomach. Every now and again, Rayner elaborated on something Dimitri said, Dimitri carefully not looking at him on the boulder beside his. He just kept talking, eventually letting Rayner take over to explain how he'd been changing his appearance to spy on both the Sun and Ash people in the castle.

"The Sun soldiers are starting to turn on Othin," he said. "They're not enjoying being subject to his unreasonable whims. The Ash citizens, however, are becoming hopeful."

"All because of your schemes?" Lynne asked, intrigued as she picked at the toe of her boot.

"Othin's easy to manipulate once you know him," Dimitri said. "Deardryn kept him so far removed from rule back in the Sun Kingdom that all he knows is what he *wants* to do, which is usually the most brute-force way forward. So, if you find a way to spin some positive outcomes while conveniently not mentioning all the ways it could go wrong?"

"It's just a matter of setting him loose," Rayner finished.

The square-jawed man seated across from Dimitri toyed with the dagger through his belt. "I've heard that he's been threatening the soldiers and their families in the central kingdom not to get involved."

"That's part of our plan," Cadmus said, perfectly cool on Dimitri's other side. "We've sent Ash Royals to their homes to act as decoys. With Othin's control over the central kingdom, the danger to those soldiers and their families outweighs the reward of recruiting them. So, we've told them to cooperate with Othin. Othin then gets to think he's stomped out our army, we get to continue building outside of the central kingdom, and hopefully, those citizens are safer now that Othin thinks he has them under control."

Lynne nodded slowly. For a few minutes longer, she and her soldiers went back and forth with Cadmus, Dimitri sagging as he was let off the hook.

After what felt like an eternity to the knot in Dimitri's stomach, the three soldiers turned to one another in a silent conversation. Finally, Lynne turned back to Cadmus.

"The reward appears to outweigh the risk to my soldiers," she told him, bowing her head. "We will join your army, Your Majesty."

Dimitri nearly slid off his boulder in relief. He wrapped his arms around his middle as the group rose, Rois coming forward to help coordinate their forces.

"You all right?"

Dimitri jumped as Rayner touched his arm, his insides ripping apart as he wanted to lean into his touch, but not knowing if he should. He nodded jerkily. And the line between Rayner's brows said he didn't believe him.

But he *would* be all right. He'd made it through that conversation. Their army was building.

Dimitri touched his enka bracelet as Cadmus and Rois returned, Cadmus offering his hands. He just had to make it through the day. Then, he could get his answers.

Chapter 71

The rest of Dimitri's day was uneventful. Even after his plan was set, he couldn't stop his jitters, Rayner thankfully taking that as a sign he should leave Dimitri alone.

By the time the sky had darkened outside their chamber window, Dimitri was worried he was too wound up to fall asleep. But either the gods or the Crystal had pity on him, for one moment he squeezed his eyes shut in his dimly lit chamber, and the next, his eyes blinked open in the aisle of books leading to the book nook. And waiting for him a few feet ahead...

"Did it work?" Dimitri asked tentatively.

"That or you have extremely vivid dreams." Analia came toward him, wearing a black-and-silver jacket he didn't recognize. But that was her phoenix pin against her chest. And there was no denying it was her as she offered her hands, Dimitri allowing her to squeeze his own.

"So, Flashfire," he said, tension melting from his shoulders, "you really mastered Sylas's magic, huh?"

"Mastered might be a stretch," she said, leading him toward the book nook. "Although, after Laness told me the gist of everything going on, I thought I'd test how far my skills can go."

"What do you..." Dimitri began, the magic of the nook's entrance tingling over his skin. Then, his eyes widened.

Aaron, Sabi, and Patryclas lounged on Sabi's large red floor pillows. The three didn't seem to notice as he and Analia entered, Sabi's words coming at top speed as she scrutinized Aaron across from her. Gods, the nook even smelled like ink and lavender, just as he remembered.

Dimitri turned to a smiling Analia, awestruck. "How did you do this?"

"I went one by one. These dreams aren't set in someone's mind, but a bridge in between. So, I made bridges upon bridges."

Dimitri shook his head, at a loss for words. Sabi, meanwhile, had plenty.

"I can't believe you're a Star Royal," she said, bracing her hands on the floor and leaning toward Aaron. "So many history books are now erroneous because of you. How does it feel to know you've invalidated countless historians?"

Aaron toyed with the corner of his pillow, looking like he was trying incredibly hard not to smirk. "I like to think of it as subverting expectations."

Sabi huffed a laugh, surprisingly unperturbed by all her inaccurate information. "Well, you certainly have the pride of a Royal. That, and you're too pretty not to be one."

Aaron looked like a child given the gift he'd always dreamed of.

"Oh gods, Sabi, you can't tell him that," Dimitri groaned, coming to take the pillow beside hers. "He's barely tolerable as is."

Sabi looked up, her expression brightening as she finally noticed him. Aaron, meanwhile, turned to Analia.

"Anna," he whined, "Dima's trying to take my compliment."

"Don't worry," Analia said, coming to join him on his pillow. "You're very pretty, no matter what he says."

"See, why did that sound sarcastic?" Aaron turned to Patryclas, feigning a pout. "Patryclas, was that sarcastic?"

Patryclas sat quietly in between Sabi and Aaron, looking like a spectator at a highly entertaining performance. "No, Aaron," he said, struggling for composure. "She thinks you're very pretty."

Aaron made an unconvinced noise. Fighting back a laugh, Analia slid an arm around his neck and whispered something in his ear. And Aaron's answering grin had Dimitri certain he was content not knowing what she said.

Patryclas's green eyes sparkled as they met Dimitri's. He leaned forward to give his knee a squeeze, Sabi squinting at Analia and Aaron the way she always did before saying something she probably shouldn't.

"Now that we're all here," Patryclas said, clocking Sabi's expression, "perhaps Dimitri can tell us what's going on."

The rest of the group looked over at Dimitri, some expressions sobering noticeably easier than others. But Dimitri liked it. He needed smiles and laughter and stupid banter after the day he'd had. Still, it took him a moment to find his words.

"Well," he said, settling back against his pillow, "I really wasn't expecting to get to talk with all of you."

Aaron slid his arm around Analia's shoulders, looking prouder than if he'd pulled off the assembly himself. Dimitri didn't expect the deep, rolling ache down his body at that. But it certainly helped put him on track.

"I want to talk about your brother," he said, pointing at Analia.

Analia's brow twitched up. "How is he?"

"Cynical and mean."

With that, he launched into everything that had happened between himself and Rayner leading up to his conversation with Cadmus. The four listened intently as he talked, Patryclas rubbing his chest in the same spot Dimitri's ached, but he didn't take it away without permission. Beside him, Sabi looked like she was about to explode with questions, but remarkably, she kept her mouth shut. And all throughout his story, Aaron and Analia traded quiet looks that had Dimitri certain he was either reading the situation accurately, or utterly wrong.

"And I don't know what to do," he finished, the amount of time he'd been speaking having nothing to do with the scratchiness in his throat. "I don't know what actions are supposed to be forgiven and which aren't, or how much you can expect people to change, or anything else."

Patryclas rested a finger against his lips, deep in thought. Sabi, however, exploded the moment he was done.

"He finally apologized to you?" she demanded.

Dimitri shrank back into his pillow. "He did. And it was a good one."

"Well, it's about time," Sabi huffed, throwing up her hands.

Dimitri didn't know why her reaction irked him. "Does that mean you think I'm not supposed to forgive him?"

"Well, I wouldn't go *that* far. If there are rules to when you should and shouldn't forgive someone, I haven't read them."

She looked at Patryclas for confirmation.

"No," he said, running a hand down Sabi's dark curls. "There are no rules to forgiveness."

"Do you believe his apology?" Aaron asked curiously.

Dimitri's response was immediate and true. "Yes. But now Cadmus has me thinking I'm making a mistake because look how nice and thoughtful Deardryn can come off when she wants to."

Sabi's face twisted in a glower. But it was Patryclas's almost imperceptible flinch that hurt.

Dimitri dropped his gaze to the carpet, tracing the toe of his boot through the thick gray fibers. "I just... I don't want to fall into the same trap again." There were more words, words on everything he was afraid to lose, but he couldn't bring himself to speak them aloud. Instead, he looked over at Analia, thoughtfully playing with Aaron's fingers. "You're surprisingly quiet," he commented.

Analia shrugged. "I'm just thinking about how I last saw you two. You were so hurt and angry. I was ready to singe him for you."

Aaron and Sabi made identical noises of appreciation. Analia patted Aaron's head to quiet him, her lips twitching. Turning back to Dimitri, she said, "I'm just wondering where all of that went."

Honestly, so was he. He chewed on his thumbnail, trying to find the moment he let it all go. But there wasn't one.

"It just... faded." Dimitri shifted, trying to find the words. "Aaron and I talked about how you two gave me a chance back in Sun, and how I stepped up, so I decided to give that chance to Rayner. And he kept stepping up. He helped me, didn't betray me when he had the chance, explained to me why he did what he did and how he was going to change. But most of all, I got tired of being angry."

Dimitri wasn't expecting that last part. He rose to his feet, going to straighten the books on the nearest bookcase.

"I don't like being angry," he mumbled, acutely aware of the eyes on his back. "I've been angry for so long, and it hurts."

"Like you're killing yourself from the inside out," Analia murmured.

Dimitri glanced back in time to see Aaron pull her closer, Analia leaning into him as he kissed her temple. And it finally sunk in that those two had found a new rhythm. One that didn't involve him.

He expected the realization to hurt. Instead, it sent his mind back to that morning in the sand with Rayner. Because that softened, adoring look in Aaron's eyes was the same look Rayner had given Dimitri. As if he saw all of the broken pieces Dimitri was juggling and wanted nothing more than to take them away. Hold on to them for as long as Dimitri needed.

"It's more than that," he said, his skin warming as he turned back to the books. "I didn't want to be angry with *him* anymore. I still remember what he did, and I don't think it was right, but I also understand why he did it. What I don't know is if that's supposed to change anything."

"This isn't a right or wrong question, Dima," Patryclas said. "There's no universal rule or truth to follow. There's just how you feel."

"You can read my emotions," Dimitri muttered. "You tell me what I'm feeling."

"That's not how this works and you know it."

Dimitri made a face, his insides squirming. Because he had a lot of feelings. Some he didn't recognize, didn't want to name.

"Do you forgive him?" Sabi asked.

Dimitri snapped out of his thoughts and pivoted on his heel. "What?"

"We keep talking about anger and hurt and whatever, but it seems like the straightforward question is whether or not you forgive him."

"That's what I'm trying to figure out," Dimitri whined.

"Technically," Aaron said, "you've been trying to figure out if you're *supposed* to forgive him, which is irrelevant."

Dimitri grumbled under his breath, their collective gazes having him wanting to turn back to the books and hide. But Patryclas caught his eye, his smile feeling like solid ground.

"Ignoring everything Cadmus said," he said, "have you forgiven Rayner?"

The book nook went quiet. Dimitri reached behind him to fiddle with a book cover, the question tingling along the back of his neck. Because he didn't have an answer. And he had no idea what to make of the jumbled emotions as a result.

"I don't know," he finally said on an exhale.

"Which means you haven't," said Patryclas. "Not completely, at least."

Those words hit him harder than they should have. He opened his mouth to protest, but all he could hear was Rayner's voice whispering through his mind. *I won't choose your life over mine.*

Gods, how had everything become such a mess? He slumped back to his cushion, the brush of Analia's fingers along his ankle as he passed having the back of his throat burning.

"So, what do I do?" he asked, hugging his knees to his chest.

Sabi, Analia, and Aaron traded uncertain looks. But Patryclas maintained his perfect posture, his finger returning to his lips.

"I think," he said, "forgiveness is the most painful process a person can go through. When someone wrongs us, it's easy to be angry with them. It's hard to realize that we're actually hurt. And it's devastating to realize we're hurt because we've lost something we will never get back.

"To me, forgiveness means letting something die. And while feeling that grief is unimaginable, the hope of finding something better in that forgiveness makes it worth it. So, this isn't a question of should or shouldn't. You have to decide if that grief is worth it."

Patryclas stretched out his booted foot, resting it against Dimitri's. And Dimitri clung to that point of contact as his world rumbled beneath his feet.

He wasn't sure why. After all, Rayner had asked if they could start over back in his Starlight bedroom. They'd found their own rhythm.

But reaching for it was starting to feel like twisting a knife in his gut.

Dimitri rubbed his eyes, then looked over at a fidgeting Sabi. "Do you forgive him?"

"Me?" Sabi's eyebrows shot up. "Well, I've forgiven him for the wrongs he's done to me. But whether or not I forgive him for what he did to you is up to you."

Aaron hummed, seeming to enjoy that approach. Turning to Analia, he said, "We don't forgive Iphen, in case you were wondering."

Analia let out a startled laugh, then immediately elbowed him. "Not the time, Aaron."

But despite all odds, Dimitri's lips stretched in a tired smile. Laness and Branten had filled him in on that situation. And while it wasn't much, it was just enough to have him able to think around that dark wave rising up inside him.

"I have to think about it," he decided.

"I think that's perfectly acceptable," Patryclas told him.

Dimitri nodded, feeling a little more grounded in the next steps he had to take. He looked up from his fidgeting fingers, his response cutting off as he noticed the blur around Aaron. Aaron, following Dimitri's gaze, let out a curse.

"Why am I always the first to wake up?" he complained. Shaking his head, he looked back at Dimitri, the red pillow visible through his chest. "Whatever you decide, we're behind you. Housing or burial arrangements can be made at any time."

Patryclas cleared his throat. But Aaron was already gone.

Analia's expression dimmed, her hand coming to rest on the pillow where Aaron had reclined. "The rest of our connections are still strong if you want to keep going," she offered.

"Yes," Dimitri sighed, slumping back against his pillow. "But let's talk about anything other than Rayner."

Sabi sat up straight, her moment having finally arrived. For the next several minutes, she regaled them with all of the interesting facts from the books she'd been reading, eventually letting Analia and Patryclas have a turn to tell a few stories of their own. All casual. Nothing about wars or evil queens or traitorous friends, the fist squeezing Dimitri's throat starting to relax.

He might not know what to do about Rayner, but at least he felt comfortable trusting his own judgment.

Eventually, Sabi's image started to fade, quickly followed by Patryclas. Just before he disappeared, he pressed a kiss to the top of Dimitri's head, Analia smiling as they were left alone.

"I'm probably going in a second," she said, rising from her pillow with a stretch. "Keep an eye on Cadmus for me, all right?"

Dimitri nodded. He rose as well, reaching for Analia before she could even open her arms. She sighed, resting her head against his shoulder, her arms tight around him.

"You'll figure it out," she promised.

Dimitri nodded and closed his eyes. And when he finally opened them once more, he was back in his chambers. And he had a decision to make.

Chapter 72

Analia woke with a splash. Her eyes snapped open, lukewarm water sloshing around her flailing limbs as she struggled to process what was going on.

Somehow, she'd ended up in her tub. Steam hissed up from the rapidly rising water, Aaron's hand cradling the back of her head to keep her face above the surface. She looked over at him kneeling beside the tub, water still burbling from the faucet.

"What's going on?" she spluttered.

Aaron watched her closely, the corners of his eyes tight. "How do you feel?" he asked.

"Confused as to why I'm in the tub."

Aaron cracked a smile, the dim light casting shadows across the relaxing muscles in his shoulders. "Well, that certainly sounds like you."

He rested the back of his free hand against her forehead, his skin pleasantly cool. Now that she thought about it, her body was uncomfortably warm. And how was there steam when the water was nowhere near hot enough?

Analia frowned. She reached behind her, her suspicions confirmed as the icy water from the faucet spilled over her fingers.

"I'm burning," she informed him.

"Believe it or not, you're much cooler than you were a minute ago."

"Really?" Analia sat up, Aaron's hand tightening around the back of her head like he was reluctant to let her move. But he settled on a shrug.

"Turns out," he said, fingers skimming down to her bare shoulder, "I woke up first because of the heat radiating off of you. It wasn't terrible at first, but you kept getting hotter. So, I started the tub just in case. And good thing I did."

He squeezed her shoulder, Analia turning over the new information. The only other times she overheated like that was when doing Aaron's radiating magic technique, and when she'd released her magic to find the damper in the Human Kingdom. And if it happened while she was asleep...

"I wonder if to access Sylas's magic, I subconsciously tried to burn through all my flames first," she mused.

"Well," Aaron said, "you *did* say all the times you accidentally summoned other Blessings was when you were upset—which usually means you were exceedingly warm."

Analia flicked some water at him. Aaron dodged, then lightly tugged her hair. For a moment, the two shared a grin, Analia's smile softening as her eyes scanned over his face.

"Were you worried?" she asked.

To her surprise, Aaron's smile turned crooked. "I'm appalled to report I've become accustomed to you worrying me."

"That's probably for the best," she mumbled.

Aaron laughed. And the tension behind Analia's collarbones relaxed as she found no mask, no careful control obscuring his expression. Just a quiet curiosity, his network a gentle glide across her senses.

"I also think," he said, playing with her hair, "exploring your new self-combusting tendency can wait until the morning."

"Fair enough." Analia drew her fingers through the now pleasantly warm water, her gaze finding its way back to Aaron's face. Down to his mouth. The flexing muscles in his arms and shoulders as he shifted against the ledge. "You know," she said, drawing out the words. "Since we're already here..."

She looked up at him through her lashes. Aaron arched a brow, something like hunger sparking in his eyes. "Again?"

"Why not? We're already awake, and the water's warm now—"

Analia broke off with a laugh as Aaron kissed her, water splashing as he climbed in to join her.

Analia woke later that morning already turning over thoughts on her accidental overheating. Aaron sleepily convinced her to eat before diving into any experiments, which she reluctantly agreed to. But as soon as both their plates were cleared, she took his hand and towed him out the back door.

"Why are we going here?" Aaron asked, rubbing his eyes as she led him through the birch grove.

"Because," she said, "I'm not sure how the second part of my plan will go, and I figured it was best we keep it away from the public."

"How reassuring."

"Have I mentioned how beautiful your eyes look with that jacket?"

Aaron looked down at his black-and-blue jacket with a smile. Then, he frowned. Just for the corners of his mouth to creep up again. "Well played, my shooting star."

"It's still true." Pausing at the top of the hollow, Analia turned to kiss the corner of his mouth. And she loved the sparkle in his eyes as she led him down the grassy slope.

"All right," he said, plopping down on his usual patch of moss. "What's first?"

"That's the easy part." Analia pulled the Crystal's casing from her pocket, placing it on their small wooden table. "All we're doing is seeing if I overheat while using Sylas's magic awake."

Aaron sat up as Analia came to crouch at his feet, his head cocking as she nudged his legs apart. But he had no complaints as she shifted to sit between his thighs, settling back against his chest.

"So far, I like this plan," he said, sliding his arms around her waist.

"I thought you would," Analia laughed. "All you have to do is let me know if I get warmer."

Aaron nodded, shifting her against him. He slipped his hand beneath her shirt, warm fingers trailing up her stomach to her ribs.

"Aaron," Analia complained, twisting to look at him.

"What?" he asked innocently. "I'm being meticulous." He kissed her nose. "For research." He kissed her chin, and Analia's composure cracked.

"You bounce out of your moods impressively fast," she informed him.

"Give it time, I haven't heard the second part of your plan yet." Aaron nuzzled her cheek. Then, he nudged her forward once more, resting his head against hers to watch.

Analia smiled to herself, not having noticed her own apprehension until it was drifting away. Then, seeing no reason to stall, she reached for her magic.

As usual, the first thing she encountered was her flames. They rose up to meet her, their heat flickering across her mental hand. But the rest of her magic was deeper, beyond the well in the cavern below, spreading so wide and deep she didn't immediately encounter any.

But she knew the melody of the shadows. Soft and low, like the promise of distant thunder. And asleep or not, her training had paid off, for as she lifted her hand, a thin ribbon of shadows laced between her fingers.

"Well done," Aaron murmured.

"Am I warmer?" she asked, unable to tell with the icy shadows across her hand and the warmth of Aaron's chest at her back.

"Barely." Aaron's fingers traced her ribs, his voice softening into something thoughtful. "I don't think I would have noticed if I wasn't already touching you. It's also so slow I might be mistaken, but you seem to still be getting warmer."

"Huh." Analia played with her ribbon of shadows, Aaron's free hand coming up to poke it like a curious cat. "It would make sense that my temperature is still increasing," she decided. "When I reach for this magic, I have to drag it up through my flames, so maybe some of that magic is getting released in the process."

"Well," Aaron mused, "you were holding that dream for a long time last night before you reached dangerous levels. Seems like these extra Blessings come with a limit." He paused. "Can you summon my magic?"

Analia let her shadows wink out, intrigued. "Let's find out."

She settled back against his chest, closing her eyes. In theory, summoning his magic should have been easier than Sylas's. She knew the cool, silken melody like her own reflection, not having to think before it was playing through her mind. Yet, the more she tried to focus on Aaron's magic, the more her attention was drawn to the quiet network behind her.

She tried to block it out, her thoughts trained on her reaching mental hand. But after a few moments, she realized they had wandered back to Aaron.

"I don't think I can do it with you here," she finally said, opening her eyes. "My attention keeps going to your network instead of my own. Even if you weren't here, though, I associate it with you so much."

She shook her head. Aaron didn't seem perturbed by this. If anything, he appeared pleased as she twisted to look at him.

"Are you saying you find me distracting?" he crooned, tracing soft, lazy circles along her stomach.

A low, rolling heat stirred in Analia's veins. "I do." She trailed her fingertips along his jaw. "In fact, I think you're trying your hardest to distract me from the second part of my plan."

Aaron's hum vibrated through his chest and into her bones. "Do you think I can distract you a little longer if I list all the reasons it's probably best you can't summon my magic?"

"You can. But you'll be prolonging the inevitable."

Aaron's darkened gaze lifted over her head, undoubtedly landing on the table where the Crystal's magic field softly pulsed. He bit the inside of his cheek, considering. Then, he sighed.

"Fine. Tell me your plan so we can see just how accustomed to my worry I've become."

Analia dragged her attention away from his fingers still resting against her skin. "I love you," she offered.

"Uh-huh." He pinched her nipple, Analia hissing at the sudden spark of pleasure. Aaron chuckled, clearly pleased with himself as he shooed her to her feet.

Analia muttered under her breath as she crossed to the table, her mood instantly sobering as the Crystal's magic field slithered across her senses.

But she knew how to manage this magic. She could do this. And she hoped she had enough control to pull back if she couldn't.

"I've been thinking about Deardryn's research," she said, scooping up the Crystal's casing. "The whole point of getting me comfortable with the Crystal's magic was so I could use it to track the other shards. And now that I've built up my tolerance and we have a semblance of clues, I thought now's as good a time as any to try."

She turned to face Aaron, who'd shifted to sit with legs crossed. And all he said was, "Sounds risky."

"You seem to be taking it reasonably well," she commented, coming to sit on the cushy moss across from him.

"I trust you," he said simply.

Analia was surprisingly touched by that. She looked down at the rough gray rock in her hands, running a finger along the central crack.

"Watch my back?" she asked.

"Always." Aaron slid his hands under hers, Analia scooting closer so their knees touched.

Then, not giving herself time to second guess, she opened the casing.

Light erupted from the crack. Aaron's hands tightened around hers as the magic slammed into them, Analia's flames crackling in response. But her shield was already in place, her attention trained on Aaron's calloused fingers, his knees pressed against hers, the magic screaming in the background.

It had only been a week since the last releasing of buildup in the council room. This was nothing.

Sure enough, it barely took a minute for the light to fade away, Aaron's jaw still tight.

Now, her plan began.

Analia curled her fingers around the Crystal's smooth face, reaching a mental hand toward its magic. The same way she had reached for the casing to open it in Accalon's chambers.

And the moment she made contact, her entire being was yanked from her body by bright, white light.

Raw, unrestrained power coursed through her awareness like lightning through a storm cloud. She couldn't feel Aaron's hands, the ground beneath her, couldn't even hear the chirping of waking birds. All there was was a wrath that could have crushed her into powder.

It was the power of kings, of gods. It was a power that had built a world, just to topple it and start anew. It was *limitless.*

Yet, it had been spurned, shattered and locked away. As if it could be controlled. Forgotten.

Analia thrashed, trying to pull away. But the magic snarled around her, screaming from all sides. It would show her what they'd thought to imprison, what magic she dared to reach for.

Crystal spare her, it was too much. She had to find her way out. But there were too many melodies. Blaring, screaming, shuddering through her.

All except one.

It was so quiet, she almost couldn't make it out through the chaos as it brushed along the edge of her awareness.

Come back to me.

Instinctually, Analia reached for it, the Crystal's magic trying to drag her back. But Analia followed the melody.

Soft. Coaxing. Leading her home.

Come back to me.

Analia strained to block out the noise, the ground resolidifying beneath her. Hands cradling her face, thumbs moving back and forth along her cheekbones.

"Come back to me," Aaron whispered.

The magic screamed. But with a final yank, Analia pulled away.

Analia gasped. Her eyes flew open, needing several moments to register her surroundings, finding Aaron's face inches from hers. Calm. Steady as he watched her. Grounding her back in her body.

"There you are," he murmured. He brushed a kiss to her mouth, Analia trembling in his grip. Because the magic still slithered across her senses.

Wordlessly, she offered Aaron her hands. He looked down, his thumbs pausing their paths along her cheekbones. Then, releasing her with one hand, he took the Crystal, closed the casing, and tossed it to the opposite end of the hollow. And the moment the magic was silenced, Analia slumped forward.

Aaron murmured something as he caught her. He pulled her onto his lap, their limbs tangling as Analia buried her face in his chest.

He was solid. So wonderfully, peacefully solid.

"Are you all right?" he asked gently.

Analia nodded.

Aaron paused. "I'm assuming that didn't go as planned."

Analia shook her head.

Aaron sighed and kissed the top of her head. "Someday, things will be easy for us."

"One can dream," Analia mumbled.

Aaron chuckled, his hand tracing long, soothing lines along her spine. Analia curled her fingers into the back of his jacket, her thoughts starting to reorganize. But even as she processed what had just happened, she had no ideas as to how she could have prevented it. Nor did she have the energy to figure it out. She only snuggled into Aaron, who seemed lost in his own thoughts.

She didn't know how long it was before their quiet was interrupted by footsteps crunching toward the hollow. Analia felt Aaron look up, but she stayed where she was as his muscles remained relaxed.

"Is she all right?" Ember asked, her voice descending into the hollow.

"She's fine," Aaron promised. "Might be ready for a nap, though."

"We were all the way across the grove when we felt the Crystal's magic," came Branten's voice from nearby. "At least, I'm assuming that's what that was."

Right. Branten and Ember hadn't finished their run when Analia and Aaron had come out. Aaron quickly filled the two in on what they'd been doing, Analia finally disentangling herself and sitting up to look at them.

"Well," Branten said from where he perched on their table, "at least one of your tests went well."

"I don't blame you for hating this thing, Anna," Ember said, scratching her healer markings as she retrieved the discarded Crystal from the moss. "Every time I'm near it I get a headache."

Analia blinked, something important struggling to rise to the surface of her mind. But Aaron had gone perfectly still behind her.

"Headache, or does it make your markings itch?" he asked.

Ember paused, her head cocked. "Both, why?"

"Because you were scratching your markings the last time you were around it as well," Aaron said.

Analia and Branten shared a look, Ember's jaw going slack.

But Aaron was unnervingly calm as he said, "Em, what exactly happens when you get those rings?"

Chapter 73

Dimitri sat on the bench on Analia's turret, the dawn sky lightening above his head as he practiced his magic.

Even though he could have gotten a few more hours of sleep after his dream with Analia and the others, he couldn't force his mind to settle. Yet, when he'd dragged himself out of bed and up to the turret, he was no closer to figuring out what he wanted to do about Rayner. So, he practiced his magic instead.

During his last few training sessions with Tyce, he'd finally gotten the hang of summoning his magic to each of his fingers, slowly building it up to a flare, then bringing it back down. Now, he attempted a level higher: dual hands. He squinted down at his fingers resting on his knees, needing several seconds to coordinate the releases to both of his pinkies.

For the longest time, he'd viewed his magic like an enemy. It was something to stifle, not control. But the more he trained, the more he saw the potential in Rayner's original analysis. Not only could he help people, but maybe, the more he helped, the more worthy he could become of that woman's sacrifice. Which meant he had to get this right.

"There you are."

Dimitri's heart skipped a beat, his magic winking out as Rayner pulled himself onto the roof. He wore a rich, dark purple jacket with shiny gold buttons, his mahogany hair mussed as if he'd just woken up.

"What are you doing up here?" Dimitri asked, his attention lingering on the flecks of gold around Rayner's pupils.

"Looking for you. I woke up and you were gone." Rayner came to join him on the bench, Dimitri neither leaning into him nor away. "Has Tyce canceled your training this morning?"

"No, it's still happening after breakfast. I just woke up and couldn't fall back asleep."

All of that was true. But it was the unspoken reason why that had Dimitri's stealing a look at Rayner, his eyes lingering on his full mouth, slightly thinner compared to their months in Moon. Just as the waves in his hair were more defined.

He doubted most people would notice the changes, but he did. Just as he noticed that despite Rayner's kindness in the Moon Kingdom, he'd kept his distance.

But now, he could feel how that wall—that oath—had crumbled. He'd proved Dimitri could trust him. But was that enough to forgive him?

"Beautiful," Rayner murmured.

Dimitri's heart jolted. Rayner didn't seem to notice as he continued watching Dimitri's hands, golden light softly pulsing along his middle fingers. And Dimitri had no explanation for his prick of disappointment.

"Thanks," he mumbled, his ears burning.

"You've really developed a deft control over your magic."

The words were complimentary. But something in Rayner's tone had Dimitri giving him a sidelong look.

"Why do I sense a 'but' coming?" he asked.

Rayner smiled to himself. He straightened Dimitri's collar, tingles running down Dimitri's spine as his warm fingers brushed the side of his neck.

"You've been training so hard," Rayner said. "I have no doubt you'll save so many lives. I just worry about what will happen when you inevitably lose someone."

Of all responses, Dimitri wasn't expecting that. He opened his mouth, just to clear his throat as Rayner's gaze finally lifted to his, the earnestness there having his words die on his tongue. Gods, what was the matter with him?

"I'm not thinking about that right now," he rasped, forcing his attention to the sunlight glowing to life on his forefingers. "I can't let that fear get in my way."

"Why?" Rayner asked, soft as the magic pulsing across Dimitri's fingers.

"Because I need to be worthy."

They were such simple words. Small ones, even. But the weight they pressed along Dimitri's shoulders was indescribable.

He shifted on the bench, watching the understanding unfold across Rayner's face. And the heartbreak that followed had Dimitri's own heart squeezing.

"Oh, Dima." Rayner rested his fingers over Dimitri's, gently smothering his magic. "Your worthiness doesn't come from your record. It comes from your effort. I think many would argue that means you're already more than worthy."

Tears pricked behind Dimitri's eyes. But just like the ache in his heart, they weren't bad. They were born from something delicate, unfamiliar, that had taken root in his chest, tentatively starting to unfurl.

He looked up at Rayner, his voice surprisingly small. "Promise?"

Rayner didn't miss a beat. "Promise."

Finally, some of that weight slipped from Dimitri's shoulders. He sat back against the bench, the cool morning breeze ruffling his hair. But his attention remained locked on the fingers Rayner still rested over his own.

"Since I made you a promise," Rayner murmured, fingertips shifting down to trace the lines in Dimitri's palms, "does that mean you'll make me one?"

Dimitri nodded, not having to think twice.

"Promise me when your record is broken that you'll forgive yourself."

Magic stuttered across Dimitri's fingers. "Shouldn't I promise you that when it happens?" he asked.

"Maybe. But there's something about deciding to do it beforehand that makes it easier to go through with."

Dimitri didn't doubt that. But something about making a promise that involved him failing in the worst possible way had his insides squirming.

Rayner shifted, his knee lightly pressing against Dimitri's. And somehow, the single word rolled past Dimitri's lips. "Promise."

Rayner's answering smile had that word settling comfortably in his chest.

"I'm still going to train, though," he said, unable to help himself.

"I'd expect nothing less," Rayner replied.

He lightly tugged on Dimitri's sleeve. Then, he pulled his hand away and sat back against the bench.

Dimitri looked down at his hands, now cold and empty, having the strangest urge to offer them back to Rayner. He wanted to feel Rayner's hands, elegant as a painter's, around his once more, feel the path of his fingers exploring his skin.

He didn't understand it. He felt stupid because of it. After all, it was just a touch. But somehow, every touch from Rayner seemed to put a piece of him back together again. And every piece he regained reached for Rayner in return.

Rayner, oblivious to Dimitri's turmoil, reached into his jacket pocket, pulling out the book with the mossy green cover Dimitri hadn't seen since their fight on Aaron's roof.

Bracing a booted foot on the bench, he rested the book against his thigh, his attention on the pages as he flipped it open. Leaving Dimitri to go back to his training in peace.

Dimitri bit his cheek. Returning his attention to his hands, he reached for his magic, sliding open the curtains that had sunlight glowing to life on his thumbs.

For a few minutes, the turret remained quiet as Dimitri and Rayner went about their separate tasks. Dimitri continued to flare his magic along his fingers, but the easier it got, the more his gaze drifted to Rayner.

He stared intently down at his book, having retrieved a pen from his pocket at some point. Every now and again, he would flip the page or make a tiny marking, lightly biting the corner of his lower lip as he worked.

He really did have a nice mouth. It was one of the features that Rayner tweaked most often when changing his appearance, and Dimitri wondered why.

Why did he always prefer blue pens like the one he currently held over black ones? Why did he only pick at his breakfast, but always clear his plate at lunch and dinner? Why did he only hum to himself when he thought he was alone?

"Dima," Rayner said, his gaze still trained on his book. "You're staring at me."

He was, wasn't he? Dimitri's gaze flicked away from Rayner's face, finally noticing the sketch on Rayner's page.

"Did you draw that?" Dimitri asked, scooting closer for a better look.

"I did," Rayner said haltingly, looking like he didn't know if he wanted to angle the book toward Dimitri or away.

Dimitri scooted a little closer, electricity zinging up his arm as it grazed Rayner's. "Can I look?"

"I think you already are."

Dimitri didn't try to deny it as Rayner angled the book toward him. He peered down at the page, taking in the precise lines of the feminine face, from the delicate sweep of her cheekbones to the gentle curve of her heart-shaped lips.

"You're really talented," he said.

"Just a matter of practice," Rayner replied, ducking his head. But Dimitri could have sworn he sounded pleased.

Rayner flipped the page, a tiny thrill running down Dimitri's spine as the movement had him leaning into Rayner a little more. But he kept his gaze on the book, taking in the fully colored replica of a familiar orange-and-gray jacket.

"That's Cadmus's jacket from his reveal," Dimitri said, pointing to the page.

"It is." Rayner skimmed his fingers along the outline of the jacket, his posture relaxing. "I've gotten a feel for general Ash Kingdom appearances, but face shapes, hair colors, and other physical features only go so far."

"So, you're trying to create costumes to complete the disguise," Dimitri said.

"In theory. I have no idea how I would actually create them, but it keeps me busy."

"You've always been interested in the minute details," Dimitri murmured.

Rayner flashed a grin, undoubtedly remembering their first conversation back in his shop. Not waiting for permission, Dimitri flipped the page to another full-color drawing, this time of Aeley's dark gray dress from her confrontation with Othin in the Council Chamber.

"How did you shade that lacy part?" Dimitri asked, careful not to touch the page as he traced the neckline with a finger.

"That took some trial and error." With that, Rayner launched into his explanation of colors and shading, his words starting off uncertain as if unsure how much Dimitri cared. But as soon as he finished, Dimitri had another question ready to go. And another and another and another, Rayner's face lighting up the more he talked, making no move to stop Dimitri as he flipped through sketches.

He'd always known Rayner was talented when it came to designing physical appearances. But it wasn't until then that he realized how gifted he was with clothes as well, just as Surce had mentioned. Down to the sketches themselves. And the more excited Rayner got, the more Dimitri wanted to know, the more he wanted to prolong this moment, the light in Rayner's eyes.

He was the sun. And all Dimitri wanted was to bask in the warm glow of his rays.

By the time they reached the end of Rayner's work, the sun had finally risen in the sky. Dimitri fully leaned against Rayner's side, his fingers itching to flip to the beginning and go through the pages he'd missed. But before he could, Rayner softly closed the book.

"Come on," he said, slipping the book in his jacket pocket. "Breakfast is starting soon."

"Why don't you eat much in the mornings?" Dimitri blurted, so used to asking questions that it popped out without him thinking.

Rayner let out a startled laugh. "Have you been watching me?"

"I think we've already established I'm too interested in other people's business."

Rayner laughed again, the sound smoothing along Dimitri's senses like a balm. "It's because I get nauseous if I eat too close to waking up."

Dimitri nodded to himself, storing yet another fact away. Rayner smiled down at him, close enough his breath wafted over Dimitri's temple, his dark, earthy scent in Dimitri's nose.

But he had no desire to pull away. Because in that moment, he finally had an answer to the question that had sent him up to the roof in the first place: he was an idiot.

It wasn't a matter of *could* he forgive Rayner. He was already on his way. Now, it was his turn to try and get himself over that finish line.

Chapter 74

The last place Analia expected Ember to tell everyone about her healer markings was Surce's dismantled dress shop. Now that the seasons were changing, Surce had to switch her winter inventory for the spring, which was a surprisingly elaborate production for how small her shop was.

"Why does Mortie get to hang things up?" Branten whined, sitting with Aaron and Laness behind a rack of winter gowns needing to be placed in garment bags.

"Because Mor is the most organized out of all of you," Surce replied from a nearby row.

"Don't worry, Branten," Mor said, passing Analia and Ember's row with an armful of spring dresses. "I'm sure you'll graduate to hanging soon. After all, you haven't ripped a dress with its hanger yet."

"That was one time and Surce knows it was an accident," Laness protested, short enough that even on her stool, her head couldn't be seen over the rack.

Analia rubbed her eyes, her lingering exhaustion weighing down her amusement. Aaron hadn't been mistaken when he'd said she probably needed a nap. But more than that, she needed answers to the questions churning through her mind. And if Ember's faraway gaze as she fiddled with the lilac dress she'd hung several minutes ago said anything, she wasn't the only one.

"As much as I'd love to debate dress duties," Analia said, "we might want to get back to the Crystal making Ember's markings itch."

Ember blinked hard at the sound of her name. "Well, that's the thing," she said, returning to hanging the purple gowns draped over her arm. "I've been wracking my brain trying to figure out why that could be happening, but nothing jumps out at me. Even with the new information from Deardryn's notes."

"Was she focusing on the markings?" Aaron asked sharply.

Analia's fingers tightened around a hanger, but Ember shook her head without hesitation. "No more than anything else."

"Perhaps if you share how and why you receive your rings," Surce said, "we might notice something you haven't."

Ember took a breath to respond. Then, she bit her lip and looked away.

"Does that go against your healer's oath?" Analia asked quietly.

After all, there was a reason none of them knew the ritual already: they weren't supposed to. And Ember had already tested that line so many times to help them.

Ember bowed her head, hangers squeaking as she pushed them aside. "I don't even know anymore."

The defeat in her voice had Analia's own heart aching. She moved down the row, intending to touch Ember's shoulder as she shifted the gowns draped over her own arm. Yet, before she could, Ember shook herself off.

"Our rings are used to signify our level of training," she explained, her voice returning to a normal volume. "After you're chosen by Rosala, you kneel at the foot of her statue in your kingdom's Healer Temple and swear to uphold the vows of a healer. Yet, you're not magically bound to that oath until you become a master healer—which was one of the interesting points Deardryn brought up in her notes. That's probably the only reason my markings haven't split."

Ember paused, her mouth momentarily pinching. Analia started to speak, but Ember shook her head and continued.

"Anyway, you then start your official training, and every time you master a specialty, they tattoo a white ring around your eye."

"They?" Surce asked.

"The master healers," Ember clarified, heading for the back of the store to retrieve more gowns to hang. "We all have to take group classes to learn each of the four specialties: internal healing, external, herbology, and medical mysteries. Yet, once you find your specialty, you're also assigned a master healer of that same specialty to help hone those skills. And that's the healer who marks you. So, for me, it was Master Lenzi."

"Is there anything special about the tattoo method or ink?" Mor asked from the row behind Analia.

"Not that I'm aware of. There might be since once you've mastered all four areas of healing, you go to the Temple of Rosala to seal your oath, and your white rings transform into your kingdom's colors. The process isn't shared with apprentices, though, so for all I know, it's just a second layer of ink."

Ember shrugged helplessly, going to help Surce in the black section in front of Analia. Analia hung a lavender-and-silver gown, her mouth turning down.

She'd always assumed her knowledge of the healers had gaps because of the separation. But the fact that the healers were keeping so many secrets within their own ranks?

Analia looked down her row, catching Aaron's eye over his rack of dark gowns. He cocked a brow, the soft melody of his network flickering across her senses in a question.

"Does anyone else get itchy markings?" Laness asked.

"No," Ember said, annoyed. "Anytime I would ask, all I would get is a sneer and suggestion that it's a side effect of being human."

Branten muttered an insult that Analia was certain had Ember smirking.

"The interesting thing," Analia said, heading toward the front of the shop, "is I not only can't sense any magic from your markings, Em, but your network either. I've never been able to sense your magic."

"Really?" Ember's footsteps hurried down her own row, the two coming to meet each other in front of Aaron, Branten, and Laness's rack. "Even when I'm this close to you?"

Analia shook her head.

"Are you able to sense any other healer's magic?" Aaron asked, intrigued.

Analia had to think about that. "I haven't been around many healers since developing my sensory abilities," she finally said. "I briefly saw a Moon healer, but Sylas's network was so loud at the time I couldn't focus on anything else. But I don't remember sensing anything from Sofika, either, when she healed you from the damper blades."

Aaron hummed, pulling another dress free from the rack with a soft rustle.

Mor asked, "Could the magic in the ink block healer magic from being detectable?"

"I don't see how that would be possible," Surce murmured. "Sofika has no rings that could be blocking Analia's abilities. Besides that, the only way I've ever come across blocking a magic network is a damper, and since Ember still has access to her magic…"

Surce shook her head. Analia, however, perked up.

"I was able to detect Aaron's magic when I came in contact with his damper chain," she said.

She extended her hand, Ember nodding her permission, her eyes wide and hopeful. Behind her, Laness poked her head around the rack to watch. And holding her breath, Analia rested her fingers along the three white rings curving around Ember's eye.

For a few moments, the shop was quiet. And Analia wasn't completely surprised when there came no thrum of magic across her senses. She shook her head, Ember's shoulders slumping.

"No matter," Branten said, the same way he'd comment on the weather as he returned to his work.

"Why are you so chipper?" Laness griped, her head disappearing back around the rack.

"Because this doesn't change anything. Even if Anna *could* sense some magic in Ember's rings, we'd still have to steal a sample of the ink to test. Especially since Deardryn's shown interest in the healers."

Analia's stomach lurched.

"You realize you're proposing we break into the Temple of Rosala," Aaron said wryly. He started to unhook a dress from the rack, then paused. Looked at Analia. Back at the dress. "Surce, if I want to buy one of these, can I give you the gold now, or do I have to beg you to release it from storage?"

Analia's eyebrows rose, the gown now hidden behind the rack. Branten leaned over to get a better look.

"Black?" He clicked his tongue. "Brother, you really need to get out of your comfort zone."

"I know," Aaron sighed, "but it does such lovely things to my eyes."

Ember and Laness snickered.

"Set it aside," Surce said, having retrieved her next armful of gowns. "You can pay me later."

Aaron thanked her and slid the gown into a bag. Then, thumping Branten on the side of the head, he rose and headed down the rack, Analia following from the opposite side to steal a peek. But with a wink, Aaron shifted the bag out of her sight and went to place it on the back counter. Analia pouted, returning to her row to hang the last of her dresses.

"I believe," Mor said, his lips twitching as he came to help her, "we were talking about infiltrating Rosala's temple."

"That's not going to work," Ember said, returning to Surce's row. "The temple is warded so only healers can get in, and even then we're only able to enter once a month."

"The day of your monthly gathering?" Analia asked.

Ember nodded. "The next available day isn't for another two weeks. And the healers will be there."

Branten groaned, his head falling back.

"Well, hold on," Aaron said, coming up behind Analia. "Is the ink from your tattoos made in your own kingdoms, or is it sourced from the Temple of Rosala?"

"The latter," Ember said slowly.

Analia's hands froze on the final dress she had to hang. She turned to Aaron, Mor making a thoughtful noise nearby. "Are you suggesting we steal some ink from the Ash Healers' supply?" she asked.

Aaron's eyes sparkled. "That's exactly what I'm suggesting."

Analia's mind raced, already turning over half a dozen plans. But there was one thing she was certain of. "I'll do it."

Aaron's eyebrows shot up. "You will, will you?"

Analia's flames crackled. "We're not sending Ember in and risking her oath," she said, folding her arms. "And if it's not her, I know the Ash Kingdom better than anyone else here, I have the best—why are you grinning at me?"

"You're so fiery." Aaron shook his head admiringly, his grin growing. "Look at you, feet planted, arms folded, chin up. You look like you're about to scorch right through me to get what you want. Do you have any idea how much I had to provoke you in Sun to see even a flicker of this look?"

Analia snorted, her flames retreating slightly. "You've always craved a fiery demise."

"Oh, undoubtedly," Aaron agreed, his fingers skimming along her cheek. "I seem to be horribly unsinged, though, so you're going to have to ramp it up a bit."

Analia tried, but she couldn't suppress her laugh. And Aaron's answering smile told her he'd gotten exactly what he wanted.

"All I was going to say," he said, ruffling her hair, "is it will be risky sending you in with the Sun soldiers already on the lookout for Ash Royals. And I doubt Deardryn will let Laness get away with her rescue technique a third time."

"Not to mention," Ember said, stepping into their row, "no healer will let a Royal waltz into the heart of their school where the ink is stored."

Well, those were good points. Analia bit the inside of her cheek, Aaron and Mor exchanging a thoughtful look.

"I think you all have forgotten a crucial detail," Laness said, pushing gowns apart with a metallic scrape so she could peer through the opening. "We already have people in Ash. And one of them is a masquerader."

Analia had, in fact, forgotten that. She rubbed her face, Mor looking like the only person who had already been considering that as he continued to straighten gowns on their hangers.

"Can you get in contact?" he asked.

"What do you think I've been doing all this time?" Laness sat back on her stool, closing her garment bag with a flourish. "Dima's at the safehouse right now with the others. He says Rayner has an idea, but he'll need time to pull it all together."

"How much?" Surce asked.

Laness ran her fingers along one of the many bracelets stacked on her muscular arms, her green eyes going out of focus for a few moments. "He says they should be ready by tomorrow night."

"Tell him Analia and I can come wait in the safehouse for ink pickup whenever he's ready," Aaron said.

Analia looked up at him in surprise.

"Compromise," he said, smoothing a lock of hair behind her ear. "The last time we were separated, you came back to me broken, and I couldn't get my hands on the people who dared to touch you. And that will never happen again."

He said it so calmly, like a simple truth he'd decided long ago. Because it was. The same truth that had him bringing her hand to his lips, his kiss soft as a vow against her middle finger.

"Deal?" he murmured.

Analia nodded, her heart tripping in her chest.

Aaron offered his Phoenix Gate smile. Then, he released her hand and headed out of their row, Surce emerging to join him as he started to coordinate with Laness. Mor shrugged, then went to help Branten with all the garment bags. Finally, it was just Analia and Ember.

For a few moments, Ember watched the bustle of activity, her hand resting on the rack beside her.

"I like him," she finally said, turning to Analia.

Her approval settled in a soft glow in Analia's chest. "Yes," she agreed, her eyes lingering on Aaron. "I like him, too."

Ember went quiet, rubbing the hem of her light blue shirt between her fingers. "Everything I've ever been taught says this kingdom is wrong," she murmured. "From the Royals, to the healers, to where it's located. But I have a hard time believing that. And that somehow makes everything worse."

Analia sighed. She couldn't imagine what a shock this kingdom had been to her of all people. "Hopefully," she said, "we're going to be one step closer to figuring out why. For all of this."

Ember nodded, but Analia didn't like the quiet, lost look in her eyes. She leaned into her, the two watching Mor whack Branten with a garment bag as he tried to carry too many at once, Aaron and Laness laughing.

She just had to hope Ember could come to terms with the underbelly of the healers they were starting to uncover. And that Dimitri could handle this plan.

Chapter 75

"So," Dimitri said. "This is the Ash Kingdom Healer School."

He and Rayner stood in the school's grand entrance, healers dressed in emerald robes bustling around them as Dimitri took in the view. The floor was made from dark gray stone, nearly blending in with the black basalt walls. Three arched doorways led deeper into what Ember called the patient floor, their edges lined with sleek obsidian glass that reflected the white magical lights above.

"It's certainly... austere," Rayner replied. He adjusted his robes, courtesy of Ember's directions—through Laness—to the healer's hidden robe shop.

Dimitri murmured his agreement as he did the same, carefully concealing what he wore beneath. "Come on," he said, keeping his voice low. "We have two floors to climb."

Rayner nodded, Dimitri still not used to his square jaw and chin-length black hair. But that steady look in his eyes was all Rayner as he turned and led the way toward the wide corner staircase. As casual as could be.

Dimitri smiled to himself, effortlessly slipping into the purposeful stride he'd adopted back in the Sun Castle. Just one of the many apprentices moving about their day, their voices echoing off the high ceiling and surrounding stone.

"You're awfully calm," Rayner murmured as they reached the second floor.

"This is nothing," Dimitri said dismissively, skimming his hand over the vines wreathed around the railing. Yes, no one would be able to shadowjump in and grab them if anything went wrong, but these were *healers*. They weren't allowed to harm them. "I've wandered into far worse."

"Like where?"

"The Bend in the Sun Kingdom."

"Really?" Rayner asked, intrigued. "I've heard whispers of that place and its Silent Queen even in my shop."

Dimitri winced. The assassin queen who'd ruled over the Bend had haunted the central Sun Kingdom for decades, no one ever seeing her face, only recognizable by the poison she injected into those from noble clans.

"She disappeared over twenty years ago. By the time I visited, she was long gone."

"What were you doing there, then?"

Dimitri hesitated. Normally, this was the moment he would deflect, wanting nothing to do with the memories he'd locked behind an iron door.

But there was something about the curiosity in Rayner's eyes as Dimitri joined him on the third-floor landing. It was the same curiosity that had had Dimitri asking him question after question on the turret roof, wanting to uncover every layer of who he was, Rayner trusting him with every detail.

And to Dimitri's surprise, that memory had his words tentatively rolling free.

"It was an accident." He headed down the hall flanked by classroom doors, his voice quiet enough the passing apprentices couldn't hear. "I escaped the castle when I was thirteen. All I had was a map I had stolen from the Council Chamber, and it was no help adjusting to the kingdom's noise, the activity, people bumping into me as they passed."

Dimitri turned left as Ember had instructed, the crowd thinning around him as apprentices filtered into classrooms.

Two turns to go, Rayner enthralled beside him.

"I didn't mean to wander into the Bend. But by the time I'd realized the buildings were getting more dilapidated, the sun had set. So, I ducked into the most hospitable-looking door I could find. Which was Gritta's."

Dimitri winced, remembering the stifling heat of countless bodies, the music magically amplified loud enough he felt it in his bones. "The barkeeper must have thought I was an idiot when I stumbled up to her counter, asking for a room, not even having a copper fleck to offer. But some drunken men at a nearby table recognized my servant uniform. Said there was no way castle staff had no gold. And long story short, I ended up backed against the wall, everyone watching, no one trying to help as they reached for my pockets. And that was the first time I..."

Dimitri mimed his exploding magic. Rayner nodded, remaining quiet as they turned right.

"The light was bright enough I was able to shove away and flee while everyone was blinded. But that was the moment I knew I would never escape. Not just Deardryn, but the shame as the truth clicked into place. So, I went back to the castle."

Dimitri's voice faded, the hallway empty and quiet around him. Rayner wordlessly brushed his fingers along Dimitri's cheek, as if feeling for the cracks his words had created. But if anything, finally saying the full story aloud had some of his broken pieces smoothing back together.

Dimitri rubbed the damper blade sheathed beneath his sleeve, his gaze lifting to the right turn up ahead. Down that hall was the common room. All they had to do was sneak through the glamored hallway inside, damper its locked door, and the Sun bastard would be a little more worthy.

Dimitri reached the corner. Just to be greeted by a group of voices, the speakers coming into view beyond the common room's ajar door. And Dimitri's body turned to ice.

"Master healers," Rayner breathed.

Dimitri stared.

And Rayner grabbed his arm. He yanked him back down the hall, past a second staircase, Dimitri's shock melting into panic as they stopped at a small table tucked in an alcove. He barely had time to note the careful arrangement of crystals on a pedestal atop it before Rayner grabbed its floor-length, dark green tablecloth.

"What are you doing?" Dimitri gasped.

"This is the only place to hide." Rayner fell to his knees, ducking under the cloth. "The apprentices might not know every new healer, but the masters will."

Yes, Ember had made that abundantly clear. But the table was so small. And the voices were drawing closer.

"We won't fit," Dimitri fretted, dancing from foot to foot.

"Yes we will—oh, just come here."

Rayner's hand shot out from under the cloth. He gripped Dimitri's ankle, Dimitri instinctively turning around at the press of his fingers, falling to his knees, scooting under the cloth—gods, let there be room.

Rayner released Dimitri's ankle. He tangled his arms around his torso, pulling him back between his raised knees. "Your feet," he whispered against his ear.

Tingles raced down Dimitri's spine. He hugged his knees to his chest, grateful he was so short and scrawny. But his relief vanished as quickly as it had come as the voices rounded the corner.

"Don't. Move," Rayner breathed.

Dimitri couldn't have if he wanted to. Not as Rayner's chest curved around his back. His body warm, arms tightening around his shoulders. And Dimitri... liked it.

Dimitri immediately swatted the thought aside. He bit his cheek, forcing himself to focus on the healers' voices halfway down the hall.

They were hiding. Nothing more. One look at the wrong time, and they were done for.

So then, why did he relax into Rayner as the footsteps neared?

"Reena, you mustn't be so quick to judge," came a soft female voice.

"They shouldn't make it so easy to judge," retorted a higher voice.

Rayner rubbed his thumb along Dimitri's shoulder, Dimitri not sure who he was trying to reassure. He just hoped he would continue, his eyes closing as he inhaled something dark and earthy.

Five steps away. Four. Three.

Rayner hid his face in Dimitri's neck as the healers reached the table. His lips grazed Dimitri's skin. And Dimitri's cock twitched—oh gods.

Dimitri barely registered the healers' voices continuing down the hall without pause. Barely registered Rayner slowly lifting his face as silence descended once more. All he knew was the terror that plowed through his inexplicable calm like a battering ram.

"Coast is clear," he squeaked. He scrambled out from under the table, smacking aside the part of himself that mourned the loss of Rayner's touch.

This. Was. Not. Happening.

Rayner crawled after him, an odd look on his face. But Dimitri didn't give him time to speak as he rose and sped down the hall, around the corner, the common room coming into view.

"Dima," Rayner called, hurrying after him, "what's wrong—"

"Common room's empty because of lectures, just as Ember said." Dimitri shoved the already open door even wider, his eyes bouncing over the geometric carpet, the couches and armchairs, the emotional whiplash having him unable to stay still as he spotted the painting of Rosala on the side wall.

"I think we have to touch it," he said, scurrying toward the painting. Ember had said it was glamored so only those who knew about the hidden door could see it, just like the safehouse door.

"Dima," Rayner tried again, "I'm sorry for grabbing you; I know you don't like your space being invaded—"

"It's fine," Dimitri said, struggling for casual as he smacked his palm on the painting. "You were right, that was the only way to hide—oh look, there's the door."

Rayner started to protest. Dimitri gripped the cold metal knob that had shimmered into existence, the hidden door squeaking as he yanked it open. He quickly descended the three steep stairs, finding himself in a corridor identical to the rest. Except this one was far shorter. And the door at the end was adorned with a wreath of blood-red roses and thorny stems.

Once, Dimitri's lungs would have tightened at that. But now, all he wanted was to get out of there as he felt Rayner come up beside him, effortlessly attracting all of his attention.

"Do you feel that?" Rayner asked.

All Dimitri felt was his sanity unraveling. He took a deep breath through his nose, forcing himself to focus. Relax. Breathe.

"There's a buzz," he said, marginally calmer. "The door is warded."

Powerfully, if they could detect it without contact. But that was why he'd come prepared.

"Let's hope this works," he said, unsheathing the damper blade from his sleeve. Then, refusing to look at Rayner, he touched the blade to the door.

Immediately, the leather hilt thrummed. Dimitri waited for the wards to flare, just as Othin's shield had done when Cadmus sliced through it. But the magic remained invisible to his eye as it flooded into the damper like a river current, the tingles fading within seconds.

"I think we're clear," he said after a moment.

"Nicely done," Rayner murmured.

Dimitri's stomach did a little flip. One he shoved aside as he said, "Let's look inside."

He twisted the brass knob, Rayner leaning in for a closer look as he eased the door open. And there came no flare of magic.

Dimitri released a tiny breath. He peeked inside, the room smaller than he was expecting. A circular table painted with the same roses and thorns sat in the center of the space, an abandoned mortar and pestle placed atop it. The air was thick with spices from the herbs that hung in bundles from the ceiling, what little of the wall Dimitri could see taken up by an ancient glass-fronted cabinet.

Well, this certainly looked like the hiding spot for some magical ink.

"Only one of us can go open the cabinet," he murmured.

"I'll do it." Rayner slipped through the opening before Dimitri could respond, turning back to look at him. "Keep watch, all right?"

Dimitri started to protest. But his words faded as Rayner met his gaze, the gentle, steady look in his eyes smoothing down his nerves.

Just as it had under the table. Just as it had every other time Rayner had grounded him when he was spiraling—Crystal spare him.

Dimitri nodded jerkily. Then, he twisted toward the glamored door, his arm behind him as he kept the blade pressed to the stone.

Gods, what was the matter with him? It wasn't like he was attracted to Rayner—he didn't let himself have crushes. He'd learned early on no one could fall for the Sun King's bastard servant. So, he'd shut that part of himself off. And he'd done a fucking good job at it.

But Rayner...

Glass clinked behind him, Dimitri's grip tightening on the dagger.

Rayner might have preferred to blend into the crowd, but Dimitri would always be able to find him. There was an artistry to his face. And his eyes... Gods, it was everything he could see in their dark brown depths that Dimitri—

"Got it."

Dimitri jumped hard enough he bit his tongue. And the dagger jerked off the door.

Dimitri yelped. He whirled around, trying to reestablish contact. But it was too late.

Vivid purple magic exploded from the blade. It raced along the doorway, Rayner thankfully having already stepped through with a vial of white ink in hand. But the magic collided with Dimitri's foot.

Tingles flared across his skin, dying off as quickly as they'd come as the onyx reclaimed the magic.

Dimitri twisted toward Rayner, "What did it do?"

"I... I don't know."

Dimitri instinctually grabbed the doorknob, stepping forward so he could pull the door shut. But the door had barely clicked into place when something rustled behind him. And Dimitri barely had time to glance back before the wreath on the door unfurled.

In a blink, the thorny vines lashed out, tangling around his arms. Dimitri yelped, trying to yank away. But the thorns pierced through his robes sleeves, digging into his skin, coiling around him and pinning his arms to his torso with unnatural strength.

Gods, he was trapped; he couldn't break free.

"Give me the blade!" Rayner exclaimed.

Dimitri struggled to comprehend his words, his arms uselessly straining to break free, his heart racing fast, fast, fast—

Rayner snatched the damper blade from his hand. With a few quick moves, he slashed through the vines, purple magic flaring as they fell limply to the floor.

Dimitri gasped for breath as he doubled over, Rayner's voice fuzzy in his ears. He grabbed Dimitri's wrist, about to pull him forward. And the white lights above darkened into emerald green.

Rayner froze. His gaze drifted up to the lights, the urgency in his voice melting into dread. "It's a signal," he breathed.

Dimitri's mouth drifted open. And Rayner launched into action.

He shoved the damper blade up his sleeve, completely ignoring the sheath. Then, he propelled Dimitri down the hall, his words as fast as Dimitri's pulse. "We have to get through the common room before anyone comes and sees us—"

"I know." Dimitri squeezed his eyes shut, struggling to shove his shock aside. Focus. He had to focus.

Biting down hard on his cheek, he let the pain ground him as he pushed through the door.

Green light illuminated the common room, which remained mercifully empty. Dimitri charged inside, Rayner slamming the door shut behind him as he followed. Just before he exited the common room, Dimitri paused. Listened.

"The healers are rushing, but not panicking," he reported.

Rayner nodded, letting Dimitri lead the way into the empty hall. Swift and purposeful. Melting into the crowd as he rounded the corner, the hallway split into two flows of traffic, Dimitri not sure if the voices around him were worried or furious.

It didn't matter. They just had to keep their heads down and meet Tyce and Cadmus in the entryway. Easy—

Dimitri grunted as he caught a stray elbow to the ribs. He stumbled, knocking into a healer beside him sweeping toward the common room.

Her blonde head snapped up. Revealing ice-blue eyes ringed in orange. And a belt of steel vertebrae around her waist.

Crystal spare him.

"Apologies, Archmaster," Dimitri stammered, backing into Rayner, trying to duck his head.

Her hand flashed out quick as an adder, fingers curling around his chin.

"I don't recognize you," she said, cold and quiet.

Chills ran down Dimitri's spine. He tried to lean away, acutely aware of the voices thrumming around him. But with surprising strength, she forced his chin up.

"Did you cross our wards?" she asked. So soft. But the crowd still slowed around them, heads starting to turn.

Dimitri opened his mouth, scrambling for an explanation, a lie, *anything* that could assuage the accusations in her eyes, her gaze dropping to his arms.

"Those are puncture marks along your sleeves," she said suddenly.

Dimitri's heart jolted. And panic took over.

He desperately tried to wrench out of her grip, the crowd surging closer—gods, they were cornered. Nowhere to go, the healer's fingernails digging into his face as her free hand reached for him.

And magic the color and consistency of smoke erupted across the hallway.

The archmaster recoiled, her grip on Dimitri loosening. The crowd cried out in alarm, staggering into each other, their organized processions rapidly dissolving.

And warm fingers found Dimitri's.

"Let's go," Rayner whispered in his ear.

He pulled Dimitri through the crowd, through the magical smoke, no one noticing as Dimitri's foot found the staircase they'd passed when hiding from the healers.

Dimitri gasped, "How did you—"

"I've been blocking my magic since the lights turned green. I didn't know what color it would flare, but I got the idea from your story."

Dimitri shook his head, not stopping to marvel as he ran down the stairs. He didn't have time to slow down, even as he squinted through the last of Rayner's magic. They just kept moving, Dimitri staggering as he anticipated another step, just to discover he'd reached the landing.

He grabbed the railing, trying to right himself as the last of Rayner's magic returned to his network.

And the vines beneath his fingers shuddered.

"They're downstairs!" the archmaster shrieked.

Rayner cursed. Dimitri raced down the first-floor hallway, the classrooms replaced by patient doors.

They just had to retrace their steps from the floors above. A few hallways, and they'd be at the entrance.

But heads were starting to turn in the patient rooms. Footsteps pounded down the stairs. And Dimitri lagged, Rayner looking equally winded by his magic slamming back into his network.

They rounded the corner. Two hallways left.

"Stop them!"

Dimitri cringed as patient and healers alike flooded into the hall, a crowd forming to block their path. He grabbed a nearby cart of healer supplies and shoved, people scattering to get out of its path.

And Dimitri and Rayner ran on, careening around the next corner.

One hallway left.

Something ripped down the back of Dimitri's robes, revealing the gold jacket he wore beneath.

"Sun soldiers!" a woman shrieked behind him—presumably the one who tried to scalpel him. Since when could healers attempt to cause harm?

Well, at least that part of the plan worked.

But the healers were gaining. The entryway was so close.

Gods, Cadmus, *please.*

Analia paced around the safehouse's empty sitting room, anxiously twisting her phoenix pin against her chest.

"They should have been back ten minutes ago," she muttered.

"They'll make it," Aaron soothed, seemingly unfazed as he watched her from the couch. But Analia caught the tension in his jaw.

"I don't like," she began. Just to cut off as magic tingled across the room.

Analia twisted on her heel. And her knees nearly gave out as Tyce emerged from the shadows, Dimitri and Rayner gasping for breath as they gripped his hands.

"Thank the gods," Analia said on an exhale. She hurried closer, her eyes rapidly scanning over them. "Are you all right? What happened? Where's Cadmus?"

"Damage control," Dimitri panted. Releasing Tyce's hand, he moved to slump down on a couch, Rayner coming to collapse beside him and removing their disguises with a flick of his fingers.

Analia stifled her disappointment. She hadn't seen her brother since Deardryn threw him in a cell, hadn't gotten a chance to check on him herself.

"He told me to verify you're all right," Tyce said, not meeting her gaze. As usual.

Analia's jaw tightened. "Tell him I'm fine and I miss him," she said cooly. Then, she turned away from her cousin who never had the courage to stand up for her, discovering Aaron had come to crouch before Dimitri and Rayner.

"You two seem no worse for wear," he decided, sitting back on his heels.

Dimitri nodded tiredly. Rayner, in turn, met Analia's gaze.

"I have the ink," he said. He pulled the small vial from his pocket, something like uncertainty in his eyes as he offered it to her.

Analia glanced at Dimitri. Rayner nodded solemnly. And Analia accepted the vial.

She didn't have to look down to know what she held. It slithered across her senses, quiet and unmistakable as the sinking in her stomach.

"Well," she murmured, all attention redirecting to her. "We were right. This ink was Blessed by the Crystal."

Chapter 76

E mber had a hard time falling asleep that night.

Everyone had been waiting in the sitting room for Analia and Aaron to return, Analia not wasting any time telling them Dimitri and Rayner were all right, and she could sense the Crystal's magic in the ink. Every face around the room appeared torn between dread and hope. But Ember felt like a jolt of energy had been shot through her veins.

This was a victory. And she'd been the key.

True, Analia not being able to sense the magic in her markings—or her network—created several more questions. But at least now, they knew.

The Crystal didn't Bless inanimate objects on its own. Magical objects were created by the Blessed, and Royal magic proved the infusing process had its limits. And since Ember doubted there were any healers who possessed all the magic of the Crystal, that left one option.

Somehow, the healers had a shard. They'd learned how to direct its magic into the ink. And maybe, figuring out how and why would give her the answers she needed about her healer's oath.

Ember didn't know how long it took her to finally collapse into bed. But when she woke the following morning, that buzz remained in her veins, having her dress in record time and beating Branten downstairs for their run.

"You're up early," he yawned, trudging downstairs a few minutes later.

"Just ready to go," Ember replied, bouncing on the balls of her feet.

Branten cocked his head, something assessing in his dark brown eyes. And whatever he saw on her face had him offering a wolfish grin.

"All right, then," he said, coming to slide open the back door. "Let's see how many laps you got."

With that, he charged out into the cool spring morning, Ember close behind. Their boots pounded across the porch and down the steps, the muddy yard from her first couple of mornings now solid beneath Ember's feet as they reached the birch grove.

And Ember ran.

She and Branten had followed their route enough times that she didn't have to think before each step. Turn right at the tree stump. Hop over the undergrowth that stretched across the path. Slow down at the stretch of thick, protruding roots.

One lap down.

Branten looked over at her, clearly checking in. But Ember didn't pause. She had finally found her rhythm: her feet pounding in time with her pulse, the air cold and crisp in her lungs.

Branten matched her pace, letting out a whoop as he leaped over a fallen tree trunk. Ember laughed, noticeably less graceful as she followed, but she didn't care.

It had been so long since she felt like she had a little control. Since she felt like she had answers within reach.

"Water break," Branten panted, slowing to a walk as they reached their starting point for the second time.

Ember was tempted to keep going without him. But clearly expecting this, Branten grabbed her by the back of her shirt, his face flushed and eyes twinkling as he pulled her to a stop. And Ember knew better than to argue as he passed her a canteen from his belt.

She tipped her head back, cold, clean water blissfully sliding down her throat. Wiping her mouth with the back of her hand, she made to give the canteen back to Branten, but he shook his head.

"You carry that now," he said, sliding his own canteen back through his belt.

Ember perked up. "Really?"

"Let's see how you handle a little challenge," he taunted. Then, he headed off once more, Ember quickly sliding her canteen through her belt and following.

It took some time for her to get used to the new weight. Her pace slowed as she searched for a comfortable place for it to sit, Branten adjusting his pace to match hers. But he let her figure it out on her own. And when everything finally clicked?

Ember lost track of time as they ran. Three laps, four laps, five, Branten periodically having them stop for water breaks, seemingly amused by her newfound energy. But it was more than that.

It was clarity. With each gasping breath, her racing thoughts slowed, untangled, flowed in a single direction. And the questions that had been nagging her for over a month finally drifted to the surface without strain.

Why did the Starlight healers' deviation from traditional practices bother her so much? Why did she feel ashamed for liking their system more? Why did the idea of suffering in silence with her addiction feel safer than letting in the people who cared about her?

Six, seven, eight laps.

"All right, healer girl," Branten panted, their starting point coming into view for the ninth time. "This is where you stop."

"What do you mean?" Ember protested, rubbing the stitch in her side. "I can keep going."

"I don't doubt that. But you're going to regret it tomorrow when you're limping around trying to heal people. And Sofika scares me."

Ember struggled to laugh through her gasps. Begrudgingly, she followed Branten's lead and slowed to a stop, tipping her sweaty face toward the breeze.

She knew he was right; she shouldn't push it. But her fingers still restlessly toyed with her canteen. And looking down, Branten's face split in a knowing grin.

"Come on," he said, undergrowth crunching beneath his boots as he trudged off. "One more lap, but we do it walking."

Ember brightened. "How come?" she asked, hurrying to fall into step beside him.

"Because you're having a buzz day."

Ember's eyebrows shot up. "I don't know what that is."

"Really? You don't have some days where your mind feels so scattered and exhausted that every little task takes all the effort you have? But other days, you're buzzing with all of the energy you have?"

Well, now that he phrased it like that, *definitely*. Those former days were what drove her to devinroot, almost in tears because she had so much to do to keep up with the other apprentices, and she just... couldn't. But that morning?

"How do you know that?" she asked curiously.

"Because you're the only person in the house who fidgets and gets distracted as much as me." Branten winked, obviously entertained as Ember's jaw dropped.

Gods, he was right. She didn't think she'd ever seen Branten sit still for more than a minute at a time, always a step ahead of everyone else when making plans, even as he misplaced his boots every morning. And Ember was the same kind of disaster.

"You and I," Branten said, tapping his temple. "We don't operate like the others. Our brains turn off when we need them to turn on. That's why I love running. You're not supposed to be thinking, so naturally, everything you've been trying to think about bubbles to the surface."

He mimed rising bubbles with his fingers, Ember only able to shake her head.

"Is that why you insisted I come running with you for so long?" she asked, sinking down on the fallen trunk Branten had leaped over.

"Partially." Branten plopped down beside her. "But it was mainly because you looked like you were going through it for a while. And this family is too desperate for a healer member to let that continue."

He said it teasingly. But the quick, sincere look he stole at her from the corner of his eye hit Ember square in the chest.

She dropped her gaze to the mossy bark, her words squeezing past the lump in her throat. "After all, you're scared of Sofika."

"Damn right." Branten threw back his head with a chortle.

She'd only known him for a month, and yet he understood her in ways she'd never been able to articulate. He was the most unexpected friend she'd ever had.

A friend with only a month's worth of history, not sixteen years. A friend who didn't seem fazed by much, and was far more intuitive than she thought.

Ember's fingers curled into the soft, rotting bark, her throat threatening to close around the words. But she was still riding the high of one victory. And Crystal strike it all if she wouldn't keep that momentum going.

"Branten," she said tentatively. "Did you ever try things to help with your 'functioning differently'? Besides running, I mean."

"Of course," Branten scoffed, as if the question were ridiculous. "I probably tried too many things."

"Did you ever try devinroot?"

Branten whistled, leaning back on his hands. "Definitely. And I *definitely* wouldn't recommend. Why?"

He knew why. At least, he suspected, the glint in his eyes having Ember wiping her sweaty palms on her pants.

But she was halfway there. She had to keep going.

"Well," she said, shifting on the trunk, "remember how you said I looked like I was going through it for a while?"

He nodded.

"That's because I had been using devinroot. And then I stopped."

Branten cocked his head. But the only sound was the birds chirping above, the two so far back in the grove all Ember could see was trees. And the words rushed out of her mouth, desperate to fill the quiet, "I'm addicted to devinroot."

Ember clapped a hand over her mouth. She stared at Branten, acutely aware of her words hanging between them, his face giving nothing away.

Gods, what was he thinking? What would he say.

"I'm not surprised," Branten said casually. "That shit is terrifying. I only managed to stop because I saw what it was doing to the people around me."

Ember held her breath, waiting for more. Branten peeled off a strip of bark to fiddle with, not looking inclined to continue.

"Does that mean you think I'm 'terrifying'?" she asked hesitantly.

"You? Definitely," Branten scoffed. "You could eviscerate me with a sentence."

A small, startled laugh escaped between Ember's fingers. She lowered her hand back to her lap, struggling to make sense of the man beside her, his eyebrows wiggling as he met her gaze.

"You really don't care?" she asked.

Branten shrugged. "I'm no expert on addiction, but you seem to be doing better, so I'm assuming you found someone who is. I'll help if I can, though."

It was such a simple response. And Rosala spare her, it was everything.

Ember wrapped her arms around herself, "I haven't told anyone else in the house yet."

"Your secret's safe with me." Branten rose to his feet, then sketched an exaggerated bow.

Ember snorted, practically dizzy with relief.

"Come on, healer girl," Branten said, hopping over the trunk and continuing on their path. "We have a lap to complete."

"You know, my name is Ember," she said.

"Yes, but I like 'healer girl' more."

Branten gestured for her to hurry up. And feeling like she was waking from a dream, Ember rose and headed after him.

"I told someone," Ember announced, pushing through Sofika's study door.

Sunlight streamed through the massive window behind the carved wooden desk, the windowsill covered in small, potted succulents. Bookcases stuffed to overflowing with books and folders lined the room, the wildflowers painted across the walls peeking in between their gaps.

Sofika looked up from the stack of reports she'd been flipping through at her desk, her head tilting. "You did?"

"I told Branten on our run this morning." Ember came to take the seat across from her, her hands still shaking as the words tumbled past her lips. "It just felt right. And he wasn't fazed. There was no pity, no patronizing sympathy or concern. He just offered to help if he could. And now I'm here because I did it, but also because I really want to celebrate with devinroot, so it's here or the greenhouse."

Gods, she needed to stop talking. But her words kept coming out like water through a leak, desperate and fast and wonderful as the built-up pressure finally eased.

Sofika put down her pen, reaching across the desk to squeeze Ember's hand. "That's excellent."

Ember leaned her head back against her chair, soaking in the praise. "It was only one person," she admitted. "I still have more to tell."

"One at a time," Sofika said. "It feels good now, but don't be surprised if it's still hard to tell the next person. But it will get easier."

Ember nodded, trying to settle into the purposefully slow cadence of Sofika's voice. She gave herself a few heartbeats to calm down, her "buzz day" still tingling through her veins. Then, she gave Sofika a tentative smile. "I did it."

"You did," Sofika agreed. "And that's not all." She released Ember's hand, Ember's head cocking as Sofika flipped through her papers. "These are your and Cenn's records from your month here," she explained. "Every poultice made, every ailment healed, every patient interacted with. And both of your results are excellent."

Ember held her breath, knowing where Sofika was going, not sure if she wanted her to stop or talk faster.

"I've shared your results with the other master healers," she said, her small, hazel eyes sparkling as she looked up. "And we all agree you and Cenn have completed your apprenticeships. I was planning on bringing both of you in this afternoon to tell you, but you're already here. So, I can say congratulations now."

Sofika spread her hands on the desk, obviously waiting for a reaction. But Ember had too many at once to give.

Victory, after so many years of training. Disappointment that Master Lenzi wasn't the one to tell her. Bittersweet that the life as a master healer she'd been dreaming of looked so different now that it was hers. And as always, there was the twinge of guilt every time she embraced an aspect of the Starlight healers' ways.

"Is this bad news?" Sofika asked.

"No," Ember said quickly, clasping her hands on the table. "This is so—thank you. I just..." Ember trailed off, her mind flashing between the tree trunk, her devinroot, Deardryn's book of notes, the big house roof. "There's one more person I have to tell before I'm ready."

Sofika nodded slowly, something like pride in her eyes. "Of course."

She turned back to her papers, quiet permission for Ember to leave or continue as she wished. Ember started to rise, not ready to unpack her thoughts on her advancement. Then, she paused.

She stared at Sofika: a woman who had done so much to revolutionize the healers, who knew so much of their history and ways. Someone she'd thought to ask about Deardryn's notes weeks ago, but had been too afraid of accidentally revealing something she shouldn't. Maybe even afraid of her answers.

But if she could tell Branten about her addiction?

"Sofika," she said. "Can I ask you something random?"

Sofika hummed an affirmation, not looking up.

"I know you've never been to the Temple of Rosala," she began, gripping her hands beneath the table, "but Aaron and I were talking about how some major landmarks across Elefthia have inscriptions written on them. I was just wondering if you know of any lines written on the temple, now that I won't get to see for myself."

Sofika didn't respond immediately. Ember remained perfectly still in her seat, hoping her expression remained casual.

"There's a plaque on the door," Sofika finally mused. "The master healers from before the Shattering have mentioned it in passing. I believe it says something along the lines of, 'With blood that's cursed with ancient rage, these sketched-out tombs may be refined, if three by three by three align.'"

Sofika flipped a page. And Ember's victorious high withered, then died inside her.

Chapter 77

Aaron was fucked. In multiple ways. And none of them were the ways he would have liked.

He knew something was wrong when he bumped into Ember in the Pulse on his way back from the Council Building, her fingers digging into his arm as she told him she had news, she only had an hour for her lunch break, they had to find the others. Seeing as Branten, Mor, and Laness were all busy with their various responsibilities, that left Analia and Surce.

The good news was they were together in Surce's studio. The bad news—for Aaron—was Surce was checking measurements on Analia's new gown. And Aaron had to keep his hands to himself.

He tried his best to listen to Ember's recount of her conversation with Sofika, her footsteps bouncing off the walls as she paced around the bench where he sat. But his eyes kept wandering back to Analia.

Her dress was made from layers of dark silver lace. It clung to her torso, accentuating the small curves of her breasts, running down to the dip of her waist, flowing over her hips. But his favorite part was the sleeves. Long and tight, they were made from a single layer of the sheer, mesh-like lace, running up from her wrists and stopping at the tops of her arms. Letting him take in the creamy skin of her narrow shoulders.

"Aaron," Surce said, kneeling behind Analia to check the hem, "please refrain from visually undressing your future wife until we're done."

Analia smothered her laugh with her hand, the darkness in her expression lightening a fraction. And that word caressed along Aaron's skin, the final layer between himself and the frost threatening to coat his veins. *Wife.*

"I'd much rather continue," he said, eyes on Analia's collarbones. "Because it sounds like Ember is insinuating Deardryn not only knows the Crystal shard is in the temple, but that's where she went on her three days of 'business.'"

"I am," Ember replied matter-of-factly.

"That's what I was afraid of," Aaron sighed. Dragging his gaze from Analia, he turned to grip the back of the bench, resting his chin on his hand. "You were saying?"

Ember rolled her eyes. "What I was getting to," she said, flicking his temple as she paced past, "is with Sofika's confirmation about the lines, it seems likely Marion is correct and the middle verse is on the final hiding spot. Yet, none of those words are in Deardryn's notes. Her focus is solely directed on the healers' history and rituals."

"Which includes the ink for your markings," Surce pointed out.

"True," Analia murmured. "But that doesn't answer the question of how she knew about the ink in the first place?"

Aaron's hand flexed around the bench's wooden backing. He'd completely glazed over that fact, too intent on knowing how close Deardryn was to breathing down his kingdom's neck to consider how she'd gained that ground in the first place. And the grim set of Ember's mouth as she finally paused before him had his stomach sinking.

"Exactly," she said. "And I think she already gave you the answer, Anna."

Surce rose from behind Analia with a rustle of skirts, asking what Ember meant. But Aaron's mind had already flashed back to his sitting room. Analia on the couch beside him, filling everyone in on her time in Moon. Every research session, every detail she'd been able to squeeze out of Deardryn, the ice finally freezing over his veins.

"She told me she found the first shard because she heard a little girl's song," Analia said slowly. "The same one that Dimitri caught a part of. And that's why he recognized the lines in the scroll."

"Which means Deardryn knows the other lines and already had Marion's idea," Aaron finished grimly. He twisted in his seat, the implication in his words pressing a heavy hand across the studio.

The one advantage they had was null and void.

Gods, what did it take to get a step ahead of that woman? He met Analia's gaze, her expression dark, her fingers gripping the loom's wooden frame beside her. Only Surce appeared composed as she circled around Analia, having finished her gown inspection.

"That theory poses several new questions," she said, stashing her sparkling pins in the cup resting on her weaving stool.

"Like how does a child know about this poem?" Aaron grumbled.

"And without the scroll," Surce continued, "how would Deardryn know those words were connected to the Crystal? How would she know those words are on the Temple of Rosala in the first place?"

"She *was* chosen by Rosala," Analia pointed out. "She has no markings, so I don't know how long she attended the school. But perhaps she heard it there?"

The shadows in Aaron's mind churned faster. But Ember didn't miss a beat.

"I *doubt* it. The master healers are unreasonably protective of all information to do with the temple. I spent fourteen years in the Ash Kingdom Healer School and never heard a whisper of those words. Sofika only knew because Starlight healers no longer abide by the stipulations of our oath. And with the healer-Royal separation?" Ember shook her head. "I can't imagine any master healer would let a detail like that slip around her."

"Which means there's a chance our original conclusion is wrong," Surce mused.

"Which means we're back to wondering how much she knows," Aaron sighed, leaning back against the bench.

He really wished he could go back to staring at Analia. Admiring the smooth slope of her neck as she brushed back her hair was far more preferable than jamming pieces together in his mind, each conclusion worse than the last.

"Do any of the three days Deardryn was on 'business' match with the day the temple's wards would have been down?" he asked, rubbing his face.

Analia blinked hard as if she was already fifteen steps ahead of him. She rattled off the dates, Aaron twisting to watch Ember slowly shake her head.

"The wards should have been up those days," Ember mused.

"So then, what was she doing?" Surce wondered, turning her cup of pins between her fingers.

"And why is she researching the healers?" Analia added.

The questions formed an ache across Aaron's forehead. He dragged a hand through his hair, trying to shove the shadows aside so he could think. And while he had no answers for Analia's question, a tiny memory rose in his mind like a listless offering.

"Dimitri's stolen letter mentioned Deardryn making a surprise visit back to Sun before returning permanently," he said slowly. "Maybe that's where she went."

"Which brings us back to the question of why," Ember said, leaning against the back of the bench.

Wasn't that always where they ended up with Deardryn? Aaron's eyes drifted over the tapestries on the walls, no one having any answers to offer as his gaze snagged on an image to his right.

It depicted his kingdom from afar. The sun shone down on the scene, reflecting off the river that wound between the ridges and ravines beyond the border.

His home. His responsibility.

"I'm going to consult the scroll," Surce said, her patience cracking as she turned and swept toward the far counter. "There must be something in there that can help."

Aaron was too tired to be hopeful. Ember trailed after Surce, Aaron not catching her words. Instead, he looked over at Analia, her silver skirts rustling as she came to sit beside him. He pulled her closer, waiting for her to look to him for reassurance.

But when Analia's smoky-gray eyes met his, they weren't worried. They blazed, her hand finding his and squeezing tight.

"Deardryn will not get this kingdom," she told him. Like a fact. Like a vow. And fuck if that wasn't the lifeline he needed.

"You sound like a queen," he murmured.

He watched her closely, wondering how she'd receive the comment. And while there was certainly a flicker of caution, she kept her chin high.

"Gods, Analia," he whispered, "you have no idea—"

Aaron cut off as Ember yelped across the studio.

"That's it! That's the mark on Brenn's and Cadmus's wrists!"

Aaron and Analia exchanged a shocked look. They scrambled to their feet and hurried to the side counter, Ember pointing at the unfurled scroll in Surce's hands.

"It's reversed," she said, "but that's definitely the same asymmetrical star."

"How did we not know that was in the scroll?" Analia asked, eyes wide as she stopped beside Ember.

"I've never heard its description," Surce explained. "Ember only said there was a mark during our first dinner, and with how exhausted you looked, no one wanted to pester you with questions."

"I really didn't describe it?" Ember asked, rubbing her face.

"To be fair," Aaron said, "you had been magically sliced a few days prior, and I didn't think to share the description Anna had given me either."

He came to join Surce as she reeled in the scroll. Sure enough, that was a black, asymmetrical star—although it was upside down.

"Surce," he said, "what were you just looking at?"

"The poem," she said, rapidly unfurling the scroll once more. "I was reading through it, wondering if we could have translated the middle stanza incorrectly and that was why we couldn't think of any locations bearing the words."

Aaron's eyes flicked over the ancient parchment, his pulse speeding up as he reached the bottom. "That's the map you showed us at lunch."

Ember gestured wildly. "Accalon had us sketch that image on a map."

Aaron's gaze shot to Analia, her face paling. But she made no move to stop him as he reached for the scroll, eyes back on Surce. "May I?"

She nodded, shoving it into his hands. Aaron unfurled the scroll so the map was directly in front of him. Turning the scroll so he could see the trailing end, he adjusted the parchment until he found the star once more, the scroll crinkling and spilling across the floor.

"This is so unwieldy," he muttered, turning back to the map.

"Why do you think I've been transcribing it onto paper for you to translate?" Surce asked.

"What are you doing?" Ember interjected, restlessly fidgeting with her robes.

"This." Aaron made sure the designs were lined up, the map facing himself and Surce, the star Analia and Ember. Then, he creased the parchment at the top.

For a moment, nothing happened. He kept his eyes on the map, Ember, Surce, and Analia crowding around him to watch. And he felt Analia flinch on his left as one by one, black lines seeped through the parchment and spread across the map, forming the same star design, no longer backward or upside down.

"Crystal spare us all," Surce breathed.

Aaron's hands tightened around the scroll, his mind racing. Why was a symbol from a creature imprisoned in a volcano showing up in Talitha's scroll? And how did Accalon know about it?

One thing was for sure, though.

"Em," Analia said, unnervingly calm. "You said my uncle had you create this by drawing lines between magical locations?"

Ember nodded, fingers pressed to her lips. "That and the three major mountains. Lucilla was the one who put it together."

Aaron's heart curled in on itself. He slid his arm around Analia's waist, but her gaze remained trained on the map.

"This map," she said, "made up of magical locations, shows up in a scroll having to do with the Crystal. And the two locations where shards are known to be hidden are included in these lines."

She traced her finger along the black lines, first along the bottom left line cutting through Scarsthain on Moon and Star's border. Then, over to the bottom right leg to where the Temple of Rosala sat in the Mist Kingdom.

"We have a map," Surce said, her voice hushed. "There are several locations, but this still narrows down our search significantly."

"And since Deardryn never got her scroll open," Ember said, "she has no reason to know about this."

A small, childish part of Aaron wanted to point out that somehow, Accalon knew. But he stomped it out, not allowing himself to destroy the little hope perking up around him. He could really use some hope himself. Because staring at those lines...

"Something's going on with the mountains," he murmured. All eyes flicked to him. "Our map comes from a mark created by the creature trapped in Mt. Vasolus. Deardryn told Anna she found the scroll in Mt. Raegyr."

"Which means something is going on with Mt. Lanula," Analia said quietly. Her hand found his on her hip, squeezing tight.

Because his grandmother was there. All the women in the DovenU. Everyone potentially at risk, either from the clue hidden in the mountain, or Deardryn if she ever found out.

"One of the scrolls came from Ethelind in Mt. Lanula," Surce pointed out. "Could it simply be another scroll location?"

"But then why would the third scroll be in the Human Kingdom instead of Mt. Vasolus?" Analia asked, tracing her fingers along the line that cut through the Human Kingdom.

Surce didn't seem to have an answer to that. She paused her efforts to straighten the trailing scroll, her topaz eyes studying Aaron as if she could sense the ice he desperately shoved back.

"I'll talk to my grandmother," he said abruptly. He passed the scroll to a wide-eyed Ember, then swiftly returned to the bench and sat.

He couldn't stare at that map, that gods-damned scroll, any longer. Not when he knew Ethelind wouldn't be free to talk until the following morning.

But he couldn't shut down in the meantime. He'd spent enough time brooding while Analia was gone, his nights of going round and round leaving him lost and confused and no closer to solving the actual problem at hand. The one in front of him, not behind him in the past.

He couldn't fall into that trap again. He could not, *would* not, let Deardryn get another step closer to his kingdom.

Aaron tugged on a thread in his jacket as Surce, Ember, and Analia went back and forth a little longer. Eventually, Ember said she had to get back to the Healer Center. She headed for the bead curtain, her fingers lightly brushing Aaron's shoulder as she passed.

Surce rolled up the scroll a few minutes later, returning it to one of her many magically guarded storage bins. Then, promising to fill in the others, she swept through the beads, leaving Aaron and Analia alone.

Analia came to sit on the stool before Surce's loom, Aaron not sure if she was trying to give him space or herself. She absently twisted the phoenix pin against her chest, her eyes downcast, her mouth slightly pinched.

"Does that pensive look of yours have to do with Accalon?" he finally asked.

Analia sighed, more tired than anything. "All I can do is believe he would have told me someday." She paused, biting her lip. "I just wish I had gotten to know him more."

Aaron's heart softened. "You know the parts that mattered most."

Analia nodded. But her shoulders still slumped. He opened his arms, and she rose from the stool, coming to sit on his lap as he settled her against him.

"We'll figure it out," she said, half to herself as she traced the embroidered thread in his collar.

Aaron made a soft, indignant noise. "I was supposed to say that."

"I suppose you should have gotten to it sooner, then."

Aaron tapped her nose. "Smartass."

Analia flashed a smile, but Aaron caught the exhaustion around its edges. She leaned her head against his shoulder, revealing the tapestry of the lakeside that had been hidden behind her. And Aaron knew what he could do while waiting to meet with Ethelind.

"We need a break," he announced.

Analia didn't look up. "From what?"

"Everything. Deardryn, the Crystal, my mental spiral over my kingdom, and your worries about being queen. Because I refuse to continue existing in a reality where looking at you in that dress is helping me *regain* my sanity."

He lightly tugged on her sheer, silvery sleeve, Analia breathing out a laugh.

"So what?" she asked. "We go home and hide for an hour?"

"Of course not," Aaron scoffed. "That house is full of reminders. What we need is a place. And lucky for you, I have just the one in mind."

Analia peeked up at him curiously. Shifting her in his arms, Aaron rose from the bench, then settled her on her feet.

"Come with me?" he asked.

Analia smiled, sliding her arms around his neck. "Always."

Some of the weight eased from Aaron's chest. He kissed her forehead, whispering against her skin. "Fair warning."

Then, he pulled them into the shadows.

Chapter 78

Analia leaned into Aaron as he pulled them through the shadows, her body notice-ably heavier than when she'd first stepped into Surce's studio.

She didn't know what she had to do to get a step ahead of Deardryn. The map was a good start, but it was an answer that weighed down her chest even more. Because somehow, her uncle had known about it. And she needed to know how he was involved in all of this.

But Aaron had said they were taking a break. And while Analia didn't think she could fully shut off her mind, the sight before her as the shadows peeled back had her a lot closer than she could have hoped.

They'd appeared in a cozy hollow. Moss and other greenery covered the long, steep slope down to the base where they stood, transitioning into sand as it reached the shore of a quiet lake. It was small enough they could have walked around to the other side, with a flat, stone bridge providing quicker access.

And the water glowed a soft, electric blue.

"What is this place?" Analia asked, voice hushed with wonder as she went to kneel at the water's edge. The blue light rippled across the surface with the gentle current, Analia dipping her fingers into the warm water.

"It's called the Lake of Dreams." Aaron came to kneel beside her, smile audible in his voice. "My mom told me about it when I was young. After she died, I spent a lot of time searching through the Wild Lands, eventually finding this pocket untouched by the Ancient Ones' magic northeast of my kingdom."

Analia nodded, swirling her fingers through the water. It made sense they were a ways from Starlight. The breeze that ruffled her hair was noticeably warmer, enough she was comfortable despite her exposed shoulders. Even the greenery, the smell of growing things, was stronger, as if spring had decided to come to this hollow before anywhere else.

Analia scooped up a handful of water, tiny blue lights sparkling in her palm. "It's like a handful of stars," she said, watching the lights trickle back into the lake through her fingers.

"Beautiful," Aaron agreed.

Analia looked up at him, about to speak. But Aaron's eyes weren't on her hand. They were on her. Obvious and unashamed and adoring, that smile she'd heard in his voice flickering across his lips.

"You're staring at me," she said, her cheeks warming.

Aaron shrugged. "You have your view, I have mine." He tucked a lock of hair behind her ear, leaning in to whisper, "I hate to inform you, mine is better."

Analia's flush intensified. "I don't know," she said, her eyes wandering across his face, lingering on the soft curve of his mouth. "I'm enjoying what I'm looking at."

Aaron brightened. He shifted so he sat with his back to the water, striking a dramatic pose. Analia laughed, Aaron's answering grin brushing her lingering worries away.

She loved seeing him like this. Silly and mischievous, smiling big enough to flash the dimple in his cheek. She certainly preferred that over the dark, brooding frown that had taken over his face in Surce's studio.

She couldn't imagine the kinds of worries he had to drag himself away from—she didn't know how he managed it. But if this was what happened when they both tried?

Analia smiled up at him, the lake sparkling behind him. Now that she thought about it...

"Is this one of the paintings from the big house?" she asked.

Aaron looked as though he'd been hoping she would ask. "It is. My mom painted it, you know."

"Really?" Analia's eyes widened, Aaron's words practically bursting out of him.

"Marion told me when she visited. I had no idea my mom could paint, let alone that she was so talented. And now, it feels like I have a little more left of her than I did before."

"And you have even more here," Analia said, spreading her arms.

Aaron's eyes shone. "Exactly." Rising to his feet, he offered his hand, pulling Analia up and lacing their fingers. "Come on, there's more to see."

Analia let him lead her across the sand to the bridge. She trailed her hand over the railing, finding the weathered stone carved with flowering vines.

"How often have you come here?" she asked, tracing the lines with her nail.

"Surprisingly, not very. It's a beautiful spot, but it always felt like it was meant to be shared."

"With whom?" she asked innocently.

"I don't know," Aaron sighed contemplatively. "I was hoping you could take a look around, help me figure it out. She has to be really special."

Analia shoved him, Aaron laughing as he tapped her nose.

"I've always wanted to bring someone here," he said, his voice softening as they reached the center of the bridge. "Someone like you. A family."

He'd said it casually, but he conveniently hid his face from her as he moved to sit on a stone bench against the railing. And Analia knew he wasn't talking about the people back home.

"A family, huh?" she asked, coming to sit beside him. "I thought you said that wasn't something you thought about anymore."

It was one of the details that had made her heart hurt the most for him when listening to his story about Liss. Something she'd been meaning to ask him about.

"If you'll recall," he said wryly, "I said it was hard to think about. Not because I don't want those things, but because of how badly I do. And only recently has that felt attainable."

"Why?" Analia asked softly.

Aaron's eyes dropped to his fingers, tracing the edge of the bench between them. "Remember after our visit to the Human Kingdom and you had to help me release my magic because the buildup was too much?"

Analia nodded.

"That's what I was afraid of. An accident. But with you?" Aaron lifted his gaze, Analia's breath hitching as he skimmed his knuckles along her cheek. "You match me. I know if something were to happen, you are more than capable of handling it—not to put that responsibility on you. Having you with me is just a reassurance I never dreamed of."

His fingers trailed down her neck to her phoenix pin, the slick glide of his network brushing along her senses. Magic so deadly he had to be dampered as a child. A power he couldn't afford to lose control of.

"I think I know how that feels," she murmured. She raised her hand, midnight flames curling around her fingers. Aaron wreathed his own hand in starlight, then tapped his fingers against hers, their magics softly canceling out.

Analia sighed, looking out across the shimmering lake, the slopes of greenery on all sides, the trees lining the hollow's rim providing patches of shade. "I think this is a perfect spot for children."

Aaron's fingers paused on her pin. "You do?"

"Not for a while," she clarified. "I still want time with you all to myself. Which means you'll be stuck taking your morning tonic a while longer."

She patted his chest, her hand lingering as Aaron's gaze darkened. Focused.

"Is that so?" he asked, his voice slipping into a croon. He leaned closer, his breath wafting over her ear. "Does that mean you're hoping to practice in the meantime?"

"My constellation," she murmured, tracing his jaw with a finger. "Are you hinting you need to work on your skills?"

Aaron made a low, rumbling noise. One that had sparks igniting in Analia's blood. Refusing to let him see her flush, she rose from the bench and crossed to the opposite railing, acutely aware of his gaze scorching down her back.

"Analia Valarus," he said, tasting each syllable like a decadent wine. "What a scathing tongue you have."

He rose from the bench, Analia's pulse quickening as she felt him prowl closer.

"Last I checked," she said, "you rather enjoy my tongue."

"Oh, I do." Aaron braced his elbows on the railing to either side of her, caging her in and leaning over her shoulder. "But I think my tongue enjoys you more."

Analia shuddered, his breath hot against her neck, metal and spice wreathing around her. But he made sure no part of them touched.

"You're blushing," he crooned.

Gods, she really was. But she shook her head, even as his voice, the tease of a touch, fanned the flames in her blood.

"Such a pretty shade of pink." He tilted his head, the brush of his nose along her jaw having her lungs stuttering. "What could you possibly be imagining right now?" he wondered. "The caress of my tongue against yours with every kiss? The way I can't help but taste your skin? Or"—Analia barely stifled her moan as he sighed the word against her ear—"is it the way I worship you whenever I get to bury my head between your thighs?"

Crystal spare her, she was over her head. So completely, maddeningly over her head.

"You're awfully quiet," Aaron murmured, his lips feathering up her neck. "Tell me, my shooting star, what do you want?"

He tilted her face with a hand, his tongue rolling beneath the corner of her jaw. Analia's whimper broke free. She arched against him, the ache between her thighs flaring as she felt him, hard and ready against her ass—gods, yes.

Aaron pressed her back against the railing, his arms keeping her in place as he pulled away once more.

"Apologies," he said unsteadily, running his thumb along her lower lip. "I didn't catch your words."

Analia sucked his finger into her mouth. Aaron swore, all teasing forgotten as he pressed against her. She sucked him in deeper, swirling her tongue along the rough, calloused length of his finger, his hand shaking by the time she let him withdraw.

Analia grabbed his wrist, whispering against his wet skin. "Touch me."

The words were an order. And Aaron seemed to have no desire to disobey. "Done."

He yanked his hand away, popping open the button securing her gown with a flick of his finger. He pushed her sleeves down her arms, shoving off her dress, her underwear, everything until she was bare and flushed and blazing before him. She tried to turn, but he pinned her back against the railing.

"No," he growled. He pointed down at the glowing water, their reflections staring back at them. "You're going to watch as I make you cum."

Analia opened her mouth. And her response was snatched away as Aaron dragged his tongue along her shoulder blade—Crystal fucking spare her.

"Gods, Analia," he said, his hand finding her breast. "You are a masterpiece."

He rolled her nipple between his fingers, already peaked and aching. Analia arched into his touch with a moan, Aaron swearing his approval against her shoulder.

She stared down at her reflection, her eyes wide, her lips parted, a breathless sound slipping free as Aaron found the spot on her neck that had all thoughts scattering from her mind.

She needed more of him. She was overwhelmed by him. The circle of his fingers, the hot, wet kisses he left on her neck, the contrast between the cool breeze against her skin and the heat radiating through the fabric between them—why was there *fabric?*

Analia twisted her head. Aaron allowed the movement, presumably thinking she was about to kiss him. But she used the momentum to flip them around, pressing him back against the railing.

Aaron's eyes widened, looking surprised and thoroughly onboard as she gripped the front of his shirt.

"Clothes off," she ordered, breathing hard.

Aaron glanced down like he couldn't fathom why his clothes were still there. He pulled out of her grip, stripping in record time, his arms tangling around her as her mouth collided with his.

Aaron's kiss flared across Analia's senses. His hands flashed across her back, her shoulders, her ass as if he couldn't decide where he wanted to touch her first. And Analia needed him everywhere. She needed friction, she needed to feel his hiss against her mouth again as she ground against him.

But Aaron had other ideas. He pushed off the railing, pressing her back, back, back, the back of her legs bumping rough stone.

"Sit," he ordered, low and breathless.

Analia couldn't have resisted if she wanted. She sank down on the bench, her legs shaking as Aaron knelt before her. He pushed her thighs apart, his gaze dragging down her drenched center with a hunger that had her mind spinning.

"What are you doing?" she asked unsteadily.

"Exactly what I promised," he murmured. He trailed his lips along her inner thigh, Analia's pulse stumbling through her veins as he moved higher, higher, higher, his breath fanning over her core as he whispered, "I'm showing Her Majesty the respect she deserves."

Analia's lips parted. And Aaron dragged his tongue up her center.

Analia's head fell back against the railing with a moan. Aaron hauled her legs over his shoulders, pulling her closer. And he devoured her. Worshipped her like a man at an altar, each scorching sweep of his tongue an offering, every kiss a vow he was desperate to make again and again.

Analia plowed her fingers through his hair, struggling to breathe through the surge of pleasure. She writhed against his face, chasing the sensation, that pleasure rising higher as Aaron moaned his approval.

He was the King of Starlight. Heir of Death. The most lethal, formidable man across Elefthia. And he was on his knees. For her.

"You are *mine*," she gasped, her fingers tightening in his hair.

Aaron's hand seized around her thigh. He sealed his lips around her clit, giving a long, hard suck. And the release that tore through Analia's body felt like the first blaze of a bonfire, her cry tearing past her lips like a plume of smoke.

She slumped back against the railing, her pulse staggering through her veins. But Aaron wasn't done. He pulled her harder against him, his mouth relentless. Starved. Analia no longer aware of the sounds she made as he drove her up and up and up and over the edge once more.

Analia gasped for breath, barely aware of the stone beneath her, her fingers still tangled in Aaron's hair. She just knew he finally pulled back, pressing a tender kiss to the inside of her thigh. And gods, he was going to be the death of her as he looked up, the hunger in his eyes searing through the haze across her mind.

He slid his arms around her waist, nipping along her jaw until he reached her ear. "On your knees," he whispered.

Gods, *please.*

Aaron helped her down onto her knees, bending her over the bench and resting her weight in her elbows. Her body shook in his grip, from the anticipation or sensory overload as his warm mouth traveled up her spine, she didn't know.

"Ready?" he breathed against her neck.

Analia nodded, all attention zeroed in on the press of his head against her entrance. And Crystal Bless that man, he didn't make her wait. He shoved inside her with one hard thrust, dropping his head to her shoulder as he moaned a curse. Analia bit down on her knuckles, unable to breathe around the stretch, the ache, how deep he pushed inside her.

Aaron flexed his hips. And if Analia wasn't already dead, she would be soon.

Aaron didn't waste time, every thrust fast and hard, his urgency tingling through Analia's blood. In those moments, there was no bridge beneath her. No lap of the lake. No schemes and threats and worries waiting for her outside the hollow.

There was just him. His mouth on her neck and shoulders. The brush of his chest across her back. The way he shifted, thrusting into the spot that had stars dancing across her vision and his name tumbling past her lips like a curse, a plea, a prayer.

Analia ground against him, "Aaron, I need—"

Aaron didn't let her finish. His hand slid between her thighs, his fingers stroking and coaxing. And flames bathed Analia's skin as she sobbed her release, flaring hotter as Aaron bit down on her shoulder and followed her over the edge.

She pressed her face to the stone, all concept of time scorched away. Only filtering back in when she felt Aaron sit up.

He gathered her to his chest, Analia limp in his arms. Eventually, she blinked her eyes open, finding him smiling down at her.

"I like break day," he whispered.

Analia breathed a laugh, burying her face in the crook of his neck. "Me, too."

The two spent the rest of the day in the lake's hollow. They alternated between the shore and the water, talking and laughing and lazily touching each other. Every time Analia started to ask if they should go back, Aaron found a new way to distract her, usually resulting in her toes curling.

By the time the sun had set, she couldn't remember why her thoughts had been so tangled. Not when this was all she wanted. His company, his thoughts, his smiles, his safety, every emotion that sparkled in his starlight eyes when he looked at her. Not when every question led back to the same answer. The only answer.

"Aaron," she murmured. The two lay entwined on the grassy slope, clothes on, Aaron's mouth warm against her shoulder.

Aaron hummed, not looking up.

"Ask me again."

Aaron froze. His eyes flicked up to hers, wide and alert. Hopeful as he asked, "We're thinking of the same question, yes?"

Analia nodded. And the smile that bloomed on his lips could have lit up universes. He sat up, reaching for his discarded jacket.

"You have it with you?" Analia asked, sitting up as well.

"I've been trying out being an optimist," he said, fishing the black velvet box from his jacket pocket. "The difference is disconcerting."

Analia's lips twitched. She proffered her hand, her fingers starting to shake as he turned back to her. Not from nerves. But the thoughtful look on his face as he studied the open box, quiet settling around them.

"I've been thinking a lot about what this ring means," he finally said, turning the moonstone ring between his fingers. "How it's a promise to protect you, cherish you. And I find it insulting."

Analia's lips parted. But her words trailed off as Aaron finally looked at her, eyes alight with all the stars in the sky.

"It's insulting to think it's an option I could deny when the moment I saw you in the tapestries, I knew you were special. And the second you laid eyes on me, my heart knew it was yours. Because the Crystal may have gifted me with death, but you Blessed me with the desire to be alive.

"Your smile makes me feel whole again. Your laugh reminds me there is hope in the darkness. Every look, every touch, every kiss I become more certain. All I want is to be there when you show the world what the fire in your eyes can do.

"I don't kneel here asking you to be my wife, or even my queen. I'm telling you you are my everything. I don't care if all of Elefthia separates us, or if we're ripped apart by war or worse. I will always love you. And I will never stop searching for you."

He finally claimed her hand, tears silently spilling down Analia's cheeks. "Marry me," he whispered. Not a question. A statement, just as he promised. And Analia knew her answer.

"You," she said, wiping her eyes. "You are my answer. Every option, every choice. I don't care if we're alone at a lakeside or entangled in the chaos that always seems to follow us. You are my home. My something to hold onto. You are the only thing I need. Because as long as I have you, I have everything."

Aaron's eyes shone. And Analia, the hollow, the world, held their breath as he slid the ring on her middle finger.

No facades. No schemes. Only them.

Aaron brought her hand to his lips, whispering against her ring. "Everything."

And it was. That moment... was everything.

Chapter 79

Dimitri had to get it together.

Ever since the incident under the table, he'd steered clear of Rayner. Not because he thought that moment meant anything—or because he started getting flustered any time Rayner looked at him. But because he had to prove it had been a fluke. Nothing more.

So, he wandered the castle, his eyes lingering on every man he passed, imagining what it would have been like if it had been him instead.

The two cramped together. His body cocooned around Dimitri's. The heat of his breath on his neck.

And nothing. He remained as disinterested as ever—which was fucking ridiculous. He could pop a hard on for the dumbest reason, for *no* reason, which was why that moment under the table was *meaningless.*

Dimitri scowled, picking at the crumbling stone of his window seat. He was just starting to think the whole thing was pointless when a passing servant caught his eye.

Dark brown eyes, curly reddish-brown hair, a fuller face and not quite full mouth. He had that slightly ageless look of the younger Blessed where Dimitri couldn't tell if he was in his late twenties or almost one hundred.

But Dimitri could imagine him under that table just fine.

The two remaining as still as possible. His arms tight around Dimitri, barely breathing, something dark and earthy in Dimitri's nose—Crystal fuck him, the servant reminded him of Rayner.

Dimitri ripped his gaze away, snarling under his breath at his half-hard cock.

He didn't have a crush. And he was going to prove it.

"**I**f I get wet because of you," Dimitri called, "I'll kill you."

He stood in the woods beyond the Ash Castle's walls, a narrow stream gently burbling beneath his feet as he hopped from stepping stone to stepping stone. Tyce had decided they needed to up his training, seeing as he was getting better at controlling his magic, but he still had to consciously think about it. Thus, he'd brought Dimitri to the river, where he had to follow Tyce's orders to summon and release his magic while trying not to fall in the stream.

"The water probably wouldn't even reach your waist," Tyce chided, lounging on a mossy rock on the bank behind Dimitri. "It's five steps, you can handle it—magic's out."

Dimitri hissed as a pebble bounced off the back of his shoulder. He quickly resummoned his magic to his hand, angling it so Tyce could see.

"No pausing your stepping," Tyce called.

"*You* pause your stepping," Dimitri grumbled, hopping onto the next stepping stone.

Across from him, Rayner's snickered. He perched in the bough of a tree a few feet off the ground, only partially paying attention to Dimitri's lesson as he scanned their mossy surroundings.

Dimitri's gaze wandered down to the purple lines peeking out from the neckline of his shirt, imagining the lightly-muscled torso beneath, his skin warm—

"Magic."

Dimitri jerked his gaze away as another pebble hit his back, his face flushed.

"Can I at least push you in, too, if I fall?" he whined, resummoning his magic and stepping onto the next rock. "You have to be used to it by now after all your training."

"Oh, I never had to hop across the stream," Tyce said. "The water would definitely extinguish my flames, but there's too much of a risk that those flames would find something else to ignite. Ash Royals train in a gravel arena behind the castle."

"Of course you do." Dimitri hopped on to solid ground, the moss wonderfully soft and stable beneath his boots. But Tyce wouldn't let him pause for long.

He turned back to the rocks, finding Tyce smiling lazily at him from his boulder on the opposite bank.

"If it makes you feel better," he said, "I once lost control of my flames when I was ten, and my brother threw dust and gravel at me until they were extinguished. By the time he was done with me, I looked like something you'd pull out from under a long-forgotten couch."

Dimitri snorted. He carefully hopped onto the first rock and summoned his magic to his fingers, his gaze briefly flicking over Tyce. His square jaw, his inviting brown eyes, Dimitri's mind wondering back to that table.

Tyce was probably the perfect person for him. He was sincere and patient, balancing out Dimitri's suspicious, anxious nature. He didn't mind the moments Dimitri's tongue was a little sharp, his easygoing nature leaving Dimitri feeling like he didn't have to be ready to bristle.

But still, there was nothing. No spark, no electricity that crackled through his veins.

"Magic," Tyce called. He flicked another pebble just as Dimitri hopped to the next stone.

The pebble hit his chest, right as he landed. And Dimitri's foot slipped.

Rayner audibly sucked in a breath. Dimitri waved his arms, desperate to regain his footing. Tyce started to rise.

But Dimitri regained his balance, his lungs deflating with a sigh of relief.

"Are you all right?" Rayner demanded.

Dimitri twisted around, finding Rayner's knuckles white around the branch beside him, leaning forward where he perched.

"He's fine," Tyce said easily, settling back on his rock.

Rayner didn't spare him a glance, all attention locked on Dimitri. Dimitri gave a jerky nod, his heart stumbling.

Tyce was right: he was fine. But that concern in Rayner's eyes... Gods, it felt so good to have someone care, even about the little moments, instead of brushing him aside.

Rayner's grip on the branch relaxed. He eased back in the tree, Dimitri realizing he was still staring at Rayner's face. A warm, heady buzz rolling through his veins, his eyes wandering along the gold flecks around Rayner's pupils, the slope of his nose, lingering on his mouth—gods damn it all.

Dimitri whipped forward, almost losing his balance once again. But he hopped to the next stone, not having to think before golden light rapidly flashed across his fingers.

"How are your military efforts going?" he asked Tyce, desperate for a distraction.

Tyce's mouth pinched. "It's... going," he hedged.

Dimitri didn't have to ask what that meant. Yes, Othin was storming through the castle, searching for the soldiers who had infiltrated the Healer School without orders, the guards just as furious at how relentlessly Othin pushed them with patrols. But now that Deardryn was back in Sun, not only was her presence a looming threat, but so was her ability to bring in as many soldiers as she liked in a blink. Meanwhile...

"The towns are so small," Tyce murmured, sifting through his handful of pebbles. "Yes, they're agreeing to fight with us, but with how large the central kingdom is, it will take time to gather enough forces to stand a chance. And we're losing time and resources every day."

Dimitri opened and closed his mouth wordlessly. What was he supposed to say to a man who had lost his kingdom, was making progress to get it back, but that progress might not be enough?

"Release it all down your arm," Tyce said abruptly, his heavy expression smoothing over.

So, as much as Tyce liked to care about other people's worries, he didn't let them see his own. Well, he supposed that wasn't surprising with a man raised to be an authority figure. Still...

Dimitri flared his magic, hopping onto solid ground. He crossed the couple paces to Tyce's boulder, nudging him with his boot until Tyce looked up at him.

"We'll get your kingdom back," Dimitri promised.

Tyce stared up at him, his hair turned to flame in the sunlight, something like indecision warring across his face. For a few moments, the only sound was the rustle of the wind through the trees. But finally, he trailed his fingers down the back of Dimitri's hand. "We will."

Dimitri grinned, rather pleased with his consoling efforts. Just for Tyce to tug his index finger.

"All the way down your arm, Dima. Training isn't done yet."

Dimitri's head fell back with an exaggerated sigh. He turned back to the rocks, sunlight flaring down his left arm as he hopped onto the first rock. And that light stuttered as he spotted Rayner watching him, his concern having hardened into stone.

But Dimitri wasn't supposed to care. They were friends, nothing more. Besides, he had bigger things to worry about.

For the next twenty minutes, Dimitri hopped back and forth along the stepping stones, Tyce calling orders, the breeze cool against the sweat across Dimitri's brow. At some point, he fell into a rhythm, allowing his mind to wander as he summoned and stepped.

Clearly, they needed to do more than assemble an army if they were going to take back the central kingdom. They needed to get a step ahead. Just as they had when Dimitri stole Othin's letter.

Dimitri shrank the sunlight glowing around his hand, his mind flashing back to the magic flaring across his fingertips in Othin's wardrobe.

"I think I'm going to need that damper blade back," he said, hopping onto Tyce's side of the river.

Tyce's thick brows lifted. "How come?"

"Othin is going to have to meet with the healers soon," Dimitri said, coming to pick at the moss on Tyce's boulder. "After all, sending soldiers into the Healer Temple uninvited would be a violation of the healer-Royal separation. But while Othin is the Sun King, he's not the Sun *Royal*. He can argue that technicality indefinitely. Meaning he won't be in his chambers with whatever he's hiding in his wardrobe for an extended period of time."

Tyce's face split in a slow grin. "You're devious," he said. He ruffled Dimitri's hair, not noticing Dimitri's eye twitch as he faded into the shadows.

Within moments, he returned exactly where he'd sat, a damper blade now glinting in his hand. "Let us know what you find," he said, passing it to Dimitri.

Dimitri gave a sarcastic salute.

The two talked a bit longer, Dimitri not bothering to return to his training. Eventually, Tyce rose to his feet with a stretch.

"I should get back to the safehouse, see if I have a town to visit." He extended his hand to Dimitri, but he shook his head.

"I want to stay out here a bit longer."

Tyce shrugged. "In that case," he said, resting his hand on Dimitri's arm, "good luck."

He paused, his hand lingering. Just long enough for Dimitri to notice. But before he could say anything, Tyce disappeared.

Huh. Dimitri looked down at his arm, then turned, finding Rayner still stone-faced in his tree.

"What was that?" Dimitri asked, puzzled.

"Don't play cute, Dimitri," Rayner said, sounding torn between tired and annoyed.

"I'm not!" Dimitri protested.

"He was flirting with you." Rayner hopped down from his tree and landed with a quiet rustle, his nose scrunched.

Dimitri stared. First at Rayner. Down at himself. Back over at Rayner.

"Why?" he asked.

Rayner made a noise that might have been disbelief. "There are endless answers to that question."

Dimitri shook his head, the concept not computing in his brain. "Tyce *likes* me?"

"You know, for someone who mocks Analia so relentlessly for missing Aaron's signs..."

Dimitri flipped him a rude hand gesture, "That's different." That didn't involve himself.

"Do you not like him?" Rayner asked, almost managing casual.

Up until that morning, he'd never considered it. But now, he slowly shook his head.

"Tyce is the second son of a low branch Ash Royal," he murmured. "There's no way he could possibly understand me."

He clamped his mouth shut before the rest of that thought could pop out. *Like you do.* But Rayner's closed off expression slowly opened once more as if he'd heard the words anyway. And Crystal strike him down, that look had a flush creeping across Dimitri's skin.

"So," Dimitri said, hopping on the first stepping stone. "All that touching, people like that?"

"Some do," Rayner replied, easing back against his tree. "Most will tell you only from people they like, and *especially* only when that touch is invited. But you don't seem to like it when people enter your personal space."

"I don't mind with some people," Dimitri mumbled.

Rayner smiled to himself. His gaze wandered over Dimitri's face, Dimitri stumbling as he landed on the moss before him. Coincidentally. Just as it was the exertion that had his pulse quickening, momentarily losing himself in the warm brown of Rayner's eyes, wondering what would happen if he was never found—no.

"There are so many poems about this in my book," Dimitri blurted, quickly skirting around Rayner to face his tree. "I've read about it so much... But it doesn't make sense."

"Are you not interested in it at all?" Rayner inquired.

His answer should have been no.

"I am," he mumbled, his ears burning.

"All right then," Rayner said. "We just have to figure out what you *do* like."

"Like what?" Dimitri muttered.

"Dima," Rayner purred, softening the syllables in his name into velvet. "Are you asking me to demonstrate options?"

He stepped closer, sending a thrill down Dimitri's spine. Once again, his answer should have been no. It really, really should have been no.

But Dimitri's body had a mind of its own: turning him to face Rayner, blood rushing through his veins, the word rolling past his lips. "Maybe."

Rayner's breath caught. His eyes darkened, dragging down Dimitri's face, his chest, Dimitri's cock stirring—this wasn't happening.

But he couldn't deny how his heart staggered as Rayner whispered, "Close your eyes."

Dimitri immediately complied. His senses strained across the distance between them, growing smaller as Rayner stepped closer, closer, Dimitri's back hitting the trunk behind him—gods, don't let Rayner look down.

"There are multiple ways to flirt with someone," Rayner began, his low, thoughtful voice sliding through Dimitri's veins like smoke. "Lingering looks. Body language. Acts of service. But I always come back to words and touch."

Rayner leaned in, Dimitri's body starting to shake.

"When you like someone," he murmured, his breath hot against Dimitri's temple, "it can be agonizing to keep those feelings to yourself. All you want is to steal a touch, let the words slip free, finally get an answer. But the possibility that answer won't be what you want is enough to have you suffer in silence. But sometimes..." Rayner sighed the word along Dimitri's jaw, sending him squirming. "Someone breaks. There's a touch. There's a high, finally feeling what you've been craving for so long, realizing it's even better than you imagined. But it's also so quick.

"Sometimes, it's just a taste." Rayner's warm fingers glanced off of Dimitri's wrist. "Other times, it's longer." His hand lingered on Dimitri's chest as it rose and fell unevenly. "And every time, all you can think about are the possibilities. What will they do next? What do you *want* them to do next? Would they do it if you asked? It sounds nerve-racking put like that, and it is. But it's also... exhilarating."

Rayner leaned even closer, Dimitri's skin unbearably tight as Rayner braced a hand on the trunk beside his head. "The high of stealing a touch in return. The electricity that runs through your body when they find that one thing that drives you insane. Like their fingers in your hair. Or their hand trailing down your chest. Or their lips on your neck." Rayner tilted his head, his lips barely grazing the spot below Dimitri's ear.

Dimitri's head fell back against the trunk, the whisper of a whimper breaking from his lips. And a jolt ran down his spine.

His eyes snapped open, finding Rayner's face inches away, his eyes wide and dark and burning with a hunger that had Dimitri wanting to grab him, drag him closer until nothing existed outside of the press of his body against his own. And that was the exact reason he cringed away, his words high-pitched and fast.

"I get it."

He tried to squirm away, but Rayner slid his hand down the trunk, blocking him. And Dimitri wanted to die as his gaze dragged down his body, finding the spot where his cock strained against his pants.

"You certainly do," Rayner murmured.

Dimitri wished the tree would swallow him whole. He tried to escape the other direction, but Rayner leaned in once more, his whisper hot against Dimitri's ear.

"I like that I turn you on."

Every thought scattered from Dimitri's mind. He stared at Rayner, wanting—gods, he wanted everything. But before he could look down, Rayner pushed away from him and turned away.

"Come on," he called, perfectly nonchalant as he strolled downstream. "We should get back to the castle."

Dimitri spluttered. His nails dug into the bark, his cock throbbing, his mind hazy with the ghost of Rayner's words.

Crystal spare him, he was in trouble. So much fucking trouble.

Chapter 80

Ember looked around the empty music shop, feeling as though she'd stepped back in time.

Thick, blue-gray carpet covered the floor. Shelf after shelf of shiny brass instruments took up the center of the room, protective cases and maintenance supplies neatly organized around them. The walls had been transformed into a mosaic of music notes, partially obscured by everything from harps, to lutes, to violins, even a piano, everything cast in the silver light of the balls of magic inset in the ceiling.

"What do you think?" Analia asked, stepping through the door behind her.

Ember tipped back her head, breathing in the slick, distinctive smell of wood polish. "I'm thinking I clearly haven't explored the Mirage enough."

Analia made a small, delighted noise. Letting the door swing shut behind her, she headed deeper into the shop, Ember still looking around as she followed.

"It's so quiet," Ember murmured, trailing her fingers over shelves as she passed.

"That's my doing," Analia explained, turning down one of the aisles. "You know Councilwoman Jeneva? I've been spending more time with her trying to figure out the Crystal, and turns out, her sister owns this shop. So, I asked if we could arrange a private visit."

"Anything for the future Starlight Queen," Ember said, wiggling her eyebrows.

Analia scoffed, the diamonds on her ring sparkling in the light as she waved Ember off.

After she and Aaron had disappeared the afternoon and evening prior, Aaron had Laness spread the word they were having a family breakfast. Ember hadn't thought much of it, too caught up in her brooding over yet another secret from the healers. But her mood brightened as Aaron and Analia pushed through the dining room door, Aaron triumphantly lifting Analia's hand as he declared he "Wore her down."

"I'm just glad that didn't include Branten tackling me into the wall with a hug," Analia laughed.

"Aaron's fine," Ember said breezily. "He's Blessed, he can take it. Besides, he's known Branten long enough to not be surprised by his exuberance."

Just as Ember hadn't been surprised that same exuberance had shocked Analia out of her uncomfortable shifting as she laughed, visibly relaxing into the shower of congratulations. Even now, her eyes sparkled as she passed Ember a tuning hammer from the shelf.

She deserved to enjoy this. Which was the precise reason Ember had tabled her plans to tell her about her addiction that afternoon. Even as the words churned inside her, just as desperate to be set free as they were to be locked away.

"At any rate," Analia said, "that's partially why I brought you here."

Ember brushed the thoughts aside. "Are you hoping for a song about how pretty your betrothed is?" she asked.

"He wishes." Analia grinned over her shoulder, leading the way to the side wall. Yet, as they reached the harps, her voice softened. "One of the things that has scared me most about becoming queen is losing myself in the crown. And if yesterday with Aaron proved anything, it's that I need moments to remember who I am. And I thought after being thrust into a foreign healer system in a hidden kingdom that shouldn't exist, you might enjoy some normalcy, too."

Analia looked at her hopefully. Ember reflexively ran her fingers along the closest harp's strings, filling the shop with a soft thrum. *Normalcy.*

"If you want normal," she said, "then you need a cloak hood to hide under, and I need a music teacher to harass."

Analia snorted, soothing the rolling ache through Ember's bones she didn't have the courage to examine yet.

"Well," Analia said, slinging a nineteen-string harp over her shoulder, "while I have no cloak, you can harass me as much as you like."

"That's not as fun," Ember whined, selecting her own harp. "You actually know what you're doing. Where are you going?" she added, hurrying past cushy stools as Analia headed for the opposite side of the shop.

"There are practice rooms up here." Analia stepped onto the rickety staircase tucked in the back corner, the wood squeaking beneath Ember's feet as she followed.

Sure enough, the stairs led to a landing with three doors. Analia pushed through the one on the right, revealing an intimate practice room.

It didn't consist of much, just a few stools and music stands, the carpet replaced by hardwood to assist with acoustics. Even though it didn't look like their old practice room, Ember had no problem slipping back into their usual routine.

Analia taking the stool on Ember's left. Their idle conversation as they tested their strings, punctuated by comments of it sounding too flat or sharp, neither of them minding as they slipped into silence to focus. And the longer it went on, the deeper that ache in Ember's bones became, the soft pluck of strings sending her mind back to that word. *Normalcy.*

A few weeks ago, she would have clung to that offer for dear life. A taste of normal was all she'd wanted back in Ash.

Yet, when she thought about what normal was, she didn't think of her routine back in the Healer School. Not her work in the apothecary. Not even her hours hiding in music halls with Analia and their harps.

She thought about her morning runs with Branten. Her lunches with the Starlight apprentices on the Healer Center roof. Walking through Aaron's house, wondering who she'd find sprawled on the sitting room couch.

Ember bit her lip, that ache radiating into a longing for fuzzy leaves. Because she knew normal could change over time. She just didn't think its past versions were supposed to hurt the more she understood them.

"How have your visits to Marisa's studio been going?" Analia asked.

Ember blinked hard, realizing Analia had shifted from testing her strings into an actual song. It was one of the first they'd ever learned: a slow, simple lullaby.

"I'm enjoying it," she said, her fingers instinctually plucking the harmony. "Cenn has been teasing me relentlessly because I can make advanced poultices without breaking a sweat, and yet I'm constantly defeated by a pottery wheel. But I paint better than him, so I still win."

"He should know by now that taunting you will only result in you beating him."

Ember's lips flickered in a smile. Even though she'd only gone with Cenn to the studio a handful of times, it felt good to have something that was hers.

"I'm glad you're starting to build your own life here," Analia said, eyes on her hands. "You deserve to have more than just the group you got sucked into by default."

"I like the family."

"I'm glad. I just... Are you happy here?"

Ember wasn't expecting that question. She looked down at her fingers, feeling that same quiet offer Analia had extended to her on the big house's roof.

If Sofika was there, she would tell her this was her moment to tell Analia about her devinroot. Take that final step and prove to herself she was ready to be a master healer. But this moment wasn't just about her.

Ember's fingers wandered across the strings, Analia quickly picking up the melody and filling the practice room with a dark, haunted waltz. The perfect depiction of how Ember had been feeling for she couldn't remember how long. And if the roles were reversed, if this was how Analia had been feeling, and she'd been keeping it from her to protect Ember's mood? She didn't know if she would be heartbroken or furious.

"Are we keeping today light and fun because we're celebrating?" she asked tentatively.

Analia shook her head. "Today is what it needs to be."

Rosala spare her, how did seven words leave her cracked wide open? She pulled her harp closer, the words balancing on the tip of her tongue, feeling like the final step before reaching the edge of a cliff. But if she could rely on anyone to be solid ground, it was Analia.

"Remember how I used to grow devinroot in my back room in the apothecary?" she asked, unable to meet Analia's eye.

Analia nodded. "It can be used in some poultices, right?"

"It can," Ember hedged. She paused. "I also used it on its own."

Ember stole a peek at Analia, who shrugged. "That hasn't exactly been a secret between us."

No, but the aftermath was.

Ember's fingers stumbled on a string, but she quickly recovered.

"You know how I used it to help me focus?"

Another nod.

"Well," Ember said, her hands starting to sweat, "when you left with Aaron and I got suspended from the Healer School, I started needing more. And when Sun invaded Ash, I needed even more. And eventually, I *needed* it."

Ember swallowed, not sure when the two had stopped playing. But now, Analia's level gaze was focused on her, no distractions. No noise to camouflage Ember's words as she said, "I'm addicted to devinroot. I haven't used any in almost two months, but I'm still addicted. And Sofika and Cenn have been helping me."

The final words escaped Ember's lips in a rush, desperate to be out. And even though there was a pure, wonderful release in finally setting those words free, she still held her breath as she waited for a response.

Analia, in turn, took a moment to soak it all in. She thoughtfully rubbed the wooden frame of her harp, Ember's pulse jittering through her veins as she waited. Finally, Analia nodded to herself.

"What do I need to know?" she asked.

Ember's eyes stung. She rubbed her tears away, letting out a choked little laugh as she realized she had no idea. "Don't let me touch devinroot?"

"Funny, I managed to get that far on my own."

Ember laughed in earnest, her mind fuzzy and spinning with relief. Her secret was out. Analia was still there.

But a small, uncertain part of herself couldn't help but ask, "Do you not care at all?"

"Of course I care," Analia retorted, lightly kicking Ember's shin. "I hate that this is something you have to deal with, and I can't fathom how you've kept this to yourself for so long. But I'm glad you told me. Especially since I'm going to need your help to not spiral over officially becoming queen, and I like to think helping you with this can even us out a bit."

Ember grinned, wrapping her arms around herself. "You're not going to spiral," she said, absolutely certain.

"And you're not going back to devinroot," Analia replied, equally certain.

Gods, she hoped so. Especially since she had a feeling the healers had a few more surprises to survive. But for now...

"Well," she said, sitting back on her cushy stool, "now that that's out of the way, I require all details from your little 'break day.'"

Analia's face screwed up like she couldn't decide if she wanted to smirk or hide. She repositioned her hands on her harp, about to speak. Just to pause as the air between them shimmered.

Laness appeared a moment later, dressed in all black, her tanned face pale.

Ember's stomach shifted.

"Laness?" Analia asked, surprised. "What are you doing here?"

"I'm so sorry," Laness said, her dappled green gaze bouncing between Ember and Analia. "You deserve a moment of peace. But I need you."

"Can it wait?" Analia asked. "We were in the middle of something."

Laness fidgeted with the enka bracelet peeking out from her jacket sleeve, her eyes wide and apologetic.

"Go," Ember said, the word momentarily clogging her throat. "We can talk more later."

"Are you sure?"

Ember was sure she was tired of her happy moments getting squashed. But based on Laness's expression, keeping Analia away would only make matters worse.

"I'll see you back home," she promised.

Analia bit her lip. Then, setting her harp on the floor, she rose and came to give Ember a quick hug.

Not saying anything. Not needing to.

Then, she pulled away, extending her hand to Laness. And all Ember could do was watch the two disappear, their farewells sounding more like "Danger" to her instincts.

Chapter 81

"Here they come," Aaron said.

He and Branten stood in the center of Mt. Lanula's internal courtyard, Aaron having shadowjumped them and their wagons of supplies a few minutes before. The Dovenesses were so accustomed to his monthly drop-off that the few women moving along the pathways carved into the rocky walls barely spared them a glance. Even the dozens of winllows drifting through the air seemed unfazed, the orbs of light casting a rainbow glow across the wide-open space.

Technically, Aaron wasn't expected until that afternoon. But with everything looming over his kingdom, his fraying nerves couldn't wait. So, he'd left right after breakfast. And as the two figures emerged from one of the countless shadowy pathways leading deeper into the mountain, he could only hope he was about to get at least *one* answer.

"Look who it is," Ethelind drawled, pushing back the hood of her gray-and-white robes as she approached. "My grandson, arriving early without so much as a heads-up."

"Apologies," said Aaron innocently. "If my resources are such an inconvenience, I can take them back. No trouble at all."

Ethelind let out a dry cackle. She patted his cheek, her weathered, regal face cast in blue by a passing winllow.

"Smart-mouthed boy."

Aaron started to protest, but she turned to Branten, openly snickering beside him. "You're looking tall."

Branten puffed out his chest. "And I feel it." His gaze drifted over Ethelind's head, finding Hyla silently lingering behind her.

The Doveness wore her magical body suit, the colors shifting to camouflage her tall, lean frame to her surroundings. Only her long black braids, dark brown complexion, and high, elegant cheekbones remained unobscured.

Branten opened his mouth. But Hyla stopped him with a glare. Her black eyes dragged down his face, his chest, all the way down to his boots before slowly making their way up again.

"No," she said, flat and firm.

Aaron winced. But Branten's eyes sparkled.

"You don't know what I was going to ask!" he insisted.

"I didn't know you were going to ask a question, and yet, my answer still applies."

"Well, that's a relief. I was going to ask if you'd like me to back off while you deal with the wagons. I'm so glad you'd like my help."

Hyla's nostrils flared, looking like she was ready to throw him off the mountain's peak. Branten grinned as if he'd love to see her try. Grabbing a wagon's handle, he sauntered toward the closest path, "I got this one, it's heavy."

Hyla snarled something under her breath. She marched forward, snatching the handle from his hand. "Stay in your weight class, runt."

She hauled the wagon away, not glancing back as she reached the pathway entrance. Branten claimed a second wagon, looking like a child set free in a sweets shop as he waved to Aaron and Ethelind, wagon wheels rattling over stone as he disappeared after Hyla.

Ethelind folded her arms. "Do I need to revoke his visitor privileges?"

"He's harmless," Aaron said breezily. "I would say he could stand to be knocked down a peg by Hyla kicking his ass, but I think he would enjoy that."

Ethelind scoffed. She reached for the handle on the remaining wagon, sounding genuinely curious as she asked, "Why *did* you bring him today? You usually come alone."

"Can't a man want a moment alone to tell his grandmother of his betrothal?"

Ethelind's steel-gray eyes widened. She dropped the handle with a clatter, drowned out by her voice as she exclaimed, "Aaron Stelingente, it's about time!"

Aaron cringed away from her echoing voice. "Why does your congratulations sound like a scolding?"

"Because it partially is." Ethelind shook her head, visibly torn between exasperation and affection. But she slid her arm across his back, her voice softening into a normal volume as she said, "Congratulations, my darling. She's exactly what you and the kingdom need."

The smallest light flickered to life in Aaron's chest. He leaned into Ethelind, soaking in the contact.

"We don't have a coronation date," he said. "Anna will choose when she's ready."

"Good." Ethelind ran her hand up his back, her gaze lifting to his face. Studying him. "So," she said. "What's wrong?"

Gods, she knew him too well. Aaron bit his cheek, his eyes flicking around to check no one was in hearing range.

"I have to ask you about the reward you gave Analia," he said carefully.

Ethelind's expression darkened. Her hand came to grip his shoulder, "Leave the wagon. Hyla will know what to do with it."

With that, she pulled him into the shadows. And Aaron didn't know if he was relieved or the furthest thing from it as her study materialized around him a moment later.

The stone chamber was sparse, only hosting a desk, a few shelves, and a window overlooking the mountainside. Ethelind preferred not to be cooped up all day, leaving Aaron little to distract himself with as she released him and briskly circled her desk.

"So," she said, taking a seat. "What have you found in the scroll?"

"Nothing good," Aaron sighed, sinking down in the chair across from her. He made to go on, knowing he had to tell her everything. But the words stuck in his throat, his muscles tightening as if bracing for a blow. "How did you get one of the scrolls?" he asked instead.

Ethelind's eyebrows flicked up. She sat back in her creaky wooden chair, rolling her lips as if trying to decide what to say.

"The scroll has been a secret in our family for generations," she finally said. "Your father gave it to me a few days before the Shattering, saying I wasn't to tell anyone of its existence until I passed it along to you. Normally, I would have been the one to give it to him, but my father skipped me when I ran off to the DovenU."

Aaron nodded to himself. Ethelind didn't like to talk about how she'd escaped the crown by fleeing to the DovenU, just for her family to drag her back to Star after her sister—and only sibling—passed from a sudden illness. Back then, the Royals still cared about the primary bloodline, meaning even if she didn't take the crown, she needed to produce an heir. And even though Ethelind was fond of her husband and adored Hester, she still fled back to Mt. Lanula when Hester was grown and could tell her to go be happy.

"Hester had no information on what the scroll said," Ethelind went on, drawing Aaron from his thoughts. "All he'd been told was if anyone came looking for it, he had to make sure they were worthy."

"That's... vague," Aaron said after a moment.

Ethelind shrugged.

"Is that also why you had me learn the forgotten tongue?" he asked.

"No, that was simply part of Star Royal tradition—although now that I say that, perhaps it was started for a reason."

Ethelind tilted her head thoughtfully. Aaron bit the inside of his cheek, the image slowly piecing together in his mind having his stomach sinking.

"Well then," Ethelind said, reclaiming Aaron's attention as her expression cleared. "Are you going to tell me your bad news now?"

Aaron screwed up his face. Ethelind tapped her fingers on the table, not breaking his stare. Never the first to cave.

Aaron sighed. "It's the contents of the scroll," he said.

Then, he told her everything. Their translations, Analia stealing Deardryn's shard, the possibility she might have already found the second. Each word seemed to rob him of something vital, the grim set of Ethelind's mouth having him wanting to curl in on himself even more. Because saying it all out loud didn't so much make it feel real as it did hopeless.

"We realized that the mark cuts through the two Crystal hiding places we know of," he said, dragging his hand through his hair. "Yet, when Accalon had Ember and the others draw the map, he used different symbols to mark *just* the mountains. And so far, the creature in Mt. Vasolus makes bargains through that mark, and Deardryn apparently found the scroll in Mt. Raegyr at a great cost. And since we know the other scrolls were *not* hidden in the remaining mountains, that likely means..."

"There's something in my mountain," Ethelind said bluntly.

Aaron dropped his gaze to the table, picking at a chip in the wood. "Do you have any idea what it might be?"

Ethelind was quiet for several moments. She rose from her seat and drifted over to the window, her fingers resting against the glass. Aaron held his breath, his magic stirring inside him.

"Accalon came to this mountain once," she finally said.

Aaron jolted upright. "He did?"

"About twenty-five years ago, right when I started slowly transitioning back into the DovenU."

"And you didn't tell Analia?"

"When would I have done that?" Ethelind asked pointedly. "When I was sending her into a trial, or when she came to recuperate here after you broke her heart?"

Ethelind didn't tear her gaze from the mountain range, but Aaron still felt her glare like a knife down his spine. He knew she had a point. But that rush of indignation on Analia's behalf was so much better than the sinking feeling dragging down his stomach.

"You're right," he mumbled.

Ethelind snorted something that sounded a lot like "I know," Aaron's jaw clenching as he bit back his retort.

"So, why did he come?" he asked instead.

"He said he was studying magic." Ethelind traced her fingers along the window-pane, her voice lost in memories. "I don't know how he made it here through the Wild Lands, especially since he was king at the time and couldn't afford to be gone for long. But there he was, casual as could be at the border, looking like he was delighted to see me as I stormed over to demand what he was doing. He was an infuriating man, too polite and charming for his own good. And my gods could he spin a story."

"Anna's the same way," Aaron murmured.

"Indeed." Ethelind finally turned from the window, boosting herself up to sit on the sill. "He didn't tell me much, insisting it was better I didn't know. But that didn't stop him from asking question after question about the magic of the mountain. Normally, I wouldn't have entertained such queries. But I've always considered myself to be a good judge of character. And something told me I could trust him.

"So, I told him how the mountain has a mind of its own. How there are some passageways even I haven't explored. And eventually, he asked if he could verify a theory."

"And you let him?" Aaron asked, startled.

Ethelind ran the toe of her boot along the floor. "I was careful not to reveal the DovenU to him, only telling him this mountain was a sanctuary to be respected. He swore to me on the Crystal and gods he wouldn't disrupt anything. So, I made sure everyone was tucked away, and I led him into the courtyard, where he quickly disappeared down a passageway. And it was a long, long time before he returned, his face pale, gripping the pin on his tunic that Analia now wears.

"I asked what happened, but he shook his head, saying we were safe and not to go poking around. Then, he left. And that was the last I ever saw of him."

Ethelind settled back against the window, story complete. And Aaron's thoughts swirled so fast he could barely track them.

"Did you figure out what he found?" he asked.

"No," Ethelind said as if the question was ridiculous. "He told me we were safe and not to go snooping around."

"And you *listened* to him?"

"Some magics are not to be poked at. You of all people should know that after going through the Underground."

Aaron's jaw clenched, arguments fizzing against his lips. But Ethelind brushed them aside with a sharp sweep of her hand.

"This mountain is kind to my girls," she said, hopping off the ledge and returning to her seat. "Our legends describe how inhospitable it was before Oharrah proved herself to the mountain. And I won't disrupt that peace. And neither will you. Not until you have stronger evidence than some lines on a map."

"Those lines have cut through two known hiding spots of the Crystal *and* all locations connected to the scrolls," Aaron argued, his knuckles turning white around the edge of the table.

"They also cut through countless other locations, and yet, there's only one shard left to find." Ethelind leaned toward him, unflinching as Aaron's magic flickered across his fingers. "Keep digging through the scroll. We already know the shard isn't here, so figure out what is before you charge in blindly. *That's* how you protect your kingdom and the DovenU—which is your top priority."

"Why do you think I'm telling you all of this?" Aaron regretted the harshness in his tone the moment he heard it.

Ethelind narrowed her eyes, but she didn't say anything as he pushed out of his chair, following her footsteps over to the window. He gripped the smooth stone ledge, trying to soothe his magic, trying to regain control.

Something important was in this mountain. He could feel it. And Ethelind was saying *no?*

"What's going on with you?" Ethelind asked. "You make risky decisions, but never rash ones."

"I do when those are all I have left," he muttered.

Gods, he sounded like a child. He felt like one, too, as Ethelind came to join him at the window, nudging his shoulder until he finally looked at her.

"You and I both know this doesn't have to do with the mountain," she said, surprisingly gentle. "What's going on?"

Aaron squeezed his eyes shut, hating the burn in the back of his throat. All he wanted was to stay silent, still, keep holding himself together because he didn't know how much of him would break off if he even twitched. But if anyone could outlast his silences, it was Ethelind.

"Deardryn is coming for our kingdom," he finally managed, opening his eyes. "Branten told me I've been too stuck in the past, turning over every decision I've made that could have brought us here. But when I look forward, I see no way out. All I see is Deardryn finding Starlight, destroying its secret, the sanctuary you and my people entrusted me to protect, and I just need to do *something.*"

The final words dragged through his throat like broken glass. He looked down as Ethelind rested her hand over his on the sill, her skin warm, his hands shaking.

"You've been raised in the afterglow of so many extreme gestures," she murmured. "You grew up in a kingdom Talitha established in secrecy, delegating countless resources to keep it that way. You came here after your father jumped almost an entire kingdom's-worth of people here during a war, sacrificing himself in the process. Your mother charged onto the battlefield to avenge her family, bringing a war to an end, and losing her life to do so."

"They were heroes," Aaron rasped, rubbing his eyes with his free hand.

"Yes, they were. But I worry those grand gestures have become—not normalized to you, but expected. Like anything less than is unacceptable."

Aaron looked away, the truth in her words stinging across his skin. Ethelind gripped his hand, leaning in front of him and demanding his attention.

"What do all of these heroic acts have in common?" she asked.

"The well-being of the kingdom," Aaron mumbled.

"Exactly. You weren't entrusted with keeping the kingdom a secret. You were entrusted with the safety of the people. This moment was inevitable from the moment Talitha established her base, and it was accelerated when your father brought everyone here. You're not a failure of a king because it happened during your rule. But if you're more concerned about maintaining the kingdom's secret than protecting the people, you're not going to be making the best decisions *for* the kingdom. So take a deep breath, let yourself have your moment—because Crystal knows you need those when wearing a crown—and find the path forward."

Her steely gaze pierced into his, giving no room for argument. And Aaron didn't so much as break as he did sag.

He pressed his forehead against the cool windowpane, wishing he was back at the lake with Analia, pretending none of this existed. Because somehow, Ethelind had found the heart of every worry, every twinge of guilt, and struck home.

Ethelind sighed, removing her hand from his to run it down his back. "Shall I stay or leave you to your moment?" she asked.

"Stay," Aaron said immediately.

Ethelind patted his shoulder. Then, she withdrew her hand. And she remained quietly beside him as his "moment" played out.

Find your path forward. He already felt like he'd searched everywhere: translating the scroll, getting the council involved, running himself ragged maintaining the wards, organizing patrols, turning over every possible move Deardryn could make. Mt. Lanula was his only remaining option, and Ethelind was right. They had to be smart about it.

Which only left the quiet, unbearably heavy option he'd been desperately fending off.

"Starlight is going to be revealed," he murmured. A statement, not a question. He turned his head against the glass, catching Ethelind nod.

"What are you going to do about it, Your Majesty?"

Brace himself for the moment it happened. But beyond that...

"Stop trying to prevent it and start preparing for when it happens," he said.

Ethelind's look of approval was the worst thing he'd ever felt.

"I'm also changing the big house's sitting room," he muttered.

Ethelind barked out a laugh. "It's about time." She reached up, patting his cheek. "Go be king. And make sure Hyla hasn't killed Branten."

Aaron offered a tired salute, having no idea how he would force himself down the path he'd found. He supposed one step at a time. So, with a farewell, he faded into the shadows. Just as his enka bracelet buzzed across his wrist.

As soon as you're done with Ethelind, came Laness's voice, *come to the Council Building. We need you.*

Chapter 82

Analia was not prepared for this.

Laness pulled her out of the thick, earthy darkness on the same rocky ledge where Lev and his squadron had cornered her and Aaron months before, the rush of the river's current echoing far below. Her eyes flashed around, flames crackling in anticipation. But the half a dozen soldiers before her wore black fighting leathers.

They clustered together in a tight ring, weapons and metal reinforcements glinting, a few soldiers keeping watch from the tree line. And throughout it all, there was the wailing.

"What's going on?" she demanded, striding toward the group of soldiers.

"See for yourself, Your Majesty," said the closest soldier, a fair-haired man Analia knew was named Tamen.

Analia started to tell him that wasn't her title. But Tamen shifted, allowing her to peer through the gap between himself and the curly-haired woman beside him. And her words choked off.

A man with shoulder-length black hair crouched in the center of the Starlight soldiers' ring. He twisted from side to side, his dark eyes rolling, his hands clawing at his ears as he rambled something Analia couldn't discern. But she had no problem recognizing the white and gold of his fighting leathers.

"We found him wandering along the border," Tamen explained, his voice faraway in Analia's ears.

"What's wrong with him?" she breathed.

"My Blessing." The curly-haired woman stepped forward, bowing her head to Analia. "My name is Layce, Your Majesty. I'm able to deprive others of their senses, and currently am stifling his sight, smell, taste, and hearing. I tried to take away touch, but he started thrashing, and we didn't want to accidentally harm him before receiving any orders."

That made sense. But why had Laness brought *her* there?

"I would have gotten Aaron," Laness said, anticipating her question as she joined them. "But he's busy with the DovenU."

"So, you got me," Analia finished.

Crystal spare her, there was too much to process. Her friend had just told her she was addicted to a magical plant, a Sun soldier was on their border, these soldiers were calling her Your Majesty, Laness was finding her to give orders—there was a *Sun soldier* at their border.

"Apologies," Analia said, raising her hands. "This isn't my decision to make."

"You're betrothed to His Majesty, aren't you?" Tamen asked. "That's his ring on your finger."

"Well, yes, but I'm not crowned—"

"His Majesty wouldn't have given you that ring if he didn't already trust you to rule," Layce said, brushing back her red-gold curls with her dagger hilt.

Gods, she knew that. Aaron believed in her in ways she hadn't known possible. But wanting her to be queen someday and being comfortable with her currently giving orders on his behalf were two completely different things.

Analia subtly wiped the sweat from her palms on her pants, struggling to maintain her composure. She couldn't overstep. But she couldn't think over the wailing, the implication of this man's presence, her lungs squeezing.

"I..." Analia began.

"Analia!" the Sun man shrieked, drawing out each syllable as he lurched forward. "Bring Analia here!"

Analia's blood went cold.

"There's also that," Layce said softly.

"He's been saying he needs to talk to you from the moment we found him," a third Starlight soldier said, running his thumb along his sword. "Says he won't talk to anyone other than you."

Analia shot Laness a look, unable to tell if she fiddled with her weapons belt out of guilt or nerves. But it didn't matter.

Regardless of what she thought, what she wanted, she was involved. Because that was what Deardryn had decided.

Just for a moment, everything slowed. Every thought, every concern, every uncertainty, all settling inside her like a pile of kindling. And finally, Analia didn't hesitate to let her flames ignite.

"Give him his hearing back," she ordered.

An ancient part of herself dared Layce to roll her eyes. But she nodded and flicked her fingers without pause, Analia's steady blaze burning hotter as she sensed the gentle melody of Layce's magic twine around the man's head.

Immediately, he went still. A predator picking up a scent. Then, he gasped, lunging for the closest soldier.

"I can hear the wind and the river, I can feel you nearby. Where's Analia?"

The Starlight soldier kicked him away, the man making a keening noise as he toppled back into the center of the ring. "Where is Analia?"

"I'm here." Analia stepped forward, Tamen reaching out to stop her. But she gave him a reassuring nod, the soldiers silently shifting back to let her crouch just out of the Sun man's reach. "You asked for me?"

He twisted toward her voice, hands grasping, "How do I know you're Analia?"

"Touch her and you'll lose your hands," Tamen spat.

Analia startled. She was so used to indifferent guards outside of Aaron. She never would have expected their protection, respect, to help push back her shoulders. Even as the man's face twisted in a sneer.

"Drop your hands, soldier," Laness said softly, stepping up behind Analia.

He hesitated, fingertips inches from Analia's arm.

"So," he panted, drawing out the word like the slide of a blade. "There's more of you. We're up to twelve."

"Congratulations," Analia drawled. "You know how to count. I'm sure Deardryn will be thrilled to know you found twelve people on a random ridge in the Wild Lands."

"Yes, especially since those people are wearing high-quality fighting leathers and carrying pristine weapons. Almost kingdom grade, wouldn't you say?"

Analia's lip curled, soldiers tensing around her. "Tell me what she wants," she said, "or the next place you'll explore is the bottom of the river."

"How do I know you're Analia?"

"Because these are my flames." Analia snatched the hand inching toward her once more, making sure he could feel her skin growing hotter, hotter, hotter.

The man yelped. He tried to wrench free of her grip, but Analia held on tight.

"What does she want?" she asked, slow. Quiet. Lethal.

But the man didn't flinch. He licked his chapped lips, Analia only just realizing how young he looked beneath his dark beard.

"Her Majesty said I was to only tell you in private," he finally said. He leaned closer, not minding Analia's warning flare of heat. "What say you? Get rid of your guards and we can talk."

His fingers grazed her shoulder. Analia gestured to Layce with her free hand, and she snapped her fingers with a quick flare of magic.

"No!" the Sun soldier shrieked. He lunged for Analia, Laness yanking her out of the way just in time.

She toppled onto the rocks, her palms stinging as two soldiers she didn't know surged forward. The Sun man screeched as they grappled, demanding they give him his senses back, give him Analia, the Starlight soldiers finally pinning him to the ground with their boots on his back.

"Are you all right?" Laness gasped, green eyes wide.

"Fine." Analia rose to her feet, her heart pounding against her ribs. Not from the Sun soldier. But Deardryn.

Taunting her. Threatening her home.

And Analia was *done* letting Deardryn loom over her every move.

She turned to Tamen, his knuckles white on his sword hilt. "How long ago did you find him?"

"Less than ten minutes," he reported. "The glamor kept him from crossing the border—the fool was mumbling something about endless ridges when we found him. But he definitely seemed to know what he was looking for."

Analia's stomach dipped. She looked around at the group, expecting to find the same dread tapping against her awareness. And while each face was certainly unsettled, more than that was the fury that had her own blood singing.

Analia nodded, offering her hand to Laness and pulling her to her feet. "You're able to roottravel with multiple people, right?"

"Short distances, yes," she confirmed. "What are you thinking?"

Once, Analia would have been thinking so many things she would have been paralyzed. But now, the words flew past her lips.

"You, Layce, and I are taking our new friend back to the Council Building. Let Surce know through your bracelets to meet us there, we're going to need an interrogator. As for the rest of you—" Analia pivoted to look at the soldiers, all of whom snapped to attention, even those at the tree line. "We need two groups. One is going to keep watch on the border and make sure no one else is hanging around. The rest of you go to the river. We need to figure out how he got here and if anyone else is with him. Laness, can you contact the captains and have another patrol dispatched?"

"Already on it," Laness said, twisting the enka bracelets peeking out from her black sleeve.

"Good." Analia's eyes swept over the guards, all watching her expectantly. "We'll keep you updated."

The soldiers nodded. Then, they tapped their weapons together in a metallic salute, the sound buzzing through their words like a harmony. "Yes, Your Majesty."

With that, they launched into movement. Layce came forward to relieve the soldiers pinning down the Sun man, his wail still echoing as Layce pressed her boot between his shoulder blades. It only took a few quick words before the others separated into their groups, each splitting off in different directions, their boots near silent on the rocks as they disappeared into the trees.

If anyone was going to find any strays, it was them. Still...

"We have merchants arriving today, don't we?" Analia asked, looking between Laness and Layce.

"We do," Laness confirmed, tucking a lock of chin-length brown hair behind her ear.

"I want to talk to them as well," Analia decided. "They might have seen something on the river, maybe even heard something suspicious from their trade partners."

"Wise call, Your Majesty," Layce said, kicking away the Sun man's grasping hand.

The title still prickled across Analia's skin. But she could get used to it. Although there was already someone who had that title, and he wasn't there.

"Layce," Analia said, "can you get him on his feet?"

Layce snorted as if that were a stupid question. She bent down to drag the man to his feet, letting out a hiss as he whipped his head back into her nose. The two grappled, Analia taking the opportunity to turn to Laness.

"Have you told him yet?" she asked, quiet enough only Laness could hear over the scuffle.

She shook her head. "I was waiting until we had a plan."

Analia couldn't decide if she was relieved or heartbroken. Gods, all she wanted was to keep Aaron far, far away, spare him from the devastation as long as she could. But she couldn't shield him from this. He had to—*deserved* to—know.

"Tell him to come as soon as he's done with Ethelind," she said, her words weighing down her heart. "Don't tell him why, though. I need to be there when he finds out his worst nightmare might be coming true."

Laness bit her lip to stop it from trembling. Analia turned to Layce to give her a moment, the soldier now on his feet with wrists between his shoulder blades.

"You did good here," Laness finally said, her voice small.

Analia folded her arms, her blaze a steady crackle through her veins.

"I'm just getting started."

Chapter 83

Dimitri marched through the Ash Castle halls, Rayner following close behind.

Just as he'd suspected, Othin had stormed down to the Council Chamber to meet with the archmaster healers first thing that morning, leaving his chambers deserted. And Dimitri had the damper blade that could bring everything to an end.

Finally, he wouldn't just get a leg up on his father. He would win. And it didn't hurt that it also provided a distraction from the tension that fizzed between himself and Rayner.

Not the kind he was used to. This was the pull of a magnet, drawing his gaze to the tension around Rayner's mouth, remembering the ghost of his lips across his neck—*no*.

Dimitri shoved the thoughts aside as he rounded the corner, finding Joshel, dressed in his gold-and-white fighting leathers, leaning beside Othin's door halfway down the hall.

"Should I be surprised to see you two?" he asked, rubbing his face.

Dimitri's lips parted, a response already on his tongue. But he paused. Really looked at Joshel. The exhaustion weighing down his eyelids, the faintly curious look in his pale blue eyes, his casual stance as he pushed off the wall.

"You know we're up to something," Dimitri said slowly, pausing before the guard.

Rayner coughed. But Joshel shrugged.

"From everything I saw in the Sun Castle," he said, "you hate King Othin. Even if he's your only form of protection, it doesn't seem like you have any reason to want to help him. Yet, you've become his most requested advisor."

His gaze met Dimitri's, waiting for him to deny it.

Dimitri picked at his nails. "You would think it's your job as a guard to inform your king of your suspicions."

Joshel bit his lip. Rayner shifted uncertainly, but he remained quiet, letting the indecision war across Joshel's face.

Just when Dimitri thought the silence would snap...

"I don't like what we're doing here," Joshel mumbled. "Invading a kingdom for an unknown reason, killing one little girl and locking another in a cell, hovering over the Ash citizens. I became a guard to protect my Royals, not inspire fear in innocent people trying to live their lives. And I... I don't like the orders I'm being given."

Joshel rubbed the back of his neck, his eyes downcast as if he'd admitted treason. Maybe he had. After all, his morals had enabled Dimitri's schemes.

Dimitri looked at Rayner, wanting to silently confer. But the pure, unconcealed look of understanding on Rayner's face as he nodded to Joshel had his thoughts drifting away.

"You don't have to lie for us," Rayner said softly. "You don't even have to stall for us. But if you let us inside one more time, we might be able to finally bring this to an end." He bowed his head, as earnest as Dimitri had ever seen him. "It's up to you."

Where did that come from? Dimitri's eyes bounced between Rayner and the uncertain guard, completely at a loss. But sure enough, Joshel's shoulders slumped.

"I won't protect you if he comes," he warned, stepping away from the door.

"You can drag us out if you want," Dimitri replied, still taken aback. But not wanting to give Joshel a chance to change his mind, he gripped the silver knob, giving a twist and stepping inside.

Just as he expected, the chamber was silent and empty. Rayner murmured something to Joshel as he softly shut the door behind them, Dimitri too consumed by his tightening shoulders to notice. Gods, his father's presence was everywhere.

"Come on," he said, heading for the wardrobe tucked in the back right corner. "I don't want to be here when Othin's done throwing his fit."

He pulled open the carved wooden doors, barely sparing the mess of clothing a glance as he dropped to his knees. He'd been reaching toward the back when the shield tingled across his fingers, and since he didn't know if Othin would be notified if anything crossed his shield...

Dimitri unsheathed the damper blade tucked in his boot, his senses pricking as Rayner came up behind him.

"Is this the Sun King's wardrobe?" he asked, clearly disgusted as he thumbed through Othin's tunics. "My gods. Just because it's expensive doesn't mean it's fashionable—is that embroidery supposed to look like *dragon scales?*"

"If you'll recall," Dimitri said absently, poking his dagger through the clutter, "we're supposed to be looking for whatever Othin's hiding in here."

"Clearly, it's not taste."

"Says the man who spends hours staring at himself in the mirror."

"That's not taste, that's vanity, and he doesn't have that either."

Dimitri snickered, needing several moments to realize his shoulders had relaxed. He looked up at Rayner, finding that same faint smile from the Full Moon Festival flickering across his lips. As if he'd won a point in a secret game. And as the leather hilt in Dimitri's hand tingled, Othin's magic traveling down the blade, Dimitri wanted to give him all the points he had.

"I think I found it," he said, dragging his gaze back to the wardrobe.

"What is it?"

Dimitri squeezed his eyes shut as Rayner crouched beside him, filling his nose with something dark and earthy. He had to get it together.

"Let's find out." Resting the blade on the wardrobe's bottom, Dimitri reached inside with both hands, feeling around until he found a wooden chest the length of his forearm. He tried to lift it, finding it lighter than he expected as he pulled it free.

"Pretty," Rayner commented, eyeing the gold, metallic sun painted in the center of the lid, its rays extending out along the chest.

"He must not have picked it out," Dimitri replied.

Rayner grinned. And Dimitri couldn't help cradling the point of his own to his chest.

"Well," he went on, "might as well open it."

Rayner looked as though he were about to respond. But finding the small metal latch, Dimitri flicked it open, his other hand lifting the lid.

And a buzz that had nothing to do with Rayner fizzed through his veins as he looked down at the neatly stacked pages within. The top page addressed to Othin.

"Looks like we found S's letters," Rayner murmured.

Yes, and a lot of them.

Dimitri skimmed his fingers down the width of the stack, thick enough they had no chance to get through everything in the short amount of time they had. He looked up at Rayner, the crease between his brows telling Dimitri he'd reached the same conclusion.

"It will be three days before she writes another letter," Dimitri reminded him.

Part of him hoped Rayner would immediately shut him down, tell him it was far too risky.

But Rayner's nod was firm as he sat back on his heels. "We'll just have to pray he doesn't check before he has another to add to the pile."

And that they would be able to sneak the letters back inside.

Dimitri didn't speak the thought aloud. He just retrieved the letters, shut the box, and moved to replace it in the wardrobe.

Dimitri sat on his chamber floor, Rayner across from him as they sifted through the letters. Thankfully, Joshel had turned his face away as they exited Othin's chambers, not trying to stop them from taking the stack of letters—although convincing him to let them return it was bound to be an interesting conversation. But that was a problem for later.

Now, Dimitri skimmed through page after page, he and Rayner having split the pile between them. But he quickly realized S's letters weren't as helpful as he'd hoped.

They mostly consisted of short, mundane details from her day, seemingly at Othin's request. If Dimitri hadn't known better, he would have suspected she was only replying out of obligation.

"Have you found anything useful?" he asked, setting yet another page beside him, carefully maintaining the original order.

"She's glad Deardryn is home and no longer has to listen to the councilmen left in charge in her absence," Rayner offered. He slumped back against his bed frame, absently tapping the damper blade against the floor as he read. "Do we know who S is?"

"Yes," Dimitri said tersely.

Rayner's eyebrows flicked up. But clearly seeing Dimitri had no interest in elaborating, he let it go with a shrug.

"Based on her responses," he said, "we'd have more luck reading through Othin's letters and all his complaints. But maybe if we can find the response to the letter we *did* steal..."

Rayner trailed off, pages rustling. Dimitri determinedly kept his gaze on his own sheets, trying to focus on the elegant—if not sometimes shaky—handwriting. Yet, even as he skimmed, his mind wandered back to Rayner.

The reason they'd gotten into Othin's chamber. The look of understanding on his face as he spoke to Joshel.

"Can I ask you something?" he blurted.

Rayner started, but he only missed a beat. "Of course."

"Why did you seem to understand what Joshel was talking about back in the corridor?"

Something in Rayner's expression closed. He dropped his gaze, Dimitri not expecting a response. But he only remained quiet for a few moments before murmuring, "I was thinking about Scarsthain. How I got there."

Dimitri perked up. He'd been wanting to ask about that for weeks now, but it didn't seem like a story he should pry for. Even as it dangled in front of him, right in reach.

Rayner lifted his gaze, then breathed a laugh. "You're adorable."

Dimitri spluttered. "I what?"

"You're visibly squirming with how badly you want to ask."

Dimitri tried to protest, his ears burning. But Rayner raised a hand.

"It's all right." He placed the page he was reading on the stack to his left, his expression growing thoughtful as he retrieved another letter.

Dimitri held his breath. Finally, Rayner began.

"I grew up in a small farm town outside the central Moon Kingdom. Despite producing a decent harvest, my town was nowhere near wealthy. But my family was. We didn't have to depend on crops for gold when we could change our appearances and steal from those in neighboring towns.

"My mother did her best to shield my sister and I from the family business. If she had her way, we would have grown up completely ignorant and left before we could get dragged in. But my father always said I had potential. And when I was thirteen, he gave me my first assignment. Assume the identity of the baker's son a few towns over and smuggle as much food as possible.

"Turns out, I was a natural. I only needed an hour of observation before I could mimic a person's tone, their gestures, their body language. I was quick on my feet if anyone became suspicious. I could stifle my guilt as easily as I could swipe a pouch of gold because that's what it took to keep my family alive. All until my final assignment."

Rayner went quiet, his gaze lost in memories. Dimitri leaned toward him like a flower toward the sun, even as his heart sank.

"My father didn't tell me what we were doing," Rayner finally said, his head drooping. "It wasn't until we snuck into the inn a few towns over that I started to worry. And I was terrified as my father broke into the room where a seventeen-year-old boy, same age as myself, was sleeping before his visit to the Royals to discuss a future engagement. And I was to kill him and take his place."

Dimitri caught his breath.

Rayner hugged his knees to his chest. "I don't know if his guards heard us come through the window or our scuffle. But they burst inside. My father fled. I was captured. And since the Royals were never able to find him, Sylas's father, who was king at the time, decided I would bear both our punishments.

"This was seven years after the Shattering, things were... harsher then. Nevertheless, I was sent to Scarsthain that night. And for the next year..."

Rayner trailed off. His gaze fixed on something far away, his body stilling into stone. And Dimitri had never been more terrified than he was watching the blank, empty look hollow out his eyes.

"Don't," he choked out, scrambling closer, finding his hand. "Please, I don't want to know, don't go there. Come back."

His voice was so small. He squeezed Rayner's hand, not knowing what else to do.

But slowly, Rayner's gaze found his. Focused. He flipped his free hand, his arms still wrapped around his knees. Dimitri tangled their fingers, Rayner's grip tightening like Dimitri was the lifeline pulling him home—he never should have pried.

"You can stop," Dimitri whispered, practically begged.

Rayner shook his head, breaking Dimitri's heart even more as he forced his mouth to open.

"I lost the wraiths in the river when I escaped," he rasped, steadier than Dimitri expected. "I don't remember what happened until a young master healer fished me out of the water. I know he knew who I was. I was in tattered clothes, emaciated, the wraiths had reported an escaped prisoner. But instead of turning me in, he brought me back to his home and did everything he could to heal me. Feeding me, talking to me even though it was weeks before I could respond. I'm alive because of him.

"But eventually, the other healers found out. He tried to protect me, saying his oath decreed he help anyone in need. But the healers said that didn't apply to people like me. So, they exiled him. And the last thing I saw before they brought me to the Royals was the purple rings split at the corners of his eyes.

"I should have been dead after that. But for some reason, Sylas fought for me. He said I was a boy, and there was no justice in having me pay for another man's choices. So, we made our oath: my eternal loyalty to the kingdom and Royals in exchange for Sylas's protection. And that might be where it ended for everyone else, but not me."

Rayner slipped his arms free from his knees, Dimitri's arms twisting awkwardly. But he wouldn't have let go if the gods demanded as Rayner brought his hand to his lips.

"I spent ninety years drifting through shadows, barely surviving, not always wanting to. But then you showed up. And in a lifetime of nightmares and misery and doubts, you're like seeing in color again. You're a relentless buzz that feels everything so much—and I know you hate it, but I love it because it makes you so alive. It makes *me* feel alive. And you sitting here, listening to me after everything I've done? You make me want to be better."

"You are," Dimitri whispered, his eyes stinging.

Rayner's throat bobbed. He pulled Dimitri closer, their arms tangling between them, the golden flecks in Rayner's eyes blazing like tiny embers. "What are you thinking about?" he whispered.

Dimitri could barely breathe out the word. "You."

"What about me?"

Every place they touched. How for the second time, Dimitri had initiated their contact. And just like their moment on his bed, he never wanted it to end.

"I'm thinking about how angry I am you had to go through that," he said, staring into his eyes. "I hate how alone you were. How you had no one to take care of you. And all I want is to take your pain away."

"Why?" Rayner asked, soft and broken.

"Because you're Rayner," he said simply. And it was. As simple as the lock and key tattooed on their shoulders.

Rayner released a harsh breath. And Dimitri didn't know which one of them moved first.

He released Rayner's hand, fisting his fingers in the front of his tunic. Rayner pushed him back on the floor, sending papers scattering.

But Dimitri didn't care. He didn't know how to care as Rayner landed on top of him, his mouth finally finding his neck. Not in the whisper of a touch. This was all hot, starving intent, his lips soft, each kiss deep enough to drown in.

Dimitri's head lulled, blood rushing to his cock as he moaned. Gods, this was so much better than he'd imagined. So intoxicatingly, world-shatteringly better as Rayner cursed against his neck, his hand curving around Dimitri's face.

So tender. Light enough Dimitri could pull away if he wanted, just as he'd gone for his neck as if giving him time to back out.

But Dimitri didn't want him to stop. He wanted the heat radiating off Rayner's skin, the graze of his chest against his as he braced his weight in his elbows, he wanted *him.*

But he had never done this before.

Dimitri hesitantly rested his hand on the back of Rayner's neck, shuddering at how soft his hair was against his fingers.

"Dima, *more,*" Rayner groaned. He flicked his tongue around Dimitri's earlobe, sucking it into his mouth.

Dimitri's soul momentarily left his body. His hand moved on its own, plunging into Rayner's hair, Rayner's moan of approval sending him spinning out of control.

"I need to feel you," Dimitri gasped, tugging on his shoulder. "Please, I need—"

Dimitri cut off with a gasp as Rayner let more of his weight drop, the hard length of him pressing against Dimitri's thigh. He squirmed, Rayner kissing down his neck, shoving his collar aside, his mouth hot and wet on Dimitri's shoulder. And Dimitri lived, died, and was reborn in the flames that seared down his body.

"Gods, Dima," Rayner panted, pulling Dimitri's face to his. "Tell me this is real. Tell me that you want this." He leaned in, whispering a breath away from Dimitri's mouth. "Tell me you want me."

Dimitri would say whatever he wanted. His lips parted, Rayner's heart pounding against his chest, a light in his eyes Dimitri had never seen before. But the word that tumbled through Dimitri's mind wasn't yes.

I won't choose your life over mine.

Rayner waited, his thumb caressing along Dimitri's cheekbone. But Dimitri couldn't speak.

He could only watch as that light in Rayner's eyes flickered.

Then dimmed.

Then went out completely.

"You don't trust me," Rayner whispered.

Dimitri's heart shattered.

"I do!" he gasped, his hand tightening on Rayner's shoulder.

"But you don't forgive me. Not completely."

"I..." Dimitri tried to force out the word, a sob rising in his throat as it refused to come.

Rayner sadly shook his head. "It's all right, Dimitri," he said, destroying him even more as he sat up. "I'll be all right. But I can't keep trying to redeem myself to someone who doesn't want it."

"But I do—you have!" Dimitri struggled into a sitting position. "You have in more ways than I can count."

"Then why don't you forgive me?" he asked. So simply. So lost.

All Dimitri wanted was to give him an answer, tell him he meant more to him than any arrangement of words could convey. But the one word he needed refused to come. And Dimitri's tears spilled free as Rayner scooted away.

"I'm sorry," he sobbed, reaching for him. "I can get there, I just need time."

"That's the thing," Rayner said gently. "You don't deserve to have to."

Rayner turned away, hiding his face as he started to collect their papers.

Because that was why they had come. To get a step ahead of Othin. Dimitri was there, demolished on the ground, because of Othin. This was all because of fucking Othin.

Dimitri grabbed the closest page, ready to tear it in half. But a word jumped out at him. He wiped his eyes, quickly skimming the page.

And for one blissful moment, the fear that skittered down his spine distracted him from the wreckage in his chest.

"Rayner," he whispered.

Rayner raised a hand, "Dima, it's fine, you don't—"

"Rayner," Dimitri said louder, his voice shaking. "The patrols at Mt. Vasolus are collecting obsidian."

Rayner froze. He turned slowly to face Dimitri, the letter in his hand falling to the ground. Because Dimitri had told him about Deardryn summoning Devourists to collect her rings. The obsidian needed to summon them.

"Deardryn is building an army," Dimitri breathed.

And the rest of his world collapsed.

Chapter 84

Aaron pulled Branten out of the shadows in the Council Building entryway, ready for the threat as his eyes flashed around the gray marble. But he recognized all of the people before him.

Analia, Marion, and Jeneva huddled together twenty paces away, heads bowed in conversation. Laness shifted restlessly off to the side, biting her nails as her other hand moved from bracelet to bracelet on her muscular arm.

Never a good sign. But the ice barely had time to form in Aaron's veins before Analia turned. And the quiet, steady blaze in her eyes took his breath away.

"Good," she said, striding toward him and Branten, Laness close behind. "You're here."

Branten began, "What's going on—"

"I'll tell you on the way," Laness said hurriedly, "we need you at the riverbank."

Branten's expression darkened. He glanced at Aaron, Aaron's stomach sinking as he realized neither of them believed she was talking about one of the rivers running through the kingdom. But before either could speak, Laness grabbed Branten's hand, and they disappeared.

Aaron turned to Analia, ice clogging his throat. "Anna...?"

"I want to check the map in the hallway one more time," she called over her shoulder. "I'll fill His Majesty in while we look."

His Majesty?

Aaron started to interject, his nerves nearing their breaking point. But Analia grabbed his hand, marching him past the spiral glass staircase, between silver pillars, pushing through one of the many heavy metal doors, letting it clang shut behind them.

"Analia," Aaron said, speeding up to match her pace, "what's going on?"

Analia didn't break her stride. But her formal tone finally softened into something familiar as she said, "I have to tell you something. And you deserve ten seconds to be Aaron before you have to become the Starlight King."

She continued to pull him down the hall, Aaron not trying to resist. Because there was only one reason Analia would act this way.

Aaron's eyes landed on the massive painting of his kingdom hanging on the wall up ahead, frost crackling around his heart like a shield as he remembered Surce's similar tapestry with the sun shining on his border. But Analia didn't spare the map a glance. She pushed open the closest door, Aaron barely having time to register it was a storage closet before she pulled him inside and shut the door.

Aaron glanced around the cramped space. Forgotten clutter lay in heaps to his left, dust and mildew filling his nose.

Analia stepped closer to him, still holding his hand as her eyes roved over his face in the dim light. And the tenderness, heartache, that softened the blaze in her eyes had Aaron's knees shaking.

"You know what I'm going to say, don't you?" she asked. She ran her thumb along his icy knuckles, Aaron not sure if he craved her warmth or wanted to shrink away.

"I think I need to hear it regardless," he rasped.

He hoped she would bow her head, take a steadying breath, anything to prolong the reality where he could be wrong. Where he could pretend the moment he'd told Ethelind he would come to terms with hadn't arrived far sooner than he was ready for.

But Analia squared her shoulders as if ready to take on whatever burden he gave her. And she stared directly into his eyes as she said, "A patrol discovered a Sun man on the same ridge we found Lev and his soldiers. He doesn't seem to have crossed the border, but it sounds like he knew what he was looking for. And he has a message for me."

Analia studied his face, clearly waiting for a reaction.

But Aaron didn't break. He didn't tremble. And he didn't so much as set the ice free as he let it settle over him.

It hardened around his heart, sealing all anguish away for later. It frosted over his mind, slowing his thoughts, banishing the shadows, leaving him with a cold, wicked clarity.

Analia found his other hand, squeezing as tight as she could. Her hands so warm, thawing a narrow pathway through the ice, just for her.

Aaron looked down at their hands, then up at her questioningly.

"You looked like you were freezing over and needed something to hold on to," she explained.

Gods, what had he done to deserve her.

"My shooting star," he sighed, bowing his head, resting his forehead against hers. "Thank you."

Analia released one of his hands, drawing her fingers down his cheek. "You're still icy," she murmured.

Aaron's lips flickered in a wry smile. "That's because when I fall in this pit, I'll need more than ten seconds to drag myself out again."

"I'll help you."

"I know," Aaron said, brushing his nose against hers. "But right now, we have to deal with this."

Analia nodded. Aaron braced himself for the moment she pulled away. Instead, Analia touched his cheek.

"I love you," she said, as if they were the only words she could think to offer. And to Aaron, they were all he needed.

"And I you." He stole a quick kiss, the warmth of her mouth thawing him the perfect amount, the ice still cold in his veins. "Now, tell me everything."

By the time the two made it back to the entryway, Aaron was all caught up. He was also thoroughly impressed with every decision Analia had made—especially thinking to summon the merchants. Informing the council was a good touch as well, especially since he would have dragged his feet if it were up to him.

Before he could tell her this, Jeneva bustled toward them. Her azure eyes flicked between Analia and Aaron uncertainly, finally landing on Aaron as she said, "Branten thinks the man is Blessed with scouting magic. They're struggling to find a trail—"

"I'm not here," Aaron interrupted.

"What?" Jeneva and Analia stared, the former confused, the latter exasperated. But Aaron waved a hand.

"Don't talk to *me*. Talk to the Royal who's been handling this from the start."

"Apologies," Jeneva said, her eyes bouncing between Aaron, Analia, her ring, back to Aaron. "I didn't realize..." Not bothering to finish her thought, Jeneva shook her head, then turned to Analia as if nothing had happened. "Branten's asking to send a Blessed tracker to see if they can detect anything."

"Send two," Analia said, not missing a beat. "One might miss something the other will catch."

Excellent decision.

"Yes, Your Majesty." Jeneva bowed her head, first to Analia, then Aaron. Then, she hurried off, already gripping the enka bracelet Laness had given her gods knew when.

"People keep calling me Your Majesty," Analia mumbled, half to herself.

"It suits you," Aaron replied.

Analia rolled her lips, but Aaron still caught her satisfied smirk. And fuck, he might not need his ice to stay calm after all if watching her rule was an option.

"Your Majesties," Marion called, footsteps echoing off the marble as she approached. "The merchants are on their way."

Analia nodded, then looked at Aaron. "What do you want to do?"

"I want to hear your thoughts," he said, lounging back against a pillar.

Analia looked like she was struggling not to roll her eyes. But when Analia got going, she couldn't help herself.

"I think we need to split up. One of us talks to the merchants, the other the council to decide how we want to proceed."

"I'll take the council," Aaron volunteered.

"Which means I have the merchants," Analia said. She nodded, satisfied with their arrangements. And Aaron didn't get a chance to wish her luck before she pivoted on her heel and swept back across the entryway, going to greet the small group of merchants who had just arrived at the door.

Aaron looked at Marion with a grin. "She's a natural," he said, the words delicious on his tongue. Because he'd always known. All she'd needed was a chance to prove it to herself.

"She certainly is," Marion agreed, following him as he pushed off the pillar and headed for yet another metal door. "And what are you?"

"Oh, I'm a disaster waiting to happen," Aaron said cheerfully. "But I always thrive until the crisis is over."

He pulled open the shiny silver door, waving Marion ahead of him. And from that point on, Aaron's day became a haze.

Talking to the council, everyone agreeing this couldn't go ignored. Trading updates with Analia as they passed in the hall, Aaron going to meet with the trackers in a different room, Analia off to confer with the council about the increased attention and questions from the merchants' trade partners. Laness did her best to pass updates along with her bracelets, Surce apparently not getting far with her interrogation.

By the time Aaron left his meeting with the trackers, learning that the Sun man had purposefully stashed his boat halfway up the river to travel undetected on foot, his jaw was tight with fury. A cold, quiet fury that had his magic snarling through his veins.

"Surce says she's gotten as much out of him as she can."

It took Aaron a moment to realize the voice wasn't in his head. Another to realize it wasn't Laness's. He paused halfway down the hall, his eyebrows flicking up as Mor approached from the opposite direction.

"I thought you were with the humans," he said.

"Not when our home is in danger. I've been helping Branten organize patrols." The two met in the center of the hall, Mor's face uncharacteristically tight. "You holding up?"

Aaron nodded once. "You?"

Mor shrugged. Neither of them were convincing.

"At any rate," Mor said, dragging a hand through his hair, "Laness sent me because her magic is running low. But Surce thinks it's time we send in Anna."

"Then let's go," Analia said, rounding the corner ahead of them, her hair now hastily braided over her shoulder.

At any other time, Aaron would have asked if she was sure. But now, he only reached for her hand. "Ready when you are."

Analia looked at Mor, who flicked his golden hand, already looking lost in thought. Then, she nodded to Aaron. And offering a farewell to his brother, Aaron pulled himself and Analia into the shadows.

Despite Surce bringing Rayner to her studio for her interrogations, Aaron didn't head there. That was a rare situation where they had reason to believe he could be trusted. But now, as the shadows faded around him, Aaron knew this was *exactly* where that man belonged.

The black stone chamber was located beneath the Council Building across from the Royal vault. The air was thick with the metallic scent of old blood, the torches in each corner of the small chamber highlighting the rusty stains around the drain in the floor. And chained to the opposing wall, breathing hard and face gleaming with sweat, was the Sun man.

"Aren't you a stubborn one," Aaron purred. His gaze moved over the man, finding no physical injuries—the blood always resulted from his turn to interrogate. But he liked that haunted, glassy look in his dark eyes. Even as they looked right past Surce seated in a chair before him, over Aaron, landing on Analia.

"Princess Analia Valarus," he panted, his chains rattling as he tugged against his restraints. "You should know I don't respond well to playing hard to get."

Aaron glanced at Analia, not sure how she'd react to all of this. But Analia folded her arms, her attention on Surce as she turned in her seat to face them.

"What has he told you?" she asked.

"A few weeks ago," Surce began, tired and calm, "Deardryn shadowjumped this man to the Moon Kingdom and sent him down the river with a message only for your ears. He has refused to provide his name, the topic of that message, or any other details."

"I take my job seriously," he interjected.

"He's dampered, and has been checked for any magical objects or modes of communication," Surce finished as if the man hadn't spoken.

Analia nodded. "In that case," she said, turning to the man, "I think it's time you finally start talking."

"Uh-uh," he said, jerking his chin at Surce. "Lady Mind Games goes. Same with cheekbones over there."

"My name," Aaron said, as cold as the magic he let flicker around his shoulders, "is Aaron Stelingente. I think you want to talk to me, too."

That certainly got the man's attention. He leaned forward as far as his chains allowed, something like hunger darkening his bloodshot eyes. Aaron held his gaze, neither of them moving as Surce rose and glided toward the exit, the heavy iron door thudding shut behind her, the lock clicking into place. Only then did the man's attention shift to Analia.

"Her Majesty sends her regards," he said. Something about his voice reminded Aaron of bugs skittering across his skin.

Analia didn't reply. She walked around the chair to stand before him, her arms folded.

"I'm sure you're curious why," he prodded.

Analia remained silent. The man squirmed, looking for a reaction, Aaron chuckling as he stepped back into the shadows lining the room.

"She's found your little kingdom," he went on. "She sent me to inform you she'll be waiting on the riverbank where I left my boat two afternoons from now. She wants to talk."

Aaron's magic seethed. Still, Analia remained silent.

"She also said," the man continued, growing louder, "if you have any hope of peace, you'll return me to her in one piece."

"One piece, huh?" Analia finally asked, chillingly quiet. "That makes sense."

The man sneered, relaxing back in his chains.

"Then again," Analia said, "it's amazing what healers can do these days."

His eyes widened. Analia's hand shot out, closing around his throat. And the man's screams echoed off the stone as fire danced across her fingers like ghosts around a tombstone.

Aaron drifted closer, drawn by the smell of burning flesh, the man trying to jerk away. But Analia waited a few moments before finally releasing him, her fingers burned around his throat as he gasped.

"This is not a game you want to play," she hissed, leaning in close.

"I agree," Aaron said, stepping up behind her. Then, he slammed his glowing hand on the man's chest. Starlight surged through his skin, his ribcage, rotting his heart in seconds.

Aaron stepped back. And the man sagged in his chains. Dead.

Analia stared at the Sun man for a few moments. Aaron's magic snarled around him, his brow already lifted challengingly as she finally turned to him.

But Analia wasn't reproachful. Not even angry.

She was furious. The kind of fury that wasn't to be placated, but survived, her eyes blazing with a fire that could build and destroy worlds.

"Deardryn doesn't get to decide the rules anymore," she told him. Steady. Unstoppable. Glorious.

Aaron nodded once. Then, he looked back at the man, taking in his slack face, his mangled throat. And Aaron *wished* killing him made him feel even a fraction better.

Aaron stepped out of the shadows in his bedroom hours later, Analia's hand mercifully warm in his. He didn't remember the endless discussions that had followed him killing the Sun man. He didn't particularly care to.

All that mattered was Deardryn was coming. His icy cocoon was almost completely melted. And the council had agreed whether he and Analia met with Deardryn was up to them.

Analia started to release his hand, the blaze in her eyes having faded into exhaustion long ago.

"Anna?" he asked, her name coming out tired and small.

She paused, her eyelids heavy as she looked up at him. "Yes?"

Aaron swallowed hard. "Will you just... sit with me?"

After the endless questions that day, he didn't know how that one felt like the most vital. Maybe not just for him, either, for Analia's lips parted, her voice shaking. "Always."

She nudged him down on the edge of their bed, wrapping her arms around him, her body so warm. Thawing the last of the ice.

Aaron closed his eyes, burying his face in her hair.

And finally, he broke.

PART 4: CORONATION

Chapter 85

Ember didn't think the sitting room had ever been so quiet. She and the rest of the family sat scattered across the couches, having abandoned their breakfasts once they'd realized no one was hungry. Not just because between the five of them, they'd been able to piece together everything that had happened the day before. But also because no one had seen Aaron or Analia since.

Ember chewed on her thumbnail, wanting to break the heavy silence, but having no idea what to say. There hadn't been anything anyone could say to console her when Deardryn invaded the Ash Kingdom. She couldn't fathom going through that grief of losing a home not once, but potentially twice. So, she remained silent, her gaze downcast.

"Can you detect anything from their bracelets, Laness?" Surce finally asked.

Laness flinched, Surce's soft voice uncomfortably loud in the quiet. "Aaron's blocking me out as usual," she murmured, twisting one of her many enka bracelets. "But Anna's... calm. I don't know if I should poke, though, and ask—"

"I hear something," Branten blurted.

Ember straightened. Branten flashed Laness an apologetic look, but she waved him off, the suffocating mood across the sitting room lifting a fraction as a door creaked open upstairs. Footsteps moving down the hall.

Analia was the first to appear at the top of the stairs. She wore a sleeveless silver tunic and leggings, her phoenix pin peeking out from behind her hair. Ember could have sworn she did the smallest double take when she realized the silent sitting room was in fact occupied, but she continued downstairs without pause.

Revealing Aaron behind her. And the dead look in his eyes had Ember's breath catching.

"I'm assuming by your silence we don't have to fill you in on what happened," Analia said, reclaiming her attention as she reached the foot of the stairs.

"We've pieced it together," Mor hedged. He stole a quick look at Aaron, Branten's knee bouncing beside Ember's as he clearly struggled not to do the same.

Gods, within seconds, their dark, brooding mood had pulled taut enough Ember could snap it with a flick of her fingers.

"Have you decided what we're going to do?" Surce asked.

"There's no choice," Aaron said, coming to slump down next to her, Analia sitting on his other side. "We have to meet with Deardryn. Otherwise, she'll keep sending soldiers until she breaks through our wards."

"Confirming we're here will result in the same," Branten mumbled, unusually sober.

"True," Analia said. "But at least in talking to her, we can try to negotiate—if not throw her off our trail."

No one seemed particularly hopeful about that. They all looked to Aaron, clearly anticipating him to elaborate. But he only dropped his gaze to the hand Analia rested on his knee. And that tension slackened into silence once more.

Gods, Ember had never realized how heavily Aaron set the tone of the house.

If he was hopeful, they were hopeful. If he said they could figure it out, they believed it. Even his moods meant something. Because if he could overcome the dread, the uncertainties, undoubtedly swirling in their own minds, they could, too.

He was their something to hold on to. And based on the curl of his shoulders, he had nothing they could grasp.

Analia studied Aaron for a long moment, her fingers gently brushing his. Then, she turned back to the others.

"If we're going to pull this off," she said, fixing her posture, "we're going to need three groups. One goes to talk with Deardryn, one stays behind to watch the kingdom, and the third goes to Rosala's temple to find that shard."

"The temple is warded," Surce murmured, eyeing Branten as he retrieved a pen from the low table to play with.

"When has that stopped us?" Analia replied.

A few shrugs, everyone looking away.

"I'll go to the temple," Ember volunteered. She forced her fidgeting fingers to still in her lap as all attention flicked to her, Analia flashing her a grateful look.

"Are you sure you want to lead that group?" Mor asked, not unkindly from Branten's other side. "Your oath seems to have strict parameters around when you're allowed to visit, and the last thing we want is for you to risk your healer status to help us."

Ember started to reply, just to catch the nods all around the room. And a lump formed in her throat.

Because they believed she had an oath worth saving. One that, based on everything she'd seen, would only come into play if she returned to the Ash Kingdom.

Back to being an apprentice, unable to share all the knowledge she'd learned. But did she want that?

"If everything I've done so far hasn't broken my rings," she managed, "visiting a temple should be no problem."

Branten and Analia shared an uncertain glance. But Ember swallowed hard and pushed back her shoulders, her voice coming stronger.

"No Royal is permitted to enter the temple, but my markings seem to give me my own Crystal-sensing abilities, so I'll be able to tell if it's there. And since Aaron has to shadowjump Anna to meet Deardryn, Laness's roottravel will be the fastest way to get there."

Laness nodded slowly, her boot softly knocking against the table's leg as she thought. "It's a longer journey than to the Moon Kingdom, but I think I should be able to get us there by tomorrow afternoon if we leave soon."

"I can shadowjump you two most of the way there tomorrow morning," Aaron murmured.

Everyone perked up, all eyes flashing to him. But Analia didn't give them time to dwell on his exhaustion as he rubbed his eyes.

"That works. We can send you off with a few damper daggers as well. Hopefully, they'll be just as good at blocking temple wards as chamber wards."

"The healers will *love* that," Branten said with a faint grin.

"Good news," Analia replied, "they'll be returned to their original places the moment the daggers are removed."

Branten made a noise as if he slightly wished they wouldn't, and Ember's and Laness's lips twitched.

"All right," Analia said, her ring sparkling in the light as she tucked her hair behind her ear. "Who's staying to watch the kingdom?"

"Me," Surce said immediately. "I want to be able to consult my tapestries as the missions progress."

"Which means I'll be keeping watch on the border," Branten said, his boots thudding on the table as he stretched. Surce pushed them off, Branten whining in protest, Mor muttering a curse and elbowing Branten as his knee knocked into him.

Analia watched the exchange, struggling to stifle her smile. "We'll send a patrol to assist."

Branten brought a hand to his chest as if mortally insulted.

"Oh, please," Ember said, "you've already decided to assemble help."

"Shhh," Laness whispered. "You have to let him protest so he thinks he has a say."

Branten started to respond, his eyes gleaming.

"Which leaves me to join Anna and Aaron," Mor said loudly.

"Yes," Analia agreed, smirking as Branten flopped back against the couch in defeat. "Just as I wanted."

She looked over at Aaron, who was already nodding.

But something about that arrangement bothered Ember.

"Shouldn't we keep the patrol on the border and send Branten with you?" she asked Analia. "I know Mor is the best choice for negotiations and is plenty lethal, but standard guarding procedures would have one guard per Royal."

"She's clever," Laness said approvingly.

"Deardryn won't know Mor is there," Aaron explained.

"Besides," Branten drawled, twirling his pen, "Mortie is the last person you want to encounter when things get dicey."

A small, self-satisfied smirk flickered across Mor's lips. One that had Ember wondering if she had misjudged him.

"I promise," he said, shifting to look at her fully, "I'll have no problem watching both of their backs."

He flicked his golden fingers, Branten whining in protest as his pen vanished, then reappeared in Mor's hand. He winked at Ember. And Ember sank back against the couch with a nod.

With that settled, everyone looked to Analia.

"All right, then," she said, a spark kindling to life in her eyes. "It's settled. We've got the rest of the day to prepare."

She looked around the group. And Ember watched as that spark caught, traveling from face to face, even Aaron sitting up a little straighter as they all nodded. Then, they got to work.

Branten rose and went to confer with Surce, Mor following Laness over to the map of Elefthia someone had hung on the side wall. Within moments, the sitting room was alive with the usual clamor of voices, twining around Ember in perfect harmony as she beamed at Analia.

She had completely shifted the tides. And based on the ghost of pride in Aaron's eyes, he'd realized it, too.

He brushed his knuckles along her cheek, saying something too quiet for Ember to catch. Analia said something in response, Aaron shaking his head. Then, he kissed her temple and rose.

Ember caught his eye as he passed her and mouthed, "You all right?"

Aaron nodded, then quietly slipped out the door. But of course, everyone noticed.

"He's fine," Analia said with a stretch. "He wanted to go for a walk and think about how to approach our meeting with Deardryn. Not even worthy of brooding in his mom's room."

The room gave a collective shrug. Then, they returned to what they were doing. And Ember couldn't help her grin as she leaned across the couch toward Analia.

"That was quite the rally, Your Majesty," she said confidentially.

Analia snorted. Rising from the couch, she gestured for Ember to do the same.

"Come on," she said, heading for the stairs. "I'll give you the damper blades now while I'm thinking about it."

Ember dutifully rose and headed after her.

They had one day to plan. One day, and she would be at the Temple of Rosala. The pinnacle of every healer's journey, the heart of their oaths.

And maybe, she wouldn't just find the Crystal shard there. Maybe, she would finally find the answers she needed to decide where to go next.

Return to Ash, or stay in Starlight?

Chapter 86

Aaron walked through his sleepy kingdom streets, struggling not to feel like he was looking at a memorial.

Even though Analia had declared Deardryn didn't make the rules anymore, it was hard not to see it that way. If he truly had a choice, he wouldn't meet with her. He wouldn't jeopardize his kingdom's secret to appease her. Yes, Ethelind was right, that secret couldn't be his priority, but it was entangled in what was.

His people's safety. A safety Analia had spent the morning so beautifully organizing to preserve. Meanwhile, he'd been staring at the path forward, unable to move.

Aaron sighed and rubbed his face, dully noting Zella coming down the street toward him. The head librarian had her nose buried in the books she held in each hand, seemingly checking information between the two.

"Zella," he called, "you're about three steps away from walking into a pole."

Zella startled. Her large tawny eyes bounced up from her books, flashing around the street, finally settling on him as she frowned.

"There's no pole," she said.

"No, but there could have been." Aaron reached her side, ignoring Zella's scoff as he nudged up a book to read the title. "Marble carving?"

Zella jutted out her chin, her indignation wavering. And as always, her excitement over her latest read won out.

"I know, I wasn't expecting to like it either. But I was organizing the section, and one of them popped out at me, and here we are." Zella gestured with her books, pages rustling.

Aaron's lips twitched in the ghost of a smile. "Does that mean I should get out of your way and leave you to it?"

"It *means* you should walk me back to the library and indulge my prattling," she retorted.

"It would be my honor." Aaron sketched a bow, slipping two slender daggers from his boots. Then, he stole Zella's books, marked the pages with his blades, and flipped them shut to carry.

Zella squawked, "Those are mine!"

"If you're walking with me, you're not walking into a pole." Turning, Aaron headed back the way he'd come, calling over his shoulder. "You did this to yourself."

Zella tried, but she couldn't suppress her laugh.

"Such a cocky boy," she said, hurrying after him. "I hope you know stealing my books means I get to ask why I caught you with that brooding look on your face."

Aaron's faint flicker of amusement caught.

Gods, all he wanted was to brush her off. He couldn't keep talking about it over and over again, his mind silently continuing the cycle until he thought he would unravel completely.

But judging by the look on Zella's face as they turned the corner, the thought alone had his "brooding look" sliding back into place.

Aaron sighed, checking to make sure the few people nearby weren't in hearing range.

"I had to make a difficult decision today," he murmured.

"Ah." Zella nodded sagely. "Does it have to do with what happened at the Council Building yesterday?"

Aaron's eyebrows shot up, and Zella made a grab for her books. He swatted her hands away, Zella giving him a melodramatic pout. One that had the beginnings of his icy irritation melting once more.

Still, he couldn't bring himself to look at her as he murmured, "Rumors certainly spread fast around here."

"Oh, but rarely accurately," Zella said dismissively. "There were some that thought you brought your healer friend here because Analia was secretly having your child, and that's why she hadn't been seen for weeks."

"Really?" Strangely, Aaron didn't mind that rumor as much.

Zella laughed. She started to respond, a passing dark-haired man cutting her off as he called, "Don't forget to tell His Majesty you started that rumor."

"Really?" Aaron looked back at Zella, incredibly intrigued to hear her response.

"What?" she asked, unapologetic. "I get to have some fun every now and again."

Aaron laughed. He shifted Zella's books away from her, expecting her to use his distraction to her advantage. But Zella made no grabs for the books as she smiled up at him.

"There you are," she said softly. "I've been missing that smile." She turned onto the library's street, Aaron blinking hard as he drifted after her. "I don't need to know what happened in that Council Building. But this decision that has you all twisted into knots... Is it because you're uncertain about your choice, or because it was a hard one?"

"The latter," Aaron sighed.

"Good. That usually means you're on the right path."

Gods, he hoped so.

"I suppose it's all a matter of perspective," he murmured, echoing his words from the library all those weeks ago. Zella's eyes sparkled up at him as if he'd found the most important answer of all.

"Exactly," she said. "Although, sometimes that perspective comes best with a distraction."

Pausing at the foot of the white marble steps before the library's front doors, she angled her head toward him. "Would you like to come in? I'm sure I can find some records for you to organize."

Once, Aaron would have taken her up on that offer in a heartbeat. But now, he looked up at the library.

The tall, circular building had always reminded him of a tower, the stone smooth and sleek, decorated with banks of windows that reflected the light. If they were in one of the fairytales from his children's books, it would be where the captured Royal would sit and wait to be rescued.

"Not this time," Aaron decided. "I want to walk around some more."

Zella seemed pleased by this. "In that case," she said, "I expect a visit soon. And bring Analia."

"Why, so you can make up another rumor?"

"I was actually planning on stopping a few. But now..." Zella grinned, outstretching her hands and wiggling her fingers.

Aaron rolled his eyes and handed her her books. Zella promptly reopened them, passed Aaron his daggers, and returned to her reading as she headed back into the library. Then, he was alone. Turning over his own words as a cloud shifted above, allowing the sun to warm the back of his neck.

It's all a matter of perspective.

He didn't think there was any shifting his perspective on Deardryn. Yet, as he turned to continue through the Pulse, the streets slowly getting busier as the morning went on, his heart didn't ache at the sight of everything he could lose.

He thought of his people whispering rumors amongst each other, everyone knowing where they originated. The way everyone recognized the people they passed as they went about their days, exchanging nods and greetings, sometimes stopping to chat. The way he'd felt like his world was slipping through his fingers, just for Zella to make plans with him for the future.

Aaron paused to watch as a trio of girls, no older than twelve, strolled passed Sofika's central garden. With a squeal, the blonde girl on the left noticed the pair of finches that had come to investigate the bird bath, the girls shushing each other as they clustered together to watch.

This was why he loved his kingdom. The people. The community. The way they had made it through the darkest times but could still find the joy in the smallest details.

This wasn't a kingdom. It was a home. And it was his job not to look at it as everything he had to lose, but everything he had to protect.

Which meant he'd been wrong. Going to see Deardryn *was* his choice. His choice not to hide and hope he could build his tower walls thick enough no one could get through. A choice that had his feet turning around and bringing him home.

"There you are," Analia said. She sat on the edge of their bed, setting the map she'd been examining aside as he stepped through their bedroom door. "How was your walk?"

"Enlightening."

Analia tilted her head, her smoky gaze studying him as he came to sink down beside her. "Should I ask?"

Aaron sighed, running a hand through his hair. But he finally felt certain of his words as he said, "This kingdom is our home. Which means we do what we must to keep it safe. Even if that means letting its secret come tumbling down."

His words settled between them, dark and heavy. Not leaving much room for conversation.

But Analia was only quiet for a moment before she asked, "What if you didn't have to carry that burden alone?"

Something in her tone had Aaron's gaze lifting to hers. Finding no uncertainty, no hesitation. Just a resolve that had the breath freezing in his lungs.

"Anna," he said, their bedroom quiet around them. "Why do I get the feeling we're not talking hypotheticals?"

"Because," she said, not releasing his gaze. "I've been thinking, too. And I think we should get married. Tonight."

A nalia patiently waited for Aaron's stunned expression to clear. For him to unfreeze. And when his mouth finally opened, he only managed a single word.

"Why?"

Analia didn't mean to laugh at that. She smothered the noise with her hand, Aaron's eyes sparkling as his shock melted away.

"Anna," he said, finally sounding like himself, "where is this coming from?"

"Me," she said simply.

In the hour Aaron had been walking through their kingdom, she had been pacing around their room. Turning over every decision they could make, each path forward, every potential outcome. And while Aaron's walk had helped calm some of his doubts, hers had ignited a spark. One that burned brighter, warmer, as she remembered the one answer she always had.

"I don't want to face Deardryn as your betrothed," she told him. "I don't want to be just another citizen, because you're right. This is our home—*my* home. The people already see me as their queen. And I'm tired of breaking myself trying to become what people expect of me.

"I worked myself to the bone trying to summon magic I didn't have so I could appease the Ash Kingdom. I walked away from a crown that was mine by right because they didn't want me. I spent a month in the Moon Kingdom agonizing over proving myself a worthy opponent to Deardryn, and even after stealing the shard, I've been spiraling trying to avoid becoming the queen she thinks I'll inevitably be.

"But what *I* want is to be queen of the kingdom I love. I want to walk into that meeting with you as a united front. Your equal. Your wife. And I know I can do this. So, marry me."

Analia stared up at him, that spark inside her crackling with her uncle's voice from long ago.

When head, heart, and gut are aligned, that is when the path is clearest.

He was right. This was her path. All fog and foliage that had blinded her to it now cleared away. And Aaron's look of awe had that certainty settling in her chest.

He slowly shook his head, his gaze lifting to the ceiling as if he needed someone, *something*, to confirm he wasn't the only one seeing this.

"Mesmerizing," he murmured. "Absolutely mesmerizing."

Analia didn't dare let her grin free yet. "I hope that's a euphemism for yes."

Aaron chuckled. "My shooting star, it's a euphemism for everything from 'I love you' to 'Dear gods, yes.'" He slid off the bed and onto his knees, that heavy, resolved look on his face from when he'd first entered now alive and shining with a pride that took Analia's breath away. "I might have this kingdom's magic," he told her, "but you are the hope we need." He took her hand, bringing it to his lips. "Light up the world."

Analia's eyes stung. She looked down at him kneeling before her, his head bowed, his lips warm against her fingers.

Her present. Her future. The past crumbling to ash behind her.

"I suppose this is extremely short notice for a wedding," she said.

Aaron laughed. "We can save that for another time. Luckily for you, the important parts are already ready."

Analia cocked her head. Aaron winked, pressing a quick kiss to her fingers before releasing her hand and standing. He crossed to his wardrobe, Analia rising and drifting over to watch as he rifled around. Finally, he pulled out yet another black velvet box. Larger than the first. And when he lifted the lid, Analia's hand drifted to her chest.

The crown was made from hammered, silver metal. Thin, elegant filigree wreathed around its delicate peaks, their paths sparkling with tiny diamonds and crystals like a sky full of shooting stars. And every path converged on the large, polished diamond in its center.

"Aaron..." she murmured, tracing one of the silver points.

"You didn't think Ember and I would stop at a ring?"

Aaron flashed a grin, thoroughly pleased with himself. Analia couldn't blame him.

"You truly thought of everything." Analia traced the central diamond, loving how her wonder had Aaron's face lighting up. "How long have you had this?"

"Not long enough to find a better hiding spot. This one took more time than your ring."

"I see."

Analia hesitated. Part of her thought she should keep her question to herself, not wanting to sound ungrateful. But this was Aaron.

"Does that mean I don't have time to make a tweak?"

"We'll make time," Aaron replied immediately. He shifted the box to one hand, his free hand curling around her hip as he leaned in conspiratorially. "What are we thinking?"

Gods, she loved that man. Analia told him her idea through a tiny laugh, Aaron gazing at her like she was the brightest star in the sky by the time she was done.

"I think that's perfect," he whispered.

Analia's heart sang.

"Come on," he went on, taking her hand. "We have a crown to alter by tonight."

Analia nodded, flipping the box shut for him with her free hand. With that, he whispered a warning, and pulled her into the shadows.

Chapter 87

D imitri walked through the Ash Castle halls. Slowly. In control. Not knowing how he still existed when it had been a day since Rayner had looked at him, and Dimitri's heart had shattered along its scar tissue lines.

All he had wanted to do was hunt Othin down so he could scream at him. Scream until his throat was raw and there were no emotions left in his body.

This. Was. His. Fault.

But he couldn't blow his cover. Not after it had taken quite the argument with Joshel to sneak the letters back into Othin's chambers, their scheme seemingly pulled off. Meaning, he'd had to wait. But now, there was nothing stopping him from shoving through the Throne Room door, his magic pulsing deep in his stomach.

As usual, the chamber was empty outside of Othin. He prowled back and forth in front of the obsidian glass throne, his footsteps bouncing off the dark stone walls like a war drum.

At the scrape of the door opening, he whipped around, his amber eyes finding Dimitri. His nose wrinkled.

"Not now, Dimitri," he said, resuming his pacing. Dismissing him without a second thought. Like it was instinct for him not to care, even when there was no one to notice.

Dimitri's hand curled around the edge of the thick stone door, ready to let his tirade loose. But the fury he'd been patiently stoking had fizzled into a spark. And his voice was barely a whisper as he asked, "Why did you do this to me?"

"I don't have time for this. My advisors are on their way to discuss who could have broken into my chambers."

So, they hadn't put the letters back in order.

Dimitri knew he should care. Yet, he couldn't tear his gaze from Othin, his shadow looming tall and broad behind him as he paced back and forth before the Everflame sconces, not noticing the small black eyes peering out of the nearest flame.

Gods, where were *his* flames? It had taken everything he had not to confront Othin the past day. Yet, standing there, all he wanted was to curl in on himself and hide.

Because it wasn't just his heart that had crumbled in that chamber. It was his ability to deny just how badly Othin had broken him.

"Dimitri!" Othin roared. "Get! Out!"

"How could you *do this* to me?" Dimitri exploded, sounding more like a sob as he finally pushed inside, the door slamming shut behind him. "How could you allow me to exist, just to brush me aside like I'm disposable? How could you tell me you love me, just to treat me like I'm worthless—"

"Dimitri—"

"Don't you realize what that's done to me? I'm scared to let anyone care about me because what if I do something that makes them stop? I'm *terrified* of caring about anyone because what if they turn out to be like you—"

"Dimitri—"

"No!" Dimitri yelled, stomping his foot. "You don't get to ignore me anymore! I can't keep hurting people—*I* hurt. So, you have to tell me why you did this to me."

Dimitri's chest heaved, his fists clenched tight enough to hurt. He craned his neck back to look at Othin, only just realizing how deep he'd marched into the chamber; deep enough Othin could have reached out and touched him. If he was Patryclas, his hand would have already been extending to smooth down Dimitri's hair, squeeze his shoulder, pull him into an embrace.

But Othin's hands tugged his black-and-gold cloak back into place. And a muscle in his jaw jumped under his dark beard as he struggled for composure.

"Well?" Dimitri spat.

Othin's nostrils flared. But it was with an unnerving calm that he said, "Come."

"I'm not a fucking dog."

"No," Othin shot back. "You're a little boy demanding answers. So, you can either come and listen, or you can leave."

Othin turned and marched to the throne, Dimitri's magic pulsing hot and fast. He didn't want to stand before Othin on the throne like some gods-damned servant. Especially not after Othin sat and snapped his fingers at him.

But Othin was right. He had Dimitri's answers.

"Promise you'll tell me everything?" Dimitri asked, folding his arms.

"Are you questioning my integrity?"

"Have you given me any reason not to?"

Dimitri didn't like the look in Othin's eyes as they narrowed. Like he was slowly piecing something together.

"Fine," he grunted. "Consider it payment for all your advisements these past months."

Dimitri's lips flattened. But still, he came to stiffly stand before the throne.

Othin took his time finding a comfortable position, the only sound the crackling Everflame sconces. And just when Dimitri was about to call the whole thing off...

"Deardryn and I didn't marry for love—wipe that sneer from your face or I'll stop here. Good. As I was saying, her parents had been trying to arrange a marriage with my clan for years thanks to our social power, with conversations continuing into the Shattering War when Deardryn took the crown. Eventually, the marriage became a peace offering after my father disobeyed her during the war. And fifty years later, when I was in my thirties, we were married.

"Ask any Sun Royal, and they'll say it ends there. But I know better. Deardryn arranged our marriage out of revenge. It was her way of keeping the Gardelle clan and our shielding magic under her thumb."

"Why?" Dimitri mumbled, rolling an imaginary pebble with his boot. "What did your father do?"

"He refused to tell me." Othin shrugged, but Dimitri caught his mouth pinch. "At any rate, Deardryn and I were married. I *tried* to make the best of things, I let her feel desired. But Deardryn wanted nothing to do with me. I was an acquaintance at best, kept out of every political meeting, allowed no opinions regarding her—I had to sleep in a different room in our chambers, for the Crystal's sake. The only time I existed to her was when she needed to keep my father in line.

"Twenty years into our marriage, we hated each other. But we also needed an heir. It took several years of misery, what with Blessed women's three cycles a year. But finally, Pryanth was born."

Dimitri didn't know how to read the emotions that crossed Othin's face. He didn't particularly care to as he struggled not to roll his eyes.

"In the beginning," Othin finally continued, sobering considerably, "Pryanth was the light in my otherwise bleak existence. But Deardryn quickly limited my access to him. It reached the point I could only see him when she was present."

"Probably didn't want him to end up like you," Dimitri muttered.

Othin's head snapped up, "What was that?"

"That must have been so hard for you," Dimitri deadpanned, unable to completely conceal his sarcasm. But Othin eased back in the throne, pacified.

"Eventually, I started pacing the castle halls, just wanting to see my son. And one day, someone stopped me as I passed and asked what was wrong. Up until that point, I hadn't interacted with her much, not only because she preferred to blend into the background, but because she was the one person Deardryn loved as much as Pryanth. Naturally, I wanted nothing to do with her. But that day, she listened to me vent. She validated my frustrations. And when she eventually turned to go, I wanted to call her back and talk to her more.

"From that point on, I started looking for her in the halls. When Deardryn wouldn't leave me alone with Pryanth, I instead sought her out. And after a few months, I realized I had married the wrong Royal."

Othin smiled to himself. A dreamy, faraway smile that had Dimitri swallowing bile. He wished he could also swallow the question balancing on the tip of his tongue.

But he'd come here for answers. And this was one of the most important ones.

"Who was she?" he managed.

Othin's gaze refocused on him. "You know who."

He did. He'd gotten his confirmation the moment he read Othin's letter and the initial attached. But he had to hear it aloud for it to be real.

"Tell me anyway."

Othin rolled his lips, his leather boots squeaking against the throne as he shifted. Finally, his amber eyes met his. "Saura."

Deardryn's younger sister.

Dimitri took a deep breath through his nose, waiting for impact. One more parent that never paid him any mind. But the blow never came. All there was... was nothing.

"Keep going," Dimitri said, his shoulders slumping.

Othin pursed his lips as if he'd been hoping for more. But with a shrug, he continued.

"I could tell Saura cared about me as well. But she would never do anything to hurt her sister. So, I went to Deardryn myself. Told her she could give less of a shit about me and our marriage, but the least she could do was let Saura be happy. I'll never forget the look of disgust she gave me. Yet, she didn't say a word. Just went in search of Saura to verify my story, Pryanth asleep in her arms. And a long time later, the two returned.

"Deardryn said now that she had an heir, she had no use for me. I was free to be with her sister. But out of respect for Pryanth and her own privacy, we had to be discreet. And we were. For three blissful years. And then you happened."

Dimitri didn't know what hurt more: Othin's scowl, or the way he said "you" as if Dimitri was the worst day of his life. He wrapped his arms around himself, trying to hold in his magic, his sobs.

Othin didn't seem to notice. He shoved to his feet, knocking into Dimitri as he resumed his pacing.

"I should have been thrilled to have a child with the woman I loved. But Deardryn ruined it for me. Shrieking at me how could I, look what I'd done—as if she didn't know what we were doing. She then confined Saura to her bed for her entire pregnancy, not wanting anyone to find out. And when you were born?"

Othin pivoted toward Dimitri, Dimitri flinching back as he leaned in close. "You were the worst thing that happened to me. You were a reminder of everything I could have had. I wanted to toss you on the streets and try to forget you. But Deardryn insisted we keep you. Because she wanted me to never be able to forget what I did. I had the audacity to love another woman and our child more than her and Pryanth. And while I tried to convince myself I could love them, they were my duty, I always went back to you and Saura. And that agony?"

Othin gripped the front of Dimitri's tunic, practically spitting the words. "That is an agony you will *never* understand. So, don't come crying to me about how you hurt."

For a few seconds, Dimitri stared into Othin's face. A few blissful, numb seconds, all he knew was Othin's wine-sour breath. The vein bulging in his temple. Then, his mouth remembered how to open.

"You can't be serious," he said. Othin's face twisted in a snarl, but Dimitri went on, louder this time, "Are you fucking *serious?*"

He shoved Othin's chest, Othin stumbling back in surprise. "You've destroyed the lives of every person you've come in contact with. You've made no efforts to improve *any* of those situations outside of blaming Deardryn. All because you had an amicable marriage with a wife that didn't want to fuck you. And you think *you're the victim?* You, who killed an innocent woman to cover your tracks?"

Othin spluttered under Dimitri's tirade, his face purple with rage. Just to pause. "I didn't kill an innocent woman," he retorted.

Dimitri thought his head was going to explode. "The entire castle knows you killed the random woman you pretended was my mother—"

"You think that's true?" Othin swiped aside the finger Dimitri jabbed at him, then raked a hand through his dark hair. "Yes, we killed a woman. But she was a criminal. She'd been evading our soldiers for decades while systematically picking off the noble clans. But we finally caught her a week before you were born."

Dimitri's mouth opened and closed several times, his heart pounding in his ears. Because he knew the faceless woman who targeted noble clans. He'd just told the story to Rayner days prior. But it was still several seconds before the words could click into place in his mind.

"Are you saying," Dimitri said slowly, disbelievingly, "you killed the Silent Queen from the Bend?"

Othin threw up his hands, "Of course! It was a win-win. The people think we sent a message about my affair, and the Silent Queen gets to disappear into the night, with the possibility of her return scaring off any potential replacements."

Dimitri shook his head, numbness spreading from his head to his toes.

"Honestly, Dimitri," Othin said, "we're not monsters."

A quiet part of Dimitri wanted to scream that he was. They all were. But he couldn't. He could only stare, wide-eyed, at the man who flipped his world upside down.

The woman he had grieved for was an assassin. Unworthy of his guilt, his shame, his self-loathing. The sacrifice he had been relentlessly trying to prove himself worthy of was a sham.

"What's the matter, Dimitri?" Othin purred, stepping closer once more. "It's not like you to have no words."

The back of Dimitri's neck tingled.

"After all," he went on, "look at how many words you've given me these past few months. I certainly would have hoped you'd find some extras to tuck away after going through my letters last night."

Dimitri's heart stopped. And the smug, triumphant look on Othin's face brought it back to life with a vengeance.

"Really?" he asked, jutting up his chin. "You're going to try to make me the monster? What did you have to do to put it together?"

"Get you worked up enough you would confess." Othin smiled down at him, almost pitying. "You may think I'm a foolish king, Dima, but I still know more than you."

Dimitri started to spit a retort, but Othin raised his voice over his. "Guards!"

The door banged open. Dimitri twisted, barely able to suck in a breath before the unit of Sun soldiers had swarmed around him, Joshel's apologetic face directly across from him.

"Take him to the dungeon," Othin said, returning to lounge on the throne.

"No!" Dimitri thrashed as hands latched onto him from all sides. So many hands, his magic pulsing faster, building with his panic—gods, it was just like Gritta's.

The night everything changed for him. The night he'd realized he'd had to keep this secret to survive. Maybe even because, deep down, he wanted to protect the father he still held out hope for.

A guard grabbed his wrists, yanking them behind his back.

But Othin had never tried to protect him. Saura—he didn't know what to feel about her. And the woman he had desperately tried to deny his identity for was worse than he could ever be.

"We've got him, Your Majesty," a male guard reported. He tugged on Dimitri's wrists, Dimitri's boots sliding across the stone as they hauled him toward the door.

Othin watched from his throne, arms folded.

Dimitri's magic flared inside him.

He met Othin's gaze.

And he watched Othin's expression go slack as he finally let his magic free.

Golden light exploded across the Throne Room. The guards yelled in alarm, some flinching back, a few hands releasing him to shield their eyes. That was all Dimitri needed.

In a flurry of elbows and knees, he wrenched free of their grips, his magic a languid thrum across the chamber.

"Grab him!" a guard yelled.

But Dimitri had already scurried over to the wall, finding the sconce he'd noted when first walking in.

"Spark," he whispered. "Is Tyce—"

"He's coming," they hissed back.

"He's over there!"

"Find him!" Othin roared.

Dimitri opened the curtains blocking his magic wide as they could go. Sunlight spread across every inch of the once gloomy chamber, bright and golden and unmistakable. And that light flared a little bit brighter as a warm hand found his.

"Let's go," Tyce whispered.

Then, guards and Othin yelling, footsteps pounding on stone, he pulled Dimitri into the shadows. His cover blown; his identity revealed.

And Dimitri was fucking relieved.

Chapter 88

By the time the safehouse's floor solidified beneath Dimitri's feet, he was shaking too hard to stand. He crumpled to his knees, something other than panic humming through his veins as he struggled to catch his breath.

"Dima," Tyce gasped, crouching before him as exclamations moved around the room. "What's wrong?"

"Where's Rayner? Othin's going to go after him now that he knows I'm a spy, we have to get him out—"

"He's already here."

"He what?"

"I brought him here earlier today because Rois needed an appearance change," Tyce explained, finding Dimitri's free hand with his own. "He's fine."

It took several seconds for Dimitri to process his words. Another for the rush in his veins to respond. "Oh," he said, quieter now. "Oh, that's good."

"It is," Tyce agreed. "I'll go retrieve your things as soon as Spark tells me the coast is clear. Everything will be all right."

He rubbed his thumbs along the backs of Dimitri's hands, Dimitri realizing golden magic still flickered across his skin. But he didn't try to stifle it. Even as he looked around at the handful of Royals who had moved to call up to the others through the hallway door, several pairs of footsteps hurrying downstairs.

This was who he was. They already knew. And he had more pressing matters as his pulse stuttered with the ghost of Othin's words, Tyce clearly trying to help. Maybe even comfort him.

But, staring down at Tyce's large hands cradling his own, Dimitri felt... nothing.

His touch didn't slow Dimitri down, no matter how fast his mind spun. His voice wasn't the sun that lit up even his darkest moods. His presence wasn't the home Dimitri never thought he could have.

"Tyce," he said regretfully, his voice low enough the Royals couldn't hear, "I like you."

Tyce's brown eyes bounced up to his. But that wasn't hope on his face. It was something far more reserved as he said, "Why do I sense a 'but' coming?"

Dimitri wanted nothing more than to duck his head, snatch his words back before he could even set them free. He hated this. Hated doing this to someone he considered a friend.

But that was just it. They were friends. And he couldn't hurt his friend by dragging him along.

"Because," Dimitri sighed, feeling like the worst person in the world, "I don't *like* you."

Gods, it sounded so much worse out loud. So blunt and graceless. Especially as Tyce's shoulders slumped.

"I'm sorry," Dimitri said, wanting to squeeze Tyce's hands, not sure if that would make things worse, doing an odd sort of shuffle on his knees as he deliberated.

He felt like an idiot. But the smallest glimmer of amusement sparkled in Tyce's eyes.

"It's all right, Dima," he said. "I figured you were interested in someone else."

"Really?"

Tyce nodded, his gaze flicking to the hallway door as the rest of the Royals shoved through. Rayner was among them, pushing to the front, rapidly scanning the sitting room until he found Dimitri.

Their eyes locked. The intensity in Rayner's gaze crackled across the distance between them, Dimitri only remembering to take a breath as Tyce softly laughed beside him. He tore his gaze away, searching for apologies.

"It's fine," Tyce promised, seeming to genuinely mean it as he finally released Dimitri's hands. "I had to try just in case, you know?"

Tyce flashed a tiny smile. Dimitri didn't know how he managed to make his mouth move, forming a noise of agreement.

That... was it? He'd been anticipating Tyce to yell at him—he was always yelled at when he did something wrong, and the twisting in his stomach certainly felt like he had.

But Tyce was so calm. Disappointed at the worst. And Dimitri was spared from deciding if he should thank him or apologize even more as Rayner arrived.

"Hey," he said, sliding to his knees. "What happened—you're sparking. Are you all right?"

His eyes flashed over Dimitri, searching for injuries, his fingers brushing over Dimitri's as the last of his magic winked out. And for the second time in a minute, Dimitri felt as though he'd been smacked between the eyes.

Just a day earlier, he'd caused the light in Rayner's eyes to go out. But there he was, making sure he was all right, his knees pressing against Dimitri's thigh as if needing the reassurance himself.

"I'm fine," he managed. But he was more than that.

He had finally revealed who he was to the Sun people. Rumors had undoubtedly started to spread. And yet, he was surrounded by people who cared instead of hated. Who helped instead of harmed. And he was one of them.

"What's going on?" Cadmus called over the voices, finally striding through the hallway door.

Dimitri glanced at Tyce, finding he had silently disappeared. He opened his mouth, having no idea where to begin. But Fayela spared him the effort.

"Spark came here in a panic a few minutes ago," she reported, coming to meet Cadmus in the center of the room. "They said Tyce had to go to the Throne Room immediately, and moments later, he and Dimitri were stumbling to the floor. We tried to ask what was going on, but Spark kept telling us to wait until you arrived."

Gods, Dimitri loved that little sprite. He sat up straight, bracing himself for Cadmus's icy stare to land on him as he demanded an explanation.

But Cadmus was perfectly calm as he nodded to himself. Turning from Fayela, he crossed the room, Dimitri and Rayner exchanging a look as he came to kneel in Tyce's original spot. And Dimitri could have sworn the ghost of something familiar flickered in his blue eyes.

"What happened?" he asked quietly.

Dimitri didn't know if that was the best reaction he could have hoped for or the worst. He looked around, all eyes watching him intently, even the seven-year-old girl. And seeing no reason to drag things out, he said, "Othin figured me out. I was able to confirm the 'S' he was writing to is Saura, and I revealed who I am in front of his soldiers, so that chaos should give us some time. But Rayner and I can't go back to the castle."

Rayner's mouth drifted open. But Dimitri could only stare at Cadmus, waiting for the fury that had been building behind his eyes the past two months to finally erupt.

Cadmus reached into his pocket, pulling out his phoenix charm. He thoughtfully turned it between his fingers, the sitting room deathly silent as they watched.

Dimitri held his breath, his hands starting to shake in his lap.

"If we've lost our spies," Cadmus finally said, "then we need to finish building our army. Now."

Dimitri didn't move, waiting for the jab. But Cadmus's expression remained blank as he rose, crossing to the nearby rickety dining room table where a map of the Ash Kingdom was constantly laid out. Then, he got to work.

One by one, he assigned each Royal to visit a town they hadn't already negotiated forces from. Tyce reappeared in the shadows beside Dimitri about halfway through, giving both him and Rayner a nod as he tossed them their packs and went to join the others at the table.

"Everyone is going to have to pitch in," Cadmus said, figurines softly clinking as he rearranged them on the map. "Even you, Tenley."

"Cadmus, she's seven," Fayela argued, hand on her sister's shoulder.

"Exactly. It will mean something to the captains to see even she is out trying to help. You can take her with you tomorrow morning."

Fayela started to argue. Cadmus met her gaze, Dimitri wincing as their silent argument fizzed between them.

Finally, Fayela nodded, her jaw tight. And Cadmus briskly turned away.

"As for the non-Royals," he went on, "Dimitri and Rayner can't go back to the castle, so that leaves Rois. Rayner, I want you to change his appearance first thing tomorrow morning so he can sneak back into the castle. Hopefully, he can assess what kind of damage Dimitri's stunt has caused."

There it was.

"Do you still have your stolen Sun uniforms?" Rois asked, leaning against a chair.

"I do," Rayner replied.

"Good, I'll be needing that."

So, Rois was planning on going through the front door. Well, if anyone had the arrogance to pull that off, it was certainly him and that sword he casually readjusted through his belt.

"As for Rayner and Dimitri," Cadmus said, "you'll be staying here. As far as Othin is aware, you two have completely disappeared. Let's keep it that way."

Cadmus's eyes lingered on Dimitri, who squirmed guiltily. Seemingly appeased by this, Cadmus turned back to his map. He swiftly delivered the last of his orders, only looking up to take in his family's nods. Then, with a brief dismissal, he faded into the shadows.

Left alone, the Royals exchanged a variety of looks, most unsettled. Clearly, despite Cadmus's plan, they knew without their spies, and Othin now onto them, this wasn't going to end well.

But with nothing else to do, they split off. The majority headed for the stairs, a few to the couches, their voices picking up around Dimitri once more.

"I know that's not all that happened today," Rayner whispered in his ear.

Dimitri jumped, realizing he'd been chewing on his thumbnail. "You 'know,' huh?"

"You didn't look panicked when I got here. You were rattled." Rayner leaned closer, Dimitri's breath stuttering in his lungs. "What did Othin tell you?"

Gods, he knew Dimitri too well. He had no doubt Rayner caught every twitch as Othin's words resurfaced in his mind, Dimitri acutely aware of how easy it would be to shift, and he'd be leaning into him.

But after everything Dimitri had put him through?

"I shouldn't dump all that on you," he said, pulling away.

"Hey." Rayner caught his wrist, the warmth of his fingers spreading across Dimitri's skin. "I'm still your friend. No matter what."

Crystal spare him, if Tyce had experienced even a fraction of the demolition in Dimitri's chest at that word, he'd spend the rest of his life groveling for forgiveness.

Rayner's fingers gave a squeeze. And Dimitri's mouth opened on its own.

He told him everything: his confirmation about Saura, the truth about the woman who died for him, his voice low enough the Royals talking on the couches across the room couldn't hear. And he didn't sob. He didn't explode. He soaked in every emotion that moved across Rayner's face, polishing and smoothing each broken piece of himself and fitting them back together.

By the time he finished, Rayner shook his head, looking at a loss for words.

"That's just... Wow," he finally said.

Dimitri nodded, his heart skipping faster as his words rose up his throat.

"You seem surprisingly calm," Rayner commented.

"Because it doesn't matter," Dimitri said, leaning toward him. "Don't you see? The expectations I was holding myself to because of that woman, everything Othin forced me to be. None of it matters."

Dimitri gripped Rayner's knees, eagerly staring up into his face.

But that was dread in Rayner's eyes as he began, "Dima, what are you saying—"

"I'm saying I care about you," Dimitri blurted, barely keeping his voice low. "I'm sorry I froze yesterday, I wasn't—this is new for me. But I want it. I want this."

Dimitri gestured back and forth between them, feeling as inarticulate as he had when talking to Tyce. He needed Rayner to understand, needed to find the words that would express how being with him made him want to believe in the possibilities instead of always expecting the worst. How watching Rayner grow beyond everything his past had tried to break him into gave Dimitri hope he could do the same.

But there was still the smallest part of him that had his mouth going dry. Only able to focus on the eyes flicking over to him in interest. And Rayner raised his hands.

"Dima, stop."

Dimitri had never snapped his mouth shut faster at such quiet words.

"I'm sorry," Rayner went on, dragging a hand through his hair. "I just... You have no idea how badly I want to hear those words. But you just went through *a lot*. And I can't get my hopes up over something you say amid that rush, just for you to regret it later."

"But I—"

"Not now." Rayner's voice was as gentle as the fingers he brushed along Dimitri's cheek. Then, he rose and turned to head back through the hallway door.

And Dimitri hated, hated with every fiber of his being, that such a wonderful, thoughtful, sensitive person had been forced into hiding for so long.

But he wouldn't chase after him. He'd wait until the rush was over, just as Rayner asked. Then, he would do everything he could to reassure Rayner he meant it.

All Dimitri wanted was him.

Chapter 89

Analia stood at her bathing room counter, frowning at her latest attempt to braid her hair in the mirror. She didn't know why she was struggling so much. It wasn't like she'd never had to get ready for a formal event before—it wasn't even her first coronation. But something was off.

Analia lightly tapped her fingers on the counter, her large eyes appearing more prominent than she was used to thanks to the dark, precise lines of kohl along her lashlines. Gods, she wasn't sure about that anymore either. She should have taken Ember, Surce, and Laness up on their offer to help her get ready, Laness still bouncing with excitement at the news. But at the time, she'd thought she wanted some quiet with Aaron.

He, of course, had only needed a few minutes to get ready. At some point, he'd come to sit on their tub's ledge behind her, amusing himself by poking through her small jewelry box and muttering, "Is this all you have? Why haven't I fixed this? Oh, that's pretty, my gold better have paid for it."

Analia didn't know when his voice had drifted into the background of her mind. She didn't realize it had quieted altogether until she felt him step up behind her.

"Can I make a suggestion?" he asked, sliding his arms around her waist and resting his chin on her shoulder.

Analia studied their reflection in the mirror, the contrast between his formal black jacket and her plain silver tunic and unraveling braids almost comical. "I'll take anything at this point," she sighed.

Aaron's chuckle was warm against her neck. "I was just thinking," he said, running his fingers through her hair, "that the only time you braid your hair is when you're in fighting leathers or some sort of Royal badassery is afoot. And while I'm unfairly attracted to that, I adore *my* Analia more."

Aaron finished combing out her braids and situated her hair over her shoulders, the black, intricately carved ring on his middle finger glinting in the light. Analia's gaze returned to the mirror, that nagging feeling settling back down, taking the tension in her shoulders with it.

"No masks," she murmured, her hand finding his as it returned to her hip.

"Just us," he agreed, leaning his cheek against hers.

Analia sighed, closing her eyes. This was right. Right person, right path, right way forward. It might have taken her longer than she would have liked to realize it, but the fact that her hair was her biggest worry was all the proof she needed.

This was her kingdom. She had a crown to claim.

And of course, that was when the hammering on their bedroom door began.

"Open up, Aaron!" Laness's muffled voice yelled. "We've been patient long enough!"

"We're indecent," Aaron called back.

Analia let out a squawk and elbowed him in the ribs, Aaron's grin flashing in the mirror.

"Nice try," Laness said. "You forgot to block me out while you were admiring Anna's reflection."

"It's unlocked!" came Ember's voice.

Aaron cursed under his breath. He barely had time to release Analia and turn before the door burst open.

Ember, Laness, and Surce shoved inside in a tangle of voices, already dressed in their black-and-silver gowns, Branten and Mor bringing up the rear.

"What are they doing here?" Aaron asked, eyeing his brothers.

"Reinforcements," Ember announced.

Aaron began, "Why would you need—hey!"

"Time to go, brother," Branten crowed.

Analia hid her laugh behind her hand as Branten and Mor bundled Aaron out of the bathing room, Aaron protesting all the way, Mor giving Analia a little wave before they disappeared beyond the doorway.

"Finally," Laness said, her head falling back.

"We appear to have come just in time," Surce added, peeking inside the garment bag Analia had hung on a towel hook.

"You're planning on smudging that, right?" Ember asked in a hushed tone, twirling her finger around her eye.

She knew she'd drawn those lines too sharp. Analia started to reply, just to be drowned out by Branten's noise of disbelief from the bedroom.

"He's got a ring," Mor called, as if it were a damning piece of evidence.

"What?"

Analia flushed as Surce, Ember, and Laness wheeled on her, looking just as disbelieving as Branten had sounded. "It wasn't planned," she offered guiltily.

"Well," Aaron interjected from the bedroom.

Branten shushed him, appearing in the bathing room doorway with Mor a moment later to join the expectant crowd. Analia ducked her head, but she caught her smile in the mirror.

"My coronation is all about the kingdom," she explained, searching for the right words. "But we didn't want the foundation of my rule to be the kingdom, too."

"Our marriage is about us," Aaron said, stepping out of the shadows beside her and taking her hand. "So, it was just us."

And lucky for them, the wedding temple was on their way to dropping off her crown for alterations.

Analia leaned her head against Aaron's shoulder, the memory a warm glow spreading through her chest. One only the two of them would ever know.

Ember's and Surce's expressions softened, Mor nodding slowly behind them. Leaving Laness and Branten.

The two looked at each other. Over to Analia and Aaron. Back to each other, unmistakably exasperated.

Analia braced herself, ready to release her speech of apologies and explanations.

Finally, Laness jabbed a finger at Aaron.

"You two are impossible," she declared. Then, she grabbed Analia and pulled her into a hug.

Aaron released her hand to let her hug Laness back, the two exchanging a grin. And Analia quickly lost herself in the wave of congratulations and hugs and complaints that followed.

At some point, Branten and Mor took the opportunity to haul Aaron from the room once again, Aaron's sigh rising above the noise.

"Bye, Anna!" Branten called, the bedroom door swinging open.

"Don't let her forget her pin!" Aaron ordered, right before the door shut.

Ember brought a hand to her heart as the room quieted, pretending to swoon. "If he turns out to be evil," she said, "I might have to kill him myself."

Laness snickered, Surce hiding her smile behind her hand.

Analia wrapped her arms around herself, turning back to her mirror.

"I've already dealt with an evil husband," she said, staring into her reflected eyes. "Trust me, Aaron is anything but."

Analia blinked in the return of light as Laness pulled her, Ember, and Surce out of the earthy darkness of her magic. The three had gotten Analia ready in record time, none of them allowing her to overthink their creative decisions, the sky through her bedroom windows a dusky purple by the time they finished.

Now, her gaze moved around the dimly lit room in the Council Building.

She stood at the edge of a large, circular floor. Thin, elegant lines carved through the gray stone, forming a map of stars and constellations, only interrupted by the central white marble altar seated in its center, a familiar black box resting atop it. Three steep steps encircled the floor, leading up to a second level lined with witness chairs.

Based on the number, Analia assumed a select portion of citizens were typically invited to watch. But now, only the councilmen sat front and center, their postures surprisingly relaxed as they softly talked amongst themselves.

Undoubtedly sensing her gaze, Jeneva looked up, her heart-shaped face brightening as she spotted Analia. "Beautiful," she mouthed, flashing a thumbs up.

The slight tightness in Analia's lungs eased. She mouthed a thanks, spotting Branten and Mor taking their seats from the corner of her eye.

Mor looked as pristine as always in his sleek black jacket, but Analia couldn't remember the last time she'd seen Branten so put together. No weapons, his reddish-brown hair neatly combed, not a hole or fraying edge in sight on his silver jacket as it stretched across his broad chest and shoulders.

But Analia didn't pause to admire. Not as a soft, slick melody glided over her senses, drawing her gaze directly across from her. Finding Aaron waiting for her on the opposite side of the altar.

He wore the same black jacket from their bathing room, metallic silver threads weaving stars across the sleeve cuffs. His black crown already sat atop his head, the diamonds and sapphires forming tiny constellations along the band flashing in the faint light. And Analia would never be able to describe the thrum as their eyes finally met.

It traveled down the length of her body like the first notes of a symphony, following the path of Aaron's gaze, his pupils slowly swallowing the starlight in his eyes as he drank her in.

The curve of her mouth. The diamond studs in her ears. The slope of her collarbones, noting her phoenix pin, breathing a curse as he reached her gown.

The gauzy material couldn't decide if it was black or darkest gray. It drifted around her as she moved like a plume of smoke, the material sparkling with countless tiny stars. The moment she'd glimpsed it inside the garment bag, she'd known why he'd picked it out when they were organizing Surce's shop.

"My shooting star," he murmured, finally coming toward her, shaking his head. "I know I'm a smartass, but what did I do to deserve you taunting me like this?"

Analia was vaguely aware of Ember, Laness, and Surce quietly retreating to join the others in their seats.

"Taunting?" she repeated, coming to meet him at the altar.

"You're right." Aaron slipped his hand around her waist, his voice dropping to a whisper. "Should I have called you breathtaking?" He kissed the skin below her ear. "Or mesmerizing?" He kissed her temple. "Or perhaps unfathomably beautiful."

His lips found the corner of her mouth, lifting into a smile under his kiss.

"You're pretty handsome yourself," she said, running her fingers along his shoulder.

Aaron grinned against her jaw. "What a pair."

Analia breathed out a laugh. If this was what her coronation would consist of, she would handle it happily. She didn't even notice the tingle of magic beside her.

"Why am I not surprised my grandson decided to get married in secret?"

Analia's fluttering eyelids snapped open. Ethelind stepped out of the shadows beside her, bringing with her the smell of stone and mountain air. She wore a long, flowing black gown in place of her usual gray-and-white robes, her sandy-brown hair in a twist, her hands on her hips as she looked at them accusingly.

Aaron winced, then pulled back. "I'm sorry?" he tried.

Ethelind ignored him. Snatching his hand, she looked down at the ring on his middle finger, shook her head, and let his hand drop. "Aaron Stelingente, you better put this one through less grief than you do me."

Aaron started to protest, Ethelind ignoring him as she pulled Analia into a hug. "Thank the gods it's you," she muttered, half to herself as she patted Analia's shoulder.

Analia's lips parted, a lump forming in her throat. She stared at Ethelind as she released her, needing a few moments before her words could finally squeeze free. "We'll do a reenactment at the wedding... Whenever that happens."

"You better."

Ethelind touched her hair. Her eyes moved between Analia and Aaron, the steely gray softening a fraction.

"Well then," she said, returning to her usual briskness. "Shall we begin?"

"We?" Analia repeated. "I thought Aaron was giving me my crown."

Now that she thought about it, Aaron had been unusually vague when describing the ceremony to her that afternoon. She looked to him questioningly, finding a secretive smile on his lips as he returned to the other side of the altar, Ethelind coming to stand between them and facing the small crowd.

"This ceremony is a bit unusual," Ethelind explained. "Usually, the reigning Royal presents their spouse with their crown and to the kingdom. But we have two Royals here."

"And I'm not interested in the power disparity in the other kingdoms," Aaron added. "I don't care if you're a Royal or a random citizen I met on the street. You're my equal in every right. Which means you receive your crown from the same person I did."

He reached across the altar, his cool fingers lacing with hers. And that blaze in his eyes... It refused any thanks, any questions of doubt. There was just a certainty that could hold together worlds.

Gods, she loved that man. Analia nodded, equally as certain.

"Then let's begin," she said.

Ethelind's face flashed with approval. She folded her hands on the altar, her gaze sweeping over the hushed onlookers, Analia realizing her presence was the reason so few had been invited. The kingdom might know their former queen resided with the DovenU, but that didn't mean they needed the reminder.

But this was right. These were the only witnesses she needed as Aaron released her hand, and Ethelind finally began.

"The Starlight Kingdom has never been a kingdom of words," she said, her voice echoing around the silent room. "It is a sanctuary. Forged from our people's dreams. Sustained by hope. And protected by the actions of those who swear to lead."

Ethelind's gaze met Analia's, her spine straightening.

"Do you, Analia Valarus, swear on the Crystal and the gods to cherish the people of this kingdom? Stand with them through the darkness and the light? Defend them with every breath in your lungs? And carry their lives and their dreams in your heart?"

Analia didn't hesitate. "I swear it."

"Kneel."

Analia sank to her knees, the room holding its breath, every gaze unwavering. Ethelind opened the box on the altar. Inside sat the crown Aaron had made for her, the same dark silver color, same delicate peaks, same diamonds sparkling along the twining filament like shooting stars. But where the massive central diamond once sat was now a circular piece of obsidian glass.

Analia looked up at Ethelind, the rightness clicking along her mind, her heart, down to her gut. This was where she was supposed to be. This was where she *wanted* to be. And she didn't look away as Ethelind settled the crown on her head.

Heavy. Demanding. Her neck steady under its weight.

Ethelind stepped back, taking a moment to take in the sight. And Analia could have sworn her eyes shone as she smiled.

"Rise," she said. "Princess of Ash, and crowned Queen of Starlight."

Analia's flames flared inside her, as warm as the metal pin against her chest. She smoothly rose to her feet, Aaron radiant across from her, anticipation crackling over the silent crowd to her left. He gestured for her to look, Analia holding her breath as she turned.

Her eyes moved over every face, taking in her council. Her family. Her people.

Together, each member of the crowd slid from their seats and on to one knee, their heads bowed, their voices rising up around her like plumes of smoke.

"Your Majesty."

Chapter 90

“Where are we going?” Analia laughed, stumbling after Aaron as he pulled her down one of the Council Building's countless halls. They'd barely had time to emerge from the shadows before he was off, the roar of the kingdom's applause still buzzing through Analia's veins.

The first few minutes following her being crowned queen had passed in a blur of cheers and her family's tangled limbs, Aaron laughing off to the side as he enjoyed the chaos. The council members were noticeably more subdued when they finally got a turn with her, but even Samuel and Jasper bowed, Jeneva mouthing “Fuck yes!” to her when they weren't looking.

Eventually, the crowd herded her up the three steep steps, everyone talking at once as they flooded toward the back of the room. Thankfully, Aaron decided to take pity on her before she could be crushed on her way through the door.

“Go on ahead,” he said, stepping out of the nearby darkness and claiming her hand. “We'll meet you on the balcony.”

Surce was the only one who bothered to give an affirmative, the others still talking as they continued through the door. Ethelind brought up the rear, affectionately fixing Analia's askew crown before disappearing after the others. Then, she and Aaron were alone.

“You enjoying yourself?” Analia asked dryly, the sudden quiet jarring in her ears.

“I'll have you know I am *suffering*,” Aaron said indignantly. “You have no idea how much restraint it's requiring to not mess up your hair or that pretty dress before you've been presented to the kingdom.”

Analia grinned big enough her face hurt.

"Really?" she asked, bracing her free hand on his chest and leaning in. "How *hard* is it?"

She brushed her mouth over the corner of his, Aaron groaning and nudging her away.

"My merciless shooting star, it's your presentation, not mine."

Analia smirked, waiting for his retaliation. But he only tucked a lock of hair behind her ear, his fingers not even lingering against her neck. Restraint indeed. Leaving her mind clear enough to consider his words.

"What if my presentation wasn't on the balcony?" she asked.

Aaron tilted his head curiously. And Analia loved the flash of his dimple as she told him her idea.

With a whispered warning, he pulled her into the shadows. He didn't immediately guide them out of the darkness, keeping them in the state in between where Analia could just make out the ground beneath her feet and Surce's amplified voice over the noise of countless people.

Introducing her. The crowd roaring their approval. And finally, Aaron let the shadows peel back, the two standing on the Council Building's roof, the cold night air kissing Analia's skin.

It took a few moments for the crowd—gods, there were so many people below—to look up. Past the sweeping balcony where Surce stood, up to the railed-off roof. Finally spotting her. And Analia would never forget the explosion of noise below.

Claiming her. Welcoming her as one of their own. Their queen.

Analia didn't know how long she stood up there with Aaron, waving to the crowd, Aaron basking in the noise beside her. She just knew he waited for her to tell him when she'd had her fill. Then, he pulled her into the shadows.

Now, Aaron's fingers squeezed hers as he led her around the corner.

"We're going here," he said, pushing open a door on his right. He tugged her inside, Analia catching a glimpse of a vaguely familiar guest room, the pale blue bedspread matching the accents on the dark gray carpet.

Then, the door shut. And Aaron pinned her back against it, his mouth hot and consuming on hers.

All the buzzing energy from the crowd ignited in Analia's veins. She hauled him closer, their teeth clashing, Analia trying to wrap her calf around his, just to be stopped by her skirts.

Crystal strike her down. She shoved off Aaron's jacket, her fingers starved for his skin as they roved over his arms, Aaron lightly sucking on her tongue and sending her mind stuttering.

"Gods, Analia," he panted, dragging his mouth along her jaw. "Do you have any idea how long I've been waiting for this?"

He ran his hands up her sides, his teeth grazing the tight skin of her neck. Analia gasped, pressing her hips into him—why were they still dressed? Why were there layers between her and the stiff length of his cock against her hip?

"It must have been so painful," she crooned, sliding her hand down his chest. "You've had to wait an entire evening."

"Oh, Analia, it's been far longer than that."

Aaron snatched her hand before she could drag it up his cock. Claiming her other wrist, he pinned them above her head, her back arching as he leaned in close.

"Do you not recognize this room?"

His voice hazed over her skin like smoke. Analia forced her gaze from the flush across his cheekbones, struggling to think as she took in the room. Familiar, just as she'd thought.

"Is this the room I went to after our first council meeting?" she asked.

Aaron's hum of approval rumbled through her core, rousing an ache between her thighs.

"Very good." His free hand curved around her breast, his thumb caressing along her nipple through the material. Taking his time. "That gnat kept us separated when all I wanted was to see you. Tell you how fucking magnificent you'd been in that meeting."

He leaned closer, Analia trembling in his grip. "All I could think about was pinning you to that bed until you believed me. Whether it was because of my mouth, my fingers, or my cock."

He pinched her nipple. Pleasure sparked across Analia's senses. She desperately tugged against his grip on her wrists, grinding against him, his moan harmonizing with hers.

In one quick move, he spun her around, releasing her wrists to find the tie holding her gown shut. "What should I do with this ribbon, Analia?" he asked against her ear.

"Fucking pull it," she spat.

Aaron's snarl of approval rushed through her veins. Quickly followed by the wave of fire as his lips brushed her neck, pulling the ribbon free with his teeth. She shoved the gauzy material down her body, his hand spasming around her hip as he realized she wore nothing beneath—"My fucking gods, Analia."

Analia kicked her dress aside and twisted around, not having time to assist as Aaron stripped, tossing his crown on the bed behind him. She started to remove her own, but Aaron stopped her with a glare. "Don't you dare."

Aaron's words sent a heady buzz through Analia's veins. He pressed her back against the door, running his calloused hands up her thighs, fingers digging into her ass as he lifted her, her legs wrapping around him.

"Analia, Analia, Analia," he said, burying his face in her neck, breathing her in. "Where could I possibly begin with you?"

Analia shifted against him, infuriatingly close to where she ached for him. "You are so annoying," she whined.

"Annoying?" Aaron repeated, offended. "But I try so hard to please."

He ducked his head, Analia's breath catching as he sucked her nipple into his mouth. He swirled his tongue, his mouth hot and wet and—gods, she needed more of him.

"Aaron," she whined, her hand fisting in his hair.

Aaron hummed innocently, his hand coming to mirror his tongue on the other side. Slow. Idle. Driving her out of her mind as his teeth grazed over her sensitive peak.

"Aaron, *please.*"

Aaron's chuckle vibrated through her bones. He came up to nestle his face against her neck once more, his thumb still circling.

"What do you want, Analia?" he crooned. "Do you want me to take you slow and deep against this door?"

He rolled his hips, a slow, deliberate move that had Analia's senses dying and coming back to life.

"Perhaps you're not interested in the anticipation," he said. "Maybe I pull you down on my face and we test how much that headboard can take."

He pressed a searing kiss to the spot where her neck met her shoulder. Analia gasped, the heat of his words, his mouth, his cock against her core barreling through her veins, white hot, her hips grinding against him. Aaron groaned, pressing her harder against the door.

"Use your words," he breathed. "What is your command, Your Majesty?"

Crystal fucking spare her. Analia's nails dug into his shoulders, dragging him against her. "On your knees," she ground out.

Gods, that look in his eyes. It was sheer starvation, his pupils swallowing the starlight into darkness.

But he still took the time to make sure she was steady on her feet as he set her down. Paused long enough as he knelt to grin up at her, pulling her leg over his shoulder. Then, his mouth was on her.

Analia's head thudded back against the door with a moan, Aaron's mouth a blaze that consumed her everywhere at once. His tongue swirling around her clit, sucking her between his lips, kissing down until he could press into her entrance.

He claimed her. Every movement was a brand, searing with the echo of his words.

Just us.

Analia ground against his face, the door rattling behind her as she gripped the knob, trying to keep herself upright. And the flames in her blood burned. Hotter, hotter, hotter—

Aaron snatched her hand from the knob, bringing it to his hair. Analia's fingers curled tight, struggling to turn her ragged breaths into words, a plea. Just for a cry to escape her lips as Aaron's fingers joined his mouth, pushing inside her and dragging over that perfect spot. And Analia's release was hot, and blinding, and tore through her like the ripping of a book page.

She sagged against the door, breathing hard, heat flashing across her skin. And Aaron didn't pause.

His fingers dug into her thigh, giving her no time to recover as he devoured her. Piece by piece. Slamming a third finger inside her as he thrust in and out, the stretch having Analia seeing stars—how was she already this close again?

She didn't know. She didn't know anything as Aaron gave a hard suck on her clit, and the second wave struck.

Analia sobbed a cry, no thoughts surviving her release. There was only instinct. And the dark, swirling desire as Aaron's eyes darted up to her, checking in.

Analia shoved him. He fell back on the carpet, his arms coming up to catch her as she landed on top of him, his lips swollen and glistening.

"Round three?" she panted. She dragged her hand up his cock in a long, tight pump, Aaron hissing out a breath as the muscles in his stomach flexed.

He slid his hands down to her hips, not bothering to respond. He only guided her over his cock, Analia sitting back, quick and smooth. Aaron jolted beneath her, spitting out a curse.

"Fucking stunning," he moaned.

Analia rocked her hips, reveling in the fullness, Aaron's heart pounding beneath her palms. She leaned down, whispering against his mouth. "Mine."

And she watched as whatever shreds of control he had snapped. He gripped her hips, his own arching as she moved up and down his length. Fast, hard, as relentless as his mouth had been before, his cock thrusting deep enough her thoughts turned to stars.

She was in control now. And she needed to feel him come undone, needed it as bad as the release winding tighter and tighter in her core.

Aaron's hands flashed over her stomach, her back, her breasts, his cock throbbing inside her. He pulled her back down to him, her crown toppling off her head and onto the carpet as his lips captured hers. Starved. Demanding. His mouth still tasting of her pleasure.

"I love you," he breathed. He snapped his hips up, meeting her as she sat down hard. And while Analia didn't know which of them fell apart first, she knew she came back together with Aaron's moan in her ear and his rigid arms around her, gathering her back into one piece.

Analia dropped her head to his chest, flushed and shaking too hard to move. Aaron gently lifted her off his cock, settling her back against his chest and holding her tight.

For several moments they stayed like that, the only sound their uneven breathing. Aaron combed his fingers through the hair at the nape of her neck, his pulse slowly settling beneath her ear.

Analia sighed, her eyelids fluttering shut. She was just starting to wonder how bad it would really be if they stayed like that indefinitely, when a tiny rumble moved through Aaron's chest.

She lifted her head, confused. Their eyes met. And his snicker broke free.

"What?" she asked, laughing slightly.

"We didn't even make it to the bed." Aaron rubbed his hand back and forth along the dark carpet, utterly entertained.

Analia snorted, Aaron's answering grin having her dissolving into laughter. He quickly joined in, the entire situation ridiculous and nowhere near as funny as they thought it was. But Analia laughed anyway, hard enough her stomach ached.

By the time the two finally quieted, a weight Analia hadn't initially noticed had lightened across her shoulders. But she could have sworn she saw its ghost in Aaron's eyes as he brushed his thumb along her lower lip.

"Promise me we'll still laugh like this after tomorrow," he said, quieter than before. "No matter what happens."

Analia's smile slipped. Finally, the thoughts of what lay outside that suite door filtered back in.

Their meeting with Deardryn. The tenuous secret of their home.

She took Aaron's hand, bringing it to her heart. "I'll make sure of it."

"You will, will you?" he asked.

"I like your dimple too much not to." Analia rested her finger against his cheek, his dimple forming under her touch as he smiled.

"Good." Aaron nestled her back down against his chest, kissing the top of her head. Then, he murmured a warning and pulled them into the shadows, reemerging a moment later on the suite bed. He nudged her onto her side, tucking her back against him as he curled around her.

Soon, they would have to return home and prepare for the day to come. They would have to leave this moment behind. But in the meantime, Analia closed her eyes, snuggling into metal and spice.

Aaron. Her husband. And she was the Queen of Starlight.

Chapter 91

Gravel crunched beneath Analia's boots as she and Aaron hiked along the riverbank. It was her first official day as queen, and she wore no crown. No fancy gown. Didn't even have a guard to shadow her as Mor silently slipped into the forest on her left.

She was just Analia. And she was ready for this meeting.

"Well," Aaron murmured, shielding his eyes as he studied the bend in the river fifty feet ahead. "There's the boat."

"And Deardryn's not alone," Analia replied. "See those six guards on board? I can sense networks from all of them."

"To think she doesn't trust us to be civil," Aaron muttered.

Analia cast him a sidelong look, finding the same grim set to his mouth she'd noted the last time she stole a glance at him. It had first appeared when he'd returned from shadowjumping Laness and Ember across the Wild Lands a few hours prior and hadn't budged since. But his network remained a calm, even glide across her senses. And all things considered, that was the best she could have hoped for.

"Come on," she said. "Let's get this over with."

Aaron nodded. He let her take the lead, Analia increasing her pace as her eyes scanned the riverbank, following the languid thrum of Sun magic. And there she was.

Deardryn sat on a large tree stump at the forest's edge. She wore a silky olive-green gown, her body partially angled away from them as she studied something in her hands.

"I didn't think the Sun Queen traveled with so little security," Analia called.

Deardryn raised her head, Analia coming close enough to realize she'd been examining a small bouquet of blue irises she must have picked by the riverside.

"Funny," she said. "I was expecting a similar remark from Aaron."

"We're taking turns," Aaron drawled.

Deardryn laughed to herself. Setting her bouquet aside, she gracefully rose to her feet, waving off her guards as they started forward from the boat.

"I'm pleased you decided to join me," she said, coming to meet Analia and Aaron halfway. "I see you dressed for the occasion."

Her honey eyes flicked over Aaron's black tunic and pants, over to Analia's slightly more formal midnight-blue shirt, Analia not sure if her mouth twitched with amusement or disapproval.

"Apologies," she said. "Your messenger didn't leave us with much time to prepare."

"Yes, and I see he's not with you. Is it fair to assume you disposed of him?"

"Would you have let him live?" Analia asked. She paused a few feet from Deardryn, her arms tightly folded, Aaron silent and tense beside her.

If that Sun man was to be believed, this was the moment their brittle peace would snap. Deardryn's guards would surge forward, undoubtedly trying to overwhelm them with combat and restraining Blessings, their conversation destroyed before it had begun.

But Analia didn't flinch. She held Deardryn's considering gaze, making no move to disturb their silence.

Even as it stretched. Pulled taut. Her flames as calm as the soft lap of the river's current beside her.

And for the first time, the gleam of approval in Deardryn's eyes felt like a victory rather than a knife to the heart.

"Excellent," Deardryn murmured. "You continue to be a quick learner." She dropped Analia's gaze, her eyes landing on Analia's tightly folded arms. "Your ring is beautiful, my dear."

Aaron's fingers flexed at his sides. Analia rolled her eyes.

"What do you want, Deardryn?" she asked.

"To pay you a compliment," Deardryn said, quietly exasperated. "I swear on the Crystal and gods, you won't be backing yourself into any corners or admitting any weakness by accepting it. It's a beautiful ring. Just as you make a formidable queen."

So, that was what she was getting at. Analia started to remind her there needed to be a kingdom for her to be a queen. But Deardryn didn't give her the chance as she turned in a whisper of silk.

"Contrary to what you may believe," she said, heading back toward her stump, "I haven't come here intending to harm you. All I want is a conversation."

She settled on her stump, Aaron and Analia tensing as she reached behind it. Just for her to lift a corked bottle of white wine, her other hand retrieving a glass.

"What do you say?" she asked, uncorking the wine with a pop. "Shall we discuss?"

"**S**omething doesn't feel right," Ember murmured.

She and Laness tromped through a lush forest, the final enka flower patch before the temple already a ways behind them. It was by far the most hospitable area they'd appeared in that morning as Laness roottraveled them across the Wild Lands, Ember struggling to forget the blackened trees and dark, malevolent power that had skittered through her bones.

But it wasn't those memories that bothered her. Not the crunch of foliage beneath their boots or the birds singing above either. It was something else...

"I'm not surprised," Laness said, looking up from her map. "The temple is just up ahead. It's bound to stir up some feelings after hearing for fourteen years the first time you'd come here would be with your master healers."

"Maybe," Ember murmured, unconvinced. Even if that was true, it didn't account for not even a whisper of itchiness across her markings.

She didn't expect them to respond to the Crystal from so far away. But surely, if they were so close to the temple, they would react to the wards. After all, her markings had been itchy long before she ever encountered the Crystal, meaning it was likely the magic she responded to, not the Crystal itself. Unless there was another variable she wasn't aware of.

Ember frowned, an ache forming across her forehead as the trees thinned up ahead. And something sickly sweet burned her nose.

Ember gagged. She threw her elbow over her nose, unable to completely block out the drug-laced smoke. And the cravings that had finally started to settle inside her snapped to attention.

"Who's smoking a pipe out here?" Laness demanded, wrinkling her nose.

Ember shrugged helplessly, her pulse staggering through her veins.

It wasn't devinroot. She was all right. But the faint lightheaded feeling that smoke gave her was too familiar not to have her spiraling back to a simpler time. One where relentless worries could be quelled with an inhale—no.

"Let's go figure it out," she said, bracing herself as she lowered her elbow. And not giving herself time to dwell, she unsheathed the damper blade from her belt.

Laness mirrored her movement, the two sticking out their blades before them as they cautiously approached the tree line. In all likelihood, the wards were on the temple itself, not the surrounding clearing. Still, Ember couldn't help her surprise as they stepped into the clearing and nothing stirred, her eyes restlessly looking around.

The large, circular area was more of a garden. Neatly trimmed hedges lined the white pebble pathways, the greenery decorated with small pink blossoms. Pale stone archways curved over each of the four paths, carved to resemble the symbol of each healer specialty: roses for herbology, vertebrae for internal healing, scalpels for external healing, and intricate loops for medical mysteries, all twined with flowering vines. But her attention went straight to the violet smoke rings.

Ember traced their path, locating the figure in black in the center of the garden. Sitting on the pristine white stone steps leading up to the short, golden temple.

"Absolutely not," she growled.

Laness extended a hand to stop her. But Ember had already marched off, her grip painfully tight on her dagger.

She didn't care about her questionable oath. This was a sacred spot. She wouldn't let it become someone's smoking ground.

"Hey!" she called, turning onto the final path. "This temple is for those who worship Rosala, not their pipes."

"Something tells me I know more about that than you, princess," drawled a low, velveteen voice.

Ember glared, coming close enough to make out the man's face as he lifted his head. Well, the lower half not obscured by a black, metallic mask, matching his jacket and thick, wavy hair.

Handsome, in a wolfish way.

"Ember, stop!" Laness called, pebbles clattering as she caught up with her. "You have no idea what you could be running into—who are you?"

"Starlight fighting leathers," he purred, his ink-blue eyes lazily flicking over Laness. "Nice."

Laness recoiled with a hiss. Ember stumbled to a halt a dozen paces from the stairs, her jaw dropping.

He *knew* about them? But how? He clearly wasn't one of Aaron's men.

"Laness," she said, eyes bouncing between Laness's raised damper dagger and the man, "who is he?"

Laness didn't reply.

"Usually," he said, "I don't reveal my identity to strangers. But I've always had a weakness for beautiful women."

Ember's nostrils flared, even as her cheeks warmed. The man latched onto her blush with glittering eyes, visibly savoring the moment as he lifted his mask.

Light skin. High cheekbones and an angular jaw, balanced by arched eyebrows, a silver stud gleaming in the left one. And four purple rings around each of his eyes, split at the corners.

Ember felt faint.

"Marcos Vensada," he said, drinking her in as he slipped his mask in his jacket pocket. "I'd say at your service, but I'd hate to start off our acquaintance with a lie."

Ember's jaw dropped. "You're Marcos?" she demanded.

Laness cursed under her breath, Marcos not sparing her or the blade she aimed at him a glance.

"You know," he said with a stretch, "it's considered rude to use such insolent tones when addressing a master."

"Did you say that to the girl you broke your rings with?" Ember retorted.

"Who said it was a girl?"

Ember didn't expect that to trip her up. Nor for her heart to skip a beat as Marcos's eyes lazily trailed over her face, noting her markings, lingering on her mouth.

"Based on *your* rings," he murmured, "you've only imagined the kind of things I've whispered. Or do the healers have you so crushed beneath their thumb you've been too afraid to try?"

Ember's blood sizzled. She stepped forward, a retort burning against her lips.

"Ember, stop," Laness hissed, grabbing her arm and yanking her back.

"Oh," Marcos said, drawing out the syllable with delight. "I've struck a nerve. Don't worry, princess, I can give you all the material you need."

Laness's hand tightened around Ember's arm. But Ember only stared, shaking her head in disgust.

She couldn't believe *this* was the healer talented enough to make Mor's hand. A healer she'd said she would love to learn from. Meanwhile, he couldn't be bothered to remove his pipe from the plaque beside him.

With blood that's cursed with ancient rage, these sketched-out tombs may be refined, if three by three by three align.

Ember quickly looked away from the plaque, struggling to keep her expression composed as the words buzzed through her veins. Their theory was correct. The shard was here.

"You've had your fun, Marcos," Laness said, releasing Ember's arm and crossing the dozen paces between them. "If you'll excuse us, we have business to attend to."

"But it's not a meeting day," Marcos said, feigning concern.

"And I'm an apprentice and she's a nymph," retorted Ember. "You know this isn't official business."

"Especially since you have those damper blades to block the wards," Marcos agreed, looking up at her through his lashes. "Tell me, how does someone so inexperienced have such passionate desires?"

Rosala spare her, he made *everything* sound sexual.

Ember ignored him, following Laness over to the opposite end of the stairs from Marcos. The nymph tapped her blade against the railing, then the step, a line forming between her brows as nothing happened.

"The wards are on the door," Marcos offered.

Ember and Laness ignored him, their daggers out as they ascended the stairs.

"You don't need to bother with that," Marcos went on, twisting around to watch them. "Healers can enter any time."

What? Ember's mouth opened of its own accord, but she quickly snapped it shut. She wouldn't indulge him. Even if he'd slapped her with yet another secret. And her markings continued not to itch.

"I'm not surprised you didn't know," Marcos said. "Apprentices don't get to know anything. They only choke down their orders, training, obeying, forgetting what it's like to question—"

"What did all that questioning get you?" Ember demanded, whirling to face him.

Marcos met her gaze. "Freedom."

The word shuddered down Ember's spine.

"How do we know you're not trying to get us caught?" Laness cut in, folding her arms.

Ember waited for him to retort they could press the dampers to the door either way. Instead, Marcos released a heavy sigh.

"Fine." He rose to his feet, abandoning his pipe as he sauntered up the stairs. "I'll show you inside. But only the novice."

"Why?" Laness demanded.

"Because while healers can enter whenever they like, there's a reason wards keep everyone else out."

Ember said, "You've been exiled. Why do you care?"

"Imagine what my reasons could be and pick your favorite."

Marcos leaned around her to open the door, no part of him touching her, Ember's skin crawling regardless. With a quick twist of the gold, rose-shaped knob, the door popped open, Marcos's breath warm on Ember's ear. "What do you say?"

Ember tensed. She glanced at Laness, clearly just as displeased with their new arrangement.

But Marcos was inviting her inside. A man who, at one point, had been a master healer. And one that clearly knew what was waiting inside.

"Fine," Ember said curtly. She slid her damper blade back through her belt, digging her elbow into Marcos's stomach in the process. He grunted, taking an automatic step back.

"Sorry," she simpered over her shoulder. Then, she pushed through the door and marched inside.

Chapter 92

Analia couldn't believe this was what Deardryn had intended when she'd request-ed a meeting.

The three of them sat on tree stumps at the edge of the forest. After taking an obvious sip from her own glass, Deardryn passed Analia the wine bottle, Analia begrudgingly filling first her glass, then Aaron's. Even though the Sun guards remained with their boat upstream and out of hearing range, Analia was still acutely aware of their stares.

"You know," she said, turning her glass between her fingers, "if you *just* wanted to drink and catch up, Aaron could have shadowjumped us to your castle."

"It would be more hospitable if we had a table and servants to tend to us, wouldn't it?" Deardryn mused. She lifted her glass to her lips, glancing at Aaron over the rim. "You're unusually quiet."

"I don't like being threatened," he said flatly.

Analia did a quick check-in, his magic still a quiet melody across her senses.

Deardryn nodded to herself. She leaned forward to adjust the blue irises she'd arranged in a bucket between them like a makeshift centerpiece, letting the silence descend between them.

Thick. Heavy.

Analia sipped her wine, finding it fruity with just enough tartness, unsurprised Deardryn had picked something she would like. Just as unsurprised by her usual tactics.

But she'd sit in that silence as long as Deardryn liked. She had nothing to prove, nothing to defend. And she hardened herself against the approving gleam in Deardryn's eyes as she finally sat back on her stump.

"We all know the reason I requested this meeting," she began, setting her wine beside her feet. "You return the Crystal shard Analia stole, and in exchange, I will permit your kingdom to continue existing in secret."

Aaron's lips flattened.

"You're really set on there being a kingdom," Analia said, crossing her legs. "You've traveled through the Wild Lands to get here. You've seen how our legends are wrong and there are several pockets untouched by the Ancient One's magic. But they're just that. Pockets. They're not big enough for an entire kingdom."

"And yet," Deardryn said, "your 'pocket' is so heavily glamored and warded that the three patrols I've sent have failed to see anything before our communication was cut off."

"We prefer people to knock before entering," Aaron drawled.

Analia could have sworn Deardryn's lips twitched.

"That withstanding," she said, "it doesn't explain what happened to all of the Star citizens after the Shattering War."

The ice that crackled in Aaron's network chilled Analia's blood. But she kept her expression blank as Deardryn leaned toward her, her eyes gleaming as though she'd discovered a fascinating bit of research.

"I know the other kingdoms prefer to consider matters closed," she said. "After all, the smaller towns can easily be written off as collateral. And while we eliminated everyone in the Star Castle, there were still Star forces that had disappeared a few days prior, and I know it wasn't because we defeated them—"

"Those are *people*," Aaron broke in. Quietly. Icily. Still in control as his network stirred, lacing through his words as he said, "Show some respect."

Analia's heart gave a long, aching squeeze. Her hand found Aaron's clenched around the edge of his stump, her fingers gently prying his free so he could squeeze her hand instead.

Not to rein him in. But to try and soften the anguish hidden on his face that only she could see.

Indeed, Deardryn didn't seem to notice as she studied him, the faintest line between her brows. And to Analia's shock, she bowed her head.

"You're correct," she said. "I apologize." She paused, waiting until Aaron's grip on his glass eased, his network still swirling. "That, however, is my point. The Star Kingdom was made up of people. And while the other kingdoms presume the survivors fled and melted into the remaining kingdoms, I have never discovered someone who claims to be from Star."

"I think this speech proves exactly why," Analia said flatly.

"True. But I knew Hester and Elspeth. They loved their people as much as Aaron clearly does. And I refuse to believe they would have left them to die."

Analia started to reply, quickly weighing arguments and denials. But Deardryn brushed her words aside with a wave of her hand.

"We've wasted enough time discussing this," she said, reclaiming her glass from the ground. "I have the evidence I need, and there is nothing you can do to change my mind about your kingdom."

"Meaning," Aaron said, releasing Analia's hand to fold his arms, "you've brought us here to threaten us, knowing we wouldn't tell you anything, let alone give you the Crystal. Seems like you're the one wasting time."

Analia didn't know how to read the flicker of emotion across Deardryn's face. But the pure cunning in her eyes as she turned to Analia had her insides shifting.

"Bold words from a king," she commented. "Have you ever noticed how on a chessboard, the king holds the most amount of value, and yet, the queen holds the most amount of potential? The king might hide behind his pieces, calling orders, but it is the queen who executes. Sneaking around the board, claiming and defending pieces until victory is had. Some say this is what makes the pieces equal. Yet, the king serves no one. And who is the queen conquering on behalf of?"

Aaron visibly struggled to remain quiet, his network hissing along Analia's senses.

Analia narrowed her eyes. "What are you playing at, Deardryn?" she asked.

"I'm simply pointing out everything you have been reduced to." Deardryn leaned toward her, a serpent readying to strike. "Do you know why I never let Othin into my council? It's because the pieces on my side of the board are *mine*. Mine to protect, mine to order, mine to rule over. I play on behalf of myself. Just as you did when scheming in the Moon Castle.

"I thought that independence would carry into your queenship. Yet, here you are. Sitting beside your king, having to soothe his temper. Letting him make decisions for you. But this isn't his decision."

Analia's flames crackled. She settled them with a mental hand, making no move to stop Deardryn's words, a quiet intensity simmering in her gaze.

"*You* stole that shard. You are the one who decides what happens to it. And I expected you to realize that." Deardryn's hand stretched, barely able to graze Analia's knee. "You are supposed to be a Royal. Not a queen obedient to a king who bows to no one—"

Deardryn cut off with a tiny gasp.

Analia first registered the blood trickling down Deardryn's temple, then the thud as the dagger that had scraped past her head imbedded itself in the trunk behind her.

"Do not touch my wife," Aaron seethed.

Chills raced down Analia's spine. She and Deardryn slowly turned to look at him, another dagger already in his hand, power rumbling off him like the opening scenes of a nightmare.

"You..." Deardryn said, easing her hand back.

"You're done," Aaron told her, colder than death. "You don't get to look at her, you don't get to talk to her, you don't get to say her gods-damned name. She already won. She stole the Crystal, and she beat you. You don't get to antagonize her into another round so you can try to salvage your pride.

"You *lost* to her. Which means now, you get to deal with me. Not because I'm a king giving her orders. But because I bow *to her*. And my next dagger goes in your throat."

His gaze pierced into hers, Deardryn clearly taken aback. But Analia was much more than that as she stared at him, her lips parted silently.

Because that wasn't Aaron. It wasn't even the Starlight King.

It was the Heir of Death. His gaze as lethal as the blade he held in his hand, his vow forged from the ice that had imprisoned him for decades.

But as he looked at Analia, she realized that vow wasn't for Deardryn. It was for her. Offered across a battlefield of memories, memories that allowed her to find him beyond the cold as she stared into his eyes.

Aaron. He was still in there. And he was in control.

"Well," Deardryn said, almost believably disappointed. "I was hoping to do this peacefully. But now..."

Deardryn flicked her fingers. Aaron grabbed Analia's hand in a flash, pulling them into the shadows.

But the riverbank had barely started to fade when Aaron hissed, the stump resolidifying beneath Analia. And magic tingled across her senses as a ring of brilliant blue light raced across the ground around them, forming a circle.

A shield. Trapping them within.

Ember turned in a slow circle, taking in the temple.

Rows of balconies encircled the wide-open room, reminiscent of a theater's mezzanine. The walls were covered in paintings of healers in their emerald robes, their faces turned away, the view focused on the patients they healed. But Ember's attention went straight to the golden statue of Rosala.

She stood in the center of the room, dressed in her own robes with arms spread, the upper half of her face obscured by a mask carved with roses and vines. Before her sat a marble altar, the green shot through with veins of white and gold.

"Welcome to the Temple of Rosala," Marcos said, closing the door behind them.

Ember glanced back at him, waiting for the jab. But while the cunning, watchful look still glinted in his deep blue eyes, his smirk had softened. Almost wistfully.

"What?" Ember asked. "No innuendos?"

"While you were correct regarding my contempt for the healers, I still respect Rosala."

Marcos stepped around her and headed deeper into the room, questions clamoring through Ember's mind as she trailed after him. But there was no time for them. Not as she reached the altar, and the faintest itch whispered along her markings.

"Unfortunately for you," Marcos said, clasping his hands behind his back and staring up at Rosala, "since you got to make your analysis of me, that means it's my turn."

Ember tore her gaze from the narrow back door she'd originally missed. "I'm not telling you why I'm here."

"Don't worry, I can make my own assumptions. Based on your companion, you're either an astonishingly stupid Star healer, or you somehow stumbled upon the Starlight Kingdom. I must say, I'm partial to the latter. I'd hate to learn you've spent a century discovering it's possible to unlock your collar, just to leave it on."

"I'm sorry not everyone takes their oaths as flippantly as you do," Ember snapped.

"Ah, it *is* the latter. Don't worry, the guilt gets easier with time. Although it can take a while to work through the anger."

Marcos cast her a sidelong look, Ember's face burning—what was the matter with her? She'd seen the Starlight healers continue to heal, be chosen, outside the bounds of their traditions. She'd come to terms with her oath not meaning as much as she thought. But hearing Marcos refer to her oath as something to control her rather than aid her...

"You make a lot of empty, snide remarks," she told him, almost steadily.

Marcos opened his mouth to respond. Then, he looked away, reaching out to trace the thin scratch running along Rosala's golden palm.

"I do, don't I?" he murmured. "You would think I would want to blather on about my reasons."

He scratched his face, his fingers lingering on the purple lines along his eye. His gaze met hers. And tingles rushed through Ember's blood.

Was he hinting his markings itched? No, he couldn't be. She didn't know of any Blessed healer who had experienced that reaction, and he still looked like he was in his late twenties despite creating Mor's hand over eighty years ago.

He had to be Blessed. So then, what was he trying to tell her?

"Should I bother finding out?" she asked, watching him closely.

"Well, secrets are always more enjoyable to discuss with those who share them."

Marcos turned, leaning against the altar with a lazy grin. But Ember's attention went to his fingers, softly drumming on the marble. Long enough for an adult to lay on, directly under Rosala's gaze.

"What happens during the master healer ceremony?" she blurted. "You know, since I won't be able to experience it myself."

The thought alone had Ember's eye twitch. But it was the approving gleam in Marcos's eyes that had cracks spiderwebbing across her chest.

"The ceremony is far more boring than you'd think," he began, pushing off the altar. "Sometimes, there are meetings where no apprentices graduate, others only a handful. But on the visit I was made a master healer, there were twenty of us."

Marcos gestured up to the balconies, Ember not daring to breathe. "We go kingdom by kingdom, everyone watching from above as the archmasters stand where we are now and call the apprentices forward. Each apprentice then gets to swear their oath, one final time. Then, they lie on the altar, Rosala looking down at them as the archmasters retattoo their rings."

Marcos paused, his eyes carefully fixed on the balconies. Giving her time to interject.

Ember rubbed her fingertips together, practically feeling the sharp ache of the needle around her eye, the echo of her voice from long ago. She'd spent fourteen years dreaming about where that moment would bring her. Now, listening to Marcos describe it, she didn't so much as long for it as she did scrutinize it. And that loss hurt most of all.

"Is there anything special about the ink?" she managed.

"You already know," Marcos replied.

Those cracks furrowed deeper.

Ember forced herself to take a step toward the back door, the faint itch along her markings increasing.

Something magical was in that room. Marcos was clearly encouraging her to inquire. Meaning he either knew something and couldn't say, or he was trying to get her to reveal what she knew. And Ember couldn't bring herself to care which anymore.

"The ink is stored in that back room," she finally said, gesturing to the door.

Marcos snorted. "Of course. You wouldn't want to leave that out where anyone could grab it."

"Because it's valuable," Ember said, her words unbearably bitter. "That's why only the archmasters are on the floor when the apprentices are marked. Only they can go into that room. Only they can know the ink is Blessed by the Crystal. And that Blessing prevents anyone who finds out from sharing that information with those who don't already know.

I'm assuming that's why apprentices get marked as well, even though they're not magically bound until graduating."

Ember stared into his face, silently begging him to deny it. But Marcos's mouth flickered in a smile, not a drop of shock on his face. And the cracks across Ember's chest groaned as the truth finally hit home.

Marcos started to speak.

Ember twisted on her heel, marching toward the back door, cracks deepening with every pound of her heart.

She had to get away from him. She couldn't survive hearing anything else.

"That's why we have the healer-Royal separation," Marcos called, jogging after her. "It wasn't to enable neutral healing. It was so the Royals wouldn't know that Helia Oshar entrusted us with a shard."

"Stop," Ember choked out.

But Marcos kept going as if his words couldn't escape fast enough. "All those things we swear to. Celibacy, loneliness, neutrality, how much wine we can drink, those aren't Rosala's wishes. It doesn't help us become better healers. It forces loyalty. Minimizes the risk of us asking questions. And we're trained to despise those who break free of the system because they are the greatest threat of all—"

"Marcos, *stop*—"

"They brand our obedience into our flesh—"

"Stop it!" Ember screamed. She shoved open the back door, barely able to see through her tears as she staggered inside.

She wanted to scream that he was a liar. That he was everything the healers said an exile would be. This. Wasn't. Real.

But the tiny back room was taken up by a shelf filled with row after row of white ink vials. And itchiness flared across her markings—those gods-damned markings. The symbols of everything she had accomplished, her proof that no matter what the other healers said, Rosala still chose her. She still saw *her*.

But they were just a tool. A way to force her into secrecy against her will, even after she'd given up *everything* to receive them.

Ember gripped one of the wooden shelves, doubling over and gasping for breath. And her mind spun. Faster and faster, questions blurring into each other, the same realization screaming through it all.

The Starlight healers didn't have a different way of doing things. They had broken free. And everything Ember had built her life, her opinions, herself, upon was a lie.

"Ember," Marcos said, his fingers grazing her shoulder, "I didn't mean—"

"Don't *touch* me!" Ember snarled. She whipped around, Marcos leaning away and raising his hands defensively.

But Ember didn't stop. She stalked toward him, backing him against the wall, coming close enough to smell drug-laced smoke—holy Crystal above she needed devinroot.

"You don't talk anymore," she hissed, gripping the front of his jacket. "You shouldn't even know *any* of this, unless you were an archmaster."

"I wasn't—"

"No talking—"

"But I got suspicious after how my rings split and I started poking around."

Marcos stared into her eyes, his breath hot and uneven on her mouth. Begging her to ask about his comment.

But Ember was tired of playing his games, the healers' games, the Defiants' games. All she wanted was to grab the shard and go.

"Marcos," she ground out, "where is the Crystal?"

Marcos averted his gaze. And Ember didn't need to hear his words. Didn't need to watch his lips form his response to know.

But she couldn't look away. Not as Marcos said, almost gently, "It's been taken."

Ember didn't think. She screamed, "Laness!"

Chapter 93

Analia pivoted on her heel, taking in the six Sun soldiers that had come to form an arc before her and Aaron. Spears glinted over each of their shoulders, daggers hanging at their belts. And a shield crackled at her feet forming a circle about five paces wide in any direction.

"Really, Deardryn?" Aaron asked, his network hissing across Analia's senses. "You're *that* desperate to keep us here?"

"I am," Deardryn said matter-of-factly, peering over the shoulders of the guards in front of her. "As you can imagine, this is an important matter to me."

Analia's senses raced along the shield, searching for where the magic was weakest.

"I knew you wouldn't be receptive," Deardryn went on. "I apologize for such forceful methods."

With the guards so close, the magic didn't have to stretch far enough for there to be a serious variation. But since it originated from the man in front of her and to the left, that meant across from him where no other guards stood...

"The shield won't hurt you, but it *will* prevent you from leaving. Courtesy of my brother-in-law."

"Nice to meet you," Aaron said. He flicked his fingers, a whip of starlight lashing toward the dark-haired man.

The shield flared a brilliant blue as the magics collided, a thrum buzzing through the air. Then, the starlight ricocheted back toward Analia.

Analia yelped and ducked behind Aaron just in time. Aaron gasped, his magic winking out before it could bounce off the shield once more. And the guards stiffened as they realized who they were dealing with.

"I tried to warn you," Deardryn chided.

Analia fell to her knees behind Aaron. Tuning out the rest of Deardryn's words, she summoned her flames to her fingers, dragging them through the gravel.

"Nice try, Analia," Deardryn called. "Your magic might not rebound, but your plan still won't work. For while you can't cross the shield, we can."

Analia's only warning was a languid thrum. She scrambled to her feet, throwing up her arm as golden light arced between the Sun soldiers, over the shield, brightening to a blinding flash as it barreled into her.

Analia's flames snarled.

But the Sun magic made no moves to attack. It wreathed around her curiously, its tingles rolling across her skin.

Analia shuddered, even as she kept the memories tightly locked away. And when the magic finally cleared...

"This *again?*" Aaron complained.

Golden shackles bound his ankles together. A far thicker band of light pinned his arms to his sides, preventing his elbows from bending. But Analia remained unbound.

"Apologies," Deardryn said. "You've always been my greatest leverage."

Analia barely heard her through the roaring in her ears. She stepped toward Aaron, midnight flames crackling to life on her fingers.

Deardryn clicked her tongue. "You'll need a large amount of fire to overpower my bonds, and at that point, my magic won't be the only thing that burns. Judging by the look on Aaron's face, he's realized he can't unleash the power necessary to break through without harming you either."

Aaron didn't reply, silver light flickering across his bonds. But Deardryn's magic held.

Magic briefly crackled outside the shield. And it had been a long, long time since Analia made no attempts to stifle the fury laced through her flames. It seared through her blood, screaming for vengeance with every pound of her pulse.

She stared past the group of soldiers, the flurry of looks they exchanged louder than any whisper. But her attention was only for Deardryn.

"You will never get that shard," Analia promised. Perfectly, lethally, in control.

Something like satisfaction flashed across Deardryn's face. Before Analia could wonder, Aaron's shackles flared. He sucked in a breath, his muscles going rigid.

"Perhaps you should hear my terms before making any decisions," Deardryn offered.

Analia's flames snarled. She folded her arms, refusing to reply, Deardryn not waiting for one.

"You have two choices," she said, her guards shifting so she could step closer. "You can give me the shard and come willingly with me back to my kingdom where we will continue our research, and Aaron will get to live. I'll even keep him in the dungeon so you can visit as much as you like. Or, I can take you and the shard by force, and you will watch Aaron die."

Her shackles flared brighter.

Something snapped.

And Aaron stifled a curse.

Analia's heart jolted. Her eyes darted over him, searching for the broken bone—gods, this was her uncle's chamber all over again. Oddly so.

Why would Deardryn want to take her back with her after she'd already stolen the shard once? Why offer to keep Aaron alive?

"I'm disappointed, Analia," Deardryn said, twisting one of her many golden bracelets. "You came all this way to have a conversation with me, and you are completely unprepared."

Analia's jaw tightened.

"My magic wasn't blocked by a damper on you, nor has it found one on Aaron. I presume it's because you've dampered me once before with Sabina's help and didn't expect it to work a second time. But to not even bring the blades as a last resort?" Deardryn shook her head. "The crown has dulled your potential."

The words thudded between them, the final move before checkmate.

But Analia's mind didn't race for a way out. Her flames didn't snap their leash. Instead, a slow, savage grin stretched across her lips.

"What?" Deardryn asked, her eyes narrowing.

"I'm just thinking about what you told me back in the Moon Castle," she said. "How overconfidence is the fatal flaw of any ruler. Yet, here you are, convinced I made a mistake. Just as I expected."

Analia raised a hand behind her back.

Deardryn's face paled.

And with a quick flare of magic, Mor's relocated damper blade fell on the mark she had made in the gravel behind Aaron. And the shield disappeared.

The shielder recoiled in surprise. A second soldier shoved Deardryn back, the rest of the guards reaching for their weapons, their exclamations echoing around the riverside as they realized half were missing. One drew his spear, spitting a curse as it disappeared with a quick flash of magic.

Aaron opened his hand, the spear reappearing in his grip. Just as Analia grabbed the damper blade and twisted, pressing it to his shackles.

The sunlight disappeared.

The shielder raised his hands, blue light flaring as he tried to replace the shield. Aaron lunged for him, gold and silver light flashing from the damper blade as he broke contact.

And Analia's flames erupted.

They spilled out of her in a wave of black and blue, their wrath roaring in her ears, barreling through the line of soldiers one by one. One, two, three, four, five, six. Her flames too hot for them to have time to scream, the damper blade disappearing in her grip.

And Analia didn't flinch. She didn't turn away from her carnage.

She rose again: her flames dying down, revealing Deardryn's destroyed bucket of irises, the charred remains of her victims. The cost of her crown. And as she stepped out of the smoke and embers, she wasn't *just* Analia.

She was the Starlight Queen. One who strove for peace, but showed no mercy to those who threatened it. A queen still finding her way, but who would do whatever it took to protect her home.

She was a Royal. And Deardryn finally seemed to understand that as she stared at her from fifteen feet away.

Her olive-green gown singed. Her face flushed from the lingering heat. And a damper blade pressed to her throat as Aaron restrained her from behind.

"I told you this was where my next dagger was going," he hissed.

Analia's blood hummed. Deardryn didn't seem to hear him, her eyes moving over her dead soldiers, the smell of burned flesh and leather filling the air.

"You killed them," she said, disbelieving.

"You and I both know there was no chance they would walk away from the riverside alive," Analia said. "You've been hoping we would spare you the trouble."

Deardryn didn't try to deny it. She shook her head a fraction, Aaron pressing the blade harder to her throat.

"This was an excellent scheme, my dear," she said. "You kept your soldier with relocation magic away so I wouldn't notice, allowing them to disarm my soldiers and free you when the time was right."

Not to mention give Aaron the damper after he pretended to lunge for one of the soldiers, instead shadowjumping out of range of Analia's flames and preventing Deardryn from escaping.

"I knew you'd find a way to disarm us of any dampers," Analia said. "Especially since, with your husband's Blessing, it would be easy for you to bring along someone Blessed with shielding. So, I deprived you of a chance to get one of our dampers, and kept them just a gesture away if I'd miscalculated."

And it had worked. But she hadn't won yet.

"Well then," Deardryn said, as casual as a comment on the weather. "You have me captured. Shall I expect you to kill me?"

She didn't seem nearly as bothered by this as she should. Analia just shook her head.

"Now, you hear *our* terms." She crossed the distance between them, Deardryn starting to tilt her head in interest before she remembered the blade at her throat. "Clearly," Analia said, "the Crystal's secret has been compromised, and you have information. So, we're going to bring you with us, and you're going to tell us everything you know so we can find the other shards and hide them again."

Deardryn's brows rose. Over her shoulder, Aaron nodded grimly.

They had decided on this the night before. Half the family wanted to kill her and bury the information with her corpse, but Analia knew she was more useful alive. Which brought them to this moment.

"Unfortunately," Analia said, "there's no other choice for you to pick. And we've been known to resort to torture if necessary."

"I see," Deardryn murmured.

She took a long moment to study Analia, Analia keeping her chin high, carefully staying out of reach as Deardryn slowly, non-threateningly, raised her hand. Aaron allowed the movement, Deardryn scratching the corner of her eye.

"I apologize for insinuating you were anything other than the formidable queen I first identified," she said. "They were merely jabs, as I'm sure you're aware. But unfortunately, I cannot allow this scheme to progress."

Deardryn tilted her wrist, causing the golden bracelets, always stacked on her wrist for as long as Analia had known her, to slide down. Revealing the edge of three black, curving lines on the inside of her wrist.

Analia's heart stopped. Aaron's eyes widened.

And Deardryn moved in a blur.

Grabbing Aaron's wrist with one hand, she gripped his forearm with the other and bent forward, twisting under the gap between his arm and his torso.

Golden light erupted from the damper blade. But instead of returning to Deardryn's network, it exploded out.

Analia gasped. She dove out of the way, skidding on her knees and throwing up an arm as the magic flooded toward her, rising up like a cresting wave.

There was no time to summon her flames. No way to avoid the Sun magic's path.

Analia squeezed her eyes shut, bracing for the blow.

And something warm and solid collided with her. Arms wrapped around her waist, pulling her into the shadows just in time.

Analia's fingers fisted in Aaron's tunic. And she didn't have time to right herself as they emerged farther downstream, the carried force sending them tumbling down the riverbank.

Gravel scratched along Analia's arms, grit stinging her eyes.

Aaron managed to stop them before they hit the water. He shot upright, his eyes darting over her, "Are you—"

"I'm fine. Did you—"

"No," he said, fast and firm. "If it's a choice between killing Deardryn and saving you, I'm choosing you. Every time."

He helped her sit up, his movements as fast and jerky as Analia's pulse as he brushed the gravel from her back.

"What did she break," Analia asked, her hands shaking as she reached for him. "I heard a snap."

"My finger." Aaron raised his left hand, his pinky starting to swell. "It was clean, I can splint it with the supplies in Mor's pack, I'm fine."

Analia started to respond.

Footsteps raced along the riverbank toward them.

Analia jumped, her head whipping around fast enough her neck ached.

"There you are!" Mor exclaimed, skidding down the slope to join them. "What *happened?*"

"Deardryn has a mark," Analia blurted.

Mor's jaw dropped, Aaron's magic surging.

Mor began, "But how—"

"I don't know." Analia tugged on the ends of her hair, her mind spinning with countless questions. And they all came to a grinding halt as her enka bracelet tingled across her wrist.

Deardryn got the shard from the temple, and Branten just got in contact. You have to get back to the kingdom. Now.

Chapter 94

Dimitri paced around the safehouse's sitting room, Rayner sketching in his book on the couch. He'd known from the moment he blew his cover he would have to hide out for a while. But he hadn't anticipated the boredom as he did so, the house quiet and empty as Rois, the Royals, and their spouses went about their missions.

"Do you think," Dimitri began.

The front door flew open.

Dimitri's heart jolted. He whipped around, sunlight flaring in his stomach.

Othin couldn't have found him already. He couldn't have picked the one time there were no Royals to shadowjump him and Rayner away—

"Where's my son?" Aeley demanded, the door swinging shut behind her as she swept inside.

Dimitri's panic caught in his throat. He jabbed a finger at Aeley, spluttering for several seconds before finally demanding, "What are you doing here?"

"How did you know we're here?" Rayner asked, upright and alert on the couch.

"Please," Aeley said, shoving her golden hair behind her ear as she searched the room. "Othin caught you all here, meaning it's the perfect place to hide in the aftermath. And since his traitorous advisor has been directing his attention *away* from this house, he has decided to check again. Today."

Aeley glared at Dimitri. He scuttled back, bumping into a chair at the rickety dining table.

"How do you know this?" Rayner pressed. "I thought after *you* revealed yourself, Othin has been keeping you out of his inner circle."

"He has. But he's a fool if he thought that would be enough to keep information from me. Almost as foolish as all of you for not including me in your schemes."

The mild bite to her words had Dimitri's insides squirming. "Cadmus didn't want to risk anyone seeing all of us talking," he mumbled. "What are you looking for?"

"Cinder." Aeley peered into an Everflame sconce, humming in approval as the sprite appeared with a crackle in the flames. "How is my distraction going?"

"Othin is unleashing all of his anger on Ronun and his 'unreasonable questions,' just as you predicted," she reported with a bow.

"You're scheming with the fire sprites, too?" Rayner asked, rising from the couch to join Dimitri at the table.

"Of course," Aeley said impatiently. "You have no idea how much I've been helping you all. Now, where is my son?"

"He's not here," Dimitri said. "He and all the other Royals are visiting towns to build an army, and Rois is infiltrating the castle."

"Figures," Aeley muttered.

She came to study the map on the table behind Dimitri, Dimitri not sure if he was more unsettled by Othin's plans or Aeley's icy efficiency.

"We have to get a message to him that this house is no longer secure," she said. "I should be able to hide you two until someone can shadowjump you away—"

"Spark," Rayner said suddenly. "What aren't you saying?"

Dimitri and Aeley started, Aeley seeming just as unaware of Spark's presence as Dimitri. But Rayner's gaze was fixed on a corner sconce, Spark's huddled form barely distinguishable in the flames.

Under everyone's stares, they curled into a tighter ball. "I was ordered not to say anything unless asked," they mumbled.

Aeley's eyes narrowed. With a crackle, Cinder disappeared on her sconce, Spark's Everflame flaring brighter as she came to huddle beside them. And that little gesture had Dimitri's stomach sinking.

"Spark," he said, taking a few steps toward them, "what did Cadmus tell you not to say?"

Spark wavered, their body darkening to red, then brightening to yellow, finally flickering back to their usual orange.

Dimitri stepped closer.

And Spark's words came out in a rush, "He went to Mt. Vasolus to release Lucilla's ashes."

Dimitri sucked in a breath, Laness's warning from Ember blaring loud and clear in his mind.

"He can't go there," Aeley hissed, gripping the table.

Rayner, eyes wide, began, "You know—"

"Of course I know! Cadmus told the council the moment he got his mark, and I saw it on Brenn's wrist after his coronation."

"Did he tell you before shadowjumping?" Dimitri asked, hurrying forward and offering his hands.

"No," Spark said. "He went on foot."

"What?" Aeley exclaimed.

"He's begging to get caught," Rayner hissed. "What is he thinking?"

Dimitri didn't know. But as the sprites hopped onto his hands, their little bodies warm against his fingers as he rushed back to the table, he knew it didn't matter.

"We have to stop him," he said.

"He's probably already there," Aeley said, anxiously tugging the ends of her hair. "Mt. Vasolus is just barely within walking distance. And if he shadowjumped to the top?"

"He might not have," Rayner said, sounding like he was trying to convince himself. "And if he's going to the top on foot, that hike will take him a while."

"Which means we have to go," Dimitri said. He placed the sprites on the table beside the map, his mouth struggling to keep up with his racing thoughts. "Aeley, how did you get here?"

"Carriage," she said.

Rayner shot her an incredulous look, but Dimitri nodded.

"That's smart. Make no attempts to hide your leaving and Othin is less likely to care. Where'd you park it?"

"A few streets over in front of a dress shop. I left through the back door and used the alleyways to get here. No one saw me leave, and everyone will see me return through the shop's front door."

"Good," Dimitri said. "We're coming with you. Your carriage is the second fastest way to get to the volcano. Rayner, can you—"

"Already on it," Rayner said, running his fingers along his jaw, creating a harsh line.

"What do you mean, 'second fastest'?" Aeley asked. Crystal fuck him, that looked like a glint of respect in her eyes.

He turned to Spark and Cinder, huddling together with heads bowed. "Don't feel bad," he said, softening his tone. "You were following orders. And you've been invaluable these past months. Are you willing to help, one more time?"

"Of course," Spark and Cinder squeaked, clasping their hands before them.

"Thank you." Dimitri turned to Aeley. "Can you show Spark the quickest path to Mt. Vasolus on the map?"

Aeley nodded, immediately trailing her finger along streets, cutting through the square to the volcano beyond.

"All right," Dimitri said. "Cinder, you're coming with us. Spark, tell Rois that's the path we'll be following. Then, have him find Joshel. I have a message for him."

Dimitri quickly relayed his words, Aeley's eyebrows shooting up, Rayner completely unsurprised. Spark nodded once Dimitri was done, hopping over to a sconce and disappearing with a crackle. And Dimitri could only pray he hadn't initiated the dumbest plan in existence.

The first thing Analia registered as Aaron pulled her and Mor out of the shadows on the Council Building's roof was the screams.

Beyond the lake, the Starlight forces in their black fighting leathers struggled to hold back a far larger wave of soldiers in white and gold, weapons and magic flashing in the afternoon sun. Analia was too far away to sense if the wards still held. But she had no problem finding the source of the panic in the streets below.

"How does she have so many?" Mor asked, gripping the railing encircling the roof in horror.

Analia shook her head, lost for words. Because there, sweeping through the Pulse, citizens' screams echoing as they fled, was a unit of Devourists.

She counted twelve of the tall, humanoid figures. Their black cloaks rippled behind them as they scattered down streets, gray-black bones poking out from their patches of dark, scaly skin.

"They're from the obsidian she's been collecting in Ash," Aaron spat.

He raked his injured hand through his hair, the other squeezing Analia's tight enough to hurt.

But she didn't try to pull away. Not just because, based on the snarling of his network, he was barely keeping his fury in check. But because she needed the pain, needed it to pull her out of the shock threatening to root her to the spot.

She had to think. Fast.

"Deardryn must have sent them to track down the Crystal," she said, her lungs tight. "Her soldiers at the border are there to keep our own distracted so they can't impede the hunt."

Who would have thought her paranoia that morning would pay off—although it was only a matter of time before the Devourists would sense the Crystal's casing in Mor's jacket pocket.

"They clearly don't have orders not to stop for a snack," he seethed. He pointed with a golden finger, chills racing down Analia's spine as a Devourist grabbed a woman trying to escape across the silver bridge into the business sector.

She screamed, desperately holding onto the railing as it pulled her toward its black-lipped mouth. Just for a ribbon of starlight to slam into its chest, sending it flying back into a building's facade.

Analia twisted toward Aaron. Cold radiated off him in waves, his hand still raised, starlight wreathing around his hand and crackling along the splint binding his pinky and ring fingers together.

He'd made that shot a hundred feet away. Flawlessly. But there was only so much power he could extend over that distance. And the tension in his jaw suggested he knew he needed a lot more to stop the glowing core in the demon's chest from stitching back together.

But at least the woman had escaped across the bridge and into the shadows, Analia's heart racing as the Devourist staggered in a dazed circle.

It would straighten soon enough. It and the others would hunt whatever Blessed got in their path as they looked for the Crystal.

Her home was violated. Her people turned into pawns to be sacrificed for Deardryn's scheme. All in the light of day.

Analia turned back to Aaron and Mor. And she reveled in the eruption of heat across her skin, her flames scorching away her shock, leaving nothing but certainty in their wake.

"We have to split up," she said. "Aaron, you have to repair whatever damage has been dealt to our wards and get rid of those soldiers."

Aaron nodded once. "And you?"

"Mor and I will deal with the Devourists."

She looked at Mor for confirmation. And it wasn't her friend, even her family, who bowed to her. It was the soldier forged by the Underground. "As you wish."

Analia's flames snarled in satisfaction.

"Where do you want me to drop you two?" Aaron asked.

"Starlight Bridge," she said, pointing to the silver bridge where the Devourist was rallying.

"Done."

Mor extended his hand, clearly expecting Aaron to pull them into the shadows. But Aaron turned to Analia, drawing her closer, his free hand tightening around her hip.

"You come back to me," he ordered, the blaze in his eyes underscored by the yells and screams below.

"I'm always searching," she promised.

Aaron kissed her hard and fast, his mouth unnaturally cold. Good. They were going to need that power, that rage, if they were going to make it through this.

"Stay alive, you two," he said, offering his injured hand to Mor. Then, he pulled them into the shadows.

Ember paced around the temple's main room, Marcos warily tracking her from where he sat on the altar.

"Well," Laness said, descending the balcony stairs, "he's telling the truth. I've checked the entire temple, and the shard isn't here."

"I'm so glad you believe me," Marcos muttered.

"Don't be petulant; I told Aaron as soon as I heard."

"Yes, just like you informed him of the invasion. What terrible timing, that."

"Watch it, Marcos," Laness warned. "My damper blade might be blocking the wards on the door, but I still have Ember's."

Ember didn't look up at the sound of her name, her feet carrying her round and round. Just as they'd been doing ever since Laness burst into the temple, taking one look at her face before swiping the dagger from her belt.

But Ember didn't care. She couldn't care as Laness demanded Marcos tell her everything, his words breaking her all over again.

"I don't know why you're threatening me," Marcos complained. "If it weren't for me, you wouldn't know the Crystal was stolen in the first place."

"You really think we wouldn't have been able to deduce that ourselves?" Laness asked, folding her arms as she stopped before him.

"You wouldn't know that it was stolen before the last meeting, nor that the healers haven't noticed yet because they haven't needed to make more ink—my gods, Ember, would you just sit down?"

"Bite me," Ember spat, not slowing.

Marcos started to retort—

"You did this to her," Laness snapped. Turning her back on him, she hurried to fall into step beside Ember, her tone softening into something gentle. "Em, we have to head back to the kingdom; they're going to need us. But I need to make sure you're all right first. So, what can I do?"

Ember had the strangest urge to laugh. Laness was offering her help? As if there was anything anyone could do to piece her back together. Even Sofika had barely dragged her back from the brink the last time she spun out like this.

Gods, Sofika had given her so many tools to deal with her addiction. But no amount of routines or busy schedules could fix this.

Be curious.

"Leave her be," Marcos said, pointedly not looking at them as he played with his mask. "This isn't something you fix."

"Be quiet," Laness hissed. She turned back to Ember, her fingers brushing hers. "Em, talk to me."

We're dealing with your mind. And when you leave it alone, it builds up until there's nowhere left to go.

"You want to know what I'm feeling?" Ember asked, unbearably tight.

Laness nodded cautiously. And the pressure that had been steadily building in Ember's chest finally erupted.

"I feel betrayed, because everything I've been taught to respect is a lie. I'm devastated because my life no longer feels like it's my own. And I'm angry.

"So unbelievably angry because I spent *years* in a system that broke me down into nothing, to the point I've made decisions I can't come back from. I'm furious because the Starlight Kingdom has proven it wasn't necessary. And I hate it was all for *nothing*."

Ember wanted to spit the words like they were poison. Instead, they staggered and fell from her lips, graceless as the tears that spilled down her cheeks.

Laness stared up at her, completely lost for words. And for some reason, that made the burning, agonizing ripping in Ember's chest feel a fraction better.

"Do you need to be left alone?" Laness finally asked.

Ember nodded, finally coming to a stop as she wrapped her arms around herself.

"All right."

Laness gently touched her hand. Then, with the righteous indignation of someone far taller than herself, she turned on Marcos.

"You're coming with us."

Marcos's dark brow winged up. "Am I?"

"You already know the Starlight Kingdom is more hospitable than any inn you could skulk in. Free food, a bed to sleep in, safety. All in exchange for information."

"Why do you think I have any interest in helping you, amenities or not?" Marcos drawled.

"Because you waited on those steps for someone you could tell about the Crystal," Laness replied. "I might not know why, but you care."

Marcos didn't respond immediately. He flipped his mask between his fingers, Ember finally noticing through her silent tears the intricate designs hammered into the metal. Reminiscent of the loops carved on one of the archways out in the garden.

"Fine," he sighed, slipping the mask over his face. "I'll come. But I only talk to healers. And no guards."

"Of course," Laness said sweetly. "You'll have a room all to yourself in a nice, big house."

Marcos rolled his eyes. But he didn't pull his hand away as Laness came to claim it, leading him off the altar and back toward Ember.

"Are you ready to go?" Laness asked her.

Ember nodded, wordlessly taking her other hand.

Just before Laness pulled her into the thick, earthy darkness, Ember took a final look around the temple. The place she had so desperately hoped would have the answers she needed. And it had.

Her oath was meaningless. The life she had so badly wanted to get back to, even when it didn't look like what she'd imagined, was over.

The temple started to fade.

Did she want to go back to Ash? No.

Chapter 95

Everything was going well until Dimitri heard the bells.

Somehow, he and Rayner—with their new appearances—had made it back to the carriage with Aeley no problem. They moved at a decent pace through the kingdom streets, the gray curtains cracked so Dimitri could peek through, Rayner quiet beside him, Aeley softly talking to Cinder perched on the candle she'd set in an ornate holder.

He'd just started to believe they'd be able to make it without Rois.

Then, the clock tower's tolls began.

One, two, three, Dimitri's stomach sinking as he counted the slow, echoing chimes. Continuing past the current hour.

"Don't tell me," he said.

"Summoning chimes," Aeley confirmed, her face paling. "Othin is calling a meeting."

Rayner blew out a breath, his head dropping into his hands.

Dimitri pushed the curtains open wider, watching as the people on the streets slowed to a stop, their heads turning toward the clock tower. Summoning everyone to the square. Directly in their path. And Dimitri had never seen such a widespread look of disgust as the Ash citizens sighed and headed for the square as slow as humanly possible.

"Crystal spare us," Dimitri breathed.

"Why is he calling a meeting?" Rayner asked, shifting in his seat to peer out Dimitri's window. "I thought he was going to invade the safehouse."

"I should have known," Aeley muttered. "He *always* makes a grand display after his plans have been ruined."

"But he doesn't have any captives to threaten," Dimitri said. Unless...

Dimitri shuddered, banishing the thought.

"We have to go faster," he said, returning to the front window. But people were filtering in from the side streets, joining the main path, their carriage slowing as the crowd grew around them.

"Can we make it onto a side road?" Rayner asked. "If everyone is taking this path, that should leave the rest open."

"There's no way we can maneuver over to one," Dimitri said, scanning the crowd.

"Besides," Aeley said, "there's no direct side path to Mt. Vasolus."

"It would be faster than this," Rayner argued.

But they had told Spark to have Rois look for them on this path. Spark was supposed to find them and direct them to Rois if that wouldn't work.

Dimitri tugged on a loose thread in his sleeve, cringing as the clock tower continued to boom. Summoning on Othin's behalf. Meaning Rois's chances of being discrete had shrunk to almost zero if he'd managed to—

Dimitri cursed as the crowd overflowed into their path, blocking the carriage. Meanwhile, Cadmus was getting closer to the top of the volcano—assuming Othin's men hadn't already caught him.

"There," Aeley said.

Dimitri jumped, not having heard her move to the front window. He quickly looked to where she was pointing, spotting a narrow alleyway about twenty feet ahead.

"Cinder," she said, "find Spark. Tell them that we've abandoned the carriage and are taking the torchside path."

Dimitri's eyes widened.

Cinder nodded and bowed on her wick. Then, she disappeared with a crackle.

"Thank the gods for those sprites," Aeley said, pulling up her smoky-gray cloak hood. Then, before Dimitri or Rayner could react to her plan, she pulled open the carriage door and stepped into the crowd.

Dimitri cursed.

"I guess that means we're going," he muttered.

Rayner smiled weakly. "After you."

Grumbling under his breath, Dimitri scrambled out of the practically stationary carriage, accidentally hopping down onto someone's foot. Ignoring their protest, he turned to the carriage driver, calling over the voices and clock tower tolls. "Keep heading for the square."

The driver, a young woman with short brown hair, gave him a salute. Then, Dimitri did what he did best: annoy the fuck out of people.

He shoved through the crowd, muttering apologies and pardons, dissolving into curses as elbows and shoulders banged into him from all sides. But he was clearing a path. And to his disgust, reaching the alleyway Aeley had indicated was the easiest part of his day.

"Come," Aeley said, brushing past him without so much as a thanks.

Dimitri started to snap a response, Rayner stumbling out of the crowd beside him. But Aeley took off down the dim path, moving faster than he would have expected. And Dimitri wouldn't be the fool who slowed her down as he and Rayner raced after her.

The faster they went, the faster they could get to Cadmus. But Aeley wasn't lying when she said the back paths weren't direct.

Dimitri and Rayner followed her around maze-like turns, the few people they passed eyeing them curiously. And to Dimitri's horror, the clock tower chimes grew farther away. Gods, they had to go all the way around the square? They would never catch up to Cadmus.

"Over here!"

Dimitri's head snapped to the side, spotting Spark frantically waving from a nearby sconce.

"This way," they said. Then, they disappeared, the flames on a sconce farther down the path flaring a brilliant gold.

"Nice," Rayner panted.

Dimitri didn't have the breath to respond. He just followed the sconces, Aeley's dark cloak leading the way around corners. One, two, three, Dimitri about to cry with how much time they were wasting. Finally, the alleyways opened up.

Dimitri glanced around what appeared to be a small, empty lot, presumably for a future hidden shop. But now, it was occupied by a brilliant gold-and-white carriage. The two sun dragons harnessed to the front radiated a dry heat. And sitting in the driver's seat...

"What the fuck are you doing!" Dimitri exclaimed, skidding to a stop before the carriage. "I told you to have Joshel steal this."

"Change of plans," Rois said, now black-haired and gripping the dragons' reins. "Othin decided to take this carriage to get to his little assembly. So, I had Joshel put me in charge of watching it while everyone's busy. I had to take the back way to avoid the guards stationed around the square from noticing, but it's only a matter of time before they realize it's gone."

Crystal fucking spare him.

"Do you even know how to steer this thing?" Rayner demanded, having gone surprisingly pale.

"I'm figuring it out."

Aeley's sigh was pure exasperation. Not sparing even a muttered complaint, she marched over to the carriage, yanked open the door, and climbed inside. Shrugging, Rois turned his attention back to the restless dragons.

And having nothing left to do, Dimitri headed after Aeley. But Rayner grabbed his hand.

"Dima, you have to go," he said, low and fast.

Dimitri thought his eyes might pop out of his head. "What?"

"This was already a risky plan. But now, stealing the carriage like this? There's no way we're not getting caught. And after what you've done, there's no chance Othin will let you walk away alive."

Chills raced down Dimitri's spine. But he released Rayner's hand, folding his arms, "I'm not abandoning you and Cadmus—"

"Dima, *please.* I won't choose this mission over you. I have to know you're all right."

Rayner raked a hand through his hair, something like anguish shining in his eyes.

But all Dimitri felt was a thrum. It raced through his body like the first rumbles of an earthquake, bringing with it the echo of Rayner's voice from long ago.

I won't choose your life over mine.

They were words that had haunted him. Grounded him. Tethered him to the past back in Othin's chambers, even as it destroyed him. It was the reason a part of himself always cautioned him to hold back.

And that rumble crushed those words to powder.

Dimitri stared at Rayner, finally seeing everything that lay beyond that barrier.

Tell me it's real. Tell me you want this. Tell me you want me.

"It's real," he breathed.

Rayner blinked. "What?"

Dimitri kissed him. So quick, his mouth on Rayner's there and gone in a blink, Dimitri not realizing what he'd done until he was already stumbling back, clapping a hand to his mouth in horror.

"Oh gods," he gasped. Heat flooded across his skin, growing hotter as Rayner stared at him in a daze. "Rayner, I'm sor—"

Rayner pushed him back against the carriage, grabbing Dimitri's hand and dragging it away as his mouth collided with his. Dimitri's entire being funneled into that moment, Rayner's kiss hitting him like an explosion.

It blazed through every wall, every defense, lit up the darkest corners of himself until there was nowhere to hide.

There was just Rayner. His sun. And Dimitri was free, and falling, and found.

He didn't know how his hand found its way into Rayner's thick curls, the other fisting in the back of his tunic. But holy Crystal above, he was glad they had as Rayner moaned against his mouth, the sound rushing straight to his cock. Rayner pressed him harder against the carriage, tilting Dimitri's face to give himself better access, his tongue tangling with Dimitri's.

Dimitri didn't recognize the small, choked whimper that escaped his lips. Gods, he didn't recognize any of this. But that didn't stop his noise of protest as Rayner pulled back, his heart throbbing throughout his body. Pounding harder as he saw the flush across Rayner's cheeks, his eyes dark and luminous.

"You," Rayner said unsteadily, "have terrible timing."

His words swam through Dimitri's mind. But Rayner didn't need a response. He nipped Dimitri's lower lip, Dimitri's bones igniting and liquifying as Rayner fit his mouth to his once more.

Slower. Deeper. Kissing him like he was savoring the taste, his mouth warm and sweet and tingling through Dimitri's blood.

"If you two don't mind," Aeley called from inside the carriage.

Dimitri jolted back. He stared at Rayner, that horror creeping back in as he finally remembered where they were. The time they were wasting.

Rayner chuckled, that light alive and blazing in his eyes. He turned his head, his mouth brushing over Dimitri's ear. "We're talking about this later."

Dimitri nodded shakily. And he had never mourned the loss of a touch more as Rayner finally pulled back, utterly unashamed as he climbed into the carriage. Leaving Dimitri to figure out how to function again.

"About time, sunshine," Rois called from the driver's seat.

"Please," Dimitri said, finally finding his voice. "We were giving you time to figure out what you're doing."

"Uh-huh." Rois winked, Dimitri grumbling to himself as he slowly remembered how to move.

He turned to climb into the carriage, calling before Rayner could speak, "I'm not abandoning you after that."

He closed the door behind him with a decisive click, Rayner appearing torn between exasperation and amusement where he sat. But he didn't protest as Dimitri came to sit beside him. And Dimitri could only hope those seconds wouldn't come back to haunt him.

Chapter 96

Aaron didn't consider himself an easily angered person. Irritated, maybe. Moody, definitely. But his temper moved glacially, freezing him one minute at a time, so slowly he didn't notice until the ice had encased him, and he was ready to tear down the world.

And he would start with the fucking Sun soldiers.

Aaron emerged from the shadows at the northernmost point of his border—at least, where his border once stood. Now, there was no slick greeting from his wards across his icy cocoon. There was only the buzz of combat, lacing through the clang of clashing weapons and the yell of soldiers.

"Thank the fucking gods you're here," Branten yelled from nearby. His combat Blessing thrummed around him as he manned the frontlines, exactly where Aaron knew he would be.

"What's going on?" Aaron demanded. "What happened to my wards?"

"Gone."

Branten twisted as a Sun soldier lunged for Aaron, but Aaron had already drawn a dagger and ducked under the soldier's guard. He stabbed through the man's eye, his scream coursing through Aaron's veins.

"Turns out," Branten continued, completely unfazed, "Deardryn doesn't need a damper blocking your wards when she has a squadron of fucking demons that can suck the magic away."

"They consumed them all?"

"Right after they ate the glamor up at the ridge. Turn."

Aaron twisted, driving his elbow into the stomach of an approaching guard. Sweeping out his foot, he tripped a second, raising his dagger just in time to deflect a third man's spear with a clang. By the time he drew a second dagger from his boot, Branten had already dispatched them all, his sword stained red.

But there were so many more. They flooded down the ridge's forested slope, the trees slowing them down before they reached the line of waiting Starlight soldiers. But also providing a place to hide as they retreated, taking a minute to recuperate before charging back in. And Aaron's fury peaked as he spotted black fighting leathers among the fallen.

"How did they get here?" he demanded, frost crackling along his hands.

"We don't know. Our lookouts along the river only spotted Deardryn's boat, but there were nowhere near this many soldiers on board."

"She must have shadowjumped them once she reached the meeting spot," Aaron growled. "She would have had to send them in a loop through the woods so Anna couldn't detect them."

That, or this had been planned far longer than Aaron realized. After all, there was no way Deardryn could shadowjump this many people from the Sun Kingdom... Could she?

Aaron didn't have time to consider as two men charged toward him. Branten barreled into them, sending them flying almost too fast to track.

"Where are the rest of our soldiers?" Aaron asked as Branten turned back.

"I had to spread them out. Deardryn sent five more patrols around the border to keep us busy."

All while the Devourists continued ahead. Terrorizing his people. Shrinking his forces even more as Branten undoubtedly sent a unit to deal with them. And if even one group of Sun soldiers broke through...

Aaron caught the glint of metal in his peripheral vision. He instinctively raised his arm, forgetting he wore no fighting leathers, the sword slicing along his forearm.

Aaron hissed, the pain intensifying as he clumsily fended the soldier off with the dagger in his injured hand.

He couldn't fight like this. But he couldn't leave his people to die.

His magic swirled through his frozen veins, reminding him of the one option he had. The option he had told himself he would never rely on again after what happened last time.

But that very oath had led to him getting captured by the humans during the war. A story that would likely repeat—if not kill him—if he upheld it now.

Dead. Right alongside his people, his kingdom. His charges he had sworn on his crown to protect, that vow stronger than any promise he could make to himself.

This was his purpose. His duty.

Aaron stepped forward, taking the first step down that path he found back in Ethelind's study. Then, he spread his arms.

Silver light shimmered to life before him like the edges of a mirage. It expanded, rose, soldiers across the ridge turning to him. And Aaron let that magic loose.

Starlight rolled across the battlefield like a bank of fog, leeching color from the world, absorbing all warmth until there was nothing but cold. As cold as the blood in Aaron's veins as his magic spread up the slope.

He'd had enough training since the war to spare all nature and wildlife, his only target the fleeing soldiers. His own forces quickly retreated, dropping to one knee and crossing their weapons in front of them. And no one dared to tear their gaze from the ridge as the screams began.

Never long. But always there as Aaron rotted the hundreds of soldiers before him. Easily.

That part of himself that had cracked open an eye on the riverbank stirred, reaching for control.

Aaron shoved it back, his magic finally dissipating. Leaving nothing but corpses behind.

Then, there was silence.

Slowly, his soldiers turned to him, still braced on one knee. And in a synchronized wave, they bowed.

All except Branten. He stood with his arms folded, his face bloodied, his dark, assessing eyes piercing into Aaron's.

"I'm still here," Aaron said cooly.

Branten's lips pursed. But he nodded. Not looking back, he waved for his soldiers to rise, their murmurs tapping against Aaron's ice.

"You have to save your magic for the wards," Branten told him, lowering his voice. "We can help get rid of the soldiers, but only you can reestablish our safety."

"I can do both."

"And stay in control while doing it?" Branten challenged.

Aaron gave a sharp nod.

"Promise me," Branten insisted.

"I promise." The words stuck to the ice in Aaron's throat. But seemingly deciding to trust him, Branten turned back to their forces.

"Our work's not done," he called. "His Majesty and I will shadowjump to the next group. Join us on foot as fast as you can."

The soldiers gave a resounding affirmative. Then, they charged off around the ridge to Aaron's right, hundreds of boots pounding toward the echo of clashing weapons.

Aaron sliced a strip off the front of his tunic with his dagger, wrapping his bloody arm. Then, he knelt to replenish the wards, his magic crackling impatiently.

The Heir of Death had awakened. And there was no putting him back to sleep.

Analia didn't have time to tell Mor her plan before the Devourist's head snapped toward them. It streaked across the polished silver bridge, fast as a midnight wind. But Mor's reflexes were faster.

He curled his fingers, and a nearby eight-foot statue of Talitha disappeared, reappearing directly in the Devourist's path. The two collided with a crash and a howl, the Devourist stumbling back and gripping its face.

"What's the plan?" Mor yelled.

"Move it again!"

Mor did as ordered, and Analia charged forward, raising her hand. Midnight flames roared across the bridge, slamming into the Devourist's chest.

The Devourist released a bone-chilling screech. It tried to retreat as Analia's flames found the glowing crystal core where its heart should be, its black cloak igniting in the process. But Talitha's statue appeared behind it, blocking its path. And the last thing Analia saw was its empty eye sockets lock onto her as the Devourist exploded into a cloud of obsidian dust.

Analia let her flames wink out, struggling to catch her breath.

"You all right?" Mor asked, coming to join her.

"Fine," Analia panted. "Just took more magic than I was expecting."

And she'd already used a decent amount on the riverbank. But the magic she had left would have to do.

"That was quick thinking with the statue," she went on, finally catching her breath. "If your Blessing wasn't exclusive to inanimate objects, I would ask you to toss them all into the river."

Mor snorted. He started to reply, just to cut off as a scream echoed deeper in the Pulse. Both their heads snapped toward the sound, but they were too far away to find the source, Analia's insides twisting at the possibilities.

"We should get going," he said grimly.

Analia nodded. "Pass me the Crystal."

Mor, knowing better than to inquire, wordlessly pulled the Crystal's casing from an inside pocket in his indigo jacket, then offered it to her. Analia cracked the stone the tiniest bit, allowing a thin trickle of white light to slither free. Then, she took off into the Pulse, Mor close behind.

"Is this the plan?" he asked, following her around a toppled statue. "Lure them to you all at once?"

"No. There's no way I would be able to take them all out before one of them got to me. So, we go one by one and pray too many don't get attracted by the Crystal at once."

The fact that her plan hinged on a prayer was far from comforting. But it was all she had as she and Mor raced through their ransacked kingdom, her flames blazing hotter at every point of damage.

The doors ripped off their hinges, revealing the destroyed shops inside. Tables along the riverside walkways that had been barreled into and shattered, glass shards glinting in the sunlight. The crashes and screams echoing around her.

Luckily, her flames' next outlet came sweeping down the street toward them, panicked citizens not recognizing Analia or Mor as they scrambled out of its way.

Analia raised her hand, beckoning with burning fingers. The Devourist hissed at her insolence, then lunged across the fifty feet between them.

Immediately, it stumbled over a large flowerpot that appeared in its path, its cloak disappearing a moment later. Analia sent her flames roaring toward its core, no longer hidden.

The Devourist's shriek echoed off the surrounding buildings. It tried to dodge to the left, Mor blocking it with a toppled fountain. It went right, one of the ripped-free doors appearing in its path. Analia moved her flames back and forth, keeping them on the core, a bead of sweat rolling down her temple.

She needed more magic. More, more, more...

With a last shriek, the Devourist finally broke apart into dust.

Two down, ten to go.

Breathing hard, Analia checked in on her flames. Still plenty in her well, crackling with anticipation. But her pulse pounded through her veins, exhaustion creeping over her and pressing on her shoulders.

"You need a minute?" Mor asked.

Analia looked around at the fleeing citizens, finally realizing who she was after seeing her flames. A few bowed their heads to her as they passed, others sobbing their thanks, the terror in the air thick as blood.

"We don't have a minute," she said. Forcing her lungs to fill, she turned to yell after the crowd. "Head for the Council Building! Find the council members, they'll take care of you. And stick together!"

Only a few affirmations rose over the noise, but the crowd thankfully headed off in the right direction. And that was all Analia could hope for.

"You don't think gathering everyone together will create one big target?" Mor asked, his voice low. Not trying to criticize. Just pointing out another angle.

"It's either that or leave them on the streets," Analia replied. "At least the Council Building has some fortifications."

Memories of black marks on necks flashed through Analia's mind.

Mor nodded. And Analia sprinted off once more, wanting to get as far away from those images as possible. But she was moving slower than before, her body heavy from all the magic she'd used.

But her work wasn't done yet. So, she and Mor ran on, calling over the citizens' tangle of voices as they went.

"Go to the Council Building!"

"Don't go off alone!"

"You have to aim for the cores in their chests. Use all the magic you have."

"Don't let it get its mouth on you."

Thankfully, most of the people they passed seemed to process their words. But Analia didn't have time to check on the rest as a third Devourist swooped down the long, central street, its slitted nostrils aimed toward the Crystal Analia held aloft.

She skidded to a stop, Mor panting beside her as he raised a hand. One of the wooden benches from Sofika's nearby garden materialized in the Devourist's path.

The demon gripped the back of the bench, flipping over it and landing on its feet, continuing forward without pause. Thirty feet away.

Analia cursed. She sent a wave of midnight flames barreling into its chest, Mor's eyes darting as he searched for something to move.

The Devourist ducked just in time, trying to get under her flames. Revealing a second demon streaking down the street toward them.

"Mor," she ground out, struggling to keep her flames on the first demon as it weaved across the street.

"I got it."

Mor rushed up a nearby shop's steps. A moment later, a thick, wooden shelf filled with colorful bedding appeared in the second Devourist's path. The shelf was too tall and wide for Analia to see the collision, but the crash tore through the square.

"Anna!" Mor yelled.

Analia twisted back toward her flames, just in time for the flying rib bone to smack her temple. She staggered, her flames wavering as pain flared across her face. And with a shriek, the Devourist burst free from her flames and plowed into her.

Analia flew back several feet. Her back collided with something hard, the Devourist pinning her against what she vaguely realized was Surce's dress shop, its skeletal fingers digging into her arms.

Analia squirmed. She tried to get her hand on its core, her flames skittering along its gray-black bones. Gods, she was trapped.

The Devourist ducked its head, its cold, rancid breath in her nose. Analia futilely tried to kick it away, spotting Mor racing toward her.

He was too far away.

The Devourist's mouth brushed her neck.

Analia braced herself.

And the Devourist made a choking noise.

It staggered back, clawing at the neck of its cloak. And Analia's jaw dropped as the black threads rapidly unraveled, coming back together to tighten around the Devourist's throat. Analia quickly raised her hand, heat flaring across her face as her flames consumed the Devourist, shattering it to dust.

Analia coughed, obsidian raining down around her. But she didn't look away. Not as the dust swirled before her, its darkness slowly carried away on the wind.

Revealing Surce.

Chapter 97

"What are you doing here?" Analia gasped.

Surce smiled slightly where she stood before her, clearly pleased by her reception. "My tapestries said the kingdom needed me." She brushed the dust from Analia's face, her bronze fingers gentle and precise.

"Anna!" Mor skidded to a stop beside her, hazel eyes wide. "I'm sorry, I got distracted with the second Devourist. Did it get you?"

"I'm fine," Analia promised, allowing Mor to turn her chin from side to side, checking her neck for himself.

Relief flooded his face as he found no black mark marring her skin.

"Thank the gods for you," he said, turning to Surce.

Surce bowed her head in acknowledgement, her black-and-silver gown dusted with obsidian. "Usually," she said, "I prefer to stay out of combat. But my magic has yet to shed any blood today. Only obsidian."

"Does that mean you can help us?" Analia asked.

Surce nodded. Then, she twisted her wrist, Analia only just noticing the black threads looped around it like a bracelet, the ends trailing like a leash.

The fourth Devourist came staggering toward them, its cloak wrapped around it like a cocoon. It snarled, trying and failing to break free. Analia destroyed it with a wave of flames.

Eight to go. But Analia was running out of energy. And the crack on her temple from the Devourist's rib bone had a headache piercing across her forehead.

"I can't keep running," she said, realizing she was still slumped against Surce's shop.

"So, what do we do?" Mor asked.

Analia looked down at the Crystal casing in her hand. Over to the Pulse's square, spotting the stage the ruhari had gathered on all those months ago during the releasing.

"We switch plans," she said, her stomach sinking. "We have to get to that stage."

Dimitri gripped the hand bar above his seat in the Sun carriage, presumably installed in case of turbulence while flying. He, however, doubted *this* was what the designers had had in mind.

"Crystal spare us, Rois, you should have gotten Joshel!" he yelled, almost sliding out of his seat as the carriage jerked to the side.

"He wasn't available!" Rois yelled back from the outdoor driver's seat, his voice tinny through the interconnected amplifier beneath the front window.

Dimitri started to retort, another lurch upward having him biting his tongue instead.

"I miss shadowjumping," he complained, tasting metal.

"Believe me," Aeley said from the back of the carriage, "if any Royals were close enough to send a sprite, I would have."

"But Cadmus purposefully kept them out of range," Rayner said grimly, his hand squeezing Dimitri's knee.

Ever since their kiss—which Dimitri still couldn't wrap his mind around—Rayner had ensured some part of them touched. As if he needed the constant reminder it was real. And even if Dimitri had the mental capacity to process everything happening, he wouldn't have any complaints.

"We're here!" Rois called.

Dimitri craned his neck, hope daring to flare in his chest as Mt. Vasolus loomed before them. Rois yanked them into a wide, ascending loop, scanning the volcano face for Cadmus, Dimitri's stomach sliding with the movement.

Gods, let him be there. Don't let him have reached the top.

"There!" Rayner yelled. He jabbed a finger, Dimitri dizzy with relief as he spotted Cadmus about halfway up the mountain, the wind blowing back his dark gray cloak hood as he climbed. They just had to get a little higher, a little closer, and—

"Dragons!" Aeley reported.

Dimitri's body turned to ice. He twisted in his seat to look out the back window, Aeley having flung all the gold-and-white curtains back to scan their surroundings.

A trio of sun dragons streaked toward them from the square, the golden scales encasing their long, serpentine bodies flashing in the sunlight.

"Crystal spare us," Rayner breathed.

Dimitri barely heard him as his mind raced.

Those dragons weren't burdened by a carriage. They were directed by Sun soldiers that knew how to fly. At the speed they were going, they had a few minutes tops before they were on them.

"We have to get to Cadmus," Dimitri said, pushing to his feet and stumbling to the front window. "If we can convince him to come back, he can shadowjump all of us away and abandon the carriage."

Meaning the Sun men wouldn't catch them. Dimitri wouldn't have to face his father who very well might want to kill him.

Dimitri glanced back to check Rayner's and Aeley's reactions. Just to grab the window ledge for dear life as Rois yanked them into a steep climb, not waiting for group approval.

Gods, Dimitri's stomach was not made for this. He gritted his teeth, wedging his boot against the doorframe as his feet slid along the carriage, the floor tilting back, to the left, back even more.

But by some miracle, Rois got them about ten feet above Cadmus and to the side.

Cadmus whipped around as Rois leveled them out, his head snapping up to the carriage. And Dimitri, having nothing but impulses left, opened the closest window. Which happened to be the door.

"Cadmus!" he yelled, "you have to come with us! There are sun dragons coming!"

"This is none of your concern," Cadmus yelled back, his cloak swirling around him in the wind.

"Then why have you done everything in your power to get caught?"

Cadmus's eyes narrowed dangerously.

"Dragons are a minute out," Rayner reported.

Crystal fuck him.

"Cadmus," Aeley called, joining Dimitri at the door. "You don't have to do this alone. We can do it together."

Dimitri looked over to see Aeley extend her wrist through the door, the phoenix charm on her bracelet flashing in the light.

"Come with us, and we'll release Lucilla together," Aeley said, her voice catching.

Dimitri held his breath as Cadmus looked at his mother. Beyond the carriage.

His face twisted in a sneer. And before Dimitri could yell, he faded into the shadows.

"Look out!" Rayner yelled.

Rois whipped the carriage to the left, narrowly avoiding the sun dragon that tried to smash into them from behind. And Dimitri and Aeley went tumbling away from the door.

Aeley caught herself on a hand bar, her icy composure cracking as she ordered Rois to the top of the volcano. Dimitri collided with his seat with a grunt, wind roaring through the unlatched door.

"Dima!" Rayner scrambled over to him, taking his hands and bringing them up to the bar, quickly grasping his own.

"The dragon," Dimitri gasped.

"We clipped it with the carriage when we turned, it's slowing down. But the other two are coming. We have to get to the top."

"What do you think I'm doing?" Rois's tinny voice demanded. "You all better hold on."

With that, Rois pulled them back into a steep climb. Dimitri's entire body flew toward the back of the carriage, Rayner finding something to brace his foot against as Dimitri pressed into his side. Aeley twisted around at the front to take in all the windows, snapping orders at Rois to "Go left, up, straighten out," her golden hair whipping around her face in the wind.

Gods, the dragons were practically on top of them. The only thing they had going for them was that Rois's lackluster steering made them just unpredictable enough to keep them on the climb. But even with the dragons' speed, they needed time to crest the top.

Five hundred feet to go.

A dragon arced toward them on either side, trying to cage them in. Rois kept them moving at the same speed, Dimitri screaming at him to hurry. Then, he jerked them to a stop, Dimitri's stomach bouncing, the dragons streaking over the carriage on a collision course.

One of the dragons swerved to the side, just in time. It twisted back to face the carriage, just to find it had shot past, climbing higher.

Four hundred feet. Three hundred.

The third dragon appeared out of nowhere, swiping a claw at Rois from the side. Rois ducked, the carriage door banging open and shut as he tried to evade. But while the dragon missed Rois, it slammed into one of the dragons pulling the carriage, sending them careening to the side.

Dimitri opened his mouth, unable to hear if he screamed over the wind as they rolled onto their side, jerked upright, overcorrected. Rayner lost whatever foothold he had, sending both himself and Dimitri scrambling for purchase, Dimitri gripping the hand bar hard enough to hurt.

Gods, Rois, come on...

Finally, the carriage straightened out. Dimitri peeked out the window, finding Rois hunched over in his seat, the carriage ascending slower than before.

Two hundred feet left. One hundred.

Dimitri squeezed his eyes shut, unable to watch as they dodged and weaved. Still climbing higher... higher...

And he sobbed with relief as he felt the carriage level out.

"There he is!" Aeley yelled.

Dimitri pried open his eyes, not sure if he was relieved or enraged. Because there was Cadmus at the volcano's peak. Standing as casual as could be while sun dragons circled above him, his phoenix charm flashing in his extended palm.

"New plan," Dimitri spat, stumbling to the door. "You bring the carriage beside Cadmus, and I yank him inside."

Rois didn't reply. But the carriage swooped into a dive, Dimitri gripping the doorframe, his gaze fixed on Cadmus.

Rayner came to stand beside him, holding a bar with one hand and Dimitri with the other, ready to brace him as he pulled Cadmus in.

Five more seconds. Four, three, two—

A dragon plunged toward them.

Rois swerved to the right.

The door slammed into Dimitri.

Dimitri lost his grip. He tumbled through the opening, Rayner crying out as he tried to tighten his hold, just to topple after him.

Dimitri landed on the volcano's peak a few feet below with a thud, the breath whooshing out of his lungs. He scrambled into a sitting position, his ribs shrieking in protest.

"You all right?" Rayner gasped, sitting up beside him.

Dimitri nodded, trying to breathe as shallowly as possible. "You?"

"Fine."

But Dimitri caught the way he gingerly pulled his wrist to his chest. Above, the sun dragons circled, forcing the carriage to take off once more, leaving them stranded. And ten feet away, Cadmus stood at the mouth of the volcano, his back partially turned to them as he watched the last of his sister's ashes disappear.

Dimitri's temper seethed. He staggered to his feet, taking Rayner's uninjured hand to help him do the same. He sent a quick flash of his magic through Rayner's network, knowing it wouldn't do much.

But Rayner brushed his thumb along Dimitri's hand in thanks. And Dimitri towed him behind him as he marched toward Cadmus.

"Cadmus fucking Valarus," he spat. "You got to release your sister's ashes, and you're not giving in to that voice today. So let's fucking go."

Cadmus slowly turned to face him, Dimitri thirsting for a fight.

But that wasn't the icy glare he expected. Not even his distracted, faraway stare. That was the Cadmus he remembered: the tension across his face relaxed, his eyes wide with anguish.

"You have to go," he pleaded.

Behind him, the sun carriage approached.

"You have to fight it," Dimitri said, stepping closer. "I felt it in your magic network. It feeds on your anger. I know you have so much to be angry about, but think about how much more there will be if you let it win."

"Dimitri—"

"You still have Analia," Rayner said, his voice tight with pain. "You lost one sister, but you still have her. You still have hope of getting back your home. This kingdom is counting on you."

Cadmus wavered.

The sun dragons pulling the carriage reached out with their front claws, almost in reach.

And an enemy sun dragon plowed into the carriage from the side.

Cadmus whipped around at the resounding crash, watching the Sun carriage topple through the air. Dimitri tried to lunge for him, his ribs screaming. And when Cadmus glanced back at him...

"Dimitri, run!" Rayner yelled, yanking him back.

Cadmus raised his hand. And Dimitri would never forget the icy wrath in his eyes as he turned and stumbled after Rayner. Knowing it was too late as the volcano rumbled beneath his feet.

And fire erupted behind him.

The explosion knocked Dimitri and Rayner off their feet, flames roaring their freedom, their heat whooshing over Dimitri's back in a mighty exhale.

They were dead.

The carriage was out of control.

They stood no chance of outrunning the lava's path as it rushed down the volcano, causing Crystal knew what kind of damage once it hit the kingdom below.

And Cadmus...

Dimitri squeezed his eyes shut, waiting for impact. Just for something to clamp around his middle.

Dimitri gasped at the flare of pain across his ribs, his eyes snapping open once more. And he was flying.

One of the sun dragons pulling the carriage held him aloft in its claw. Dimitri frantically twisted in its grip, barely registering his relief as he spotted Rayner hanging from the second dragon's grip.

But the three enemy dragons circled around them, forming an escort. Herding them back toward the Ash Castle, undoubtedly where Othin waited. And behind them...

Dimitri looked over his shoulder, golden lava still reaching toward the sky in an endless tirade.

For the first time in millennia, Mt. Vasolus had erupted when there wasn't a new ruler to be crowned. Claiming the past one all the same. The eruption far larger than the one Analia had described to him when talking about Brenn's coronation.

But just like that day, instead of spilling down the volcano's face, the fire slowly retreated back into the volcano.

And Dimitri could have sworn a low, velveteen laugh echoed in the roar of the flames.

Chapter 98

Aaron didn't enjoy killing. But he couldn't deny he was fucking designed for it.

As soon as he and Branten emerged from the shadows at the second attack point, the hum of combat vibrated through his icy cocoon. His magic swirled, poised to turn this battlefield into a graveyard.

But Branten was right: his priority had to be the wards. So, he reluctantly turned away, kneeling on the outskirts of the fighting and pressing his hand to the muddy ground.

Preserve his magic. Replenish the wards. That was his job. Even as Branten's feet twisted in the mud beside him as he fought off attackers, his combat Blessing making each move precise and brutal.

He didn't need Aaron. But gods, Aaron needed the release as he rose a few minutes later, the section of wards restored and his magic begging for a fight.

"Come on," Branten panted, wiping the blood from his clearly broken nose. "Next point."

"I can't leave them," Aaron said, drifting toward the fighting.

"All our forces from the first point are coming, they'll be fine."

"But what about in the meantime?" Aaron pressed. "How many people will die waiting for that help? This group is smaller, and I have the magic."

Branten bit his lip, his obvious worry having the frozen clarity across Aaron's mind growing colder.

"I don't take orders from you," he said, almost a growl. Then, he stalked around Branten, not looking back as Branten twisted to watch him spread his arms. And the lethal satisfaction as his soldiers hurried back and the Sun forces screamed was worse than any drug.

It was life. Life for him to claim, to spare, the power dancing along his fingertips like a will-o-the-wisp in the night.

This. Was. Power.

And the part of himself that was terrified of it grew a little quieter as his magic winked out, leaving his people unscathed. Just in time for the soldiers from the first group to come thundering into view along the ridge.

Branten had been right. But Aaron didn't remember how to care as he barked an order for the two squadrons to meet them at the third point, Branten's face pale as Aaron grabbed his arm and yanked him into the shadows. Using even more of his magic. But he had so much left as they reemerged, as endless as his fury as he took in the carnage around him.

This was his home. His to defend. His to avenge.

Aaron slapped his hand on the ground, not hearing Branten as he replenished the wards.

This was how he'd felt back during the Starlight War. Buzzing. Lethal. Willing to do whatever it took to protect what was his.

Aaron rose as soon as the section of wards was complete, not giving Branten time to speak before raising his hands. Magic—so much magic—rolled off him in waves. It chilled the air, whispering the promise of death as it swept across the ridge encircling his kingdom, Sun soldiers falling in its wake.

He was unstoppable. Why had he locked this part of himself away?

The thought had barely formed when images struggled to the surface of his mind.

Him kneeling in a ring of bodies, many wearing black leathers. The air metallic in his nose from blood and residual magic.

A small, desperate part of himself strained for that memory, trying to drag it into focus. But it slipped away across the ice.

All he knew was there were two spots left. His army was growing bigger. And Branten gripped him by the shoulders, shaking him hard enough his teeth rattled.

But Aaron didn't hear his yells. He pulled Branten into the shadows, already crouching to replenish the wards as they emerged at the fourth spot.

Ice slid across the ground like a knife across skin. Aaron ducked and twisted to avoid Branten's snatching hands, trying to stop him from turning on the Sun soldiers as he finished.

The Heir of Death left no survivors. Even if his magic had to be quick, faster than a blink as Branten tackled him to the dirt.

"Finish the wards," he snarled, digging a knee into Aaron's back.

Aaron thrashed, spitting out foul-tasting mud. He hadn't gotten all the soldiers.

"The fucking wards, Aaron!" Branten grabbed his wrists, Aaron's shoulders twinging as he dragged them behind his back. "You promised."

That word was so small, barely cracking the ice. But it was enough to have Aaron slip into the shadows, telling himself he would come back for the rest. He wouldn't stop until every Sun soldier lay dead across the ridge.

The ground resolidified beneath him. Aaron tried to throw Branten off his back, his teeth grinding as Branten's hold didn't falter. He sat up, dragging Aaron up with him, the two grappling until Aaron was firmly pinned in Branten's grip.

"You're lucky I won't let your men see you pinned on your face," he growled. "Now, *fix the wards.*"

Aaron snapped his head back, Branten leaning away as he anticipated the move. Taking Aaron's hand, he pinned it to the ground, starlight snarling out of him without his permission.

Aaron's fingers spasmed into the dirt, trying to remember why that scared him, only finding ice. There was too much gold on the ridge. He had to—

"You're done." Branten ripped Aaron's hand from the ground, starlight still streaming from his fingers.

Not as much as before. He was running out of magic, even as its fury drew from an endless well.

"I have to stop them," Aaron hissed, straining against Branten's hold.

"No."

Aaron didn't know if he screamed or if it was his magic. He twisted his hand, trying to direct it toward the Sun soldiers. But Branten jerked his arm, forcing that hand in front of Aaron's face.

"Look at your ring," Branten ordered.

"No."

"Look at your ring! That's *Analia's* ring."

Her name jolted down his ice-coated spine.

"Go to Analia," Branten told him, his fingers painfully tight. "Our forces are more than large enough to handle the rest. Find. Analia."

Aaron's chest heaved, struggling to process his words. All he knew was her name. Cracking along the ice. Nowhere near enough.

"Branten," he said, pitifully small.

"Find. Analia."

Aaron stared at the black, metallic band on his middle finger, clinging to the image. Her ring. The one she had given to Aaron. Not this.

The Heir of Death snarled at him to look back at the Sun soldiers, his voice reverberating through the ice. But there was just enough of himself left to force those cracks wider. Enough for him to nod.

Then, Aaron faded into the shadows, the Heir of Death far from back to sleep.

Analia stood on the wide, circular stage in the Pulse's square, Surce's back pressed to hers, Mor standing a few paces in front of her and to the side.

"You sure you want to do this?" he asked, rubbing his golden wrist.

"It's the last plan we have," Analia said.

Surce remained silent behind her, presumably scanning the streets in anticipation. They'd already cleared away the citizens, Analia praying the Councilmen were ready to take care of the influx of people sent to their building. With that done, there was no reason to stall. So, Analia opened the Crystal's casing and raised it high.

Brilliant white light flared from the stone, illuminating the square and refracting rainbows across the destruction. Surce stiffened as the magic flooded over them, Analia's shield already up and ready. But she couldn't deny the howling of the magic had the pain across her temple sharpening, her teeth grinding as she struggled to keep her shield in place.

Thankfully, the Crystal hadn't had too much time to accumulate buildup. Within a minute, the light had started to dwindle, Analia's legs shaking as it finally winked out entirely.

But there was no time to recover. For, right on cue, the Devourists flooded into the square.

They came from all sides, sweeping through side streets, emerging from store fronts, joining together in a hissing mass as they streaked toward the stage.

One, two, three, four, five.

"Surce?" Analia asked, cradling the Crystal to her chest.

"Three from behind," she reported.

So, they were all accounted for. Meaning now, the true test began.

Analia's eyes went to the first quick flare of magic, a chunk of broken marble the size of a shield appearing in the air and falling to the ground with a crash in the center of the Devourists' group. They scattered, chunks of marble, stone, wood, anything Mor could spot raining down on them.

Separating them. Herding them away from the stage. And cornering one in the triangle formed between a bakery and a statue.

Analia sent a wave of midnight flames flooding toward it, the crackle of her fire nearly drowning out the Devourist's screech. But Analia destroyed the core before it could flee.

Seven left. Analia's flames dangerously low.

Surce called her name, Analia realizing she'd been swaying on her feet. She pivoted, spotting the Devourist trapped in its own cloak that Surce whipped around the stage toward her. She dredged up her magic, nearly falling to her knees as she turned the demon to obsidian dust.

Six left. Barely enough flames for the next, her headache dragging its sharpened point down her face and through her bones.

She had to make this work. Mor and Surce didn't have the power required to kill them. This was up to her.

She shakily turned back to the crowd before her, struggling to tune out the Crystal's magic field slithering across her senses. Mor had managed to hit one of the Devourists with his raining debris, the demon groggily trying to rise from its knees twenty feet away.

Analia dragged up her flames, her heart sinking at how small the wave was as it engulfed the Devourist. She tried to summon more, crying out as pain lanced across her chest.

Mor's head whipped toward her, "Anna—"

"They're coming!" she gasped.

Mor quickly turned back to the remaining three Devourists on his side, cursing as they dove through his obstacles, making it within ten feet of the stage before he shoved them back with a well-placed door. Analia gritted her teeth, black spots dancing across her vision as she strained for a spark. Just a little more.

Finally, the Devourist shattered under her magic. And Analia's flames winked out.

She was empty. There were still five left. And she could sense Mor's and Surce's networks dwindling.

The Crystal pulsed in her palm, soft and gentle as a poisoned kiss. Analia shook her head at it, immediately regretting it as the stage tilted beneath her feet.

She'd tried to touch that power once. And this was not the place to try again. Which left one option.

"Surce," she said, trying not to groan. "Send your final two over here."

Analia could tell by the straightening of Surce's posture against her back that she was gearing up to argue.

"Do it!" Analia snapped.

Surce didn't reply. But one by one, she whipped the tangled Devourists around the stage by the trailing threads of their cloaks, the demons thrashing and snarling.

Analia planted her feet, trying to steady herself. Then, she reached for her magic. Beyond the empty well where her flames once slumbered, into the cavern below. Searching for the soft rumble of impending thunder.

Analia raised a shaky hand. And a column of icy shadows snaked toward the first Devourist.

Powerful. Shattering it in seconds. Analia tried to direct the magic toward the second Devourist, just for a flash of heat across her body to send her doubling over.

She staggered toward the edge of the stage, trying and failing to regain her balance. Her foot met empty air.

And Mor grabbed her just in time. He pulled her to him, bracing her with an arm around her waist.

"Anna," he said, panic creeping into his voice. "You're *really* warm."

A dazed, almost delirious, part of her noted that meant it must not be released flames that had her overheating after all. It was the price of the magic. But she had another good blast in her.

"I'll be fine," she wheezed.

She twisted in his grip toward the final entangled Devourist, ready to break it into dust. But she couldn't force her mind to move. She was stuck, paralyzed with exhaustion as crashes and snarls pounded through her ears.

Tingles ran across her wrist from her enka bracelet. *Anna,* Laness said, *whatever you're doing, you need to stop. Now.*

Gods, she wanted to. She really, really wanted to. But there were four left. No one to match them.

With a victorious screech, the entangled Devourist twisted its knee, stepping down hard on Surce's leash. Surce stumbled, yanked forward by the tension. Giving the Devourist just enough slack to snap its arms out in one quick movement, breaking the threads. Then, it lunged for the stage.

Analia yelped. She didn't remember calling on her shadows, but they were there, lashing out from her hand in a lethal whip and slicing into the Devourist's core.

The Devourist exploded at the base of the stage.

Three left.

Analia crumpled to her knees.

Mor tried to catch her, but a Devourist broke free. It's talon-like nails scraped along the stage, inches from Analia's own hands.

Mor stomped down hard with his boot, the Devourist hissing as it snatched its hand back, Mor kicking it away and barely avoiding the heart-racingly fast hand that tried to grab his foot in return.

"Analia, you must stop," Surce gasped, falling to her knees beside her.

Analia's teeth chattered despite the blaze across her skin. She didn't try to fight as Surce dragged her back toward the center of the stage, her shaky fingers finding her bracelet.

We need Aaron, she mouthed. *Tell him we need him at the square.*

He was the only one strong enough to destroy three Devourists. Assuming he hadn't already used up all his magic defending the border.

Laness didn't reply immediately. Analia braced her free hand on the stage, the Crystal pulsing in the other like a heartbeat as Surce went to help Mor. But the Devourists had learned quickly.

The three separated, forcing Mor to target them one at a time. They stayed away from any structures he could block them against, their arms snapping out like wings any time Surce tried to tangle them up.

White light flickered insistently across the Crystal's face. No. She couldn't risk it.

Her bracelet buzzed. *Aaron is... busy.*

Something in Laness's tone had Analia's stomach drop. Crystal spare her, what was she supposed to do?

Analia struggled to sit upright, reaching for her bracelet. Just as Mor let out a yell.

He stumbled back, blood gushing between his fingers as he gripped his face, the bone that had hit him clattering to the stage. Surce twisted toward him, her hand outstretched.

But the Devourist was faster. It lunged onto the stage, tackling Mor to the ground and landing on top of him, its mouth latching onto his neck.

Mor went rigid. Analia's lips formed his name, no noise coming out. Surce desperately looked between Mor, the remaining Devourists, and Analia, black threads whipping in front of her. But she couldn't keep them back for long.

The Crystal vibrated in Analia's fingers.

She was on her own. Three Devourists left, Mor running out of time, Surce soon to follow, her kingdom destroyed around her. And Aaron couldn't come to save her this time.

A Devourist broke free of the web of threads, grabbing Surce's wrist.

And Analia reached for the one option she had left.

The moment her mental hand made contact, the Crystal's victory shrieked through her being. It snatched away the feeling of the stage beneath her knees, the snarling Devourists, only leaving the wave of white light and wrath.

Finally, its time had come. It could finish the destruction that had been started that day. The Devourists, the kingdoms, the people themselves. Destroy it all and rebuild from the rubble that remained. Perhaps this time, they would know better than to claim its power for themselves.

Analia desperately tried to block out the noise, the scattered fragments of her mind searching for those early days in Deardryn's study. Back when she'd first faced this magic, realizing she needed a distraction—no, not a distraction. An anchor.

That's what she'd been searching for. From the moment she'd found her uncle's corpse, haunting her even through the Moon Castle halls. An anchor for who she was, how she wanted to rule, the person she strived to be.

The Crystal snarled, demanding her attention.

Analia focused on the stage she barely felt beneath her knees. A stage placed in the center of her home, the riverside walkways and sparkling bridges coming into hazy focus in her mind.

The people moving about their days, laughing with each other, the air sugary sweet with the newest pastry from Rosalina's. Back to the house, Laness weeding her aggressive front garden. Inside, to where Mor tended a sizzling pan on the stove, Surce examining a tapestry on the island behind him. Back to the birch grove, where Branten and Ember verbally sniped at each other while they ran.

And over to the training hollow, where he waited for her.

The Crystal's magic hammered against her shield of memories, Analia becoming aware of its smooth face against her fingers.

He was the anchor that had taken her uncle's place, even back in the Sun Kingdom. Pushing her. Believing in her. Giving her something to hold on to.

But it was time she became her own anchor.

Back in the Moon Kingdom, she'd thought that meant standing alone. Even after she'd realized that wasn't true, she'd been paralyzed by just how not alone she was. She'd been picked apart and questioned and conditioned to second-guess herself for so long, she'd never realized the answer she'd been searching for was the simplest of all.

All she had to do was trust herself.

And she knew Aaron would be least surprised of all that, kneeling on that stage, the Crystal's magic screaming through her mind and a trio of Devourists bearing down on her, she found her footing immediately.

Analia opened her eyes, forcing the white light away until the square hazily appeared before her. Just in time to spot the Devourist as it grabbed her, talons digging into her wrists.

Analia looked up into its empty eye sockets. Then, she let the Crystal's magic erupt.

Blinding white light exploded across the square. The Devourist instantly dissolved into obsidian dust that coated her skin, no match for the magic in her palm. But neither was the kingdom.

Analia tightened her fingers around the Crystal, struggling to rein it in, direct it away from the buildings—so easily toppled. But their targets were the Devourists' cores.

The magic resisted like a toddler digging in their heels during a tantrum. But slowly, Analia dragged it back toward the stage. Over to the Devourist on top of Mor, shattering it in seconds, pulling the magic away kicking and screaming before it could do the same to Mor.

One more.

Analia gritted her teeth, magic pulsing through her as she dragged it to her right. Finding the Devourist recoiling away from Surce, still on her feet.

And in an explosion of obsidian dust, it was gone.

Analia had no idea how she managed to close the casing, the magic winking out with a final, furious howl. She just knew as soon as it was gone, the rock tumbled from her fingers.

Analia crumpled forward, barely catching herself on her elbows, her muscles completely limp. There was nothing left inside her.

But the square was silent. She'd done it.

Analia closed her eyes, vaguely aware of Surce rushing to her, asking if she was all right.

"Mor," she groaned. "I'm fine, go to Mor."

"He's unconscious, but his breathing is steady." Surce's hand brushed over Analia's hair, Analia sagging into the stage even more.

"Take him to the healers. Through your beads in the shop. I'll be fine here."

"But—"

"That's an order." It barely sounded like a moan.

But Surce, her displeasure palpable, retracted her hand. Analia listened as she went to Mor, not having enough of herself left to hear how she managed to get him away. She just knew the moment she was alone.

For a long time, Analia remained like that. Half sprawled on the stage, eyes closed, trying to remember how to move. Eventually, she managed to push herself onto her hands and knees, then into a sitting position. She braced her hands on the stage, struggling to keep herself upright.

And finally, magic tingled behind her.

Analia didn't bother glancing back. She'd know that magic anywhere. Even as he didn't say a word. He only knelt behind her, gathering her to his chest, shaking almost as bad as she was.

And something in Analia's chest collapsed. She gripped Aaron's tunic, his skin icy through the fabric. And the furious, relentless churn of the dregs of his network had her wanting to cry.

She had to reel him in. But she had nothing left. Absolutely nothing.

Analia struggled to sit up, tasting ash and dust. But Aaron gently nudged her head back against his shoulder. He turned his own head, burying his face in her hair.

And slowly, remarkably, his network settled.

Analia curled into him, a sob lodging in her throat. But she didn't have the energy to let it free. She just held on to him, her eyes moving around the square as Aaron's lips found her forehead.

Their secret destroyed. Their sanctuary turned into a battlefield.

And even though neither of them made a sound, Analia could taste salt on her lips. And she didn't know if it was from her tears or Aaron's.

Chapter 99

The next several hours were some of the worst in Analia's life.

She didn't know how long it took Aaron to finally whisper a warning on the stage and pull them into the shadows, reappearing in their bedroom and carrying her to bed. Analia protested all the way, telling him there was too much work that had to be done for her to rest. He, in turn, said only one of them needed to be on their feet, she'd used far more magic than him, and she wasn't going anywhere until her body cooled.

With that, he nestled the duvet around her. And Analia was asleep before he had time to straighten.

If Aaron had gotten his way, she would have slept through the rest of the day and into the following morning. But she woke only a few hours later, coated in a cold sweat and shaking from nightmares she couldn't remember.

But she was back to a normal temperature. So, sliding out of bed, she dressed in a tunic and pants that didn't reek of smoke and decay, braided her hair, and was off.

Analia wasn't surprised the Healer Center had become the central hub of activity. Battered soldiers pushed in and out of the side doors, their voices low and skin speckled with green paste. Healers bustled through the color-coded patient halls, Analia spotting their green robes through the main door whenever an apprentice would slip into the waiting area to update the crowd that had formed.

What was surprising was Ember had taken on the role of director. She sat at the large corner desk, gesturing for family members to go sit on the couches, asking others to wait while she skimmed through the papers in front of her.

"I'm surprised you're not with the other healers," Analia said, making her way through the crowd toward her.

Ember offered a tired shrug. "I shouldn't be in a healer room right now. I've had a long day."

That certainly looked to be true. The light from the wide bank of windows highlighted the pale pallor of her skin, her lower lip red and cracked as if she'd been biting it. Analia instinctively started to ask if she was all right, just to cut off as she remembered that was the most ridiculous question she could ask.

"Did Aaron come retrieve you?" she asked instead.

Ember nodded. "Laness was able to get us a decent way back before she had to stop and wait for him. She'd already been roottraveling all that morning, and it took even more magic to bring back a third person."

"Third?"

Ember's lips briefly flattened. "Laness will fill you in. She's through the door on your right. But I think there are people here who want to talk to you first."

She gestured over Analia's shoulder, and she turned.

At some point, the crowd had shifted to look at her, their murmured conversations dying down as they got her attention. Analia took one look at their bruised skin, their quiet, tear-streaked faces. Then, she lightly stroked the back of Ember's hand and stepped forward to greet the crowd.

Analia didn't know how much time she spent in that waiting room talking with her people. Reassuring them she and Aaron were taking care of it, they were safe, listening to their fears and stories. A surprising number thanked her, having witnessed her, Mor, and eventually Surce's run through the kingdom.

They had every right to blame this invasion on her. It came mere months after she, the first outsider to ever step foot in their kingdom, first arrived. But instead, they turned her into their lifeline. And Analia would let them grab hold as long as they needed.

By the time someone tapped her shoulder, Analia's heart felt like a massive bruise.

"The council is requesting you, Your Majesty," Tamen said apologetically. The blond soldier still wore his fighting leathers, some left over green paste clinging to the skin around his eye.

Analia nodded. She turned back to the waiting area, about to apologize. But they waved her away, many wiping their eyes, the teenage girl she'd been talking to giving her a final hug before releasing her. And all Analia could think as she followed Tamen through a side door was that they didn't deserve this. None of them.

The thought hollowed out her chest. But it also pushed back her shoulders as she reached Sofika's study. She swept through the door, Tamen bowing to her before softly shutting it behind her, the small group inside looking up at the noise.

"Where's Aaron?" she asked, looking around.

The five council members had evidently given up trying to cram their chairs around Sofika's desk, instead forming a loose arc around the room.

"He's dealing with reports," Laness said, sitting off to the side with an exhausted Branten.

Jasper grunted, "He said you'd be here sooner or later, and we should carry on until you arrived."

Of course he did. Analia came to take the empty chair beside Marion's, making a mental note to track Aaron down as soon as she left this meeting.

"In that case," she said, "I must have a lot to be filled in on."

Gods did she.

Laness went first, recounting everything they'd learned from the Temple of Rosala. Analia wasn't nearly as surprised as she should have been that Marcos was the one to shatter the illusion of the healer's oath, nor that he had stipulations surrounding the rest of his knowledge. She'd deal with him later. She was more interested in making sure Ember was handling the news all right.

But for now, she had to manage her dull sense of wrath as Laness detailed the missing Crystal. Especially as she realized Deardryn's random visit to the Sun Kingdom while "on business" was so she could hide it there.

Jasper sucked in a breath between his teeth at the news, the rest of the council visibly dismayed. But no one made to speak as Branten took up the story, explaining how Deardryn had sent her Devourists to a more eastern part of the wards than her other patrols. His soldiers reported barely having time to notice the dark figures at the base of the ridge before they pushed through the glamor, only pausing for a few moments to consume the border before streaking into the kingdom. Then, the Sun soldiers arrived.

"My scouts say there were no survivors," Branten finished, having carefully skirted around Aaron's involvement in dealing with the Sun soldiers. "We got every Devourist and person that could have escaped to tell the story of our kingdom."

"That doesn't explain how they found it in the first place," Samuel said, having risen from his chair to obsessively straighten the piles of papers on Sofika's desk.

"Well," Jeneva said, "the Devourists consume and track by magic, right? Deardryn probably sent them to the last spot she knew her patrols visited, and they tracked our glamor and wards from there."

No one looked happy about that possibility. But an even worse one rose to the surface of Analia's mind.

"Has anyone checked in with the Human Kingdom?" she asked.

"Mor's there now," Laness replied, turning the enka bracelets on her wrists.

Analia nearly slumped under her rush of relief. "He's all right?"

"He's banged up," Branten rasped. "Won't be using any magic for a minute, but he's fine."

"Last I heard," Laness added, "he said everyone was fine and the wards remained intact—although the humans are even more wound up than they've been the past few months."

Wonderful.

"That makes sense," Marion mused, softly tapping her fingers on her chair. "The humans rely on no magic other than their wards. Of course the demons would aim for a kingdom humming with Blessed and Demiblessed."

"Maybe," Analia murmured. She hesitated, not wanting to destroy the fragile hope that had perked up across the room. But if she was right...

"What are you thinking, Your Majesty?" Iphen asked across from her, unusually somber.

Analia sighed. "I'm thinking that if Deardryn has a shard, she might have been able to use it to track ours any of the times we've opened it in this kingdom. Which could explain how she managed to transport so many soldiers here."

"She's been doing it gradually over time," Jeneva breathed.

"And her coming down the river on her boat was to throw us off," Branten growled. He rose from his chair, looking like he was ready to kick a hole through the wall.

"Branten," Analia said, "go gather a squadron to check out the area around our wards. See if you can find where these soldiers were making camp. Hopefully, there's nothing and we're wrong."

Branten gave a short affirmative. He marched to the door, his heavy boots thudding on the wood floor as he exited.

Analia's enka bracelet tingled faintly. *Good call.*

Thanks, she thought back, not looking at Laness. *How are you holding up? Do I need to come up with a reason to get you out of here, too?*

I've got more energy than the rest of you.

Well, that wasn't hard.

You should know, Laness went on, sounding regretful. *Cadmus went to Mt. Vasolus. Dima tried to stop him, but it... it was too late. He, Rayner, Rois, and Aeley are now in the dungeon, although they don't seem in immediate danger.*

Analia prayed she kept the horror off her face. She surreptitiously hugged her stomach, tasting bile as she thought about her brother—she didn't even know what could be happening to him with that mark.

And now, Deardryn had one as well. But when could she have gone to the volcano?

"In the meantime," Jasper said, startling Analia out of her thoughts. "You and His Majesty will have to make a public address."

Gods, add it to the list of things she had to do. But he was right. The kingdom needed to see their Royals.

Analia nodded heavily, a headache forming behind her eyes. "I'll track down Aaron." She rose from her chair, muscles protesting all the way. "Laness?"

"I'll stay here," she said, drawing her feet up on her chair. "Keep everyone up to date on what's happening."

Analia nodded. Then, flashing Marion a look that clearly said, *You're in charge,* she headed for the door.

Analia inhaled the sharp, leafy scent of antiseptic paste, trying to ignore the moans and cries of pain as she headed down the sky-blue hallway. She couldn't imagine what was happening in the wings dedicated to more severe cases, her glimpses into the rooms she passed having her heart breaking.

Layce, the soldier that had helped her with the Sun messenger, gritted her teeth as a healer tended to the crisscrossing lacerations running down her face. The young boy who apprenticed in Rosalina's bakery bit the knuckles of his free hand as another healer fixed his broken hand. So many more, Analia wishing she knew how to summon Deardryn's magic so she could do something to help. Especially as she peeked into the last room on the right.

Aaron sat on one of the wooden chairs beside the patient bed. His shoulders hunched over the stack of reports in his lap, his eyes unbearably faraway. He didn't seem to notice she was there as she softly tapped on the door, his heavy gaze only lifting to hers once she'd taken the chair beside his and touched his knee.

"How is he?" she asked, nodding to the bed.

Brookston lay fast asleep beneath the covers, his hand tucked under his cheek, green paste covering the left third of his forehead.

"He'll be fine," Aaron said on an exhale, setting his reports on the floor. "Strong pulse, steady breathing. Apparently, he got clipped by some falling debris when Evena was rushing everyone back to Nova House—I already checked, it wasn't from you or Mor."

"Thank the gods," Analia breathed.

"The healers said he should wake up any minute now." Aaron shrugged. But all Analia could see was exhaustion in his eyes.

"And how are you?" she asked, combing her fingers through his hair.

Aaron tipped his head back into her touch, his words impossibly simple. "This was supposed to be a safe place."

Analia's lips parted. But she had no words. No words could ever make this right. She could only mouth, "I know," her hand sliding from his hair so she could wrap an arm around his shoulders. Aaron gripped the edge of her chair and pulled her closer, Analia coming to lean against his side.

And that was the worst silence she had ever felt in her life.

Analia blinked hard, her eyes drifting back to Brookston. Gods, he looked so small when not bursting with energy.

This was what Deardryn had taken from them. Safety. Innocence. Joy. Peace.

Finally, Analia found her one certainty in this destruction. She wouldn't stop until her kingdom got all that back.

"The council says we should make an appearance soon," she murmured.

"I thought as much." Aaron rubbed his eyes, about to go on. Just as Brookston let out a tiny moan.

Aaron immediately leaned toward him, murmuring and stroking his disheveled curls as he stirred. For a moment, Analia thought his eyes would open. Then, he screwed up his face and squeezed them shut once more.

"Head hurts," he mumbled, smushing his face into his pillow.

"I know," Aaron soothed. "You got an impressive bump on your forehead."

He glanced at Analia. She quietly rose, slipping from the room and checking the healer's name marked on the door.

Cenn. Thank the Crystal. Not just because she spotted him exiting another room farther down the hall.

Analia called his name. He looked up, the tired fog clearing from his eyes as he headed for her.

"Your Majesty," he said, inclining his head.

"Analia," she corrected. "Brookston just woke up."

"Really?" Cenn perked up. "How did he seem?"

"Groggy but alert."

"That's the best news I've gotten all day." He turned, about to enter the room, but Analia stopped him with a touch to his arm.

"I know you must have endless things to do," she said apologetically. "But have you... Have you had a chance to talk with Ember?"

Analia fiddled with the hem of her shirt, hoping she wasn't crossing any lines. But Cenn's smile was kind.

"She already talked to me. We're looking out for each other."

Analia blew out a relieved breath. "Good."

She hesitated, having so much more she wanted to say to him. But Cenn patted her hand as if he already understood. Then, he led the way into Brookston's room.

"I hear someone is awake," he said by way of greeting, going to perch on the bed.

At some point, Brookston had crawled into Aaron's lap, his face hidden in his shoulder. Aaron gently shifted him around to face Cenn, Brookston sounding unusually withdrawn as he said, "I am."

"Excellent."

Cenn started in on his exam, Aaron looking over at Analia as she came to stand at his shoulder.

"Two hours until our address?" he asked, soft enough only she could hear.

"I'll tell the council."

Aaron nodded. He took a breath to say more, his silver eyes moving first to the reports on the floor, then back to Brookston.

"I'll take care of these," Analia said, stooping to retrieve the papers.

"You don't have to do that," he said quickly.

"Consider this your nap break."

Aaron's lips twitched the tiniest bit. Analia kissed his temple, then ruffled Brookston's hair as he counted Cenn's raised fingers. Finally, mouthing a thank you to Cenn, she slipped from the room.

She had work to do.

Chapter 100

Two hours. That was all the time Aaron had given himself to wallow in everything that had been taken that day. Part of him thought it was too much time after the hours he'd already spent in that chair, alternating between checking on Brookston, going over reports and giving orders, and staring off into space as he tried to process what said reports described.

Details on the damages in the Pulse, ranging from cracked fountains to entire buildings ravaged. An ever-growing list of injuries and fatalities, his hands shaking every time he thought about how close Mor had been to being one of those numbers.

Thankfully, Surce had gotten him to the healers, and he'd woken up a few minutes before Aaron arrived. He found him pestering his assigned healers to release him; he was fine, he had work to do. Aaron still wondered if he'd made a mistake letting him go, the black mark on his neck seared into his memory even after Mor hid it behind his jacket collar. But that was why he had Laness sending him hourly updates on him. Just as she was keeping him up to date on Marcos's "conversation" with Surce.

He'd gone to retrieve Ember and Laness from the Wild Lands not long after freeing Mor, hissing a curse as he realized Marcos was with them. But he trusted Laness. If she said they needed to bring him back with them, he would. And he would have eyes on him at all fucking times.

Aaron sighed, shifting a sleeping Brookston against his chest. At this point, he didn't know who was comforting whom: Aaron consciously matching his breathing to Brookston's slow, even breaths, snuggling him closer whenever he squirmed from a nightmare, his little hand gripping Aaron's sleeve.

He'd changed out of his mud-stained clothes after debating Analia into bed, but he could have sworn he could still smell the metallic scent of his magic. If he was honest, that was what haunted him the most.

All the lives he had taken on that ridge. He'd ordered the scouts assessing the border to count every person that had been killed by his magic, his mind swirling in the meantime.

How many families had been destroyed because of him? How many friends would have a hole forever carved in their hearts because of his magic? How many soldiers had known the situation they were marching into, and how many had simply been following orders? How many of those soldiers didn't approve of those orders?

Logically, he knew no one could be allowed to walk away alive after what they'd seen. He himself had killed several people over the decades for that very reason. But there was a certain kind of grief that came from not being in control when making that decision.

So, he asked for the numbers. And that would be his reminder as to why he could never let this happen again. It would also be his punishment. He wouldn't tell anyone about that part, though. He knew Analia would somehow put it together. He'd talk about it then.

For now, he sat in Brookston's dim patient room, watching the sun slowly disappear beyond the horizon, the noise of the Healer Center through the ajar door sounding so far away.

"I want to go home," Brookston mumbled into his chest.

Aaron blinked hard, not having realized Brookston had woken up.

"I know," he murmured, rubbing his back. "But Cenn said he wanted to keep you here overnight, remember?"

Aaron kept Cenn's tacked on, "Just in case," to himself.

"Why did Evena leave?" Brookston persisted.

It took Aaron a moment to remember Evena coming in the first place—sometime after Analia had left. "She's coming back," he promised. "She has a lot of people to take care of right now."

"I want to be with them," Brookston sniffled.

Gods, break his heart more why didn't he. Aaron stroked his hair, not sure what to say. But he was spared by the door softly opening.

Brookston hopefully peeked over Aaron's shoulder, Aaron craning his neck to watch Analia slip inside. She hadn't bothered changing out of her black-and-silver tunic, his reports tucked under her arm, the only sign that she was about to address their people the neat braid over her shoulder. The fact she didn't try to dress up the event with a fancy gown or expensive jewels had Aaron loving her even more.

"Is it time?" he asked.

Analia nodded. She came to kneel beside Aaron's chair, Brookston tracking her with round eyes.

"How are you feeling?" she asked him, bracing a hand on Aaron's thigh.

"I don't want Aaron to go," he said fiercely, tightening his grip on Aaron's shirt.

Analia's brow twitched up. She looked at Aaron, but he hadn't realized Brookston had heard their plans either.

"It won't be for long," he said, starting to lift Brookston back onto his bed. "I'll be back soon—"

"No." Brookston whined the word into several syllables, his blue eyes teary as he clung to him.

Aaron exchanged a look with Analia, but she appeared just as lost as he was.

"You won't even notice I'm gone," Aaron tried again. "Just close your eyes, and I'll be back when you wake up—"

"No. I don't want to be alone again."

"I can have Evena or Cenn come sit with you—"

"No!"

Brookston wriggled out of Aaron's hold and back onto his lap, burying his face in his shoulder and hugging him tight as he could.

Gods, what was he supposed to do? He had to reassure his kingdom, give them something to hold on to. But there was already someone desperately clinging on.

Brookston was scared to be alone. And if his little gasps meant anything, he was working his way up to a full-blown meltdown.

"What if *I* stay with you?" Analia asked.

Brookston quieted for a moment. He turned his head to peek at her, seeming just as surprised as Aaron by the offer.

"But you have to go, too," Brookston sniffled.

"You would think that," she said, "seeing as I'm queen now. But as a queen, I care more about taking care of my people than formalities and appearances. And right now, it seems like you need someone. I might not be Aaron, but many would argue I'm actually better."

Brookston hiccuped. "Really?"

Analia shielded the side of her mouth facing Aaron with a hand, making a shushing gesture with the other. "He hasn't come to terms with it yet."

Brookston giggled, still tearier than usual. But in that moment, the only thing Aaron loved more was Analia's answering grin.

"Are you *sure?*" he asked. "You deserve to be there as much as I do. We can find someone to stay here."

"This is our kingdom now," she said, rising to her feet with a stretch. "We take care of everyone together. And right now, you're needed out there, and I'm needed in here. We can trade places next time."

"I'd like to stand *with* you."

Analia shrugged. "I'll have to check my schedule." She tossed her stack of reports on the patient bed, then reached for Brookston. Brookston stretched toward her in return, Aaron already forgotten. And there were no words that could describe the emotion unfurling in Aaron's chest.

Rising to his feet, he passed Brookston to Analia, letting her take his seat. For a moment, he allowed himself to watch her, completely settled in her choice as Brookston geared up to tell her the full, detailed story of what happened to his head. Then, he leaned down, Brookston politely pausing as Aaron slid an arm around her shoulders.

"I think I just fell in love with you all over again," he whispered in her ear.

Analia smiled to herself, her hand curving around his cheek. "Do you know what you're going to say?" she asked.

Aaron nodded, the decision having settled in his chest the moment he first sat in that chair.

Analia stared into his eyes, seeming pleased by what she saw.

"I'm proud of you," she whispered.

Fuck if that wasn't a punch to the gut.

She turned his face to hers, whispering against his mouth, "And I'm not telling you the soldier count."

Of course she wasn't.

"That's probably for the best," he sighed. He pressed a quick kiss to her lips, then ruffled Brookston's hair. Finally, he faded into the shadows.

Aaron reappeared a moment later in the Council Building, not needing directions to know where to go. Indeed, the five councilmen waited for him beside the glass balcony door, Surce, Branten, Laness, and Mor all clustered together in the corner of the small staging room.

He wasn't surprised by the exhaustion etched across their faces. They could probably see the same in his own. And maybe that was why they all only exchanged a long, heavy look as Jeneva came forward to offer him the circular amplifier.

Aaron thanked her and clipped it to his shirt, Marion stepping up behind him to settle his crown on his head. Just as heavy as always. But there was something gratifying about the lack of questions as he headed for the balcony door, as if the council finally trusted him to make a decision that wouldn't end in disaster.

Aaron sighed as he stepped outside, the voices from the crowd below swelling on the cool evening breeze. Nowhere near as loud as addresses past. They couldn't even bring themselves to applaud, and, looking out across the kingdom, Aaron didn't blame them.

Their once beautiful, carefully crafted home had a sector of destruction in its heart. Even when they rebuilt the statues and fountains and buildings, the atmosphere would be forever changed. Because the safety of secrecy wasn't something they could ever get back.

Talitha had known that. His father had known that. Even Ethelind had known that. But they had also known it was a safety that came with an expiration date.

This wasn't his fault. It was his to fix. And now, it was up to him to find something stronger than that secrecy.

Aaron looked up at the dusky sky, the moon and some stars already out, the sun a sliver above the horizon. He waited for it to fully disappear. And only then did he step up to the edge of the large, grand balcony and look down at his people.

"Hello."

He paused, waiting for the voices to die down, all attention landing on him.

"It's almost unfathomable how trivial that sounds now," he said, his thoughtful voice softly echoing. "How can such a simple greeting still exist after everything you have gone through today? You've had to watch your home be invaded, violated, and tarnished. You've had to experience the terror of fleeing for your lives through streets that were supposed to be your safe place. You've had to face the unimaginable grief of learning someone you love has been injured or killed.

"Parents, siblings, friends, lovers, children. No one was left unscathed today, even if they bear no scrapes or bruises. When put that way, it's rather insulting to start this speech with such a useless greeting."

Aaron's lip curled slightly. "I don't say all of this to try and tell you how you're feeling, or dig any of those wounds deeper. I say this because this is how I'm feeling. I'm heartbroken and angry and have been desperately searching for any semblance of control, and if you feel this way, I understand you, and I detest that you understand me, too.

"This attack was unwarranted. You did not deserve to lose everything you have lost today. It isn't fair, and I'll be the last person to tell you otherwise."

Aaron paused, allowing the murmurs to spread across the crowd, his eyes moving from face to face.

"Analia was going to join me here today," he finally said, tracing the cold metal railing with his fingers. "I wanted to stand here with her and show you all your Royals were a united front that would fix everything. But she's back at the Healer Center. She's taking care of the people she can help. And watching her, I realized something. Yes, we have to fix what happened today. We can't let this destruction, this loss, go without justice. And we won't. But in order to do that, we need to take care of ourselves first.

"I know for many of you, you're probably barely hearing me over the fear. But try to hear this." Aaron leaned forward, feeling the crowd's attention move with him. "I understand if all you want to do is fall apart. I'm not telling you you shouldn't. I'm asking you not to fall apart forever. Because we drove out the invaders today. We won, even if it doesn't feel that way. And we can't let the stories of those who should still be here go unsung. We can't let the legacy of this kingdom crumble without justice. We don't forget.

"Today, we mourn. But tomorrow, we rebuild."

Aaron didn't expect applause as his words faded off. He didn't expect acknowledgment of any kind. But slowly, one by one, every person that had gathered at the foot of the Council Building dropped to one knee and bowed their heads. And in that silence, Aaron knew they didn't kneel for him. They kneeled for the home he would do everything in his power to restore.

Aaron turned, that decision he'd made in Brookston's room grounding in his chest as he headed back into the staging room. He didn't stop to talk to the council or his family as they stepped toward him, only pausing long enough to take off his crown and amplifier. Then, he headed for the door, meeting Branten's eye as he passed.

"I want a full report on our military ranks and prospects in my hands tomorrow morning," he said, the room fading into shadows around him. "Everything from our most seasoned captains to those still in the Underground. Reassemble our troops. Tell them to prepare for war."

Author's Note

Thank you so much for reading *Kingdom of Dreams and Decay!* This one was definitely a roller coaster, and I hope you enjoyed the ride as much as I did writing it. If so, I would appreciate it so much if you left a review on Goodreads or Amazon. Reviews play a crucial role in helping books find their way into readers' hands, and leaving even just a star rating means more to us authors than you'll ever know.

KODAD started out as a book about coming to terms with our pasts and stepping into our power and identity. As I started writing, it became more of a story about the burdens and sacrifices of responsibility. But now, at the end, I'm realizing this is the story of the in-between. It's that pesky stage where we've started to emerge from the darkness and are now struggling to find the steps forward that will take us into the light. It's the part of the story that, interestingly, we spend the most amount of time navigating, yet designate the least amount of time to when recounting to others.

As a writer, I get it. On a neurological level, researchers have found our brains prefer stories with forward progression and satisfying endings, and the in-between is anything but that. It's blurry and confusing and often consists of just as many steps backward as forward. But all of those steps are essential to getting us out of the darkness and into the light. For it's in that dim, hazy fog that we find our choices. And more importantly, the courage to go through with them.

I hope in reading Analia's, Aaron's, Dimitri's, and Ember's in-betweens, you've found a little more light in your darkness. The in-between can take time to navigate—why do you think this book is so long? But there is always light waiting at the end. As for these characters, you can read about the light—and darkness—they'll encounter next in book four, *Kingdom of Vows and Vengeance,* coming soon.

In the meantime, if you'd like to keep up with me and all my future books, plus get some free, exclusive bonus chapters, you can subscribe to my newsletter at www.abigail ehrhardt.com now. I can't wait to see you there!

Glossary

The Ancient Ones: three dark, malevolent beings that ruled over Elefthia during ancient times.

Ash Kingdom: founded by Azar Valarus, this kingdom is ruled over by the Ash Royals and is known for its forges, creativity, and volcanoes, specifically Mt. Vasolus.

Ash Royal: descendants of Azar Valarus—one of the Defiants and rulers of the Ash Kingdom. All are Blessed with fire magic, which can range in a variety of colors.

The Belt: a string of volcanoes located in the Ash Kingdom.

The Bend: a network of drug dens, brothels, and other nefarious businesses on the outskirts of the Sun Kingdom.

Bless: the act of bestowing Blessings.

Blessed: the humans—and their descendants—whom the Crystal gifted magic to. All Blessed are guaranteed to have an extended life span, faster healing, and heightened strength and reflexes, as well as the same magic as their parents. It's a fifty-fifty chance for either magic if both parents have magic.

Blessing: a word that has become synonymous with a person's magic, extended life span, faster healing, and heightened strength and reflexes.

Copper fleck: the smallest unit of currency.

The Crystal: the Ancient Ones' most powerful weapon. Translucent and palm-sized, the Crystal is responsible for magic flooding Elefthia, bestowing Blessings, and sealing away the Ancient Ones. At some point during Talitha's reign, it disappeared.

Crystal Guard: existing in all kingdoms, the Crystal guard is made up of the seven strongest warriors in each kingdom, charged with protecting the Royals.

Damper: created from onyx, after various carvings and charms, a damper can act like a magical plug, drawing all of a person's magic to itself and not releasing it until removed. The longer the damper is worn, the longer it takes for the magic to return.

Darmanten: one of the five major gods, he is the god of day and night.

The Defiants: seven humans that stepped up during the war against the Ancient Ones, ultimately sealing the Ancient Ones away, enabling the Crystal to release magic into Elefthia, and founding the seven kingdoms.

Demiblessed: those with one Blessed, one human parent.

Devinroot: a plant that grows off of magic and is a highly addictive stimulant.

Devourist: the demons that made up the majority of the Ancient Ones' army.

Doveness: the name of a member of the DovenU.

The DovenU: a secret tribe of female warriors located in Mt. Lanula.

Elefthia: the name of the continent the once seven, now six kingdoms are found on.

Elladine: one of the five gods, she is the goddess of death and younger sister of Rosala and Kierra.

Enka flowers: a flower whose magic can create communication pathways between people.

Everflame: a flame created by Azar, which cannot be extinguished and provides the majority of the Ash Kingdom's magically powered light.

Ferrin: one of the five gods, he is the god of time and prophecy.

Gold piece: the highest unit of currency.

Gritta's: a drug den in the Sun Kingdom.

Healers: Blessed, Demiblessed, and, in extremely rare cases, humans, that have been chosen by Rosala to receive healer magic from the Crystal. Healers swear vows of celibacy and political neutrality.

Healer markings (sometimes referred to as "markings" or "rings"): the rings inked around a healer's eyes, which depict their level of training. There are four rings: herbology, internal, external, and mystery, which are marked in white as apprentices, but turn the healer's kingdom's colors upon completion of their apprenticeship.

Human: while Royals, Blessed, Demiblessed, and healers are all human, the term has predominantly come to refer to magicless humans, or to the race as a collective.

Kierra: one of the five gods, she is the goddess of life, and older sister of Rosala and Elladine.

Magic network: the internal network that a Blessed's or Demiblessed's magic runs through.

Mist Kingdom: founded by Noelani Sai, the Mist Kingdom is ruled by the Mist Royals and is considered to be the most devout of the kingdoms.

Mist Royal: descendants of Noelani Sai—one of the Defiants—Mist Royals rule over the Mist Kingdom. All are Blessed with water magic.

Moon Kingdom: founded by Mahina Ruanega, the Moon Kingdom is ruled by the Moon Royals and is known for its bogs, tattoos, and secretive people.

Moon Royal: descendants of Mahina Ruanega—one of the Defiants—Moon Royals rule over the Moon Kingdom. They possess Blessings that allow them to manipulate darkness—although they are intentionally vague about what that specifically entails.

Mt. Lanula: one of the three major mountains of Elefthia, located in the Wild Lands.

Mt. Raegyr: one of the three major mountains of Elefthia, located in the center of the Star Kingdom.

Mt. Vasolus: one of the three major mountains of Elefthia, Vasolus is a volcano located in the Ash Kingdom.

Nymphs: appearing incredibly human-like outside of their slit pupils and pointed ears, nymphs derive their life source from a specific plant—although they have a general affinity for all plants.

The Phoenix Gate: the gate in the center of the wall surrounding the Ash Castle, created by King Accalon Valarus during the early years of his kingship.

Pulsepearl: a small pink pearl that is the source of a wraith's magic and life force. They also enable the holder to relocate to any location where there is another pulsepearl.

Rosala: one of the five gods, she is the goddess of healing, and older sister of Elladine, and younger sister of Kierra.

Royal: the descendants of the seven Defiants and rulers of the once seven, now six kingdoms of Elefthia.

Sand Kingdom: founded by Theistan Rubarena, the Sand Kingdom is ruled over by the Sand Royals, and is known for its red deserts, and general practice of not using animals for work or food.

Sand Royal: descendants of Theistan Rubarena—one of the Defiants—Sand Royals rule the Sand Kingdom. They are Blessed with earth manipulation.

Scarsthain: the highest-security prison in Elefthia, located on the border between Star and Moon territory. It's home to the foulest, most deadly of criminals, and is known for its brutality.

Scarsworn dagger: ceremonial daggers only found in the Moon Kingdom that allow people to make magical, blood-based oaths that manifest as tattoos on the swearers' skin.

The Serpent's Tail: one of the three major rivers of Elefthia, which runs from the Wind Kingdom at the northeast, down to the Sun Kingdom, southeast to the Mist Kingdom, and then southwest to the Moon Kingdom.

The Shattering: the climax of the seven-year war between the Star Kingdom and the six kingdoms. The Star Royal line was completely eradicated after Royals from all six kingdoms sent a deadly blast of magic through the Star Castle, so powerful that King Hester's bone fragments were all that survived. This effectively ended the Star Kingdom's rule over the other kingdoms.

Silver chip: the unit of currency valued higher than a copper fleck, and lower than a gold piece.

Solemnai: a celebration that happens every three months in the Sun Kingdom. The tradition was started by Queen Deardryn Oshar to help bridge the gap between the commoners and Royals.

The Solstice Ceremony: occurring once a year, the Solstice Ceremony takes place at the foot of Mt. Raegyr. Here, the reigning Royal from each kingdom releases a blast of magic into the ground to maintain the magic flow across Elefthia.

Soul gate: the Soul Gate can only be opened on the Summer Solstice and the days following and preceding. Each gate can only be opened by the magic of the reigning Royal, and permits direct access to the Star Kingdom where the Solstice Ceremony takes place.

Star Kingdom: founded by Talitha Stelingente, the Star Kingdom was once ruled by the Star Royals. After the Shattering, it became the one piece of neutral ground the six kingdoms could gather on.

Star Royal: descendants of Talitha Stelingente—leader of the Defiants—and rulers of the Star Kingdom. Star Royals are given the Blessing of death.

Sun dragon: dragons that are exclusively found in the Sun Kingdom. Their bodies are long and serpentine, covered in scales in varying shades of gold that are as strong as steel. They have small, white wings, short, stubby legs, and large, golden eyes.

Sun Kingdom: founded by Helia Oshar, the Sun Kingdom is ruled by the Sun Royals, and is known for its research, scholars, and library full of forbidden texts.

Sun Royal: descendants of Helia Oshar—one of the Defiants—Sun Royals rule over the Sun Kingdom. Their Blessings revolve around the life force, enabling them to heal the minds, souls, life forces, and magic networks that healer magic cannot reach.

Sunstone: golden fist-sized stones that can sense Sun magic and glow in response. They provide most of the magic-based light in the Sun Kingdom.

The Unleashing: the moment that the Defiants procured the Crystal and used it to release magic into Elefthia for the first time.

The Wild Lands: the southernmost section of Elefthia, where the Crystal dumped all of the Ancient Ones' dark, malevolent power. It is wisely left alone as a result.

Wind Kingdom: founded by Raiden Cruchendai, the Wind Kingdom is ruled by Wind Royals, and is known for its mountains and cold temperatures.

Wind Royal: descendants of Raiden Cruchendai—one of the Defiants—Wind Royals rule over the Wind Kingdom. Their Blessings revolve around air manipulation.

Wraiths: predominately found in the Moon Kingdom, wraiths are spectral beings that commonly possess the offered bodies of recently deceased humans. Their known to have all-black eyes, a chill that radiates off of them, and their magic and life force are connected to their pulsepearls.

The Wraithhouse: the largest religious sanctuary for wraith-kind, located in the central Moon Kingdom.

Xenol: a plant that is able to eat away a person's magic, and eventually, a person's life force.

Acknowledgments

Coming to the end of this book feels like a fever dream. I started writing KODAD July 2024 after a year of only working on revisions, and to say I felt rusty was an understatement. I also wrote, revised, and passed this off to my editor in a little less than a year. So, needless to say, this was a labor of love... emphasis on labor. That being said, there are so many people I need to thank for polishing this monster into the cohesive story it is today.

First and foremost, I have to thank Auntie Vikki. The Queen of Continuity, Master of Punctuation, Knower of Distances. I genuinely don't know what I would have done if I didn't have your eagle eyes spotting all of my plotholes, and also your top-tier problem solving skills helping to fill them in. Thank you, thank you, thank you for continuing to love these stories as much as I do, and for lending me all your copy editing and proofreader knowledge!

In that same vein, a massive thanks to my badass beta readers, Cat, Marlena, Kyra, and KJ, for all of your reactions and suggestions. Extra thanks to Kyra, PA extraordinaire, for so kindly sacrificing some of your sanity to help manage my own.

I also have to thank my editor, Noah, for all of your polishing and catching all the instances I forgot to use a question mark instead of a period. I really wish I had an explanation for that one, but I don't.

So much thanks to my art team, Liz Heaven from Ravenpagesdesign and Maria Spada. Liz, I genuinely don't know how you keep outdoing yourself with these covers, and getting to collaborate with you is one of the highlights of my job. Maria, I'm still in awe how quickly and perfectly you put the under jacket design together. It's absolutely stunning!

Major thanks to my friends Christi, Kylee, and Kenna for being my number one hype team and taking every opportunity to mention my books to strangers. It sends me into a panic every time, and I love you all for it.

To my family—you fucking traitors. I told you *not* to read the spicy chapters in KOSAS, not to have a casual family convo about it around the kitchen table. I suppose this is the price for having a supportive family and built-in hype team, so thank you and I love you all... But also how dare you?

Finally, to you, dear reader. Thank you for taking a chance on my books, for loving these characters, and for following their journeys. You make all the hard moments worthwhile.

About the Author

Abigail Ehrhardt has been writing absurdly elaborate stories since she was nine years old, to the point her teachers had to confine her plots to forty-five minute time frames. It still didn't help. Now, her stories are just as fantastical, just as intricate, but (hopefully) a lot easier to follow.

As a baby, Abigail was diagnosed with bilateral retinoblastoma, a rare cancer of the retinas. After having one eye removed and the other severely damaged, she quickly realized books were her key to unlocking a world that was no longer designed for her. Now, she writes stories of her own, featuring a healthy dose of magic, romance, and wounded dreamers.

You can find her in Connecticut, where she's probably hoarding nail polish, adopting far too many plants, and becoming more emotionally attached to the side characters than protagonists of whatever book she's reading.

instagram.com/abigailehrhardt.author/

facebook.com/profile.php?id=61553660026246

tiktok.com/abigailehrhardt.author